To: Beverley

A Star's Legacy

Volume One of *The Magdala Trilogy:*
A Six-Part Epic Depicting a Plausible Life of
Mary Magdalene and Her Times

Peter Longley

*With best Wishes
always —*

iUniverse, Inc.
New York   Bloomington

A Star's Legacy
Volume One of The Magdala Trilogy: A Six-Part Epic Depicting
a Plausible Life of Mary Magdalene and Her Times

iUniverse books may be ordered through booksellers or by contacting:

iUniverse
1663 Liberty Drive
Bloomington, IN 47403
www.iuniverse.com
1-800-Authors (1-800-288-4677)

ISBN: 978-1-4401-4256-7 (pbk)
ISBN: 978-1-4401-4254-3 (cloth)
ISBN: 978-1-4401-4255-0 (ebk)

Printed in the United States of America

iUniverse rev. date: 7/7/09

Dedicated to the memory of

My father

Charles William Hovenden Longley

And in memory of

My mother

Dorothy Enid Longley

INTRODUCTION

A Star's Legacy is the first part of a trilogy of novels that include *Beyond the Olive Grove* and *The Mist of God*, all speculating on the plausible life and times of Mary Magdalene. The series traces the lives of a fictitious Roman named Linus Flavian and the quasi-historical persons of Joshua of Nazareth, Maria of Magdala, and their son Ben Joshua.

    Star of Wonder, the first part of *A Star's Legacy*, is a novel set in the turbulent Jewish state from 7 B.C., in the latter years of King Herod the Great, up to his death in 4 B.C. The intrigues and hopes of the Jewish state and its people are revealed at a time when global prosperity and trade is paramount in the region, fostered by the rapidly growing influence of the Roman Empire. For a few months in the winter of 5 B.C., an unusual heavenly body in the form of an elongated star travels across the Middle East in a westerly direction. The characters in this novel, both Jewish and Roman, all form their own opinions about what this heavenly sign could mean and adapt their interpretation to their goals and aims. Central to this is the character Miriam, who sees the star and other mystical night experiences, as signs from God that a child she is carrying will have a special purpose for the Jewish people. Others foster her viewpoint, although their own beliefs about the star are different. In the innocence of her youth, Miriam is caught up in a political plot. After her child Joshua is born, the plot places her life and that of the child in danger. In order to protect her vision for this child, she is forced to flee Judea.

Children of Destiny, the second part of *A Star's Legacy*, deals with the childhood, adolescent years, and early adulthood of Linus, Joshua and Maria, all of whom were born at the time of the mysterious star. These are the years which Christianity and history have generally termed 'the missing years' in the life of Jesus.

The second novel in the Magdala trilogy, *Beyond the Olive Grove*, deals with the adult life of Joshua as well as the continuing lives of Linus and Maria. They express an unusual interpretation of the known life of Jesus Christ. The third novel, *The Mist of God*, continues this challenging interpretation, taking the reader from Judea to Gaul, Rome, India and Asia Minor. This is a bold and different look at the birth of Christianity and the possibility that the true teachings of Jesus have been distorted or lost. *The Mist of God* also introduces the fourth character, Ben Joshua, a child born of Joshua and Maria.

Although the Christian story, as handed down through generations of believers, is recognizable throughout this trilogy, the interpretation and handling of history is decidedly different, reflecting the forefront of a diligent search for the true Historical Jesus at a time when world consciousness is in turmoil and change. The novels are a rich blend of Jewish, Roman, and Greek traditions that mingle at times with Asiatic thought. They open with a messianic plot that results in the birth of Joshua into a little-known family with some biblical historicity. I have molded real historical persons with fictitious and semi-fictitious characters. As much as possible, I've given those characters, who are biblically historic, their true Aramaic names rather than the Greek and Latin translations with which we are more familiar. The result is a refreshingly different look at the biblical first century A.D. and of the circumstances and characters of this well-known story.

The opening events happen against a backdrop of anti-Roman zealot rebellion and the various interpretations of the passage of that moving star, or comet, which was easily visible throughout the Middle East in the tumultuous last year of King Herod the Great. Joshua of Nazareth, known to us as Jesus Christ, is generally considered by most scholars to have been born shortly before the death of King Herod the Great in 4 B.C. I have followed this preference for dating events in these novels.

At the birth of Christ, the Roman Empire had only recently come to the area of Judea. Not all the known Western world was encompassed within its walls, but Roman influence was as far-reaching as its Oriental counterpart in China. China and Rome had trade connections with India. Given that the Americas were unknown, it can be said that at no time in history had the world seemed more as one than two thousand years ago. This is a striking parallel to today's global reach.

It was at this time that the Roman calendar was created. The old calendar had been updated first by Julius Caesar and then by Augustus. The two additional months that they conceived gave us our present twelve-month calendar. Julius and Augustus are immortalized in the summer months of July and August. With only minor adjustments, the Augustinian calendar has become the measure that unites our world today. Two thousand years ago was the start of the 'Pax Romana', an extraordinary concept of global peace based on the passage of goods in free trade, and again, a striking parallel with the hopes of our present era.

Two thousand years ago also saw a world afraid of change and fearful of the new Roman order, one that spawned apocalyptic prophecies and resistance movements, along with the fledgling religion that became Christianity. But the prophets of apocalypse were proved wrong. The world did not end. Christianity was not the swan song of an old belief system, but became the foundation of two thousand years of Western civilization. So the world today unanimously dates its calendar from the legendary birth of Jesus Christ. But the wheel turns full circle. At the start of the Third Millennium, we see a revival of those same apocalyptic fears and resistance movements as the world parallels its past. As we potentially approach unity and a new order, we find ourselves also afraid of change, listening once more to prophets of doom.

PETER LONGLEY
December 2008

ACKNOWLEDGEMENTS

I am indebted to many who have contributed to my thinking and enabled me to embark on this work. Scholastically, I stand in the tradition of the great Anglican twentieth-century theologian John A. T. Robinson and my contemporaries, Robert Funk, Marcus Borg, Don Cupitt, John Dominic Crossan, Elaine Pagels and A.N. Wilson. I have admired the critical stance of Bishop John Shelby Spong, who treads new frontiers in Christo-centric thought. Philosophically, I have learned much from such contemporary writers as Deepak Chopra, Harry Palmer, author of the *Avatar* materials, and Neale Donald Walsch, author of *Conversations with God*. All of us owe a debt to Albert Einstein, Stephen Hawking and others for the advance of quantum physics that has so dramatically changed our thought patterns and practices as we look to the future in this Third Millennium.

Specifically, in regard to the text of this novel, I acknowledge the patient reading and encouragement I received from Waldemar Hansen, author of *The Peacock Throne*, who was my predecessor as World Cruise Port Lecturer on board the ocean liner *Queen Elizabeth 2*. I am also grateful to Rabbi Harry Roth and The Venerable Canon Robert N. Willing, chaplains on board the *Queen Elizabeth 2*, for their support in the early stages of writing and their sound advice on some of the religious practices I have described. I am also indebted to the Reverend Lawrence H. Waddy for input on aspects of the Graeco-Roman world in the first century.

A number of people have assisted in editorial work on this book, including Jessica Colville and Linda Anderson. I am also grateful to Anthony J. W. Benson and James A. Veitch, Associate Professor, Victoria University, Wellington, New Zealand, for their encouragement and promotional work on my introductory novel to this series, *Two Thousand Years Later* (Hovenden Press 1996), and to John Lewis for his support of *The Magdala Trilogy* and for introducing me to Robert W. Middlemiss. Bob Middlemiss has not only honed my technical and editorial skills, but has proved to be a good friend who understands the deeper implications of the goals I am aiming at in the series. I thank my late father, Charles William Hovenden Longley, for his encouragement and spiritual insights, and my godfather, Oliver Gyles Longley, C.B.E., who never gave up on me. Despite my breach of orthodoxy, he has always believed in my vocation. Finally, I sincerely thank Kazumi Masuda, Bettine Clemen and Nicole Glenn for their endless support and patience with me through half a lifetime of research in bringing this project to fruition. I have tried to create a framework for the teaching and healing ministry of Jesus and a plausible life of Mary Magdalene that can be more popularly acceptable in the philosophical and spiritual thinking of the Third Millennium. Scholastically, I have advanced on my own background as a graduate in theology from Cambridge University in the 1960's, much of the discussion and interest engendered from using the tools of textual criticism advanced by scholars of the Jesus Seminar.

PETER LONGLEY
December 2008

A
Star's
Legacy

"O—Star of wonder, star of night,

Star with royal beauty bright,

Westward leading, still proceeding,

Guide us to thy perfect light."

John H. Hopkins

Part One

Star of Wonder

CHAPTER ONE

On the road to Sepphoris

Jonathon lost consciousness as he felt the nails tearing at his hands on the crossbar. The last sound he heard was his friend Mosheh's cries as the Roman soldiers tied him down and reached for their bloodied mallets.

When consciousness returned, Jonathon saw only a watery world in hues of yellow and orange. His wooden death post rose from the ground. As the cross was raised, Jonathon's body pulled on the thongs holding his arms. Agonizing pain came from the gaping wounds in his hands. He felt as if he was going to fall.

He could see Mosheh hanging helplessly from a post across the way, his head drooping.

"Roman bastards!" Jonathon shouted.

A man used a mallet to drive pegs and stones into the posthole. The cross jarred with every blow, pulling on the torn muscles of Jonathon's tortured body.

When Jonathon's cross was secured, the soldiers snapped their whips at the line of convicted men. Jonathon could see Matthew, his young brother, among them.

After the initial agony and shock, a stunned calm came over Jonathon. His body adjusted to the discomfort and, although suspended, found its natural resting point on the cruciform frame. The sun beat down. Flies gathered in the congealing blood of his wounds.

We failed, he thought.

Then the pain returned, throbbing in his wounded hands and feet. Worst of all was the strain on his lungs against the weight of his chest. He fought to breathe.

Jonathon forced his mind away from the dreadful pain. He remembered carefree days of the previous summer. He had spent them in the hills outside Nazareth with Mosheh and Matthew, where they'd sharpened their skills with slingshots against Benjamin Levi's sheep. Dinah was often waiting for them when they got home. They'd never decided which one of them was going to marry her. All of this was before they had enrolled with Ahab's zealots.

Who will tell Mother and Dinah that Ahab killed us? He's no better than the Romans! he thought.

A buzzard flew overhead awaiting the pickings of death.

Pain shot through Jonathon's body again. He dropped his head to find relief. The bright color of a field poppy caught his attention from the ground below.

* * *

Between the clefts of rock in the hilly, spring landscape, wildflowers held their heads toward the midday sun. Purple, white and yellow, hints of blue, the red of the poppies, all mingled on the carpet of gray-green. Here and there in fields, patches of vines showed their first bright green shoots.

Two youths, Samuel and Caleb, were climbing through the hidden cover of this scrub. Caleb first saw the crosses.

"Samuel! They're crucifying them!" he shouted.

Samuel looked up from the sage and stones. He could see the crosses.

Caleb pulled at him.

"Get down! They might see you. They might kill us, too, if we get too close."

Samuel eased back down into the scrub. The boys slithered off to some rocks where they were hidden from the rough workers and scarlet-tunicked overlords—these men responsible for conducting this act of Roman oppression. The sound of carpentry, the clamor of winches and hammers, drifted toward them, overriding the screams and cries of those being crucified.

Caleb and Samuel had become caught up in the excitement of the zealot movement. The boys expected to join. The anguish of losing a family member through the activities of the freedom fighters hadn't cast its somber shadow on their young lives. After the zealots raided Sepphoris, there had been excitement in Nazareth when a Roman centurion was killed on the road to the north. But there were some among the Nazareth crowd, like the rich man Joachim ben Judah, who had condemned the killing as a senseless move not worthy of the cause. The youngsters had little knowledge of the failed attack on the Roman garrison at Sepphoris. In the curfew that followed the raid, it was difficult to hear news of those who had fallen to the Romans they had hoped to slaughter.

Caleb and Samuel realized they were among the first from Nazareth to know their fate. They watched the crosses being raised up along the roadway. Some of the crucified were little older than they were; others were men their fathers admired.

Caleb and Samuel watched how it was done. A post was lying a mere two hundred cubits in front of them. First, two or three rough men— probably slaves or members of the gladiatorial school in Sepphoris—dug a hole in the stony ground. Roman guards brought the prisoners closer to the site. Leather thongs tied their arms to heavy planks. There was no way they could escape. If they fell under the weight of their burden, the guards kicked them and lashed with their whips until they struggled back to their feet.

The screams of one victim reached Caleb and Samuel. He had been thrown to the ground. The man was kicking out with the little strength he could muster. With ease, the laborers grabbed his flailing legs and tied them together. They fastened them to the post nearest the hole. Then they tied additional thongs of leather and rope around the intersection of the beams. The cross was lashed and framed the man's head.

"It's Matthew!" Samuel exclaimed, fright tightening his stomach.

"Quiet!" Caleb ordered, craning his neck to see.

The soldiers called forward a brute of a man with a scarred face. Taking a heavy nail and a mallet, ignoring the screams of the prisoner, he drove the nail through the flesh and bones of the victim's feet until they were secure within the post. Then he hammered two more nails through the prisoner's hands just below where his wrists and forearms had been bound to the crossbar. Blood coated the mallet head as the nails secured the prisoner to the beam.

Caleb momentarily looked away. He put his arm around Samuel's shoulder. But mesmerized, the boys continued to watch.

Six laborers tied ropes to the crossbeam of the post. They pulled on the ropes, raising the cross until it slipped into the crude hole in the ground. They pulled again until the cross stood against the blue spring sky. With the aid of a mallet, one of the Roman laborers secured the upright post in the ground with large, compacted, loose stones. Matthew, still screaming, hung on the rough-hewn cross. The group advanced fifty cubits down the road. The next hole was ready. The soldiers reached for another prisoner.

It was a long time before Caleb and Samuel dared to move from their safe hiding place in the scrub. They waited, as the midday sun baked their backs, until the procession of prisoners, soldiers, and slave laborers had moved well from their sight. The youngsters escaped by crawling among the rocks and thickets to a small, unkempt vineyard. There, along the shelter of a stone wall, they were able to escape the terrible scene they had witnessed. They traveled for some time through scented wildflowers in the direction of Nazareth. Their progress was slow.

The track they followed rose up from the provincial capital to higher ground. It gradually led to the hollow that formed the backdrop to the village of Nazareth. Slithering in the scrub, Caleb and Samuel reached the summit. From there, they could see the road ahead was tranquil. There were no soldiers, no screaming prisoners or sounds of mallets, no cracks of the whip. It was as it had always been—a simple stony track with the beauty of the Galilean hills in spring sloping away on either side. It must have been at least midafternoon before either Caleb or Samuel saw or heard any sign of life beyond the buzzing of spring insects, but at length, they spotted a lone Roman soldier, wearing a plumed helmet and riding a magnificent white horse, coming toward them from Nazareth to Sepphoris. He didn't seem to be in any hurry or to be on any kind of official business. Caleb and Samuel had vowed death to all Romans after what they had witnessed earlier in the day. Caleb spat on the ground and cursed the horseman. Samuel reached for his slingshot.

"No!" whispered Caleb. "It'll serve no purpose."

Samuel lowered his weapon and frowned at his friend.

"What if you miss him? We'd be caught. He has a horse and we're on foot. We'd end up joining all those others along the roadside and we'd achieve nothing. It's better for us to be informers and tell the others what we've seen. They'll know what to do. Perhaps they'll reward us."

Samuel put away his slingshot.

"You're a rotten shot anyway," Caleb continued. "What makes you think you could hit that Roman from this distance? You can't even hit the doves flying out from Benjamin Levi's cote!"

The two boys ran back to Nazareth to tell what they'd seen.

* * *

As he approached Sepphoris, the Roman horseman saw the first ugly cross rising out of the barren landscape. The crucified man strung up on the crossbar hung in the agony of death. Nearly one hundred now lined the roadway.

The sun gleamed on the gilt of the young centurion's helmet. Red plumes that marked his rank fluttered in the light breeze. The only sound came from the white stallion's hooves on the stones. Centurion Flavius Septimus knew as he made his way toward Sepphoris that his idyll was over. The lines of crosses, some upright, some tilted forward with the sagging weight of their victims, told him that he was back in the service of the Empire. Something dreadful must have happened while he had been away in Magdala.

As he pulled up his horse, Flavius Septimus was torn between duty and compassion. He thought of Esther, the Hebrew whore with whom he had shared contentment over the past few weeks. He remembered her fragrance, the warm breath of her, and the sensuous caverns of her naked body. He'd explored all of her when she'd taken him daily in her arms. Flavius didn't like to think about who else had held that naked flesh and experienced Esther's sensual warmth. After all, Esther made her living satisfying men. Flavius had always visited Esther at sundown, a special time for him. Now, in the light of the setting sun, he remembered the dirty, olive oil smell that permeated Esther's couch. Her hands had felt good on his flesh. Her gentle massage had become a habitual end to his days, culminating when their bodies entwined into one. Esther's face, tense on the threshold of fulfillment, shimmered in his memory. Their pleasure was in stark contrast to the dying victims who hung on these roadside crosses. Yet, Flavius reflected, they were as Hebrew as Esther. It was his duty as a centurion for Flavius to uphold the law and order of Rome. To these dying men, he was the enemy. Yet in his heart he was carrying love for a Hebrew whore. Was he betraying the Empire? Had he betrayed Copernia, his aristocratic young bride? But she was back in Tuscany. *Should momentary contentment, happiness, and inner peace be signs of betrayal?* he mused. He looked up at the faces of the crucified. A deep pain gnawed at him.

Flavius rode on in silence. Some of the crucified men had died. Others were able to muster enough life to spit at him. Some cried out:

"Murderer!" "Unclean pig!" and "Death to all Romans!"

They screamed their pathetic cries in Aramaic. Although he was still learning this language, Flavius' previous experiences in Syria had taught him enough. He was an enemy in a land he loved.

Flavius Septimus was the son of Lucius Flavius, the Governor of Tuscany. He had been sent to Sepphoris from the Syrian headquarters where he'd served in Damascus under Quirinius. He was a representative of Roman power, the real power in this land ruled only in name by that Semitic prince of the desert, King Herod of the house of Antipater. Herod, in his treaties with Rome, had established provincial capitals to remind his people of his links with the power of the Empire. Sepphoris, a little to the northwest of Nazareth, was the Galilean capital. These crosses on either side of the roadway, leading to the new city, were gaunt reminders of that powerful alliance between King Herod and Rome.

What has happened? Flavius asked himself. *There must have been a serious uprising.*

His guilt was compounded by the feeling that he'd failed in his duty. Where had he been when Rome needed him? He'd been on the shores of the lake, planning his future and dallying in Esther's arms. But he loved Galilee, with its gentle hills, and the blue waters of Lake Gennesaret. The landscape above Magdala reminded him of the country estate in Tuscany that had been his childhood home. Cypress trees, rambling banks of honeysuckle, trumpet flowers, and groves of citrus fruits tumbled down the hillside to the little village of flat-topped houses beside the great lake. There, Hebrew villagers lived, tending their nets and spinning their wool, going about the simple business of living.

Why would people of Galilee want to rise up against Rome when Rome protects them and their idyllic lifestyle? Flavius thought, as he looked at the relentless lines of crosses. From his point of view, the whole world belonged to Rome. *Rome is the very symbol of security, good commerce, order and strength. Men throughout this world, from Hispania in the west to Syria in the east, beg for the prize of citizenship and live in peace. Why would anyone want to rebel?*

Flavius knew he might be called upon to fight the Parthians, or those beyond the reach of Rome. But here in Galilee, surely there was no reason for rebellion or warfare. Certainly, his soldiers were drilled. They guarded and supervised the building construction at Sepphoris. At times, they marched and rode as escorts for the great caravan trains making their way down from Syria to King Herod's new commercial port of Caesarea. They protected the merchants and traders who were open to brigand attack as they carried the riches of the east into the Empire. Brigands, robbers, and thieves were the riff-raff of the Empire, who could be found in any settled land. These criminals didn't threaten Rome or the government's authority, but only violated the innocent population of the Empire's lands. As a soldier, Flavius saw his role as that of protector, not warrior. He upheld the rule of law and justice for all peoples of the Empire against the vagrants who might disrupt the flow of commerce and the settled life of the Empire's world.

Now, Sepphoris was only a short distance ahead. Her glistening white marble buildings looked welcoming to Flavius. He kicked his heels, girding the stallion. Crosses of the dying faded from thought to the drumming of hooves. He needed to be briefed.

* * *

The last shafts of golden light disappeared below the western hills. Long shadows of dusk turned into early moments of night. It was that time of day when the stars shine forth from a green-blue sky, before the darkness sets in for good. In Nazareth, a new spiritual day was beginning for Joachim as he looked out over his sloping vineyards and groves. This wealthy landowner raised his bushy eyebrows that matched his graying beard to peer at the landscape. His large physique and keen deep-set eyes gave him the appearance of a patriachal, much respected man. In the small room at the back of his courtyard home, it was Joachim's custom each evening to greet the new day with prayers as the sun set and closed the old day forever. Prayer was men's business in his tradition. Anna, his beloved wife for more than thirty years, never prayed with him. At this sacred time of the day, she was busy preparing their evening meal and supervising the baking of tomorrow's bread. Joachim's family had observed these timeless evening rituals for generations. His forebears had enjoyed the privileges and riches of the priestly class in service at the Temple. His family was of royal lineage that could be traced back to the great King David who had united Israel and fulfilled the vision and command of Moses. It was King David's son, Solomon the Great, who had established the Temple in Jerusalem. To his heirs, this was forever the center of the Israelite dream and symbol of Jewish strength. There had been dark times when God had reminded His people of their frailty and failures and had caused them to suffer and fall captive to foreign powers. Always, however, the Jews had survived. The God of Israel had never abandoned His people. Jerusalem, David's city, was always restored.

Joachim stood up, feeling the weight of his heavy garments pull on his shoulders. He reflected on his past. He'd been destined for a career of probable importance in the Temple hierarchy. It all seemed so far away now as he looked out over the pleasant landscape spreading down to the vale of Esdraelon. The distant sight of Mount Tabor rose up from the valley floor as a silhouette against the evening light. There was a mystery about the hill that caused him to reflect on Mount Moriah and the Temple with its sacrificial pyre.

Since the time of Zerubbabel, sacrifices have been offered on the holy mount of God, he mused. *Sacrifices continued despite the wicked invasions by the Syrians, Egyptians, and in my own childhood, by the sacrilege of the Romans. Pompeius, like Antiochus Epiphanes a hundred years before, broke into the Holy of Holies. Father wept that day. But, despite this horror of horrors and our unsettled government, the Temple's sacrificial fires have not been quenched.*

Joachim rejoiced as he reflected on the traditions of the Davidic priesthood that he had left behind. He shrugged his shoulders, clearing his thoughts, and held out his arms to pray in the custom of men:

"Hear, O Israel. The Lord our God, the Lord is one. Praised be His name whose glorious kingdom is forever. Tell me, Lord, what is Your plan for my daughter Miriam? Can you reveal to me a little of Your purpose for her? It was a tremendous sacrifice for Anna and me to hand her over to the House of the Temple Virgins all those years ago. We did it for You, Lord. But Zechariah says soon she will have to leave. What is Your purpose for her, Lord? What is Your purpose for my little girl?"

He paused as he stood waiting to receive an answer, cocking his head on one side. No perceived answer came.

"Tell me Lord," he prayed. "When You're ready, tell me."

Then, dismissing the subject of Miriam, he continued in prayers of gratitude for all the bounty that was his.

"I know I should be grateful, Lord. You have given me so much. What tradition took from me You have restored to me in other ways. I have the best vineyards, and bountiful olives. Even Anna's herbs look promising."

He smiled.

"You have given me even more prosperity than Benjamin Levi. But Benjamin has sons, Lord. Why was I never to have a son? What did I do to upset You? After generations of service at the Temple, why was my family struck down? Did our dedication of Miriam to Your service restore us in Your sight, Lord? I know You never abandoned me, but for the sake of my father, is our family honor restored?"

Again, there was no answer, but deep inside Joachim knew the answer. Soon, he must go to Jerusalem and meet with his wife's brother-in-law, the High Priest Zechariah. *Surely Zechariah would want my input as to how he should arrange a suitable priestly marriage for my daughter,* he thought.

Darkness had now set in, and the stars were bright in a clear sky. This was Joachim's favorite time of the year. In a week or two, the sounds of crickets would fill the jasmine-scented night air. In a few days, his vineyards would be lush with fresh green leaves. Weeds that had been dormant through the short winter would need to be pulled. It would be time to round up Jason and his men and hoe the fields; time to prune the worthless limbs off the old fig tree spread out against the eastern wall. Anna's herbs outside the kitchen—mustard, dill, rosemary, thyme, and coriander—would start to grow tall again. The mustard, now small, would grow to be the tallest of them all. He looked at the moon, little more than a crescent in the sky, and asking forgiveness for his impatience he then concluded his prayer, thanking God for his bounty.

* * *

As Anna kneaded the dough with her maid Judith, she tried to avoid thinking too much about Miriam. But it often crossed her mind how different life might have been if she could have conceived in the normal way and given to Joachim the family that he'd deserved. Somehow, it had not been God's will. *I was the cause of his downfall,* she felt.

Joachim had been sent away from the Temple by Issachar, the High Priest, dashing his own hopes of ever wearing the High Priest's crown. It was a tradition and one of the unwritten laws that all Temple priests must have children so that their lineage could continue devotion to the duties of the Temple and to the glory of God. If a priest didn't have a family, it was deemed the will of God and a sign that he must give up the priesthood. Despite Joachim ben Judah's expensive and generous gifts to the Temple and his total dedication to its ritual and worship, eleven years ago he had been called before the Council and declared unworthy. He'd been suspended from his Temple duties. At first he had been bitter, full of resentment for the unfair judgment of his Temple peers. He had searched the Temple records to find a legal precedent for his case, but to no avail. He was at that time the only priest of the Temple who had not raised children for Israel.

Anna remembered how Joachim had returned to their home in Jerusalem, feeling enraged. *At first he blamed me for my barrenness and his loss of status. Then he wept and felt abandoned by God. I beseeched him to leave Jerusalem and retire to Bethlehem. But my birthplace wasn't good enough for him. He went his own way, dwelling in the wilderness. I didn't know if I would ever see him again.*

As Joachim's anger had abated and his reason and love for Anna returned, he had acceded to her wishes. With a last look back at the smoking pyre of the sacrificial mound and the sparkling new marble of King Herod's outer Temple wall, Joachim and Anna had journeyed south to the village of Bethlehem.

Bethlehem was in the high country on the road to Hebron, but far enough from Jerusalem for the Holy City to become lost behind the rugged mountains. There, in Bethlehem, a miracle occurred.

After two decades of a barren marriage, I conceived, Anna recalled. *Miriam came into our lives!*

Joachim and Anna had returned to Jerusalem, where they presented their newborn child to the High Priest as was the custom in priestly families. The child had received the traditional Hebrew blessing, and Joachim and Anna had made a vow. With their babe in Anna's arms, they stood in the Court of the People and promised that they would dedicate their child to God. This meant that their little girl would be given to the Temple, as a symbol of purity, to be brought up in the House of the Virgins.

Four years later, they fulfilled that vow. They had taken Miriam to the Temple where she had been led away by the High Priest to a corner of the precinct where few men ever enter. *It was a desperate moment. I didn't know whether I was afraid or spiritually fulfilled*, Anna recollected. A tear or two rolled down her cheeks and fell in the dough.

"What is it, Mistress?" Judith asked.

"Miriam."

"She's with God."

"Not much longer," Anna said. "Soon the High Priest will have to find her a match. We are denied even that," she choked.

"But you always said you believed Miriam was a miracle," Judith said, "destined to be important. She'll be married to a rich priest, possibly a Sanhedrin councilor, and live in a big house."

No high-minded destiny or hope for Miriam's future, however, could eradicate the pain that Anna still felt at being separated from her child. *They had been redeemed*, Joachim had said. *God had proved his love by giving them the prosperity that they now enjoyed.*

"I would rather have been the mother I could have been for my daughter," she mumbled.

Judith kneaded the dough for Anna. She poked the loose strands of her frizzled brown hair into the folds of her headdress and wiped the dough from her hands on her gray robe. She looked at Anna quizzically, the lines on her forehead deepening.

"Mistress Anna," she asked, "maybe when Miriam leaves the Temple she can come back to us?"

Anna looked away from Judith, busying herself with the bread.

"Judith, I've told you not to ask about Miriam's future. Miriam is in God's hands. She's God's child now, not ours."

Judith was determined to push the matter further.

"But, Mistress Anna, as you say, they can't keep her at the Temple much longer. She'll be all grown up—fourteen years. How much longer can she remain one of those child virgins?"

"Judith, don't think I'm not concerned with thoughts of Miriam, but I have to try to banish them. Her father and I have no control over the will of God. We dedicated Miriam to God's service. The High Priest will decide her future. We mustn't concern ourselves about Miriam. He'll choose a young man for her."

Anna looked back at Judith and smiled from her teary face. Although Joachim's wife had put on the weight of her middle years, her skin had a freshness that contrasted to the leathery texture of her servant's. It was impossible for Anna to frown at the younger woman.

"Now, Judith," she said in a motherly sort of way, "help me get these bread cakes into the oven."

The two women performed their evening ritual and moved the flattened cakes to bake them for the next day's bread. The aroma of the rising dough soon permeated the air. When it reached a certain rich, pungent smell, Anna knew it was ready.

Joachim returned from his prayers. He pulled a piece off one of the fresh loaves, even though they were really for the next day. Somehow, when the bread was warm and doughy it tasted better.

"Not too much," Anna warned him, "too much of that fresh bread and you'll have a stomach ache."

Judith set bowls of lentil soup on the table.

* * *

Judith had joined Joachim ben Judah's household as Anna's maid when she, too, was only fourteen years. Since then, the only life she'd known was with Joachim and Anna. She'd been proud to be part of a household that served in the Temple and had felt privileged in Jerusalem each time she went to the well in the square to draw water for their daily needs. The other giggling servant girls, sitting around the well, served merchants and sundry rich Jews. Some served in houses of the Herodians or even in Roman families. There were few, however, who served in the household of a Temple priest. Joachim was one of the most respected holy men of the city.

Judith herself wasn't much concerned with matters of religion, but she enjoyed the status that her master's position gave her. She couldn't read or write, so the ancient scrolls that Joachim often brought to the house meant nothing to her. But she prepared her master's food, as her mistress bade her, according to all the rules and traditions of the Jewish people. She made sure that the right cups and utensils were always laid out at the appropriate times in the ritual of food preparation. Anna had taught her these details. Judith did these things, not for God, but because this is what she had been taught to do as Anna's maid. Her mistress' constant references to God's will fell on her shoulders like rain, running off as soon as they'd been uttered. God meant respectability to Judith. She'd a secure life in the Temple priest's household. Prayers, preparation, feasts and festivals were simply a part of her duties. This was her role in life. There had never been a serious question of Judith getting married. In her world, marriages weren't contracted and arranged as in rich men's houses. Her family held no status. Her brothers had married, but she'd no real contact with their families. Her childhood ended when she was sent to the house of Joachim ben Judah, to live in his household for the rest of her days.

Judith had never felt deprived of family life. Because her master and mistress had never had a child during those first fifteen years, the lack of family life had never been a conscious gap in Judith's simple mind. But Anna's unexpected pregnancy and the birth of Miriam had brought joy into Judith's life. Perhaps more than her mistress, she'd come under the spell of motherhood and given all her love to the pretty baby girl who had begun to grow up with them in the house at Bethlehem. She combed her hair and washed her face and often at night when Miriam awoke, she showed her the stars. The stars fascinated Judith.

"They are God's angels," she used to say to Miriam.

The arrival of Miriam had given new status to the servant girl.

After Joachim's dismissal from the Temple, Judith had felt a certain shame at the Jerusalem well. She was very happy when the family had moved to Bethlehem and her mistress had conceived. The baby gave Judith a new purpose and pride in her service to Joachim and Anna.

But her master and mistress gave away their beautiful little girl to be hidden in the Temple and to be taken away from them forever. Judith had tried to understand. Joachim and Anna were obviously good people, but their action remained a mystery to her. Judith had never forgotten

19

the little girl whom she'd adored. Some of the pain had eased when they moved north to Nazareth and started a new life. She grew to enjoy Galilee with its country smells and abundance of green. Galilee never seemed to turn as brown as the hills of Judea. And then, there was her status. She felt much better treated than any of the other servants in the village. Her home, the house of Joachim, was the most gracious, ornate, and magnificent in Nazareth. Among the maidservants both young and old, who gathered at the village well, she held her head high.

CHAPTER TWO

Nazareth's Freedom Fighters

Ahab's small house was close to the center of Nazareth, but it had its own courtyard adjacent to the street. Caleb knocked vigorously on the wooden gate. Ahab was a rough old man with an unkempt beard, who walked with a limp and leaned heavily on a stick. He had served in the armies of the Hasmoneans and even fought in the campaign against Pompeius, fruitless as that expedition had proven to be. The meddling Idumaeans had switched sides and caused the Roman victory, or at least, so Ahab always said. That was when he had injured his leg. He had little feeling for religion, but he hated the Romans and fought for the political freedom of his country. Time, and the continued failure of the freedom movement, had taken its toll on the patience of this old man who for three decades had been a leader of the zealots. Ahab abhorred the lack of fighting spirit that now permeated the movement.

"I can hear you!" he shouted when he heard the frantic knocking at his gate.

He muttered curses as he came out into the yard.

"Who goes there? Jew or foreigner?"

"Caleb—Simon's son."

"Caleb?" the old man questioned, raising his wiry eyebrows.

"Yes, sir! Caleb—Simon's son! I've news that could be important to us all. I have Samuel with me. Please let us in!"

"Oh! The young ones who were here last month?"

"Yes, sir!"

Slowly, Ahab removed the heavy board that latched his gate from the inside. He never took any chances after sundown and always barred the door. He knew he was a wanted man, especially any time there was an uprising. Ahab opened the gate and saw the faces of the two youths. He recognized his nephew Samuel.

"We can't be too careful these days," he said. "There are too many snivelling lovers of Rome around who mingle freely with our oppressors. Why, we hear Greek spoken almost as freely as Aramaic! Now, what do you want?"

Caleb and Samuel stepped over the threshold. Ahab barred the gate behind them.

"Well, what is it?" Ahab repeated.

Caleb remained the spokesman.

"The Romans, sir, they've killed many of our men. The road to Sepphoris is lined with freedom fighters. They've nailed them to wooden crosses and left them to die."

Ahab flinched and cast his eyes to the ground.

"The Sepphoris raid. Jonathon, Mosheh, and Matthew. They all left from here."

"Yes, sir! It was them we saw."

"You saw Matthew?"

"Yes, I think so," Caleb answered. "I know we saw Jonathon and Mosheh."

Ahab paused, his mind lost to fearful imaginings.

"How many did you see hanging from crosses?" he asked.

"Many, Uncle," said Samuel. "They were all the way from Sepphoris, nearly to the top of the hill."

"We kept our distance," continued Caleb, cautious now, observing the anger in Ahab's face. "We watched carefully from a safe hideout in the rocks and saw everything—the line of prisoners, the soldiers, and the men with mallets and nails. Nobody saw us. We escaped through that old vineyard with the stone wall."

"Yes, yes! I admire your bravery," cut in Ahab, "but how many were in the line of prisoners?"

"Not that many," Caleb replied, looking at Samuel for confirmation.

"By the time we got there, most of the posts had been erected and the men were already strung up."

"Later, a lone soldier rode by," said Samuel. "I wanted to kill him with my slingshot, but Caleb wouldn't let me."

Samuel looked up at his uncle.

"I'm ready to fight, sir," he said. "Is there going to be another chance? Can we join the movement? We'd make good scouts and we'd help the cause."

Ahab stroked his saliva-encrusted beard.

"Those dead and dying men are witnesses to our rebellion," he muttered.

He looked at the two youths.

"You've done well, boys, and I'm sure you'll be good members of the movement someday. But we've suffered a bad defeat. Those men you saw crucified out there were some of the best we had. The garrison at Sepphoris is weak at this time of the year, and our contacts had assured us our victory would be easy. We outnumbered those Roman bastards! Why did we lose? Something must have gone wrong."

Ahab's eyes carried great pain.

"So many good men..."

"Uncle, how should we fight back?" asked Samuel. "Would you like us to act as spies for you? Surely we can do something to help."

Ahab gripped his nephew's shoulder.

"Yes, my boy, something will be done. But I don't know what" he said. "First we must call a meeting to give word of your story. Caleb, spread the word in the upper village. You know the houses of our people. Samuel, take the lower village. There are fewer zealots down there, but be sure to include the house of Joachim ben Judah and other members of his synagogue group. I rarely agree with them, but we need their financial support."

A smile crossed Ahab's old face.

"You were right to come straight to me. You'll be freedom fighters one day and fight for our cause."

These last words elated Caleb and Samuel. After all they'd witnessed that day, they were eager to act. They left Ahab's courtyard and went their separate ways to spread the word.

"Children," muttered Ahab as he latched the gate behind them. "The movement today is run by amateurs and children. Where now is the spirit of the Maccabees? Where is the power to plunder the enemy? It's in the hands of religious maniacs, children, well-meaning busybodies, ascetics, and desert wanderers. These are people who believe our freedom will come from holy men with no stomach for fighting. They have no vision of real victory. They're the leaders now. Our good men have become brigands, without leadership or discipline. That's why we're failing. Every man is out for himself and none are really fighting for the cause."

Irritably, he shook free of his words. *Talking out loud with no one to hear—I must be growing senile*, he mused.

The old man walked inside and considered the news and loss of Jonathon, Mosheh, and Matthew. In Nazareth, they'd been the only young zealots with the stamina to go along with the Sepphoris plan. Now, his best men were vulture meat on the Sepphoris roadway.

* * *

Joachim's house on the southern outskirts of the village was built around three sides of a paved marble courtyard. A large lintel and wooden gate led in from the street to this haven that formed the center of the house. Two gnarled olive trees gave shade to the courtyard. A colonnade of pillars in the light Hellenist style surrounded the rooms that led off from this court. It shaded a pleasant portico where most of the family living took place. A fountain sparkled in the open space, fed by the small underground brook that led out from Nazareth's well. By a clever device the water was caught underneath the marble flags and confined to give pressure to the little fountain. The overflow was then piped away to become the water source for the terraces of vineyards sloping away toward Mount Tabor. To the west, the hills of history, of Megiddo and King Saul, stood guard over the plain of Jezreel. As a deeply religious man, Joachim often reflected on their magnitude and portent, while his own contribution was so small.

In some ways, Joachim's house was built in the manner of a Roman villa, but the small window openings and the flat roofing bore witness to Jewish tradition. The furnishings, by Nazareth's standards, were lavish. But they were sparse when compared with the villas of Sepphoris or the town houses of Jerusalem. Much of the comfort and warmth in winter was created by hanging richly colored draperies that gave character to the cluster of rooms around the courtyard. At night, two braziers burned outside. The glow of their embers reflected in the fountain's waters. The braziers gave heat in the winter and drew away the insects from the inner rooms in the summer.

The stars looked down on this peaceful place. They gleamed through the outstretched arms of the ancient olives.

Then, the peace of this evening scene was suddenly broken by a frantic banging on the wooden gate.

Judith ran out to see who was there. When she saw it was only a youth, she let him in.

"May I speak with your master?" Samuel asked breathlessly.

"You may. I am he," said Joachim, who had stepped out from the portico and followed Judith to the gate.

"Joachim ben Judah! Ahab wants you at his house as soon as possible for a meeting of the zealots. There's been terrible murder of our people by the Romans. Caleb and I saw the crucifixions ourselves!" the youth breathlessly sputtered out. "Ahab wants your advice."

"Tonight? Right now?"

"Yes, sir. Ahab needs you right now. We must plan revenge. Please help us, Joachim ben Judah."

"All right, my son. What's your name again? Isn't it Samuel?"

"Yes, sir."

Joachim put an arm on the lad's shoulder.

"Would you like some fruit and bread? We're about to eat. Come in and tell us what all this is about."

At the dinner table, Samuel recounted the events of the day. Joachim listened without interrupting him but with a faraway look on his face. He showed no emotion as Samuel excitedly told the older man his tale.

"All right, I'll come with you," Joachim said.

He wanted to add, *I never did approve of the Sepphoris raid. It's all for nothing and such a waste of good lives,* but the boy was too young.

He passed Samuel a bowl of pomegranates and dates.

"Let's finish our meal first," he suggested gently.

* * *

By the time Joachim and Samuel arrived at Ahab's house, most of the zealots had already gathered. Ahab's back room was pungent with the acrid smell of the one oil lamp burning on its stand. In the ruddy glow of that weak flame sat the twenty-odd men who were members of the Nazareth group. When raiding parties were planned, the numbers grew. Adventurous brigands, searching for spoils and dubious reward, would attach themselves to the cause. Here, in the dismal light and sweat of an overcrowded room, Ahab had gathered his followers. He welcomed Joachim as if they'd been long time friends, although in reality they didn't like each other.

Joachim sometimes felt ashamed of zealot motives and thought that the cause was falling under the leadership of brigands and evil men. Joachim believed in a Davidic Messiah—a new Zerubbabel—who would lift up the people of Israel from their misfortunes and malaise. In the early days of the Maccabees, the Hasmoneans had a measure of military success, but to Joachim they'd never been God's agents. They were usurpers who were not of the Royal line. All the Scriptures and the teachings of men such as Hillel and others of the Jerusalem school, in which Joachim had been so well trained, believed in a Davidic Messiah. *And when he comes, how will he grapple with this political ferment?* Joachim thought. *What will he make of this gathering and its bastardized wisdom and zeal?* He gathered his wits and listened.

"Caleb, one of our youngest members, has a lot to tell you," Ahab announced.

The youth, cowed in this threatening presence, repeated his description of the day's events. But by this time, most of the men knew about the Sepphoris debacle and the horror of the Roman retribution.

Ahab spoke again:

"Jonathon, Mosheh, and Matthew have been taken from us. I suspect other hangers-on from the hill country may have joined our party in the raid. We've suffered a severe defeat. The reports from our spies in Sepphoris must have been inaccurate. The low strength of the garrison at this time of the year must have been greatly exaggerated. Obviously, we didn't get the support that was promised from the gladiators and slaves. Our men have been butchered by the Romans. We need a plan to strike back."

Ahab looked around the smoky room.

"Kill every Roman you see!" came across the rank air.

The oil lamp flame fluttered and licked around its base.

"Yes! Death to all Romans!"

"We must ambush all roads into Sepphoris," the voice of an old brigand shouted from the back.

"Foul their water supply in Sepphoris," a member of the Synagogue party suggested.

But by and large, members of the movement remained silent. They knew their defeat and smarted under it. These bolder schemes soon diminished into the usual calls for civil disobedience and refusal to pay commodity taxes.

Some of the men favored attacks on caravans heading for Caesarea, but in the past, such action had never been successful. The better-armed Roman escorts had always overcome the would-be brigands.

Ahab looked at Joachim ben Judah. In his heart, he attributed much of the current weakness in the movement to Joachim's pacifist thoughts, but they needed Joachim's support.

Joachim kept Caleb close to him as he rose to speak:

"Brethren, I know that all of us value the freedom of our land. In our hearts, we seek revenge for the loss of those dear to us. We all knew Jonathon and Mosheh, and Matthew who recently joined us from Nain. But remember how I cautioned you on the subject of the Sepphoris raid? No good can come from such puny efforts when our nation lacks strong leaders to work on our behalf. How can we, a small group of hill people, take on the might of Rome? Indeed, Rome isn't our prime enemy in this conflict. In some ways, Rome offers us a measure of protection..."

Ahab's wizened old face took on a purple hue in the acrid smoky light. His anger coiled as his rival condemned his lifelong work.

"Rome," Joachim continued, "protects us from the threat of Parthian invasion, a fate which would be worse than what we endure now. Rome has made some of us rich in trade. We now have markets for our produce that we didn't enjoy in the warring days of the Hasmoneans."

"Traitor!" shouted the old brigand from the back. "Death to all Romans!"

"And death to all lovers of Romans, too!" muttered a man who sat close to Ahab.

For a moment, it seemed as if Joachim would be set upon, as others turned against him. The patriarch, however, was protected by his friends—members of the Synagogue group, an influential and intellectual body who only paid lip service to the zealot movement. They were at Ahab's more to take the pulse on events than to advance the cause.

"Never mind me, protect the boy," Joachim said.

"And you," a Synogogue member said.

"Watch Ahab. He will hold them in check."

And Joachim knew he was right. A move against him at this time would have ended in a bitter struggle between the Synagogue group and the brigands who sat together in the tense atmosphere of Ahab's house. Ahab himself, enraged as he was, knew that he must hold the two groups together. Joachim and the Synagogue group were his financiers, the ones who could really make things happen. They were the men whom the villagers would follow. Without their support, the brigands, and even Ahab himself, would fear for their own lives.

In a voice of false contrition, Ahab stood and called for silence. Then, he said:

"Joachim ben Judah, what plan do you have for our freedom?"

"My plea is this," replied Joachim in a voice of authority designed to sway the room. "I've supported our raids on the Romans and I've seen the cruel delight they've taken in cutting down our people. Don't think I condone their action. I love our land as much as anyone here."

"Yes, because you're rich!" jeered a voice from a darkened corner.

Joachim calmly continued:

"We can't win a war against the Romans. All we're doing is causing them to hate us. Eventually, they will destroy our way of life in retaliation. I say to all of you, it's not Rome we need to destroy…it's the Herodians."

"The Herodians?"

Surprise cast itself in the flickering light.

"Why? We hardly know of the Herodians here in Nazareth. It's the Romans who are our oppressors!" shouted the old man sitting close to Ahab.

"Our land is ruled by King Herod whether we like it or not," said Joachim. "Herod makes the laws. Herod builds our new cities. Herod executes justice. Whatever Rome does here is done with Herod's full consent. Herod is our tyrant king, and yet you tolerate him."

"Jerusalem politics!"

"We don't know Herod!"

"Herod doesn't interfere with us. We're Galileans, not men of Judea!"

The meeting erupted once more into the common battle cry—"Death to all Romans!"

Joachim bided his time until order was restored. Then, he continued:

"Whether you like it or not, I'm telling you Herod and the Herodians are our enemy. Herod's family have no right to the throne of David. They're using our land for their own profit by plundering our people and subjugating us to the Romans. We can't order resistance to the Romans while an Idumaean sits on the Jerusalem throne. He's a foreigner from the southern desert—a Jew only by adoption and not by blood."

Joachim looked around the room, relieved to find the zealots finally listening to him.

"Believe me, brethren, I've lived many years in Jerusalem and I've seen the devious work of the Herodians. They've maneuvered our High Priests, oppressed our people, and destroyed our identity. We need to aim our attack at the house of Herod."

In the sudden quiet, a question, well reasoned, offered itself.

"If this should be our plan of action, how can we play our part here in Galilee?"

"Is that you, Elias?"

"Yes, it's me."

"With good questions like that you should sit near the front."

A first scattering of laughter touched the room.

"Listen, Elias. Have you forgotten that the slaughter in Galilee in the days of your father was the work of Herod? Didn't you lose a brother in the fierce fighting at the caves? Oh yes, Herod may have used Romans to assist his forces, but Herod gave the command. Herod crushed those who supported the freedom that the Hasmonean cause fought for. Who ordered the building of Sepphoris? Who invited the Roman garrison to come in, Caesar or Herod?"

"Both!"

"Brethren," Joachim said, "our land will not be free until we're free of the Herodians. This may be sooner than you think, since they seem bent on destroying each other in family rivalry. The King is thought to be mad. My contacts at the Temple in Jerusalem are frightened by his daily rages."

"Maybe you are, too!" the chief spokesman among Joachim's opponents yelled.

Joachim paid no attention to the man.

"There are many factions amongst the Herodians. Some would gladly unite against the King. The house of Herod may destroy itself. I feel that our goal should be to destroy Herodian rule and establish the rule of our fathers through the legitimate house of David. Until the house of David takes on its rightful role, there will be no peace in Israel. It's in the Scriptures. We're living in prophesied times."

At this, the Synagogue group nodded approval, while Ahab glared across the room.

"Religious maniacs and meddlers," he muttered.

Ahab rose to challenge Joachim.

"Joachim ben Judah, if all you say is true, when will this rebellion take place and who'll be our leader? What do we know of kings and princes? What is their blood to us? We're Galileans!"

There was a cheer from the crowd, bolstering Ahab.

"We're not concerned with your High Priests and Temple officials. Your kings and priests mean nothing to us. Most of us have never even been to Jerusalem or seen the Temple there. Your philosophy and schemes have no place in the hill country. Be realistic. Our men have been slaughtered and butchered by red-tunicked Romans, and we'll have revenge!"

Ahab's arm came up.

"Who seeks revenge? Who'll continue our cause against these Roman bastards?"

"Death to all Romans!" resounded again.

"We'll fight on," said Ahab, as he felt the tide turn in his favor. "There will be another Sepphoris. When that day comes, it'll be Romans who'll die. Their bodies will be nailed to wooden crosses for the vultures to devour."

He addressed Joachim again, gesturing in triumph:

"Joachim, you're a man without courage. You lack fighting spirit. You're spoiled by the ease of your life and riches. If you're not for us, leave us. But don't deter us in our cause. We'll avenge the deaths of Jonathon, Mosheh, and Matthew. And we'll overcome these bastards!"

Most of the angry men agreed with him. But not his old rival, the patriarch intellectual of the Synagogue group. Joachim had friends in Nazareth and in other nearby villages, and Ahab needed his help. It always came back to that. Joachim was the most influential man the zealot movement had. And he was the only financier in the Nazareth group.

* * *

As Joachim walked home, shunned by the excited zealots, even the subdued Caleb, he thought about serious matters. He knew in his heart that from this evening on he could no longer support the erratic work of these uneducated freedom fighters.

There is a lesson to be learned from the repetition of history, he thought. *The hanging corpses on the road to Sepphoris are not the first defeat and won't be the last. The victory has to come some other way, perhaps through the work of a mediating messiah.* He was increasingly sure of this.

Many in the room didn't understand what I said or they openly disagreed with me. He sensed rejection. The mood was turning against him. Even some members of the Synagogue group, his closest friends, were wavering. He wondered what would materialize from their discussions if they continued to meet in the cool of his olive grove.

Surely this is the Messianic Age, he thought. *There will be divisions in the land of Israel. Hasn't this just been clearly seen in the divisions between Hyrcanus and Aristobulus and their respective heirs? Each generation of the Hasmonean family has divided itself. Now Herod and the Herodians are doing the same. The time is surely ripe, as inevitable as the grape harvest in my vineyard. The Messiah of the house of David must be at hand.*

Joachim walked over the threshold between the prayer lintels of his gate. He put the heavy latch firmly in place. The stars shone brightly above the branches of the old olives, and the courtyard fountain shimmered in the reflection of a pale moonlight. Shadow shafts pointed in the direction of the chamber where Anna lay sleeping. Joachim returned to his world of peace and beauty, but his mind remained ablaze in the turmoil of the times.

* * *

East met west within the walls of Jerusalem. Potentates, Parthians, and merchants, who traded fine silks from distant lands, paid court and tribute to Herod the Great, the King of the Jews. The palace of the Idumaean monarch glittered with color and luxury. His clever blending of Semitic traditions with Roman lifestyles was designed to make visitors feel welcome in his splendid capital. Romans and Greeks found baths, gladiatorial schools, and circus pleasures. Semitic traders and eastern visitors found gardens, traditional feasts and the smells, sights and sounds of home. To all, however, the great Temple on Mount Moriah marked Jerusalem as forever different from the other cities of the Syrian Province.

Herod had almost completed a massive reconstruction of the Temple area. He realized that he had no real understanding of Temple matters. Therefore, he hadn't attempted to destroy the basic Temple structure. Instead, he embellished the Temple with marble and granite walls, porticos, gateways, and stairways of such magnificence that even the most fanatic Jew admired his handiwork. His Temple was an anachronism dressed up in Hellenic splendor. But it was a focal point of unity and spirit in a diversely divided land.

This was Herod's Jerusalem. But in between the splendors of the Temple and the gracious villas and Roman edifices in the olive groves to the west, lay the real Jerusalem. This Jerusalem seethed with intrigue, crowded commerce, and Oriental smells of dung and beasts of burden. The streets were so narrow that the light of day barely reached the ground. This part of the city was a concentrated mass of urban humanity, many dressed in the only rags they had, living on their wits, overcrowded and underfed. The squatting vendors and urchins were a potential, menacing mob, ready to follow any zealot leader or miracle worker if they promised a dream of freedom. They were gullible, easily conned by countless soothsayers, fraudulent magicians, tricksters, and thieves, often accompanied by the cacophonous sounds of pipes and drums, mangy dogs, exotic monkeys and even hissing snakes. This was the real Jerusalem, lying in the shadow of the Temple, where sultry women with flashing eyes could be bought for a loaf of bread and a merchant's wares lost to the glint of a dagger. This Jerusalem stood beside the luxurious world of King Herod and the Romans and was maintained by unprecedented cruelty. To those huddled masses that made up this part of the city, neither the Temple nor the Herodians gave much hope or satisfaction.

Within the Temple, there was a strange aura of beauty and peace. Tradition continued in the acrid pall of sacrificial smoke that rose upward from the inner court. There was a still silence in the gracious colonnades of the outer Court of the People and a bustling activity in the vast Court of the Gentiles. Here, in an area that covered nearly half the mount, the moneychangers stretched out their grasping fingers that often supported their easy gains in the form of large rings, to trade the coins of Caesar for Temple shekels. The people had to use traditional shekels to buy sacrificial animals—the doves, geese, goats and lambs that were lined up in cages of assorted sizes. Their religion dictated it. The color, sounds, and throng of eager purchasers, hopeful beggars, and swift moving Levites and priests, intermingled with the gaggling geese, cooing doves and bleating lambs. A veritable menagerie lay within these walls.

During the three pilgrim festivals of Passover, Shabuot, and Succot, Jews from all corners of the kingdom crowded into Jerusalem and the Temple precincts, along with pilgrims from the far reaches of the hot deserts. They made their way through the hills with their children and donkeys, singing, laughing and sometimes in despair. Yom Kippur, the Day of Atonement, was the most sacred day. This was the one occasion each year when the High Priest entered the inner sanctuary of the Holy of Holies where the sacred tablets were kept in the Ark of the Covenant. This was the day the Temple virgins led the High Priest's procession out to the side gate where the Azazel goat was released. Within the Temple, this was a very solemn time, but in a matter of days the solemnity would give way to the free spirit of the feast of Succot, the ancient festival of Booths. The pilgrims would camp all over the hillsides surrounding Jerusalem, sleeping in bowers built with simple sticks and roofed with vines and palm fronds. The significance of the feast was to mark the covenant made in the wilderness thirteen hundred years earlier when the children of Israel fled Egypt under Moses's leadership. But over the centuries, the festival had fused with a harvest thanksgiving—an annual celebration in gratitude for the good gifts of the earth. The booths were built to remind the pilgrims of their ancestors' temporary desert dwellings during the days of wanderings after leaving Egypt. At this festival time of the year, the easy access to fresh grapes, new wine and the fruits of the harvest, and the released joy after Yom Kippur fasting, turned the encampments around Jerusalem bacchanalian. Succot, the most popular of the three great pilgrim festivals, brought Joachim on his next and vital visit to Jerusalem.

CHAPTER THREE

Zechariah and the House of the Virgins

.

Joachim spent the summer in intellectual fervor. At a discussion with Benjamin Levi and the Synagogue group, on a balmy evening under the old olive trees of his home, Joachim declared his vision of the Messianic Age. He had become ever more convinced that the Scriptures indicated the time of Israel's glory was fast approaching.

"It was prophesied by Isaiah," he said. "I believe that out of the present chaos, a leader will arise who will herald the Eternal Age. One raised up by God to be our spiritual leader—a new Moses. The signs all point in that direction."

Benjamin raised an eyebrow.

"What do you mean?"

"The Roman protectorship is mild. It hasn't removed the right of kingship in Israel. I'm convinced the Herodians represent the last of the troubled times and that the legitimate house of David will soon take their place. The appointed Messiah of the Lord will rule instead of the Herodians."

"But only as a puppet king."

"Rome will give our kingdom the prosperity of peace, but our kingdom will reunite tradition, the Law and the Temple. It could be the dawning of a golden age for our people."

"But there are powerful men in Jerusalem who support the Herodians."

"The Scriptures are on our side, Benjamin. We must pray. The High Priest is my wife's brother-in law, he will have an interpretation of the times. I need to feel him out. I need to go to Jerusalem and get a sense of current thinking at the Temple. The Temple must offer a better way to secure our future than making sporadic raids on Roman soldiers in the hills of Galilee."

"I thought you'd left all that behind, Joachim. You wouldn't think of leaving Nazareth? You're so well established here now."

Joachim looked across the valley toward Mount Tabor.

"How could I leave this?" he assured his friend. "I've been blessed."

"We've both been blessed."

"But I do feel I need to follow this through. It's as if God is telling me to go to Jerusalem. When I pray, I get this feeling that God is truly answering me. I see it in the stars, in the moon—God telling me I must go to Jerusalem. Have you noticed how bright the stars are these days? I've unfinished business in Jerusalem."

"It's your daughter, isn't it?" Benjamin said.

Joachim smiled.

"You're not supposed to discuss that, Levi."

But Joachim believed that Miriam was somehow a part of this. *What is Zechariah planning for her in these exciting and treacherous times?* he wondered.

Zechariah, the High Priest, a tall and heavy-set man, was married to Joachim's wife Anna's younger sister, Elizabeth. Joachim wrote a letter that he had sent to Jerusalem with a passing caravan. He asked if he and Anna could visit with Zechariah and Elizabeth at Ain Karim, the High Priest's home west of Jerusalem. There, they could celebrate the High Holy days together. Within a month, Zechariah confirmed his request.

'It has been too long, Joachim. We have many things to share. These are exciting and treacherous times,' he wrote.

Joachim reflected on the choice of words, which echoed his own. Was that, too, some small sign?

* * *

Ahab the zealot's summer had brought frustration and setback. His hopes of swift revenge for the deaths of Jonathon, Mosheh, and Matthew had been dashed. Two brigand attacks on detachments of soldiers moving from Sepphoris on the road to the north had failed. In the second attack, Ahab had encouraged Samuel, despite his youth, to join the ambush party. As a result, Samuel had been killed.

Samuel's death hit the village hard, and support for the zealots became thin. Locally, the movement flagged. Without Joachim's support, its veneer of respectability was lost. Meetings at Ahab's house ended; the single oil lamp, witness to so much zealot spirit, was snuffed out. There were few who even spoke to the wizened old rebel. Many blamed him for Samuel's death. Besides, it had been a bountiful summer, and the village looked as if it would have one of the best harvests in years. Matters close to purse and heart gripped Nazareth more than forays against the Romans.

* * *

Joachim's vineyards looked promising. The grapes were swelling and turning in the warmth of high summer. Figs, grapes, and olives all exceeded previous years, for which each evening, in his accustomed place, Joachim gave his thanks to God. He didn't grow much grain, but Benjamin Levi's fields to the east looked full in the ear. Traders from Magdala and Capernaum had passed through Nazareth on their way to Caesarea, talking of the fine crops around Lake Gennesaret. God's bounty was everywhere.

Joachim considered this agricultural plentitude to be another symbol of the dawning Messianic Age.

"It's one of the signs," he said to Anna. "We should take some of our figs and pomegranates to your sister."

"I was going to," she said, looking up at her husband. "Perhaps Zechariah can take some to Miriam."

"Perhaps," was all Joachim would reveal.

This upcoming visit to Elizabeth and Zechariah combined Joachim's need to discuss the messianic dream with the Jerusalem priesthood. Could Miriam be a part of this? *Perhaps.*

* * *

37

Judith and Anna prepared for the journey.

"Do you think we might see Miriam?" Judith asked her mistress excitedly.

"I don't know. Zechariah is her guardian. But he should be making plans for her by now."

"My master is deeply excited about this journey, isn't he? I don't quite understand his thoughts and the way he talks to me sometimes, but I know he's excited. He showed me the stars the other night and told me they are brighter than usual, as if something important is about to happen."

"He's wiser than both of us," Anna said kindly. "A man of God."

"But I wish he would talk more of Miriam. I've missed not seeing her grow up."

"So have I."

* * *

Zechariah, dressed in a rich purple robe with silver phalacteries on his arm and forehead, stroked his curly beard as he left the council hall of the Sanhedrin. King Herod had built the great religious debating chamber within the Temple walls. Following the High Priest out was Simeon, his deputy and probable heir to the High Priest's crown. Older than Zechariah, Simeon seemed small beside the giant, but his snow-white hair gave him the appearance of wisdom.

"Shammai was in good form today," the High Priest said. "He's split the Pharisees right down the middle. He knows what a touchy subject this belief in life-after-death has come to be. Shammai and Hillel really liven up the discussion."

"Possibly those who hold a more conservative view will stay with the Greek philosophies of Hillel," Simeon cautioned, "although quite a few among the Pharisees don't like the creeping influences of Greek thought. Personally, I think Hillel goes a bit too far myself. He'd like to see us use the Greek Scriptures here in the Temple!"

"Well, many more would understand the Scriptures that way. Let's face it, he has a good point. We're the only center in Israel still teaching strictly from the Hebrew Torah. Even here, the Shammai liberals keep adding Aramaic interpolations from the Prophets and other sacred writings they find in the Greek version of our Scriptures. Then, there are so many ideas that our people brought back from exile in Babylon and Persia. That's where all this life-after-death business started. The pure Torah's hard to find now with all these interpolations."

A young priest in fine robes acknowledged them, touching his forehead in salutation as he walked past.

"Isn't that Gabriel?" Zechariah asked.

"Yes. He seems a bright one. I've often seen him at the debates."

"Good looking, too."

"Very good family," Simeon acknowledged. "But, what about the work at Qumran? They're trying to preserve the pure Torah there."

"Yes, but with a lot of embellishments. They're preserving the language at Qumran. Many of the conservatives support the excellent work being done there. Some of our best scribes are now at Qumran, including my two sons from my first marriage. I don't hear much from them, but what little I do leads me to believe that there's a strong pharisaic influence in the translation of the Sacred Books. I also think zealot passion runs rampant amongst the Essenes. They're a bit extreme down there."

"But our Scriptures are safe at Qumran," Simeon noted. "If there's ever an invasion from the east, or the Romans destroy Jerusalem and the Temple, we know that our sacred Scriptures will be preserved."

Zechariah looked down at Simeon.

"Why are you so fearful of the Romans? The Romans have a liberal policy toward religious practice. They tax us, but so long as we pay tribute to Caesar and acknowledge them with a few outward gestures, like the eagle spread over the Triple Gate, the Romans leave our religion alone. Real problems with the Romans will only come if we break our alliance and try to set up an independent religious state. It's not our religious beliefs that bother the Romans; it's our national aspirations they fear."

Simeon gestured with his hands, trying to shape his words.

"How do you reconcile that with your belief in a Davidic messiah?" he asked. "The Romans will hardly accept a Jewish king. They have such close ties with the Herodians."

"The Messiah will be different," the High Priest answered.

They heard a commotion as they entered the Court of the Gentiles.

"Robbers!" a man shouted.

Zechariah looked over at the moneychangers' stalls.

A man was raising his fists in rage.

"I know what my coins are worth! You've short-changed me, you bastard!" the man shouted.

Penned lambs started bleating.

"Shall we see what that's about?" Simeon asked.

"They'll sort it out," Zechariah said, looking down at the ground in deep thought. "National aspirations are not what it is all about. That's where we've always gone wrong. The Messiah will be far more than a king or leader of a triumphant army. After David and Solomon, the kingdom was split because our kings became warriors. Later, the Hasmoneans were nationalists first and religious leaders second. I believe that the Messiah, who will sit on David's throne, will be a rallying point for the identity of our people throughout the Empire. He'll be the perfect example of everything a good Jew should be and more. He'll be the annointed one, chosen by God. He'll speak with the authority of God Himself."

"But what about us? Aren't we God's representatives for our people?"

A flock of pigeons, disturbed by their approach, flurried into the air. They wheeled around the courtyard and settled elsewhere, awaiting scraps from pilgrims.

"I don't see him as a warrior priest like Judas Maccabee," Zechariah continued. "He'll come from a priestly family, of course. But we'll still be the spiritual leaders, the guardians of our tradition. The Messiah should have a mystery about him above our duties. He'll be above the squabbling of the Sanhedrin. He'll sit on David's throne and give legitimacy once more to all that is best in our people."

The High Priest looked at Simeon with a sparkle in his eyes.

"Our people will accept a king from the house of David even under the political umbrella of Rome. It's tradition, Simeon! Tradition counts for so much in the lives of our people. But his role—it has got to be more than tradition. It has to embrace the essence of Jewish faith throughout the world. Remember, Simeon, there are more Jews today in the cities of the world than here in Judea. They say there are a vast number of Jews in Alexandria who live quite differently from us. Their synagogue is said to be almost as big as The Temple. The Messiah must be a symbol for us all."

A young boy passed by the two High Priests and stared at Zechariah in his fine robes. Zechariah watched as the child then walked toward the melee of pilgrims making deals with the moneychangers.

"Did you see the way that boy stared at me? It's one thing that still deeply bothers me."

"What?"

"Children. You know how it is round here. Elizabeth and I have been married fourteen years now, and we are still without a child. There are those among the conservative Sadducees who might use that against me. They see Elizabeth's failure to conceive as a sign from God that I should give up the High Priesthood and retire quietly to my vineyards at Ain Karim. You remember my wife's brother-in-law, Joachim, and what they did to him?"

"That was different, Zechariah. Joachim had no sons. You do."

"Yes, but not from my marriage to Elizabeth. My sons were Hannah's children. The sisters Elizabeth and Anna seem to be barren."

"Anna eventually had a child. Maybe Elizabeth will, too."

"You mean Anna's daughter, Miriam?" Zechariah said with a faraway look.

"Yes. But forgive me for asking, do you think the Messiah could actually be God? I mean if you rank him above the priesthood, above the diaspora of scattered Jews—a unifying force for Judaism throughout the world—could not God Himself be born among us? Such authority can only come from God."

Zechariah stood still. He looked around him.

"All things are possible," he said slowly.

The well-dressed young priest was walking toward them once more on his way to the Inner Court.

"There's Gabriel again," Zechariah noted. "Miriam is on my conscience these days," he continued as the priest passed by. "She's one of the oldest at the House of the Virgins. She wants to stay there forever, but I must find a spouse for her future. For Joachim's sake I have to make a good match for her."

Both men turned to look back at the young man simultaneously.

Simeon nodded his head.

"He may be your man, Zechariah. He's good-looking, fairly wealthy, and a Davidic priest."

"Gabriel," Zechariah repeated slowly, putting his arm around old Simeon's shoulders.

"Gabriel, the son of Melchizadok," Simeon said. "A very good family, but not ambitious. His late father was a close friend of mine in his earlier days."

"I shall think about it."

Gabriel disappeared into the mass of people crowding the Court of the Gentiles.

"I think I've had enough of the Sanhedrin for today," Zechariah said, returning to business. "The debates get more and more heated and I'm almost afraid to go back in. One day, they're going to ask my opinion on this life-after-death matter, and I don't really know how I'll answer them. It's sad to see so much division. That's why we need a Divine focal point—a Davidic messiah. We'll rally around him and defend our faith."

Simeon hesitated.

"I wonder if he will believe in life after death."

* * *

Shortly before Joachim and his entourage were due to arrive at Ain Karim, Elizabeth lay with Zechariah.

"You'll never believe this, Zach, but I think I'm going to have a baby," she announced.

Zechariah stared.

"I mean it."

"You really think so, Elizabeth? At our age, a child would be a miracle, like what happened with your sister Anna. Why, you're even older than Anna was when she became pregnant."

Elizabeth kissed him.

"You're the High Priest, my husband. You should believe in miracles. I've prayed for this day for so long. This child will be proof of our long-standing love and our faith in God."

Zechariah held Elizabeth close to him. His eyes were wet with tears.

"If this is true, this will be God's baby. We'll dedicate this child to God."

Elizabeth pulled from him.

"Don't take our child away, Zach. If our child's a girl, please don't send her to the House of the Virgins like Anna did. Promise me, Zach, you won't send her away."

Zechariah considered her plea. He touched her cheek as he looked into her eyes.

"Don't be afraid, dearest. I won't deprive you of motherhood."

They lay together silently for some time. Although happy with the news, Zechariah felt fearful. His first wife Hannah had died in childbirth. After fourteen happy years with Elizabeth he didn't want to lose her, too.

"Joachim and Anna will be traveling south any time now," he said at length. "Maybe we should keep this a secret. I don't think you should tell them you're going to have a baby."

"Whatever you wish," Elizabeth answered.

Joachim turned and held her. Soon, they fell asleep in each other's warmth.

* * *

At their best, Joachim's mules moved slowly, but they were able to carry a lot in their panniers. After a journey of four days, Joachim and his footsore party finally approached Ain Karim in the late afternoon.

"Is that the village?" Judith asked wearily, her leathery face marked by fatigue.

"I think so," Anna said.

This wealthy community of patrician families, many of whom, like the High Priest, spent much of the year in Jerusalem, had spacious and well-planned houses. They were similar in style to Joachim's home in Nazareth. The village lay on the outskirts of the Judean wine country where vineyards spilled down the valleys to the coastal plain. Joachim compared the bloom of these Judean grapes with his Galilean fruit. The Judean grapes looked fuller, as if they'd make better wine. Nonetheless, the Galilean harvest had been bountiful. The whole land was feverish with harvest. On the journey, they had witnessed peasants working long and hard to get the bounty gathered in time for the feast of Booths.

Joachim halted the mules at the threshing floor beside the grinding mill on the outskirts of the village. Golden autumnal light swept over the rugged hills from the west. He hugged Anna.

"Well, here we are. Well done. You see, we made the journey."

"Do you remember which is Zechariah's house?" Anna asked.

"Yes. It's at the far end of the village."

* * *

Before Joachim and Anna reached Zechariah's place, village gossips spread the word.

"They're coming!" they shouted through Zechariah's gate. "We've seen them. They must be your relatives from the north. They have mules and look like they've been traveling for days."

Elizabeth and Zechariah were waiting to greet their guests by the time Joachim and his party reached their gate. Elizabeth embraced her older sister. Zechariah held up his arms and gave his traditional Hebrew blessing. When they had all gathered in the courtyard, servants led the mules away to the back. In no time, Elizabeth was preparing them an evening meal.

Reclining on couches, Roman style, they were all anxious to talk. In only one or two days the Yom Kippur fast would begin. Time was of the essence. Joachim was anxious to discuss matters with Zechariah before the High Priest left for Jerusalem to conduct the solemn ceremonies at the Temple.

The two sisters, Elizabeth and Anna, hadn't seen each other for a long time and talked much of the old days when Joachim and Anna had lived in Bethlehem. And, when Joachim and Zechariah became deep in conversation and oblivious to the women's domestic chatter, Elizabeth brought up the subject of Miriam.

"Don't you ever regret the vow you made dedicating Miriam to the Temple?"

"Sadly, Elizabeth, you've never had a child of your own," Anna said. "You'll never know the pain of being separated from that close bond that only a mother can know."

Joachim overheard her. He looked up. Their conversation stopped.

Elizabeth glanced at Zechariah with a knowing look.

"I don't normally discuss this matter with you, do I dear?" Anna said.

Joachim picked some grapes from one of the large succulent bunches.

"Discuss what?"

"Miriam, my dear."

"No. Nor should we now."

"But why not? Miriam's no longer a child, she's fourteen!" Anna protested.

She looked across at Zechariah with pleading in her eyes.

"Zechariah, we know Miriam's your charge. That's the sacrifice we made, but can you reveal just a little? Is she pretty? Surely you can tell us something about the child we dedicated to God? She must be about ready for marriage. Have you any plans for her? She's old enough to leave the House of the Virgins."

Every time that Judith had questioned Anna on the subject of Miriam, Anna had longed to know the answers. In his daily evening prayers, Joachim looked for answers, too. Now, both of them were reclining at this table with the one man who could answer their heartfelt questions.

The High Priests were never supposed to reveal their plans for the Temple virgins. The virgins resided on the grounds of the Temple as a symbol of purity for the whole Jewish people. They were entrusted to God throughout their childhood and remained innocent and chaste. They performed certain duties on High Holy days that symbolized the supreme sacrifices their families had made by dedicating their daughters to God.

Never more than two Temple virgins were accepted by the High Priest in any given year. Since most were received between the ages of four to six, there were usually between fifteen and twenty such virgins in residence. They were schooled in piety and the sacred Scriptures. They ate only sacrificial meat and sundry produce brought to them by the Levitical eunuchs—food that had already been dedicated to God by Temple pilgrims as part of their purification. Likewise, their bread was made only from the grain stored in the Temple granaries filled from the people's tithes. The Levitical eunuchs, being emasculated men, were the only ones normally allowed within the House of the Virgins. They acted as go-betweens from the Temple to the matron of the virgins. The virgins were always dressed in white. They spent most of each day playing and praying in the house dedicated to them in the corner of the Court of the Gentiles. The only entrance to their home was from the sacred Inner Court.

All the rooms of their house faced out on a central courtyard where there was a beautiful garden. A fountain played in its midst. Olive trees grew, giving shade to the ground. Beautiful arbors of flowering vines in purple, white, and shades of pink twisted their way up the pillars and architrave of the portico. Compared with the bustle of the Court of the Gentiles outside, the House of the Virgins was a place of heavenly peace. But there were branches in the trees that invited the virgins to hide as they played children's games. Naturally, from time to time the virgins squealed as the older girls carried the younger ones around. Disciplinary action from the matron wasn't unknown, but for the most part the virgins were awed by the serenity of their home and its nearness to God.

The virgins lived in four or five spacious rooms around this courtyard. In keeping with the idea of their purity and way of life, their rooms were very simply furnished. The younger children were well cared for by the matron, who was often assisted by the older girls who performed certain domestic duties. Water was brought in to the virgins for bathing. When they weren't studying or playing, the virgins learned to spin and weave at wheels and looms around the portico. The older girls wove many of the Temple vestments, and it was considered to be a special honor to spin the purple wool. They learned how to dye the sacred colors, and those secret recipes were closely guarded.

On high festivals and Holy Days, dressed in white ceremonial robes and golden headdresses, the Temple virgins paraded with the priests who took the sacrificial items to the altar. A Levite carrying an incense burner walked before them, and another followed behind. On either side of the procession of virgins, also dressed in white, the Levitical musicians played on their lyre-like kinnors.

The virgins were called to worship by the deep notes of a large water organ—the magrepah—standing between the porch of the Inner Court and the Altar of Sacrifice. At the sound of the magrepah, the procession of virgins and accompanying musicians made their way to the center of the priestly Inner Court, facing the gathered crowd in the lower court, known as the Court of the Jews.

The Levites chanted psalms to the rhythmic sounds of frame drums, cymbals, timbrels, clappers, rattles, and other instruments. Around the sacrificial altar, trumpeters played chatzotzerah, which were peculiar to Temple worship. Other musicians played double reed pipes known as chalils, which were also commonly found in Roman temple music. This musical pageant was an expression of the Sadducean fusing of Hellenist ideas, and designed to protect their vested interest in the Temple and its lucrative income.

The virgins had not been a feature of Solomon's Temple but had developed out of Hellenist ideas as a symbol of purity. The trumpeters were more traditional, and heralded the arrival of the High Priests on the High Holy days and of the priests-in-residence on other festivals.

Each year, every Temple priest served a term taking charge of the Sanctuary area and its worship. Daily sacrifices of thanksgiving were offered by the Levitical priests, who kept the fires going at the great altar as a permanent reminder to all Jerusalem of the Temple presence in the city's midst. Ritual and ceremony had never been more glamorous than now in the magnificent new surroundings of King Herod's Temple.

As High Priest, Zechariah was responsible for this whole Temple organization. Now, as they reclined on couches in his home, he thought about how he would answer Anna's heartfelt questions. He knew more than anyone did, the status of Temple affairs. However, when challenged by his wife and sister-in-law on the subject of Miriam and the House of the Virgins, he didn't want to reveal too much. Miriam was no ordinary Temple virgin, and she posed a problem.

"Miriam's been a model virgin," Zechariah answered after reflection, easing his big frame on the cushions. "Her piety exceeds that of all the other virgins. I feel sure she's destined for a very special future in a priestly household."

Anna remained persistent.

"Have you plans for her betrothal?"

"Miriam shows no desire to be betrothed at present. She says that she's betrothed to God."

"But she can't stay at the House of the Virgins much longer. Tell me, Zach...I'm her mother. She must have reached puberty by now."

Zechariah tried to smile as he stroked his beard.

"I've considered it, but she doesn't want to leave. She may well have to come here and live with us until I can arrange her betrothal."

He took Anna's hand in his.

"Miriam's different from the others," he said. "She's very lovely, but she's shown little interest in betrothal plans. Her contemporaries are anxious to leave and be married, but not Miriam. We've made arrangements for the others, but Miriam always rejects my proposals. She seems to feel she has a more personal relationship with God and speaks of messages from God's angels."

"Messages from God—visions—these are signs of the times," Joachim said excitedly.

Zechariah turned toward him.

"Yes, I suppose they could be. But Miriam has a very lucid, and at times disturbing, imagination. Sometimes, she says angels feed her, and she spends long hours on her own talking out loud to God in intimate personal prayer. Let it suffice for me to say that Miriam glows with a unique spirituality, and whomever we choose for her has to be a very special spouse."

Zechariah let go of Anna's hand and stared blankly for a moment.

Joachim's stomach surged with excitement. *Miriam is part of God's purpose. I knew it*, he thought.

The High Priest faced his guests again.

"Joachim, leave it to me. I have some ideas. Now, tell me about your journey."

* * *

A full moon climbed upward in the night sky over Jerusalem. In the courtyard of the House of the Virgins, shafts of yellow moonbeams, separated by the branches of the olives in the courtyard, illuminated the ground of the sacred garden. It was moments such as this that captivated Miriam. The moon held a sweet mystery for her. She'd steal away from the other virgins after they'd settled down to sleep, and stand for hours, staring at the pale orb as it made its slow passage over the open courtyard. She believed that the moonlight provided ladders upon which the angels of God descended and ascended to bring her messages. This was how Jacob had communicated with God so long ago. Angels had descended to him down a ladder of light and ascended back to God.

Miriam walked out into the moonlight on this eve of the Atonement prior to the High Holy Day of Yom Kippur.

Here are my angels, she thought, as she stood bathed in a shaft of light that led up through the dancing leaves of the trees.

The moonbeams played on her young face, reflecting in the luster of her tresses of chestnut hair and casting a lemon-blue sheen on the simple white shift she wore. The light exaggerated her young breasts. The moon caught the serenity of her smile. The beams flickered.

They're coming down to me, tumbling down from heaven.

She tried to catch them in her slender hands. She listened in the night silence.

I can hear them chattering.

"Gabriel! Is that you?" she shouted in her clear, innocent young voice.

The leaves rustled.

"Yes, I'm here," her favorite angel spoke, as only she could hear.

Miriam felt a surge of spiritual power, as in the gentle sounds of the parting leaves she heard Gabriel speak.

"Miriam! You're a chosen child. God has selected you for a purpose, to be His messenger. You must listen so you can convey God's messages to the world."

Miriam stood in the moonlight frozen in silence.

The High Holy Day of Yom Kippur is a time when the people of God renew their purity, she thought. *The High Priest, acting on behalf of all the Jewish people, removes our sins in the ceremony of the Azazel goat. In the morning, I'll be part of these ceremonies. This year, I'll lead the procession. We'll take the living goat to the gateway and let it out.*

She looked down at her bare feet, dirty but demure.

My friends Jude and Rebekkah will be witnessing this for the last time before becoming betrothed. They'll be going away. But I don't want to be married. I'd rather stay here. What if I don't like the man the High Priest chooses for me?

She sighed.

"Maybe, Gabriel, he won't understand my angels."

She looked up again at the leaves and the shafts of pale light.

"Maybe when I'm married, you'll leave me, too."

She held out her hands to catch the moonbeams.

I want to remain as I am, in constant touch with the pure light of God. I don't want to lose my closeness to God just to become a wife and mother.

She stood bathed in moonlight, an aura of purity and perfection and mystery.

Jude and Rebekkah don't have this special relationship with God's angels.

They want to leave the House of the Virgins and get married to strangers, but God means me to remain with Him, pure and undefiled. My angels tell me so. But what of Gabriel's words—a messenger! Am I truly to convey God's messages to the world? And in what way can I be a messenger?

Miriam felt she could hear her angels again in the rustling of the olive leaves.

"Miriam! You're God's chosen! You're betrothed to God," they seemed to say. "This very shaft of light that bathes you now ties you directly to God. He's anointed you in the moonlight. You're His messenger. Through you and this light, all men will know God. The moonbeams that hit you now will radiate from you to touch all people."

Miriam looked up at the moon through a haze of gladdened tears. Through their crystal shimmer she observed its pulsating round edges.

"My God!" she said. "I know You've chosen me and You've sent Gabriel and his angels to me. I can feel Your power. Creator of all the stars, use me, as You will. I'm Yours. I'm one with You forever. Let it not be my will, but only what You want for me."

Miriam had no idea how God might use her. Perhaps she'd be allowed to remain at the Temple's House of the Virgins. As Miriam stood in the shaft of moonlight, she only knew that God was with her and that His angels were administering unto her. The breeze moved the trees above. Miriam saw the light carry her angels back up to God.

* * *

On the Day of Atonement, the Herodian court trumpeters announced the arrival of King Herod and his entourage as they reached the gate of the Outer Court for his annual visit to the Temple. King Herod was now nearly sixty years old. He still had a powerful physique and a cunning look. He was the perfect mesh of Semitic craft and Roman polish. He lived and ate Roman style while in his palace in Jerusalem, but when he went on campaign with his well-treated army, he camped in the nomadic style of his ancestors. He wore his hair in their style and vainly dyed it black to conceal his years. These long ringlets of thick black hair were held in place by a jewel-studded gold band that was his crown. For the Temple ceremony, he was dressed as a Semite, wearing a flowing red outer robe lined in green that covered his golden tunic. Although there was much for which the once-vigorous king should atone in his personal life, he was still popular with the ordinary people.

The views of Joachim and Zechariah were not well established amongst the merchants and artisans, who, if nothing else, thanked Herod for a period of considerable prosperity. Business had been good. The many farmers, who had descended on Jerusalem and the surrounding hills to celebrate the festival of Succot, were in a jubilant mood. Merchants and farmers thrived in their little kingdom under the shadow of Rome.

This shadow of Rome, however, was a cause of deep concern at the Temple. The magnificence of King Herod's facade was becoming dwarfed by a fortress, now half built, on the northwest corner of Mount Moriah. This building, close to the House of the Virgins, was to become home to Roman cohorts and was already referred to as the Tower of Antonia. From the tower, the Romans would be able to look into the courts of the Temple and even into the innermost court surrounding the Holy of Holies—all with the blessing of the King of the Jews—Herod.

The King's procession ended with another fanfare as Herod and his entourage mounted the royal dais set up in the center of the Outer Court. It faced the wide steps that led into the Inner Court. The King didn't abuse Temple customs. Only the priests, Levites, and Temple virgins had access to the Inner Court. This was as far as the King could go. From his vantagepoint seated on the dais, King Herod could see all the way up into the Sanctuary, past the two bronze Phoenician-style pillars known as Jachin and Boaz. The Sanctuary building was where the High Priest would intercede with God on behalf of the people. To the right, Herod could see the great water organ set up to announce the beginning of this holiest of Holy Days.

The real observance of Yom Kippur had begun for most Jews on the previous day with a fast in preparation for the forgiveness of sins. The strict holy households had officially observed the complete fast. King Herod and his Court, on the other hand, were not so devout. They had ceremonially fasted, but this hadn't stopped the King from enjoying a little fruit as he'd discussed the fate of his two ungrateful sons with some of his Roman friends.

Alexander and Aristobulus, Herod's only remaining family members carrying Hasmonean blood, were in captivity in Sebaste. He was considering having them put to death.

King Herod had observed the same full moon as Miriam did the night before. It had bathed his palace gardens in its luminous light, catching his olive trees in silver beams. It had reassured him. The kingdom was secure, or certainly would be as soon as he had executed Alexander and Aristobulus! He decided to make a new will. He'd leave the kingdom to his eldest son, Prince Antipater—son of Doris the Idumean. This would banish the Hasmonean threat forever. In the event of Antipater's death, he'd leave the kingdom to Herod-Philip, the son of yet another of his Jewish wives. The kingdom was prosperous. Rebellion was now limited to a few anti-Roman rabble-rousers in northern Galilee. Most important of all, Herod himself was once again secure in his favor with the Emperor—his liege and personal friend, Augustus Caesar. Loss of Imperial favor had been a serious threat to his ambitions, but now that favor had been restored, Herod felt his power.

I created the mighty ring of fortresses now surrounding Jerusalem, he thought as he waited in the sun.

He signaled for his servants to fan the air with palms as sweat formed on his brow.

These fortresses protect the kingdom from any possible Parthian attack or from threats by my annoying siblings in Nabatea to the southwest. Within the heart of this kingdom I've built Sebaste, making it the principal city of Samaria. In Galilee, I've created the garrison city of Sepphoris. The Romans should thank me for what I've done. Look! I've transformed this city of Jerusalem.

Herod reflected on Jerusalem and his present surroundings as he waited for the ceremony to begin.

This Temple's regarded by many to be one of the finest buildings in the whole Empire—A worthy tribute to my name. Then there are the theaters, gymnasiums, and baths. I've created civilization in this backward land. Would the Hasmoneans have built the gladiatorial schools or encouraged the good order of Roman settlement? No, never!

The King smiled with pride, looking around at the vast crowd now jockeying for place behind him.

My devotion to providing my people with sports activities and endowing this land with the glories of ancient Greece has won me respect in the Graeco-Roman world. It wasn't for naught that they made me President of the Olympic Games four years ago.

He mopped his brow, ever conscious that the black dye in his hair might run with the sweat.

My greatest challenge was the harbor at Caesarea. Nobody believed I could turn the shifting sand dunes of the Judean coast into one of the finest harbors on the Great Sea. Look what prosperity that port has given to my land and to the Roman world.

Caesarea was, indeed, Herod's crowning glory. The King had constructed, at enormous cost, a magnificent harbor on an impossible site. The traditional ports of Alexandria in Egypt and the Syrian ports of Tyre, Sidon, and Antioch had been the caravan terminals for the lucrative trade from the east. The Seleucid rulers in Syria and the Ptolomies of Egypt had grown fat on this passing commerce. Herod was well aware of the fortunes to be made in the field of trade. His own personal fortune had in part come through his mother's family in Nabatean Petra. This rose-colored rock city was an important oasis on the southern trade route from Arabia to Egypt. It was essential for all caravans to stop and water at that hollow in the desert. Nabatean treasury buildings in Petra, carved straight out of the unusual pink rock, were stocked with tribute taken from the merchants passing through. Why, even some of the jewel-encrusted vessels that Herod used at his own table had recently been extracted as booty from the Petra treasures when, two years ago, he had been forced to send his army down to help quell a Nabatean revolt, even though they were his kin.

When will these desert kingdoms realize that the alliance with Rome is their greatest security? Herod thought. *I dedicated Caesarea to the Emperor. I created a lucrative trade route for my own kingdom.*

Cleverly built halfway between the ports of Egypt and Syria, Caesarea Maritima, Herod was confident, would cause the diversion of considerable trade through his realm. The tariffs, pay-offs, and port taxes would be of enormous benefit to his country and his personal coffers. But the coast of Philistia, where Judea met the sea, was shallow, with drifting sands and no natural harbor. Great dunes ran down the coast intermittently with areas of swamp. Herod's conception and determination had been well tested. But he'd triumphed! He'd built at Caesarea the most magnificent harbor in all the Levant. He was justifiably proud of his achievement and of the benefits his scheme was already bringing to himself and to his country.

Half-Roman, half-Jew, Semitic by blood and Roman in culture, this undisputed despot sat firmly on the usurped throne of David. Now, here in the Temple, still honoring the site chosen by the shepherd king, Herod sat on his dais as the great magrepah sounded its deep notes marking the beginning of the Yom Kippur morning ceremonies.

CHAPTER FOUR

The Succot plot

The hillsides around Jerusalem were already crowded with farmers in a festive mood. To most of them, the solemn ceremonies in the Temple weren't the real reason for making their journeys to Jerusalem. Yom Kippur would only become significant to them when the High Priest opened the gate in the eastern wall and let the Azazel goat out. Those gathered on the hillside would then shoo this beast away in a mood of gaiety. Only a few would reflect on the symbolism of the custom. In shooing away the goat, they were throwing away their sins as the scapegoat took their burdens out into the wilderness. For most of them, the sight of the goat symbolized the end of the solemn day of Yom Kippur and the start of the happy festival of Succot.

Coming after the grape harvest, Succot was one of the merriest times of the year. The people celebrated the boon of their harvest, drinking their new wine. Already, long before Yom Kippur, little groups from all over Israel, and some from farther lands, were busy building natural booths of sticks, vines, and palm fronds that would become their dwellings for the festival days ahead.

* * *

In the House of the Virgins, Miriam was now the oldest among the High Priest's charges. The little ones looked up to her with awe and reverence. Her budding breasts, doe-like eyes, and slender fingers gave her the appearance of a young woman. Inevitably, she took on certain responsibilities. For Yom Kippur she was in charge of the procession and saw that all the virgins put on their best sun-bleached robes. She dressed their hair and made sure they washed their feet. When ready, she assembled them at the gate, where they waited for the sign that the procession could begin.

The Levites carried lyre-like kinnors and joined the virgins. Below, in the Outer Court, the huge crowds pressed behind King Herod and his entourage. The smoke of the High Altar twisted upward into the clear sky on this perfect autumnal day.

Miriam watched the pall of white smoke and imagined her future. A turtle dove caught her attention. It circled above the court to rest in the eaves of the Sanctuary. Then, a late season butterfly with yellow-striped wings and subtle streaks of red and green alighted on the tresses of her chestnut hair.

"Such pretty colors," remarked one of the younger virgins holding Miriam's hand.

"Can you see those delicate wings?" Miriam said. "They're the wings of an angel, a messenger from God."

The young girl frowned incredulously.

The long, low notes of the great water organ echoed from the walls of the Temple Court. Miriam checked to see that the virgins were in pairs. She smiled at them and squeezed the little hand holding hers. The Levites started to pluck their kinnors, and they began the procession.

They moved past the gate of Sacrifice, which was close to a huge ritual bronze dish. Ahead was the altar, and beyond stood Zechariah. The High Priest towered above them in his splendid robes and high crown. One of the Chief Priests held two tethered goats beside the High Priest. The Levitical choir was already lined up, chanting to the sounds of the Temple music. As the virgins approached, the trumpeters heralded their arrival with a blast from their chatzozerim. The noise was deafening.

Miriam and the virgins stopped in front of Zechariah.

Below, in the Court of the Jews, the King now sat on his dais.

The throngs of atonement pilgrims looked up at them—a sea of dark-haired humanity held back by Herodian soldiers.

This view of the masses from the restricted area of the Sanctuary Court was the closest the virgins ever came to knowing the great world outside. Miriam looked on the crowd with a certain hesitation and fear as she wondered what the High Priest might be planning for her. But then she felt God's presence enfolding her, and the fear left her.

In ceremonial fashion, Zechariah turned, took the great knife from the Chief Priest, and thrust it into the soft lower throat of the first goat, the cacophony of musical sounds drowning the beast's cries.

Miriam shivered as the fresh blood covered the blade and drenched the High Priest's hands.

Four priests held the goat. The two Chief Priests then continued with the disembowelment of the beast as Zechariah walked up the steps to the Sanctuary building to wash off the blood in a ceremonial bowl. After his ablutions, Zechariah placed incense on the great menorah that guarded the entrance to the Holy of Holies and on the six burners that lined the dark walls inside. He unleashed the long golden cord that wound around his waist and slowly parted the heavy dust-ridden drapes that concealed the sacred inner chamber. As he entered, the gold cord unraveled, leading the way back into the outer room as the veil of the Temple closed. He now stood alone in the dwelling place of God.

There was little that Zechariah could see or feel in this intimate presence. *Most people would be very surprised if they were to ever really know what's here,* he thought. *It's dank and dirty.* Zechariah stood in the dim light and looked at the Cherubim and Seraphim. *Those great gilded angels are flaking, and the wood of their spreading wings is rotting,* he observed. His eyes rested on the old wooden box that they guarded. *In King Solomon's day the Ark of the Covenant stood here,* he thought. *It contained the sacred tablets of Moses. Now, this box stands in its stead, housing mere copies of the Ten Commandments. Seeing the originals were lost in the exile to Babylon five hundred years ago, it's all really a hoax! This place isn't the dwelling place of God. Surely, such a dwelling can only be in one's heart. And yet, tradition says that only I can enter this place.*

Zechariah coughed, slightly ashamed of his feelings. The cough echoed in the eerie chamber. He could identify with Antiochus Epiphanes and the Roman commander, Pompeius. Upon entering this most holy of places, they had felt disappointed with what they found. They'd come in as conquerors, expecting to see gold, treasures, and riches, but they'd found nothing but this old box guarded by flaking wooden angels. The High Priest felt as if he should be greeted by the angel of the Lord, who would touch his lips with a burning coal, as the prophet Isaiah had described. Alas, there was no angel of the Lord. There was nothing except the musty smell of the Temple veil's decaying drapes and that same old wooden box with the gilded cherubim and seraphim standing guard. It was damp, and little light filtered in through the tattered veil. But there was just enough to see and smell the decay that was this Holy of Holies.

Thank goodness the virgins have nearly finished weaving the new Temple veil, Zechariah thought. *I fear that if I have to pull this one apart one more time the whole rotten drapery will come crashing down from its hooks.* In the silence, however, and in accordance with his bidden duty, the High Priest held out his hands in prayer and called on the Name of his God:

"Yahweh, God of Abraham, Isaac, and Jacob, leader of our people and the Lord of Moses, I, Zechariah of the tribe of Aaron, call on You at this solemn time to take away the guilt of our people and our many grievous sins. Restore us into oneness with You as we sacrifice the goat as a whole burnt offering on this day. We recall all our evil thoughts and mis-doings to You. In this act of sacrifice we ask for Your forgiveness of our sins and those of our fathers. In the name of all Israel, we seek Your forgiveness so that from this day forth we may have clean hearts, desiring to live only in Your service. We ask to be at one with You, O God, so that peace and prosperity will follow us all the days of our lives. We ask for Your guidance and leadership in all our doings. May we be an example to the world by the purity of our lives."

Zechariah looked up. Inevitably, the thought crossed his mind that he was talking to those four dusty carvings and the rather crude wooden box. *Tradition decrees that God lives in that box. I, Zechariah, am the only person privileged to enter God's house and only on this one occasion in the year. Praying to God on behalf of all the people of Israel seems no different here in the Holy of Holies than at home in my room.*

"Surely, the answer is not here," he whispered. "Surely, now is the time for the establishment of the rule of the Messiah. If there was a restored Davidic priest-king, perhaps God could be taken out of this dusty old room. The holiness of the whole kingdom could be influenced by the Messiah's example and rule. He'd be a symbol of our inner godliness."

Zechariah considered the King sitting in the Inner Court on the Royal dais. *Under the Herodians the Jewish religion and state have become separated. Why, Herod can't even enter the Sanctuary Court. It's forbidden by tradition and law. A Davidic messiah could be the High Priest of God as well as King. That's what the Hasmoneans tried to achieve, but they had the wrong kingship.*

The future must lie in the Royal house of David, as Isaiah and the prophets foretold. It would unite us again as the people of God. But how, in this world of the Herodians and their heirs, can the seed of David be established? The High Priest put his hand to his brow as his mind began to plot out his dream. *It must be through a scheme to nurture a Davidic heir secretly. The well-established Davidic Priestly families are known to the Herodians, so this seed will have to be carried by a relatively lesser family.* Zechariah's thoughts left that room of decay and rot, and settled on Miriam, ripe and pure, possessing a quintessential essence that was holy. He remembered Joachim leaning forward, his eyes bright at the thought of Miriam— 'messages from God, you mean visions?' Zechariah had dismissed them, but now he saw how perhaps the seed of a Davidic priestly family could be carried in her. *Her father is away from Jerusalem politics up in Galilee, not to be suspicious.* He stroked his beard as he looked at the dark images of the dank cherubim. *What about this Gabriel, the young priest that Simeon recommends? He should be ready to settle down. He's only superficially active in Temple affairs. He really doesn't have to know much about the Davidic plan. If Miriam conceives through his seed, a Davidic messiah could be born whom we could mould to our future needs. Gabriel's ineffectual. He's only on the fringe of the Temple hierarchy. The Herodians will never suspect such a union.*

The High Priest wound the ends of his beard around his fingers and smiled. He linked his thoughts on Miriam and the birth of a possible messiah with his own situation. *My wife is going to have my child, after all these barren years. What's the reason for this miracle? Surely, it must mean something at this stage in my long devoted life.*

Suddenly, there in the musty, dank room that only his high priestly predecessors and the barbarians Antiochus and Pompeius had seen, it dawned on Zechariah that Elizabeth's child really must be a sign from

God to tell him of something great that God wanted him to do. *Perhaps it's God's will that I should bring about the union that would conceive the future Messiah. Isaiah envisioned angels with hot coals flying from the place where the cherubim stand in this very chamber. That was God's sign to the prophet—Isaiah's close encounter with the Almighty.* With gathering confidence, Zechariah now felt he was in the presence of God, for the Lord had shown him a sign as well. His miracle child, too, would be a child of the Messianic Age, a forerunner of the Messiah of the house of David. *This is God's sign to me,* he thought.

Zechariah, intoxicated with insight, his blood pumping in excitement, shook himself, drawing back to the present and the crowd outside who were waiting for him. He stretched out his arms and prayed as he had never prayed before:

"Yahweh, O God and Father, I come into Your benign presence to lift my voice in penitent prayer. The Day of Atonement sends me a message from on high, calling me in love to return to You. May it be Your will, O Master of Israel, that I may hear and heed Your signs and Your voice? You have given me the understanding to distinguish between good and evil and have bestowed upon me freedom of will to choose between them. Often, I have disregarded Your signs and words and strayed from Your path. But, in Your mercy, O God, give me the means of turning from my evil ways and of coming back onto the path You want me to follow."

The High Priest paused, his face racked with strain, sweat beading his brow.

"Give me strength, O my God, to cast out the complacency and self-righteousness that have blinded my eyes and led me to my failings and misconduct," he continued. "Forgive my sins, O merciful Father! May I find tranquility for my troubled soul. Help me to look into my own heart and thus come to know myself and Your purpose for Your chosen ones. O God and Father of us all, hear my prayer and in Your mercy show me my destiny."

After his private petition, Zechariah moved on to the solemn prayers in Hebrew that gave atonement for the sins of all Israel. Meanwhile, the Levitical priests, to the sounds of trumpets, cymbals, and other rhythmic Temple music, cut up the carcass of the dead goat and prepared the sacrifice for the fire.

* * *

By now, the sun had risen higher. A bead or two of sweat masked Herod's proud face and he felt black dye oozing around his scalp.

"Faster! More air!" he shouted to the slaves waving their fanned palms.

There was no shade in the Court of the Jews, and the High Priest seemed to have been an unusually long time in the Sanctuary. *Zechariah might have been murdered or poisoned*, the King thought. *The High Priest has as many enemies as friends in the scheming rivalry of that volatile group.* In the Court circles in which Herod moved, internal politics were often resolved in such a way.

* * *

Finally, Zechariah emerged from the Sanctuary building and carefully rewound the golden cord about his waist. All was ready for the offering to God. In a loud voice, the High Priest called out from the Sanctuary steps:

"Hear, O Israel: The Lord our God, the Lord is one. Praised be His name whose glorious kingdom is forever."

Part High Priest, and part, calculating showman, Zechariah looked around the crowd in a dignified way and adjusted his heavy crown.

"Our God and God of our fathers, pardon our transgressions, remove our guilt and blot out our iniquities on this day of Atonement as You had promised: 'I, even I, blot out your iniquities for my own sake, and your sins I will remember no more.'"

At this point, the portions of the dissected goat were arranged on the smoldering altar, and an acrid fatty smoke moved upward into the clear autumnal air.

"God evaporates our sins like a cloud and our transgressions like a mist," continued the High Priest. "Return to God because He has redeemed us. For on this day, we shall be forgiven and cleansed from all our sins. Before the Lord, as manifest in these Temple virgins present before us, we shall all be pure."

As the greasy smoke rose upward, Zechariah took the other goat from the waiting Chief Priest. This was the Azazel—the scapegoat. Holding his hand on the goat's head, Zechariah solemnly transferred the sins of all the people of Israel onto the goat. Then, in procession with the virgins, the Levites, and to the sounds of the Temple music, the High Priest led the goat out from the Sanctuary, through the inner Court of the Jews and across the outer Court of the Gentiles to a small exit in the eastern wall. There, opening the gate to the cheers of the waiting pilgrims, Zechariah released the Azazel.

The scapegoat ran out into the vale of Kidron, jeered on by the crowd. The Temple gate closed and the official ceremonies came to an end.

* * *

Anna and Elizabeth stayed at Ain Karim throughout the Day of Atonement. They fasted in the traditional way and started to dress their booths in the vineyards. Joachim had already built the frames. The crowds were not as obvious at this distance from the city. There was less chance of petty theft and more chance to observe the harvest festival of Succot in the sincerity of their hearts. It truly had been a good year. There was much for which to give thanks to God.

Zechariah had strained his voice while shouting the Shemah and the prayer of Atonement from the Sanctuary steps. He'd experienced a growing hoarseness as the day went on that he attributed to the unhealthy musty air in the Holy of Holies.

"Elizabeth, I don't feel very well," he complained on his return with Joachim to Ain Karim in the late afternoon of the following day.

"What's the matter?"

"My throat's sore. I'd better lie down and rest."

Holding Elizabeth's hand, he asked her to fetch him some honey and herbs.

"Joachim can help you finish off the booths?" he suggested.

In the cool of his chamber, he wrapped himself up in a woolen blanket before lying on his old straw pallet.

Elizabeth prepared a potion of honey and herbs. Zechariah was exhausted from the journey along the crowded roadway and from his exertions at the Temple ceremonies the previous day. After he drank the potion, he fell asleep and drifted into a dream…

He was back in the dark dank chamber with those golden angels. The seraphim started to flap their wings in a pulsating rhythm. Their gold leaf coating flaked off, drifting to the floor. Then, grasping the ceremonial tongs, one of the seraphim took a burning coal from a brazier, the only light in this dreamlike recreation of the Holy of Holies. Flying through the air with the coal glowing between the tongs, in the semi-darkness of the chamber, the seraph came toward Zechariah. He tried to back away, but the red-hot coal came closer…closer…ever closer. Fear gripped Zechariah. The hot coal touched his lips…

Zechariah awoke in a sweat. He tried to scream out and call Elizabeth as the aftershock of the nightmare haunted him, but no sound came forth. He had been struck completely dumb.

* * *

A detachment of Roman soldiers under the command of two junior officers, Justin and Spartus, left Jerusalem by the Northern gate and set out on the winding road across the vale of Kidron towards Bethpage, Bethany, and Jericho. Justin and Spartus rode beside each other at the head of this marching column. They were in no particular hurry since they were merely on a routine patrol.

Jericho was down in the lush valley of the Jordan. There, King Herod had built his sumptuous spring palace surrounded by orchards and vineyards. Roman soldiers on the Jericho patrol were always pleased to arrive in this valley of plenty after a period of serving in the capital. Jerusalem had its delights but was tense; Jericho seemed like a relaxation center to the soldiers. Close to Jericho were sulfur baths, which the Romans always enjoyed. The sulfurous waters and the fresh fruits, fine dates, and good living of the Jordan valley were constant barrack room talk. But the steep and rocky road down to Jericho was not safe for travelers. Robbers and bandits were constantly found in the area. The spoils of their victims were hidden away in cave dwellings. This was a dangerous road for Roman soldiers, too. They could easily be attacked by zealots, as they passed within easy range of hidden missiles slung from well-aimed slingshots or hurled from overhanging precipes.

As the patrol of soldiers set out on this autumn morning, their thoughts were not so much on wayside robbers and political zealots as on the strange sight of bacchanalian revelry all around. Some of the soldiers laughed and pointed, until Justin called for silence in the ranks. The whole Kidron valley and its hillsides, rising up past the Mount of Olives, over to Bethpage and Bethany, and the hills toward Ramah to the north and Herodium to the south, were littered with pilgrims. The scene was reminiscent of a vast Tuscan country fair with rustic tents made out of simple sticks, vines, palm fronds, and olive branches. The inhabitants of these temporary dwellings were enjoying an endless picnic—swapping yarns, drinking fresh new wine, and tending little fires for cooking their flat bread. It was a happy scene.

The pilgrims were far too concerned with their own affairs to pay any attention to the Roman soldiers. The sounds of braying donkeys and bleating goats filled the air, while Hebrew women filled pots and jars with water from the trickling brook that wound its way south through the vale of Kidron.

"Not a bad religion," commented Spartus, as they pulled up their horses to survey the scene.

"I think the Jews call this the feast of Tents," Justin said, as his horse pawed at the ground and shook its mane. "It's a sort of harvest thanksgiving."

"It looks like Saturnalia to me. A good excuse for a party. This scene reminds me of the wine festivals in Greece. Were you ever stationed in Greece?"

Justin smiled.

"I wasn't that lucky. The best post I had was a short period in Ephesus over in Asia Minor. That was very pleasant. It certainly beat Gaul. Have you been in Gaul? It's not only dangerous, but the climate's awful!"

"No, but I was in Hispania six years ago. It was quite civilized. The west's very different from the east. I don't like it very much here."

The two soldiers kicked their horses on to a jingle of bridles and leather, as the column of men marched behind them. They continued to swap notes in a worldly way, good naturedly trying to top each other's travels in the service of the Empire.

* * *

Many miles to the north, another, more senior officer of the Roman army, made his way across country from Sepphoris to Magdala. Flavius Septimus was going to inspect the progress on his villa, and pay a last visit to Esther, his Hebrew whore. Copernia, his high-born Tuscan bride, would be joining him at Magdala in the spring, and his duty would then be to his marriage and family status. Copernia had been anxious about leaving the comforts of Tuscany. Flavius hoped her arrival would be eased by his building her a suitable villa to welcome her to Galilee, but temporarily his thoughts were on Esther, *that woman of great passion and skill*. He could not wait to see her welcoming eyes, the caress of her smile, before she enfolded her legs around him and took him in.

* * *

Joachim helped Anna prepare the booths below Zechariah's home. There were three spacious bowers he'd carefully staked before he left for Jerusalem.

"You've done a fine job," Joachim said to Anna, as he admired the weaving of vines that she had accomplished in his absence. Together, they wove more palm fronds into the mesh.

"Did you see Miriam?" Anna asked.

"I think so. Well…yes, I'm sure I did. Zechariah said she was the oldest of the virgins and would be leading the procession. But if it was her, that golden hair is now a deep chestnut."

"Is she pretty?"

"From where I was… I would say so. She's quite mature. I mean you can definitely tell she's a woman. She has a woman's shape."

"Long legs and budding breasts?"

"Yes, she's very slender, and in those flimsy sheaths they wear, her breasts definitely showed."

Anna hugged Joachim and snuggled up to him as they admired the booths.

"We did well, didn't we," she said.

"Yes, but I would suggest we take the one in the middle; it's the best. The one on the left could probably use another palm frond and the one on the right's a little crooked."

He kissed Anna.

"I'm like a child again."

Anna backed away and looked at him quizzically.

"A child?"

"Yes. We shall sleep again under the stars. Do you remember the first time you slept under the stars?"

"Oh, yes! And the cool smell of the night air. I didn't get this night catarrh then like I do now. As children, Elizabeth and I would watch the stars for an omen of good tidings!"

Anna bent down and started to weave another palm frond into the left-hand booth.

"So, when did Zach start to feel ill?" she asked.

"On the road. He's just very tired. Yom Kippur is the hardest festival—it's not just the physical strain but also the emotional strain. He's acting as the intermediary between God and our people. In some ways, he takes on the burdens of our sins even though they are ceremonially put upon the Azazel goat. After all, he's the one and only person who actually transfers our transgressions to the beast. It must be very emotional."

"So you don't really think he's sick."

"No. He'll be fine after a good night's rest. It was a busy time for all of us as I recall. There are always so many pilgrims at the Temple asking for atonement sacrifices of lambs, goats, doves, and fowl, as if the Azazel was not enough. We used to spend hours in the rooms around the Sanctuary preparing these sacrifices and blessing their donors. It's very hectic."

He patted her shoulder.

"I'm sure your brother-in-law will feel better in the morning," he said.

Already, as the sun was setting, the great new harvest moon was rising like an orange ball in the eastern sky.

Joachim pointed to it.

"Look at the moon. I don't think I've ever seen it look so big. Something very significant is about to happen, my love. We are witnesses to changing times."

Joachim and Anna made their way back up through the vineyard to the outer wall of the house. The sand-colored stones glowed in the last ruddy embers of the fading light.

Joachim stopped.

"It's time for my prayers," he said.

He'd greet Succot with his usual evening prayers, knowing that after a feast in the home, the family would leave their house to dwell in the wilderness as their ancestors had done in the days of Moses. Unlike the days of Moses, however, when food was restricted to the dew and manna that greeted the Israelites each morning during their Sinai wanderings, Joachim and Zechariah had an abundance of fruit, bread, and special cakes to enjoy in their booths. This was always such an exciting time of the year for those who were rich or poor, pilgrim or priest.

"How much time do I have?" Joachim asked.

"As long as it takes me to help my sister prepare supper."

Joachim smiled, but it held fatigue.

"I've time for my prayers. That's really all I need to know."

"And you are finding it difficult in somebody else's house, my husband."

Joachim nodded, his tired eyes offering their love.

"And you know me too well, my wife."

Judith heard Joachim open the wicket gate in the garden wall. She ran out to meet them.

"Mistress, your sister wishes to see you right away," she said.

Anna followed Judith back to the kitchen where Elizabeth was soaking some linens in cold water.

"Is it Zach?" Anna said.

"He's getting worse. He's feverish. I don't think he'll be fit to come down to the vineyard with us tonight. I'm sure he's just exhausted, but I'm concerned."

"Joachim says it must be the strain of the Temple ceremonies. He remembers it was always exhausting, not only for the High Priest, who's charged with emotion at Yom Kippur, but for all of the priests and Levites."

* * *

In the privacy of his room, Joachim prayed for Zechariah. Then, he thanked God for the harvest. He prayed for Anna, Elizabeth, and Judith. And of course, as always, he prayed for Miriam.

It would be nice for Miriam to live with Zechariah and Elizabeth, he thought. *It's peaceful here at Ain Karim, much better for her after leaving the seclusion of the House of the Virgins than the bustle of Jerusalem. Whoever Zechariah chooses for her will be a lucky man. She is more beautiful than I could ever have imagined. It's no wonder she has visions of angels—she is an angel. But what are Zechariah's intentions? What are his betrothal arrangements for Miriam? I know she will have to go wherever the High Priest decides. Zach's a good man. I'm sure that he'll do his best for her.*

Joachim coughed and stood, holding his arms out in front of him.

He began to recite the familiar evening prayers he'd learned and studied all those years ago at the Temple school.

* * *

Later, Joachim, Anna and Elizabeth ate their evening meal while Zechariah lay restless in his chamber. They were all strangely quiet as they fed on a hot pot of earthy vegetables and thought about the High Priest.

The harvest moon had now climbed up high in the night sky and lost its orange glow, casting instead its familiar lemon light into the High Priest's atrium. Zechariah's household always dined around the atrium porch on the eve of Succot. It gave them a feeling of being outside, as they started to celebrate the harvest festival and the feast of Booths. Later, they would go down to the olive and vine bowers, the makeshift dwellings or 'tents' that Joachim and Anna had prepared, and start the observance of the Mosaic custom, recalling the days of their ancestors wandering in the wilderness. Elizabeth and Anna had the cakes, fruit, wine, and sweetmeats prepared in woven baskets. They'd carry torches to light their way down the stony path that led from the wicket gate to their encampment. Elizabeth decided she'd stay behind this first night to take care of Zechariah, but she sent her maid, Hannah, along with Judith to carry the baskets and jars. Anna and Joachim lit torches after supper, and prepared to make their way out into the night.

"Send Zach our blessing," Joachim said as they stood at the gate.

Elizabeth and Anna embraced.

"Join us as soon as you can, Sister," Anna said. "I'm sure Zach's just exhausted. He'll be fine in the morning."

By the light of the torches and increasing brilliance of the moon, the family descended to the place that Joachim and Anna had prepared. Nature's silence enveloped them as they established their camp. A galaxy of stars offered their mystery in the darker depths of the periphery of the heavens.

* * *

When Zechariah awoke, Elizabeth took more cool linens and gently washed his body.

"You still have a fever, my husband, but this will comfort you a little."

The High Priest watched her, his eyes too bright and holding a fear in their depths.

"Are you in pain?"

He shook his head.

"Your throat—is it still sore?"

He took her hand, nodding.

"I'll get you some warm honey and herbs," she suggested.

He closed his eyes, then opened them, suddenly restless.

"What is it, Zach?"

In frustration, he pointed to a wax tablet.

Elizabeth picked up the tablet and brought it over.

Taking the stylus, Zechariah wrote in Aramaic: 'This is a sign from God.' Zechariah was too weak to write anything else.

Elizabeth studied the Aramaic, written but distorted by fever. She remembered how he'd said the same thing about her pregnancy.

"Do you think this child of ours, conceived so miraculously, is linked to your lack of speech?" she asked.

Zechariah nodded.

Elizabeth dropped the cool linen.

"Why has God chosen us in this way?" she asked, anger in her words. "Why are you, a good man, being punished?"

The nausea of her pregnancy took her. It had been a long and difficult night and she'd nursed Zechariah alone. Lack of sleep and emotional upheaval now brought on morning sickness. Dawn was streaking the eastern sky and as the sun began to rise, Elizabeth forced down her own discomfort to bathe her husband with the linens.

"We must comfort each other," she said.

Zechariah twisted his head from side to side, anguish etched in his features.

"We have been touched by God, Zach. I feel His presence, I feel His control. Can this be good, my husband? Can this be good?"

But the High Priest could offer no words, for his wife or himself. The rising sun hurt his eyes. Elizabeth leaned across him, her soft bosom comforting him as she applied the cooling linens.

* * *

Anna hadn't slept well under the stars. Joachim was peaked by their curiosity. He always enjoyed the night air at the season of Succot, but for Anna it had a damp heaviness that upset her sinuses. She was the first to rise and pour water from the jars to quench her thirst and wash her face. In clearing her sinuses, she awakened Judith, a light sleeper who was easily disturbed. The maid joined her.

"Have Mistress Elizabeth and Master Zechariah come down?" Judith asked.

"No, Judith. Their booth is still empty. I'm worried about them. Why don't you go back up to the house and see how they are?"

"All right, but let me light the fire first so we can do our baking here in the open."

"Don't bother with that, Judith," said Anna, breathing in the heavy air. "It's more important to check on my sister and Zechariah. I don't want to leave here until Joachim wakes up. I can light the fire and start to prepare the dough. Anyway, we still have plenty to eat."

Judith set off up the path toward the garden wall. It had seemed much farther when they had come down the night before, guided by their torches in the moonlight. In reality, they were only a few hundred cubits down the hill, almost within sight of the house.

Anna began to put together the kindling in the hearth of flat stones that Joachim had prepared for them. She worked quietly in her discomfort, drawing satisfaction from this festival of Booths, its reliable rhythms, solace, and celebration of God's bounty.

* * *

The wicket gate wasn't closed when Judith got there. She slipped in and crossed the courtyard to the house. Upon entering Elizabeth and Zechariah's chamber, she found them asleep. She quietly gathered the linen cloths and brought a fresh jar of water. Her eye caught the wax tablet beside the pallet, the stylus and the markings beyond her understanding. Obviously, Elizabeth had been up nursing the High Priest and had finally fallen asleep. Satisfied, Judith left the chamber and made her way to the kitchen to prepare some food for them when they awoke. Hannah, Elizabeth's maid, had left to go to her own booth with friends from the village, so Judith took charge.

But Judith wished she could have stayed in Nazareth, as nothing seemed to be going right for them here. She'd looked forward to coming south because she wanted to visit Jerusalem, but Joachim and Anna never seemed to want to go to the city. Judith had been to Jerusalem with them in past years and she remembered its excitement. *The Temple is such a spectacular building. I love the bustle of the Court of the Gentiles with all the bazaars. Hopefully, before we leave Judea, Joachim will take us back there. I can join them in making selection of a sacrifice.* As Judith reflected on the Temple, she thought again of Miriam. *Zechariah wasn't the High Priest when Joachim and Anna gave Miriam to be a Temple virgin. But he promised them then, because of his relationship to the family, that he'd try to see good care was taken of their little girl. She's my little girl, too! Miriam was my charge!*

She started the oven fire and prepared warm honey and herbs for Zechariah.

Judith carried the potion into Zechariah's chamber. Elizabeth was now awake. At first the older woman was flustered to see Judith. But she spoke to the maid politely:

"He's been very sick through the night, but I think he's better now. I'm not feeling very well myself."

She looked around.

"Thank you for the fresh water. That was very thoughtful."

"Can I get you some honey and herbs, too?"

"No, Judith. But you know what I'd really like?"

"I'll get it for you if I can."

"I'd like some fresh figs in warm goat's milk. See if we have any in the storeroom."

Judith had never seen Elizabeth prepare figs in warm goat's milk during their brief stay. Nor, for that matter, had Judith prepared such a dish for her sister in all her years in Nazareth. But she didn't see any reason why she should turn down Elizabeth's request.

When Judith went to the storeroom, it crossed her mind that this was a strange request. *But who am I to question my mistress's sister's taste?* she thought. *Obviously the High Priest's fever has broken. He looks much better than last night.*

After Zechariah woke up, as much as he tried, he still couldn't speak. He stared at his wife in utter helplessness—a High Priest who could not pray, encourage or rebuke.

Judith returned with the two dishes.

Nodding her thanks to Judith, Elizabeth fed Zechariah the hot honey and dried dipping herbs before tackling her own request.

* * *

"**Did you watch the** stars last night, Anna?" Joachim asked as he savoured the warming sunrise.

"I couldn't, Joachim. My breathing was difficult."

She stared pointedly at him.

"Did you witness anything?"

Joachim shook his head.

"Not last night, but I feel it in my bones, Anna. I feel something in my bones."

He looked around.

"Where's Judith?"

"I sent her to the house to check on Zechariah. She's late getting back."

"How long is it now since she left?" he asked.

"She's been gone an hour or more. I expected her back long ago with news of how they are. Do you think we should go up?"

Anna was looking for an excuse to get away from the harvest bugs.

"I don't like to break with tradition," Joachim answered. "But if you're really concerned, we can go as long as we return to stay out overnight. Let's assume that no news means all is well. If there's really something wrong, Judith would have returned."

As the sun rose up to its midmorning height, there was still no sign of Judith. Anna and Joachim began to retrace their steps back to the house, where they found her in Zechariah's room. The High Priest was sitting up, looking more himself again. But now, it was Elizabeth who appeared pale and weak.

"O Mistress Anna," Judith called, "Mistress Elizabeth's been taken poorly today. She's felt sick all morning. I tried to give her some figs in warm goat's milk, but she wouldn't eat any more than one."

"Figs in warm goat's milk!" exclaimed Anna with surprise. "Why did you try to give her such a strange dish? My sister always hated figs as a child. Surely some honey and herbs would have been far more sensible."

"Yes, but she wasn't so sick when she asked for the figs, Mistress. I followed her wishes. I thought it a little strange."

"Very strange! When did Elizabeth begin to feel sick?"

"After I prepared the figs. I came back and she was gagging and wanting to vomit. She said she was all right and that it would pass in a moment. She did get better, she fed Master Zechariah. Then, I gave her the figs. She was pleased when she saw that I'd gotten her what she wanted, but she could only manage to eat one before she felt like vomiting again. It's been like this all morning. She gets better and then feels sick all over again."

Anna looked worriedly at Zechariah.

"What is it, Zach? What's wrong?"

Zechariah pointed to the wax tablet, nodding frantically.

Joachim picked it up. Zechariah's message still showed in bold Aramaic letters imprinted in the wax: 'This is a sign from God.'

Zechariah pointed to his mouth and shook his head. He smoothed the wax with the stylus and wrote again in a bold script: 'I can't speak. God has taken away my voice. This is the sign of a miracle.'

Elizabeth rallied a little and sat up, glad to see Joachim and Anna.

"Joachim! Zechariah can't talk. He thinks God's punishing him for some unknown reason," she said. "He had a bad fever all night. His throat's parched. He'll be all right tomorrow, he's just weak now."

Zechariah waved his arms frantically. He took the wax tablet back from Joachim and smoothed it out, replacing his previous message with one word: 'No!'

Then he nodded toward his wife, who looked at him fearfully. Elizabeth took Zechariah's hand.

"Anna, I think I'm going to have a baby," she said.

Tears welled in her eyes.

"Elizabeth! After all these years!" Anna exclaimed. Then, she embraced her. The truth was out. A feeling of joy and warmth replaced the previous tension.

Zechariah managed a smile before worry took him again.

"Anna, Zechariah feels as you did when you found yourself miraculously pregnant with Miriam," Elizabeth explained. "He believes that our child will be special, a gift to us from God. He believes that his sickness and loss of speech is a sign from God to confirm this miracle. Anna, I'm a fair age now and I was barren!"

Zechariah was busy flattening the wax again. He then wrote in bold letters once more: 'God has struck me dumb to seal His covenant with us.' Smoothing the tablet once more, he continued: 'Our child will herald the Messianic Age. This is God's sign of the coming kingdom!'

Joachim pressed Zechariah's arm.

"I understand, Zach. I hear you and I understand. I've had thoughts of my own about the Messiah and his coming. Last night I watched the stars for a sign…"

"Perhaps your loss of speech is an early sign!" Anna said, interrupting her husband in her gathering excitement.

"We talked at the Nazareth Synagogue group," Joachim added. "All agree the Messianic Age is about to begin."

Zechariah turned again to his tablet, his stylus poised, then he gently laid it down and smiled at Joachim. There was no need for words. All was understood. The High Priest rested, content. The signs were in place.

King Herod's family is fighting over succession, Joachim mused. *Roman legions have overrun Israel following the invasion of Pompeius. The new Temple at Jerusalem provides a fine center for Judaism that can be respected throughout the known world. With the fall of the Herodians, Davidic rule could return and be protected by Rome, giving birth to a Messianic Age when the chosen people of God will again become the center of the world.* Joachim had so wanted to discuss all these things with Zechariah. Now, he was even more anxious to talk, and hoped that the High Priest would soon recover. Obviously, they were thinking along the same lines.

As Joachim pondered these matters, Anna held her sister in her arms, rejoicing that Elizabeth could conceive, even now that Zechariah was so well on in years.

Elizabeth seemed relieved she no longer had to hide her secret. She wasn't concerned with Zechariah and Joachim's lofty thoughts and messianic dreams. She was consumed with joy.

Anna and Judith took good care of Zechariah and Elizabeth throughout the rest of the day. By evening, they all felt well enough to celebrate Succot in the traditional manner. They made their way down to the booths in the vineyard. Zechariah carried with him his wax tablet and stylus, for there was so much he now wanted to communicate with Joachim. Judith made sure she brought down a supply of fresh figs and a skin of goat's milk. Elizabeth rested as Anna and Judith warmed the milk at their outdoor hearth. Crickets and frogs began an evening chorus to greet another Jewish day.

Anna looked across at Elizabeth.

"How are the figs?" she asked.

Elizabeth smiled.

"Good…Very good."

"You didn't like them as a child."

"I know."

Elizabeth ran a hand over her still flat belly.

"Perhaps my child wants figs."

"Perhaps."

Anna looked across at Joachim and Zechariah.

"Look at them pray, Elizabeth. Such devout and good men."

Elizabeth nodded.

"I wonder when Zach will speak again?" Anna remarked.

"When God is ready, I suppose."

Anna took the warm goat's milk from Judith and gave it to her sister.

"Let me help you with this," she said, propping her sister up.

Elizabeth sipped the milk.

"So much talk of signs! I think my child is a sign," Elizabeth suggested.

Anna looked at her thoughtfully.

"I think you're right. But I wonder about Miriam. There is something about my child, also."

She paused, then dismissed her thought with a shrug.

"We must leave interpretation to the men," she said.

Elizabeth smiled.

"Tradition!"

Joachim and Zechariah prayed long into the night, occasionally casting their eyes to the stars.

* * *

King Herod was in a pensive mood as he stared out of the window across the public pleasure gardens of his Jerusalem Palace. The King's tent for Succot was dominant in the scene, but he only used the tent ceremonially at the beginning of the feast of Booths. The massive frame of this once athletic king was shrouded in the red and yellow robes of his rank. Although he put on a brave front, the lines in his sun-wizened face and the sadness in his once sparkling Arabic eyes gave way to a greater truth—the King was losing control of his kingdom.

Salome, Herod's sister, sat close by. Salome had dark hair like her brother, which she, too, had dyed black and pinned up in the Roman style. Her cheeks were painted in a cosmetic rouge that highlit her dark, penetrating eyes. A mean countenance stretched over those angular bones. She was dressed in pink and green robes that would have been more suited on a younger frame. A lady-in-waiting stood behind her. At court, Salome held remarkable powers of persuasion over the aging monarch and was the one courtesan who knew how to win his favor, even at times when his temper flared, which nowadays it did often. Salome was more aware than others of her brother's malady, and now she watched him closely.

The King suffered from the early stages of a common disease of the Levant believed in the villages to be caused by advancing age. The disease struck people at random, regardless of background or class. Because more peasants died younger than the better-educated Jews, it seemed more prevalent among the affluent establishment. Herod's once virile body was decaying. He suffered from manic depression and mental disorders. He was losing his sense of balance. Salome could always interpret the signs—a long period of silence with the King, like now, gazing out from his window, blind to the world around him—then a forthcoming outburst. The scheming Salome carefully laid her groundwork. As King Herod decayed, so would she manipulate him and gain control and political power.

Abruptly, Herod broke his mood and summoned Royal guards. Without raising himself from his chair, he gave an order to their commanding officer:

"Take the road to Sebaste in Samaria. I'll have papers prepared. My sons Alexander and Aristobolus are held at our fortress there. They are to be put to death. See to it that their end is clean, for they are of our royal blood. Although I commit them to death, I don't wish to make a spectacle of this. Sebaste, like Sepphoris in Galilee, is a Roman city. There are few Jews there who would or could stir up rebellion against our decisions. These Jews, however, are wary people."

He glared at Salome.

"Some are looking for a weakness in our house. I've even heard rumors that some want to see me dead. There are zealots and Pharisees who speak of a Davidic revival and a fulfillment of messianic dreams. I'll let them know who's king. I'll address the multitudes at the Temple as soon as I hear you've accomplished your task."

"What will you say, Herod?" Salome asked when the guards left.

"I'll proclaim Prince Antipater, my eldest son, as my successor and Herod-Philip as my next heir. My mind is made up. The justice of the court in Berytus will be fulfilled."

Salome nodded with approval, glad to be completely up to date on the King's moves. All that she'd planned and worked toward was coming to fruition. She and Doris, Antipater's disgraced mother, had risen to the apex of power. The King was losing his mind, but, fortunately for them, not his despotic cruelty, which still had its uses.

"Bring Ptolemy to me," the King commanded.

Salome left.

A few minutes later, a man with fuzzy white hair and a long straight nose followed Salome back into the chamber. His drab, gray tunic contrasted with the opulence of the King's robe. In his hand, he carried scrolls of papyrus. After bowing before the monarch, the scribe sat at a table, flattened the scrolls with weights and dipped his writing instrument in an oily, sooty compound kept in a small jar.

Salome, her angular face echoing the severity of her thoughts, stood behind Ptolemy.

The King stood at the window without even looking at his scribe.

"Prepare two warrants of death," the King commanded. "Draw up formal papers for the execution of the Princes Alexander and Aristobolus and forward the referrals to Rome and to Governor Saturninus in Damascus."

He paused, his hand shaking slightly.

"The matter is finished," he continued. "Justice will be carried out as approved by the Roman court in Berytus. It is our order and our command that these executions take place."

Ptolemy, who had served the King through the many crises in his family affairs, would have liked to advise the King of his error, but he knew Salome was looking over his shoulder and was probably the originator of the murders. As he wrote out the warrants in a bold hand, his thoughts reflected the opposite. *It should not be the murdered bodies of Alexander and Aristobolus that the King should seek, but the heads of three others—Salome, his sister; Pheroras, her brother, who is an equally guilty palace schemer in her entourage; and Doris the Idumean.* Duty bound, however, he obeyed in personal fear of the King's wrath. He knew, as did Salome, that as soon as these death sentences were executed the King would turn on all around him in a fit of rage. It was one of the symptoms of his disease that was ever becoming more frequent.

The orders were drawn up, and Salome presented the papyri to the King.

Herod signed the parchments, and the death sentences became official. Caesar had given the King all authority over his own family, his heirs, and the internal government of his kingdom. The seal of Herod turned murder into law.

"Give these to the Captain of the guard," the King ordered.

Ptolemy bowed and left, a knot forming in his stomach.

Salome watched with a cruel detachment as the familiar signs engulfed the sickening king. At first, there was remorse. The King began to weep. For many years Alexander and Aristobolus, his sons by his second wife Mariamme, the Jewess whom he had scandalously put to death for intrigue a few years before, had been the hope of his throne. He'd never trusted Antipater—Doris' son. For years, he'd banished Antipater and his mother. He'd lavished all his care in education, statesmanship, and kingship upon the two boys whom he had hoped to be his heirs. They'd been schooled in Rome and were used to dealing with the Imperial Court. Herod knew from long years of experience how important that was. He'd been swiftly reminded of this during the recent brief period when he, too, had fallen out of favor with the Emperor. Imperial favor was the key to maintaining his role along the Great Sea's eastern seaboard known as the Levant. The alliance of his throne and Rome had been and was still the mainstay of his success.

Still rational in most aspects of government, the King believed in the rumored treacherous plotting of Alexander and Aristobulus and those around them. He'd tortured their close associates to make them confess their crimes. Even Herod's barber had been implicated in a plan to slit Herod's royal throat. Salome herself had schemed to falsely accuse the two princes of all these plots. She'd even cleverly arranged for Aristobulus to marry her daughter who informed her of the princes' scheming. This palace intrigue had brought reports to the King that Aristobulus was plotting his early removal. It cut deep into Herod's vanity when he heard this wayward son considered him a dotard who dyed his gray hair black. Injury to his self-worth festered along with the King's physical condition, and he succumbed to all of Salome's schemes.

Beset by troubled and quarreling relatives, Herod desired unity and peace among his heirs. With each revelation of betrayal and deceit, the King became more morose. He wept for those he destroyed among his kith and kin, but his pride forced him to carry out his purge. In the growing depression and pain of his decaying sickness, remorse turned to rage, and rage to madness. Then followed a calm.

Salome watched her brother go through these sick phases after he'd ordered the executions of his relatives. She watched, untouched by them, her darker reaches beneath her silk and jewels celebrating her gathering power.

When life again had its uneasy calm, Herod called for an assembly in the Court of the Gentiles to announce the new succession. By this time, the strangled corpses of Alexander and Aristobulus, tossed in the back of a cart, had been taken from Sebaste to the family mausoleum at Alexandrium.

* * *

Joachim waited patiently as Zechariah worked the stylus across the tablet. These had been good days despite the High Priest's affliction. They had experienced the days of Succot, with their nourishing of the spirit and lifting of the heart, and they had their growing closeness as they thought deeply on the Messianic Age and the Messiah of God. By word and wax tablet, with knowing glances and intuitive insights, the two men explored the future, now imminent, now firing their very souls.

'Our respective wives are destined by God to foster children of messianic importance,' wrote Zechariah in his developed Aramaic abbreviations.

"Because Anna and Elizabeth are of the Davidic line?" Joachim said.

Zechariah nodded. His hand gripped the stylus: 'Our children have both been conceived as rare births. A Divine miracle which we must heed.'

Joachim selected a date from a wooden platter and chewed on it thoughtfully.

"A Divine miracle for the messianic purpose," he repeated.

Zechariah's dark eyes glowed with fervor. He moved the stylus again across the wax tablet: 'I do not fully understand Miriam, but something is there, Joachim—enough to make me concerned about her betrothal— and to whom she should be betrothed.'

"It is her obsession with angels, isn't it?"

'Yes, Joachim. But as we look for signs, we must recognize her, we must fathom her ways, which could be holy in their message.'

"That is strange, coming from you, a believer in the solidity of the Temple, dismissing pharisaic ideas about angels and demons."

Zechariah looked uncomfortable, screwing up one eye. 'They're not Jewish,' he wrote. 'There are too many eastern thoughts from the Persisans and Parthians invading our faith.'

"The cult of Mithras. It bothers me sometimes, too, Zechariah. Schools of Mithras are spreading throughout the Greek-speaking world. I fear, as the gentiles embrace these superstitions, Rome will look on Mithras with more favor than Judaism. We might lose our status as a *religio licita.*"

'We Sadducees are in somewhat of a tight corner on this one,' the High Priest wrote.

"Politics, Zach. If the Messiah is as you believe, he will be a binding force above the politics of the Sanhedrin."

Zechariah put the wax tablet aside and slowly nodded in agreement. Then, he pointed at the platter of dates.

Joachim handed it to the High Priest, who took two or three of the succulent fruits.

It was surprising with their cumbersome communication that the two men were able to discuss so much.

* * *

Anna and Elizabeth took no part in their menfolks' deliberations. When not completing the daily chores, which were far harder to accomplish at the campsite than in the comfort of the house, the two sisters and Judith pondered on the coming birth of Elizabeth's baby.

"I'm so excited for you, Sister," Anna said as they collected driftwood for the fire. "A baby in our family again."

Elizabeth beamed:

"A son or daughter for me and a nephew or niece for you."

Judith fed the fire.

"When you visit Mistress Anna in Galilee, I can look after the baby, just like I used to look after Miriam," she suggested.

"Yes, Elizabeth, you will have to visit us," Anna agreed. "All these years you've never come up north to Galilee."

"It's very beautiful there," Judith interjected. "We have the finest house in the village."

The flames caught the new kindling.

* * *

Zechariah hinted to Joachim that in his plan for Miriam he saw a very special messianic role.

'God is guiding me,' he wrote boldly. 'My loss of speech makes me only more determined to believe that Elizabeth's pregnancy is part of His purpose, too.'

"Miriam and your child will be cousins," Joachim noted.

'Yes. Our families have been chosen. You are redeemed, Joachim. My son and your daughter are part of this.'

"But, Miriam will be some fifteen years older than your son, and what if your child is another girl?"

Zachariah vigorously erased the wax.

'No, he will be a boy,' he wrote.

Joachim chuckled.

"Zach, you've got a plan, haven't you?" he said.

Zechariah looked around to see that the women were out of earshot.

'Yes,' he wrote. 'Miriam could be the mother of the Messiah.'

Joachim got closer to him, his heart pounding with excitement and fear.

'I have a priest in mind,' Zechariah revealed. 'Good looking, from a good family, but sufficiently low key not to attract attention. Rarely debates, just listens.'

"Yes…" Joachim said, wondering how far the wily High Priest was prepared to go.

'The Messiah must be of good Davidic blood, yours, Joachim, and that of this young priest.'

"Go on…"

Zechariah smoothed out the wax with the back of his stylus to create a fresh tablet.

'The seed will be carried secretly. Only you and I will know,' he wrote slowly. 'When the time comes, let the zealots overthrow the Herodians. Then, Miriam's son can be proclaimed a new Davidic king.'

"But what if the child's a girl?"

'This is God's plan. The child will be a boy.'

Then, grinning, Zachariah wrote as an afterthought:

'Cleopatra was a girl.'

"I understand about the Davidic king," Joachim agreed. "That has been the trouble ever since we gained our independence from Syria. Judas Maccabee was Davidic, but the Hasmoneans and the Herodians are of very mixed blood. Herod's really a Nabatean."

'A wily fox from the desert hole of Petra,' Zechariah agreed.

He smoothed the tablet again as if he had something important to say. Joachim watched as the High Priest hastily wrote:

'Miriam's child could be the fulfillment of Isaiah's prophecy.'

Joachim put his arm on Zechariah's shoulder.

'The Lord will give us a sign,' Zechariah continued. 'Behold a young woman shall conceive and bear a son. To us a child will be born; to us a son will be given. The government will be upon his shoulder, and his name will be called Wonderful Counselor, Mighty God, Everlasting Father, Prince of Peace.'

At this point Zechariah had filled the wax tablet and handed it to Joachim. Joachim read it a little uneasily and handed the tablet back. Zechariah smoothed out the wax again and completed the quote:

'Of the increase of his government and of peace, there will be no end.

He will sit upon the throne of David and will establish and uphold his kingdom with justice and with righteousness for evermore.'

"Zach, I don't want to dampen your enthusiasm, but you sound a bit like the Pharisees in the Sanhedrin or my rabbi up in Nazareth. Anything can be backed by scriptural quotes if we look for them."

'The prophets are great teachers.'

"Yes, but they are not the authors of the Torah. Their words are not binding for legal interpretation. What if these words of Isaiah are just referring to the birth of a male heir at the Royal Court? I mean, I agree with your scheme. I'm just not sure I want to place this scripture on it."

Zechariah reached for another date.

'You sound like a true Saduccee,' he scratched in the wax. 'Besides, wasn't the Torah revised in the time of Ezra? Tradition is one thing, but the Messiah will be above tradition.'

On this matter, Zechariah and Joachim differed, but it wasn't a stumbling block for Zechariah in the interpretation of his scheme. He simply dropped the subject of prophetic interpretation and interpolation and continued to explore with Joachim his ideas on how to find the best Davidic spouse for Miriam.

'The priest I have in mind is Gabriel,' he wrote.

Zechariah didn't wish to divulge much more to Joachim at this time. The light in the High Priest's eyes was enough to convince Joachim that his Davidic plan was already well-established.

"Let's join the women. We can talk more later," Joachim said nervously, the messianic plot now becoming a little too close to his own life for his comfort and ease.

* * *

Within two days, Joachim decided to leave Zechariah's house.

"I need to take Anna and Judith to Jerusalem before we return to Galilee," he suggested.

Zechariah entrusted Joachim with the important task of informing the old Chief Priest, Simeon, that he must fulfill all the High Priestly duties until Zechariah could speak again. Despite constant dosing with sweet honey and herbs, Zechariah's voice had remained mute. Elizabeth continued her craving for figs in warm goat's milk and only suffered once more from the morning sickness that had bothered her so much after the night she had stayed up nursing Zechariah.

Their mules packed up with good Judean grapes, some excellent figs, and a variety of personal gifts, Joachim and Anna said goodbye to their relatives. Joachim and Judith led the three mules while Anna walked beside them as they made their way out through the village and on up the road to Jerusalem.

CHAPTER FIVE

Esther and Gabriel

Many Succot pilgrims were now on their way home. Their camels, donkeys and mules thronged the road. Joachim's little mule train was running against this traffic, so progress toward Jerusalem was slow, but the life around them was exciting. Carts were laden with produce and goods picked up in the Holy City. There was still a festive spirit as these pilgrims wound their way along the stony track.

Because of this throng, it took Joachim and his family a full day to reach Jerusalem's city walls. They stayed at an inn outside. The inn was simple—a flat-roofed house where they were served an adequate but plain meal. Joachim blessed their food. After the sustenance, they settled down for the night.

Unable to sleep, Judith slipped out to enjoy the excitement of the bustling crowds. Even at nighttime the pilgrims were still moving along the road. Some carried torches; many were in half-drunken stupors, beating their animals. Behind them, the city lay shadowed by the waning moon, which a week before had been the glory of the sky. The stars gleamed in the clear night air. Judith sat beside the road for some time and took in the sights and sounds.

By morning, the crowds had dispersed and the bacchanalian festivities of Succot were over. In the city, business returned to normal.

The patricians living in the Roman western extremities were pleased that the bustle and danger of this rabble had ended.

Joachim made arrangements to stay at the inn another night so he could conduct his business that day and give Anna and Judith the chance to make holy sacrifices. They set out in the direction of Mount Moriah and the Temple.

They passed by the great aqueduct of Herod snaking its way through the olive patches, gardens, and villas of the patrician dwellings. Its arches were Roman. King Herod had adopted the Greek style in most of his architecture, but the aqueduct followed the perfected style of Roman engineering that transformed sanitation and urban living throughout the Empire, and it was a symbol of the new order.

Closer to the center of the city, all manner of transport was found. Camels belonging to merchants and travelers competed for space with donkeys and mules. Horses drew swift chariots driven by proud Romans and Herodian patricians, scattering geese and hens from their path. The smell of dyes, tanning vats, and goats mingled with spices and the sweet perfumes of fragrant gardens, preserved by King Herod in many parts of his remodeled city. But from whatever approach the traveler came, always gleaming white on its hill was the crowning glory of Herod's capital—the Temple. Judith loved the bustle and excitement of it all, although in truth she knew Joachim and Anna would have preferred to be on the road north, returning to Galilee and their quieter life.

The long walk made them thirsty. When they reached the steps leading up to the Triple gate, Anna saw a beggar woman who was selling cups of water. She asked Joachim if they could stop and drink from the beggar's bowl.

"Certainly, my dear," Joachim said, and he reached into his purse for two small coins.

The ragged woman took the money and poured water into a wooden cup from her jealously guarded supply.

Joachim tasted the water and spat it out.

"It's bitter!" he yelled, wiping the residue from his mouth. "Don't touch it."

The beggar, having safely pocketed the coins, just gave a toothless grin.

Ahead, lay the bazaar of the Court of the Gentiles, with its cages of animals, along with the moneychangers and cunning traders who knew how to fleece gullible pilgrims. Anyone could enter the Court of the Gentiles, and it seemed like the whole world did. There were Jews and Greeks, Parthians and Syrians, people from Asia Minor, and visitors from Rome and Egypt. It was hard to pick out Aramaic, the native tongue, in the bevy of languages all around. Greek seemed the most universal. It was in Greek and Latin that inscriptions could be found warning strangers not to enter the Inner and Sanctuary courts of the Temple. These tablets of stone clearly stated: 'Let no stranger come within the barrier and the court which surrounds the Temple Sanctuary. Every captured trespasser will be responsible for his ensuing death.'

Joachim changed his coins for the obligatory Temple shekels. Anna and Judith helped him select two goats for sacrifice. For an additional fee, an elderly gentleman who was hanging around at the moneychanger's stall, offered to lead the goats up to the inner Sanctuary for them. Joachim agreed to the sum and parted with his shekels.

In the outer court of the Sanctuary there was a lot less hustle and bustle and fewer beggars and racketeers. In this strictly Jewish area, less Greek was spoken, although there were some Jewish visitors who spoke the educated Greek of the free cities of the Graeco-Roman world. At the far end, stood the heavy gilded doors, guarding the steps leading into the priestly court and the Sanctuary building.

"This is where the King comes on the High Holy Days," Joachim explained to Judith. "These doors are open at Yom Kippur so that the King, who can't go further than this, can watch the ceremonies from a dais right here where we're standing. I'll go up and call for one of the Levitical assistants to take our goats."

Joachim went to one of the two side doors while Anna and Judith remained with the goat man.

Two of the Levitical priests came out. One took away the goats so they could be slaughtered and sacrificed in the traditional way.

Foul odors of decaying flesh and entrails hung on the air drifting over the Temple precinct. Judith tugged on Anna's dress.

"This smell's dreadful!" she whispered.

Anna's troubled sinuses blocked out the worst of the odors, but she nodded in agreement.

"I much prefer the excitement of the bazaar in the other area," Judith stated.

Although nearly twenty years had passed, the Temple odors were reminders of Joachim's priestly past. He greeted the smells and sounds as if he'd only left yesterday.

Once the goats had been taken away, Joachim asked the other priest if he could arrange for him to speak with the Chief Priest.

"Simeon's not here," the man said.

"Well, where can I find him, then? I need to speak with him urgently."

Joachim pulled out his parchment.

"Look, I have a message for him from the High Priest Zechariah," he explained.

"He's over in the Sanhedrin Council Chamber. He could be there all day."

Temple business was very matter-of-fact to most of these Levites. As the Temple servants, they acted primarily as sacrificial butchers, performing a necessary function, but they were not policy makers or part of the hierarchy.

During this conversation, the goat man disappeared. He, no doubt, was already seeking out the next gullible-looking pilgrim to whom he could sell his services.

Joachim, Anna, and Judith crossed the inner Court of the Jews to the far corner where the large building that housed the Council Chamber of the Sanhedrin stood. There, they met Simeon.

The Chief Priest was taking a rest from the debate inside and had come out for a little fresh air. Simeon's snow-white hair framed a kindly face; he held his head high with a great dignity and sincerity. Joachim had always liked this older man who had been senior to him in his own Temple days, but Anna and Judith weren't interested in listening to the two men reminisce. They left to trade shekels for trinkets in brass, gold, silver, and bronze in the open market bazaar.

There, they found jewelry in the Hebrew style along with fashionable Roman-mode pins for sale. All manner of brass and silver vessels, pots, and urns for food preparation were also available. Anna and Judith purchased a souvenir or two.

Judith was particularly interested in one of the Hebrew-style brooches and held it up to her shoulder.

"How does this look, Mistress Anna?" she asked, as she tried to look dignified, even though she was smiling like an excited girl.

"Pretty, Judith. Would you like me to buy it for you?"

"Oh, would you, Mistress!"

* * *

Joachim smiled at Simeon.

"I do believe your hair is whiter."

Simeon grinned.

"Perhaps it will make me look wiser."

"You have always been wise, Simeon."

Joachim took out the scroll that contained Zechariah's messages.

"Please read this."

Simeon's kindly face shadowed as he read. Then, he looked up and said:

"Zechariah wants me to fulfill the duties of High Priest. But why?"

"He's lost his voice," Joachim said carefully, "I'm sure this assignment will be only temporary."

He did not endow his words with any spiritual portent, giving no hint of a sign from God in the silenced vocal chords.

"He must take lots of warm honey," Simeon said.

Joachim nodded.

"He receives the best of care. So, I can report back to Zechariah that all is well and understood?"

"Of course," Simeon agreed suspiciously. "But are you sure this is nothing more than a sore throat?"

Joachim nodded.

"Well, I'll inform the Sanhedrin immediately," Simeon said.

As he turned away, he looked back at Joachim.

"I always enjoyed your company, your wisdom, your modesty. I miss you and those old days," he said. "How long will you be in Jerusalem?"

"We're leaving right away," Joachim replied. "Remember, I'm a farmer now."

Simeon smiled.

"Yes…" he said.

"You serve the Temple well, Simeon," Joachim acknowledged, and then they parted.

He watched Simeon make his way through the crowds.

Joachim went in search of Anna and Judith.

"Joachim," Anna called as she saw him approach. "Look at these brooches."

Joachim looked at his wife's purchases, then glanced at Judith.

"Ah, that new brooch looks good at your shoulder."

"Mistress Anna bought it for me. It's so beautiful," Judith said pirouetting before him.

Joachim put his arm around his wife's waist.

"We must start back for the inn," he said, but his thoughts were on Zechariah and his great plans worked out by spoken word and writing stylus.

* * *

Flavius Septimus, the Sepphoris centurion, looked out over the landscape of his fledgling Galilean estate. He was proud of his new home above the growing fishing community of Magdala. This view reminded him of his Tuscan roots. Tall cypress trees broke the arid autumnal day with their dark green tones. The late afternoon sun played on the rocks and stones that littered the hillside above the villa, then hid behind the shadow of the western hills

I hope Copernia will like it here, he thought. *But, I'll have to give up Esther.*

Flavius' father, the Governor of Tuscany, had been a member of the Curia in Rome and Copernia, Flavius' young bride, was the niece of Senator Tarquinius, the most revered member of the Senate and a close ally of Caesar Augustus. It had been quite a match in Roman society when these two illustrious families had come together. And now, with the zealots under control, Copernia could come to live with him in Galilee.

He looked out again at the beauty of the land. Other houses were not far away. Several members of the militia had sought the peace and tranquility of the Galilean lake. Some came from Sebaste in Samaria and others, like Flavius, were from the Roman community in Sepphoris. A number of Jewish patricians, Herodian retirees and enthusiastic

Hellenists, had also seen the potential of this land and taken up residence scattered along the hillsides to the south of Magdala.

Copernia…Yes, you will like it here, he thought, but his loyalty swung like a pendulum.

Thoughts of Esther embraced his hungry body. *Maybe I could visit her just one more time,* he mused. He walked round to the front of the villa with its view over the village out onto to lake with its distant Gadarene shore. *At least I should visit her and explain,* he thought.

He then turned to inspect the progress on his home. The main structure of the villa was complete. Flavius opened the sturdy gate that led into the outer courtyard on the south side of the building. Lack of running water prevented the customary Italianate fountain but, on a hexagonal plinth in the center of this court, Flavius observed his statue of Hermes had been mounted to gracefully greet visitors. Olive trees gave shade, and marble slabs paved the ground. Flavius approved. He crossed to enter the villa by the vestibule, which looked quite luxurious with a magnificent mosaic floor depicting tritons and sea monsters. Beyond, cast in the shadows of the late afternoon, was an open terrace surrounded on three sides by pillars in the Greek style. This inner garden had that same vista to the east that looked out over the tops of the whitewashed houses of Magdala to the lake. The great cliffs on the far side of the water glowed pink in the fading day. *They always seem closer toward sunset,* he said to himself, *at midday they seem to recede into a faint purple haze on the horizon.* Flavius noted that the work on the architrave was not finished. Portions of the proposed marble frieze lay in sections among the purple weeds where he planned to have this terrace garden.

I should build a pergola along that open wall for honeysuckle, trumpet vines, and jasmine. They would tumble down to the road below, bringing color throughout the seasons of the year. His imagination anticipated the future perfume emanating from those Mediterranean hues. *Copernia will love this,* he thought. He crossed back to the vestibule, feelings for Esther receding in the excitement of his new home.

The triton motif followed on from the vestibule into the large central chamber that would be the dining room, but the mosaic tiles were not yet completed. However, Flavius noted that the niches for statues he'd ordered to be sent up from Caesarea were ready. Reaching the central atrium, he saw a lot of masonry lying around, but the centurion was pleased with the progress on the rooms that led off from this courtyard. There were five chambers with two further ones down a passage that formed the north wall of the garden terrace. To the south, forming the west wall of the entrance court, were the offices, kitchen rooms, and the all-important storerooms.

It's a pretty large villa, the biggest up here, he concluded. *Copernia should like it… She's only been used to the finest in Italia. It's so hard to know how she'll respond to my military lifestyle here. I'm doing my best…I'm creating a Tuscan villa for her right here in Galilee!*

He walked through the domestic wing and came out into the daylight at the back. Shielding his eyes from the setting sun, he looked up at the gently sloping hill before pacing out a flat area. *This will be Copernia's herb garden. It could all be behind a retaining wall, which will square off the villa as in those country houses of Tuscany.*

Flavius was pleased. He'd employed a master mason from Caesarea to supervise the work and was amazed at the quality of craftsmanship that this Roman master was getting from the Hebrew artisans of the village. In only nine months, they'd accomplished a great deal.

But, as the sun set below the western hills, Flavius Septimus could not stop himself making his way down to the village. He knew that Esther would hold herself for him, forgoing on even other regular customers. She would be ready for him. His passions mounted, and once inside the brothel he was rewarded.

Esther stood in quiet shadow smiling at him, her silhouette lush in the flickering lamplight.

"My Roman soldier," she murmured, as if it had only been yesterday, and as she stepped into a penumbral light she ran a delicate hand from her bosom to her thigh, her long nails trailing down the fabric of her dress. The flesh of her breasts swelled over the cool fabric restraint. Her eyes never left Flavius' face, willing him to her, until she had him close and had drawn his hand to her belly. In sinewy strokes, she moved against his tunic.

"Come with me. It's been too long," she said huskily.

She led him to her cushioned bench, still enfolding his hand to her belly, then moving up to her fleshy breasts.

"Be patient," she murmured, as he pulled down the fabric to release her lush bosoms. "All is for you…all in good time."

But he could not hold back. Torn by guilt, he stripped her roaming her heavy flesh, plundering an Earth Mother, soaking in her sweat and heaving breaths.

"What is it, my Roman?" Esther said, startled.

"I've missed you," he answered, sounding desperate.

He was spreading her now, insistent, plunging. Esther arched her back as he entered her.

"It is more than that, Roman," she said suspiciously.

But he wasn't listening. He lost himself in her, sloughing off guilt concerning Copernia and cries of crucified men, until he fell against her in his own cry, and lay quiet in the dark.

Esther stroked his back, running her fingertips down his spine to the pooling sweat.

"My Roman soldier," she said, almost to herself.

Flavius was quiet for some time. When he spoke, it was of the past.

"Remember when we first met?" he said.

Her finger curled in his sweat, slippery in the dark.

"It was on the lakeshore south of the village."

"You pulled open your robe and let me see your breasts."

"And you spoke Aramaic."

His laugh was a hot breath against her flesh.

"Not very well, I'm afraid."

"At least you tried, and it's much better now—very good in fact."

"I was lonely," Flavius said.

"And so was I."

Flavius pulled on his tunic and tied the cord that held it in place.

"I'll be leaving tomorrow," he told Esther as she lay back, stroking her breasts.

"No more visits?" she asked suspiciously.

"Not for a while, maybe never. I have to go back to my duties."

Esther turned away. She pulled the dirty cover over her.

"What if I have a child?" she said.

Flavius reached into his pouch and pulled out four denarii.

"For you," was all he answered.

For the first time, he became conscious of the pungent odors of the whore's room and of the stale, musky smell of other men's desires. As guilt closed in, he realized that he was a Roman first and a lover second. Esther would be losing a comforting friend.

Esther didn't know her centurion was soon to be promoted to tribune and become the Commander of the Sepphoris garrison. Duty and a shared life with Copernia now rose foremost in Flavius' mind. He was to be a man of importance in the Levant. This meant that he could no longer dally with this Hebrew whore. He had a duty to uphold his position and a conscience that dictated he must be faithful to his young and beautiful bride.

He quietly left the house with its smells of wasted joy and walked along the beach. Flavius Septimus had grown up. He now stood for all that was best in the power of Rome. From now on he would soar with the eagles.

* * *

While Flavius visited Esther, those two other Roman soldiers, Justin and Spartus, were enjoying different delights on the shores of the great salt lake to the south. The Jericho patrol was almost a pleasure trip. No bandits or brigands working the steep road from Jerusalem to Jericho had attacked. The criminals' targets were, after all, lone travelers or small mule trains of unsuspecting traders from the Peraea and the Decapolis, with goods for Jerusalem who couldn't fight back. Occasionally, the soldiers of the Jericho patrols would come across the victims of such brigand attacks— festering, half-dead bodies lying in the roadway stripped of all that had any value. It was the patrol's duty to pick up such unfortunates and bring them to medical care in Jerusalem or Jericho or even the smaller villages of Bethany or Bethpage. More often than not, they found such victims already expired. They buried them beside the stony track leading down to the Jordan valley.

The two or three days spent in Jericho by these small police patrols were always times of rest and recreation. On the shores of the lake, known as the Salt Sea, and by some as the Dead Sea, were the sulfur baths where Justin and Spartus now sat, enjoying the healing balm of the bubbling warm waters.

"This is the life," Justin said. "Judea's not so bad."

"Wait and see," Spartus replied. "Never trust these Semites."

The mineral content was high, and all invaders had found the health benefits of these waters. But the Romans, more than any before them, had educated the Herodians and Hellenists to the joys of these sulfur springs, as well as their medicinal benefits. The Herodians, in conjunction with their Roman advisors, constructed magnificent baths close to where the Jordan river emptied itself into the great salt lake. This was at the express command of King Herod, who had been advised to use the mineral waters. Herod had enjoyed such luxuries on his many travels in the Empire and sought to duplicate them close to his favorite palace. He spent more and more of his time at Jericho. It was the most Roman of all his royal residences, but it was also to him the most lovely.

The Herodian Baths south of Jericho were built in white marble. This kept the rooms cool in the summer heat. The open courts, where the baths themselves were located, let in shafts of white light that played through the pillars. Everything was spotlessly clean.

As the gray bubbles burst around them, Spartus and Justin talked further about the privileges their military careers had given them. The sulfur baths were a luxury that, at home, would hardly have been theirs. Both men came from humble origins. The hot sun blazed down on the shores of the Salt Sea even during this autumnal season. The tepid waters of the bubbling springs felt very relaxing and surprisingly refreshing to the two soldiers, at least when compared with the searing heat outside. They looked forward, too, to the delight of massage and body cleansing at the skilled hands of those whom Herod had appointed to his Royal Baths. In a way, this special spot on the shores of the Salt Sea was an example of the serene security linking Herod and Rome.

* * *

Joachim had his three mules, along with two donkeys he had purchased for Anna and Judith, packed up early so that his family could get in a full day's travel. Most of the time he led the train on foot, only occasionally riding one of the mules. They skirted around the northwest corner of Jerusalem, passing close to the walls on the outside track leading past the small skull-shaped hill locally named Golgotha. Traditionally, the stoning and execution of criminals of all sorts took place on this spot. Stoning was a death penalty that lay within the jurisdiction of both the High Priestly courts and the Herodians. Crucifixion was administered only by Roman jurisprudence. Golgatha was a desolate place, without olives or date palms to give shelter. It was merely a rocky outcrop outside the city walls. Evidence of a recent stoning was clearly visible.

"Our people can be just as cruel as the Romans," Joachim noted as they passed the bloodied stones.

Not far away, two vultures were pecking at a shallow grave.

"What might the poor fellow have done?" Anna asked.

"Anything. Stolen a loaf of bread in the crowded market. Defecated in the Temple courts. Who knows?"

Not far beyond Golgotha, the track met up with the newly paved road running north from Jerusalem to Sebaste. This was one of several highways that Roman engineering had brought to Herod's kingdom. A highway already linked Caesarea with Sebaste.

"The new road does make a difference," Anna said as their party moved swiftly along.

"Look back if you want to see the Temple one more time," Joachim suggested.

Anna and Judith pulled up the donkeys and looked over their shoulders. Over the next rise, Jerusalem, with its Temple surrounded by Herod's new buildings, disappeared into the backdrop of the Judean hills.

Joachim watched the village threshing floors, now busy as Judean peasants flayed their last remaining ears of wheat and spelt, separating the chaff from the grain. Like those at Ain Karim, these were usually close to the roadway, making it easier for the delivery of the golden sheaths. Many a millstone was also hard at work to secure the end product of the successful harvest.

They stopped to water the animals. A toothless peasant helped Joachim raise the bucket from the well.

"What an unusual year," Joachim said.

"A good sh…spring harvest and a good harvest of late sh…summer wheat. God is…sh good," the man whistled and lisped as he lowered the bucket again while the donkeys slaked their thirst.

Soon, they were on their way once more, Joachim now riding the lead mule and the two women again astride their donkeys. Periodic flocks of sheep at times slowed them down as wily old shepherds herded them along to more verdant pastures. Goats ran wild. Flocks of geese, cocks, and hens strutted the little streets of the villages as if they owned them. It was obvious the holiday was over. Agriculture was on the move again.

The following day, shortly before the family arrived in Sebaste, a detachment of Herodian guards on their way back to Jerusalem hurriedly passed them. Armor gleamed in the sun. The guards' faces were like stone. Their swift horses caused Joachim's mules and old donkey to veer off the roadway.

"They seem in a dreadful hurry!" Anna said.

"Just the Herodian Guard, my dear," Joachim assured her, as he pulled the mules and the donkey back on line. "They probably want to show off their horsemanship. They're getting more like the Romans every day."

The family traveled on, making it to Sebaste in the golden light of early evening. There, they found accommodations for the night similar to the little inn outside Jerusalem.

Sebaste was essentially a Greek city built by King Herod for the government of Samaria. The Samaritans were despised by the Judeans in a hatred that went back seven hundred years. It was often the source of bitter quarrels. For this reason, the city was very much a garrison town, housing both Herodian and Roman militias. But Herod took a lot of trouble to see that the Greek cities, which he built, were to his credit in the eyes of all Roman visitors. Herod's cities impressed visitors with their spacious, colonnaded streets, libraries, baths, gymnasiums, and amphitheaters. Sebaste was probably, apart from Caesarea, Herod's most classic city. It was totally different from the ancient villages Joachim and Anna had passed since leaving Jerusalem. The buildings, none more than a decade in use, reminded Joachim of Sepphoris, although much of Sepphoris was still under construction.

Anna and Judith needed provisions, so Joachim stopped awhile. At a street tavern, pungent with camel dung, he heard a rumor or two, which he mulled over as he sipped on his warm wine.

"Yes, Alexander and Aristobulus, the two princes."

"Put to death."

"They carried them off in an open cart."

"They were arrested on charges of plotting against the King. They were executed by members of the Herodian Guard."

"They had a warrant and all."

"I'm glad I'm not of the Royal blood."

One of the gossiping men whistled at a serving girl.

"More wine" he called out, pointing at empty goblets. "So who will be the bastard's heir now?" he continued.

"Probably Antipater, the one banished to Rome."

Joachim thought differently. *Herod never favored Antipater,* he mused. *It was he who banished Antipater and his mother from Judea.*

"It could be Herod Philip."

Joachim silently nodded in agreement and smiled. *Such confusion in the King's remaining family can only help Zechariah's grandiose plan,* he thought. *Maybe Zechariah's scheme really can come to fruition. Perhaps in these fast moving times a Davidic messiah can become King on Herod's death.*

The thought scared him. *My own family is implicated in Zechariah's plot. Zechariah suggested that our daughter Miriam should be the mother of the future king! This is something I can't discuss openly with Anna. Her family might be deeply implemented, too! Apart from Miriam being Anna's only child, Anna's own sister, Elizabeth, is part of Zechariah's scheme!*

Joachim looked around the street tavern. Discussions on the Messianic Age had seemed so exciting when purely academic. Now that the lives of kith and kin were involved, he began to think Zechariah might have gone too far. Thoughts raced through his mind against the background of tavern chatter. *Who is Gabriel, Miriam's future spouse? What influence will Elizabeth and Zechariah have over Miriam if she lives with them? Will they fill our daughter with prophetic ideas and lead her into believing in this destiny? What influence will Elizabeth's child, Zechariah's 'Elijah,' have on Miriam and Gabriel's child? They'll be almost contemporaries, cousins of the same age.*

Joachim reflected on the possible fate that might come to his family and friends. He forgot the grandeur of their messianic dream and hoped King Herod would sort out his family affairs. *Things are going too well. There's prosperity throughout the land. It might be wiser to accept the 'status quo,' as the Romans call it, and hope that Herod will find a strong heir to ascend his throne. This rumor that the popular Herodian princes, Alexander and Aristobulus, have been put to death isn't comforting. It brings the reality of the messianic dream just a little too close.*

Joachim left the tavern, trying not to draw any attention to himself.

Judeans rarely spoke to Samaritans, but their wine was comforting in his belly.

In this nervous state of mind, Joachim led his family back to Nazareth. They stayed one more night along the way, stopping at the village of Nain.

The following day, while descending into the vale of Esdraelon, they joined forces with a small caravan making its way up north from Caesarea.

"What's in those two carts?" Judith asked, seeing body parts protruding from the straw.

"Statues, Judith," Joachim said. "The drivers say they are headed for the village of Magdala. Probably imported for some wealthy Roman. I've heard there are lots of Romans building along the western shore of the lake."

These days, whoever is king of the Jews, he thought, *must assuredly be allied to the might of Rome.*

* * *

There was a knock at the High Priest's gate. Elizabeth looked up from her couch on the porch. Zechariah was in his chamber. Their servant Hannah went to see who was there.

"Soldiers!" Hannah gasped when she opened the gate.

Elizabeth could see that the men who stood outside wore tunics of the Herodian Guard, their daggers gleaming in the sun.

"I need to speak with your master, Zechariah the High Priest," the Captain of the guard asked.

Elizabeth had already called Zechariah, who came out to meet them.

"Zechariah the High Priest?" the Captain asked.

Zechariah nodded, still unable to speak.

"Zechariah, you are commanded to return to Jerusalem. The King is to make a Proclamation at the Temple. He requests your presence."

Again, Zechariah merely nodded.

"He can't speak," Elizabeth interceded for her husband. "He has some problem with his voice right now."

The Captain raised his eyebrows as he looked at the High Priest.

"The Proclamation will be read at the Temple in two days. This is by the order of the King."

The Captain impatiently turned to shout an order to the small detachment of guards. Without looking back, the officer joined his men.

Early the next day, Zechariah obeyed, setting off for Jerusalem, leaving Elizabeth to rest at home.

It was King Herod's political genius to use the Temple as a platform for major State pronouncements. He always made such announcements flanked by the High Priest and his entourage along with the Chief Priest, the President of the Sanhedrin. This had the effect of binding the people behind his wishes. As on the international scene, when Herod had used the power of Rome to back his monarchy, he used the power of the High Priestly office to cement his power at home. His system worked.

Zechariah had no bad feelings about going back to Jerusalem. He wouldn't be able to make any speeches himself, or even pronounce the traditional Hebrew blessing over the King and people, but Simeon would be beside him and would take care of those ceremonial details.

* * *

King Herod, flanked by Zechariah and Simeon with the other Chief Priest and officials of the Sanhedrin, stood on the curved steps in front of the great, gilded doors leading from the Temple's Sanctuary court. Herodian guards had hastily summoned the citizens of Jerusalem together and formed a cordon around the steps to keep the curious crowd at a safe distance. The King's trumpeter, and his Chief Scribe Ptolemy, were standing ready at the base of the steps. Once all were assembled by protocol, the trumpeter played a fanfare. Ptolemy presented the King with a scroll. In a loud voice that echoed in the acoustics of the Outer Court, the King read his prepared speech:

"Citizens of Jerusalem! Men of Israel! We are gathered together here in the Court of the Jews in the presence of the High Priests and leaders of the Sanhedrin Council to make an announcement of great importance to our future and for that of our kingdom. Whereas, we have previously made public the succession of the kingdom, it is now our intention to make certain changes, legally noted and in immediate effect. Our son Herod Antipater, son of Doris of Idumea, we now name our heir and, should he not survive us, we name Herod-Philip, son of Mariamme, to be next in succession. This decision has been made necessary through the changes incurred by the rebellion of our sons Alexander and Aristobolus whom, in accordance with the power invested in us, we have put to death."

Herod looked around. There was tension in the air, a pregnant silence from the crowd.

"A House divided against itself is not worthy of the throne," he continued. "We ask, therefore, that you support our succession, give allegiance to Prince Antipater, and continue to enjoy the peace and prosperity that has been given to you by the house of Herod and our Emperor, Augustus Caesar. We ask for your continued loyalty throughout the tenure of our reign, and wish it to be known that peace and unity have been returned to your Royal house."

The King handed the scroll back to Ptolemy, and held his head up imperiously.

All eyes then turned to Simeon and Zechariah, who stood with outstretched hands. Simeon solemnly pronounced the priestly blessing:

"The Lord bless you and keep you. The Lord make His face to shine upon you and be gracious to you. The Lord lift up His face to you and give you peace."

As he did so, Zechariah felt the power of the system. *In the presence of the King, these familiar Hebrew words link God with kingship, priesthood, and people in a powerful and timeless bond. It would be even more effective,* he thought, *if the king was of God's chosen lineage—a descendent of King David.*

Later that evening, after the crowds diminished, Zechariah stood alone outside his chambers in the Inner Court. Leaning against a marbled column, he looked up at the night sky. *It is time to implement the plan,* he thought. *This additional weakening of the house of Herod signals the time is right.*

* * *

Miriam was the only Temple virgin ready for betrothal who had not been matched. Zechariah summoned the unsuspecting Gabriel to the High Priest's palace.

The ruddy faced young priest, dressed in fine robes and wearing silver phylacteries, more for show than their religious symbolism, excitedly entered Zechariah's chamber.

Simeon, standing behind the seated High Priest, acted as Zechariah's voice:

"We have called you here because we have noticed you as a promising young member of the Sanhedrin. We have a proposition for you."

Gabriel smiled at the recognition. He felt a sense of oncoming power.

"We would like to offer you the chance to become betrothed to one of our Temple virgins—the virgin Miriam. Such matches we do not make lightly. We select husbands for our virgins very carefully."

The good-looking and relatively unknown young priest was flattered by the High Priest's intentions. He felt it an honor to be considered as a suitable spouse for any Temple virgin.

"How old is she?" he asked.

"Almost fourteen. Miriam is a very sweet and beautiful young lady. I am sure she will make you a wonderful wife."

Zechariah nodded in agreement.

"I'm honored, sir," Gabriel said. "How soon can I meet her?"

"We'll arrange it soon. We'll send for you."

Gabriel left in good spirits, anticipating prestige and political influence as outcomes of this happy fortune.

He met the two High Priests at the old Hasmonean palace on several further occasions before meeting his proposed bride. Through Simeon's interpretation, Zechariah subtly revealed his plan.

"You've been chosen because of your Davidic ancestry and relative obscurity," the old man explained. "It is the High Priest's desire that through this marriage, Miriam will conceive and carry future Davidic seed."

To Gabriel, this seemed a pleasant enough task until Zechariah, through Simeon, carefully explained the serious political implications of the plan.

"So, you believe my son will inherit Herod's throne?" Gabriel said with mixed emotions.

He liked the idea of power and privilege, but he feared the dangers of the intrigue.

"You will be protected," Simeon assured him. "One of the reasons you have been selected is your relative obscurity. You will be able to live a normal life. The house of Herod is likely to implode on itself. When this happens we will call on your son. It's God's will. The dawn is coming of a new and exciting time for our people."

"When can I see Miriam?"

"When we feel you are happy with this arrangement. We understand that it carries some pressure of personal responsibility."

"It does, but what if I don't like the virgin?"

"You will," Simeon assured him.

* * *

The young couple's first brief meeting was arranged at the chambers of the High Priest in the Court of the Jews.

The matron came out into the garden of the House of the Virgins where Miriam was weaving wool for the new Temple veil.

"The High Priest has called for you, Miriam. Put on your clean white dress."

Miriam put down the shuttle.

"Does this mean he is going to tell me I am to get married?" she asked.

"I don't know, but that would be what I would suspect. It's time, Miriam. Your stay with us can not be much longer."

Miriam put her arms around the matron. Tears formed in her eyes.

"It's all right, Miriam," the matron assured her. "The High Priest will make a great choice for you. Now, go and get dressed."

Miriam left for the dormitory.

When she was ready, the matron brushed Miriam's long chesnut hair and washed her feet.

"Here, today you must wear sandals," she said, as she handed her a pair of thonged shoes.

The matron then took her out into the Temple Court and escorted her to the High Priest's chambers.

Gabriel was already there. He looked Miriam over as the matron brought her in.

"Sit down, Miriam," Simeon said in a kindly voice as Zechariah stood up, his head almost touching the low ceiling. He stretched out an arm in the direction of each of the young people.

"Gabriel, this is Miriam," Simeon said.

"Miriam," he continued, "Gabriel is a promising young priest and we would like you to consider him as a suitable spouse."

She looked at the young man who smiled amiably. Her beauty obviously satisfied him. Her skin was smooth and clear. Her hair hung in long tresses, framing her oval face. She had large eyes that were filled with wonder, warmth, and trust. Her lips looked soft. Her complexion was fair, unlike the olive skin of most girls. His ruddy complexion turned even brighter.

Miriam noted Gabriel had a muscular body, he was clean-shaven and he had sparkling deep-set blue eyes. His hair was dark in thick, tight curls. He looked very different from the older Levitical priests and Temple eunuchs. Miriam's innocent beauty had never been touched. But her body, developing in perfect proportions as she stood on the threshold of womanhood, felt a tinge of excitement that she had never before experienced.

Gabriel gazed at her and continued to stare after her when she was escorted out.

Not knowing why, she instinctively looked back to see Gabriel one more time.

Zechariah felt inner satisfaction. He was now convinced of the perfection of his match. *God seems to be smiling on our messianic dream. Here, surely, is the perfect union for the dawn of the Messianic Age,* he concluded.

* * *

Miriam had mixed feelings after her meeting with Gabriel. She had wanted to stay at the House of the Virgins and dedicate her life to God. But when one of her friends, Jude, asked her about Gabriel, Miriam shyly looked away.

"Is he handsome?"

"He's..." She held her stomach. "He's different."

"What do you mean?"

"I don't know, Jude. My stomach aches. How did you feel when the High Priest introduced you to your betrothed?"

"Very excited. I can't wait to get out of this place. I don't know why you are so attached to this prison."

"This is God's house, Jude. We were all dedicated to God. What God wants is what we must do."

Miriam still felt betrothed to God. Although new sensations were welling within her, Miriam's mystical marriage was still in the moonbeams that she saw in the courtyard.

For over a year now, every month as the moon rose high and full, Miriam had listened to the messages from God that she continued to believe her angels sent as they climbed up and down heavenly stairs. That evening, she walked out into the courtyard and addressed her favorite angel:

"Gabriel, what will happen to me when I leave this place?"

She noted the coincidence in the name she felt belonged to her spiritual confidant and that of the young man the High Priest had chosen for her. Her heart raced. *Now, you will always be with me, Gabriel... Gabriel...angel and husband.*

The fragrance of junipers filled the night air.

Her perceived angel called her name in the whispering of the olive leaves. When she caught his spiritual energy in her heart, Miriam felt power and strength well up within her confused body.

Nobody at the House of the Virgins understood Miriam's visions and fantasies. The matron and the High Priest both dismissed as adolescent fantasies the girl's claims that God talked to her in the moonbeams.

Now, Miriam was experiencing her first glow of adolescent desires that fused with her visions. At times, she wanted to suppress them, and be the vulnerable child of God she conceived herself to be, but at other moments, curious excitement overcame her.

Zechariah believed Gabriel would lead Miriam into adulthood with his worldly wisdom. And as the young couple continued to meet, Miriam became more enthusiastic about her prospects. Gabriel, although ten years older than she, did spark within her a glowing feeling of contentment that was a new sensation. She decided her angel must now be in the form of this young man with the same name.

"Can Gabriel be an angel?" she said naively to Zechariah on their next meeting.

Zechariah still had no conviction on the subject of angels.

"If you choose to make him so," he said, using his innate wisdom.

Sometimes, while alone in the garden at the House of the Virgins communing with God, Miriam believed she saw Gabriel's face in the moonbeams' light. Her emotions became confused, but her total dedication to God remained steadfast.

Zechariah brought Miriam and Gabriel together as often as he dared. At first, their meetings in the Temple's Inner Court office were brief and well chaperoned. Later, the High Priest arranged for them to meet at the old Hasmonean palace, and they would take walks together out to the Mount of Olives. Miriam's response to Gabriel was one of wonder rather than love and affection. She began to look forward to Gabriel's visits, but in his presence she became quiet and shy. She confided her growing feelings for the handsome youth only when talking to her angels. *Jude only speaks of her spouse as the future father of her children*, she thought to herself. *I don't see Gabriel in this way.* Her feelings for him were linked imperviously with her feelings for God.

"I feel as if I want to be enveloped by Him as I am here in the moonlight," she said to her angels, her heart pounding. "I want to be bathed in His light as I am in your light."

The olives swayed in the breeze, causing the waning moon to flicker a response.

"You are a child of God. Whatever happens you will always be a child of God," her angels reassured her.

She felt security in her future.

* * *

Gabriel held Miriam's hand and stared ahead of him at the Temple Mount, its pyre of sacrificial smoke drifting over the city. A breeze stirred the fanned fronds of the palms of the lush grove where a small brook babbled over its stony path down to the Kidron. These walks in the hills with the virgin were beginning to pall. His initial pride in being selected as a spouse for one of the Temple virgins waned at the prospect of life with one so other-worldly, so far removed from the flesh and blood life of the city. Guilt also gnawed at him as he remembered the perfumed sweetness of his tryst in the brothel the night before. *Will I always have to seek satisfaction that way if I marry the High Priest's angel?* he thought.

Miriam did not seem to respond to his touch; they never kissed. She lived in her own dream where butterflies and insects held more meaning.

At twenty-four years of age, Gabriel with his charm and good looks, was used to being the center of any party.

Miriam turned to him and smiled. It was a sweet smile, but Gabriel feared what it prefaced.

"Leanna is so sweet, Gabriel. She's my favorite among the young virgins. She likes to snuggle up to me at night. Sometimes, she just sits beside me and feeds me my wool."

"Miriam, you are about to leave the House of the Virgins. Have you no thoughts about your new life?"

"God will take care of me."

"And what about me?"

She looked at him.

"God will take care of you, too. We are God's children."

"And what if God does not take care of us? He doesn't take much care of the beggars in the streets of the city."

"Oh, God will always take care of me. He tells me so in the moonlight. I hear Him when the wind blows through the trees. He sends His angels to me. He sent you to me."

Gabriel felt frustrated that he could find no way to break her childish nature, but her latter remark fired his passion for her innocent beauty. Her lithe young figure and doe-like eyes aroused his sexual desires enough for him to feel he could fulfil his role. Make her pregnant had been the High Priest's message. That was his task. *Maybe that's all the High Priest really wants of me*, he thought. He had led her to this lush grove at the foot of the Mount of Olives intentionally. Known as Gethsemane, he knew this to be a romantic spot favored by young blades of the city. As he walked Miriam down the hillside toward the grove, he held her narrow waist, seeking her response. Now, he stood up and pulled her to him. He'd held out long enough. He wanted her body, not her conversation. He kissed her on the cheek and stroked her chestnut tresses of hair.

Miriam felt her nipples harden, but knew not why. She sensed her heart beating faster. But still, she pulled away.

"Gabriel!" she squealed. "What are you doing?"

"What any man would do with an angel!"

His lips met hers.

Miriam didn't know how to respond as Gabriel pushed his tongue into her mouth. This taste of kissing wasn't what Miriam had expected. It disgusted her, but she didn't resist. She tried to imagine her moonbeams, but they faded. She couldn't hear her angel's voice.

Gabriel's hand cupped her breast. Miriam's hardened nipple responded with a strange, tingling sensation. Gabriel released her mouth.

As he gently massaged her bosom, she felt more relaxed. The sensation felt good, unlike that thrusting tongue in her mouth. She didn't know why, but the feel of Gabriel's hand made her smile. The moonbeams danced again.

Gabriel was aroused. The frustration of having this unattainable beauty paraded before him must end. She was his now. She was the dumb High Priest's gift. He'd no longer have to chatter about moonbeams, angels, and messages from God. The High Priest had informed him he wanted him to pass his seed through this virgin. *It is time to obey this command.*

He picked Miriam up in his arms and carried her to a grassy glade. Miriam laughed and kicked her legs.

"Put me down, Gabriel!" she squealed. "Put me down!"

This was like the games she played with the little ones in the virgin's courtyard.

Gabriel put her down, almost throwing her to the ground. He pulled at her shift and tugged at his tunic. His manner changed. The game got rough. Gabriel ripped off his loincloth. He showed her a man's flesh, rigid, matching the ruddy complexion of his face. Miriam began to struggle, but Gabriel pushed her back down. With one hand, he squashed her left breast, as the other pinned down her arm. It hurt. Gabriel pushed himself onto her innocent body.

"I'll show you moonbeams and angels," he said, "and all the stars of heaven!"

Gabriel thrust at her, pinning Miriam's legs with the weight of his body. He slid against her flesh. He tried to enter her, but the lips of her womanhood were tight.

Miriam screamed.

Nobody was nearby to hear.

Gabriel thrust again. He pierced her vaginal lips.

She resisted him.

He was too strong. The sky seemed to darken. Gabriel pumped at

Miriam with a frenzied look on his face. She pushed at him with all her might and tried to bite his arm. Her teeth caught his wrist.

Gabriel drew out of her body but rushed at her again.

"No, not now!" he cried as he came to his climax.

The warmth of Gabriel's fluid spurted over the smooth flat of Miriam's belly and ran in sticky blobs between her legs. He fell on her body and entered the girl again. Though he was spent, he kept Miriam pinned down, even as she fought for breath. He seemed to be locked on top of her for an eternity. Finally, the sounds of the garden returned. Birds were chirping. The small brook babbled as it tumbled over pebbles.

Miriam, imploding, withdrawing, lost, abandoned, empty, could say nothing. Her angel Gabriel had deserted her. Gabriel was not in this man. She was too stunned to cry and too naïve to know what had happened. The only relief was that her ordeal seemed to be over.

"I'm sorry," Gabriel said, when he released his body from her. "I couldn't help myself. You're beautiful. I wanted you so much. Please forgive me for what I've done."

Tears formed in Gabriel's eyes.

"Just leave me alone," Miriam said. "I don't want to be betrothed to you or anyone else. My angels will take care of me. I'm betrothed to God and God alone."

Gabriel straightened Miriam's dress. His flesh had shrunk. He wound back his loincloth. He held out his hand to Miriam and pulled her up.

"I'm sorry," he repeated. "Let me take you home."

Miriam didn't say a word as they retraced their steps along the path from Gethsemane, across the Kidron and back to the walls of Jerusalem. Her white shift wasn't torn, but it showed marks of her struggle in the green stains of the grass on which they had lain. Gabriel took her to the High Priest's house, where he left her and disappeared into the obscurity of the city.

Miriam remained silent, sore, and bleeding. Afraid to speak to Zechariah, she sought consolation communicating with God, watching his angels in the flickering moonbeams and waiting for His advice for her troubled mind.

* * *

Seated at a heavy table in his private room at the Hasmonean Palace, Zechariah considered his plan. *Elizabeth is now five months pregnant. It's a miracle. We will have a son. God has chosen us to be the instruments of the Messianic Age. Gabriel and Miriam will also have a son. God is guiding me. These cousins will be the hope of a new Israel. My son will be a great teacher; he will prepare people for the time when Miriam's son can freely be proclaimed the legitimate Davidic King of the Jews.* He took a sip on a goblet of wine and felt inner satisfaction.

A servant entered.

"There's a man to see you, sir."

"Who?"

"Gabriel, the priest who was here the other day, sir."

"Show him in."

A few minutes later the servant returned with Gabriel.

Zechariah saw that Gabriel was agitated, his face even redder than his normal, handsome, ruddy complexion.

He waved the servant away.

"I want nothing more to do with this betrothal," Gabriel said. "It will not work with this virgin—not for me."

"But our agreement?"

"What agreement? You made me a proposition. I took you up on it. The young woman is beautiful. It's not that. She has no conversation. She doesn't seem real. I need a woman who's real, sir. I'm a man of flesh and blood. Talk of children snuggling up to her in bed, and helping her weave, a fixation on angels and moonbeams—It's not for me—I can't handle her any more."

"She'll grow up. Give it more time."

Zechariah poured him a goblet of wine.

"No. I've made up my mind. I don't want to be part of your scheme. Find someone else for your virgin. Ask somebody else to 'get her pregnant.'"

Zechariah leaned back nervously. There was a tense silence between them. He sipped on his wine, set down the cup and stood up, towering over Gabriel.

"Very well, leave, but you are to say nothing—nothing about getting her pregnant. Understand?"

"I really couldn't care if she gets pregnant or not. Miriam's your problem, sir, not mine."

Zechariah regained his composure.

"I'm sorry it has not worked out. I will not force her upon you."

Gabriel left.

Zechariah picked up his goblet again and drained its content in a series of gulps. *Oh Simeon,* he said to himself, *obviously Gabriel was not suitable. I need to find somebody else, and quickly.*

* * *

In Bethlehem, the traditional birthplace of King David to the south of Jerusalem, there lived a carpenter named Joseph. His family had been there for generations. Through the Temple archives, Zechariah had traced the lineage of minor Temple priests of the Davidic line to Joseph's family. Joseph was among many descendents of the royal line whose ancestry had long since been forgotten. Like many such Davidic families, Joseph's had fallen from positions of privilege and prestige to become ordinary citizens, even peasants. Joseph wasn't recorded in the carefully kept Temple records, but a certain Matthan was, and he'd lived in Bethlehem. Zechariah recalled meeting the man many years earlier when visiting Joachim in the days he had lived in Bethlehem. They'd been young Temple priests then. When Zechariah sent out his scouts to Bethlehem to investigate the descendents of Matthan, they discovered that Matthan's grandson Joseph was still living in the village. Jacob, Joseph's father, also a carpenter by trade, had several sons. Only Joseph had remained in Bethlehem. Matthan had long since passed away, but leaders of the Bethlehem Synagogue were able to tell the Temple servants where to find Joseph.

Through this research, Zechariah learned that Joseph had been married to a Bethlehem girl named Martha, who had given him four children from this marriage, three boys and a girl. Martha had apparently died about three years earlier. Joseph's oldest son was named Jacob, a young man with a serious nature who wasn't as interested in his father's trade as Joseph would have liked. Jacob had learned a little Greek and was resented by his brothers for his scholastic leanings. They called him 'James', thinking they were mocking him by changing his Hebrew name to something that resembled the language of the hated Roman foreigners. He liked the name, however, and kept it.

Ruth, Joseph's daughter, was the youngest in his family. She'd recently turned five. Her brothers were between ten and fourteen. Joseph tried to get James and Amos, his second son, to work with him on his carpentry projects. Unlike his older brother, Amos showed some promise. Since Joseph had lost his wife, James had taken on a lot of the responsibility for raising the family. Little Ruth missed her mother terribly, even after three years. She was encouraged by her big brother to take over some of her mother's domestic duties. She often tried to bake the simple cakes and bread that were the family's sustenance, sometimes burning them. Ruth often went to the well to fetch water, although the jar was very heavy for her, and James sometimes had to help her carry it home.

It was Joseph's third son Jonah who was the problem child. Jonah had been seven when his mother had passed away. He'd been the most affected by the tragedy. At ten, he'd become a rebellious youth and planned to leave home to live on his own. He constantly disobeyed his older brothers and father. Ruth was afraid of him, because he bullied her. The problem became so bad that Joseph finally sought the help of his widowed cousin, Bathsheba. For about a year Bathsheba had lived with his family and brought some domestic order into Joseph's chaotic household.

Zechariah sent his Temple servants to Bethlehem. They peered into Joseph's carpentry shop. It took up most of the road frontage of the small square house.

Joseph, a robust man with large clumsy-looking hands, looked up from chiseling a plank. His dark beard was flecked in sawdust.

"Are you Joseph, the son of Jacob, the son of Matthan?" their leader asked.

"What do you want with me?"

He set aside the plank and picked up a mallet.

"Come with us to Jerusalem to meet Zechariah the High Priest."

"What is this? I'm an innocent man. Can't you see I have a family? Is my son in some sort of trouble?"

"Not that we know of. Our orders are simply to request that you come with us. The High Priest needs your services."

The Temple servants weren't armed and made no overture to treat

Joseph roughly. Joseph's fear subsided, and he set the mallet aside. He was a good man. He'd always said his evening prayers and regularly attended the Bethlehem synagogue.

Since Martha's death, he'd had no time for anything. It was as much as he could do to keep up with the back orders in his trade. The amount of building work had increased since his father's time. Orders for carpentry outpaced his capacity to produce.

"I haven't time," he said.

The Temple servants were persistent. They produced a small bag of silver coins to assure Joseph that due compensation would be made.

At this point, Bathsheba became curious to know what all this was about. Seeing the bag of coins, she said:

"Oh, Joseph! What's there to lose? I'll be here with the children. You can give Amos some simple tasks to perform while you're gone. He's getting more skilled every day. He repaired our old benches effectively."

She smiled encouragingly.

Amos was becoming quite an accomplished joiner now that he'd worked with Joseph for a year. Soon Joseph would be able to give him major work in the carpenter's shop. If James had half of Amos' ability, they'd now have a thriving business, but James made far too many mistakes and preferred his academic studies. James could read and write. It looked as if neither Amos nor Jonah would ever achieve that goal. James attended the synagogue school, and the Rabbi had commented to Joseph that he had a very bright son. Amos and Jonah had left their schooling and received their education in the streets. Bathsheba, struggling with Joseph's sons, had done her best to start educating Ruth into the domestic chores that would be her life's role. Life in Joseph's house was not easy. Joseph wiped his hands and patted Bathsheba's shoulder.

"All right. I'll go."

He exchanged the carpenter's tunic for his best robe. Then, he surprisingly embraced his cousin Bathsheba.

"Take care of the family. I'm sure I'll only be gone a few days," he said. "I'll see the new Temple in all its glory. I can come back and tell you all about it."

* * *

Zechariah put down the scroll he was reading when a servant announced that the carpenter from Bethlehem had arrived. The High Priest stood up and pointed to his empty goblet. The servant nodded and left. Walking over to the window, Zechariah looked down into the courtyard.

The guards had dismounted, but a dark-haired, middle-aged man in a rough, brown robe was still astride a pathetic-looking mule. *That must be him,* he thought. *Matthan's grandson.* He raised his eyes upward. *God, is this the one?* He watched the man slide off the mule. *He looks much older than Gabriel, about twenty years older than Miriam. Obviously, he comes from a much simpler background. There might be advantages to this. This man will take the virgin into relative obscurity should any suspicion of the messianic plot arise. If this man marries Miriam, nobody will suspect that a child of such a union could possibly be the Davidic Messiah and a future King of the Jews. It will be easy to hide the seed of the house of David in this lowly background far removed from Jerusalem politics and the suspicions of the Herodians.*

The servant came back with a jar of wine and two goblets. Zechariah handed him his wax tablet on which he had written: 'Send the man to me along with my steward.'

After a scribe had interpreted the message for the servant, Joseph was escorted by Zechariah's steward in to the High Priest's presence. Taller than Gabriel, Joseph still looked small beside Zechariah as the High Priest beckoned for his steward to serve his guest wine. Zechariah noted Joseph's simple dress that still smelled of the mule's sweat, but the man had a humble kindly face.

Simplicity seems to be Miriam's way, he thought. *Maybe the kind face of this middle-aged carpenter will appeal to her strange mysticism and innocence. Apparently, Joseph already has a family. Miriam might like that. She's proven herself to be good at helping out with the young Temple virgins. Joseph's children would be about her own age. She will probably identify with them.*

Zechariah felt a new hope in the carpenter. *All is not lost. God is still in charge.* Communicating through his steward with his wax tablet, he outlined to Joseph his intent.

"You want me to marry one of the Temple virgins?" Joseph said incredulously.

Zechariah nodded.

A surprised grin came over Joseph's face.

"How will I support her?"

Zechariah wrote for his steward to pass on: 'We will help you.'

Incredulous but curious, Joseph looked up at the High Priest.

"Is she beautiful?" he asked.

Zechariah's face matched that of his guest.

"Very beautiful," his steward answered.

The High Priest felt a great relief. Joseph was interested. He believed God had intervened in leading him to Joseph and considered his original selection of Gabriel to have been a secular mistake.

* * *

Joseph felt a little self-conscious in the striped blue-gray robe that Zechariah's servant had provided for him. They had suggested he bathe in the Hasmonean baths; it was some five years since he had immersed himself in warm water. He was used to a quick bucket of water thrown over his torso at the village well. *They are really serious about this*, he thought. *They really want me to marry this young woman.*

The servant came back to his room.

"The High Priest would like to see you now."

Joseph followed the man to the large room overlooking the courtyard.

Zechariah smiled when he saw Joseph in his new robe with a clean, fresh face. He beckoned for him to sit at the heavy table and poured him wine.

A minute or two later the door opened again and Miriam was escorted in.

Zechariah, whose perceptions seemed to have become sharper in his mute state, watched Joseph. The man seemed to lean back uncomfortably, but never took his eyes off Miriam—her simple beauty enhanced by a white dress that contrasted with her long chestnut ringlets. Zechariah silently turned his attention to Miriam. She looked perplexed, her eyes dashing from Joseph's calloused hands to his kindly face.

After the bath, the slight graying of Joseph's dark hair gave him a softness and calm honesty. Miriam seemed to warm to that. In appearance, Joseph was everything that Gabriel was not. Miriam had no illusions now about good looks and affluent clothing. She had expressed her feelings to Zechariah about that. It was as much as he could do to persuade her to meet Joseph. *'I don't want to be married,'* she had said. *'I'm married to God.'* Zechariah guessed that Gabriel must have done something to upset her. Miriam had retreated into herself. Zechariah, now, beckoned to Joseph to introduce himself.

"Shalom," he said nervously. "The High Priest thought I would like to meet you."

Miriam looked Joseph in the eye and then smiled.

"Yes. He wants me to meet you, too."

Zechariah relaxed. He could see they were open.

"Can I offer her some wine?" Joseph asked.

Zechariah nodded.

Miriam took only a sip.

* * *

As they shared more moments together, Miriam reminded Joseph of his younger life with Martha before they had their family. *Will she be able to handle my family?* He wondered. *She will be about their age! She'll be like a big sister to Ruth, and maybe she will tame the tearaway Jonah.* Joseph warmed to her more as an adopted daughter than as a potential spouse. *Bathsheba will still be there to run the house,* he consoled himself.

Zechariah was afraid to say too much to Joseph about his ultimate plan. *The simple man might become frightened,* he concluded. Nonetheless, the High Priest was now convinced that he was executing God's will in this messianic plan. God would reveal his purposes to Joseph in due course. It was enough for now that he had explained to Joseph that it was one of his responsibilities as the High Priest to find suitable spouses for the Temple virgins. The steward read Zechariah's message to Joseph:

"I found your grandfather's name by tracing the lineage of David in the Temple archives. I needed to arrange a marriage between Miriam and a Davidic family. It's a requirement for the virgins, you know."

Joseph believed him.

Joseph felt more comfortable, too, as he freely discussed his children with Miriam. This seemed to be their common ground. Obviously, Miriam liked children. She could help him with his.

Zechariah observed that although she expressed to him her desire to stay at the House of the Virgins as an assistant to the matron, she seemed much happier at the thought of living with this man than with Gabriel. Zechariah, with his clever coaxing, had gotten his way.

Joseph agreed to consider the proposal, but first he needed to return to Bethlehem and complete his back orders. Zechariah sent him back with gifts of clothing and wine.

That night, Zechariah walked out on his terrace overlooking the city. The ghostly light of the full moon made Herod's new buildings gleam as he himself glowed. *Joseph is infinitely more suitable than Gabriel,* he thought. *Simple, too. He won't question me. God is guiding us again. The messianic dream is alive once more. Tomorrow, I will take Miriam to Ain Karim.*

* * *

Miriam walked out into the courtyard at the House of the Virgins, knowing this would be for the last time. In the moonlight, she prayed: *Tomorrow I have to go away to the High Priest's house in the country. Please send your angels with me. I'll pray in the moonlight there just like I have here.* Miriam's emotions were a mixture of fear, excitement, regret, and wonder. She often thought like a child, but her body told her that she wasn't childlike. She looked down and felt her budding breasts that seemed somehow exaggerated in the shadows of the moonlight. She'd noticed how the Levitical priests and Temple servants treated her differently than when she was younger. She'd seen the way they looked at her. Her stomach tightened as she remembered her experience with Gabriel. *Joseph will be more gentle with me,* she thought. She wanted to deny that adolescence and womanhood were upon her, but she knew they were.

As she stood in the moonlight, Miriam reflected on the time of the full moon the month before when she'd celebrated her last Passover at the Temple. This time, the matron, a middle-aged Jewess who always wore a blue robe and headress, had asked her to help hide the crumbs of leaven. *She said I was now too old to hunt for them and that I must help her now organize these Passover games.* After she and the matron had hidden the leaven, they had watched as all the young virgins tried to find the crumbs, searching through every room in the house. Miriam smiled: *Leanne pulled at my dress. It was so hard to tell her I couldn't help her. But that wouldn't have been fair.* Once all the crumbs had been gathered, they were ceremonially burned. Only the flat unleavened matzohs could be eaten during the following seven days. This was in preparation for Passover. "*Hide the flat matzoh,*" Matron said to me. "*Then, send the young ones out to find it.*" *This was the beginning of the serious Passover observance.* Every year, the matron explained that the matzoh flat bread that hadn't been leavened was to remind the virgins, and indeed all Jews, that when their ancestors prepared to leave Egypt with Moses, there'd been no time to make normal bread and wait for it to rise. In haste, they'd taken the flat matzohs with them for their journey. Miriam had felt a pride in hiding the matzoh. This last Passover had meant so much more to her—no longer a game, but now a religious ceremony. Now, a month later, she was about to start a new cycle in her life's journey.

She called on her angel, Gabriel. He flickered down the shaft of light while the wind rustled the leaves of the old olive trees.

"Gabriel! Gabriel! There you are!" she called out in a voice that was neither child nor adult. "Gabriel, please stay with me. I don't want you to ever leave me. Will you stay with me wherever I go? Will I still be able to find you in the moonlight at the High Priest's house? Will you be with me when I have to live with Joseph and his family?"

The wind stirred the trees again, and a full moonbeam fell down on Miriam, making her glow in its translucent light. It seemed that a whole choir of angels had descended from above and alighted upon her. Some of the dead leaves that lay on the marble slabs at her feet rustled and swirled in a little dance as they caught the eerie light. This seemed to give her the answer she was hoping to hear.

"Yes, Miriam. We'll be with you wherever you go," they seemed to say. "You're a child of God. No matter where you are, God will always be with you."

In her heart, Miriam heard the angels sing:

"Holy! Holy! Holy!"

Her heart beat with emotion. She felt she could hear Gabriel's voice. She looked up through the parted branches of the gnarled trees at the smiling face of the moon.

"Greetings, Miriam!" the voice said. "The Lord is with you! Don't be afraid, for you've found favor with God. If you have a child, you must name him Joshua. Any child of yours will be like a son of God bathed in light. He'll rule over God's kingdom forever because God's kingdom has no end."

The leaves sprang back in the night breeze and broke the full flow of the moon's light. Once again, the angels seemed to flicker up and down the scattered beams.

Miriam stood, awestruck in the power of her emotions. *I'll give Joseph a son, and he'll be great, just as Gabriel said. Gabriel and the angels will stay with us and our family forever. God will lead me wherever I must go.*

Every time the wind opened the leaves above, the shaft of full moonlight bathed Miriam in celestial light and she heard music. She was totally mesmerized by the moment. With a mixture of fear, elation, apprehension, and joy, tears rolled down her cheeks. She felt one with God, united to Him in His power and majesty. God could use her in whatever way He wished, because she was His and His forever.

Clouds began to pass over the full moon. The strength of the light weakened, leaving only a silver outline around the passing clouds. The courtyard faded into darkness. The rustling of dead leaves increased. The breeze stiffened and moved the upper limbs of the old trees in a ghostly silhouette. The air chilled, and the sounds of night returned.

Before going back to the warmth and safety of the virgins' bedchamber, Miriam knelt down with her hands across her chest and cried out to her God:

"Look after me, Lord, for you've chosen me. Do with me whatever you like, but take care of me!"

Total darkness then engulfed the courtyard. The silver lining around the clouds disappeared. The first drops of rain splattered on the marble slabs.

* * *

Spring rain fell outside the windows of the Commander's Quarters in Sepphoris. The parade ground was muddy. Flavius Septimus, pleased with his promotion, looked from his balcony at the scene made all the more dismal by the early approach of evening. The noise of horses attracted his attention. A dispatch rider from Damascus arrived.

The man dismounted. Soldiers took his horse. Flavius prepared to meet him, adjusting his uniform and seating himself at the table that served as his desk. He heard the man being escorted up the stone stairs.

"Greetings!" the man said on entering the room, "Hail Caesar!"

"Hail Caesar!" Flavius replied.

Opening his leather dispatch bag, the man put four scrolls on the table. Flavius recognized three of them to be routine information from the Syrian Governor, but the fourth was from Rome. It was sealed with Senator Tarquin's token, and the scroll was edged in purple.

"They'll take care of you in the Centurions' dormitory," Flavius said. "Make sure you use the hot baths while you are here. You must be soaked through."

The dispatch rider smiled.

"I will. Your baths are very good here."

He turned to leave, but at the door, looked back at the Commander.

"Hail Caesar!" he snapped.

"Hail Caesar!" Flavius repeated.

It was taking Flavius a while to get used to this imperial form of address that now went with his rank. *I am truly Caesar's representative in Galilee now*, he chuckled to himself. He picked up the Senator's scroll.

'Young Flavius,' he read.

How he hated Copernia's illustrious uncle's way of addressing him.

> 'Copernia will be traveling to the Province of Syria this month. I have arranged passage for her on a comfortable boat heading for your new port of Caesarea. With fair winds, she should arrive in Judea the middle of next month. I am sending this by Imperial post to Damascus. You should receive this a week or two before her arrival. By the way, congratulations on your promotion. Your father would have been proud of you.'

It was signed: 'Tarquinius.'

Flavius Septimus was in Caesarea for over two weeks before the large vessel from Ostia was sighted on the horizon. He had checked daily with the agents on ships from Rome. All ships so far this spring had either come up from Alexandria or down from Antioch.

"She's a big one," the agent said as he squinted out to sea. "She'll almost certainly be the first from Rome."

Flavius went back to his inn and proudly changed into his official uniform as a Tribune in the service of Caesar. By the time he returned to the inner harbor, he could see the large galley. Her sail was now lowered, and the muffled sound of the slave master's drum wafted across the water.

The feathered plumes of his Tribune's helmet swayed in the sea breeze that brought a salty tang to his face.

Caesarea was a magnificent gateway to the Levant. Copernia's first impressions of Judea would be highly favorable. The architecture and ambience were decidedly Roman, as was the dress of so many on the quayside. The new marble of the splendid colonnades around the warehouses, the paved walls of the inner and outer harbors, and the hustle and bustle of maritime life would remind her of Ostia. There was little that was Semitic about Herod's port city. Flavius was so glad that he was here to greet her. All thoughts of Esther were temporarily banished as he kept his eyes on the approaching vessel. The drum stopped. The oars rested. With a splash, the anchor fell into the waters of the outer harbor.

Men shouted as they prepared a lighter to meet the galley. For a moment, Flavius considered riding out on the lighter, but the agent assured him that he was outside the right warehouse for this delivery.

"Better for you to stay here, they'll be some time out there loading her up."

It wasn't possible to bring such a large, heavily laden Roman vessel into the inner harbor because of the sandy shallows. The breakwater wall, built to precision by Herod's stonemasons, gave shelter and protection to the vessels anchored in the outer harbor awating their turn to unload their goods.

The sun felt warm on Flavius' back as he waited.

At last, the ferrying lighter came back into the inner harbor. Flavius spotted Copernia standing on the prow of the raft-like boat. She looked as lovely as he remembered her. Her olive Latin complexion had been enhanced by the sunshine of a pleasant voyage. Somehow, the olive skin of the Tuscan women was less weathered and coarse than that of the Hebrews. Despite her bulky traveling clothes, Flavius saw the beauty of his wife's form, and the grace and poise that belonged to this aristocrat of the Tuscan Province. Seeing her again, made him feel even more guilty that he'd sated his needs with Esther.

Copernia recognized him. She waved as the breeze blew through her hair. Several large chests and boxes were stacked behind her on the lighter. Soon, the pontoon boat was alongside. Flavius extended his hand to help Copernia up the steps. Her eyes glistened with tears of joy.

On the bustling dockside, a little self conscious in his new uniform, Flavius put his arm around her slender waist:

"Welcome to Judea," he said rather pompously.

She smiled.

"It doesn't look so bad. I expected a backwater, but this place looks grander than Ostia."

"Ostia's a port of merchants," Flavius said as he swept up his arm proudly. "This is Caesarea, the gateway to the Levant."

Copernia tried to pick up her damp skirts that hung heavily.

"Where will they put my things, Flavius?"

Four dockworkers were already moving the heavy chests.

"Don't worry, my lady," the agent said. "I have all that under control. They are to be carted to Magdala—right, sir?"

"Right. Just as soon as you can get them there, but pack them well. My wife has some breakable items there—like those statues. Use plenty of straw."

"Magdala's one of those villages south of Capernaum—Taricheae right?"

"Right," Flavius repeated.

The man grinned:

"Taricheae and Capernaum…Where the fish come from. Those flat fish are very special."

Flavius looked at Copernia.

"Well, what do you think? You see the Temple up there. It's not quite finished yet, but we should go up and place an offering in gratitude for your safe voyage."

King Herod had built and dedicated the temple at the head of the inner harbor to his patron, Caesar Augustus. Masons were still working on parts of the frieze, which meant that one side was hidden by scaffolds and planks. Flavius, with his arm still firmly around Copernia's waist, took her to the temple. After offering thanks, Flavius and Copernia went to a Taverna situated on the outskirts of the town.

Finally, by the light of a single lamp and to the sounds of the tavern crowd below, they kissed. At first, it was gentle, not passionate, befitting their patrician background. Flavius still felt pangs of guilt as he held his wife. The memory of the cheap fragrance of the whore's bedchamber stood sharply in contrast to Copernia's sweet scent. The silky refinement of his wife's smooth Latin skin was so different from the abused softness of Esther's body.

"I've missed you," Copernia said.

Flavius was not sure what to say as his conscience gnawed at him. Better to show his response with more passion, he thought. He buried his head in the comfort of her breasts and tried to forget Esther.

Copernia pulled him closer, but Flavius could not forget Esther's passion.

When they made love, Copernia was more passive in response, but more loving in her joy than her Hebrew rival.

"You looked so magnificent in your new uniform," his wife said, stroking his chest after she reached fulfillment. "I think I can be happy here."

"Wait till you see your new home. It's beautiful on the lake, Copernia. It'll remind you of Tuscany."

Exhausted, the couple lay in each other's arms. *I have a duty to Copernia now*, Flavius thought, while his wife slept. He kissed her gently and then slept, too.

CHAPTER SIX

The future is sealed

In the tradition of Jewish betrothal, Miriam was to wait awhile before marrying Joseph. She'd stay with Zechariah and Elizabeth at Ain Karim and become accustomed to life in the outside world. Miriam only had to perform the most basic of domestic duties in the House of the Virgins. The High Priest decided that Elizabeth should train Miriam in the household skills she'd need. It was unlikely in her forthcoming marriage to a man like Joseph that Miriam would ever have a maid, so it was necessary for her to learn all the intricate rules of food preparation. She needed to know how to gather produce and cook or preserve it in the traditional way.

Meanwhile, Joseph set about the task of preparing his family for Miriam's arrival in Bethlehem. His greatest wish was that the new arrangement wouldn't upset Bathsheba. She could be a big help to Miriam since she knew all the household skills, but Bathsheba was very territorial about her position.

Miriam looked with awe at all the sights on the road from Jerusalem to Ain Karim. She didn't remember the countryside that she must have seen in her youngest years. Seeing bullock carts, camels, and oxen was a fresh and new experience. She'd never watched seed being sown or oxen ploughing. The sight of birds following a plough and swooping down for the scattered seeds that fell by the wayside from a sower's bag was exhilarating and exciting. She loved the simple square houses that made up the small villages. Each house was built of sand-colored limestone and had a flat roof that could be reached by a flight of stone steps. The people used these flat roofs for living space. They wove and spun in the sunshine while others slept under awnings, resting from their labors.

This short journey was the most wonderful experience Miriam had ever had. But when they arrived at Zechariah's house at Ain Karim, some of the novelty diminished. The villa reminded Miriam more of the House of the Virgins, with its courtyard in the Hellenistic style, than of the flat-topped peasant homes they'd passed throughout the day.

But after Elizabeth welcomed her with open arms, Miriam felt at home. Elizabeth was in her sixth month of pregnancy and obviously showing. This, too, was a new experience for Miriam, who showed great adolescent curiosity in her aunt's condition. Elizabeth explained that her baby would be due in about three months or less, and that at times she felt really tired. She told Miriam that the worst stages had been at the very beginning, when she'd felt sick and craved strange foods. Miriam was fascinated by all that Elizabeth said. She reflected upon her vision of Gabriel and the angels in the moonlight. *Gabriel said that I'd have a baby.* She wanted to learn all that she could from Elizabeth.

"How do you know you're going to have a baby?" Miriam asked.

"You just know," Elizabeth said, taking Miriam's head onto her chest. "Very quickly your body begins to respond. You feel different. Soon after that feeling, your body tells you you're pregnant."

Miriam had been frightened the year before when she'd begun to experience menstruation. It was rare that the matron of the virgins had to explain as much as she did to Miriam. Most of the virgins left the Temple on the threshold of puberty. At first, Miriam thought she'd cut herself while climbing on the olive trees in the courtyard, playing with some of the younger children. The bleeding, however, didn't heal. She'd asked the matron for help. When the bleeding stopped, she thought she'd been cured. But it came back again the next month. Miriam cried. She didn't believe the matron when she'd assured her with the words:

"This makes us women and no longer children."

Miriam was making bread with her aunt when she asked about Zechariah's dumbness:

"Will he ever talk again?"

"I hope so, Miriam. He believes he will. I believe his lack of speech is a sign from God."

She placed Miriam's floured hand on her belly.

"Zechariah does, too. This child of mine is a miracle baby. I was never expected to have a child, but the Lord has determined that I should. This baby's God's baby, Miriam. God chose us, and in doing so gave us a sign. Zechariah will speak again. His dumbness is just a sign from God that our baby is to be someone special."

"God gives us so many signs," Miriam said.

But Miriam had been at Zechariah's house for less than a month when it occurred to her God must have taken away the sign of her womanhood. The monthly bleeding stopped.

Elizabeth had explained a great deal to Miriam in their female chats about pregnancy. She'd allowed Miriam to feel the little movements of life within her own womb. However, she hadn't mentioned the true function of a woman's menstrual cycle. So Miriam didn't equate her irregularity with pregnancy. Instead, she thought she must have failed or sinned in some way, and God had taken away her womanhood.

As they were picking herbs together from the little garden outside the kitchen, Miriam brought up the subject.

"Aunt Elizabeth, does God punish us for our sins?"

"Well, that depends. Sometimes, God seems to punish us, and deep in our hearts we know why He's done so. That's when guilt shows itself. If we repent and feel sorry, God removes that guilty feeling and makes us whole and happy again."

"What if we don't know we've sinned?"

"Well, sometimes, we think we don't know. That's because we're too proud to let ourselves know. We become blind to our faults and the things we might have done wrong."

"Elizabeth, I think I've sinned in some way," Miriam said slowly.

Tears welled in her great brown eyes.

"I don't know what I've done wrong. Maybe I've been blinded by all the new things I'm learning. I've neglected something I should have done."

"God doesn't punish innocent young people like you, Miriam," Elizabeth said, putting an arm around her shoulder. "You have to do something very wrong for God to punish you. You have to hurt someone deeply or deceive people for your own gain."

Elizabeth smiled at Miriam.

"I don't think you've offended God in those ways. God's not going to punish you for small things, like having wandering thoughts when you're praying, or forgetting small details in the food preparation. God loves you, as your Father. He doesn't want to punish you unless He must for your own good."

Miriam was now in tears. Elizabeth's embrace didn't comfort her. She blurted out the truth:

"Elizabeth! God's taken away the sign of my womanhood. He's made me like a child again."

She fell into Elizabeth's arms.

Miriam clung to her, greedily taking in her warmth, pressing herself like a babe to her bosom, urgently burying herself into the warmth and flesh.

Elizabeth took her in, recognizing Miriam's needs for closeness and maternal comfort.

"My dear girl. The House of the Virgins must have been terrible for you."

"No! Oh, no! I loved it there. I was doing God's work!" Miriam shivered in her anxiety.

"Of course, Miriam, of course. I simply meant you needed closeness, to be held and touched. We all need that, especially as you are now a young woman."

"But, Aunt Elizabeth, I still haven't bled in the usual way." she said, as her tears wet Elizabeth's bosom.

"Sometimes, at your age that happens. You're still growing into womanhood. Your bleeding will probably come again soon. Promise you'll tell me when it returns. Then you'll know God isn't punishing you."

Temporarily, Miriam was satisfied. She began to see the bleeding more as a bodily function than as some sign from God.

"I'm so glad I have you to talk with," she said .

Elizabeth smiled, delicately pressing away Miriam's tears with her thumb.

Two more weeks passed, however, and Miriam began to feel nauseated and lethargic. Complaining of sickness, she sought Elizabeth.

"I don't feel well. There's been no sign of the bleeding. I'm afraid. There's something wrong. Help me. Maybe I'm dying."

This time, Elizabeth pondered on the unthinkable possibility that her naïve niece might be pregnant and not even know how she got that way. She comforted Miriam as well as she could without revealing the horrifying thoughts in her mind.

Elizabeth straightened the straw pallet on the floor and turned to her niece.

"Miriam, lie down awhile on this pallet. I'm going to make you an herbal drink. I won't be long. Then you can sleep."

Elizabeth hastened to look for Zechariah.

"Zach," she whispered when she found him, "I think Miriam's pregnant! She's feeling sick and has shown no sign of her womanhood for nearly two months."

Zechariah struggled to speak, but his utterances were incomprehensible. He gave up and reached for his stylus and wax tablet. He wrote: 'It could be Gabriel!'

Zechariah had felt unhappy about Gabriel since the young priest had withdrawn his support. Possibly, the spoiled youth had taken advantage of Miriam's innocence. He remembered the grass stains on her dress. *Did he rape her?* he asked himself. Zechariah was a little afraid of Gabriel, who now had vital knowledge of the High Priest's messianic plan. All could be exposed by this good-looking, self-confident, charmer. He was likely to brag to others that the High Priest had selected him to be Miriam's spouse. Zechariah's finger tapped the wax tablet vigorously, blurring Gabriel's name with his accusation.

Elizabeth looked at him in horror. She knew nothing of Zechariah's messianic plan beyond their joint belief that their expected child was a special gift to them from God.

"Who is Gabriel? What is going on?" she asked.

'A potential spouse,' wrote Zechariah. He smoothed the wax and continued: 'I selected him before Joseph, but he let me down.'

Zechariah hadn't been able to share much with his wife over the past three or four months because of his incapacity to speak. 'Are you sure she's pregnant?' he wrote.

"No, but it's a possibility. Miriam's confided in me that she's afraid God might be punishing her for some terrible sin she thinks she's committed. If Gabriel took advantage of her, she might think she's a sinner. Zach, if this is true, it's terrible. Miriam's only a child in so many ways, she still has so much to learn. She's not ready to be a mother."

Elizabeth began to cry.

Zechariah's first concern was for the dire consequences to them all if his messianic plot was talked about to the wrong people. He squeezed the wax tablet as he considered the possibilities, cleared it, and then started to write again: 'We must be sure she's pregnant.'

Elizabeth nodded through her tears.

At first, Elizabeth and Zechariah tried to cheer up Miriam without revealing their true thoughts on her condition. It wasn't long, however, before Miriam started to crave raw green peppers from the garden. Miriam's continued nausea and the passing of more time with no sign of her menstruation eventually convinced Elizabeth of the reality of the situation. Unquestionably, Miriam was going to have a baby.

Zechariah was now faced with the painful duty of trying to find out the details from Miriam. He had to do this through Elizabeth because of his impediment. Not altogether to his surprise, the truth he suspected began to emerge.

"Miriam," Elizabeth said in a kindly way, as the girl lay on her pallet in a nauseous state, "you're going to have a baby. We'll take care of you, but there are certain things we really have to know."

Elizabeth expected fear, remorse, guilt, and tears, but Miriam beamed, lifting herself up, and excitedly asked:

"How soon?"

"In about seven months, I would think. It's hard to tell unless you can give us some information."

"What do you need to know?"

"Miriam, who is the baby's father? Was it Gabriel?"

"Gabriel told me I might have a baby," Miriam said.

A joyous smile crossed her face.

"In the moonlit courtyard, at the House of the Virgins, Gabriel said if I had a baby he'd be a son of God and a great king! Gabriel said that I'm favored by God and He'd look after me forever!"

In her joy, she remembered the virgins' garden, the lustrous warm orb of the moon, the dancing moonbeams and Gabriel's heavenly presence.

When his wife reported her findings to him, Zechariah's anger increased. It had never occurred to him that Gabriel would trespass within the forbidden House of the Virgins. *How did he get past the matron?* he thought. *It is no wonder that Miriam thinks she has committed some kind of sin.*

Zechariah nervously stroked his beard. Then, he started to write: 'Tell Miriam it's all right. Her baby will be great, a gift from God to us all.'

Elizabeth passed on the message.

Miriam lay back on her pallet. A warm glow emanated from her happy face. She was in another world and was no longer afraid, knowing Gabriel had been there in the moonbeams. She'd be at one with God forever. She smiled contentedly, closed her eyes, and fell asleep.

Elizabeth didn't understand her niece's serenity. *How can you be so calm if the man deserted you after probably raping you?* she thought.

Zechariah faced a crisis. He'd have to explain everything to Joseph. He needed to silence the priest Gabriel and would probably have to bribe the bastard to keep him quiet. How could he go to Jerusalem now? He needed to be with Elizabeth until their own son was safely born.

Pressures built up all around Zechariah. He held Elizabeth. She felt the powerful tension racking his body. As his lungs heaved, Zechariah called out to God in his anguish:

"Ma Ga!"

"Zach!" Elizabeth shouted in surprise.

"Ma Ga!"

"Zach! You can speak!"

"Ma Ga!" pressed from his lips, a whisper this time.

He took Elizabeth by the hand. Exhausted, they rested.

* * *

In the days that followed, Zechariah set up a small loom on the porch so Miriam could weave. Elizabeth, her pregnancy now restricting her household activities, sat with Miriam feeding her yarn.

"I really hear these messages," Miriam said excitedly as she passed the shuttle through the fibrous cords. "I know God speaks to me. I know exactly what He is saying to me, but I just know it. I don't really hear a voice, but I know what He is saying somehow. Gabriel told me many things. He relays messages from God. He told me I will have a son and I must name him Joshua. He'll be a king and rule forever."

"Gabriel?"

"Yes. The matron said Gabriel is an archangel. He's my angel. All the angels sing to me. I hear them in the moonlight—also, in the rustling of the leaves. But they seem to say much more in the moonlight."

"Slow down, Miriam. You're speaking too fast."

"I hope they speak to me here, Aunt Elizabeth. Gabriel hasn't spoken to me since I came here. Is that a sign I've done something wrong?"

Elizabeth listened to it all, but could only conclude that her niece was confused and trying to hide in a fantasy what must have happened. *Did Gabriel make improper advances on her?* she wondered. *Did he make her pregnant? I know Zach thinks so.* Elizabeth, knowing how naïve and sincere Miriam was, found it hard to believe that the virgin could have freely given herself to this man she wanted to disguise as her angel. She fed her niece more wool.

"God has chosen you in some special way, Miriam, just like He's chosen me," she said. "He will forgive you for anything you've done. He forgave King David because He chose him. If your baby is to be a king ruling forever, He will forgive you, too."

Miriam smiled.

"I don't really worry about it any more. I thank God for selecting me as His chosen one. My child is God's special gift to me. I can be a mother, and also a sister to all Joseph's children. Do you like Joseph?"

"I haven't met him yet, but I'm sure I will."

Elizabeth, as her own time came nearer, observed Miriam's growing maturity. Since discovering the truth of her pregnancy, Miriam's childlike world was falling away, leaving in its place a great spiritual intensity and fervor. She was becoming more responsible, deeply concerned that she'd be a worthy mother of the son whom she claimed was from God. An astute and fast learner, the mother-to-be added earthly, simple domestic tasks to her spiritual calling. The innocent was becoming a powerful presence.

But Miriam continued to speak warmly of her Gabriel, even if somewhat mysteriously. It puzzled Elizabeth. At the same time, Miriam showed an ever greater interest in the serious proposal of her marriage to Joseph the carpenter. Miriam expressed a growing desire to care for the carpenter and his family.

Elizabeth worried deep in her heart about Miriam's optimism and confusion if her child really was the result of Gabriel's indiscretion— possibly a monstrous rape. *But what of my own child? Zach and I both believe the child in my own womb is a gift from God,* she mused. *What's happening to us all? What's happening?* She sought out Zechariah.

"Wha hav happ....hav happ…" Zechariah said, reaching for his wax tablet. It was still easier for him to write than speak. 'Miriam's child is still a child of God. Our son and Miriam's son are divine gifts to our people,' he wrote. 'But now, nobody should know.' He smoothed the wax.

"Do you think Gabriel knows?"

Zechariah picked up the stylus.

'Not yet, but he might find out. I will have to keep him quiet. Leave that with me,' he wrote.

"How will Joseph take this news?"

Zechariah stared ahead for a moment, then, wrote feverishly again: 'We must get him here. I will have to explain to him. They must marry, Elizabeth. They must.'

* * *

Zechariah sent messengers to Bethlehem inviting Joseph to Ain Karim. But Joseph wasn't really ready to take in Miriam. He needed to enlarge his simple home at the carpenter's shop. He didn't want to curtail the freedom of his sons and daughter. At the same time, he needed to provide his bride with personal privacy.

Then, there were problems with Bathsheba. He felt he needed her to run his household. Miriam would have so much to learn. She hadn't any experience of normal domestic family life. Bathsheba could teach her. Yet, Joseph suspected Bathsheba was jealous of sharing his household with Miriam.

In the midst of this uncertainty, Temple messengers arrived again. This time Joseph was summoned to go with them to the High Priest's house at Ain Karim.

Joseph arrived at Ain Karim on the day when Elizabeth had gone into labor. The High Priest's household was focussed on the imminent birth of her baby. The village midwife was already present. Despite Elizabeth's age, everything appeared to be progressing normally. Miriam, too, with remarkable newfound strength and wisdom, soothed Elizabeth as she came into her ordeal.

When the High Priest received Joseph, to the carpenter's surprise Zechariah greeted him with a semblance of speech.

"Osef, wel cum," he said slowly. "Cum, cum, cum in."

The High Priest then stuttered an attempted explanation that his wife was giving birth. From a distance, Joseph could see the hushed activities in the room where Elizabeth lay, but Zechariah led him off into an adjacent room. He continued to try to converse, but his nervous stutter made him unintelligible.

Miriam, unaware of Joseph's arrival, continued to comfort Elizabeth.

"More water and linens," called the midwife.

Miriam and Hannah handed her what they had.

"Nearly there. Just a little more," the midwife encouraged Elizabeth in the discomfort of her birthing.

Elizabeth pushed her pelvic muscles as hard as she could.

At last, the baby was born. In her advanced years, Elizabeth had conceived and given birth to her first child, a baby boy.

Zechariah heard the shouts of the women and the first cry of his son. Tears ran down his face. Running out with Joseph to Elizabeth's chamber, he cried out with joy:

"Ma Ga! Ma God! A son!"

His speech was almost normal.

"Osef! A son!" he cried again, embracing Joseph.

Elizabeth smiled weakly. She was still in great pain. Not only had she given birth to a son, but Zechariah's voice was returning.

After his first burst of joy, Zechariah lost his speech control and fell back into stutter.

When asked what name should be given to the child, Elizabeth answered:

"Zechariah."

Zechariah shook his head in agitation. As the Patriarch, it was his choice of name that would count in any case.

"No! No Zech, no Zech!"

He took up his wax tablet and wrote: 'His name is to be Jon.'

"Jon?" the women exclaimed as they stood bloodied and tired.

Jon or Jonah had never been family names.

"Jon," answered Zechariah, his impediment miraculously leaving him again.

Joseph was amazed at what he'd just witnessed. The High Priest, who hadn't been able to speak for nearly nine months, was speaking. The miraculous recovery had come precisely at the time of the birth of his son.

Zechariah himself called it a miracle, his occasional stutters becoming less and less obvious.

"This has to be a si..si..gn from God. Jon, our son, will prepare the way for the Mess..mes..i..ah. He will fulfill the role of Elijah and pr.. prepare the way for our future Davidic king," he announced.

Elizabeth held Miriam close to her as if they shared a secret.

Joseph could now see them. Miriam still had the same sweet smile he remembered, but she looked different. There was a new decorum to her, her innocence replaced with a wisdom.

The midwife cleaned the baby as Elizabeth waited for the joyous moment when she'd hold the infant in her arms.

Elizabeth looked up at Miriam and stroked the girl's forehead with the back of her hand in a weak gesture of affection.

"Blessed are you among all women and blessed is the child within you, too," she said. Holding Miriam's hand, she continued to speak to her in a serious and personal way:

"God has given us the privilege of having you here with us, because it is the fulfillment of His plan. Blessed are you for believing in God's messages. Your child will be everything you expect. He will be great. All generations shall call you the blessed one, because you will be the mother of the Messiah."

Miriam cried with joy.

Joseph heard just enough to be disturbed.

As he listened to Elizabeth pouring out her emotions to Miriam, who knelt beside her with her face buried in the older woman's arms, he began to glean that Miriam was pregnant.

Elizabeth looked up.

"Is that Joseph?" she said.

"Yes, Joseph's here," Zechariah answered.

Miriam turned and stared at the carpenter incredulously.

Zechariah observed Joseph's reaction.

"Be careful," he cautioned them all. "Don't sp..speak of a miracle or of its implications to anyone now. This must remain our secret. Let it suffice to just say that we have been bl..blessed."

The midwife handed baby Jon to his mother. The room filled with joy as Elizabeth rocked the newborn child.

Joseph stood awkwardly.

Zechariah sensed Joseph's feelings.

"Joseph, can I talk to you for a moment? You arrived at a propitious moment."

They went outside on the porch.

"Joseph. This is why I've asked you to come here. We've discovered that Miriam's also going to have a baby. She's now in her third month. Naturally we don't think you're the father."

"Certainly not! What's all this about?" the puzzled carpenter asked with mixed emotions of anger and fear.

Zechariah gathered and formed his words carefully. His throat ached from the effort.

"We think, from what Miriam tells us, that the father is Gabriel, a man I'd selected for betrothal to Miriam. He ran out on us."

"Why didn't you tell me that before?" Joseph shouted. "I don't believe what I'm hearing! You came to me with all those stories about my family being descendents of David to cover up some mistake in your choice for Miriam. You cheat!"

"Joseph, I swear to you I had no idea the virgin had been violated when I called you to Jerusalem."

"You didn't want her to marry this other man, though!"

"Sometimes, our first choice isn't the best. But this whole business of Miriam's pregnancy has come as a complete surprise to us."

"A surprise to you! What about me? I have my family to think about! It's been hard enough to sell them on your crazy scheme as it is! Do I tell them I'm marrying a Temple prostitute on the orders of the High Priest?"

Zechariah flinched.

"I don't know what to say to you," Joseph continued. "Why have you chosen to destroy my life?"

"Please listen, Joseph," the High Priest pleaded, putting an arm around the carpenter's shoulder. "The important thing here is that Miriam doesn't want to marry Gabriel. She wants to join your family in Bethlehem. She's pleaded with us to honor our betrothal plan. Joseph, although the decision's yours, it's my belief that God has selected you to be Miriam's spouse. God has selected Miriam to be the mother of a special child who might be the salvation of Israel and create the dawn of a new age in our history. I believe my newborn son, Jon, will prepare the way for Miriam's child. You've seen the miracle God has shown us here. I was dumb. Yet as soon as Jon was born, I could speak. That's only one of the signs we'll witness, if this really is the dawn of the Messianic Age. God's using us, Joseph."

"Yes, but the child won't be mine!" Joseph shouted.

"I know, Joseph, but in some ways that's what's so clever about God's plan. Let's forget who the father of this child is and accept him as God's child, our future Messiah. If he's Gabriel's son, he'll still be of Davidic blood. If you, an unknown and good person, can bring up Miriam's precious child, the Messiah will be raised secretly. No powers, no Jerusalem factions or jealous Herodian princes, need ever know where the true Davidic heir is hidden. You can enjoy a normal family life. If Miriam's child is eventually called to David's throne, we'll be prepared."

Joseph frowned. Being only a simple carpenter in the presence of the spiritual leader of the land, he didn't know how to express his fear or sense of being betrayed.

"Sir," he said in a slightly calmer voice, "how can I accept such a situation? My family would make a laughing stock out of me. You're asking me to feed two extra mouths when I can barely feed my family as it is. It's all right for you with your wealth and position, but I'm a poor man. I can only live a simple life."

"Is it money you're going to need?" Zechariah asked.

"No. It would be better to call off this betrothal. How can you expect me to take on this responsibility?"

"Joseph, please bear with us and accept Miriam into your family. She wants to be with you. You'll be a far better father to her child than Gabriel would ever be. Do it for Miriam, not for me."

"How can you say, 'Do it for Miriam'? You're the reason Miriam's in trouble."

Zechariah looked around to see they were still alone. The women were all busy celebrating, except Miriam. Miriam had followed them to the door and was watching. Zechariah took Joseph out into the courtyard.

"Joseph," he said in a more tender way, "we have to put this all in the hands of God. Miriam has dedicated herself to God. She's full of goodness and grace. She believes that her child will be a son of God. She even says she'll name him Joshua because that's God's wish. Miriam believes this child will be special because God has told her so in angelic visions. Joseph, she really wants you to share in the glory of this God-given child. As I believe in the special role of Jon, my newborn son, so Miriam believes in the role of her son. Incidentally, the two children will be cousins. Elizabeth is Miriam's mother's sister."

The look on Joseph's face showed his disdain for Zechariah's plotting.

"I will name my own son, if he is to be my son!" he said contemptuously.

"Joseph, we'll help you in every way we can. We'll send money for Miriam's child. We wouldn't dream of you taking on this responsibility alone. I really do believe you should take Miriam and give your home to her and her child. Do this for God, not for me."

Joseph shook his head.

"I'm not sure. Give me time to think about this. You're asking too much of me."

They returned inside, neither of them quite sure if the matter was resolved.

* * *

Over the next few days, while Elizabeth recovered from her confinement and Zechariah became absorbed with young Jon, Joseph and Miriam spent time together, walking through the verdant vineyards of early summer overlooking the coastal plain. The days were warm and bright, and recently hatched multi-colored butterflies fluttered along the paths.

Miriam didn't tell Joseph that the young Temple priest had raped her. When pressed by Joseph on her relationship with the young man, she replied:

"I never slept with him. I don't believe Gabriel the priest made me pregnant. It's most unlikely. It was my angels who told me I was going to have a baby."

She stopped and looked at the butterflies.

"Joseph, these are my angels."

Miriam held out her hand. A large yellow butterfly with the color of the full moon alighted on her finger and spread out its wings.

"My angel Gabriel promised he'd be with me forever. In the moonlight, he gave me God's message. My baby will be God's baby, Joseph. We are God's chosen family. Gabriel told me so, and in time he'll reveal more of God's intentions for us."

The big yellow butterfly fluttered its wings while resting on Miriam's finger.

"Look, Joseph. You see how the butterfly agrees."

Joseph wondered at the innocent simplicity and yet total belief and sincerity of this girl to whom he'd become betrothed.

The big yellow butterfly flew away and joined the others. A host of yellow butterflies then flew around Miriam and Joseph, like a choir of angels. Miriam stood in awe, looking up at Joseph with her big round hazel eyes and her hair blowing lightly in the breeze.

"Can you hear them, Joseph?" she said joyfully. "They're singing 'Holy! Holy! Holy!' They're Gabriel's angels. They'll protect us and my child wherever we go."

Joseph melted at the sheer delight and innocence of this wide-eyed maiden. He didn't believe in her story about the butterflies, but he loved her for it. Nonetheless, he recognized a new mystical power in her, and a purpose. *Ruth would like the story of the butterflies*, he thought. *But someone needs to take care of Miriam. Why not me? Her spiritual presence might be good for all of us, even Jonah.*

"What did you say you want to name him?" he asked.

Miriam looked up at Joseph, wide eyed.

"Joshua," she said.

"So be it, then."

From that moment on, he knew that, whatever the truth of her story, he wanted to protect her, love her, and make her his own.

It was to Zechariah's great relief that Joseph agreed to marry Miriam. For propriety, however, Joseph thought it better that Miriam should finish her pregnancy at Elizabeth and Zechariah's house. It would give him more time to prepare his own family for the shock that lay ahead.

Joseph and Miriam were married in a very simple ceremony on a hillside outside Ain Karim. It was a beautiful summer's day when Zechariah brought them together. A host of yellow butterflies fluttered all around them. Elizabeth, holding baby Jon, and Elizabeth's maid Hannah standing with them, witnessed the happy event.

* * *

On an afternoon that same summer, on a hillside overlooking the village of Magdala in Galilee, Tribune Flavius Septimus, the Sepphoris Roman garrison commander, and his wife, Copernia, sat on a tussock admiring the view over the blue waters of the Galilean lake. Copernia lay her head down in Flavius' lap. Buzzing insects were enjoying the warm balm of the sun-filled landscape. She looked up adoringly into the eyes of the man she loved.

"Flavius," she whispered. "I'm with child."

Flavius pulled her up and stared at her before lightly kissing her on the lips.

"You are?"

"Yes!"

"But that's wonderful!"

Flavius put his arm around Copernia and held her tight.

Below them, their villa stood picturesque in a cleft of the hillside, looking so Tuscan.

"Our first child will be born here, Copernia, in the house I designed for you in Galilee. Don't you now love this land as much as I do? We're so lucky!"

She stood up.

"No, I don't love your land," she said pointedly and with Tuscan pride, "but I love you!"

Flavius watched her now, against the hillside, her hair moving to the light breeze. Their first child would be born at the villa he'd designed, overlooking the shores of the lake. His family would be raised in the land he loved. That's what he wanted. They would live in security and peace in the Empire he served. For a moment, Esther shimmered sensually behind his eyes. *No, that's over,* he thought.

"What are you thinking?" Copernia asked.

"Only that I love you, Copernia," he whispered. "Would you like to come back with me to Sepphoris?"

"To the city."

"Just for a while. You can enjoy provincial Roman life."

She smiled.

"It is beautiful here, Flavius. But I would rather be with you."

CHAPTER SEVEN

The Star

Melchar and Belshazzar slept. The cool comfort of the night sky enveloped their drovers' encampment. Earlier in the evening, a small fire had been a source of light and life as the men had swapped yarns about their travels. Now, it had dimmed to a few struggling embers. Rough poles, staked into the desert sands, held the meager goatskins that provided the men with shelter. Their camels grunted, chewing on the night air, their nostrils flaring.

In the darkness, a lone desert scorpion made its way down from the dunes and raised its barbed tail toward the leathered face of one of the camels. The beast flinched. It raised its head and neck, letting out a deep, bellowing cry. The scorpion scurried back into the shadowy sands. The sound of the camel's cry awoke Melchar and Belshazzar.

The two merchants crawled to the opening of their tent to check on the disturbance. When different drovers met to share an encampment, they rarely trusted one another. Many a box of precious stones or spices had changed hands under the cloak of a night sky. In the desert, it was every man for himself. Melchar, with his hand on his knife, looked out.

"Anything out there?" whispered Belshazzar.

"Nothing that I can see."

The camel, so recently threatened by the dreaded scorpion, resumed its monotonous chewing on the air.

Melchar surveyed the scene. Everything seemed normal. White dunes picked up the pale light reflecting from a crescent moon. The partial orb was surrounded by vivid desert stars. Melchar's eyes adjusted to the dim light. The camels were now calm. There was no sign of a thief. The tents were silent. Their fellow drovers were asleep.

Belshazzar crawled back to his blanket, but Melchar, now fully awake and still suspicious, stood up and walked out.

The camels eyed him. These beasts of burden were Melchar's life—the means of his livelihood. He had spices and gems for Petra from the traders of Chaldea. In Petra, he'd trade them with the rich merchants for an additional camel, then possibly hire himself out to take further goods on to Egypt or up into Herod's kingdom. Such had been the pattern of his life from boyhood. The desert was his world.

Melchar looked up at the heavens. He knew all the constellations and how to use them to navigate his camel trains along the desert routes. At any time of the year he could survey the stars and know where he was. They gave him security. In their wisdom, he saw a changing, but permanent guideline to the destiny of his life.

Then, Melchar looked toward the desert horizon, beyond the dunes, and out to the east along the route he and Belshazzar had traveled the previous day. Something caught his eye that seemed different. Way low on the far horizon there was a star Melchar didn't recognize. It seemed larger than normal, but fainter in brilliance. At times, it seemed to almost disappear, as if it was blinking. Then it would reappear like a thin line far out to the east. Melchar stared at the phenomenon for a while. The star was so faint that it strained his eyes for him to oberve its blink. The star troubled him, drawing an unease from him, his desert instinct grappling with what he saw, his religious notion of gods and destiny plucking at him. His skin reacted to the cool night air. Camels offered moon shadows on the pale night sand. He shuddered.

* * *

After his speech had fully recovered, Zechariah returned to Jerusalem. He sat with Simeon on the terrace of the Hasmonean Palace as his deputy filled him in on the Sanhedrin debates.

"You know, Simeon, I am no longer sure the debates are that important," he said confidentially. "We are on the threshold of a new era.

Our whole belief structure may be on the verge of change. God is leading His people once again—not me, not you—God."

Simeon leaned toward him, his white hair startling in bright sunlight.

"What do you mean?"

"God has given me my son, Simeon. Elizabeth, who was considered barren, conceived. It was no accident. God showed us that when He struck me dumb. My speech returned exactly when my son was born."

"It is miraculous," Simeon admitted.

Zechariah stood up. He looked even taller than Simeon remembered, holding his head high and proud.

"This is the dawn of the Messianic Age, Simeon. Miriam will also have a son. Her child will be the hope of all Israel."

His mind had eased over the problem of Joseph. He felt Miriam's spouse, this fundamentally decent carpenter, now understood. At last, the problem of her betrothal had been successfully solved. His plot to save his people had itself been saved. He felt confident that the Davidic seed would be carried secretly in the child to be born in the house of Joseph at Bethlehem where nobody would be suspicious. The only problem he still had to face was how to silence Gabriel.

Simeon raised his curly white eyebrows.

"Gabriel's child?" he asked.

"Maybe, but ordained by God. Miriam was meant to have this child. Joseph, the carpenter from Bethlehem has agreed to marry her. He knows she is with child, but the child will have a secure and loving home away from intrigue and gossip. Now, have you seen Gabriel? I need to watch that young man closely."

Simeon looked concerned, deep furrows forming in his forehead.

"Does he know he got the virgin pregnant?"

"I doubt it, but if he raped her as we suspect, it may cross his mind. I'm more concerned that he could be spreading bad rumors about my plans to hasten the Messianic Age."

"Your plans or God's plans?"

The High Priest looked down at his elderly partner.

"God's plans...but I have become the agent of their execution. It's in the Scriptures, Simeon: 'And there shall come forth a rod out of the stem of Jesse, and a branch shall grow out of his roots. And the spirit of the Lord shall rest upon him, the spirit of wisdom and understanding.'"

"Isaiah."

"Yes, Simeon: 'Unto us a child is born, unto us a son is given, and the government shall be upon his shoulder. His name shall be called Wonderful, Counselor, The Mighty God, The Everlasting Father, The Prince of Peace.' God's son, Simeon—the Messiah."

Simeon felt Zechariah's enthusiasm. He, too, knew the Scriptures.

"Isaiah also said: 'The people who walk in darkness will see a great light: they that dwell in the land of the shadow of death, upon them will the light shine,'" Simeon added.

"This is the time for the light, Simeon. Before we die we will see the light."

A warm breeze blew across the terrace, catching the long sleeves of the High Priest's green robe.

"Wine, Simeon, or would you prefer a goblet of cool water? I think that's my choice."

They went inside.

* * *

Zechariah started to receive alarming reports from his spies, eager men of his household that posted themselves around the council chamber of the Sanhedrin.

After a session, he was sitting on the wall bench of his small office beside the chamber, a room that also housed a number of sacred scrolls in wooden boxes along one wall, when one of his spies crept in to see him.

"Gabriel was talking to some of the other young priests, sir. He was boasting how he had rejected the Temple virgin," the man said.

"Exactly what was he saying?"

"Something about the Davidic priesthood preserving the royal line. He said you were a revolutionary."

Zechariah nervously clenched his fists.

"Did he!"

"He said he didn't want to be part of some political plot."

"Anything else?"

"Yes. I followed him into the city a couple of nights ago. He frequents a brothel in the Roman quarter."

Not surprising, Zechariah thought. *What did he call himself, a man of flesh and blood? If only I'd known all these things before I asked him,* he recalled.

"So, what happened there?"

The spy laughed nervously.

"I didn't go in. But after a while he came out with several young blades from the western city. They went to a tavern and drank heavily. Then, Gabriel made some comment about the virgin's breasts, 'little buds with hard nipples,'" he said. "They all laughed."

The man hesitated as if he wanted to say more.

"Carry on."

"He said she lacked passion, sir."

Zechariah thought for a moment.

"Is he still in the chamber?"

"I think so, sir."

"Bring him to me. I need to talk to him. Just say I need to talk to him."

* * *

At first, Zechariah greeted Gabriel cordially.

"Sit down. I just want to ask you a couple of questions," he said calmly, trying to make Gabriel comfortable. "Would you like a cup of water?"

Gabriel's normally ruddy complexion was somewhat pale. He seemed scared of the High Priest just as Zechariah was nervous around him. He accepted the cup and drank.

"It has reached my ears," Zechariah said slowly, "that you have been talking freely about my plan to marry the virgin off to a member of the Davidic priesthood to preserve the royal line."

"Well, isn't that what you told me?" Gabriel said. "You said that my royal seed would be carried secretly by the virgin. When the time came, you would establish a revival of the Davidic monarchy."

"Yes, I did say something like that, but you were sworn to secrecy."

"Well, I haven't said anything. It seemed a stupid idea to me anyway. I might have thought more of it, if things had been better for my part of the bargain. The virgin was full of extraordinary fantasies. She had no understanding of the real world. You were asking too much of me."

"I didn't ask that you should rape the virgin and defile her before your marriage, Gabriel!"

Sweat formed on the back of Gabriel's hands and neck.

"Is that what she told you? What are you saying? What proof do you have?"

"You've been talking, Gabriel. Brothels and drink loosen your tongue. Your loose tongue may destroy us all. I could have you imprisoned for what you've done. Your crime of rape won't go unnoticed by God, but for all our sakes it's important it remains a secret from other men. You violated the chosen virgin. You took advantage of me and of your priestly office. I took you into my confidence, yet now you're making a laughing stock out of me within these very walls."

Zechariah raised his voice:

"I forbade you in the name of God to discuss this with any living soul, but now I'm hearing stories. Your monstrous crime is enough. You're an impetuous fool without responsibility for yourself or what I entrusted to you in the name of God. Your passions will be judged by God, but your breach of trust could destroy both of us. Think, Gabriel, and remain silent!"

Gabriel's frustration turned to anger.

"What do you mean, I violated the virgin? How dare you suggest such a thing! You're the schemer! You're the one who came to me with this whole stupid idea. You asked me to marry the child. I'd never waste my time with her. I'd rather have my affairs with harlots in the brothel than marry such a naïve creature. You must be mad! You're becoming a senile old man, just like Simeon."

"Hold your tongue, Gabriel! You violated the virgin and you know it. She's pregnant and has named you the father."

Zechariah looked piercingly at Gabriel.

"What? I never laid a hand on her!" Gabriel shouted. "She's a dreamer. She lives in a world of her own imagination."

He laughed.

"When we were together all she ever talked about was visions of God, angels, moonbeams and butterflies. Do you believe her word against mine?"

"Yes, Gabriel. I do," the High Priest said, but he remembered his very own wife's doubts. *If Miriam really is to be the mother of the Messiah, Gabriel could just be some soiling presence ultimately of no consequence.*

"You're madder than I thought! Who'd want to violate the virgin anyway? She has no knowledge of the world or how to please a man. Do you think I'm a rapist? Do you think I can't get enough of that elsewhere without having to resort to violence? You're mad! Did you call me here to accuse me of rape? How dare you!"

Zechariah didn't move.

"Rapist you are, Gabriel! You've brought shame on your profession and name. How can I not believe Miriam? She lives in my house; she's my charge, and I know she's been violated. It has to be you. You probably raped her in the forbidden court of the House of the Virgins. You're the only man who's ever been in her presence there save the eunuchs and Temple servants."

"This accusation is outrageous!" Gabriel retorted. "I've never been inside the House of the Virgins!"

He stood up to his full height and stabbed his finger at Zechariah.

"You've had access to her, you lying bastard!" he said. "You did it. You've proven to the world how, as a senile old man, you could sire a son. The whole city's talking about that! You had access to the House of the Virgins, and you've doted on that moon-eyed creature for months! Now, I understand! You've covered me in blame."

A confident smirk came over Gabriel's angry face from the strength of his accusation and his gathering belief that he was right.

"This all fits in with your plan to pass the seed of the House of David secretly! I'll get you for this! High Priest or no High Priest, I'll destroy you! I know you for what you are—a cunning, scheming, bastard! If the future house of David rests in your blood, then God help us all!"

Zechariah was taken aback. It hadn't occurred to him that anyone might think Miriam's developing child could be his. What defense would he have against such a scandalous rumor?

"Gabriel, what is it worth to you?" Zechariah asked. "Only we know the truth, and that is that Miriam is pregnant. Whatever our opinions of each other, we can't let the circumstances of this out. It's too dangerous. Can we come to some agreement? Let's say one hundred shekels?"

Zechariah turned to the wall of scrolls. From behind one he pulled out a small leather bag that clinked with silver.

"Now you're offering me a bribe to hide your heinous crimes? What manner of a High Priest are you?" Gabriel shouted. "Do you think I'd take your silver to cover your sinful pleasures in raping the innocent virgin? Keep your silver for the Roman brothel and let the whole world know you for what you are!"

"Gabriel!" Zechariah said firmly. "I can call my guard and imprison you for offenses against God's Holy Temple. I'll offer you two hundred shekels. Can we talk business?"

But Gabriel was reckless, intoxicated with the power given him over the High Priest.

"How low are you going to stoop, O mighty High Priest? How much is it worth to you that I keep silent? Is it worth your High Priest's crown? You treacherous schemer!"

"Four hundred shekels," Zechariah said.

"Four hundred shekels! You'd offer me Temple silver to cleanse your soul? You vile creature!"

But as Gabriel spoke, this bribe tugged at his cunning brain.

"Five hundred shekels, no less," Gabriel countered.

Zechariah continued to outstare his opponent.

"Four hundred."

"Five hundred, I say."

"Four hundred and fifty shekels; that's my final offer. Either you accept this and keep silent or I'll arrest you for dishonor in your Temple duties."

Gabriel looked back into the eyes of his foe.

"You're forcing my hand with a bribe. I'll hate you for this for the rest of your days. Cursed be you, Zechariah! Cursed be your son! You're no better than swine!"

Zechariah reached for another bag and counted out the silver coins. He hoped Gabriel would uphold his end of their deal. Zechariah was frightened, but he believed his plot had been saved. And yet...and yet... Gabriel's adamant protests that he had not raped her...What of that? And Elizabeth's troubling thoughts of the Messiah's coming, troubling because these thoughts came to her from Miriam, not from him, her husband and High Priest. Zechariah felt a profound unease as he thought of his grand scheme.

Gabriel watched intensely as Zechariah counted the coins. *What if the virgin is carrying my child?* he thought. *I know I was not inside her, but what if...* A shiver ran down his spine. *What if...*

He took the money and ran from the Temple precinct.

* * *

Flavius Septimus looked at his wife propped against the pillows beside him. He wondered how much longer they could enjoy making love in her advancing pregnancy. Delaying his pleasure, he laid his hand lightly on her naked stomach and kissed her on the forehead.

"Our son, Copernia," he said. "Who knows, he might be a future Governor of Syria!"

"Oh, Flavius! Why governor of Syria? You're obsessed with Syria!"

"The Herodians won't be here forever, my dear. Even if they remain titular kings, the presence of the Empire is becoming stronger here. The message I received from Sepphoris today shows who really runs the Levant."

"What was it, Flavius?"

"It was an edict from Quirinius in Damascus. All Syria, including the kingdom of King Herod, is to come under an Imperial census. Every man is to be accounted for and his trade recorded. Isn't it wonderful to see the order that's in our world today?"

Copernia sighed.

"Is that all? I thought it might have been something a little more exciting."

Despite the beauty that Flavius had created for her on the hillside above the lake, his young wife still yearned for Tuscany and the security of being at the center of the Empire rather than on this uncertain fringe. *Can nothing I do for her make her happy?* he mused. In that moment of frustration, thoughts of Esther danced before him. But Copernia placed her hand on his and pressed it against the life stirring in her womb again.

"Governor of Syria would be an honor, Flavius," she said, "but what if he could be Governor of Tuscany like his grandfather or a senator like my uncle Tarquinius? Wouldn't that be better than Syria, much though

I love being with you here? Our son must have the best of everything, Flavius. He'll be educated to be a leader in the Empire."

Flavius got off the bed and poured himself a goblet of wine, the sweat of his naked body glistening in the lamplight.

"Don't belittle Syria, Copernia. Syria is on the brink of greatness. This is the crossroads where the wealth of the Orient spills into the Empire. Now that we've established law and order in the Levant, this is where fortunes can be made. Herod's no fool. His port at Caesarea is no accidental dream. This is the gateway to the East, and it's now securely in Roman hands. Herod gets fat on trade tariffs, but Caesar will only use Herod and his fickle family as long as it's expedient for him to do so. Mark my words, Copernia, in time we will have direct government here, and our son could be the first Prefect or Procurator."

Copernia smiled.

"Procurator of Judea first, then Governor of Syria," she said, "but ultimately a senator in Rome!"

Flavius drank, put down his goblet and returned to the bed.

"Always your dreams take you to Rome and the Senate," he said disparagingly.

Her hand rubbed her belly.

"Not me—him! Dreams for him!"

Her smile faded. She propped herself up on one arm.

"Are you disappointed?" she said. "Surely not. How could you be disappointed?"

Flavius kissed her lightly on her cheek.

"Not disappointed. Perhaps I want only for you to love our home more."

"It is beautiful here, Flavius," Copernia repeated, "but it's so quiet. Do I go on too much about Rome and Tuscany?"

"Perhaps," Flavius replied.

Later, Flavius and Copernia stood in their terrace garden and watched the approach of evening. The glow of the butter lamps collecting the evening insects replaced the hazy light of the fading day. The stars cascaded against a night sky that was rapidly crossing the lake and capturing the hills of Galilee in its cooling folds. Rising above the shore of the Gadarene country on the far side of the lake, a bright streak appeared that Copernia hadn't seen before. Many drovers traveling along the caravan routes from the east had told stories of a strange star in recent weeks.

"Look, Flavius! There's the star," Copernia said.

"What star, sweetness?"

"The one you were talking about, my love."

"Oh, the star in the east that the caravan merchants keep speaking of."

Flavius looked at the cone of light shining just above the Gadarene hills.

"Yes, I see what you mean. It isn't really like a star; it's more of a streak in the sky."

"What do the soothsayers say, Flavius? Surely, someone has tried to explain this phenomenon. What have you heard in Sepphoris?"

"Only what I've already told you, dearest. Many travelers have mentioned a large star in the east, but nobody has gotten too excited about it yet."

"I'm excited! This could be a sign! Our son might be born under this very star. Perhaps that will confirm he's to be a future Senator or even Emperor!"

"Don't get too carried away, Copernia."

Copernia pulled away from him, folding her arms, watching the strange star's progress. It touched her deeply; indescribable feelings moved inside her, chilling her blood with strange excitement. She looked up at her man with satisfaction written all over her face. The star was on her side. Her son would be more than a Prefect, Procurator of Judea or Governor of Syria. Her son would be destined for the purple lined toga of real government.

Leah, their Hebrew maid, called Flavius and Copernia in for their dinner. They left the terrace and its night sounds. Flavius Septimus had done his best to help Copernia feel at home in this foreign land by making their villa a mirage of Tuscany in the Galilean hills. Statuettes Flavius had bought in Caesarea, placed in their wall niches, caught the soft glow of the lamps. Comfortably reclining, Flavius and Copernia enjoyed the fruits that the dark-haired, deep-eyed maiden served to them, preliminary to their evening meal when sweetmeats and savories would follow. But a mood had taken them, some touch of the heavens and the star cradled there. They ate in silence. Leah kept her distance, but peered out at the night, searching its secrets.

* * *

Flanked by two guards, King Herod adjusted his red robe as he sat bethroned on his dais in the Hall of Audience at the Royal Palace. Princess Salome sat beside him in a sleek green dress with a gold cord at her waist, and an elaborate gilded hairpiece, studded with emeralds, crowning her angular face. The heavy room boasted massive pillars on which braziers burned. The space was sparsely furnished.

"Call in the soothsayers," Herod shouted to his chamberlain.

Ptolemy opened the door guarded by two more of the king's men, dressed in their gray and red uniforms, daggers gleaming in their waistbands.

An assorted collection of scribes, scholars, astrologers and soothsayers, carefully selected by Ptolemy for their advice, entered the room and sat on cushions before the dais.

Ptolemy approached the King and bowed.

"Tell them I'm curious to know more about the mysterious star in the East," Herod said.

A series of platitudes rose from the soothsayers.

"It honors your Majesty."—"It's a symbol of prosperity."—"It is protecting the trade routes leading to our land."

Salome leaned toward the King.

"Ask them what it means for your succession?" she whispered.

The soothsayers were clever enough to make any interpretation favorable to the King.

"Your heirs will reign forever and ever," came the predictable answer.

The King held his stomach and winced in pain. He was short of breath and he felt sharp spasms in his chest and abdomen. He knew he was not invincible. His malady increased daily. *The scholars and astrologers are keeping quiet; maybe they know more than these foolish soothsayers,* he thought. The star had risen higher in the heavens, although it still wasn't the dominant body. Herod was afraid the star might be read to predict some harm to himself and his family. Lately, Herod's periods of breathing difficulty and bouts of abdominal pain had increased.

"What say you scholars and astrologers?" he bellowed.

A learned man stood up.

"The star is unusual, Your Majesty. It is obviously moving. It may not in fact be a star at all, but a moving heavenly body. It has the appearance of leading a trail of light."

"Elijah's chariot," one of the scholars chimed in. "It is Elijah bringing in the golden age of our people. It is time for the Scriptures to be fulfilled."

The astrologers were less ready to make predictions at this stage, but led the King to believe that the passage of this star through the heavens would eventually reveal some important truth. They claimed that when the star was closest, it would have maximum power and influence over their lives. By their calculations, they predicted this position to be at least two lunar months away.

As Herod mused over the astrologers' conclusions, there was a scuffling sound at the entrance to the great hall. The guards blocked the entrance. Ptolemy ran to see what it was about. A man dressed in drab civilian clothes and carrying a large imperial scroll, surrounded by an escort of Roman guards, stood in the doorway.

"Who goes there?" Ptolemy asked.

"I demand an audience with King Herod. I have an important message from Damascus."

Ptolemy nodded to the Herodian guard, who stood back.

"Follow me," Ptolemy said to the Romans.

"Your Majesty, a messenger from Damascus," he announced.

Herod stroked his black beard, twirling his fingers in the ends. As he did so, the dye rubbed off on his hands and revealed the truth of his advancing age and the sign of his vanity.

Salome adjusted her gilt and emerald hairpiece and watched Herod with a look of concern. It was a bad sign when Herod pulled at his beard. Usually it signified a fit of rage.

"More news of trouble in Galilee, I presume," the King said. "You Roman officials don't seem to be able to control the brigands. In my younger days I'd have marched up there and ended this ahead of my own soldiers. We need a stronger troop of the Herodian Guard there. Perhaps we can station troops in Sepphoris alongside Romans. Those Galileans will be the death of us all. All troubles seem to start in Galilee."

The messenger, his traveling clothes in contrast to the splendid dress of Herod and Salome, greeted the King respectfully. Then, opening the scroll he was carrying, he formally addressed the monarch in a more condescending tone:

"Your Majesty. Acting on orders from Augustus Caesar, in the name of Quirinius, I bring you this proclamation."

The messenger read in a pompous voice:

"To Herod of Judea, Greetings! I, Quirinius of the Province of Syria, do hereby command that all male subjects of your kingdom are to be numbered in compliance with the wishes of His Imperial Majesty, Augustus Caesar. They are to be recorded for the annals of the Empire as to their trade and profession, each according to his own city. The census is to be arranged and the information collected before the spring of the seven hundredth and forty-ninth year of the glory of Rome. The details are to be forwarded through Tribune Flavius Septimus, Commander of our Sepphoris garrison, to Damascus where the Syrian Province will keep copies of the records and forward the same to Rome. I remain, your close colleague and servant of the Emperor, Quirinius, Governor of Syria."

The messenger bowed.

Herod tried to rise from his chair, but momentary pain held him back.

"Quirinius of Syria!" he screamed. "Am I a vassal to this new Governor of Syria? I deal directly with Rome! I take counsel with Rome and Rome alone! Was I not in Rome a close friend of the Emperor? Did not Augustus Caesar restore me to my former glory? Is Damascus greater than Jerusalem? Who is Quirinius to send me such messages? I was respected by Saturninus. Let Caesar bring to me what's necessary. My people to be numbered! For what purpose? To give more power to Quirinius and those in Damascus? I am King of Judea! I have control of Samaria, Galilee, and the provinces beyond the Jordan! Quirinius has no direct control in my kingdom. Caesar must deal directly with me! Do I not provide for Caesar's legions within my realm? Do I not collect Caesar's share of taxes from the port tariffs at Caesarea? What right has Quirinius to interfere? He commands the Roman legions through my pleasure only. I don't take orders from Quirinius! This is an insult to my majesty!"

"Sire," said Ptolemy, "perhaps it's not such a bad thing for our kingdom to be recorded for the annals of Rome. We might capitalize on the information for our own purposes. We'll be arranging the numbering of our people, not Quirinius."

"Silence, Ptolemy! Sometimes, you're a fool! Don't you see this makes a mockery of my majesty? Tell Quirinius I will not accept such demands. I'll answer only to Caesar!"

King Herod yelled at the Syrian messenger:

"Idiot! Take your scroll and return it to Damascus."

The Roman held his ground.

"I speak for the Emperor, Your Majesty," he said. "My master sends this edict in the name of the Emperor."

"In the name of the Emperor of Syria?" shouted the King.

"No, your Majesty! The Emperor of Rome! Your favor with Caesar is well known to my master."

"Is it known well enough that I could have him removed from Damascus?"

The messenger took a pace backwards, and the Roman soldiers accompanying him rushed forward to avert further confrontation.

"Your Majesty, I don't doubt your influence with the Emperor," the messenger said, "but these are Caesar's orders."

Another bout of sharp pain pierced the King's abdomen and chest. He doubled up in his chair in agony.

"Leave my kingdom!" he gasped. "Leave now, before I call out my guards and arrest you for insubordination."

The King then choked, collapsed on the floor, and began to cry out in delirious tones.

King Herod's bodyguards rushed forward to pick him up.

The messenger placed the scroll in Ptolemy's outstretched hand. Joining his Roman guards, he gave an order. The soldiers, their faces masked, their bodies rigid, escorted the messenger from the chamber and back into the more rational world outside.

"Out!" Ptolemy shouted to the assembled scholars, astrologers and soothsayers.

Salome showed no emotion. She smoothed her sleek green dress and followed the bodyguards as they helped her ailing brother back to his private apartment. *It will not be long,* she thought.

* * *

The last rays of sunlight played on Mount Tabor. They gave a golden light to the hazy outcrop. Joachim stood in his usual place of prayer overlooking the Vale of Esdraelon, thinking back over recent events, studying them, divining as best he could God's will. Before him, the harvest of the valley was for the most part gathered. But it was not quite as bountiful as the year before, because a plague of locusts had damaged the summer wheat. *Yet, despite that*, he mused, *leading my mules around the outskirts of Jerusalem, there were busy threshing floors, hardy crops being flayed by peasants.* It had been a rare harvest of spring cereals. *Life can be capricious.* For some unknown reason, Joachim thought about Golgotha—the bloodied rocks from recent stonings—the way he had led his small party around it, keeping the women's heads turned away. *Yes, life can be capricious.*

Looking out from his favorite prayer spot, Joachim watched the shadows of the evening clouds run over the fair land below him. *Miriam, now pregnant. My daughter of the gentle heart and wondrous dreams. Miriam of the House of the Virgins—what of her now? And what of me?* He looked at his circumstances honestly. He could say he was still one of the most respected men in Nazareth. People had also accorded him respect and perhaps affection when he went down to Judea to celebrate the High Holy days and the festival of Booths. *Zechariah's letter promised us he will arrange for us to see Miriam and meet her proposed husband—this man named Joseph*, he consoled himself.

As he held out his arms to pray, Joachim smiled at the good feeling he and Anna had about their coming grandchild. They would enjoy their roles as grandparents. They could lavish all the love they had held back when they had given Miriam over to the House of the Virgins. *Even Judith is excited*, he thought, as he recalled their servant's reaction. *She, too, will offer her quiet and innocent love.*

Humbly, Joachim began his prayers, finding in them the profound comfort and hope that had served him all these years. He prayed to God for all those things in his life he could not change; he asked for divine guidance in all matters where he was required to shape his destiny, and the destiny of those who relied on his wisdom. He prayed for Miriam and Joseph. His words carried across the valley as darkness shrouded him.

Finally, he prayed they would have a safe journey. It was time to accept Zechariah's invitation, time to meet Miriam and Joseph. Overhead, stars offered a first gleaming. One star, way out on the eastern horizon, looked different. *That's odd,* he noted.

The morning of their departure from Nazareth saw feverish activity at Joachim's house. Joachim had decided to take three donkeys and two mules with them on the journey. He'd purchased the extra donkey from Benjamin Levi. Anna and Judith were busy packing.

"Did you put in that blue cloth with the white and gray, Judith?" Anna asked.

"Yes, Mistress."

"Good. I couldn't find it where I left it. That blue cloth's precious. It's a gift from the Levis. It would make up into a beautiful head shawl for Miriam. The material is so much finer than that coarse gray."

"It's very pretty, Mistress Anna. I hope Miriam will like it," Judith answered.

Anna went in to the dark storeroom to pick up a prepared box of jars and pots. She called out to Judith to come in and help her.

"We must strap this box on one of the mules' backs," she suggested. "We don't want the jars to crack."

One of the lads from the village assisted with the ropes, and the wooden box containing the eight kitchen jars was secured to the saddle. The jars were decorated with Greek-style motifs, recent purchases from Sepphoris. The other mule was already laden with heavy panniers, holding figs and dates, sacks of flour and grain, and honey in covered crocks.

Anna returned to the house to fetch a beautiful orange and rust colored hanging blanket that she'd decided, at the last minute, Miriam might like for her future home in Bethlehem. She also picked up a woolen blanket for her nephew, baby Jon.

Joachim led the donkeys in from the farmyard. One donkey was already laden with the needs for their journey, which included three straw-filled bags for sleeping pallets and two bags of fodder for the animals. Since they might not make it to Samaria in less than two days, Joachim prepared for his family to sleep out under the stars.

The sun rose over the little courtyard, catching the trickle of water in the fountain and brightening the silvery leaves of the gnarled, old olive trees. Joachim had the mules and donkeys roped together. They were ready to leave.

After paying the lads from the village who'd helped them pack, Joachim led Judith and Anna out on the two riding donkeys with the baggage train following. The gate was latched behind them, and they set off down the hill. It would be a long walk on the road south, but Joachim was still strong and proudly led the way.

The Roman road down from Nazareth was busy with travelers, although most of the carts and donkeys were moving against them, coming up from Caesarea. It was easy traveling downhill into the valley, but when they turned off this road they had to take the rough track up to Nain. It became apparent by mid-afternoon that they would need to make their first camp somewhere beyond that village on the hilly road to Samaria. They found a site about five miles south of Nain. It was a good, flat, grassy area. By nightfall they were weary, footsore, and ready for sleep. The discomforts of a night in the open were forgotten in the delight of resting on their straw pallets. Joachim soon fell asleep, but Anna, plagued by her respiratory problems in the night air, looked up at the stars.

Judith couldn't sleep either. Thoughts of Miriam raced through her mind, too. *Will Miriam remember me?* she wondered, as she tossed on the straw pallet, trying to get comfortable. *It's been more than ten years. Will she be a pretty young bride? She was so lively as an infant. I still don't understand why it was good for God to have Miriam at the Temple. Why couldn't she have lived with us in Nazareth?* She reflected on their happy life in Nazareth. *I'm sure Miriam knows nothing of the seasons and the harvest. She's never danced with the girls in the village or had friends to gossip with around the well. There are so many joyous things she's missed. I feel sorry for her. Perhaps I can bring her some of those simple joys.*

Doubts also crowded Judith's mind.

What if Miriam doesn't want to remember me? What if she's become proud and without feelings? Perhaps she'll feel ashamed of me now that she's living in the High Priest's grand house. Her mind will be on this man she's going to marry and her future with his family. She won't remember her mother's maid.

Cold chills ran down Judith's back. A tear welled, and a lump formed in the back of her throat. She realized her happiest days, her own youth, had been spent with the baby Miriam.

Judith looked up at the stars for comfort. Lying flat on her back, she could see the whole canopy of the heavens. The moon showed as a crescent on the horizon. Succot was still two weeks away and the full moon of harvest hadn't yet formed. The individual stars seemed extra bright, and a stellar haze spread through the heavens like smoke caught in a beam of light. Some stars winked in and out around the soft glow of this milky way. Farther out, lone constellations stood out against the blackness of the night. On the outer reaches of the eastern horizon, Judith caught sight of a single star that was different from the others. It didn't look like a star at all. It had a stellar sparkle at its apex, but there seemed to be added length to its form, making a trail of light pointing upward. It didn't appear to be moving, but it had a mystery and wonder to it that set it apart from all the other celestial bodies in that clear night sky. Getting up, Judith shook herself, and stood mesmerized as she studied this star, her eyes bright in the darkness.

Joachim was snoring, but Anna, still wide awake, called out:

"What is it?"

"Over there, Mistress. There, see that beautiful star."

Anna sat up.

"Where?"

Judith pointed to the eastern horizon.

"Over there."

"Joachim can probably tell you what star it is. Ask him in the morning."

In the morning, it was gone. Judith mentioned it to Joachim as they were packing up the mules. But her master wasn't that interested.

"I noticed it the other day. It's odd," was all he said.

He was more concerned to make up for lost time and advance their journey. The subject of the star gave way to hard roads, weary limbs, and the hot breath of tired animals.

* * *

Elizabeth watched Miriam at work. Miriam seemed far away, almost in a trance, as she fed her shuttle through the threads on her loom. *She could weave blindfolded*, Elizabeth thought. *I wonder what is going through her mind. Such a very special, precious child.* Miriam found the work therapeutic during the latter days of her pregnancy. By rote, she tied more purple wool onto her shuttle and started the process again.

Elizabeth replenished her basket of yarn.

"You're the fastest and neatest weaver I've ever seen," she said. "Zechariah will be delighted at the progress you've made. They certainly taught you well. I would think we must have enough material now to complete the Temple veil. If the virgins in the Temple are working nearly as fast as you, Zechariah should be able to hang it soon after Yom Kippur."

"Oh, I'm not really that fast," Miriam said. "Naomi is much faster than me. I'm sure she's made more cloth. The matron used to say that Naomi worked quicker, but that I was neater."

"Ah! But, did Naomi always get to work with the purple wool?"

"Well, not always," Miriam admitted, her face blushing with a shy smile. "They always seemed to give me the purple wool, perhaps because I was the oldest."

"Or, perhaps because they knew you were destined to be very special," Elizabeth suggested. "The purple is only used for the best garments or draperies. That's why we have to use it for the new Temple veil. Zechariah says the old one is in such rotten condition now that he's almost afraid to open it on Yom Kippur for fear it will fall down at his touch. How fitting it is that the mother of a future prince of Judah should be the one to weave the greater part of the veil of the Holy of Holies."

Miriam put the shuttle down and looked up at Elizabeth.

"Perhaps we should not speak like this," she said.

"But it's true, isn't it? Don't you feel it, Miriam?"

Miriam was silent for some time. She stared at the purple veil's developing form.

"I feel many things. I struggle with many things. But, yes, it is true: I know that I am a holy vessel."

She looked at Elizabeth with a cool insight beyond her years, perhaps a rebirth of herself even as her child grew within her.

"But we should be careful how we speak of it," she continued.

Suddenly she smiled.

"Most times I don't feel like some princess, and Joseph's hardly a prince. I love him, that is true, but he builds houses and works as a carpenter. He doesn't wear fine robes like King Herod."

Elizabeth's mouth firmed in censure.

"Now you mock me."

"Not at all. But I suppose I once thought Gabriel to be like a prince. That feeling's gone though. Shouldn't we get back to our weaving?"

The click and sweep of the loom filled the room.

"Miriam?"

"Yes?"

"How did Gabriel know the baby would be a boy?"

"Because it must be a boy to carry God's word."

"Careful, Miriam, the wool is catching!"

"Sorry. My mind is elsewhere."

Miriam smiled, then returned to her weaving.

Elizabeth sat down beside Miriam at the loom.

"I knew that my child was going to be a boy. I told Zechariah again and again that we would have a boy."

Then hastily she got up.

"Speaking of Jon, I'd better see if he's hungry. You'll get used to that when you have your baby. They take all your time. You won't be able to weave much then. But I'd stop now if I were you, the best of the light's gone."

Elizabeth left to find Jon and his wet nurse from the village.

Miriam felt her child kick within her. A radiant smile crept across her face, and she placed her hand over the curve of her belly. She glowed with the excitement of approaching sanctified motherhood.

* * *

The donkeys clip-clopped downhill toward the white marble slabs of the new Roman road that ran from Caesarea to Sebaste.

"Look, Joachim, they've finished the road!" Anna exclaimed.

"So, I see. Traveling is becoming easier. The Romans do know how to build roads and fine cities. Mark my words, Anna, in a generation we won't know our own land."

Where the narrow road that had led Joachim's family across the hill country met this new gleaming white ribbon of marble, purple thistles proudly waved in the breeze.

The donkeys edged out onto the side paving. A fast-moving, horse-drawn chariot took a Roman official on his business from Samaria down to the coast. The Roman was dressed in a toga, his face clean-shaven, and his hair short and curly. His appearance was quite different from that of Joachim, who wore his long traveling robes and sported a beard that straggled from his aging face.

"Oh, Mistress Anna," Judith said excitedly. "They travel so fast on this new road. Why, it's dangerous. That man almost knocked us down."

"They will knock us down," responded Joachim. "But they'll also build us up. We can't fight Rome. Rome is now a part of our world."

The donkeys and the mule train turned to the left as Joachim led them out onto the highway. They headed on up to Sebaste, King Herod's Hellenistic capital of Samaria.

* * *

Melchar and Belshazzar, the two Chaldean merchants, made their camels kneel. Dismounting, they led them into the narrow gorge that protects the exotic city of Petra from the outside world. Wisps of desert fog drifted across the hollow where outcrops of pink rock broke the surface of the monotonous stony desert. Within that mysterious hollow lay the Nabatean stronghold, one of the richest of the desert cities.

"At last," muttered Belshazzar, already thinking of the trading ahead of them.

"Yes! This was a long haul," Melchar agreed. "I think it'll be profitable, though. We need to make sure we trade all the silks here so that the small-time merchants can take them on to Alexandria. You get the two extra camels we need as quickly as possible. Then we'll travel on, with the jewels and spices, up to Herod's kingdom."

"Will we ship out of Caesarea this time?" Belshazzar asked.

"I think it'll be easier than Alexandria. There are too many middlemen eating up the profits in Egypt. It's not like it was in my father's time. The Romans have a much firmer grip than Cleopatra's agents did. But I think we might be able to do some business with the Herodians. We'll need that to offset the Roman pickings at Caesarea."

"I'll leave the business to you, Melchar. You speak Greek. But I know I can always pick a better camel."

They led their heavily laden beasts in between the rocky walls that shut out the desert light. The fringe of colorful protective cloths and the loose ends of ropes tying the panniers together, swayed with the rhythm of each camel as they plodded on in single file, each roped to the one in front, a train of hairy humps. The smell of fresh dung from earlier passing traffic seemed trapped in the canyon. At times, the way was so narrow that should camels be making their way out they would barely pass. Then, rounding a final turn, the light of the Treasury court became visible to them beyond the narrow exit. They'd reached the hidden city. Rich hues of reds and pinks caught the sunlight that played on the surrounding cliffs.

The square was bustling. Apart from prosperous looking merchants in bright kaftans and assorted turbans, and tax collectors in blue and silver Nabatean tunics, an army of bare-chested slaves chipped away at the opposite cliff. Work was commencing on a new façade.

"The Treasury house," a drover explained. "They say it will be the new wonder of the city."

Melchar looked up at the men, working high up on a wooden scaffold. Below them, the crew had started hollowing out a huge cavern. The scale of the project was staggering.

"How long will it take them?" he asked.

"A lifetime," the old drover said. "I won't live to see its completion."

The merchant train halted in front of the tax collectors' tables, Nabatean guards keeping a wary eye from behind.

"What are you carrying and what will you be trading?" one of the tax collectors asked Belshazzar.

"We'll be trading silks, from Cathay and India, for camels."

Documents duly marked and tariffs agreed upon, the string of heavily laden camels was allowed to proceed along the well-worn road that led to the inner city. High up on the cliff walls, conduits carried fresh spring water along the same route. Several large, carved openings in the rock's face led into memorial chambers and tombs of wealthy Nabatean families. A Greek theater nestled below them. After about a mile, the street turned to the left, revealing the central plain where Petra spawned its city. There was the bustle of trade on every side.

Camels fought for space with mules, donkeys, oxen, and carts, all carrying wares to the central market square. This was the business heart of Petra where desert deals were made and lost. It was the caravan crossroad that most suited Melchar's slick tongue and astute eye. The cry of a desperate merchant, selling his last wares for the hope of a camel, mingled with the superior claps and gestures of rich Petra salesmen, their rings flashing in the sun while they grew fat on the failures of such lesser men. There was excitement in the air even as one man's misfortune became another man's gain. This was desert law—an eye for an eye and a tooth for a tooth. To Melchar, this was the most exciting place in the world, for he loved the art of the deal.

"Belshazzar! We'll outwit the fat ones this time," he said. "We have the best silks Petra has ever seen. When we make our pitch in the market place, we'll become rich."

Belshazzar grinned.

"I trust you, Melchar. But I'll pick the camels! If you were to choose our camels, we'd never make it back to Chaldea!"

"It's a deal, my friend," replied the eager merchant.

Then, Melchar fell silent as he remembered the star.

"I know we'll do well," he said at length. "That strange star followed us all the way from Chaldea to Petra. It's an omen of our good fortune. Haven't you noticed, Belshazzar, how it's getting bigger and brighter each night?"

"I sleep at night, Melchar, you know that. Perhaps tonight I'll pay more attention to it."

"It means success for us, Belshazzar. I feel it in my aging bones."

The crowds thronged around them. Belshazzar made sure the precious silks were well hidden from thieving hands. He adjusted the ropes on the panniers of the lead camels.

Beggars and rich merchants jostled each other in the streets. Everywhere, arms were flying in the air, hands reaching out in gestures. The pungent odors of camel dung, ass urine, and body sweat, mingled with the rich tang of leather and spice. The street opened out into the Agora—the market square. A Doric colonnade with pavements of marble, like those at the entrance to the theater and in the Treasury Square, acknowledged the Hellenic influence.

At last, the two merchants were at the center of activity. This was where fortunes could be made.

* * *

The cluster of sandstone buildings that made up the village of Ain Karim was a welcome sight to Joachim and Anna after their journey. Exhausted, they stopped at the well to refresh themselves, washing the dust from their faces before meeting their hosts.

Zechariah and Elizabeth were well aware how close they were. The village gossips had long since gathered at their door to inform them of the approaching mule train. The whole village was curious about the Temple virgin now living at the High Priest's house. All comings and goings there were cause for gossip and rumor.

The mules took a draft of water from the drinking trough beside the well. Judith bathed her mistress's feet and then washed her own. A crowd of curious village youths gathered around them.

"Where are you from?" one of them asked.

A dirty-faced boy with a ruddy complexion put out his hand, begging for coins.

"What are all these pots for?" he asked, tugging at Anna's robe.

"They are for my daughter. We haven't seen her for a long time. She's married now and needs things for her new home."

"She's the one who married Joseph, the old man from Bethlehem, isn't she?" chimed in the ruddy-faced youth.

"Yes, that's right!" Elizabeth said.

"Is Miriam pretty?" Judith asked.

"She's pretty, but she doesn't come out much," the youth answered, before another voice from the back of the group remarked on the fact that Miriam was expecting a baby.

"Yes! She's going to have a baby," a maiden echoed. "Some people don't think the baby's Joseph's. That's why they keep her locked up in the High Priest's house. Nobody's too sure who the father is!"

One of the young girls laughed.

"I don't think it could be Joseph. He's too old."

"Nonsense, Susannah! Look how the High Priest had a baby boy and he looks even older than Joseph."

"Don't be silly, Jonathon. Elizabeth had the baby, not the High Priest! Maybe he wasn't the father, either. Strange things happen in that house."

They started arguing among themselves as to whom the father might have been until Anna began to cry at the village youths' unkindness.

"I heard that the virgin, locked up in the High Priest's house, was raped," said an older woman who had been listening to the youths, "by a rich man from Jerusalem."

Joachim hurriedly gathered the lead ropes of the refreshed donkeys and mules.

"Let's move on," he said in a reassuring and calm voice. "Don't worry about what they say. Elizabeth will be waiting for us and we'll be made very welcome."

They moved off down the street toward the big wall at the end that marked the entrance to the High Priest's house.

When they reached the open gate, Elizabeth and Zechariah stood with arms outstretched in welcome. A young maiden with a mystical smile and flowing curls of chestnut hair stood beside them. There was a freshness in the look on her beautiful face, and a luster in her eyes; and there was a calm, a repose, as well as tears of joy.

"Greetings, Joachim! God bless you!" said Zechariah as he lightly kissed him on both cheeks. "Welcome, Sister. Welcome to you both."

He embraced Anna, then turned to the young maiden.

"Miriam, this is your mother and father," he said.

Tears burst from Miriam as she looked into the eyes of the mother whom she had not seen since she was four.

"Miriam!" was all Anna could say. "Oh, Miriam!"

She took her daughter into her arms.

Over a meal carefully planned for their arrival, Zechariah told them that Joseph would be coming to Ain Karim in a few days.

"Joseph will complete our family gathering. You'll love him. He's very quiet but is one of the kindest men I've ever met."

"Yes," Miriam said. "He loves me, and we'll be very happy. I can't wait for you to meet him."

Joachim turned to Zechariah.

"We noticed this strange star on our journey down. It seemed to be the talk of Samaria. Actually, I sleep well under the stars and didn't pay it a lot of attention, but fascination with it kept these two awake."

Anna smiled at her husband's skepticism.

"It is very unusual," she said.

"Well, Joachim, I move slowly on these things," Zechariah answered, putting an arm on his shoulder. "In Jerusalem, people are excited and agitated about it, too. You can see it much better from Jerusalem, especially from the higher ground with open views across the Jordan valley to the east. Here, it's not so easy to see, as the hills slope the other way. King Herod's asked for astrological interpretations."

He started to laugh.

"The soothsayers are hoodwinking the Romans with all sorts of strange predictions."

"But what about you, Zach?" pressed Joachim. "You're our High Priest and a man of God. Do you think this could be one of the signs we're waiting for? You know, the signs we talked about."

Miriam looked at Elizabeth. She smiled as Elizabeth nodded.

Zechariah looked around nervously, then continued:

"Some think it might be a sign pointing out the fall of the house of Herod. The Herodians are certainly very nervous about its appearance. The Romans are already predicting an increase in their power and influence. You know, maybe I shouldn't tell you yet, but I will anyway. The Romans are already planning a massive census of our people. We're to be accounted for as residents of the Empire. Quirinius, the Roman Governor of Syria, has issued the decree for all our citizens, not just those of Roman Syria, but here in Judea, Samaria and Galilee, too. We must register our names, professions, and trades to Imperial officials in our towns and villages of birth."

"That can't please Herod too much," commented Joachim.

"Well, it certainly belittles his power. If Quirinius can issue decrees over Herod in the name of Caesar, Herod no longer really has control. There is a rumor that he flew into a rage when the messenger brought him the news—that, and the fact that he's sick, and given to periodic pain."

"Do the zealots know about this? I certainly never heard anything in Nazareth. Maybe this star will herald a great victory for them. Possibly, a new rebellion will be planned. But whatever, Zach, I hope you and I are wise enough to know that Rome is here to stay."

He paused to study Zechariah's reaction. Zechariah showed little response, only staring blankly at Joachim.

"Incidentally, have you seen the new road to Caesarea?" Joachim said, wisely changing the subject. "It's magnificent! You know it really would almost be better for us now to travel to Jerusalem by going down to

Caesarea and then up to Samaria, just to stay on these new roads. You can travel so much faster on the Roman roads. I think we could have cut at least half a day off our journey if we'd done that."

"Well, Joachim, you speak of roads, but I have to consider the new tower for the Roman guard that overlooks the Temple. It's going up too fast. Soon, the Romans will have such a strong presence in Jerusalem that everyone will see Herod as a mere puppet in Caesar's hands."

"What will that do for us?" asked Joachim. "Do you still believe in your messianic dream?"

Zechariah glanced at Miriam. In turn, Miriam again sought strength from Elizabeth.

"I do, Joachim, but not if it falls in the wrong hands," Zechariah answered.

"You mean the zealots?"

Elizabeth and Miriam seemed to be whispering to each other.

"Yes, but I think we are boring the women."

He looked at Miriam again. With a kindly smile he changed the subject:

"Miriam's done the major part of the weaving for the new Temple veil. Why don't you show Anna and Joachim some of your handiwork?"

She stood with great poise as if she were somewhere else, a mystical, almost whimsical look on her face. Joachim and Anna could clearly see her swelling belly under her loose white shift.

"I'll fetch the section I finished yesterday," she said, serenely walking from the table, as if she knew that her child, God's child fulfilling the words of the Scriptures, was to be the Messiah.

"Miriam's the best weaver we have," Zechariah continued. "She was always clever with her hands, but this autumn during her confinement, she's more than proved her skills. I think I'll be able to hang the new Temple veil shortly after Yom Kippur or at least well before Passover. You know, in truth, Joachim, I'm afraid when I go into the Holy of Holies that the veil will fall at my touch."

Joachim laughed.

"If the Temple veil were to fall, it would be read by everyone as a sign from God. It's just like this star. We're living in uncertain times, Zach. I'm not sure whether the world as we know it is on the brink of something great or a total disaster, but in the name of the God of

Abraham, Isaac, and Jacob, I certainly hope that it's something great. It may be hard for us to understand, but know that a new world is about to dawn for us. I think I believe in that star. At first, I thought it a trifle, but now I see how much excitement it is causing, I'm starting to think more about it myself."

Miriam returned with samples of her weaving. She showed them to her mother. The purple wool was closely woven and finely crafted.

"That's beautiful work," Anna said. "They taught you well in the Temple house."

Elizabeth stood behind her sister and looked at Miriam.

Miriam smiled back at her as if light shone from her.

"We'll talk later," Zechariah said to Joachim.

The conversation then turned to domestic matters and the joy of reunion.

Only Judith seemed unhappy. She had so longed to see Miriam, but Miriam didn't seem to recognize her. The little girl she had once held and to whom she had taught her first words was all grown up, and more, perhaps...Judith tried to suppress her feelings as she watched Miriam drape the lovely purple weave across her slender arms. There was something ethereal about her. *She is from another world,* Judith thought. *She's other worldly, so removed from me. She will never joke and laugh and dream with me. She's a child of the High Priest now, a child of the Temple. No...a woman, a priestess.*

* * *

Joseph the carpenter patted his donkey's rump as the beast plodded slowly toward the sandstone dwellings of Ain Karim. It had been difficult for him to explain to Bathsheba and his own children the reality of his marriage to Miriam. Bathsheba had been unquestionably jealous. James had coolly tolerated his father's decision, going about his daily tasks in a perfunctory way, but obviously feeling disturbed by the news. He'd buried himself in his studies at the Rabbinical school in Bethlehem and talked little with any of them when he returned home in the evenings. Amos had probably been the most receptive, due to his naturally happy disposition. He had helped his father in the remodeling of their home for Miriam.

Jonah, a dark-skinned strapping youth, belligerent and independent of spirit, was still upset over his mother's death and hated his Aunt Bathsheba. He'd run away from home several times and on more than one occasion had ended up in trouble. He'd said he'd leave for good if his father ever brought Miriam home to live with them. Bathsheba had no more control over Jonah than Joseph did. It seemed that Jonah hated everyone and everything. Joseph had talked to the rabbi about his problem child, but to no avail. The rabbi, whose main interest in Joseph's family was in cultivating James as a scholar, merely shrugged his shoulders, held out his hands, and smiled, saying:

"He's only a boy, Joseph. He's only a boy."

Joseph had an uncomfortable feeling that the rabbi didn't approve of his marriage, either. The man certainly hadn't expressed excitement at the prospect of meeting Joseph's new bride.

It was only Joseph's youngest child, Ruth, who'd showed any enthusiasm. Bathsheba attributed the girl's excitement to the fact that Ruth had always had to feel and say the opposite of her brother Jonah.

Joseph's household was filled with unrest, held in check only by Bathsheba's domestic influence. Joseph was nervous about bringing Miriam home. As his donkey moved closer to the village, he felt a strong desire to stay there and never return to Bethlehem.

A crowd of youths gathered around Joseph and accompanied him down the widening street toward the long wall of the High Priest's house. They patted his donkey and pulled on the lead rope.

"You're the old man who married the virgin, aren't you?" asked a bright-eyed youngster in high-pitched Aramaic. "I remember you!"

"Yes! We remember you!" the others agreed.

"Have you come back for her?" the ringleader asked in a more authoritarian tone. "They keep her locked up in that house. We hardly ever see her."

"Oh, no. They don't lock her up, young man," Joseph answered. "It's just that Miriam can't get out much now."

"Because she's going to have a baby," one of them teased. "Is that the reason?"

"Is it your baby?" the ringleader asked. "Some people say it's not your baby."

"Yes, some people say she was going to have a baby before you married her," another chimed in. "Is that true, mister? There's something funny about that baby. Everyone's talking about it."

"Boys! Miriam's my wife. None of this should be any concern of yours. Let's hear no more of your gossip. Be off with you!"

The boys giggled nervously. They let go of the donkey's rope and stood back as Joseph kicked the beast forward.

Miriam had a premonition Joseph was near. She stood outside Zechariah's open wooden gate. Anna and Elizabeth observed her and spoke quietly on the porch:

"You see, Anna, how she stands, so self-possessed."

"She holds herself well, Elizabeth, but that's from her training in the House of the Virgins."

"No. It's more, I tell you. This baby..."

"What about the baby?"

Elizabeth watched Miriam.

"I have such mixed thoughts," she said. "I think of her rape, and then I think of this child separate from the rape, as if there is some blessing to her, some anointed presence."

"You mean her imaginings, her butterflies, her talks with angels?"

"I just wonder if they are imaginings, Anna. We talked one day, while she was weaving the new purple veil. There was, there was..."

"There was what, Sister?" Anna asked, growing exasperated.

"There was something holy in her, something I can't describe—only feel."

The two women looked at Miriam standing by the gate.

"Joseph will be here soon," Elizabeth said.

"How do you know?"

"Because Miriam is there, waiting for him. She knows."

When Miriam heard the donkey bray and saw Joseph approaching, she stood up and ran toward him.

Joseph dismounted and held out his arm to her.

They embraced one another. It was the embrace of a father for his favorite daughter, but, nevertheless, it carried a message of love that could be seen in Miriam's eyes. They led the donkey through the gate, and Joseph felt relieved to be in the safe and secure world of Zechariah's home.

Elizabeth stepped out into the courtyard full of curiosity, Anna following.

"Anna! I thought it must be. Here he is! This is Joseph, Miriam's husband," Elizabeth said throwing her arms around the carpenter.

"Joseph! How well you look. We're so glad to have you back with us."

When Judith heard the commotion, she came out to meet Miriam's husband, too.

"Oh, Judith. This is Joseph," Anna said. "Go down to the grove there and tell Joachim and Zechariah Joseph's here."

Judith turned to leave the courtyard by the other gate. Zechariah and Joachim were down in the vineyards. It was the time of the grape harvest, and often Zechariah liked to supervise the work, showing that he was both a farmer as well as the High Priest. Joachim checked Zechariah's grapes with interest, commenting on the differences between these Judean grapes and his own in Galilee. Finding her master and the High Priest, she cried out:

"Mistress Anna wants to let you know that Mister Joseph's here!"

Zechariah looked up.

"Oh, Joachim! We must go up immediately. I didn't think he'd be here so soon. Judith! Ask Hannah to pour out some wine from the good vat. We'll celebrate tonight."

Judith returned to the house ahead of the two men.

Joachim put his arm on Zechariah's shoulder.

"Zach, it's done," he said. "All is now achieved. Our little family's intact and our secret's secure. Gabriel's name will never pass my lips again."

Together, they climbed up the stony path, leaning on their sturdy staffs. When they entered the familiar courtyard, Zechariah blessed his family, and Joachim embraced his son-in-law, who seemed only a few years younger than he.

* * *

Flavius Septimus gazed out from his terrace above Magdala. The unusual star was clearly visible. There was still no sound of a newborn child within the illuminated walls of his comfortable villa. He'd sent Gladius, his slave, to fetch a Hebrew midwife from Magdala early that morning, when Copernia had gone into labor. Now, ten hours later, there was still

172

no news. Periodically, Copernia's maidservant ran out for fresh linens and clean water, which Gladius assisted in supplying.

Gladius handed the maid-servant the fresh towels, then stood in the vestibule and looked out at his master. He was proud to be a slave to such a man—if he had to be a slave at all. His master was strong and respected, and those strengths fell onto him by association. Gladius always thought back to the day the year before when this commanding officer of the Sepphoris garrison had purchased him, rescuing him from the arena.

And Gladius knew he gave good service. He knew he was a good-looking, strong and virile, not yet disfigured in mortal combats. In gratitude, Gladius dedicated his life to Flavius Septimus, and now, seeing his master concerned about Copernia and the birth of his child, he worried.

Gladius quietly went to the doorway and looked up at the night sky. The harvest moon was beginning to wane, and the Hebrew festival of Booths, regarded by the Romans as 'that annual time of bacchanalian revelry', was coming to an end. His calm Gallic eyes watched the strange star that rivalled the moon as the most dominant feature of the night sky. It had climbed much higher now, and the trail of sparkling light emanating from its center was more obvious. It was the most unusual heavenly body Gladius had ever seen.

"Are there enough towels and water for my wife, Gladius?" Flavius asked from the terrace.

"Yes, Master. She is comfortable."

"I see you are watching the star."

"Yes, Master."

"Like most people in this part of the world."

"Yes, Master."

"What do you make of it?"

"A sign…Master. Of what, I don't know."

"Soothsayers and sorcerers are predicting startling events."

Gladius hesitated.

"These are uncertain times, Master."

Flavius smiled.

"Yes indeed, Gladius. Now please check on my coming child, to be born under this star."

At the Roman barracks in Sepphoris, the common belief was that the star heralded the fall of the house of Herod. The King was reported to be ill, some said with an incurable malady similar to the dropsy that seemed to plague many of the Hebrews. It seemed to spare neither peasant nor king and usually struck those who had been most athletic and virile in their early life.

The officers had discussed if this could be the meaning of the star. *Was the house of Herod in such disarray that it might fall with the death of the King?* Flavius thought. *Would this be the moment, when as Roman authorities, they would step in forever and make Judea, Samaria and Galilee a true province of the Empire?*

Flavius pondered on these things as he looked up at the portentous phenomenon nightly making its journey across the heavens. *This is a great omen for the birth of my son,* he thought. *He, too, could be great. Possibly the Prefect or Procurator of such a new Roman province? Jerusalem, Sebaste, Sepphoris could all be his; Syria or even beyond could be his. Perhaps it's all foretold here in the heavens. Perhaps I'm going to be blessed with this good fortune.* The thought then crossed his mind that the child about to be born in his home might be a girl. *What would I do with a girl? This is no place to bring up a girl.* He tugged at his tunic. *If that happens, I'll have no choice but to send her to Tuscany to be brought up by her grandparents as a Tuscan patrician.* He thought of Copernia. *She might say she needs to go back to Tuscany with her!* He beat a clenched fist on the balustrade.

"It's so important that my child's a boy. That star must be shining for me. My child will be a boy!"

The cry of a newborn child came from the lighted chamber.

Flavius trembled.

A moment later the midwife came out.

"Flavius Septimus, you have a son," she said in Aramaic, as she held up the infant in a bundle of linens.

Gladius was behind her, repeating the news in Latin.

"Master! The Mistress has born a son!"

"A son!" cried Flavius. "The first in a new line of rulers in the service of the Empire. Linus, that's what I'll call him—Linus Flavian, the first in his line!"

He turned to Gladius.

"Pour wine for everybody! This is a great day in my household. Linus

Flavian, my son, has been born under the sign of this great star! Tonight, Gladius, further greatness has come to our house."

The midwife hurried back to the lighted chamber.

Copernia took the baby into her arms as she lay on her bed. A sweet smile of satisfaction crossed her exhausted, but proud, Tuscan face. She had born Flavius Septimus a son.

* * *

Dirt, dust, and dung rose up in the air at the Petra camel lots. Dealers beat the ungainly beasts to get them to make the right moves for the drovers. The dust-covered men shouted and the camels bellowed.

"I'll take those two," Belshazzar said.

The sharp-eyed dealer with whom he was negotiating bowed before handing Belshazzar the lead ropes. The man gave his final command to the ungainly beasts, hitting them with a switch to move them out of his yard.

Belshazzar proudly led his purchases out into the bustling market street. Hides hung from poles, and woolen hangings and awnings gave shelter from the sun. In their shade, eager merchants bargained with the wise and foolish. But Belshazzar knew his two new camels were worth every cheap, colored stone with which he'd parted. He was sure Melchar would be pleased. The camels were sturdy, obedient, and well trained. They were long-distance camels that would stand parching journeys across the deserts to and from the lands of Persia and Chaldea.

Melchar was still negotiating for the best deal he could raise on their silks. The price was good, but not as high as he had expected. Unfortunately, other drovers had brought in a shipment of silk earlier in the week, and the market was somewhat saturated.

"You know you can double your trade in Egypt with these quality silks, my friend," Melchar pleaded. "I can't offer them to you for less than the stated price."

Then, his sharp eye caught the glint of gold coins in two old wooden boxes. He pointed at them.

"I'll trade them for those two boxes of gold pieces. Is that a deal?"

"That's too much. You want to keep me a poor man?" the wily dealer retorted.

"You're not poor, my friend. It's well-known you're the swiftest dealer on the market here. But I trust you. I know you'll market my silk well. Those boxes of gold pieces for these bales of silk is a fair price. You won't let Melchar down now, will you? I could trade with others, but I always come to you. You're a wise man and you know a good deal."

Melchar paused, but kept his eyes pierced on the merchant as the man awkwardly shuffled from foot to foot. Then, in a more demanding voice he struck his deal:

"These four bales of silk for those two boxes of gold pieces!"

"Melchar! You drive a hard bargain!" the dealer exclaimed. "You know very well the market price of this gold in the hands of those greedy Romans. If I had the means of carrying this gold to Judea and Caesarea, I wouldn't be a poor man."

He noticed Belshazzar holding his camels.

"Ah! Here's Belshazzar. See how your trusted friend has traded stones for camels? I'll tell you what, Melchar. I'll take your silks for the boxes of gold pieces, but I'm asking you for some extra stones from Belshazzar."

The dealer turned to Belshazzar, who was grinning from ear to ear, obviously proud of his success at the camel station.

"You hawked for two fine beasts there, Belshazzar. What say you to helping an old friend here? How about some colored stones to add to these silks? Melchar drives too hard a bargain."

"Melchar knows what he's doing, you old thief. I don't part with my stones for anybody," Belshazzar answered.

Then, ignoring the dealer who was shaking his head in self-pity, he continued to show off his camels to his partner.

"What say you, Melchar? How do you like them? The best that I could get."

"You did well," Melchar answered, scratching at his forehead. "However, I can see we're wasting our time here. These silks are too precious to be wasted on a fool."

Looking at the dealer for the last time, he continued with the voice of victory:

"The silks for these boxes of gold pieces, no more and no less!"

The old dealer shook his head again.

"You rob me, Melchar," he said. "I'll always be poor if I trade with you."

But Melchar stood his ground.

"Come on, you old fool. You know exactly where to replace these gold pieces. The day you'll be a poor man is the day I'll stop coming to Petra."

Then, looking away from the dithering merchant, Melchar addressed his partner:

"Start to pack up the silk, Belshazzar. We must be on our way."

Belshazzar pretended to reach for the bales, while Melchar made his deal:

"All four bales of silks for your two boxes of gold pieces, my friend. Yes or no?"

The game was over. The dealer broke his act. A sheepish smile smarmed across his face.

"Take the gold! It must be the effect of that star in the heavens affecting me! Go! I agree to the silks."

The negotiations over, the dealer and Melchar embraced.

Belshazzar left the silks where they were and picked up the heavy, studded boxes of gold pieces. The last of their silks had now been exchanged.

The pickings had been good. The camel train they led out of Petra numbered six beasts rather than four. The panniers that had held the precious silks were now heavily laden with boxes of gold, bags of precious stones, and jars of frankincense gum. The inexpensive stones they'd carried from Chaldea had served as useful currency since they'd exchanged them for ones of far better quality. If a man was sharp and stood his ground, he could always leave Petra with a profit. Melchar and Belshazzar were proud of their achievements.

The incredible, sun drenched, pink city was soon behind them. The camels made their way through the narrow passage in the rock walls to gradually climb up into the white light of the surrounding desert. Thistles vied with loose stones and outcrops of the rosy rocks in an otherwise flat and bleak landscape. Melchar and Belshazzar set out for the northwest in hopes of having equally successful trades in Herod's kingdom.

By nightfall, the camel train reached an area of date palms surrounding a small oasis where the beasts could be watered. The different drovers in the group separated to look after their own. Several, staked claim to areas under the palms, but Melchar and Belshazzar slept in the open, closely guarding their precious cargo and beasts of burden.

While traveling, many of the drovers spoke of the great star. Even the natural majesty of the rocks, the dramatic cliffs, and the bustle and excitement of Petra, had not detracted from the star's strange fascination. Now, Belshazzar and Melchar could stare at the star in all its wonder as it occupied the black night against a waning harvest moon. It was unlike any heavenly body they had seen.

Melchar was in awe.

"Belshazzar, my friend," he said. "That star is surely bigger and higher than it was before. Look at that trail of light! It disturbs me, the way it seems to move."

"Yes. It's as if it's trailing us. It's been with us all the way from Chaldea and has grown in brightness as we've made our journey. Perhaps it's trying to tell us something. It doesn't have to be a bad sign, Melchar. It might be a sign of good things to come. We did well in Petra, didn't we? Perhaps under this same bright light we'll do well in Herod's kingdom."

"We ought to. We've got the best in gold and stones that I can ever remember carrying. They sparkle like that star, Belshazzar. They glow with our good fortune."

The two men gazed up at the light in the heavens. The head of the star was glowing and permanent, but the trail of light seemed to come and go.

CHAPTER EIGHT

The Soothsayer

Gabriel, dressed in a red and green robe that picked up his complexion, took his usual seat in the Sanhedrin, close by a pillar and not far from the door. He didn't stay for many of the theological debates. But a few minutes in the cool of the Sanhedrin chamber gave him a chance to catch up with Temple gossip. From his seat, he could scan the assembly and easily hear the whisperings of neighbors. These days, the chamber bristled with rumors. Gabriel was even more curious about Temple intrigue now that he knew something of Zechariah's plans. Sadducean leadership was being challenged. The Pharisees were ready for a political revolt. Their uncomfortable alliance with King Herod was fading fast as they witnessed his growing sickness.

Gamaliel, an outspoken Pharisee, started to talk softly to his neighbor:

"You saw how the King looked at Yom Kippur?"

"So short of breath and stooping."

"He looked close to death."

Ah…the succession, Gabriel thought.

"Will Antipater succeed?"

"I don't think so, not if Salome has anything to do with it."

"Salome!"

"She'd never stand for Antipater to rule. She loves Herod's weakness.

It gives her power. She's able to manipulate Antipas, but Antipater with his influential Roman friends is too much for her."

Salome is already in control, Gabriel agreed.

"How long do you give the King?"

"Long enough. I think he has the dropsy—the old man's plague. He could linger on for a year, or possibly two. Long enough for us to be ready."

"The destruction of the house of Herod?"

"Total!" Gamaliel answered.

Gabriel pricked up his ears. But the momentum was stopped as the two gossips were forced to stand, to allow a group of councilors to pass and take their seats further along the bench. Once they had settled down, the intriguing conversation started again:

"Do you think Salome will destroy Antipater before the death of the King?"

"I'm sure of it. She is wily, that woman," Gamaliel said, nodding his head, a wry smile coming across his face. "She's ambitious and her mind is a scheming trap."

"A pharisaic state then?"

"Yes, my friend."

The rebel Pharisee put his arm around Gabriel's neighbor. They looked intently at each other.

"Without the Sadducean High Priesthood?"

"Possibly. Zechariah's too weak a politician to head the movement, and Simeon's far too old. The new generation will forge a government that needs no monarch or High Priest—a rabbinical Jewish state."

"What of Rome?"

"Rome's a shadow, my friend," Gamaliel whispered.

"A very uncomfortable shadow."

"Yes, uncomfortable. But Rome doesn't have any desire to interfere with our faith. Rome may well encourage such a theocracy within the state, one that's run by the synagogues and not by the Temple. It's the Temple, High Priests, Sadducean power, and unfaithful kings that Rome fears. Rome doesn't understand us, our Law or our theology. These things she'll leave well alone. That's the secret of our movement. We'll be victorious when the rebellion comes. It's the house of Herod that we need to overthrow."

Gabriel reflected on the comment.

Gamaliel's right about Rome, he thought.

The shofar sounded, long and deep. The Sanhedrin came to order. Chatter and whispers came to a halt. The business of the day was announced—a continued discussion over pharisaic interpretation of certain Davidic psalms. Gabriel quietly slipped away.

In the world outside, the young priest surveyed the bustle of the Temple's outer court. In the far corner, close to the House of the Virgins, Gabriel could see the tower of the new Roman barracks rising above the walls. *Roman soldiers will soon be able to look right into the Temple,* he thought, *into the courtyard of the Virgins' House.* That thought reminded Gabriel of Miriam. As always, when he reflected on her, guilt pulled at the muscles of his stomach. *I should have just told the High Priest I wanted release from our agreement. I didn't have to rape the virgin. But she needed to know I'm a man of flesh and blood. I just couldn't take that sweet talk about angels and moonbeams any more.* He could never be sure that what the High Priest had said wasn't true. *Maybe my rash action did lead to the virgin becoming pregnant. Maybe she is carrying my child. It could be just one of those unhappy accidents.* He consoled himself with the thought that his full intentions had been thwarted. *But it's almost impossible... such a slim chance...I wasn't even inside her when I climaxed.* He thought of his encounter with the High Priest and felt lighter. *He might have raped her, too. I scared him to death when I suggested that. He felt he had to bribe me to keep it quiet.*

Pungent smells and the cries of animals drifted toward him from the pens beyond the moneychangers. Pilgrims lined up to exchange currencies for Temple shekels to pay the merchants selling off the sacrificial animals. The system benefited the Temple treasury. Other visitors, including many gentile foreigners, stood around, admiring the Greek structure of this Herodian masterpiece. The white marble colonnade of the portico surrounding the Great Court's outer walls stood out boldly against the blue sky. Jewish families were celebrating the rituals—purification rites, circumcisions, and coming manhood. Babies cried, men prayed, women expressed pride and joy. The Temple was the apex of the religious life of the land.

Mount Moriah has such a look of permanence despite the creeping Roman presence and these seeds of pharisaic revolt, Gabriel noted.

He wandered deeper into the complex, into the outer Courtyard of the Jews. Ahead, were the great bronze doors that led into the Priest's Court and Sanctuary. It was much quieter here. There was only a handful of people in this outer court.

"The King sat here just two weeks ago," Gabriel muttered to himself. "He did look weak. Of course, Salome was with him. I wonder what damage she can do before it's all over? I have to agree, the house of Herod is doomed."

He thought again of High Priest Zechariah's solution. *I haven't heard about restoration of a Davidic monarchy in the Sanhedrin gossip, only the destruction of the Herodians. Maybe I should credit Zechariah with more cunning than I have. He suggested that the Davidic seed should be carried secretly through an unknown virgin like Miriam. That secret seed could have been mine. Maybe it is.* He stood motionless as the insight took him. *I could be the father of our future King!*

Gabriel smiled to himself, dismissing the idea. The stupidity of the suggestion amused him, as he now saw it in political perspective. *Surely the Romans would never tolerate such a kingdom. They'll be only too pleased to get rid of the Herodians, but once they do they'll want to take over the full responsibility of government, probably better government than we now have. Of course, there are lots of fools and zealots out there who think we can overthrow the Romans and expect another Maccabean victory. That'll never happen.*

Gabriel looked up at the growing fortress tower, surrounded in wooden scaffolding with an army of slaves walking the planks. It could be seen from almost any part of the Temple. The noise of construction merged with the noise of the Great Court behind him. *Rome is surely here to stay*, he concluded.

A man, dressed in a robe of many colors, wearing gold earrings and sporting several gaudy rings on his fingers, seemed to appear from nowhere.

"Greetings, my friend," he said. "Are you a stranger here?"

Somewhat surprised, Gabriel started to laugh.

"No, stranger. Who are you? What's your business here?"

"I'm a soothsayer, sir."

The man looked directly into Gabriel's eyes.

"I have the power to predict your future," the man said. "Here, in this holiest of places, I can predict your future. I have the power from God."

"You have the power from God?"

Gabriel chuckled.

"I'm a priest of God. How about that?" Gabriel informed the soothsayer.

"Yes, sir! You don't take me seriously. I have the power to predict. I could see you're a man of education and background. I get a strong message concerning you. I was watching as you crossed this courtyard. You're a man who thinks deeply."

"Well, what do you say, soothsayer? Can you predict my future?"

"I singled you out, sir, because God told me you're a man with a purpose; a man with a mission to fulfill."

"God told you this? You're telling me God singled me out from all the crowds that you meet each day?"

Gabriel waved a mocking hand at the activities around them.

"What's on your mind, soothsayer? If you're a charlatan I can have you removed from the Temple, because, you see, I have the power of authority! But, speak on."

"No, sir. You must believe me. Our paths have crossed for a purpose. You carry a heavy burden. You've a message of utmost importance to give to the world, but you're afraid. You're holding back your message, and the deceit is destroying you."

Feelings of guilt mixed with curiosity rose within Gabriel. He chafed at the secrecy imposed by the High Priest when he'd accepted the bribe. He wondered: *What could this soothsayer know about Zechariah's messianic plot?*

Sweat beads formed on Gabriel's back and brow. Chills ran down his spine.

"What sort of a message do you think I hold? To whom shall I reveal my message?" he asked.

"The world is at a crossroads, sir. The star in the night sky tells us the time has come."

"Everyone observes the star, soothsayer, and reads his own fortune. But for me, it's the time for what?"

"A new order—a new kingdom."

"Whose kingdom?"

"God's kingdom, my friend. Ruled by God for God's people."

The soothsayer held his head on one side, observing Gabriel. He fidgeted with one of the rings on his spindly fingers.

"A kingdom more powerful than Herod's?" Gabriel asked.

"Much more powerful."

Gabriel felt the chills return.

"More powerful than the Romans?"

"Yes, my friend, even more powerful than Rome."

"Are you telling me my message is to tell the world that Rome will fall and that the power of the Romans will crack?" Gabriel asked.

"Empires come and go, my friend," said the soothsayer. "You know a secret more powerful than Empires."

Gabriel started to tremble.

"So, what is this secret then?"

Guilt gnawed at his stomach as he thought of his fateful tryst with Miriam in the garden at Gethsemane. *How does this man know that I might have passed the Davidic seed?* he mused.

"Let me look closer at you," continued the soothsayer.

The stranger squinted, then looked piercingly at Gabriel.

"You're basically a conceited, but honest man. Your eyes tell me you don't mean any harm. But you lack real purpose in life. You've wasted your youth on trivial affairs and traded your good looks for prestige and position. Show me your hands."

Not really knowing why he was giving this soothsayer the time of day, but intimidated by the accuracy of the man's statements, Gabriel held out his hands.

The soothsayer grabbed them and with his bony fingers traced the lines of his palms. He looked intent. Gabriel felt weakened, allowing the soothsayer to draw out the last of his resistance.

"Yes. I don't make many mistakes. I can see it all in your hands."

The soothsayer looked up at Gabriel.

"These hands haven't known hard work or heavy labor."

The man then studied Gabriel's palms.

"Your hands are clearly marked and reveal to me the truth, as I suspected. You're a messenger. You'll tell the world of some great event. The star that hovers over Jerusalem these nights tells us the time is right. I predict the event concerns a child."

The man then returned his gaze to Gabriel's face.

"You're a priest of the Temple," he said. "You know the Scriptures?"

Gabriel nodded uncomfortably. He was not a great student of the Scriptures and never had made it much of his business to study in the rabbinical schools.

"Do you remember the words of the prophet," the soothsayer continued, "and how it was written: 'A virgin shall be with child and give birth to a son, and they shall call him Emmanuel, which means God with us.'? You remember that prophecy, don't you, sir?"

"Yes, er... yes," Gabriel answered, not with recollection, but now deeply anxious.

"You falter in your reply, sir. A definite sign that you're the one."

Gabriel stepped back from this intruder who had invaded the secrets of his mind. He could still feel the power of the soothsayer's grip on his hands, and he longed now to be free of this interrogation.

"Who are you?" he challenged. "Why do you trouble me with these things? Has Zechariah, the High Priest, sent you to seek me out? Why do you bother me? He's fed you all these facts, hasn't he? Does that old man think he can scare me? He's a scheming bastard. He framed me! He paid me off with Temple silver and now he's sent you to scare me to death."

The soothsayer watched him with cunning eyes.

"No, sir. I know nothing of the High Priest. It's under the star, my friend. You must tell the world what you know, because I believe it's important. I only know that when I first saw you, I knew you were the one."

"Tell my message to whom?"

The soothsayer shrugged his shoulders, an oddly innocent gesture.

"That, my friend, is up to you. My power doesn't reveal all things. I've passed the power to you. It's up to you to use it as you think best. I've found the man I've been looking for. You're the one. Go! Tell it on the mountain. You know the secret that's locked within your heart."

The soothsayer bowed deeply, his spindly fingers clasped together.

Gabriel, stunned and frightened, watched as the man turned and left, disappearing into the throng of Temple visitors, there to move among the pilgrims and ply his strange trade beside the other unlicensed hawkers of the Temple area. So many were capitalizing on the fears invoked by the ever-present star of the recent night skies.

* * *

Zechariah looked up at the two Temple eunuchs who were hanging the new veil in the Sanctuary. One emasculated man was lithe and sinewy, the other rather overweight. *I hope he doesn't fall*, he thought. These temple servants had already attached the first five rings to curved hooks that held the drape in place. Zechariah hoped and prayed the disintegrating old veil wouldn't fall while they hung its replacement. If an accident were to happen it wouldn't be his fault, but it was a sacred rule that nobody with the exception of the High Priest, not even a Temple eunuch, should ever see the Holy of Holies—the sacred interior of God's dwelling place. As each new ring was added, the rich color of the cloth, woven in segments by the Temple virgins, unfolded in its purple majesty. Ring by ring, the old, gray, and acrid remains of the last Temple veil fell to the ground in a musty pile of dust. If Zechariah's reign as High Priest would be remembered for nothing else, he was determined it would be for hanging this new veil.

After Zechariah left, the eunuch who'd been dismantling the old rings said in an effeminate, high-pitched voice:

"Let's peak inside."

His friend looked down to be sure the High Priest had really gone.

"All right, open it up."

The larger of the two eunuchs pulled the rotting fabric apart.

"This old veil stinks," he said as the must and dust settled.

"What can you see?"

"It's too dark," the big man replied. "I can't see anything. Hold the new drape up a bit higher to let in more light."

His companion hoisted up the newly woven material so he could pull it to one side.

"Is that better?" he asked.

"I still can't see anything."

"Wait a moment. Your eyes will become accustomed to the dark," the other eunuch suggested. "Can you see anything now?"

"Not really."

"Let me take a look," his friend said impatiently, as he strained over from his ladder to look through the narrow opening between the felled veil and the newly hung material. "Oh, I see what you mean. It's very dark."

"Maybe there's nothing there. Just the invisible God," the fat one replied before peering into the gloom again.

Slowly, the ghostly form of the cherubim and seraphim loomed in the dull aspect of his changing vision.

"I can see something now," he called back.

"What?"

"Two angels, carved in wood, or they might be beasts. They have wings."

"Let me see!" the other eunuch said, as he peeked in through the drapes again.

He was disappointed.

"Just two old carved statues! Is that all that's here?"

"Quick! Let's close it up!" whispered the fat one. "If the High Priest catches us he'll punish us severely."

The two eunuchs closed the drapes and methodically continued with their steady task of pulling up the new material, hooking it on to the staves, and hacking away the semi-rotten rings that held up the old veil.

* * *

Like a bellowing cow, the shofar resounded in the crisp autumnal air, calling the people of Ain Karim to their synagogue. Rich and poor made their way side by side to the familiar meeting place. The synagogue was fast becoming the focal point of their village life.

Joseph and Joachim were on their way up from Zechariah's vineyards.

"That's unusual," Joseph said, examining a cut on his hand from their recent work. "What can it mean? Why are they calling us to the synagogue? It's not the Sabbath or a Holy Day."

He licked his wound.

"Who knows? They want to tell us something. Maybe they've concluded what that star foretells," Joachim suggested.

He laughed.

"We hear something new every day."

"Yes," Joachim agreed. "Some people seem to think it heralds the end of the world, but I don't believe those scaremongers. I'd like to think it means a new beginning."

"Perhaps the King's dead. You remember how Zechariah described His Majesty at the Yom Kippur ceremonies."

Joseph and Joachim joined with other men of Ain Karim as they made their way toward the synagogue for this unusual meeting. By the time they got there, a bustling crowd had already gathered. Laborers, merchants, and passersby mingled with the established families. Joachim and Joseph took their seats along the outside wall in the area customarily reserved for the High Priest's party.

"If this is something important, it's a shame Zechariah isn't here," Joachim said.

"He seemed concerned to get back to Jerusalem in a hurry."

"Temple business, Joseph. I remember the pressures. Zechariah's been concerned at how the Pharisees are taking over the debates there. I think he feels he needs to express more Saduccean leadership in the Sanhedrin. He wants to retain control, be at the center of things. His recent impediment and the birth of Jon kept him rather isolated."

A temporary hush came over the gathered crowd when the rabbi of Ain Karim, dressed in traditional black and white, came in through the synagogue's side door. But whispering recommenced when they saw the gray tunic of a member of the Herodian guard accompanying him. Standing before the assembled crowd, the rabbi held up a scroll.

"I have an important announcement," he declared.

Silence resumed as he looked around.

"Listen carefully. This is a proclamation from the King."

He began to read to them in a serious and deliberate tone:

"Citizens of Judea, Greetings. Wherewith we act on the behalf of Augustus Caesar, we command that all male citizens of Judea must register their names, kinfolk, and trade with the authorities in their hometowns and villages. This census is to be executed within the next two phases of the moon. Every male over the age of twelve is expected to make this registration for the annals of the Roman Empire. Required details are needed on citizenship, age, trade, and family affiliation. This census is part of a total Imperial census and will be fulfilled at our command on behalf of Caesar Augustus. Witnessed on this day by our hand, Herod, the King."

Members of the gathering huddled and talked to each other, occasionally looking over their shoulders at the rabbi.

Someone shouted:

"This is about taxation for Rome!"

"Roman bastards!" shouted out an elderly zealot.

But most of the citizens of Ain Karim left the synagogue as they had entered—bemused, not really any the wiser, and not particularly concerned.

"Most of those there have never left this village," Joachim said. "They married in Ain Karim and will die here. Their lives are woven around the agriculture of this village. It's the same in Nazareth. They know only the world of vineyards, the threshing floor and the village well."

"It's the same in Bethlehem," Joseph agreed.

"I know, Joseph. Remember, I once lived in Bethlehem. It's no great problem for these people to be asked to leave their names, ages, and professions with the synagogue authorities. The rabbi probably knows most such details in any case and will take care of things for them."

Details as to how and when to make this declaration seemed of little importance.

"I thought we might hear something a little more significant," Joseph said.

Others around them were already more interested in the ever-present and ever-growing streak of starlight now easily visible in the night sky.

"Well, it may be more significant than you think," replied Miriam's father. "Little by little, the Roman Empire is taking over from Herod. It's more obvious up in my country than it is down here in Judea. We're going to see changes. This is only the start."

"What do you mean, Joachim?"

"Well, with increased Roman power and the probable fall of the Herodians, who knows what other changes we may see? These could be exciting times. Everybody else believes in that star, so why not us?"

Joseph nodded, rubbing at the cut on his hand.

"You should wash that cut before it gets worse. Working in the vineyard doesn't help it."

"It's nothing. But, about the star and Miriam."

"Ah, yes. Miriam," Joachim repeated.

"She has changed profoundly, perhaps more than I understand."

"And her new composure has affected Elizabeth and Anna, too." Joachim stood still and hesitated, before continuing. "It's as if her humiliation by Gabriel is now blotted from her mind. Now, she moves and acts in prayer and watches the star, believing that this star is all about her."

Joseph nodded.

"As perhaps we should." He looked up. "I don't understand, but there is something about that star."

"So the star could be for us…for Miriam?" Joachim said quizzically.

"We have as much right to its mystical power as anyone else, I suppose."

"Do you believe as Elizabeth and Anna now believe, that Miriam carries God's child—the Messiah?"

Joseph raised a hand in agitation:

"Lower your voice," he said.

"Well, do you?"

"I don't know. I only know that this new way of thinking about her pregnancy is better for her. She is maturing, she offers new wisdom—far better than the naïve, inexperienced adolescent from the House of the Virgins."

As he witnessed the mutterings of the stargazers around them, Joachim answered morosely:

"Everyone is turning the star either to their own advantage or to someone else's misfortune. Tell me what you really think, Joseph. Miriam believes her child is to be someone special, more than that, it seems. So does Elizabeth. Elizabeth believes Jon was a gift from God and a sign for us all. They both think that their children have been sent to them by God."

"Sent by God, but by the seed of Gabriel," added Joseph, with more than a hint of bitterness in his voice.

"I understand your doubts, Joseph."

"I don't know what to think. I love your daughter and I'll be a good father to her child. I look forward to our life together. I'm deeply honored to join your family. Miriam's stories are part of her charm. But she tells them as if they were solid fact, when she hasn't lived in the real world. She hears voices from God, but she's been sheltered from reality. I'm not going to stop her believing in her child's destiny. Every mother feels her child is special. But I'm not sure what I believe."

"But what of Zechariah's belief that Jon and our Miriam's child will be partners in a messianic dream?"

"Whatever will be will be," Joseph said. "I'm content to build houses and take care of my family. You've been very kind to me. But I'm a simple man. I don't have the advantages of priestly men from Jerusalem. I have to work hard to produce for my family. I can't afford to build my life on dreams—even dreams about God's purpose. I'll do anything I can for Miriam's child and I'll cherish your daughter forever. She's brought a lot of joy into my life at a time when disappointment and misery had nearly engulfed me. I'm very grateful for the smallest blessings. God's gift of Miriam is the greatest blessing I'll ever receive."

"And Miriam's child will be the greatest blessing that Anna and I will ever receive," Joachim added, as he put his hand on the carpenter's shoulder. "Joseph, it's good to talk with you. You put things in the right perspective. Think about it. Anna and I will soon be grandparents. How long do you think it will be now, about a month?"

"About six weeks, I would think."

"Joseph, you'll be the father of our grandchild. We're so pleased to have you as one of the family."

The two men embraced, then walked back to Zechariah's house.

Joachim looked over his shoulder at the black sky to the east. The bright star had climbed up behind them in the advancing night, and Ain Karim took on its nocturnal look of innocent peace. The first chills of winter descended with the darkness.

* * *

Back at Zechariah's house, while Anna and Elizabeth were waiting for Joachim and Joseph to return, Miriam sat in the courtyard with Judith. A new sense of reunion was growing between these two whose lives had been separated by circumstance and station.

"Judith, I'll miss you when I go to Bethlehem," Miriam said. "You always listen to my stories and you've told me about things in my early life that I've never known, like the time you had to carry me off the roof when the thunder and lightning struck Bethlehem. It must have been a terrible storm. I don't remember it."

191

"You were very young. We used to all sleep up on the roof in the summer, but that particular night God opened the skies without warning. Perhaps God speaks in the thunder. Before He speaks, He opens the roof of the sky and lets out the light of heaven. It was very frightening."

Miriam watched her, appreciating the enthusiasm in her eyes, the delight in their friendship.

"I wish you could come to Bethlehem with me again," she said. "I suppose that's impossible, since my mother and father will need you."

Judith couldn't conceal her joy.

"Oh, Miss Miriam! I've so longed for you to say something like that. It would be wonderful to come to Bethlehem and care for your baby as I did for you. Do you think they'll let me go with you?"

"Let's ask them. But Joseph isn't wealthy. I don't know whether he can afford to have an extra person in the house. He has his own family to take care of. From what I understand, they're quite a handful. He has a cousin who helps him, but I don't think his house is very big. The house won't be anything like this one. Anyway, let's ask. I do so want you to be with me when my baby's born."

"Oh! Let's hope so!"

But then, Miriam became quiet. She looked at Judith more seriously.

"Judith, do you understand about my baby? This babe growing in my womb is sacred, it is hallowed according to the fulfilment of the Scriptures."

Judith moved uncomfortably in her seat.

"I do feel that, Miss Miriam, but…"

"But what?"

"Well, I'm just a simple woman. But I do hear all the talk of omens and signs, and I overheard Mistress Elizabeth and Mistress Anna talk of your baby."

"And what do they say?" Miriam asked, her voice now soft and kindly, but curious.

"Well, they talk of Mistress Elizabeth's boy, Jon, and of your coming baby. They say they are touched by God, that your babe…" Judith looked at the gentle swelling of Miriam's belly…"that your babe is the Messiah, just as the star says."

Miriam nodded.

"Is that what the star means to you, Judith?" she asked.

"Oh, yes. I watch it as it mysteriously moves across the heavens. And you, Miss Miriam, what do you think?"

"I agree with you. The star is a most beautiful sign of God's work inside me."

As they spoke, a cool breeze blew across the courtyard.

"Let me go and fetch you a shawl," Judith said. "These evenings are really getting chilly."

After Judith left, Miriam looked up at the night sky. The scene reminded her of the garden at the House of the Virgins. The branches of the knotted olive trees moved lightly in the breeze. Through their tracery, she could see the bright star and its trail of light. It was right above her, looking down into the courtyard.

She reflected for a moment on Judith's story about the thunder and lightning. Perhaps the star was also a gap in the heavens for God to speak through. The whole night sky reminded her of the moonbeams that had flickered up and down on that last night in the courtyard of the House of the Virgins. She could imagine the angelic messengers she'd seen in those moonbeams. They'd taken her thoughts to God and brought God's blessings back to her. It had been such a moving experience. She'd felt enveloped in God's light. Nothing had ever been emotionally as strong as the power that had surged through her young body that night. She eyed the star curiously.

"What are you trying to tell me?" she whispered. "Could everything that my angel Gabriel said to me be true? Is Jon's destiny to be linked to that of my own child? Will my son be a 'Prince of Peace' and a leader of our people, as Gabriel predicted?"

The leaves stirred. In their rustling, Miriam could hear the voices of her messengers. They were as vivid now as in the House of the Virgins. Light from the heavenly body above flickered through the leaves. She felt the same incredible power and peace she'd experienced before.

"Gabriel! Are you there?" she cried out.

Miriam felt she heard Gabriel's voice once again:

"Greetings, Miriam! You're about to have a baby. Don't be afraid, because the Lord is with you! You've found favor with God. When your baby's born, you'll call him Joshua. He'll be great and will be called a son of God. God will give him rule over His kingdom forever, because there is no end to God's kingdom."

Miriam stared at the star—entranced. It blinked at her. The mysterious trail of light flickered as she observed it through the dancing leaves.

She was still watching when Judith returned.

"Miss Miriam! Is everything all right?"

Miriam didn't answer.

"Look! I have your shawl. Let me put it around you. It's getting cold. Maybe you should come inside."

"No, Judith. Let's stay here," Miriam pleaded. "Just the two of us."

"You're trembling, Miss Miriam. Are you sure you're all right?"

Judith put her arm around the young woman.

"I'm fine, Judith. Gabriel came back," she said, pointing. "He's up there in that star, watching us. Gabriel's going to be with us wherever we go."

"Oh, Miss Miriam! You mustn't let the ghost of Gabriel haunt you like this. He's in your past. Remember how the High Priest told us not to talk about him anymore, especially around Joseph. Joseph's your husband. He'll be back soon."

"My Gabriel isn't the same as that priest in Jerusalem," Miriam said mystically.

She looked up at Judith, her brown eyes wise and compassionate in the light of the courtyard brazier.

"Nobody can take my Gabriel away. He'll always be with me. He's my guardian angel. Joseph understands about Gabriel. My Gabriel's a messenger from God. Gabriel comes to me in visions. He was here, just now, in the rustling of these trees."

"I believe you, Miss Miriam," Judith said with practical expediency. "I'll believe anything you say, but I don't want you to catch a cold. We must go inside."

Miriam pointed up at the bright star in the sky above again.

"Joshua will be born under its light," she said.

"Joshua?"

"Gabriel told me to call him Joshua."

The latch moved on the roadway gate. Joseph and Joachim entered the courtyard. They looked more like brothers than son-in-law and father-in-law. Their faces glowed in the soft light of the brazier.

Miriam got up to greet them. Joseph put his hands around her and kissed her forehead.

* * *

In the vast Temple court of the Gentiles, the priest Gabriel was searching for the soothsayer who had accosted him a few days before, seeking out the bent form with its grabbing hands, the rings and the earrings. He was afraid and yet at the same time flattered by what the soothsayer had said. He walked toward the shade of the colonnade.

What if the soothsayer is right? he thought. *What if I am a messenger from God? How can I promote my message? If I tell of the High Priest Zechariah's plans for a Davidic messiah to anyone and that old fool finds out, he'll imprison me or worse. Perhaps I should appeal to King Herod. But what use would that be when my message would almost certainly be detrimental to the Royal family? This must be how Jeremiah and the prophets felt. How difficult it is to be on the King's side, but still have to speak out against the King. 'Go! Tell it on the mountain,' this soothsayer said. But tell it to whom, and how much should I reveal?*

Gabriel leaned against a pillar and watched. He was close to the Triple Gate. Pilgrims and curious passersby were coming and going. Beggars and cripples, some charlatans, were seated on the steps waiting for an occasional prosperous merchant to add a few coins to their cause. A man dressed in fine Oriental robes, perhaps a Parthian, a Persian, or perhaps a wealthy man from Chaldea, mounted the steps and dropped three large silver coins into a cripple's bowl. The cripple nodded, trying hard not to break his vacant stare as a broad grin fought to surface on his face. The wealthy man moved on. Gabriel watched, amused as the cripple rose to his feet and ran off with the bowl and his newly won silver. The rich man disappeared into the throng of pilgrims heading toward the moneychangers.

Gabriel felt intuitively compelled to follow this well-dressed man and did so at a discreet distance. Along the way, the rich man was accosted by other beggars, some of whom received rewards for their endeavors. The message went out. Soon, a crowd of ruffians followed the man, hands stretched out in contrived pity. As they were passing the tables of the moneychangers along with the cages of birds and animals that awaited purchase for sacrifice, the crowd grew hostile, jostling each other to get closer to the wealthy merchant who was giving out the silver coins. A cart of small cages holding turtle doves overturned, liberating the doves on a swift beat of wing. In the rush and brawl that followed, Temple dealers began to beat on the beggars. The finely dressed man walked on, unheeded.

Then, all of a sudden, there was the soothsayer, the same man who had approached Gabriel a few days earlier. The soothsayer ran out in front of the rich stranger and shouted:

"Shalom!"

The merchant prince stopped, formally greeted the man, and bowed.

The soothsayer then did likewise.

"Greetings, my friend," said the soothsayer. "Are you a stranger here?"

The merchant answered in Aramaic.

"I'm Chaldean. I'm making my first visit to Jerusalem."

"I'm a soothsayer, sir. I have the power to predict your future. Here, in this Holy place, I can predict your future. I have the power from God."

"Well, what prediction would you make, soothsayer? What future have you in mind for old Caspar here?"

"Caspar, that's your name, sir?"

"Yes. I'm a merchant from the far away land of the Chaldees. I'm on my way to Rome."

"I can see you're a man of substance, sir. Let me see," the soothsayer said as he stared at Caspar with a glazed expression. "I predict great things for you. I'm sure you'll be very successful. You'll be well rewarded. However, I singled you out for a different reason. God told me you're a man with a purpose...a man with a mission to fulfill."

"Really?" Caspar said, "Your god told you I'm a man with a purpose? Well, tell me more. What purpose?"

"You have a message of utmost importance to carry to the world. It's a message of peace and love between all peoples, but you're afraid. You keep holding back your message. You don't seem to want to take political responsibility."

"What do you know, soothsayer? Peace is my message. I've traveled far in search of ways to open up new trade routes. I envision a mercantile peace for all nations such as we've not known since the time of Alexander the Greek."

"You've come to the right place, Caspar. You're the one. You must give your message to the world. The world is at a crossroads. Look at that star in the night sky. Doesn't that tell you the time has come?"

"The time for what?"

Gabriel was astounded. The soothsayer appeared to be tricking the rich man with almost exactly the same line as he had used on him just a few days before.

"The time for a new order—a new kingdom."

Others in the courtyard started to gather around the soothsayer and Caspar.

"Whose kingdom?" Caspar asked.

"A kingdom ruled by God for God's people."

"Some say the Roman Caesar is a god," Caspar noted.

"God's kingdom is more powerful than Caesar's. Empires come and go, my friend, but you know the secret of inner peace, and that's more powerful."

The soothsayer grabbed the rich man's hands.

The same firm hold, the same intensity, Gabriel noted, *it's the same routine.*

Caspar backed away.

Gabriel chuckled. *It evokes a similar response,* he observed.

"Yes. I don't make many mistakes," said the soothsayer. "I can see your future in your hands. These hands haven't known heavy labor or hard work, have they? They're clearly marked, though. They reveal to me the truth that I had hoped to find in you. You're a messenger. You'll tell the world of some great event. I predict that this event will involve a child. Sir, let me quote from the Hebrew Scriptures: 'A virgin shall be with child and give birth to a son, and he'll be called Emmanuel, which means, God with us.' That child, sir, could be your answer. Maybe through that child, you'll be able to spread your message of peace."

The rich man, now impatient and wishing to be rid of the soothsayer, reached into his purse and pushed five large silver coins into the man's hands.

The soothsayer bowed in appreciation.

"God be with you, my friend," he said. "It's under the star. You're a messenger and I'm telling you to deliver your message. You must tell the world your plans. As soon as I saw you, I knew you were the one. I've passed the power on to you. Use it wisely. It's up to you. Go! Tell it on the mountain! You know the secret that's locked within your heart."

The soothsayer turned and left Caspar standing with his arms outstretched and his mouth agape, as if some great responsibility had just fallen upon his shoulders.

Gabriel watched as the soothsayer disappeared into the crowd, no doubt to swindle more silver coins from other unsuspecting visitors.

"Caspar!" Gabriel called out.

The rich man turned with a look of surprise.

"Do I know you?" he asked.

"I was listening. I heard everything the soothsayer said. You see…he spoke to me several days ago. He told me I had a message just as he said so to you."

"He told you the same thing?"

Gabriel grinned.

"It looks as if we've been fooled, but the soothsayer may not know how surprisingly accurate his prediction could be. His remarks have greatly disturbed me, because I can see some truth in what he says."

"Carry on, my friend! Enlighten me!" said Caspar. "What's your name?"

"Gabriel, sir. Why don't we go to a tavern I know? I'd like to hear your story, too."

They left the Temple, Gabriel leading the stranger through the narrow streets of Mount Zion. Beasts of burden rubbed against sandstone walls as impatient drovers pulled them up shallow steps. Awnings, some of woven cloth and others of cured skins, shielded the sun from tables of merchant's wares, butter lamps, cooking utensils, goblets, daggers, baskets, jars and cloth of all kinds. From small cavernous rooms, came the smell of freshly baked bread. The ground was littered with dung and rotting fruit. Dogs were sniffing and scavenging among the scraps. They reached a courtyard, well protected by high stone walls. Inside, were several rough-hewn tables. The place was busy. Most of the patrons, like Caspar, were visitors to Jerusalem. The sounds of laughter and sensuous music drifted out from the tavern beyond.

They sat down at one of the outside tables. A lithe, young, dark-haired maiden approached them.

"Gabriel," she said. "So who's your good-looking friend?"

"Caspar. He needs wine. Bring us your best."

"You've been here before," Caspar said, as the young girl went in to the house.

"Drink some wine and I'll show you why."

The girl returned with two goblets. She flashed her eyes at Gabriel.

"You'd like me to dance for your friend?"

"Later, Samantha."

Samantha tilted her head seductively, then returned to the interior.

"So this is your first visit to Jerusalem," Gabriel said. "I overheard you. You said you're from Chaldea. Would you rather we converse in Greek?"

"Whatever, my friend, I speak Greek, Aramaic and Persian."

Caspar then continued, mixing Greek and Aramaic as he thought appropriate.

"Yes, I'm from Chaldea. There's a lot of talk along the caravan routes today about Judea's potential. Things are changing in Alexandria. The Romans are not as easy to deal with as the Egyptians were. By the time you pay them off there's not much profit. It might be different here."

"Why?"

"Your king is one of us. He still has strong contacts with the Nabateans. Some people are considering diverting the Alexandria trade from Petra to Judea. Your country could become the new gateway to Greece and Rome."

"Through Caesarea?"

"Yes, I hear it's a magnificent harbor. Not as big as Alexandria, of course, but with the right deal it could be more profitable for some of us."

"I've only been there twice, but it looks like a good facility. The King is very proud of his achievement there."

"Do you know King Herod?"

"No, but I move in circles that know him."

Caspar's eyes lit up. He raised his near empty goblet.

"Perhaps you can help me?" he said.

Gabriel turned and attracted Samantha's attention.

"Two more," he said, as her heavy perfume touched the air.

He addressed Caspar again:

"So, how can I help you?"

"I'm investigating this route to bring new Oriental trade to Rome. I'm on my way to Rome to make connections. Your king could help me. I want to have an audience with him. If he could arrange the right connections for me in Petra and Rome, I could bring valuable trade to Judea."

"I know King Herod's chamberlain. We've had a drink together. It might be possible for me to assist you, but I can't promise anything. According to Ptolemy, King Herod has violent mood swings these days."

"Ah, the King's chamberlain is Egyptian?"

"Well…an Alexandrian Jew."

Samantha returned with two more goblets. She set them down and put her arms around Gabriel's neck as she looked seductively at Caspar.

"You want me to dance?"

Gabriel's eyes sparkled as Caspar looked Samantha over.

"She dances well," Gabriel said. "I think you would like her."

"I'll be back," Samantha said. "The room will be free soon."

Caspar quaffed on his wine.

"She's beautiful," he noted, a smile crossing his expensive face.

"She can please you. I know."

"So you've brought me to a brothel?"

"A discreet brothel. Most of the girls will dance for a coin or two."

Caspar looked around at the international clientele.

"So, what's your business?" he asked.

"Oh, this and that. I conduct business at the Temple."

"That's a splendid building."

"It will be when it's finished."

Caspar took another sip from his goblet.

"And you know this girl?" he asked.

"Yes. I come here quite often."

"Do you also have a wife?"

"No, but I nearly got married recently."

Gabriel took a deliberate draught on his wine.

"That's what struck me as so strange when the soothsayer was talking to you," Gabriel continued. "It seemed like he was telling us both about the girl I was supposed to marry."

"Samantha?"

"No. You know, when the soothsayer talked about a virgin who's with child? I might even be the father of such a child. I was the innocent victim of a plot. Can I take you into my strictest confidence? Caspar, my life could be in danger for revealing this."

"Of course, my friend. You intrigue me."

"This plot was dreamed up by the High Priest here. The plan was for me to secretly father a baby who is of the Royal Davidic family. You see... I'm a Davidic priest. They chose me for the task. I was to be betrothed to one of the Temple virgins. I went along with it to begin with. I was being handed a young beauty. It seemed too good an opportunity to miss. In reality, it wasn't like that. The virgin was very strange. She was a sort of spiritual mystic. I couldn't understand her. She was immature, yet very desirable. I backed out of the deal, though. I swear to you, the virgin never willingly lay with me. I tried one time, but she rejected me. I suppose it's possible that at that time there is just a slight chance I impregnated her. I've since found out this moon-faced, innocent girl is with child. But I don't really know how it could have been me. Personally, I think the High Priest raped her and I was chosen to be the scapegoat."

Caspar raised a bushy eyebrow.

"What a story. But why are you telling me all this?"

"The High Priest accused me of rape on account of that minor indiscretion on my part. I barely touched her. Anyway, they selected this virgin to be the mother of the future King of the Jews."

Gabriel looked around to confirm nobody was listening to them.

"They hope to overthrow the Herodians and establish a new Davidic dynasty."

"You mean oust King Herod and his family?"

"Yes. But you're sworn to secrecy. I was paid off in silver to keep quiet."

"And you're going to pay me off by giving me Samantha?" A light came into his eyes. "Well, it's a deal. You can trust old Caspar here to keep a secret."

"They don't want Herod or the Romans," Gabriel said. "They want a king of the Royal house of David. They selected me so that the seed of my ancestors could be passed on secretly through this virgin, and nobody would know other than the High Priest and his plotters. But the virgin was too innocent. I lost interest. You know what I mean. You're a man of the world."

"You say this virgin is with child?"

"Her name's Miriam. The baby should be due very soon. It must be nearly nine months since I last saw her. She may have already had the child."

Samantha returned. She'd changed from her serving shift into a series of gossamer veils strung with gold chains and cheap stones.

"I'll dance for you now," she said.

Gabriel passed her two silver coins.

"Follow me," the sultry girl beckoned.

Samantha took them into a room decorated only with oil lamps and large, comfortable cushions. In one corner, three musicians waited with their instruments. As soon as they started to play, Samantha gyrated before them, her skin rippling to the rhythm. One by one, she removed the veils and threw the scented scarves in Caspar's direction.

Caspar picked them up and sniffed their perfume.

When she was finished Samantha was standing right in front of him. Caspar reached up and touched the flesh of her thighs.

Samantha teased him, turned, and stepped away, looking back at the wide-eyed potentate.

"Do you want to go with her?" Gabriel said.

"Do you think that's what she wants?"

"Of course. Go with her. You see, Jerusalem's not such a bad place."

Caspar stood up and adjusted his robe.

"All right, so where do we go?"

"Follow me," Samantha said in her husky voice.

Caspar then disappeared into another room.

Gabriel lay back on the cushions and stared at the ceiling, wondering if maybe he had told Caspar too much. But at least now, he also shared Caspar's secret. When Caspar returned, Gabriel put an arm around the contented potentate's shoulder and said assuringly:

"If you have nowhere to go in Jerusalem, please be my guest. I would like you to stay with me. I have a fine house on the west side, close to the King's palace."

"Why not? It would be my pleasure to stay with you. Maybe you can help me set up appointments to discuss trade," and with a wink, he added, "and other things with our Herod of Jerusalem. So, tell me about their virgin. Maybe I need to find her if what the soothsayer said means anything."

The two of them sauntered from the tavern.

"The High Priest will know where she is. As I say, I think he raped her and tried to frame me. You can probably find out from him, but don't ever mention my name. You heard all this from the soothsayer, not me. If they found out I'd told you, they'd have me imprisoned or even stoned."

"That's terrible!"

"Remember, it was a priestly plot against King Herod's family. It's true…the King hates his own family. He keeps changing his heirs. Maybe he'd be glad to know of this prophecy, but then again, he might take it as a personal afront on his own power. According to Ptolemy, you never know which way he's going to turn. Officially, King Herod and the High Priests work together. But one day Herod's championing the independence of our Jewish State, and the next he's conniving with the Romans. He's a cunning old fox."

* * *

Miriam lay on a couch, her fresh face shining in the light of an oil lamp. She was now approaching the last month of her pregnancy. Judith puffed up the cushions for her.

Joseph and Zechariah lingered over a goblet of wine after their evening meal while Anna and Elizabeth cleared things away.

"Leave the grapes," Zechariah said. "Joseph likes these grapes."

Judith left with Anna and Elizabeth. The dishes had to be washed and cleansed according to the Levitical laws. In the High Priest's house, tradition was important.

Joseph took a sprig of grapes from the bunch.

"This Roman census makes things awkward," he said. "Will it be better to go back to Bethlehem now, while Miriam can still travel, or wait until after the baby is born?"

"Traveling with a baby just a few days old might be risky. Besides, if you wait for the baby, you might miss the census."

Joseph's kind eyes twinkled at that.

"Would that really matter?" he asked.

"I'm sure they'll miss some people. I doubt it would matter very much. I don't really know. This is a Herodian and Roman task. It's not in my realm."

Miriam called to them.

"I think we should go," she said. "I'm still strong. I might be too weak to travel after my baby is born. I have a funny feeling about this, in any case. God's child should be born in the Holy City of Bethlehem—David's city."

Joseph looked at Zechariah.

"That might be a good idea," the High Priest agreed. *It might give more credence to my plan*, he thought.

Joachim, who had stretched his legs in an after-dinner walk, came back in to the dining room with Anna. Anna trimmed another lamp to give them more light.

"Joseph thinks it might be wise for them to return to Bethlehem now," Zechariah said.

Miriam sat up on the couch.

"I think so, too. I want my baby to be born in David's city."

Anna sat down beside her.

"You'll need help," she said.

"Joseph says Bathsheba will be there."

Joseph turned to Miriam.

"Don't count on her," he said. "It's as much as she can do to keep the others in order." Then, facing back to Zechariah he added, "It's not easy having a large family."

"It won't be easy for Miriam either."

Joachim sat at the table with Joseph and Zechariah.

"Anna and I were thinking about that. We would like to let Judith go with Miriam. She could stay with Miriam as long as she needs her, weeks, months, even years."

He looked at Joseph.

"We'll take care of the extra expense."

"Yes, Joseph," Miriam said excitedly. "That would be wonderful."

She called Judith.

The middle-aged servant came running in from the kitchen.

"What is it? Are you all right?"

"I couldn't be better, Judith. You're going to come with us."

"To Bethlehem?"

"Yes."

Judith sat on the couch beside Miriam and kissed her lightly on the cheek.

Joseph felt disturbed. *How will Bathsheba react to two new women in the house? She isn't happy about my marriage, and now this. Where are they all going to sleep?*

Zechariah nodded at Joachim.

"It sounds like a wonderful idea, Joseph," Zechariah said.

Joseph got up from the table and walked over to the couch.

"How soon would you like to leave?"

He looked at Judith.

"I know you will be a great help to Miriam," he confirmed with a slightly unconvincing frown.

"Let's go as soon as we can," Miriam said brightly. "I know I'll be all right. It's God's will. This is all part of God's plan—my baby will be born in David's city!"

"We had better get on our way soon, then," Joseph agreed. "I can see I have some building work to do before the baby is born!"

* * *

Joachim and Anna decided it would be best for them to leave now, too.

"We can go with them to Jerusalem," Anna explained to her sister. "Joseph can then take the mules with Miriam's dowry items on to Bethlehem. We have our two donkeys to make our way back to Galilee after registering Joachim in Jerusalem for this census."

"Not a very comfortable ride," Elizabeth said.

"It will be easier for us than for Miriam. I just hope nothing goes wrong."

"She should have the best part of another month."

It was crisp, bright, and sunny when they set out. Miriam rode Joseph's only donkey. Judith walked beside her. Joseph plodded on ahead with the lead rein. Even though it was not far, it would be a slow journey. Joachim and Anna followed, leading their two mules, which they'd loaded up with the simple, practical items of Miriam's dowry—cooking utensils, her wedding headdress, woven blankets and a bolt of blue linen.

They traveled toward Jerusalem, taking it slowly so Miriam would be in maximum comfort. But along the way, Miriam felt the baby in her womb kick out. She winced in pain.

"What's wrong?" Judith asked. "Is it the baby? My God, what if we can't get to Bethlehem?"

"I'm sure I'll be all right," Miriam said as the pain subsided. "My baby's just restless. He's never ridden a donkey before."

Judith looked up at Miriam and saw comforting radiance shining from her face.

"I'm so glad I'm able to come with you," she said.

"Me, too."

The donkey plodded on a few more paces, swaying uneasily.

"I can't help being a little nervous, Miriam," Judith confided. "I've never lived with anyone other than Mistress Anna and Master Joachim."

"Don't worry about a thing, Judith," Miriam said. "God is good. God will take care of us. I've never met my new family either. Can you believe it Judith? James and Amos are older than I am—my stepsons! I don't know what to make of Jonah, he seems to be the wild one."

She paused for a moment and then smiled back at Judith.

"Ruth, Joseph's little girl, sounds adorable. I'm sure she'll like me."

"I hope they like me, too. What about Bathsheba? You said she's Joseph's cousin?"

Miriam smiled.

"She must feel like she's married to Joseph. She's been running his home for three years. I don't know what she'll think. Don't worry what any of them think. I'll be with you. Joseph will take care of us. God will be with us. My angel Gabriel's always with me."

"You really believe in that angel, don't you?"

"Don't you believe in angels?"

"I suppose we all have angels watching over us."

The donkey stumbled on the uneven road.

Miriam flinched.

"Judith!" she cried out. "It hurts! He's really kicking hard. Perhaps I am going to have my baby. Ask Joseph how much further it is to Jerusalem."

Joseph had already turned around.

"How much further to Jerusalem, Master Joseph? Mistress Miriam's hurting."

Again, the pain subsided.

"Don't worry, Joseph. The pain's gone," Miriam said. "We must go on. This is God's purpose for us."

"We'll see Jerusalem soon," Joseph reassured her. "I know a place where we can stay near the city gates. From there it'll be easier to skirt around the city in the morning and take the road south for Bethlehem. The busy streets in the city might be too much for you."

Their party slowly shuffled on. As Joseph had predicted, the city came into view as they arrived at the brow of the next rise in the road. It was dusk when they came to the inn.

Judith recognized the flat-roofed house with its vine arbour.

"This is where we stayed before with Master Joachim and Mistress Anna," she said to Miriam.

The innkeeper had a room. It was sparsely furnished with a rough bench bed, a small table, stool, and two lampstands. Joachim accepted it. There was good stabling behind the inn. Joseph tied up the animals and fed them hay.

The inn was warm from the kitchen fire, and the innkeeper served them potage from a large cooking pot. The lentil soup, along with a goblet of wine, felt good in their bellies.

Back in their room, Anna and Miriam shared the bed. The men prepared pallets to sleep on the floor. Judith would also sleep on the floor, but she had taken a cloak and gone outside.

Joseph was soon asleep. Before settling down, Joachim joined Anna and Miriam, seating himself on the side of the bed. His eyes glinted in the soft glow of the lamp.

"You will send word to us when the baby is born?" he said. "Zechariah will know how to get a message to us."

Miriam smiled.

"We will find a way of letting you know. The rabbi in Bethlehem can write a letter for us."

Anna held Miriam.

"I'm so glad we were able to share this time together," she said. "I... er...we, never stopped talking about you all those years. We really missed you, Miriam."

"I know. I feel your love," she said. "But it was all right, Mother. I liked it at the House of the Virgins. I was there for God and now God is here for me."

"He is… He is," Joachim agreed. "God never deserted me, and He will always be with you."

"And my son…Joshua, will be a son of God."

"Joshua?" Joachim queried.

"Yes, that's what Gabriel wanted me to name him."

Joachim looked at Anna, but said nothing.

"What if you give us a granddaughter—a pretty girl like you?" Anna said, agreeing with her husband's furtive look that this was no time to open up the subject of Gabriel again. "If it should turn out to be a girl, I'm sure in time Joseph will give you a son."

Miriam looked into her mother's eyes.

"I know it's a boy. God told me. My son, Joshua, will be a child of God, chosen to be a leader—the anointed one."

Anna felt the confident poise of her daughter. *You are very sure of yourself,* she thought. *Such confidence will go a long way. You will be a great help to Joseph's family.* She kissed her on the forehead.

"You need to sleep. You will have a long day ahead of you tomorrow."

"I am sleepy," she said. "My baby needs to rest, too."

Joachim clasped Anna's hand.

"I'm very proud of you," he said. "My daughter has become a beautiful woman."

Anna extinguished the lamp.

Joseph snored.

* * *

Herod's palace was the second largest building in Jerusalem, only rivaled in magnificence and splendor by the Temple. Its massive outer walls were built in the beautiful yellow stone that gave all Jerusalem its special glow. The stone sparkled in the sun and was less abrasive to the eye than the white marble of the Greek cities.

When Gabriel and Caspar reached the outer gates, two Herodian guards crossed their spears, blocking their path.

"Name your business!" one of them said.

Gabriel, dressed in a new yellow and red robe purchased the day before in the bazaar, produced papers that Ptolemy had prepared for him. After he'd handed them over, the guard stood aside and allowed them to pass through, instructing them to wait in the inner court. Tall cypress trees grew in dark green spires within this courtyard. Marble seats surrounded a fountain. To meet King Herod, Caspar, too, had purchased a new striped robe in green and yellow, with matching headgear. It was tied at the waist with a gold silk cord.

After a short while, one of Ptolemy's agents came out and greeted them.

"Caspar of Chaldea, welcome to Jerusalem. Follow me. The King will see you now."

Gabriel stood up, but the agent reprimanded him.

"Not you, sir...just, Caspar of Chaldea. You must wait here."

Gabriel hung back while Caspar and the agent entered the palace.

The King's chamber was up a flight of steps. On arrival, they found Herod seated in a simple Roman chair. With great difficulty, Herod attempted to rise.

"Caspar of Chaldea, Your Majesty," the agent announced.

"Chaldea," the King repeated. "Welcome to Jerusalem. So what brings you here from the East?"

Caspar replied in Greek, the preferred language of court and commerce:

"Your Majesty, I bring you the opportunity of great riches from the East. I've opened up caravan routes from India to Chaldea, and I've access to new silks and treasures from Cathay. There's a wealth of new trade pouring into Chaldea from the Orient. So far, few traders have found markets across the deserts to bring these riches to Rome. I can open up such routes. I could bring you treasures that would even impress Caesar."

Caspar opened a small box he was carrying.

"Your Majesty," he continued as he presented the box to the King. "I have jewels from India. These precious stones are only fit for a king. I offer them to you as a gift from the Chaldeans."

The King's eyes lit up as he saw evidence of truth in Caspar's story of the riches in the East.

Caspar picked out some of the choicest rubies and sapphires.

"Look at these," he said.

King Herod, sick as he was, greedily seized a ruby. He turned the stone between his forefinger and thumb.

"These are only a fraction of the wealth that lies before us," Caspar continued. "Yours is a land of great opportunity. Since you built the fine harbor at Caesarea, you've made your land a potential depository of wealth bound for Rome. There could be rich pickings here, Your Majesty, that could personally benefit you and your kingdom. Why should we send this potential wealth to Rome through Antioch and Alexandria when it could come through Caesarea? Judea lies between the southern and northern trade routes. At the right price, this could be advantageous to us both."

The King looked at Caspar, all the while clutching the choice ruby.

"That's precisely why, against great odds and the ridicule of the world, I built the great harbor in the dunes. I realize the potential of Caesarea not only to serve us on the fringe of the Empire, but as you have rightly pointed out, as a gateway for entry into the Roman world."

King Herod once again studied the lustrous stone, his weakened eyes alive with greed as he held it to the light.

"I've been waiting to meet someone like you, someone who truly understands my achievements."

"And I need someone like you, Your Majesty. I need your permission to allow me to pass this lucrative trade through Judea. Your reward will be substantial, of course. But first, Your Majesty, I need your recommendations for access to those markets in Rome."

Herod made an impatient, irritated gesture.

"Things can always be arranged in Rome, but first we have to finalize agreements here—arrange things here. What advance payments can you guarantee us?"

"I can make gold reserves available to you immediately. I can present you with more rubies like those you hold in your hand. I have connections with traders in Petra. I'll persuade them to change their caravan routes from Alexandria to Caesarea."

"Now, that's good!" said the King. "How soon can we expect shipments of these Oriental treasures?"

Caspar stroked his beard and thought for a moment.

"By early summer," he said thoughtfully, "if I can negotiate the best markets in Rome. That's why I need the right introductions there."

"As I said, that can be arranged," the King answered, studying Caspar. "You're a shrewd man. I like your plans. If all you say is true, I'll give passage to your traders."

"There are riches to be enjoyed here, Your Majesty. Riches to be made in this most fortuitous year. Have you considered that star in the night sky? It could be an omen of the good fortune in our partnership."

"The star?"

"Yes, Your Majesty. That star has followed me all the way from Chaldea. It's now right above Jerusalem. A deal made between us at just this time could benefit us both."

"Caspar, I hear comments on the subject of this star daily. I would like to think this is one of the more sensible suggestions. You're a man who has traveled. What opinions have you heard on this subject?"

"This star's one of the strangest things I've ever seen. It moves. I've watched its progress from Chaldea. I'm sure it must herald some important and great event."

King Herod leaned over in his chair confidentially, ignoring a brief spasm of pain.

"Like what?"

Caspar saw that he now had the King's attention. Now, was the time to start to deliver the message.

"A new era. A new world order, perhaps," he said.

"You mean a new kingdom?" asked the King.

"A world of peace and unity, Your Majesty. Perhaps a world united under the Caesars in Rome, where trade can flourish and riches come to us all. I believe in a universal world of peace."

Herod became a little uneasy.

"What do you think this moving star means for us here in Jerusalem, especially for me?" he asked pointedly.

"It must mean great things for you. Why, only the other day I was accosted by a soothsayer in your Temple. He told me I had a message to give to the world. He seemed to think that such an era of peace was linked to the birth of a child. He thought this child would be born in your kingdom and he quoted from the Hebrew Scriptures."

The King looked at Caspar intently and beckoned with his hand for him to continue.

"This soothsayer said the child would be born to a virgin and be one of the gods living among us. Perhaps that's what this star predicts."

The King began to twirl the ends of his beard with his fingers.

"A future king in my kingdom?"

"Well, I didn't say a future king, Your Majesty, let's say, a 'prince of peace'. Such a man could be a leader or a great prophet, perhaps. Of course, you're the King. Your heirs will be kings after you. But within your kingdom, according to what the soothsayer told me, a virgin may conceive and fulfill that Scripture."

The King became deep in thought.

"Caspar, I want to know more of this. Perhaps God will bestow a great honor on my kingdom, but in these uncertain times I'd like to be sure."

"It's under the star, Your Majesty."

"Thank you, Caspar. Perhaps this star will add to our riches. Keep me informed of your travel plans. I'll instruct Ptolemy to give you letters for Rome. I can guarantee you useful introductions, but I'll expect you to keep your side of the bargain. If you find out any more about this virgin, let me know. This matter needs to be investigated."

Absently, King Herod allowed the sapphires and rubies to fall between his fingers. They gleamed in the light.

"Sire, the rewards will be good. I thank you for your interest," Caspar said, bowing and touching his forehead in respect.

* * *

Caspar left the box of sparkling rubies and sapphires for the King. The agent escorted him out. On their way down the stairs, Salome, her eyes hard and speculative, passed by. The agent subserviently acknowledged her:

"Greetings, Princess Salome."

As Caspar rejoined Gabriel in the courtyard outside, Salome entered the Royal chamber. She dismissed the king's guards.

King Herod continued to handle the gemstones.

"Come here, Salome," he said excitedly. "Look what that merchant from Chaldea gave me."

Salome peered in the box, then studied Herod.

"What did he want?"

"My patronage for trade routes through Caesarea to Rome."

Herod grasped a ruby and held it up to Salome.

"Yours, Sister," he said.

Salome took the ruby and cupped it in her hand.

"Can he be trusted? He came here with a member of the Sanhedrin."

"Who?"

"Someone Ptolemy knows. I believe his name's Gabriel."

Herod, feeling some pain, lifted himself back into his chair.

"The Chaldean said some strange things about the star."

"Like what?"

"He thought it might be a sign of some new, world order, based on peaceful trade. There, I am with him. There can be profits in that for us. But apparently, he met a soothsayer in the Temple who linked this new prosperity with the birth of a child of importance here in my kingdom."

Salome bristled. She didn't trust anything that came from the Temple.

"Don't listen to them, Herod. They don't really support us," she said.

"The High Priests and the Sanhedrin?"

"Yes. I've heard that some of the Pharisees are boldly talking about some kind of new state. This kingdom belongs to our family, Herod, and more particularly to Antipas, Archelaus and Herod Philip—not the children of the Jewess."

Herod held his stomach and coughed. When the pain had passed he said:

"Apparently the soothsayer backed his statement up with Scripture. We should be prepared, Salome. This could be the seeds of rebellion."

"I would say it is."

Herod stroked his beard.

"The child of a virgin born in our land. Let me call in the rabbinical scholars and scribes to investigate this in the Scriptures."

The following day, Salome, dressed in a sultry red dress that emphasized her painted face, watched her brother as one-by-one these holy men brought the King Scriptural quotations concerning the birth of a special child.

"That's not it," the King finally shouted. "Get out! The woman needs to be a virgin. Don't bring me any more stories about princes born long ago."

For two days, the rabbinical scholars continued to pore over their scrolls.

The astrologers and soothsayers surrounding the Royal court also became fascinated with Herod's new passion. Once again, they tried to link the story to the great star that hung above.

"Your Majesty. Because the star is now almost overhead, the theory you have proposed indicates the birth to a virgin must be imminent and close by, probably here in Jerusalem," a serious astrologer with an intelligent face advised.

"No Scripture as yet has been found to verify that theory," interrupted a skeptical scribe. "Don't put your trust in astrologers and soothsayers, Your Majesty. If there is any truth to be found in this, it will be revealed to us in the sacred Scriptures."

The astrologer scowled at the confident scribe.

The King, stressed by the time this was taking, felt the rage welling within him. Sweat formed on the backs of his hands and the nape of his neck. He wondered if the dye in his hair was running. He wiped the back of his neck with his hand. Black droplets ran on his fingers.

A young man entered the chamber carrying another Scriptural scroll. He bowed before the King.

"Your Majesty, I've found a quotation from the prophets that might satisfy your curiosity," he said.

"Speak on, young man. This time you had better have something good!"

Salome leaned forward in her chair, looking intently at the scribe.

"There's a quote here," the man continued, unravelling the scroll. "It refers to a special birth in Bethlehem of Judea."

"Bethlehem?" queried the King. "You mean that small, ragged village we pass on the road to Herodium?"

"Yes, Your Majesty. It says here in this scroll of the Prophet: 'And thou, Bethlehem, in the land of Judah, art not the least amongst the princes of Judah. From your number shall come a Governor that shall rule my people, Israel.'"

"Interesting," Herod said, twisting the rings on his fingers nervously. "Does it say that the child will be born to a virgin?"

"No, Your Majesty, but Bethlehem isn't far."

"I said she has to be a virgin!" Herod yelled.

"Perhaps the possibility can be investigated. Bethlehem was King David's village, Your Majesty. It's insignificant today, but it had a glorious past."

"If the prophecy is true," added the astrologer, "such a village so close to us here in Jerusalem would indeed be right under the star in the night sky."

Without further investigation the King called for Ptolemy. The aging advisor, who like Salome was irritated by everyone's constant search for meaning in this passing star, entered the chamber. The presence of so many soothsayers, astrologers, scribes, and scholars made him uneasy.

"Your Majesty. You called for me?" he said.

"Yes, Ptolemy. You have details on Caspar of Chaldea, the merchant prince from the Orient. He was here the other day. I need to see him again. Have him brought to us."

"Certainly, Your Majesty. He's staying in Jerusalem with a priest of the Temple named Gabriel. It was through this Gabriel's influence that the Chaldean was introduced to us."

"I know, I know…"

"I have some papers prepared for the Chaldean, but not everything necessary for his visit to Rome."

"No, Ptolemy. I don't need his papers… I have another mission for him to fulfill first."

"I'll send a messenger right away, Your Majesty."

Ptolemy bowed and left the chamber.

Later that evening, Caspar found himself once more before the King. Again, he had dressed to make an impression. He wore a bejeweled turban that was echoed in his emerald studded belt. Princess Salome, in a sultry green dress, bare at the midriff to expose the red ruby the King had given her, was seated close to her brother. When King Herod made his proposals, Salome never spoke but kept her eyes fixed on Caspar.

"Caspar of Chaldea, before I send you on your way to Rome, I'd like to ask you to do me a favor. I need to know more of the story about the virgin's child. It has come to light that there is a prophecy referring to a child who could be a 'Prince of Peace'. The Scripture refers to such a baby being born in Bethlehem, a poor village not far from here on the road to our fortress at Herodium."

Caspar looked up at Salome and caught her gaze before he answered.

"Herodium. That's your desert fortress to the south?"

"Yes. My astrologers tell me the strange star above us naturally appears above Bethlehem at this time. If this prophecy is to be fulfilled, then the child would be born directly under this celestial light. I'm sending you to Bethlehem to investigate this matter. If you can find evidence there of an unusual birth that links with the theory of the virgin, I'll reward you with further favors and assure you of the highest introductions in Rome—possibly an introduction to Caesar himself."

This last remark sent Caspar's blood pounding.

"Your Majesty, I shall be honored to conduct such an investigation on your behalf. But, you say Bethlehem is a poor village. There are probably many young girls with unwanted children there. Amongst the poor, illegitimate births are high."

The King chuckled.

"They breed like rats, but I trust you to seek the right one out. Didn't the soothsayer tell you to be a messenger? Investigate this matter and report back to me."

Realizing King Herod was determined to investigate this Bethlehem connection, Caspar agreed:

"All right, Your Majesty. I'll prepare to leave."

"Leave as soon as possible while the great star is directly overhead!" cried the King.

The excitement caused the King to strain his ailing lungs, and the chest pains returned, sending an anguished look across his face.

Salome knew the King was about to have one of his fits. The increasing frequency of his seizures was further cause for Salome's alarm. Antipater might return from Rome. Maybe the star heralded the death of her brother and the start of Antipater's reign as King. *What will then become of Antipas, Archelaus and Herod Philip?* she thought. To Salome, these political considerations were far more important than all this nonsense and superstition over prophecies and illegitimate children.

Salome watched Caspar, this source of her anger and irritation, with her mascaraed eyes full of venom.

"Don't trust him, Herod. He's in league with the priests," she said.

The King waved a hand in dismissal as he held his chest. Caspar left the Royal chamber on a sweep of his Oriental robe. He pushed Salome's presence from him. The merchant adventurer had a new mission. He was to search for the 'Prince of Peace.'

CHAPTER NINE

On the road to Bethlehem

Every rock and vantage point in the open spaces sloping down from Jerusalem's city gates was occupied by onlookers. Soothsayers and latter-day prophets, holy men and would-be astrologers mingled with the crowd, seeking coins for their opinions on this wonder of the age. Rich and poor fell under the star's spell. Roman patricians, Herodian courtiers, and Jerusalem citizens mixed with passing traders and camel drovers.

After supper at the inn, Judith had excitedly joined the crowd of stargazers outside Jerusalem's western wall. She wrapped the cloak around her that Anna had given her for this journey. The pretty brooch her mistress had selected in Jerusalem was pinned at her shoulder. She felt free, like one of the patricians. *The star has meaning for me, too,* she thought. *Look what changes have come into my life under its light.* It was the first really cold night of winter, but she was too mystified to care. She mingled with the crowd. The great streak of sparkling light was right above their heads. The heavenly body appeared much closer to them than the myriad of stars filling the crisp night sky. It was a spectacle beyond compare, fascinating yet fearful, drawing gasps from the crowd. A crescent moon, beginning to wax in the winter quarter, looked small and insignificant compared to the awesome majesty that lay right above.

Judith gazed upward in awe, but also with affection. She had watched it from the home of her master and mistress in Nazareth; she had watched it from rude camps under night skies; she had become acquainted with its portent through Miriam and her expected child—and now, here was the star at its fullest glory, its greatest power, high over their heads, while all around murmured in wonder and praise. Those around her were still trying to find its meaning, Judith knew. Hadn't she listened to the blessed Miriam? Hadn't she steadied the donkey as Miriam's blessed child kicked inside her womb? *Oh blessed night, oh blessed night!* she sang to herself. Judith's eyes filled with tears as she stared into the vast and mysterious heavens.

She was caught off guard in her joy and sense of personal adventure, as the uncertainty of her future made itself known in the depth of her feelings. Mingling with her excitement, came pangs of homesickness for the familarity of her past in Nazareth. She knew she wanted to be with Miriam and care for her baby, but she'd much rather have Miriam with them in Galilee. Judith was nervous about how much she'd enjoy life in a strange house in Bethlehem. It was her one distraction from total joy.

I wish the baby could be born in Joachim's house in Nazareth, she thought. *Life in Bethlehem will be so different, working for a tradesman rather than a rich man like Joachim. My status will be greatly diminished. It's one thing to know Joseph in Zechariah's fine house, but how will Joseph be when he's back in his own home? Then, there's Bathsheba and Joseph's children.*

But, as she looked at the star, these thoughts and worries subsided, and she was bathed again in excited joy.

* * *

North of Jerusalem and beyond Samaria, Copernia and Flavius Septimus were also stargazing in Galilee. They could see the star easily from the verandah of their villa, despite the warm glow of the braziers that took the chill from the winter air. Copernia carried Linus, their month old son, in her arms swathed in a blanket. In the aftermath of her pregnancy, she'd regained much of her figure. Flavius put his arm around her waist. He had no need for Esther now. The birth of Linus had brought him closer to Copernia. With his free hand he pointed at the star and its glittering trail of light.

"It's almost right above us now, my love," he observed.

"It's wonderful, Flavius! It has to signify something great."

"We discuss this almost every night. It does signify something great. That something is right there in your arms!"

Flavius caught the infant's hand with his little finger.

"Linus Flavian, this is your star. You'll govern this land. You'll be Caesar's friend and servant."

He looked up at Copernia and winked.

"I'm proud of your Tuscan blood, Son."

Copernia laughed.

Flavius fell into baby talk, twisting his finger in the chubby palm of the infant's tiny hand and making grimaces at him. A smile crossed the baby's face. Copernia continued to giggle as she rocked the infant in her arms.

Linus let out a brief, happy cry.

Copernia looked at her husband triumphantly.

"He's a Tuscan tiger," she said.

"I know, my dearest. I know."

They walked back into the warmth of their villa.

* * *

It was midmorning before Joseph and Miriam had everything packed up for the last part of their journey.

"Take this shawl, Miriam," Anna said as she handed Miriam a homespun garment. "It's warmer than the one you have. The nights are getting cold."

Miriam took the shawl, and they loaded the last of their humble possessions into the donkey's pannier.

"Joseph, there's barely room left on the donkey for me," Miriam said in good humor.

"Oh, you can manage."

He helped Miriam up, lifting her onto the donkey's back.

"Sit sideways and hold on to this wooden pommel."

The donkey stumbled forward a step or two, as the transfer of weight broke its stance.

"I'll need to be careful. So much is at stake," Miriam said, grasping the pommel as the donkey stumbled forward two more steps.

"It's all right," Joseph reassured her. "Judith will be beside you, and I will be right behind you with the mules. Harm will come to you if you try to walk."

"I am with you right now, Miriam," Judith said, supporting her.

"Thank you, Judith. How far do we have to go?"

"Not as far as Ain Karim to Jerusalem," Joseph assured them. "Bethlehem's less than a day's journey to the south. We'll be home tonight, even though the road's not good."

As Miriam sat, waiting on the donkey, Anna embraced her.

"Good-bye, my dearest. When you're able, you must bring the baby up to Galilee for us all to see."

Hastily she whispered:

"You are God's vessel! Your child is of God!"

She turned to Joseph.

"You're all welcome to come and stay with us any time. Take care of Miriam."

She smiled at Judith.

"Take care of that baby when he comes. We're entrusting you with the birth of our first grandchild."

But Anna's eyes conveyed more than those words.

Joachim blessed them:

"God be with you all. May God Almighty guide you and protect you."

He embraced Joseph.

With tears welling in their eyes, Joachim and Anna then waved good-bye.

Joseph tugged on the donkey, and they started to move forward, Judith watching Miriam's place on the animal's back. He handed the rope to Judith and led out the mules.

They followed the well-worn path around the city until they came to the southern gates. The relative green of the western approaches to Jerusalem gave way to arid land, falling to the south and east. Behind them, the Temple stood on Mount Moriah, glistening in the morning sunlight. The black smoke of sacrifice rose from the Sanctuary into the still cool air. On the right of Mount Moriah, the rugged outcrop of the

Mount of Olives with Mount Scopus beyond, stood as sentinels guarding the city's eastern approaches and the road to Jericho. The Bethlehem road followed a rocky ridge directly to the south. It rose from Jerusalem before dropping down beside the wastes of the Judean wilderness. This was harsh country, the last frontier before the land of milk and honey. Beyond the Judean wilderness and the rocky high country, lay the salt flats and the desert stretches that marked the western bounds of the Nabatean kingdom and the caravan routes to Petra. This road to Herodium was known as King Herod's fortress road. It guarded the southern extremes of the kingdom of the Jews.

It was about two hours before sunset when Miriam first felt the sharp pangs of impending labor. The donkey ride into this barren landscape had been difficult, and they'd stopped frequently to give Miriam a chance to rest. It was all Miriam could do to hold on to the beast, when they did make progress. Every muscle in her body was tensed into keeping her ungainly seat in the wooden sidesaddle. As her muscles pulled, she felt the unfamiliar strains from within that instinctively told her she was about to give birth to her child.

"Judith!" Miriam cried. "It's coming! My baby is coming!"

Judith saw fear in Miriam's eyes.

Joseph joined them.

"Mister Joseph," Judith said, with a surprising calm as her duties called upon her. "I think Miriam's going to have her baby. She's afraid. The journey's been too much for her. We have to stop."

The donkey willingly stopped. Joseph was calm and reassuring, but his hands trembled as he looked at Miriam's once serene face now showing anguish and tears. Martha, his first wife, had died giving birth to a stillborn child. Joseph felt a nagging, awesome responsibility for Miriam's welfare. His young wife was going to have a baby. It wasn't his baby, but if he was to believe her, this baby was to be a son of God—an angel's child. And, there were moments now, when he truly believed it. Something in Miriam's gathering serenity and strength of purpose willed him to believe. But now, like any woman about to give birth, she had human needs and fears.

Silently, Joseph prayed.

When he lifted Miriam off the donkey, his wife felt cold. Shivering in fear, Miriam buried her head in the folds of Joseph's traveling robe.

Judith took a little water from their only skin, and with the hem of her garment wiped the perspiration from Miriam's brow.

A sharp pain followed by several spasms caused Miriam to flinch. She grasped Joseph's arm.

"I'm sorry, Joseph. I can't go on!"

"Mister Joseph," Judith said, "we must find shelter."

"We're not far from Bethlehem," Joseph intimated. "The village is just over the next ridge and down in the hollow. Please help Miriam walk slowly. It'll be dark soon, but I know this road well."

Judith put her arm around Miriam and helped her. Joseph tied the donkey in with the mules. They staggered a little farther down the rocky road.

The pains kept returning, and Miriam began to feel increasingly faint.

"It's no use, Judith!" she said. "I can't go on. I must stop. Please! I might die!"

A fierce spasm overtook Miriam and she lay down on the stony track, holding herself in agony.

The sun had turned into a golden ball in the western sky. The white light on the open terrain and sandy valleys had given way to the golden glow of a winter's eve. As the sun fell lower in the west, the great star began to show brighter in the sky above. Its trail of light became visible against the hues of dusk, and it cast an awesome majesty over the desperate scene below.

Miriam in her pain stared up at it.

"The star," she gasped. "The star!"

"It's there to give you help, Miriam," Judith said. "Try to keep up your strength. We are not alone, we are in God's care."

"We cannot get her as far as Bethlehem," Joseph said quietly. "But there's a cave off the road up ahead. She can rest until morning."

"Will she be all right, Mister Joseph?"

Judith's faith wavered as she sought to protect her beloved Miriam.

"I've had four children, Judith. I know Miriam's condition will not improve. But she will be safe and sheltered in the cave."

As they were trying to get Miriam on her feet again, three shepherds appeared in the fast fading light, moving a large flock of bleating sheep across the road.

Joseph called out to them and waved his arms.

"Greetings! Shalom! Can you hear me? Please stop! We need help!"

"Yes! What do you want?" the burly leader shouted back, as the sheep bunched together.

"My wife's sick, and we can't travel. We need shelter. Can you help us move her to a nearby cave? I don't think we can make it to Bethlehem."

The shepherds came closer.

"Your wife's sick? How can we help?" the leader asked.

"Help us carry her? Maybe we can share your skins? We didn't travel in readiness for a cold night out."

"We're moving south, but in no hurry. We can share a camp. Can your wife move?"

"Only with the greatest difficulty. To be honest with you, I think she's going to have her baby tonight."

"We know that cave. It's a good shelter," the shepherd leader said.

"The cave over the hill there on the way down toward Bethlehem. It's quite spacious."

The shepherds then took charge.

"Joel! David! Help me carry her!" the leader shouted to his two companions.

The man smiled at Judith and Joseph.

* * *

Miriam was so faint she barely knew the shepherds had picked her up. The sharp spasms abated for a while. She looked up at the great star, brightening the coming night sky. Around her, the sheep bleated. The sound mixed with the summoned voices of her angels. She heard the comforting voice of Gabriel. The pain and discomfort of the world around her receded as she felt herself enveloped in a great sense of relief and calm.

Don't be afraid, Gabriel said. *Miriam, remember God has chosen you. You'll have your baby and one day he'll be recognized as Joshua—a son of God.*

Miriam closed her eyes. She felt safe and secure in the arms of the shepherds. Joseph and Judith, the donkey, the mules, their wares clattering, and the sheep bleating, followed closely behind, as they all made their way down the stony slope to the open cavern that was to be their shelter.

By the time they got there, it was completely dark. The youngest of the shepherds, Joel, immediately started a small fire at the entrance to the cave. It cast a glow on the dirty walls of ancient rock. The floor inside was well covered with the droppings of dozens of sheep. Bats hung overhead.

Joseph spread his cloak over the saddlecloth from the donkey and made as comfortable a pallet as he could for Miriam to lie on.

The pains began again and Miriam lay in agony, holding Judith's hand. Judith took more water from the precious skin and wiped Miriam's brow. The spasms increased.

"She will have her baby tonight," one of the shepherds said, his weathered face reflecting the firelight.

Judith now took charge. *Joachim and Anna made it my responsibility to see that their grandchild is safely delivered,* she decided.

"Do you have a skillet?" she asked the shepherds. "Anything that will hold water over the fire will do. We'll need some warm water to help her."

The shepherds had an all-purpose iron pot they used in their wandering life. They lent it to the cause.

Joseph started to boil some water.

The fire and the animals slowly overcame the barren coldness of the cave. Judith continued with her task.

"It's warmer now, Miriam," she said comfortingly.

The frequency of Miriam's spasms increased, and the pain became sharper. Judith tore the hem of her garment to make a gag for Miriam to bite on. Despite the sheep nuzzling up to them, Judith managed to wash Miriam and prepared her for the imminent birth.

Joseph, somewhat lost but deeply concerned, held Miriam's hand as she went into the last stages of labor.

High in the heavens the star pulsated, looked upon by vast numbers of people, some of high birth, some of low, some mighty warriors and some men of peace, some of religious fervor and others of greed, some of pure heart, and some who were evil. The star offered its awe-inspiring presence, some lodestone of fortune, desires and hopes for those feverishy watching it. But it was a young woman hidden away in a cold cave who felt she would know its glory most; who embraced the miracle.

The babe's first cry echoed against barren walls; it caused the sheep to move restlessly but not in fear, and grown and hardy men of the desert looked on, their features softened in joy.

Joseph shed his tears, while Judith clutched the infant in her arms within the simplest swaddling cloths to keep him warm. Then the babe was in Miriam's waiting arms, her pain and fatigue momentarily washed from her as she held her son—her profound reason for being on earth.

"Joseph," she said. "This is Joshua."

Beyond the cave's warmth a night sky offered its message across a vast abyss of timeless mystery.

* * *

Belshazzar and Melchar halted their camels.

Ahead, lay the festering body of an unfortunate roadside victim.

"Robbers," Belshazzar said.

Melchar looked around. The winter sun felt good on his back after a cold desert night, but who knew what might be waiting for them in the rocky landscape? He eyed the boxes of gold coins roped and bound to the panniers.

"It's hard to sleep at night while we're carrying all that gold," he said.

"Should we bury him?" Belshazzar asked.

Melchar dismounted. The body was rigid, the flesh dry.

"He's been dead a while. He's beginning to stink."

He kicked at the corpse and rolled it over. The dead man's tunic revealed the wound.

"Stabbed, I would say. Yes, stabbed."

There was no sign of life in the desert terrain, but the landscape was rocky ahead.

"They must have stolen his camel," Belshazzar said.

Melchar abandoned the corpse and remounted his camel.

"We must proceed with care."

Silently, and with watchful eyes, they pressed on and upward toward the craggy cliffs ahead. At length, they could make out the walls of a fortress way above them. Melchar looked up.

"Herodium. We're entering Herod's kingdom," he noted.

"That's Herodium?" Belshazzar repeated quizically, shading his eyes from the reflected brightness of the cliffs, "King Herod's fortress?"

"I'm sure… It must be… At last we'll be free of this desert and dust and can camp in safety and greenery and enjoy the sweeter terrain of Judea. As much as I love the desert, those sandy salt flats truly have to be some of the worst country we've ever crossed. Nothing grows there, not even thistles or scrub, and there's no majesty to the dunes as in Arabia."

Momentarily, they listened to the sounds of silence until a buzzard flew out from the crags and diverted their gaze.

"It certainly is a hostile land," Belshazzar agreed. "Isn't this where tradition says the Jews wandered around for so long before they entered Israel?"

Melchar leaned forward on his camel, adjusting his comfort.

"The land of their wanderings was farther south," he said. "Legend claims they were slaves in Egypt. Through the cunning of a man called Moses they escaped and disappeared into this desert. They got lost, and it took them forever to find their way out. But really, you can understand why. It's the worst country I know. I think it's better farther south on the route from Petra to Alexandria than up here. I don't know anywhere in all our travels that's quite like this."

They beat the camels into motion again. The ungainly beasts plodded on up the rocky road leading to the higher ground.

"The new camels are performing well," Belshazzar commented.

Herodium hung over them as they wound their way up the pass. A vast vista of white, salty sand punctured with parched rocks stretched behind them to the fortress atop of Mount Masada. As they rose higher, the deep cleft of the Salt Sea came into view in the desert valley on their right. The sun caught the greenish blue of the saline waters, making a sharp contrast with the reflected light of the barren rocks of the rift.

Belshazzar looked up at the fortress again.

"King Herod certainly has a natural stronghold to guard his kingdom. Nobody could pass through here without being watched from up there."

"They're probably watching us right now. They're wondering what brings us to Judea. These Jews are an independent and proud people, Belshazzar. You'll need to watch them when we start to do business. They'll pull you down in no time. It'll be much harder dealing with them than with those soft merchants of Petra who've grown fat on their easy profits. The Jews are fighters. We need to make private trade with their influential leaders, not the scrappers in the bazaars."

"And how do we do that?"

"We can deal directly with the King's court, or with Roman agents."

Belshazzar looked quizzical.

"How? We don't have the contacts."

"Leave it to me," Melchar said. "Remember I make the deals, you look after the camels."

Belshazzar nodded.

"That sounds like it would be safer than trying to trade in the open markets, especially with all our gold."

"Ah...You catch on quickly, my friend. Remember what they're like in Alexandria? They're probably even harder to crack in Jerusalem."

The lead camel slipped, stumbling on the loose stones of the track. It snorted in momentary panic. As the beast picked itself up again, it scattered small stones down the barren hillside. The noise echoed in the strange silence.

"I'll bet they can hear everything up there as well as see us," Belshazzar said.

As they rode higher, patches of desert thorn and thistle grew beside the stony track; sage and tussocks of grass sprouted out from the crannies of the pass. Melchar and Belshazzar could now see the circular form of the fortress. It lay atop the craggy outcrop.

Past Herodium, they entered the land of the Jews. The surrounding scrub gave way to scattered pines and little groves of cypress trees. Olives showed signs of civilization and cultivation. Belshazzar and Melchar had arrived at the place where the desert meets the sown. In a way, it was an anticlimax. After so many days of traveling, Melchar and Belshazzar had entered Herod's kingdom and passed the boundary of the Roman Empire, unheeded and unchallenged. The fortress on the hill now lay behind them. Later, they made camp at a small oasis of greenery in a hollow on the edge of the Judean wilderness.

Belshazzar and Melchar's makeshift tent was not really sufficient for the cold of the high ground. They wrapped themselves in goatskins for protection.

"You stink, Belshazzar."

"It's the goat skins."

"No, it's you, too! After so many days on the road, we probably both stink."

Their camels, also pungent from their labors, were close by. The precious cargo of gold and frankincense lay stacked at their feet, and the great star illuminated the sky above.

Belshazzar and Melchar could see it through the cracks of their crude tent.

"It's followed us all the way from Chaldea," Belshazzar said.

"And got brighter all the time. It augurs well for us."

Shortly after daybreak, the early morning sun cast its beam through the same tent opening. It struck Belshazzar's face and caused him to stir. He sat up, as if startled, but waking up he saw he was in familiar surroundings. The camels were chewing on the morning air. Everything was in order. The precious boxes of gold and frankincense lay safely at their feet. His sudden movement, however, woke Melchar.

"What disturbs you?" Melchar asked.

"It's nothing," Belshazzar replied, rubbing the sleep from his eyes. "Everything's fine. It was only a dream, a very strange one."

"What was it about?"

"You and me."

"Well, tell me, then," Melchar said.

Belshazzar turned to his friend.

"I'm not sure if I can remember it all. It kind of stopped suddenly in a blaze of light."

Melchar noticed the tent becoming brighter as the sun rose.

"What was it about?"

"Well, we were continuing on our journey. The country was stark and stony. It was just like the wilderness out there. We tried to find accommodations for the night, but the village we came to was very crowded and nobody seemed to want to help us. We tried to trade, but again there was no response. It was as if we weren't welcome. Nobody wanted to know us."

"The Jews, Belshazzar," said Melchar. "Remember, I told you yesterday. They're a hard people to deal with. We, who are not of their chosen race, can expect that kind of rebuttal, at least at first. When they see the quantities of gold and precious balms we're carrying, they'll come around to trade with us."

"There's more to my dream, though," Belshazzar said. "We gave up on the people in the village. We left in the afternoon and moved on. As darkness fell, the great star appeared just as it has every night on our recent travels. It seemed even bigger and brighter in my dream. Its trail of light seemed to change direction, pointing downward to reach the ground to form a sparkling ladder from the land to the star above. The light almost blinded us. Curious, we turned off the road to the place where the starlight fell. We really needed to pitch camp anyway, but in my dream that didn't seem to be much of a consideration. As we got nearer, we saw that the light fell on a cave. Inside, there were shepherds and angels with wings. They were singing and full of joy. In the center of the cave, there was a man and a woman, and in front of them, a young girl. The girl was cradling a newborn infant in her arms. This baby seemed to be the object of all their affections. Even the donkeys and animals sharing the cave were peacefully looking on in wonder."

"And, then?"

"Well, that's it, Melchar. In that bright light, I woke up. I can't tell you any more, but it moved me. It was beautiful. There in that cave in the light of this same bright star, there was such a strange feeling of welcome and peace. I woke up with joy in my heart, a sort of contentment that's hard to describe."

"You dreamer! The bright light was the rising sun streaming into the tent! The reality lies on the road ahead. It's time for us to get moving. We need to find that village and get some decent food. How I long for some fresh fruit! We could both do with something other than these endless locust cakes stuck together with wild honey."

The two drovers set about striking their camp and packing up the camels. The sun rose higher in the winter sky, but the air remained crisp and chilly. In the clear morning light, they could see across the wilderness of Judea. Ahead, lay clumps of trees and patches of greenery, breaking the monotony of the barren rocks.

* * *

Gabriel waited for Caspar under a brazier outside the King's palace. At length, his Chaldean friend emerged looking serious.

"What happened?" Gabriel asked, as they left the palace by an ill-lit side street.

"The King is stalling for time. He's sending me on a mission first, before I get those vital introductions. I don't know whether it's him or that calculating sister of his, but no matter, I'm not going to get anywhere with either of them until this matter is resolved."

"What matter?"

"You have to help me, Gabriel. They want me to find the virgin."

They stopped before descending steps into a busy square where night traders were selling spices and grains.

"The King's found some Hebrew sacred writings that refer to a 'Prince of Peace' being born in Bethlehem. He thinks the soothsayer's virgin could be the mother of this child. It could be your virgin."

Gabriel hastily descended the steps into the square, where the oil lamps of the stalls and the braziers on the walls cast a glow on his ruddy cheeks. Caspar, in his fine flowing robes, ran after him and caught his arm.

"Don't you see? My life will be in danger if you involve me in this matter," Gabriel pleaded. "I'm sworn to secrecy, and I've already revealed too much just to you. You don't understand the undercurrents here. It's one thing for you to carry out the King's wishes, but another to involve me. The High Priest will arrest me as soon as he finds out what's going on."

"Gabriel. Why are you so afraid of this High Priest?"

"Because I know the High Priest's plans, and they're dangerous to the Herodians."

"Do you agree with the High Priest's plans?"

"No. I don't. That's one reason why I withdrew my support. I'm not political or interested in changing the establishment. I happen to be a Davidic priest. That was an accident of my birth. I don't want to be involved in the High Priest's Davidic plan."

"But what of the soothsayer and all you told me?"

"Not here, Caspar. Let's go to the tavern."

Once they were settled in the warmth of the tavern, and Samantha, flashing her dark eyes, had served them wine, Gabriel felt more relaxed.

He leaned toward Caspar:

"Maybe a new Davidic age is about to begin. I'm not a lover of the

Herodians, but I do value my life. I'm a peaceful man. I don't mind if I live under Herod, Rome, a Davidic king, or in a pharisaic state..."

"A pharisaic state, my friend. What's that?"

Gabriel looked around. The tavern was busy, but nobody was listening.

"A state without a monarch or titular head, run by the Pharisees through the synagogues."

"And is that likely?"

"Why do you ask so many questions, Caspar? Jerusalem and the Temple are full of intrigues. There are undercurrents. I'm afraid of getting involved. I'm a man seeking only a prosperous and peaceful life."

"How can I find the virgin without you?"

"Unfortunately for you, that's your problem."

Gabriel picked up his goblet and drank.

"But Gabriel, what if the 'Prince of Peace' is not to be a rival king? What if he is to be a son of the gods, as the prophecy says?"

"A son of God here, Caspar! Can you imagine the Herodians allowing such a rival in their land?"

"But the King said he was flattered that his kingdom might be the setting for the birth of this prince. That's why he wants me to investigate the virgin. The King might like to meet you, too!"

"No...Not now, Caspar! You've done enough damage! You've put my life in jeopardy! I got you an audience with the King. I did you a favor, so you could get the contacts you need in Rome."

"But you're still curious."

Samantha approached them.

"Would you like me to dance?" she said, as she pulled a silk scarf from her bosom and twirled it around her head.

"Not tonight!" Gabriel said firmly.

Samantha scowled at him, then moved on to other potential clients.

Gabriel got closer to Caspar.

"Yes! Of course I'm curious. The soothsayer's prediction, the extraordinary star, the information I know to be true. Privately, I'll help you with your investigation in any way I can."

Caspar patted Gabriel's back and raised his goblet.

"How can I find this virgin, then?"

"She may not be in Bethlehem at all, although it would be a clever ploy of that scheming High Priest to hide her in one of the outlying villages. His plot would stand less chance of discovery there than in Jerusalem. As for the Scripture, that's only one quote from the sacred scrolls. It's out of context, picked from the scrolls at random. I can't tell you that it bears any truth."

"But the soothsayer?"

"There's something very fascinating about parts of this story, but I don't know how else I can help you other than what I've told you. Go to Bethlehem and inquire. It's not a large place. See if you can find a young maiden named Miriam, with chestnut hair, who has recently had a baby. I'll investigate here in the Temple precincts. The High Priest has to know where she is. I still say he's the father of this child, not I."

"You don't believe the child to be a son of the gods, then?"

"Zechariah involved me in his political plot. When and if the King finds out, there'll be terrible consequences. Some may believe this child to be a son of God...that's if they connect him with this Scripture. Quite possibly the spirit of God will descend on him in some special way, if he's to play any role in the destiny of our people. I'm curious, but indifferent."

He drank again and wiped his mouth with the back of his hand.

"Please understand it's too dangerous for me to go on this quest with you. What if the High Priest was to find me helping you look for Miriam? I'd be stoned to death, Caspar."

"I understand, Gabriel. Just keep me informed. I'll go on to Bethlehem alone. Maybe it's worth a try. I'll try to find your Miriam. Perhaps I'll find the 'Prince of Peace', too!"

"Good luck, my friend," Gabriel said putting his arm around Caspar's shoulder.

"Somehow we'll uncover the mystery," Caspar continued confidently. "We're partners Gabriel. You helped me, I'll protect you."

They drank together.

The next day, Caspar gathered essentials for his journey. After saddling his camel, he set off on the road south to carry out his quest.

* * *

Belshazzar and Melchar, the desert traders, arrived in Bethlehem, the small village set in a hollow with the wilderness of Judea sloping away to its right. Hill country lay to the north, but to the west, greenery spread out from the wilderness fringes. Conifers and junipers grew on the distant hills. Close by, were olive groves, cypress trees, and scrub bushes. Loose stone walls hid dormant vines. It was a warm and welcome sight.

"A land of milk and honey, Belshazzar. Now, I know we're in the land of the Jews."

"Well, let's get down to the village and enjoy some of that milk and honey. I'm parched and hungry. Perhaps tonight we'll eat well. Maybe we'll even have goat meat!"

They led their camels into what turned out to be a squalid collection of simple, flat-roofed dwellings. But there was a well, and fresh water tasted wonderful after days in the desert. Belshazzar went looking for some fruit and bread. Anything would seem good to them after their diet of locust cakes. Melchar filled their skins with the clear water, running it through his hands while the camels drank their fill.

Villagers gathered around the strangers. They eyed the big boxes.

When Belshazzar returned, he had some grapes and a pomegranate or two, but he hadn't found any bread. They walked their camels down the only street until they came to a noisy inn. Melchar went inside to ask if there might be lodgings there or anywhere in this humble little place.

Upon hearing Melchar's appalling Aramaic accent, the Judean landlord turned to his neighbor with a disapproving look.

"Roman spies!" the man muttered.

"You're not here for the tax count by any chance?" the landlord asked.

"No, sir," Melchar answered. "My companion and I require lodging overnight. We're tired and on our way to Jerusalem. We can pay you well. We need rest, a good meal, and stabling for our camels. Can you assist us?"

"There's no room here!" the man answered roughly. "The village is full of strangers. You don't sound like you're from our country either."

"No, sir. We're from Chaldea," Melchar said.

"Chaldea!" repeated the landlord's friend. "Do the Romans now send us spies from Chaldea?"

"No, sir. We're not spies. We're traders."

"No Romans here!" shouted the disgruntled man. "We don't want anything to do with Romans here!"

"But you could grow rich on this trade, sir," Melchar suggested. "You'd be the middle men here, taking profits in every direction. Your world could change. Doesn't the star that hangs over your village mean something? Doesn't it herald something special for you?"

"We've no room here," broke in the landlord. "All lodgings in Bethlehem are filled. You'd best move on while you have daylight. There are some caves north of the village. If you need shelter, they should suffice. You look like you're used to sleeping outdoors."

"Smell like it, too," added his neighbor.

"Be gone with you!" cried the landlord, waving Melchar away.

Melchar rejoined Belshazzar and shook his head.

"The village of your dreams?" he said as he spat on the ground.

Quietly, they left without even a loaf of bread. They devoured the pomegranates, spitting out the pits. Nobody smiled in Bethlehem. It was a miserable place, so different from the exciting atmosphere of bustling Petra in the Nabatean kingdom.

"You were right, Melchar. These Jews are tough," Belshazzar agreed.

"Let's move on and find these caves before it gets dark," Melchar suggested practically.

"You know something, Melchar? Bethlehem might not be a very friendly place, but didn't my dream tell of a cave under the great star just to the north of Bethlehem? I have the strangest feeling about this place. My dream's coming true!"

"We'll see, Belshazzar. Personally, I could have done with a comfortable night and a good meal. We haven't even managed to get a supply of bread, only a handful of pomegranates and a few moldy-looking grapes. These people think we're Roman agents. They're a fiercely proud, nationalistic people, these Jews."

"It's not going to be easy, Melchar. Maybe we should have gone to Alexandria."

"I'm beginning to think so. Let's get moving. This outlying village of Bethlehem is on the road to Jerusalem. Things will be better there."

They rode up the stony track that led from Bethlehem into the rocky hill country to the north. A shepherd passed by, leading a flock of dirty sheep toward Bethlehem. The sun lost its power as it dipped in the sky, becoming a great amber ball. Dusk was upon them, and the air grew cold. In the failing light, Melchar caught a glimpse of rising smoke from rocks off to their right. The rocks looked dark and menacing as twilight moved over the landscape. The great star appeared right above where they were, its brightness increasing as darkness advanced.

"Let's move off the road down to those rocks," said Melchar. "I swear that's smoke I see down there, possibly a shepherd's hearth. Maybe we'll find those promised caves."

Belshazzar and Melchar carefully made their way over the uneven ground toward the group of rocks.

"You're right, Melchar. I can see the fire now. There must be an encampment."

"Let's join them. I've had enough of this for one day," Melchar said, looking up at the star, blinking at its brightness. "Is that part of your dream, Belshazzar?"

Carefully, they led their camels down. Sheep from a large flock were bleating around the rocks.

When they got there, they found the fire burning outside an entrance into a rocky cavern. Melchar and Belshazzar stopped their camels at a discreet distance. Leaving Belshazzar with the beasts, Melchar advanced toward the cave.

Melchar thought he could hear a baby's cry. This was confirmed when he peered into the cavern, its interior glowing from the light of the shepherd's hearth. There, he saw a young woman, oddly serene in the firelight, with a baby at her breast. He could see the cave was deep. More sheep were huddled in the corners, and pungent odors of animal urine and rotting excrement wafted out from the interior.

The young woman looked up. She didn't see Melchar and called out:

"Is that you, David?"

Nobody answered.

Slightly embarrassed at the tender scene, Melchar stepped back into the shadows again, wondering what his next move should be. He heard voices from behind. One was female and the other sounded like a rough shepherd's. In front of him, lay the domestic scene he was embarrassed to interrupt, and behind, his escape route was now cut off.

He called out in response:

"Greetings! Hello there!"

The young woman continued to nurse her baby, but a man's voice answered from behind:

"Shalom, my friend! Who are you? Are you looking for shelter?"

"Yes. I was wondering if we could join you here in this cave?" Melchar asked.

"Of course," the voice answered from the shadows.

As the shepherd and woman moved closer, they became more visible. The woman was much older than the young mother in the cave. The shepherd appeared to be a burly man of middle age with rough hands and a lined face. They were both carrying thorns and sticks to kindle the fire.

"I'm sorry to trouble you," Melchar said. "My friend and I couldn't find any lodging in Bethlehem today, and we were told there was shelter out here in these caves. Do you think we could join you for the night? We have very little food, but we could bake locust cakes over your fire."

"No reason why not," answered the shepherd. "Where's your friend?"

"Up the hill there holding our camels. I'll call him down."

Melchar whistled.

Belshazzar heard him and led the camels down to the glowing light in the rocks.

"We're from Chaldea," explained Melchar in his broken Aramaic. "We're on our way to Jerusalem. This is my partner, Belshazzar."

Belshazzar tethered the camels.

They learned that the old shepherd's name was Joel. Melchar assisted Belshazzar as they carried their precious boxes into the cave. The young woman had finished feeding her baby and wrapped him in a shawl. She looked weak and tired. Soon, the infant lay asleep on a sheath of dirty hay.

The woman who'd been out with the shepherd fussed over the young mother, making her as comfortable as possible.

"Miss Miriam, you must rest now," she said. "Joseph will be back soon with fresh bread and fruit and we'll all feel better. Meanwhile, you must rest as much as you can."

Miriam looked up at the older woman.

"Thank God you're here with me, Judith," she said. "I think I might have died without you."

"I'll be with you and Joshua as long as you need me, Miss Miriam. I took care of you when you were a baby. Now, I'm going to take care of your baby. But immediately, you must sleep."

Miriam leaned back on the makeshift pallet, and the older woman covered her with a traveling blanket.

"Thank you for helping me," she whispered.

She was still too exhausted to acknowledge Belshazzar and Melchar, and she closed her eyes.

After their weeks of sleeping outdoors, the two drovers found the cavern comfortable. They spread out their hides and made themselves at home, making sure they kept their precious boxes close by. Belshazzar scooped up some of the dried dung from the cave floor and fed it into the fire. The turds glowed as the heat burned through them. Soon, the fire was hot enough for them to bake some cakes of locust flour. Another shepherd, David, joined them. The sheep huddled together for comfort and provided body warmth both for themselves and their masters.

A donkey brayed a cry from outside, and an older man and his young shepherd boy companion dismounted in the glow of the firelight. The older man carried a skin of water, and the young boy had two loaves of fresh-baked bread. Tied to the donkey was a woven sack of fruits and a skin of new wine. Judith went out to greet them.

"How is the baby, Judith? And Miriam?"

"All is well, Mister Joseph. The 'Prince of Peace' is sleeping."

"Where did those camels come from?"

"Two men from Chaldea arrived at sunset. They couldn't find any lodging in Bethlehem, so they're here. Mister Joseph, it's good to see you back."

Joseph touched her arm affectionately.

"Judith, be careful with words like 'Prince of Peace' around strangers," he warned.

"But that's what Miss Miriam calls the baby."

"All I can say is, be careful around strangers."

Belshazzar rose from prodding the locust cakes at the fire.

Melchar came out from the cave to join them. He looked up at the bright star.

"You know something," he said. "When we started our journey, that star was just a small dot on the eastern horizon. Now, it's right above us and it's so much bigger. It's followed us all the way."

"The star is the talk of Jerusalem," conceded Joseph. "It's keeping everyone guessing as to what it might mean. Personally, I don't really worry. My wife's just had her first baby right here in this cave, and my main task is to be with her and see that everything's all right. You're welcome to some of our bread and fruit."

"You were luckier than we were, sir," Melchar said with some bitterness. "We couldn't even purchase a loaf of bread in that miserable village."

"Really? Well, please, share mine," Joseph said, offering them a loaf. "Bethlehem does seem very crowded at the moment. It's because of this census. That's why we're going home. I live in the village and I was able to pick this up from my own house."

It was a joy for them all to eat the simple meal of bread and fruit and to enjoy the shared skin of wine.

Belshazzar forgot about the locust cakes. Joseph's generous fare was much more welcome.

The shepherds and the two drovers exchanged ideas on the strange night star. Belshazzar spoke of his dream.

"It's very strange. This whole scene, the cave, the baby, the young woman and even the animals, and all under this bright star—it's exactly as I saw it in my dream. It is as if I was already here."

Joseph and Judith were asleep, but Miriam couldn't help overhearing what Belshazzar was saying.

"There were shepherds like you, and angels singing. There was so much joy in the cave…a sense of peace and wonder."

"And then he woke up," Melchar said, breaking some bread from the small loaf. "All that light and everything was just the sun striking our tent. You and your dream, Belshazzar. See if you can sleep now and tell us about your dreams in the morning."

Angels singing, Miriam thought as her heart pounded with inner joy. *A sense of wonder and peace.*

The donkey broke its tether and wandered in, making itself at home close to where the baby infant lay, and chewed on the moldy hay.

The child awoke. Joshua didn't cry. His eyes found his mother's.

Miriam reached out, picked up Joshua and cradled him to her as the donkey started to eat the infant's bed. There, in the quiet of night, alone with God's gift, illuminated by the flickering flames of the fire outside, she looked around at her sleeping husband, servant and strangers. All had shared in this experience of Joshua's birth. All those here, now sleeping, had met a son of God. Miriam looked at her babe, aware of the fearsome responsibility of her role.

All of her life's experience had led her to this moment. The time in the House of the Virgins, praying and staying close to God. And then His shaping of her spirit by sharing His angels with her, to provide her with solace and protection. And then, the indescribable experience of conceiving a son of God. Yes, there had been the ugliness and violence of the priest, Gabriel. But God had protected her. As this exquisite and holy life had grown inside her womb, she had gained in insight. She was stronger now. She was certain in purpose. She was ready for the task of raising her son to serve God's plan. As the baby Joshua moved comfortably in her arms, Miriam wondered just what his destiny would be.

"Joshua, Joshua..." she murmured as she looked deeply into her son's eyes. "How wise you seem, for a babe. What are you telling me?"

She rocked him.

" My angel told me you would be a prince and a king. Zechariah said the same thing at Ain Karim. But I'm not so sure we'll become a royal family. My life with Joseph will be very simple. But you will be my 'Prince of Peace.'"

Joshua closed his eyes in newborn sleep.

"Joshua," she whispered. "You'll be someone special. I don't know how. But you're my child, Joshua. You're my son from God!"

Joseph snored. Miriam smiled at her sleeping husband, their love based on respect and care. She knew Joseph would take care of her in every way. She loved him as she did her own father. If Joseph wanted to have children by her, she would yield to him, as Elizabeth had advised, but Joseph hadn't mentioned such things. Their responsibility now was to Joshua, the child who had been promised to her by the angels. Miriam shooed the donkey away and, pulling the remaining hay closer to her pallet, gently laid Joshua down again. Then, she turned over on her pallet and pondered on these things until she fell asleep.

* * *

Caspar set out early, well dressed in his embroidered cloak, as the sun rose behind the Mount of Olives. A cock crowed to greet the new morning light, as Caspar guided his camel down the narrow streets around the great Temple walls. The air was cold and crisp. He turned his camel out onto the road heading south. He had to find the virgin and the 'Prince of Peace'. The thought of the incredible favors King Herod could grant him intoxicated him—*an introduction to the Emperor!...Augustus Caesar himself!*

About midmorning, Caspar saw the first and only travelers on that lonely road. Ahead, there was a small camel train moving toward him. There were two drovers with the lead camels and a string of three other camels. It looked to his trader's eye like a small merchant caravan. As they got closer, Caspar noted these were desert camels, not domesticated ones for agricultural purposes such as he'd seen in Egypt and parts of Judea. When they were close enough, Caspar called out to the men:

"Greetings! Shalom! Are we the only travelers on this road today?"

The lead drover waved a friendly hand.

"Greetings! You sound like a Chaldean."

"Yes, I'm Caspar of Chaldea."

By now their camels were almost side-by-side. The features of the two men weren't Semitic.

"We're Melchar and Belshazzar, also from Chaldea," Belshazzar answered, staring at Caspar's fine robes.

From this point on, they broke from speaking their poor Aramaic into their native tongue.

"What's your business?" Caspar asked.

"We're trading goods from Petra to open the way for the silks of the Orient. Chaldea can supply the Romans with many luxuries from India and Cathay."

"I know. That's precisely my business. We should make a Chaldean team here. Caspar, Melchar, and Belshazzar."

With typical desert rivalry, Melchar quickly replied:

"Why not? But let's call us Melchar, Belshazzar, and Caspar!"

They laughed and saluted each other.

"It's hard to crack the Jews," said Melchar. "We made little impression on them in Bethlehem. It may be just as difficult in Jerusalem. How's the marketplace there? We know exactly where we stand in Petra and Alexandria, but Jerusalem is new territory for us."

Caspar now had the upper hand. After all, he had influence with Herod, the King of the Jews. Herod had promised to give him letters of introduction for Rome. He was already well on the way to establishing his powerful trade network.

"If we become a team and you stay with me, we could become rich," he said. "I know people in high places in Jerusalem. We could be a good team. How many camels do you have?"

"Five."

"Yes, Caspar," joined in Belshazzar. "We have five excellent, desert camels, but I know we could buy others in Petra on our return. How many do you have in your caravan?"

"I came with only three, but I have many contacts in Chaldea. Camels are never a problem for old Caspar. Tell me about Bethlehem. I'm on my way there to do business for King Herod of the Jews. How big is the place?"

"It's only a very small village," answered Melchar.

"And a very unfriendly place," added Belshazzar.

"Well, maybe you could help me in my quest. I have a most unusual mission. I've been asked to seek out a young maiden who may have recently had a baby. This baby could be of great importance to the King. There's a prophecy that says this baby will be a great leader and a peacemaker. The prophecy says the child will be born in Bethlehem of Judea. Maybe we could search the streets of Bethlehem together."

Belshazzar and Melchar eyed each other.

"Tell us more about this prophecy," Melchar said.

"Well, the King has been informed that the Hebrew religious writings point to the birth of a child in Bethlehem as the symbol of a new age. The astrologers and soothsayers at Herod's court link this birth to the remarkable star that lights up the night sky in these parts. They say the mother of this child is a virgin—rather young. Maybe we can seek out young, unmarried mothers in Bethlehem. There are bound to be a few among the poor. Perhaps one will stand out as special and be the one."

Melchar looked at Belshazzar.

Caspar saw the look and was instantly on guard. That was a look more suited to the devious likes of Salome.

"What is it?" Caspar asked suspiciously.

"Shall I tell him, Melchar?"

Melchar shrugged. Never one to dwell on supernatural things, he added:

"Why not, you told the shepherds in the cave."

"What cave?" Caspar insisted. "What are you talking about?"

"I had a dream," Belshazzar began. "Out here in the desert. Under the sway of the star."

"Go on."

"It was a very detailed dream…We couldn't find lodging in the village, so we moved on and followed the star. It led us to a cave where there were shepherds and angels…"

"Angels?"

"Yes—and singing. This was my dream, of course."

"And then what happened?"

"This woman had a baby. All was peaceful there."

"But this was a dream," Caspar said impatiently.

"Yes—but a dream that came true."

"So you say, Belshazzar," Melchar interrupted. "How many times do I have to tell you, the light you saw was the rising sun on our tent."

"A light?"

"A wondrous light," Belshazzar said.

"And this dream came true?"

"We were with them last night. We were fed and kept warm. The babe was peaceful and sleeping."

Caspar listened. This was as fantastic as his meeting with Gabriel after the soothsayer had predicted his mission of peace.

"The cave stank, Caspar," Melchar said. "It was not the stuff of miracles."

"But the mother, Melchar!" Belshazzar exclaimed. "Have you ever seen such serenity on a woman?"

"No," Melchar admitted. "I give you that, my friend."

"And what did you say the maiden's name was?" asked Caspar.

"They called her Miriam—a Hebrew name."

"You must be kidding! My friend Gabriel told me the virgin's name was Miriam! Can you show me this cave?"

"We can go back, but they may have already moved on. If so, they'll go to Bethlehem where the older man lives."

"If this is the child," said Caspar with a gleam in his eye, "we may have found the 'Prince of Peace'. Good fortune may follow us wherever we go. Perhaps this is what the star's all about."

"Yes!" said Belshazzar, showing delight in Caspar's thinking more of his dream than practical old Melchar. "The star's directly above the cave. In my dream, the sparkling trail of light led to the cave's entrance."

Belshazzar looked at Melchar.

"Yes, Caspar. We'll take you there," Melchar said. "But don't forget, if we help you in your quest, you must live up to your end of the deal and help us in Jerusalem. We're partners now. We are three merchant princes from afar, ready to become rich by selling our goods to Rome. There's potential here, and you hold the key. Together we'll trade in Jerusalem and go to Rome."

"It's a deal," Caspar said. "I feel the strangest sensations. This could be a great day in our lives. It's as if we've been led to this place to come together. We're three Chaldeans, united in a mission and purpose."

"Belshazzar," Melchar said, resignedly, "turn the camels. Let's go back to the cave."

The three Chaldeans moved on down the now familiar road. By mid-afternoon they reached the point where they'd turned off the stony track and led their camels toward the rocks.

"They're still there!" said Belshazzar. "I can see their donkey and mule at the cave entrance."

Joseph's donkey and the mule, which had carried the precious jars and practical items from Miriam's dowry, were tethered to a stake in the ground.

Belshazzar stopped the camels, and the three merchants dismounted as their beasts made customary groaning sounds.

The shepherds had gathered up their flock and moved on.

Joseph emerged from the cave entrance.

"Belshazzar! Melchar!" Joseph called out. "Is there something wrong? Why have you come back?"

"Nothing's wrong. This could be the most important day in our lives," answered Belshazzar. "We'd like you to meet our new friend—another Chaldean. This is Caspar."

Caspar formally bowed and greeted Joseph, who in turn treated him with the reverence of a potentate, his tradesman's eyes admiring Caspar's luxuriant robes.

"Caspar is anxious to meet the young mother and her baby," continued Belshazzar. "Can we go in?"

"Of course. The baby's asleep; he is remarkedly calm and quiet. But Miriam's awake and getting stronger now. I think we'll be able to move her to Bethlehem tomorrow."

Caspar went into the cave followed by the others. It was dark inside, lacking the warmth of the fire that had glowed at night. The pungent odors revolted Caspar as he looked at sleeping bats hung upside down from the roof. The gloomy light revealed the maiden and another woman sitting with her. In front of them, on a fresh bed of hay, and wrapped in swaddling cloths, was the infant child. Caspar stared at them, his calculating gaze moving from babe to mother. *Here… here is the key to unlock untold riches through King Herod's grateful support,* he thought.

"Miriam. This is Caspar, a friend of the men who stayed with us last night," Joseph announced. "He wants to see the baby."

Caspar smiled at Miriam with a reassuring look of kindness.

The babe stared into the darkness, occasionally moving its tiny hands.

Miriam looked up at Caspar and noted his embroidered cloak. *This is no ordinary visitor,* she thought. *He's not like the shepherds or even the two drovers who stayed with us last night. This is a man of substance.*

"Greetings, your name is Miriam?" Caspar asked.

Miriam sat up.

"Yes, sir. What can I do for you?"

"I'm seeking a young maiden and her child who should be born in or near Bethlehem. According to Hebrew writings, or so I'm told, a virgin will give birth to a son and they will call him by a name that means 'God with us'. He'll be born in Bethlehem in the land of Judah, and he'll be a prince who will rule Israel. My friends here think you might be that virgin. If so, it's a special privilege for us to be here. We would like to give you gifts and acknowledge such a child as a god amongst us."

Miriam's heart raced! Her newborn baby was being acknowledged as a son of God by total strangers—men who weren't even Jews! Angel Gabriel had been right. God had given her a special role! She really might be the mother of a prince. Not a wealthy prince living in a palace, but a prince who was to lead her people—a son of God! And with that thought, a first fear moved inside her. Giving birth to a son of God was not just a profound gift, it was also a responsibility that could, in the years ahead, include risk and danger.

"Perhaps I am that virgin," Miriam said, her voice serene and quiet in the dismal cave. "This is my son, Joshua. In our language that means 'God with us'. He is a son of God."

The words echoed, offering a confident truth around the standing men. Outside, the donkey brayed loudly, and above Caspar several bats eased their dark wings before folding them back into silent warm shapes.

"A son of the gods," Caspar murmured.

Miriam nodded.

"My angels told me my child was God-sent."

"And that is a heavy responsibility," Caspar said softly, while all the time his heart drummed in his encloaked chest. *Wait until King Herod hears of this!* he thought.

"It is indeed, sir," Miriam said. "But your coming here has proved them right. God must have led you here."

"Through my dream," Belshazzar said.

"Your dream?"

"She was asleep when you talked about it last night," Melchar said.

"No, I remember, I heard you," Miriam said, nodding slowly. "So many signs, good Belshazzar, so many signs, both in the hearts and dreams of men and in the night sky."

Joseph watched her, this young woman who was his wife. How she was changing! Where was the naïve innocent from the House of the Virgins, the ravaged young woman, raped and seeded? But that ugly memory was receding even in his memory, to be replaced by this glorious, quiet event, which was fulfilling scripture and drawing to them even these merchants and rich overseers. Joseph eyed Caspar's cloak. *So many hours of carpentry to own something like that—but then what would a simple carpenter want with a cloak like that? Better to have food on the table!*

"The gods and the star, Miriam," added Belshazzar. "We believe that the heavens are heralding something special."

"Yes," said Caspar. "Your child was born under this star. A new age will dawn—an age of everlasting peace. This peace will come to all mankind because of your child. He must be the 'Prince of Peace.'"

Caspar called out to Melchar and beckoned Belshazzar to follow him.

"Let's fetch some of the gold and frankincense," he said. "We should pay homage to this prince."

The three merchants unpacked the precious boxes strapped to the camels. They carried three of the boxes with them into the cave and presented them to Miriam, placing them on the ground in front of the infant.

The baby opened his eyes. He smiled at Caspar. Tears formed in the eyes of Belshazzar. Even skeptical Melchar felt a softening in his heart. For a moment, all of them remained still and silent until Joshua gave a short cry. Miriam reached out and picked up her child. Joshua enfolded himself to his mother, seeking her breast.

Caspar was the first to speak. He knelt down and opened one of the boxes, exposing rubies.

"I've found the 'Prince of Peace,'" he said. "I bring you gifts of precious stones."

Even as he said it, Caspar's ambitious mind was calculating even greater riches to replace them.

Melchar and Belshazzar did likewise, but with some reservation at giving away some of their hard-earned profits. They displayed perfumed balm of frankincense, the precious ointment from the gum trees of Arabia, which they'd brought with them from Petra, and presented the smaller of their two boxes of gold coins. Following Caspar, they bowed before the infant and Miriam, who held Joshua close to her and accepted their obeisance as fulfillment of her special role. The reverence of these three merchants from Chaldea seemed to confirm this. *The outside world is coming to me, here in this rude cave,* Miriam pondered. *They come with gifts and words from the Scriptures.* She stirred, girding her spirit and tired body for the months and years ahead. *I must protect this son of God. That is my task: to protect and nurture and yes—serve.* Again, a small fear moved inside her. *Such responsibility. There might be danger.*

Joseph left the three visitors to walk outside.

The sun had set by now, and that strange blue light of dusk was descending on the surrounding wilderness. The great star was clearly visible in the half-light. It hung right over the cave. Judith was already outside, lighting the evening campfire. They exchanged looks of frustration.

"Are these men staying here like the shepherds?" Judith asked.

"I don't know, but I wish they'd go," Joseph answered. "I am grateful for their gifts, but Miriam needs peace and quiet."

"I wish they'd go as well," Judith said. "I don't trust these people. They're foreigners and strange."

Caspar, Melchar, and Belshazzar didn't stay. They left the precious gifts at Miriam's feet and departed from the cave, acknowledging Joseph and Judith as they left. They packed up their camels, and by the light of the great star, made their way back up the roadway and headed for lodging in Bethlehem.

Belshazzar spoke first, once they were out of earshot:

"Melchar, perhaps we should have given the larger box of gold coins."

"No, we did the right thing. Her God would want us to provide for our own needs in this inhospitable desert."

"How can you say that!" Belshazzar exclaimed. "A son of the gods and we gave him second best!"

Melchar shook his head.

"You are swayed too much by your dream."

Belshazzar turned to Caspar.

"And you, sir…you gave generously, those stones of such riches, color and value."

Caspar shrugged.

"We all gave to the child. In fact, we are the first to give to the child."

"The first?"

"If what she says is true, then there will be others."

Melchar nodded.

"These times will be difficult for them, especially for Joseph. He's such a simple man."

"An ideal place to hide a 'Prince of Peace,'" Caspar murmured.

"What did you say?"

"Nothing."

With a swirl of his embroidered cloak he said:

"Let's see if they allow me room at their inn."

* * *

It was lightly raining, the damp cold reaching into the confines of Gabriel's home. Only the kitchen was warm, where Gabriel's maid, Jude, kept the fire burning as she prepared her master his evening meal.

There was a knock on the door. Gabriel removed the wooden latch and opened up.

Caspar stood there, his embroidered cloak soaked.

"I tethered the camel at the back," he said as he gladly crossed the threshold. "Can we warm up some wine?"

"Of course, my friend. I'll arrange it right away."

"Let me get out of these wet clothes. Can you lend me a robe?"

Gabriel fetched him a heavy brown robe, then asked his maid, Jude, to heat the wine.

"There will be two of us for supper now," he said.

A little while later, Casper joined Gabriel in the warmth of the kitchen. Bowls of thick warm soup were ready for them, along with a jar of mulled wine, as they sat on stools at a rough table.

"So what do you have to tell me?" Gabriel said.

Caspar averted his eyes in the direction of the maid.

"Oh," Gabriel said wisely. "Jude, can you leave us alone?"

Jude left the kitchen, disappearing to some back area of Gabriel's house.

"We found your virgin, Gabriel," Caspar said excitedly. "She was with the child in a cave. The child had just been born. It was a very humble scene, but I'm sure she's the one. Her name was Miriam, as you said. She's convinced her son is a son of God."

"You mean she still believes in Zechariah's messianic dream, even though the old man raped her?" Gabriel yelled. "How naïve can she be? Does she think the High Priest is God?"

Caspar raised a placating hand.

"No, she's a sweet, young woman, quite dignified in her own way, and she's accepted my gifts and those of my friends because she believes she's been chosen to be the mother of this 'Prince of Peace.'"

"Who are your friends?" Gabriel asked nervously. "The less people who know about this, the better."

"Oh, they were some Chaldean merchants I met on the road. They led me to the cave. They had sheltered there the night before."

They sipped on the warm wine.

"You believe her, don't you? I can tell it from your excitement. You really believe the soothsayer and the King's advisers were right, don't you, Caspar? You're not even a Jew! How can you believe such a story? There must be a father. If it's not Zechariah, then it has to be someone appointed by him who fell for the plot I refused."

"It doesn't really matter what I think, Gabriel," Caspar said. "My business is my own. But think on this: it could have been you. Do I detect a look of guilt on your face? Is Miriam really a virgin, or was she just a naïve girl who didn't understand how she could be with child?"

He nudged Gabriel in the ribs.

"Did you violate her?"

"What? Leave me out of this!"

"What about the star? Doesn't everyone have some explanation for this phenomenon, or pin some hope on this mysterious symbol? True, some are frightened and think it is a sign of bad things to come. I see it as a good omen, Gabriel."

Gabriel's anger abated.

"But don't you think these events are merely a series of coincidences?" he suggested. "You're trying to bring meaning to the meaningless."

"Nevertheless, it was this star that really brought Melchar, Belshazzar, and me together. The child was born right under this same star, Gabriel, a future 'Prince of Peace.'"

Caspar mused over his words, savoring their portent.

"Many babies were born under that star. Even more are being born as we speak! Everyone claims some personal interpretation of this star," Gabriel countered.

"You're so skeptical, Gabriel, but then, so was I. Let's consider. I met my companions seeking the 'Prince of Peace,' and with their help and the information you gave me, we found a young girl who claims she's a virgin who has had a baby. Do you think it's coincidence that I met you when I was with the soothsayer in the Temple court? Then, you arranged my important meeting with King Herod. Was it coincidence that we learned about the virgin being in Bethlehem? Or that I met Belshazzar and Melchar on the road, and they'd slept the night before at the cave where Miriam and her child were? Gabriel, perhaps there is order to these events. Fate intrudes itself. The one unifying factor is that star! All these so-called coincidences have occurred while that star was right above us."

"It's certainly strange," Gabriel admitted. "But I'm still not convinced."

They both slurped on the thick soup and drank more of the wine.

"Frankly, neither am I. But, Gabriel, you're a Jew. You're supposed to believe in Divine guidance. Don't you offer sacrifices at your Temple because you believe you have a personal relationship with your God?"

"Who knows, Caspar? I fear I'm losing my faith. When you cannot respect your own leaders, and they're as divided as our Sanhedrin members, it's hard to find guidance."

"Miriam believes angels talk with her."

Gabriel laughed.

"She used to tell me about those angels, Caspar. She's little more than a child. I got bored with it. Surely you don't believe all that?"

Caspar looked serious.

"She is no child. Not the woman I saw in that cave. The babe must have changed her. She believes it was her God, your God, who led us to the cave. Can't your God be personal like that? Even we Chaldeans believe the gods can speak to us through these guardian angels."

"I'm not a deeply religious man, Caspar," Gabriel said, moving his stool back and facing his Chaldean friend. "I'm not a particularly good Jew. But I've become caught in the middle of something that was never my purpose to experience. If God is bringing about all these coincidences, why did he have to choose me to be part of it? I curse the day the High Priest called me to his palace. I was enjoying my life, but now I live in fear. I'm afraid of the High Priest because of his bribe. I'm afraid of the King because of my unwilling involvement in a messianic plot against him. I'm afraid of the Pharisees because I fear rebellion and Herodian and Roman repression. I'm afraid of you, Caspar, because of your disturbing interpretation of our faith. I don't like your coincidences! Too much is happening at once."

"I agree. And the star, in particular, affects us all. Do you acknowledge that your God could speak to us through this star?"

Gabriel's face clouded.

"You seem to think so, and that disturbs me. You're not a Jew, but you seem to believe the God of the Jews can affect all lives."

"I believe in a universal god," Caspar said simply. "Sometimes, He is the God of the Jews; sometimes he is one of our Chaldean gods; and sometimes he is the gods of the Romans."

"You believe Caesar to be a god, then?" Gabriel asked.

"No, but why couldn't the gods use Caesar? If Caesar can help to bring universal peace, could he not also be an instrument of the gods?"

"I suppose that is a plausible belief for Romans, but not for us here in Judea."

"Why not?"

"You know how much my people hate the Romans."

"Well, then, if not through Caesar, why not through a Jewish child as the Hebrew Scriptures have foretold? Why not through the virgin's child?"

"Virgin!" Gabriel spat out the word. "You'll trick me into belief, Caspar."

"We must consider all, Gabriel. I, too, confess to being cynical on occasion. After all, for me this whole business is about getting those introductions out of King Herod."

Caspar smiled. He got up to leave.

"I am staying at the inn outside the western gate," he said. "I promised Belshazzar and Melchar I would return tonight. Have faith in the star, Gabriel. The star's above us all. Believe in its power. We're living in exciting times, and somehow the gods are working their purposes out for all of us."

Gabriel laughed as he looked at the rain outside his door.

"If that star's above us now, it's invisible," he chuckled.

"Which side are you on?" Caspar murmured. "The love of a child or the fear of a child?"

Caspar embraced Gabriel and left.

The next day, he sought an appointment with Ptolemy. He needed to report to King Herod on his findings and collect the letters of recommendation for Rome as his reward. As soon as this was achieved, he'd be able to travel to Caesarea with Melchar and Belshazzar.

CHAPTER TEN

Rebellion

Joseph's house had four rooms and an outbuilding, where Joseph tethered the mule and donkey and stored his rough timber. One room was for the men, one for the women and Miriam's baby. The simple, stone and flat-topped home was built on the street with no protective wall. It opened to Joseph's carpenter's shop and an all-purpose provision and cooking room.

Joseph's kitchen was a busy place. Here, Judith heated water to bathe Joshua. Bathsheba baked bread and argued with Jonah. Ruth was always under foot, and Joseph, James and Amos came in and out, bringing in dust and wood shavings from the carpenter's shop. It wasn't long before Miriam confided to Judith her insecurities in Joseph's household.

"Judith, I miss the trees in the courtyard and the sound of the fountain. I miss the birds early in the morning," she said nostalgically.

"So do I. I wish you could have stayed in Nazareth at your parents' house. It's even bigger than the High Priest's house, and I miss it so much."

On a rare moment when they were alone, Joshua feeding at his mother's breast, Miriam asked:

"What do you think of Bathsheba?"

"I don't feel comfortable with her," Judith replied. "If I didn't have your companionship and Joshua to bathe and care for, I'd become depressed."

But she knew she'd asked to stay with Miriam, and she accepted her role. She knew, too, that part of Miriam's depression was natural after childbirth; she'd observed this in Elizabeth.

"This house is a lot smaller," she said. "It's difficult with Bathsheba… but…Joseph has promised to build you a loom and your own spinning wheel. We'll get used to it here. It's just different."

Beyond the kitchen area, Joseph had started to build an extra room, but the work had stopped while he'd been away. The construction was beyond the capability of James and Amos. Now, Joseph was required to fulfill back orders for the villagers before he could continue this addition.

Joseph came in from the carpenter's shop, his beard all covered in sawdust.

"When I get to it, I promise the new room will be much bigger," he said. "It'll be lit with a large window like the kitchen. When we get your loom and wheel, you'll be able to spin and weave. Then we'll build proper stone steps leading up to the enlarged roof so that by the time the warm weather comes, you'll be able to enjoy the evenings outside. It'll be a fine house when we've finished. It won't take too long."

Miriam smiled, and Joseph left to wash at the well.

Judith looked at Miriam.

"Do you think other people will bring us gifts for Joshua?" she asked out of nowhere.

"I did, but sometimes I have doubts now."

Miriam shed a tear.

"Life here is not as sacred," she said sadly. "My angels don't talk to me."

"But what about the star?" Judith said, trying to encourage her.

"It's still there. You're right. God will show us what to do. We just have to be patient."

Judith left to fetch water for the evening.

When Joseph returned, cleaned up, he took Joshua from Miriam.

"He's getting stronger every day," he noted. "Soon, we'll be able to take him to the Temple."

He smiled at his young bride.

"We should take you back to Jerusalem for purification."

"When we go, Joseph, can we see Elizabeth and Zechariah? I miss them. They'd love to see Joshua. We promised we would if we could."

"Of course, if they're in Jerusalem, but I can't go back to Ain Karim. I've got so much to do here. I'm behind in my work. Amos isn't as fast a learner as I'd hoped, although he's doing his best. James is a lost cause. He's always with the rabbi and never in the shop."

"I like James," Miriam said, "and perhaps it's good that a student of God's work should be in the same house as Joshua."

She smiled at Joseph.

"James is always very nice to me."

She looked around to see if they were still alone.

"Jonah, however, never looks me in the eye. I think he resents my being here. I can't talk to him at all."

"Nobody can, my little one," Joseph replied, returning Joshua into Miriam's arms. "Not even the rabbi can talk to Jonah. He was very badly upset by his mother's death and he's always resented his cousin, Bathsheba."

"That's what you always say, Joseph, but I'd so hoped he wouldn't resent me."

"He doesn't say much to anyone, Miriam. Maybe he's just sizing you up. Jonah really hasn't any friends. I'm sure he likes you. He's rebellious. He always takes the opposite viewpoint from the rest of us. Why, you're only a little older than him. Jonah should relate to you much more than he does to Bathsheba."

Joseph's eyes lit up.

"I have an idea. Let's bring Jonah with us when we take you to Jerusalem. He's always running away from the synagogue school, so I don't think he'll be missed. It might be a good idea to get him away from Bathsheba and give him some responsibility. He can look after the animals. He likes the animals."

"Let's take Jonah with us, then," Miriam agreed, as she wiped Joshua's mouth and tucked his blanket around him.

"How soon do you think you'll feel like going to Jerusalem? It's nearly a full day's journey, but it'll be a lot easier than our journey down."

Miriam looked up.

"Oh, I'm fine now. I think we could go any time, but you'll let Judith come with us, won't you?"

"Of course, I'm glad she's here to help you. My goodness, what would we have done without her in the cave the night Joshua was born?"

"I don't know, Joseph. I think about it even now. Mostly, I think I should have been stronger in spirit—kept my faith in God—for it was God's purpose that Joshua be born as he was. Somehow we'd have survived because Gabriel and the other angels would have made sure we did. Anyway, Judith was with us, and those shepherds, too. Everyone helped. Then those three merchants came. You know...they knew Joshua was a child of God. We really have to keep those precious gifts safe until Joshua's old enough to understand."

"We will, my little one, we will."

Joseph kissed Miriam on the forehead.

"You'll get used to this house and my wayward sons. It means a great deal to me to have you and Joshua living here. Have faith in me, Miriam. I'll take care of you."

Miriam felt a tug at her lower skirt. It was Ruth pulling at her. Ruth was smiling and looking up at her with adorable eyes.

"Miriam, can I hold Joshua's hand?" she asked.

"Of course, Ruth. Anytime you like."

"I'm happy you came here," the little red headed girl said.

Miriam knelt down. Ruth patted Joshua and took hold of his tiny hand. Fingers closed on hers, his eyes bright and gentle.

* * *

The visit of the new Governor of Syria to Sepphoris was a proud day for Tribune Flavius Septimus. He sat astride his great white stallion with the breeze brushing the red plumes of his golden helmet. Beside him was his aide, Marcellus, and behind them, the men of the Legion—the whole garrison of Sepphoris—lined up with their centurions to await the Governor's arrival.

Flavius said to his aide in a quiet voice:

"I'm glad Quirinius resigned his post in Damascus."

"And this new man...Varus...What do you think?"

Flavius smiled in the sunshine, his helmet gleaming.

"It's too early to tell at the moment, Marcellus. We shall see."

"At least he's made us his first priority."

"Yes, a good start."

But Flavius knew only too well why Varus was in Galilee this day. He wanted to see how easy it would be to absorb Galilee, Samaria and Judea into the full Syrian Province.

As if reading the Governor's mind, the aide said:

"It is well known now that King Herod has little time left."

Flavius steadied his white stallion, smoothing its neck.

"Common knowledge, indeed, Marcellus. And those heirs are noted for their vicious bickering over the succession. Not good times."

"Forgive me, sir, but perhaps Syria already controls Herod's kingdom."

"Agreed," Flavius said. "And perhaps on this grand day of pomp and trumpets, we shall learn more about it. Step back now."

The Governor's entourage came into view—a distant swirl of dust, with golden eagle standards held high, catching the sun. Flavius braced himself to suitably welcome the new authority and ride with Governor Varus back to Sepphoris. He thought of Linus and Copernia in the villa on the Galilean lake. They'd be proud of him now. As the Governor came nearer, Flavius dreamed of the day that his son Linus might head such a column as Governor of Syria.

The new Governor drew alongside, a younger man than Quirinius with a clean shaven, round face masked by the splendid helmet of his office.

Flavius put his arm to his chest:

"Hail Caesar!"

"Hail Caesar!" Varus replied with a warm smile.

Flavius immediately sensed a bond between them. They were almost contemporaries.

A trumpet blared.

Flavius opened his scroll and read his prepared welcome speech in Latin.

The Governor saluted again.

There was a fanfare, and the two leaders rode side by side to the gates of Sepphoris.

Back at the barracks, after the formal ceremonies had been concluded and the Legion inspected, Varus and Flavius relaxed in the Commander's Quarters, removing their helmets and ceremonial swords.

Over a generous supply of Galilean wine, they began to explore each other's feelings on the imminence of the Roman takeover.

"Have you met Antipas and Archelaus?" the Governor asked.

Flavius reflected on these two Herodian princes who had potentially come to power through the execution of Alexander and Aristobolus.

"No. I believe they're in Rome. I've heard that Antipater tried to poison them. Aren't they Antipater's closest rivals to Herod's throne, now that Herod-Philip has been struck off?"

"Yes," Governor Varus said. "It's ironic that Antipater took such a prominent part in the poison trial of Syllaeus in Rome. Local information has him also involved in plots against Archelaus and Philip and even against his own father."

"If Herod believes these rumors, Antipater will never inherit," Flavius said. "If you ask me, I think the King will change his will again. He'll take the side of Antipas and Archelaus, and if so, we should be able to exercise a lot of power over them. They're not well educated in statecraft like Antipater. It should be easy to control their courts. Maybe they'll try to divide the kingdom, one ruling Galilee and the other Judea."

"Whoever rules, I think we can rest assured we'll be the real power. Rome's day has come, Flavius Septimus. I like your spirit," Varus said with approval. "But I understand the King's sister Salome favors Philip. He might get the lands beyond the Jordan. Salome may be a force to reckon with. We'll be close allies here, Flavius. One day soon we'll have a reorganized Syrian Province in which you will have a stake."

Flavius felt a glowing feeling of success as he saw his ambitions and dreams rising and those for his son.

"The Levant's no backwater anymore," continued the Governor. "We need good men like you, prepared to make their lives out here. New trade routes are opening up. In all fairness, Herod's port at Caesarea is the envy of the Levant. Judea could become very important to us."

He eyed the Commander.

"Rich pickings, Flavius Septimus. Stay with me!"

"Varus! Let's drink to Caesar, the Empire, and the future Province of Judea! The groundwork is laid. To your successful Governorship and to the glory of Rome!"

The two Romans cupped each other's arms and drank from each other's goblet. No poison flowed here, only the draft of friendship.

"Eh! Flavius. These Galilean grapes make pretty good wine."

"The best. Galilee, indeed Samaria and Judea, too, are lands of opportunity, sir. This is a land of milk and honey, as the Jews used to say. You should see my vineyards on the shores of the Galilean lake. They are as good as we have in Tuscany. Maybe on your return from Jerusalem you can visit with us. I'd like you to meet my son Linus. We'll educate him to be a leader in these parts. Seriously, sir, stay with us a day or two when you return. I'd like your true impression of Herod's court and the future. Things are going to change around here."

Flavius chuckled.

"Perhaps the changes are heralded by that strange star. A drama's being played out under its bright light."

"Maybe my arrival in Damascus was due to this star," the Governor said. "The soothsayers say that because of this phenomenon, my term of office will be one of dynamic change. We're on our way, Flavius Septimus. To Caesar and the Empire!"

They drank from their goblets again.

The following day, their friendship sealed, Flavius accompanied the Governor and his entourage for a short part of his journey on the road to Sebaste. At the point where Galilee merged into Samaria, they said their goodbyes.

Governor Varus openly admired Flavius' great white stallion.

"A fine animal, and I would bet a fine friend and noble in battle, Flavius."

Flavius didn't hesitate.

"He's yours, sir. I will have him readied for you when you return home."

The two men looked at each other in gathering respect.

"Until then, Flavius."

"Watch the star," Flavius said.

"I will. It's the great equalizer: it's there for people of every rank. It keeps about me a certain humility!"

Flavius laughed as his friend ordered his entourage forward. He watched as the golden eagles escorted Varus into the distance. From here, Varus would travel through Samaria and then south to Jerusalem. There he'd make his assessment of the Herodian court. *The star, it's there for the glory of Rome,* Flavius thought.

* * *

Winter winds filled the great sail of the speeding galley. Majestically, it drove the vessel forward, easing the sweat of the slaves rowing to the beat of the drum. On board this galley, Antipater, King Herod's son and heir—or so he believed—watched the churning waves. He stood as he had stood for several hours, planning his actions and dreaming his dreams of power. His hands gripped the ballustrade as the familiar sand dunes hove into view. He could hear the crash of the breakers along the shoreline. Antipater smiled as the sailors lowered the great sail, and the galley moved forward to the rythmic oars.

Antipater drew deep breaths as he admired the white and yellow Judean stonework of Herod's Caesarea.

"I do respect your vision, my father, my King," he murmured. "From that, I will learn."

He braced himself as the galley approached the shelter of the deserted harbor, not concerned that no Herodian guard was there to welcome him, the heir apparent; neither was he concerned that no detachment of Roman soldiers were there to greet him, Caesar's friend. After all, nobody knew he was coming. The thought made him smile. This arrival was so different from the purple treatment he had received in Rome.

He watched as they passed the forlorn warehouses along the waterfront that were closed for the winter. There were only three lighters, taking on cargoes for coastal trade. Only foreigners seemed to be walking the quays. Chaldeans, Syrians, Nabateans, and Egyptians, waiting for rare winter ships to take them from the Levant to the heart of the Empire.

And then, Antipater felt uneasy. Guilt caused sweat beads to form on the nape of his neck. Now that he'd arrived in Judea again, he questioned whether his long-distance plots to establish his reign had succeeded. *My spies tell me my uncle Pheroras is dead. Did he die a natural death, or did he die from the poison I sent up by Antipilas from Egypt? Was action taken on the false evidence I gave with regard to my half-nephews Archelaus and Philip? Something's wrong. The port is too quiet.*

The galley drifted quietly to its dock. Shouts to ship oars broke the quiet as three finely dressed Chaldeans looked on from the wharf. Antipater waited, tense now, his surge of guilt making him fearful. More

261

shouts, and the drawing in of the oars, then the scrape of the galley's hull. Gently, the vessel rocked once, as if grudgingly giving up her ties with the sea.

Antipater was playing for the highest stakes, and his hands that now released the ballustrade were a murderer's hands. But then, he came from a family of murderers. At least, here, he would be fighting for power over people who hated him, rather than having to dispose of his friends.

* * *

Caspar, and his two new friends, Melchar and Belshazzar, had been disappointed on their arrival at Caesarea. No ship was ready for an immediate sailing to Italia. The great harbor with its splendid buildings, warehouses, and wharves, lay empty. A few galleys had passage to Alexandria and up north to Tyre, Sidon, and the Orontes, but none to Italia. The three Chaldean merchants took lodging in the deserted port area and awaited a ship.

The galley that brought Antipater to Caesarea gave Caspar his opportunity for a sailing to Rome. While booking passage on it, he learned how people hated Antipater, king elect of the Jews. Caspar couldn't help thinking about the 'Prince of Peace'. The more he learned from the port agents of the intrigues and mistrusts within the Herodian family circle, the more he thought about that simple scene in the cave at Bethlehem.

Caspar had gained what he needed from the Herodians—letters of introduction to the highest officials in Rome. He, along with Melchar and Belshazzar, could build the trade empire of their dreams. It didn't matter to him what lay in the future for King Herod and his heirs. The King couldn't live long; that was obvious. Whether this hated Antipater, who had brought the ship to Caesarea that Caspar so desperately needed, could safely secure the throne of his father was of no real concern to him and his friends.

Caspar watched as their precious cargoes were laden onto the waiting galley. Soon, they'd be on their way.

"What if the house of Herod falls?" Caspar asked his friends. "Do you think that's partly what the star foretells?"

"Maybe the house of Herod will be replaced by a new order, as you were told by the soothsayer," Melchar said. "But of course, Belshazzar sees the star as only for the virgin's child."

"But the soothsayer said 'a kingdom ruled by the 'Prince of Peace', the child of a virgin,'" Caspar confirmed.

Belshazzar nodded vigorously.

"Our 'Prince of Peace' from Bethlehem, Caspar. The one I saw in my dream. We found the child right under the star. Something's going to happen here. There's going to be a dramatic change in Judea, and we might have encountered its new leader. That should bring us good luck, Caspar."

Melchar shook his head.

"Look, you two dreamers. It was a very unusual and dramatic scene. But, let's be practical. If there's any change in the land of the Jews, it'll be Rome that makes the change. Even now, Rome rules this land. Rome's winning the Levant. That's why we really need to get to Rome, while we can still make use of our Herodian contacts."

"In that, Melchar, you're absolutely right," Caspar agreed. "Let's hope this ship will get us to Rome in time."

He eyed the great sail folded on its deck.

* * *

The bleakness of the winter countryside around Jerusalem, the dormant vines and hues of brown and gray, only added to Antipater's fears. The prince became even more afraid as he approached Jerusalem. Bravely, he rode as if in triumph, his entourage dressed in their finest. He'd returned expecting to claim his throne as his father retired in disease and sickness. At the very least, he'd be the regent king. Even in Sebaste, no Herodian detachment came to meet him. In loneliness, he rode those last few miles.

At the palace gates, Antipater was received, but his entourage wasn't given entry. The prince felt trapped.

What's gone wrong? he thought. *Has the King found out about my plot? Has Antiphilus been caught?*

Obstinately, Antipater soldiered on. There was only one way to find out the truth, and that was to confront the ailing King. He mounted the stairs from the inner court. Ahead, lay the familiar Royal chamber. A young Herodian guardsman, not familiar with Antipater, halted him.

"The King is in audience," he said.

"I am Prince Antipater, the heir apparent," he shouted. "I need to see my father now!"

The guard let him pass.

King Herod, looking grave, was sitting at a table with Princess Salome. A Roman, obviously a high ranking military officer, judging by his elaborate cloak and the helmet he held under his arm, stood in front of them. They appeared to be in a deep and serious conversation. They looked up, somewhat surprised when Antipater entered. Herod's bodyguard rushed forward as Antipater advanced and knelt before his father, hoping for the King's blessing. He noted the cold and cynical look in his Aunt Salome's mascaraed, calculating eyes.

The King looked at his son. Antipater could feel his father's wrath.

"Arrest this man!" Herod shouted to his bodyguard, who already had Antipater in his grasp.

Herod addressed his eldest son with fury.

"You worthless villain! I gave you everything, but you betrayed me. Nobody deceives King Herod! You've stirred up enmity in my house, reviving the spirits of the Hasmoneans! You tried to poison my brother in the last days of his noble life. Your plotting against Philip and Archelaus is known to me, but worst of all, it has reached my ears that you have attempted to destroy me before my time."

The King stood up, quivering in his fury.

"I may be riddled with worms and I may not have long to live in my suffering, but I'm still King. Antipater of Judea, before I die, you'll suffer for your crimes."

Salome nodded.

The King shouted at his bodyguard again:

"Take this man away!"

The young guard at the door took Antipater's other arm. The King called to Antipater, acknowledging the Roman official.

"Prince Antipater, this is Varus, the new Governor of Syria. Tomorrow, I'll appoint him to be your judge."

The guards led the heir apparent from the chamber. Salome's brown eyes were like agate. Carefully, she kept her triumphant heartbeat to herself.

* * *

News of Antipater's arrest swept through the Sanhedrin, urging on the pharisaic plotters, encouraging their intent on rebellion.

The chamber was crowded and councilors were still coming in. They had to stand at the back when Judas and Matthias, the upcoming leaders in the new movement, started to speak. Gabriel was at his pillar. Today he had no intention of leaving.

"Now is the time!" announced Judas. "The house of Herod is in total disarray. The High Priesthood shows its weakness in its alliance with the crumbling monarchy. Our time has come. We need to show our strength and assert our position. Let's act now! Who stands behind us?"

A large crowd of young members stood up, clenching their fists in agreement.

"We'll show them where Judaism really lies," Judas continued. "It lies within us, with the interpretation of our Law, with the rule of the synagogue, and the peaceful practice of our faith. The Temple has become a mouthpiece of Herodian opinion—not the house of God. The Temple has become a symbol of past glories—not of our present faith. Do you remember the words of the prophet Micah?"

His voice rose confidently, summoning fervor with the ancient words he dramatically read from a sacred scroll:

"Wherewith shall I come before the Lord and bow myself before the high God? Shall I come before him with burnt offerings, with calves of a year old? Will the Lord be pleased with thousands of rams, or with ten thousands of rivers of oil? Shall I give my firstborn for my transgression, the fruit of my body for the sin of my soul? He's showed you, O man, what is good; and what does the Lord require of you, but to do justly and to love mercy, and to walk humbly with your God? The Lord's voice cries out to the city and the wise man shall see your name! Hear the rod and who has appointed it!"

The young zealots shouted with enthusiasm, but a few of the older Sadducees shook their heads in horror at this break with tradition. Matthias, sensing the division, continued where his co-leader had finished.

"Friends! The Temple is part of our tradition. But the Temple needs to be freed from the insincere trappings of political compromise. This is not Herod's house. This is not the High Priest's palace. It's our house! The Temple belongs to us, as Jews, and not to the glory of the Herodians and their allies. How can we respect this central institution of our faith when the graven image of Rome hangs over our portal, and the tower of Rome grows on our northern wall?"

There were more screams of approval, and a youth stepped forward.

"Who agrees we should destroy this abomination, the eagle of Rome?"

More shouts rose from the crowd, and the meeting developed into enthusiastic support for a blow at the oppressor. Zealots and Pharisees, and even a few Sadducees, came together in common cause.

Gabriel witnessed the fervor, but as always, he had no desire to become personally involved. He quietly left the plotters behind him, choosing to go into the bright sunlight of the court of the Gentiles. He crossed the court to the Triple Gate and looked up at the carved, gilded eagle. Matthias was right. This symbol of Rome spread its wings out over all who entered the Temple.

The usual throng of pilgrims were mingling with the beggars and thieves who made their living off the fat of Temple clients. A young woman passed by, holding a child in her arms. Gabriel was sure it was Miriam, but as a stronger woman, composed, purposeful. He sucked in his breath as they looked at each other and then she passed on. An older man and a woman were accompanying her, and a young boy was pulling on their donkey. Curious, he turned and followed the little party of pilgrims.

They passed through the gates in the low walls leading into the Court of the Jews. Here, there were fewer people milling around. Gabriel could get a closer look at the young woman who was carrying the child.

It was obvious that she, too, had recognized Gabriel. She was whispering to the older man. He looked around and smiled at Gabriel, acknowledging his presence. Gabriel nodded, before walking on nonchalantly, passing them and moving toward the offices in the inner court.

In their passing, Gabriel again saw Miriam's face. *The same, yet different*, he realized. *Some maturity there. What have been her experiences to have her countenance changed like that—from one of sheltered innocence, vulnerability, to a quiet strength?*

Gabriel didn't speak, but went ahead of the little group, considering his thoughts. *But it is her! That was Miriam. And that must be her child!* He stopped in his tracks, his stomach churning. *That might be my child? I wonder who the others are? The young boy barely looks old enough to be her husband. The other two look more likely to be her parents.*

His conscience gnawed again, but he repressed it with the bitterness that he felt toward the High Priest. *The child has to be the High Priest's bastard,* he assured himself. *Maybe they're bringing the child to Zechariah. I'll follow them. Damn it! This virgin has come to affect my whole life. It seems the events of last year always catch up with me. It's my curse! She's destroying me. What have I done to deserve this?*

Gabriel waited in the shadows as the little group moved into the offices. Then he followed them toward the rooms of purification.

Miriam's here for purification, he observed. *She's here to acknowledge the safe birth of Zechariah's bastard! The hypocrisy of the structures here! Why, the Temple hierarchy whitewashes its own sins!*

Gabriel reflected on the pharisaic utterances he'd heard in the Sanhedrin Chamber. *Maybe those rebels are right. The Temple is an outdated hierarchy. It should be replaced by synagogue schools and pharisaic law. At least the Pharisees are sincere in their intentions. They just desire to keep the purity of our faith. The Temple has become too political!*

After a while, to Gabriel's surprise, the High Priest's assistant, Simeon, that kindly, white haired old man who was Zechariah's partner in Temple affairs, came out with the young woman and the other three. Simeon was carrying the child. He handed the infant back to his mother and held out his arms in prayer:

"Lord, now let your servant depart in peace, for my eyes have seen this child, Joshua, who will be the future hope of our people, the one whom You have prepared to be the light of the world and the glory of Israel."

The young woman held her baby close to her breast. She stood stalwart in the cool of the Temple's shadows. Like Zechariah, Simeon seemed to know her child was special—a potential leader of God's chosen people.

Simeon blessed them with the traditional Hebrew blessing and then turned to the woman.

"Your child will cause great controversy in this land, and your life will not be easy. You have a special charge, Miriam, but God will be with you through all trials and dangers. God bless you and Joshua. God bless Joseph, Jonah, and Judith. God bless you all."

The infant looked up at his mother. His hand reached for her.

Gabriel watched as Simeon led them out into the sunlight of the open court. There, the High Priest's right-hand-man left them.

Gabriel followed the family at a distance. An elderly woman, whom he knew to be a senile, self-proclaimed prophetess who had dedicated her life to the Temple, looked up as she swept the courts. She smiled her grotesque grin. Her laugh, when it came, was slipping into madness.

The young mother edged away from her.

As Gabriel observed the scene he nodded, even more convinced he was looking at Miriam.

"Behold! A child of God! The redeemer of Israel!" the prophetess called out.

Her words then trailed off into gibberish.

Gabriel watched the young woman clutch her child to her breast and walk quickly to reach the comfortable shelter of the pilgrim crowds. They were milling around the stalls selling sacrificial doves. The young boy followed behind them, coaxing the lazy donkey that had stubbornly halted in front of the senile old woman. Gabriel stayed where he was. He, too, was afraid. He didn't know whether to believe in his own cynicism that this child was the High Priest's bastard or his Gethsemane mistake. Either way, it bothered him that the child might really be, as Caspar had said, the 'Prince of Peace'. He watched as the young boy pulled the braying donkey forward.

The following day, the Temple became a political arena once again. King Herod was carried in on his bier to announce yet another will of succession. The King announced Antipater's disgrace and named Antipas, his son by the Samaritan, Malthake, to be his heir.

* * *

With the first breath of spring, King Herod and his entourage moved to the pleasant palace at Jericho. His physicians had recommended daily bathing in the mineral baths to help his painful body swellings. The monarch was in a state of fever almost continuously. He had the greatest difficulty in breathing due to constriction in his lungs. But Jericho gave him some measure of peace. It was his favorite palace. The first blooms of springtime were beginning to populate the fragrant gardens, while in the contrasting dungeons below the palace, Antipater was kept under house arrest following his trial by Varus of Syria. King Herod had appealed to Caesar for a decision on his sentence. For a while, Jerusalem was free of Herodian influences.

* * *

Among the members of the Sanhedrin, plotting continued. Judas and Matthias put their energies into the movement against the Roman eagle.

"With the Herodians thin in Jerusalem at this time, the hour has come for us to strike," Judas advised. "Who now stands behind us?"

There was a massive cry of general support from the younger zealots.

"I propose we establish our revolt by degrees," added Matthias. "First we should act purely in the interests of our faith. We should remove the abominations from the Temple and purify our house. Political considerations and internal reorganization of our principles can come later. Who is for the destruction of the eagle?"

A massive cheer resounded through the Sanhedrin.

"Tonight?" resumed Matthias.

The cheering continued.

The first blow of a pharisaic revolt was a simple plan soon to be executed. The destruction of the gilded eagle was to be a symbolic gesture. Although, outwardly seen as a potential blow against Rome, it was really planned as a blow against the Herodians. It was King Herod who had placed the eagle over the Triple Gate—a conciliatory measure on his part to the power of Rome. Its destruction would pose a weakness in Herodian rule and be seen by few as having much bearing on pharisaic faith. But they could justify their actions by claiming they were cleansing the Temple of pagan secular symbolism.

A band of forty pharisaic youths met outside the Triple Gate that night. Only two of the more athletic among them were required to grapple up the structure to reach the giant eagle. They hacked away with axes. Piece by piece, the great outspread wings fell to the marble portico. Souvenir hunters among the onlookers enthusiastically sought the broken wings.

No sooner was the work accomplished, when, as fate would have it, the Captain of the Roman garrison at Antonia's Tower, the fortress still under construction against the northern wall, entered the city from Kidron with a detachment of armed soldiers. The Pharisees were too intent on listening to Judas and Matthias making symbolic speeches to notice they'd been surrounded. The first of the victims was a sixteen-year-old youth. A Roman club swept him off his feet, so that he fell back, facing upward to look at his assailant. Almost simultaneously, others fell. The Romans kicked and beat them into submission. There was no escape. The Captain of the guard announced their arrest, and the soldiers tied them into groups of ten. With brutal swipes from the Roman clubs, the youths, some still clutching fragments of the Roman eagle, were dragged around the Temple to Antonia's Tower. Within twenty-four hours they were part of a Roman march from Jerusalem to Jericho.

The arrests were Roman, but the sentences needed to come from Herod. The King was briefed by the Captain of the Roman Guard in the private splendor of his Jericho Palace. The scent of jasmine, peaches and perfumed roses hung on the air in the Royal apartments that looked out over extensive gardens. Gossamer drapes swayed in the light breeze from the openings to the balcony. But the pleasantness of the surroundings was far from the torment of the King's health. Salome watched. She knew her brother was now close to madness. The message of these Roman guards might just tip the scale.

The King beat the table at which he sat with a clenched fist.

"Where was the High Priest?" he asked.

"Not among them."

"But he is in charge of Temple affairs. He's as guilty as these men."

"That is your affair," the Captain said wisely.

Herod beat the table again before rising, stooped over with one hand clutching his tortured stomach.

"They are all sentenced to death," he shouted. "Judas and Matthias are to be burned alive, the others to be executed by axe or arrows. Ptolemy, prepare the documents. No mercy is to be shown."

He slumped back into his chair.

The Guard saluted:

"Hail Caesar!"

Herod thumped his fist again:

"Hail Caesar!"

The Captain left. He had done his duty.

King Herod leered around his pain as he looked at Salome and Ptolemy.

"They took axes to hack at the eagle of Rome," he cried. "We shall use axes now to hack at their flesh until they die."

The King then turned to Ptolemy.

"Send messengers to Jerusalem. Arrest Zechariah, the High Priest and Gabriel, Caspar of Chaldea's friend. Bring them to us here in Jericho as soon as possible."

The next day, the forty spirited youths were dragged from their cells to an enclosed square of the palace yard. There, they met their appointed deaths around the burning pyres that consumed the flesh of their leaders. That evening the red of the sunset cast its magical glow over the fragrant gardens, and danced in the pools of blood that lay on the marble slabs of the yard.

* * *

A detachment of the Herodian guard knocked at the gate of the old Hasmonean Palace outside the Temple walls.

"Open up in the name of the King," their commanding officer shouted.

A servant opened the heavy door.

"Take us to Zechariah, the High Priest of the Jews," the officer said, as he crossed the threshold.

"I can't disturb him. He's at his prayers, sir," the servant said.

"Bring him here!" the officer shouted.

The servant rushed into the High Priest's chamber.

"Master!" he cried. "There are some soldiers here wishing to speak with you."

Annoyed, Zechariah turned on the man.

"You know not to disturb me at prayer. What is this?"

"Master, it's true. There are soldiers outside wanting you."

Zechariah was suspicious. He had expected some sort of Herodian or Roman repercussion for the recent, rash destruction of the outspread eagle.

"What do they want with me?" he asked.

"They want you to come out, Master. They sound impatient and angry."

Zechariah raised his hands toward heaven.

"God protect me! My hour may have come!" he said.

Turning to the servant, he continued in a calmer fashion:

"Tell them I'll be with them in a moment."

The servant left.

Zechariah sensed imminent danger. This was no time to feel the wrath of the King. Herod's irrational decisions in his increasing sickness and personal suffering were now well-known. Only the night before, news had reached the High Priest of the cruel deaths imposed on the rebellious young Pharisees. Yes, they'd taken a rash course of action. They'd been foolish. But they hadn't deserved to be hacked to pieces, pierced by arrows, and burned to death by oil soaked faggots. *If only I had paid more attention to the Sanhedrin debates,* he thought. *I could have stopped this folly. If only I had been there.*

"God Almighty!" Zechariah prayed. "Protect your old servant, Zechariah. Dear God, protect us all in these difficult times. If my time should be near, take care of Elizabeth and Jon and look after Miriam and Joshua. They're our messianic hope. Watch over them, Lord, and protect them in their innocence. If I've offended you, Lord, or if I've endangered these innocent lives, please protect them. They're innocents in a scene I've set. Spare them, Lord."

The guards rushed in impatiently.

"Are you Zechariah, High Priest of the Jews?" their leader shouted, his face flushed with malice.

"I am he."

"You're under arrest and to be taken to Jericho."

"For what reason?"

"That's no concern of ours. This is the King's command," came the leader's reply.

Zechariah was seized by three rough guards who tied his arms and gagged his mouth. He was taken from his palace to a waiting cohort of Herodian troops. They'd bound and gagged Gabriel in a similar manner.

Zechariah's fears mounted when he saw Gabriel. *So this is it,* he sensed. *Herod has found out about the messianic plot. He has tracked down both of us, and probably because of Gabriel's loose tongue.* The two priests were led out through the north gate of Jerusalem and onto the road down to Jericho. They stared at each other, unable to speak, eyes bulging and desperate as they strained against the gags. Whatever their past enmity, they now marched together as the common foe.

The Mount of Olives was ablaze with wild flowers in hues of blues, yellows, and white with sinister patches of orange and red. Zechariah reflected on them as he prepared to meet the wrath of the King. *There's a canker in Israel,* he thought, *that is ever growing. Just as these red and orange flowers increase each year in the field of yellows, blues and whites, so this canker increases to destroy the settled order of our faith. Never have we needed the Messiah more than now. The Herodians are irrational and the Romans are brutal. The Pharisees and the Sadducees seek to destroy each other, and like Elijah, I, only I am left, and they now seek to take my life.*

He looked at Gabriel, who scowled at him in anger. Zechariah thought about his messianic plot. *That man must be Joshua's father. What bitter irony that this man, who violated the virgin and has destroyed my High Priesthood, should be the father of our future king.* The thought sickened him.

The column of soldiers moved on from the Mount of Olives, passing through the villages of Bethpage and Bethany before beginning the steep descent down the winding road to Jericho.

* * *

Simeon, shocked by Zechariah's arrest and assuming the High Priest's responsibilities, called in a messenger.

Simeon's once-sparkling eyes looked fearful, set in his well-lined face and framed by his massive white beard.

"Seek out Joseph ben Judah in Bethlehem," he ordered. "When you find him, give him this message."

The scribe prepared to write.

"The High Priest Zechariah has been arrested. Flee to Egypt for a while with Miriam and Joshua. Things look bad here. You could be in danger. By the hand of Simeon, Chief Priest."

The messenger sped from Jerusalem southward through the hill country, which like the vale of Kidron, was a carpet of spring wild flowers.

* * *

Meanwhile, on the same balmy spring day, Zechariah and Gabriel were brought before the King.

King Herod hadn't slept all night. Although propped up by a mountain of pillows, his chest pains and breathing difficulties caused him to choke. The mineral baths hadn't helped him much. His flesh was diseased and foul. Death hovered over the once mighty Herod.

Salome entered his bedchamber, followed by Ptolemy carrying a scroll. She turned up her nose at the stench.

"My brother and Majesty," she said, "following our discussions I have had Ptolemy draw up a provisional plan."

"For what?"

"The succession."

The King scowled.

"Read it, then."

Ptolemy read:

"It is our opinion that Prince Antipas has not the ability to govern the whole realm. We, therefore, declare his kingdom should be the region of Galilee where there is strong Roman support for his government. It is our will, therefore, that Archelaus should be the King of Judea and Samaria, and the Princes Antipas and Philip Tetrarchs of Galilee and the lands beyond the Jordan. We appoint our beloved sister, Princess Salome, as the executor of all our estate to divide as she thinks fit for the benefit of our heirs and our kingdom."

Ptolemy laid the scroll before the King. Salome trembled for fear that her irrational brother might change his mind. Slowly, Herod took up the pen that Ptolemy proffered and, dipping it in the jar of oily ink, he affixed his signature. He looked up at Ptolemy, dismissing his sister's role.

"Satisfied? Now…get out!"

Salome sensed a cruel fit coming upon the King.

Later, when King Herod was carried on a litter into the Council Chamber of his summer palace to pass sentence on the High Priest, Salome sought to protect herself.

"Zechariah," King Herod announced, "I've summoned you before us so you can account for the insubordination of our people within the precincts of our Temple."

"God's Temple!" Zechariah replied, looking at the floor.

He tried to ignore the stench emanating from the King.

"Did God build the Temple or did we build the Temple?" asked the King. "Speak to me, Zechariah! Did God lift stone upon stone to build the Temple of the Jews?"

"Your Majesty, you built us the finest Temple that Mount Moriah has ever known, but it was dedicated to God."

"Then, why have you allowed sacrilege to take place within its very walls? Why do I have to hear of rebellion in the Sanhedrin? You're incapable of governing the Temple. You're not fit to be our High Priest. Enlighten me, Zechariah, or shall I have it forced from you? What is this rebellion? Who are the leaders?"

"Pharisees in the Sanhedrin," Zechariah replied. "You know how they've infiltrated their revolutionary ideas into the establishment."

Herod didn't seem impressed with the High Priest's reply. It seemed the King knew more. He was holding a flail in his hand, which he was running through his fingers. He beat it upon one of the pillows until the exertion brought on a paroxysm of coughing.

A servant swiftly brought him water to drink.

"You!" the King said as he recovered and addressed Gabriel. "You, Gabriel! Do you know anything about this virgin your friend Caspar from Chaldea believes to be the mother of a future king of the Jews?"

Gabriel didn't answer. He trembled in fear.

"Don't you hear me?" the King yelled. "If you don't hear me I'll have your ears removed as useless appendages. Do you know of such a virgin?"

"I know of a woman who claims to be a virgin. She has a child, Your Majesty," Gabriel managed.

"The virgin of Bethlehem?" asked Herod.

"Possibly… of Bethlehem," Gabriel stammered. "I believe her child was born in Bethlehem."

"Good! Now, we're getting somewhere," said the King. "Is this child thought to be the one to inherit my throne and to be the future King of the Jews?"

Zechariah glared at Gabriel, who remained silent.

The King observed their interplay with satisfaction.

"Do you value your ears, Gabriel?" he shouted. "Perhaps you need to be reminded."

King Herod called his guard to unsheathe his sword.

"No!" cried Gabriel, beads of cold sweat running down the back of his neck. "I confess, Your Majesty. Yes! I know of the child."

"And who is the father of this child?" continued Herod, as he motioned for his guard to rest his sword at Gabriel's neck.

"Zechariah the High Priest is the father!" shouted Gabriel, terrified, but certain he was right. *The High Priest can't harm me now*, he mused, *he's also the King's prisoner.* Gabriel turned to look at Zechariah. The High Priest appeared stunned by the accusation.

"No, Your Majesty! It was Gabriel. He raped one of the Temple virgins. He's the father of her child!" Zechariah retorted.

Herod's voice rose, sick and palsied, in a terrible rage.

"A Jewish King! An infant to be king in place of our family! Is that your plot, you scheming zealots? No wonder you started this rebellion in the Sanhedrin. You thought you could destroy my family and create a bastard king. I'll see to it your plot doesn't succeed. I'll have all male children recently born in Bethlehem put to death. And you two scheming zealots, I'll have you put to death along with them. Guards! Take them away!"

The King gave instructions for an open death warrant on all male babies to be found in Bethlehem. Members of the Herodian guard were dispatched to carry out the task. Zechariah and Gabriel were then flung into the dungeons of the Jericho palace, joining Prince Antipater.

* * *

Bathsheba, still trying to maintain her hedgemony in Joseph's household, sent Judith out to the Bethlehem well. As Judith returned with two buckets of fresh water, a stranger astride a mule came up to her and reined in his beast.

"Can you advise me where Joseph ben Judah lives?" the man asked quietly, after carefully looking around.

"You mean Joseph the carpenter?" Judith said, assuming the man wanted to place an order.

"Joseph ben Judah, whose wife is Miriam," the stranger said.

"Yes, sir."

She put the buckets down and pointed.

"It's at the end of the street, the last house on the left."

The messenger smiled at the ease with which his mission had been accomplished. He kicked his mule on down the street.

Joseph and Amos were working when the stranger arrived. The spring sunlight streamed in through the open front of the carpenter's shop. Joseph looked up from chiseling a plank. Amos likewise eyed the stranger.

"Joseph ben Judah?" asked the messenger.

"Yes. What can I do for you?"

"I have an important message for you from Simeon the Chief Priest. There's been an anti-Roman demonstration at the Temple. I don't know how you're implicated, but he advises you to leave the country with your wife and child. He wishes to inform you that Zechariah, the High Priest, has been arrested by the King. He fears for your lives as there is great unrest in Jerusalem and at the King's court. He advises you to go to Egypt where you'll be safe."

"Egypt! What have we done?" Joseph asked. "I'm a simple carpenter behind in my work. It's very inconvenient for me to leave Bethlehem now."

"I can't tell you any more. That's my message," the stranger said.

"Who is it?" Bathsheba called out.

"A man telling Father he's in danger," shouted back Amos into the dark, cavernous room behind them.

"Nothing, Bathsheba," added Joseph. "Is Miriam back there?"

Miriam came out, holding Joshua in her arms. She blinked in the sunlight of the carpenter's shop.

"This man has brought us some disturbing news," Joseph said.

The stranger remounted his mule.

"Tell us more," Joseph called up to him.

"What more can I tell you? I've been sent to you by Simeon, the High Priest. He said it was urgent, and I've relayed his advice."

"Simeon, the High Priest," repeated Miriam. "What does he want, Joseph?"

"He wants us to leave the country. He wants us to take Joshua and go to Egypt to live there for a while. Apparently, our lives are in some sort of danger. Things are not looking good here. He says Zechariah's been arrested."

"Arrested? Why? What can Zechariah possibly have done wrong?"

"Who knows, Miriam? The Temple is a place of intrigue. I don't want anything to do with their way of life."

Joseph put his arm around Miriam and held her close.

"Was anyone else arrested, young man?" he asked the messenger.

"Many zealots—young Pharisees from the Sanhedrin. They were all put to death. I've heard they were cut to pieces with axes at the command of the King. People say the King has become particularly cruel in these days of his worsening sickness. Some are now doubting his sanity. Maybe that's why the Chief Priest Simeon fears for your lives. A man called Gabriel was also arrested and taken to Jericho with the High Priest."

"Gabriel!" cried Miriam.

She turned to Joseph, tears beginning to well in her eyes.

"He's the one who didn't want to marry me. That's why he followed us."

"Could Gabriel have caused us to be in danger?" Joseph asked.

"Perhaps."

Miriam looked solemnly at her husband.

"Joseph, we must go to Egypt."

"But I've said…"

"No.! Joseph…we must go to Egypt."

Joseph looked at her face, the sternness and conviction in it.

"You have changed, Miriam. You have changed so much since…"

"Since Joshua was born?"

Joseph shook his head.

"Before then. I'm not a learned man, Miriam, but I have a good sense of what is right and wrong. In you, even though I cannot find the words, I see what is right."

He embraced her.

"As do Elizabeth and Anna, and Joachim and Zechariah," he added.

"We carry with us a son of God, Joseph, the very future of our people."

Joseph nodded as he looked down at his hands.

"A carpenter…I cut and mold wood to my will, I build, I give. But you? Look at you, Miriam…Touched by God, who creates within you…"

"We must protect Joshua. And there appears to be little time."

Joseph nodded.

"We can go to Alexandria," he suggested. "Egypt will be safe, and I know I can find work there. I've heard the city is even bigger than Jerusalem."

As he spoke, the messenger turned his mule and left.

"What do you think of him?" Joseph asked. "He heard us talk."

"In these times, we are but one more sign, my husband." Miriam smiled. "That is our protection. There is the star, it shines on all. But it is meant for us."

"And you are sure of this?"

"Why did the shepherds come? Why did the merchants come bearing gifts? Why should this star beam down on some worthless cave?"

"Because you were in it," Joseph said.

"Because Joshua was born there." Miriam touched his arm. "We must go, my husband…Now!"

"Judith," Joseph called. "Prepare food for a long journey. We shall be traveling again."

In the dark interior of their small home, Joseph and Miriam gathered up their belongings. Bathsheba said little, glad that Miriam and her baby boy would be leaving. That night, however, Ruth snuggled up to Miriam.

* * *

In the silent dankness surrounding the three prisoners in their cells, there was sudden commotion. Zechariah moved to the grill in the great door separating him from the world. In the dim light, a jailer came down the hallway, shouting fiercely at the guard on duty.

"The King is dead! The King has taken his life! Long live Antipas, the King of the Jews!"

Zechariah's knuckles whitened under the dirt as he thought about the consequences of Herod's death.

The name Antipas indecisively echoed from the dank walls. Herod's final will remained unpublished, and Antipater was as yet unaware that earlier in Jerusalem he had been formally disclaimed. The prince pounded on his cell door, ready to claim his throne.

"Release me! I am the King! Release me. At last my time has come. I'll make it worth your while in gold and silver. Let me claim my throne!" he shouted.

Zechariah felt a moment of relief. If the King was dead, there was a fair chance he'd also be released. He could return to little Jon and Elizabeth at Ain Karim.

The jailers conferred. Spurred by greed, they released the prince.

Antipater didn't get far. While making his bid for freedom, he was met by four Herodian guards. They trapped him on the stairs leading up from the dungeons. Weakened by his stay in jail, Antipater fell to the ground as the first blows hit him. He looked up only to see the gleam of the dagger that slashed his throat.

The jailers met a similar fate as they tried to escape. Their corpses, along with that of the slain prince, lay where they'd fallen in pools of their own blood.

The four soldiers disappeared as swiftly as they'd come, their orders carried out, their task accomplished.

Zechariah called out to Gabriel:

"Didn't you hear the jailers say the King is dead!"

"Yes! But didn't you see what the guards did?" answered Gabriel. "This must be the work of Salome. We'd better not get our hopes up too high. Things may not be any better for us if she's grasped all power."

The dank silence of the dungeons returned until another detachment of Herodian guards came down. They dragged the three corpses into Antipater's cell. Then the Captain unlocked Zechariah's door. The guards bound the High Priest's hands and took him away and up the stairs.

After his time in cell darkness, Zechariah was almost blinded by the sudden daylight. The soldiers led him through the palace until once again he stood in the King's chamber. The King was still alive!

Herod ranted in a rage brought on by pain, malady, and frustration. He'd tried to kill himself, but, before he could accomplish his death wish, his cousin had saved him. He cursed the man's well meaning action. The pain was too much for him. He sought only the peace of his own death.

"The High Priest, as you commanded, Your Majesty," the Captain said.

"Zechariah, the zealot," the King said. "I sentence you to death by hanging...You, and your scheming friend."

The King turned to the Captain of the guard.

"Take him away! See that he and Gabriel ben Judah are dead by sundown!"

Footsteps echoed off the walls of the narrow stairway heralding the guards' return with Zechariah. They led straight to Gabriel's cell. The guards opened the clasp on the lock and threw the High Priest in, closing the door behind him.

"What did they say?" asked Gabriel from the darkness. "Is the King dead?"

"No. Whatever our differences may be, remember we're both children of God. Prepare to die, Gabriel. We're sentenced to death by hanging."

Gabriel shook with fear, his hopes of survival dashed.

Zechariah prayed.

For the first time in a long while, Gabriel also prayed. He prayed in frustrated, silent desperation. *God of our Fathers, why have you done this to me? Is it because of my sins? Is this punishment for my licentious young life? Why, Jehovah? I'm no different from other men. Why did you single me out to be a part of this man's secret plan? Why do I have to die for a cause in which I have no interest? I didn't really harm the virgin, Lord, not even if her child is mine. I withdrew from the High Priest's scheme. Why are you punishing me for this?*

Suddenly, Gabriel laughed out loud, disturbing the pious Zechariah.

"No Herod or any High Priest will govern the Jews! No pharisaic state will ever be created! Soon it will all be over. Israel will fully belong to Rome," he shouted.

The guards, carrying torches and ropes, returned. They tied the ropes to the crossbeams in Zechariah's cell. Having set the scene for execution, they then seized Gabriel. Tying his arms behind his back, they thrust Gabriel into Zechariah's cell. They fixed the rope of execution around his neck. Gabriel struggled, but there were six guards to subdue him. They pulled on the rope. Gabriel strained to his limit to hold on to his ground support, cursing his executioners, his cries of fear demonic in the flame from the torches. They pulled again. Gabriel's toes left the ground to the snap of his neck.

Zechariah was thrust into the cell with Gabriel's corpse still suspended from the crossbeam. In the moments available to him, Zechariah looked at Gabriel, at the almost peaceful features, the quietly closed eyes and slack mouth, which almost carried a smile of release, in no way reflecting the shouts of fear and hysteria Zechariah had heard. Only the neck looked odd, bent as it was against the rope. *A good death,* he thought, *a snap of the neck and done. Perhaps that will be for me.*

As he was manhandled beneath the next rope, Zechariah prayed a last prayer to his God. As the words filled the cell in a priestly flow of reverence, he watched the soldiers haul on his rope. His massive frame held him to the ground despite the painful jerks. Then he spun, a macabre pirouette, as the rope closed around his windpipe, slowly strangling him. He twisted and kicked as blood and breath were denied him, and his lungs heaved, but still he prayed. He prayed for understanding from his God, whom he had served so faithfully, as to why he was denied a simple snap of the neck. He pursued the prayer as darkness closed in and his lungs bled. But he received no answer. Then…nothing.

* * *

Miriam looked back at Bethlehem. The houses looked less squalid from a distance. The village took on a certain charm as the sun enhanced the beauty of its yellow stones. The tall cypress trees made it look like an oasis in the landscape. Miriam thought of Elizabeth and baby Jon and wondered what they were doing. She wondered if they knew that Zechariah had been arrested. She had Joshua in front of her on Joseph's faithful old donkey. Judith rode the mule that also carried blankets and their food supplies. Joseph was seated on another donkey he'd purchased the day before. Strapped beside him was the precious box the rich men had given to Miriam in the cave at the time of Joshua's birth. It was heavy, but Miriam had insisted they bring it with them. The donkey had cost Joseph almost all his winter wages, but there was no way they could have made this desert journey on foot.

"Hopefully, south of Beersheba we'll meet up with a caravan bound for Alexandria," Joseph said. "I've heard through the rabbi that there are many Jews in Alexandria."

But Miriam was not really listening. She thought of Gabriel the priest. *Would all this have happened if I'd married him? Perhaps I should have married him. If I hadn't become so frightened and if I'd understood his needs a little better, he'd have accepted me. Was he really a zealot rebel?* Finally, she thought of God. She held Joshua closer to her.

"God would have given you to me in any case, whether I'd stayed with Gabriel or not," she whispered. "But I'm married to Joseph, and that's where our future lies."

They rode on. Bethlehem disappeared. The road began to slope toward the desert plains. By nightfall, they were well to the south. As the stars grew diamond bright and the lustrous desert moon rose, the night became as it was before Joshua was born, when everyone watched the great star. It had hung over them then. Now, the last vestiges of the star and its thin trail of light could be seen only as a speck on the western horizon.

Part Two
Children of Destiny

CHAPTER ONE

Judith's Homecoming

Sunlight caught the golden frieze on the gleaming architrave of Caesarea Maritima's Temple of Augustus. The massive structure stood as a sentinel watching over the port. In its dark shadows, two Hebrew boys silently rolled marbles in the dirt. As the boys played within this shadow of Rome, a ship from Alexandria was anchoring in the outer harbor.

On board, after nearly nine years of living with Joseph and Miriam in Egypt, Judith was returning home. In Egypt, she had helped Miriam take care of Joshua when he was young—the grandson, her master, Joachim, hadn't yet seen. Now, she stood on the deck at the aft end of that gently rocking Roman galley, coming home. A breeze caught her graying hair and flattened the folds of her simple cotton shift against her sturdy legs. The woman felt a great relief. At last, she was returning to Galilee, and would be leaving behind the dust, dirt, and clamor of Egypt. Judith had hated the flies, the heat, the endless mud, and the pungent odors of Alexandria's back streets. Breathing in the fresh air of the Levant, she looked up at the Temple of Augustus and the green hills beyond. They gave a false but welcome impression of peace and calm.

Out of Judith's earshot, a rough Roman shouted at the Hebrew boys. They looked up at the man with fear in their eyes, picked up their marbles and left the precinct.

Amos, Joseph's restless teenage son, was traveling with Judith. He joined her as they waited for the lighter from the inner harbor to ferry them ashore.

"The air smells so good!" he said, sniffing the breeze. "I don't think I'll miss Egypt at all."

Judith laughed.

"Me neither," she agreed, "but I'll miss Joshua and Miriam—even your father. Hopefully, they'll be able to follow us to Galilee soon."

Judith looked forward to performing simple daily chores at her master's comfortable home. The cramped mud-brick compound that had served as Miriam's house in Alexandria was dingy compared to her memory of Joachim ben Judah's place in Nazareth. She recalled its light and airy courtyard, splashing fountain, and fruiting fig and olive trees.

It seemed so long since that fateful night when they had fled to the safety of Egypt. Joshua was now a well-developed eight-year-old. Judith had sensed a loss of purpose now that Joshua was growing up. There was little she could really do to make life more comfortable for Miriam or Joseph's family, and James, Joseph's oldest, monopolized much of Joshua's time. Her presence with them was just an extra mouth to feed. When Joseph suggested to Amos that he should return to Israel and set up his own business, it was willingly arranged for Judith to travel with him and go back to Miriam's aging parents in Nazareth. There, she could be more help than in Alexandria.

"Are all the girls as beautiful as Miriam in Nazareth?" Amos asked.

Judith smirked.

"I'm sure there will be one just waiting for you."

His eyes lit up in his fresh young face.

"It's a shame she doesn't have a sister," he said

"You're old enough now to make your own choice. Wait and see. I'm sure there's a pretty Galilean girl just waiting for you."

A lighter arrived alongside, creating a soft thud of creaking wood.

A rough sailor helped Judith and Amos clamber down into the flat-bottomed ferry that would take them through to the inner harbor. The sailor then threw down to them their meager possessions—a cotton bundle of clothing, Amos' box of tools, and a skin for drinking water that had been given to them by Joseph.

"The air does smell sweet!" Judith agreed.

The lighter pulled away from the galley, rocking gently on light swells.

Ashore, Amos and Judith reveled in a sense of freedom. They were both happy to put Egypt behind them, with its flies and oppressive heat. For Amos, the endless task of making mud-bricks was over.

"I'll be able to have my own woodworking shop in Nazareth," he said, looking at his roughened hands. "Then, you can bring all the beautiful young girls of Nazareth to visit me there."

They left the harbor and joined a caravan that they learned would pass through Nazareth, taking goods from Caesarea to Damascus. It was a slow-moving group, consisting mostly of ox carts laden with heavy goods. Amos cut down a staff from a roadside grove. He gave it to Judith as they wearily trod the road. They soon became footsore, but nothing could distract them from the joy they felt in being home.

On their arrival in Nazareth, Judith led Amos to the familiar gate breaching the long wall that marked her master's house. She could see the branches of the old olives above the coping, and could hear the light whisper of the trickling fountain in the yard. A deep feeling of relief surged through her.

"This is it, Amos. We've come a long way."

Her dark eyes studied the gate.

"This is the house where Miriam's family lives."

"Does everything behind this wall belong to Miriam's father?" Amos asked, wide-eyed.

"Yes. It's beautiful. There's a wonderful view on the other side."

The gate was barred. Judith knocked on it with her staff. There was no response. She knocked again, harder and longer.

* * *

Anna heard the noise. She left the comfort of her couch on the porch, crossed the courtyard, and unlatched the gate.

"Judith!" she exclaimed. "Judith! Is it really you?"

She had little doubt, but Judith did look different, weary from the long journey and nearly nine years older than when Anna had last seen her. For one thing, she had put on a lot of weight in Egypt. And her hair was graying.

"Yes! It's me."

"You've come back! Why, we'd given up hope of ever seeing any of you again. What news have you? Where's Miriam, Joseph and the family?"

Judith embraced her old mistress. Joachim's wife's face was lined, and her hair was fully gray. She was shocked to see how much Mistress Anna had changed.

Amos took the staff and stood aside.

"Oh! Mistress Anna! How good to be home!" was all Judith could say as tears welled in her eyes, streaking her sunburned face.

A young boy, about Joshua's age, ran out into the courtyard and stared at the strangers.

Anna called to him.

"Jon! Go and fetch your mother! Our family's home at last!"

The boy hesitated. He had strange, piercing eyes. He studied Judith and Amos and then, as if he approved of them, he ran back into the darkened interior.

"Judith, where are they? Where's everyone else?" Anna repeated, looking anxiously for her daughter and grandchild.

"Mistress, this is Amos, Joseph's second son. He's traveled with me all the way from Egypt. He's going to stay here in Nazareth and start up a woodworking shop in preparation for Joseph and Miriam's return."

"You mean they're not with you?"

"No," she said, wiping at a last tear. "Joseph makes bricks in Alexandria, and Miriam and Joshua are still there with him."

It was hard for Anna not to display her disappointment. She wasn't going to see her grandson. Her excitement fell back inside her.

"Joshua's growing up now," Judith said. "He's about the same age as the lad who was just here. Was that Jon?"

"Yes. That was Jon."

Anna looked up again in a brave attempt to overcome her disappointment that Joshua was not with them.

"Tell me about Joshua. Is he a strong and handsome boy?"

Amos shut the gate as he admired its craftsmanship.

"He has a fair complexion, very different from Amos," Judith confided. "His hair's lighter. He works at the brick kilns, but studies a lot with James, Joseph's oldest son. One thing I really like about Joshua is his simple love of nature and the gentleness that he shows to animals. He's a very kind boy, and he laughs a lot."

Anna's sister came out to greet them. Elizabeth had lived with Joachim and Anna in Nazareth since Zechariah had been executed. Judith had only heard the accounts of those events as told to her by Joseph's sons long after Zechariah had been murdered. Apparently, soldiers of King Herod had also come at that time to Bethlehem and drowned innocent babies in the village well. Of course, Master Joseph had been warned about some kind of danger, which was why they had fled from Bethlehem and gone to Egypt. Judith knew that the family had been in danger, but she really didn't know why. All she knew was that her mistress's brother-in-law, Zechariah the High Priest, had been killed by the king's men. It was all very confusing. Now, nine years had passed. It was all enough for her to understand why the High Priest's widow had so aged.

"Elizabeth, you remember Judith," Anna said. "And this is one of Joseph's sons."

Jon returned and stood beside his mother, peering around at the strangers through half-squinting eyes—eyes perhaps too old for one so young.

"This is Jon, Judith, the little boy you helped to deliver," Elizabeth managed, her voice quavering as she thought of Zechariah and those days surrounding Jon's birth. "This is Zechariah's son, our gift from God."

Judith nodded, smiling tentatively.

Jon, in return, stared at her with no expression on his face. She couldn't help thinking that Miriam's boy was better looking and much friendlier. Jon was heavy and distant.

The little group moved out of the courtyard into the shade of the porch. The familiar smells of the old house filled Judith's senses and bridged the gap of so many years.

* * *

Joachim was more than surprised when he came up from his vineyards. He stroked his heavy beard and screwed up his eyes in near disbelief before he dropped his stick and embraced Judith.

"And who's this?" he said, looking at Amos.

The young man seemed too old to possibly be his grandson.

"This is Amos, one of Joseph's sons," Judith explained.

"And where are Miriam and my grandson?"

291

Judith looked at Anna, who came to her rescue.

"They're in Egypt," she said, trying to sound encouraging around her own disappointment. "Only Judith and this young man, Amos, have come home. But the others will be coming."

"Soon?" Joachim asked.

"We don't know, but apparently Miriam assured Judith they'll come back, and the good news is that they'll come here. Amos is going to start his own business—a woodworking shop like his father's."

"Thanks be to God!" Joachim cried out as he embraced Amos. "Blessed be God forever! My boy, we'll help you any way we can."

The evening meal that followed was the forum for a barrage of questions about the long family separation. Judith picked up a succulent date as she explained the rigors of her original journey and how they had joined up with a caravan from Petra as it crossed the desert to Memphis. Apparently, on reaching the great river Nile, they'd settled down just north of Memphis in a small, mud village named Giza. Judith's eyes glowed as she told of extraordinary monuments that rose from the desert nearby— great triangular mountains of stone, and strange, sculpted animals called sphinx that looked like lions with human features. However, it was not these great monuments that fascinated Joachim and Anna most. They wanted to know about their grandchild. They wanted to know about Joshua and their daughter Miriam.

"Joshua's a very gentle child," Judith explained. "He was a very good baby despite the hardship and travel. Oh, he cried when he got over-tired, but he really put up with a great deal in those difficult days. At Giza, he became very sick and we feared for his life."

"Sick with the fever?" Anna asked, as she served them a pottage of lentils and root vegetables.

"Yes, Mistress, but that was long ago. He had a terrible fever. He couldn't eat or drink. I don't think he knew us at that time. He was so weak that Joseph called on a village healer. There are lots of magic men in Egypt. The man held a stick over the boy's head and sang in the strangest tones. At the same time, Joseph prayed earnestly to our God. We all did. Twice Miriam thought she'd lost her precious baby boy, but God answered our prayers. Joshua recovered, and he hasn't really been seriously sick since."

She held up her wooden bowl and slurped on the pottage.

"O God of Abraham, Isaac, and Jacob, we give thanks," declared Anna as she held Joachim's hand. "So what's Joshua doing now?"

"He makes bricks with Joseph, Mistress. You should see him when he comes home all covered in mud! Joshua's also learning to be a scribe. James, Amos' older brother, teaches him to speak and write both Greek and Hebrew. We all journeyed on a boat down the river from Memphis and settled in Alexandria, a huge city, much bigger than Jerusalem. Sometimes, James takes Joshua to the big synagogue school in Alexandria. Oh, Mistress, you should see the synagogue in Alexandria! James is a rabbi there, and he says it's the most exciting place he's ever known. Apparently, Joshua's a very smart child. When James brings him home, they talk together about the things that Joshua has learned."

Judith turned to Amos.

"I think James has been a very good influence on Joshua, don't you?"

"I suppose so," Amos answered begrudgingly, looking up from his bowl, "but my brother never helps us much. I'm the one who's always had to work. James never joined us in the mud at the brick kilns, and he's useless as a carpenter."

"He's a scholar. He's very respected," Judith said.

Amos put his bowl down with a thud.

"That never bought us food, tools or even feed for the donkey and mule. At least Joshua worked with Father and me part of the time, even though it was always hard to get him to concentrate on what he was doing. He's good with the animals, though. James did teach him that."

"At least James joined us in Egypt," Judith said. "Nobody knows what happened to your other brother."

Amos laughed as he wrung his strong artisan's hands.

"Jonah! Maybe he was the sensible one and just left to go his own way, but he has no skills. At least now I'm setting myself up on my own. I have skills. Father's taught me a lot."

"We'll help you," Joachim said, wiping his mouth and beard. "I have timber and tools. We can begin soon. I think I know of a house you can use. It's quite big and nobody's living there at the moment. It's right on the square. An unpleasant old man named Ahab used to live there, but he's dead now. God bless you, Amos, you don't have to feel nervous here. I give thanks to God that we'll all be together. God's blessed old Joachim. This is a great day in the house of Ben Judah."

Judith didn't try to contradict what Amos had said. She had great respect for Amos' practical thinking, but she also knew how much James meant to Joshua and how Joseph had so often supported James' religious studies.

"Well, Mistress Anna," she said, "you'd be proud of your grandson. You'll find he looks a little like Master Joachim with similar eyes. Of course, he's too young to show a beard yet, but his hair is thick and he does have a beautiful smile, especially when he laughs."

"Oh, Joachim," Anna said, addressing the aging patriarch. "Think about it, soon we'll have all our family here. The years of waiting are over. The grandchild that Zechariah promised to us we'll finally know and see with our own eyes!"

Anna pulled a grape from a succulent bunch of Joachim's best and passed the fruit to her husband. As he helped himself, she turned to Judith.

"How soon, Judith? How soon will the family come to Nazareth?"

"Joseph didn't say, Mistress. However, he did ask Amos to set up a business here for him, didn't he, Amos?"

Amos looked up.

"Yes, that's what he suggested. 'Go to Nazareth,' he said. 'Start a carpenter's shop there so that when we return, we'll have somewhere to go.'"

He turned to Joachim.

"Joachim ben Judah, thanks for offering to help get us started."

"Amos, you're as my son," Joachim said.

He stretched out his arms and looked upward:

"Yaweh, God of our forefathers, thank You for this day," he prayed. "We are gathered together at our table in the sure knowledge that You have not forgotten us. You have blessed us not only with the fruits of the land, but You have brought back to us our family."

Relaxing his prayerful posture, he looked at his wife and clasped her hand.

"Soon, Miriam and Joshua will be with us again," he said.

Tears welled in Anna's eyes.

"Joseph, too," she said.

* * *

Amos, assisted by Elizabeth's son Jon, soon built up a small business. But Jon didn't really show any more aptitude for the job than Joshua had in Egypt. As before, Amos very definitely carried the load. Judith attended to Anna and Elizabeth's needs. Joachim seemed quite the patriarch again.

As the harvest moon heralded the passing of another fruitful season, they prepared to celebrate the feast of Booths. It would be their happiest celebration of this time-honored harvest festival that they had enjoyed in years.

Chapter Two

Doves and Eagles

After smoothing the mud in a wooden frame, Joshua shook the residue from his hand. He watched the soggy mess fall as he stood there covered in slime. All the workers around the kiln were naked and sweating. Stooping down, he put his small hands back into the great pool of sludge. With a sucking noise, the oozing mixture bubbled up. Surplus water drained off as he leaned over to mix the mud with straw and dung. The midday sun baked the dirt on his back and buttocks. Joshua had been making bricks all morning, and Joseph had been working beside him methodically. They felt confident that the overseer would be pleased with their efforts. However, the work had definitely been easier in the days before Amos had left. Amos had been more concentrated and was a faster worker than either of them.

Joshua took some mud and sculpted it into a dove. He looked at his creation, then, taking more mud, he created a second dove and sat it on the corner of his wooden mold. The doves faced each other and Joshua made a cooing sound as he animated his creations. He sat cross-legged and began to sculpt a third bird. When the third dove was completed, he leaned back and made more cooing noises. A shadow suddenly cast itself over the scene.

The heavy foot of the Egyptian overseer crushed the little birds into the ooze from which they'd been created. The overseer's heavy hand then cuffed Joshua.

The boy flinched.

"You're not here to play! Get back to your work!" the overseer shouted, pushing Joshua's young body down into the slime.

As he fell forward, Joshua landed face first. The mud completely coated him, and when he looked up he could see Joseph trying to hide a smile.

When the overseer had passed, Joseph stood up and started to laugh raucously, pointing his finger at Joshua in playful admonition.

Joshua got up out of the mud, now laughing, too. His teeth and eyes stood out in stark contrast to the dirt on his face. He wagged his finger at Joseph in return.

"I must not make mud birds!" he said playfully.

Not wishing to cause further trouble, he put his hands back into the mud and started to mix it with straw and dung, pouring it into the molds.

Father and son worked at making bricks until the sun turned golden, heralding evening. Then, released for the day, Joshua and Joseph walked along the path between the tall reeds that led back into the dirt streets of Jewish Alexandria.

Ruth greeted them. She splashed a bucket of water over Joshua to rinse off the pungent crust of mud, and they laughed together. Then she fetched another bucketful for her father.

When they had all washed, it was time for whatever food Miriam had managed to prepare for her working men—bread and a watery soup of corn husks and lentils. James was missing, but the others were too hungry to wait for him. James was always studying late at the synagogue. When he did return home, the soup was gone and the bread cold, but he still found time and energy, as he always did, to teach Joshua a word or two of Hebrew, inscribing the letters for him on a wax tablet.

The Egyptian summer lingered. It was nearing the time of Succot, but the air was still humid and warm. At Miriam's request, Joseph had built a small booth out of dried palm fronds against a wall of their mud-brick house. The incomplete bower had no roof, only walls like a fence. Joshua liked to go and sit in it. The temporary structure attracted him as a hideout. Often, he played there with Ruth. Sometimes, he slept there.

On one such evening, as Joshua lay stretched out on the bench counting the stars in the Egyptian night sky, he fixed his gaze upon a particularly brilliant one that he didn't remember seeing before. *That star's so bright,* he thought. *I wonder if it's the same as the one Mother and Judith tell me about when they speak of my birth?*

As he focused his gaze, he curiously considered those stories. *I wonder who those rich men were who brought us the box of gold? How did they know where we were? Why did they come? Why does Mother say that it was because of me? Why does she tell me that one day I might be a prince?* He thought about that for a moment. *How can I be a prince when I have to work in the mud making bricks?* He chuckled to himself. *James might be a prince one day, but I really don't think I will be.* He stared at the stars. *I'd like to be a healer, though. I'd like to mend the wings of injured doves and the legs of wounded sheep and dogs. I think the animals are really more sensible than we are. They always seem to know what they're doing. They don't seem to mind the heat or even the flies. If I'd been born an animal, I think I would have liked to have been a bird—a soaring dove. Then, I would have been able to fly so high that I could have reached heaven and seen God. He could have used me as a messenger. As a dove, I could warn everyone of bad things that might be about to happen. I could fly to God every time that there was trouble or hardship, and God would tell me what to do to put things right. Wouldn't that be wonderful?*

Joshua dozed off into a light sleep.

He dreamed.

He found himself flying like a bird, but the land over which he flew was not the reed-filled lagoon of the Nile delta or the desert sands beyond the river. The land he saw was a land of gentle hills covered with flowers in blue, red, yellow, and white. There was a lake of clear waters and little villages of clean, white houses. As he flew higher, he saw an opening in the clouds above him and heard a voice calling out to him…

Then he awoke. He couldn't remember what the voice had said.

Joshua rubbed his eyes as he tried to recall his dream, but the sounds of the crickets and bullfrogs from the reed marshes reminded him that he was at home and in no such distant land. The familiar smell of the dung-strewn streets of Alexandria filled his nostrils. Joshua sleepily climbed from the brick bench and went inside the house. But memories of a star-filled heaven offered their echoes, and a dove beat its wings.

* * *

It was a perfect Galilean day. The sun shone brightly as it rose in an azure sky. Spring flowers became a blaze on the hillside as they opened to the morning light. The lake at Magdala was still and calm. Between the cypress trees below the villa of Flavius Septimus, the white rooftops of the Hebrew houses could clearly be seen. Clustered closely in the village, they were in such contrast to the spaciousness of the Roman homes.

"Is everything loaded, Gladius?" Flavius called out to his servant from the yard gate.

Gladius lifted the last two boxes of Copernia's clothing up into the back of his master's high wagon.

"Yes, Master. We're ready to go."

Taking her son Linus by the hand, Copernia stepped out on the porch and crossed the outer courtyard. The boy was dressed in a simple tunic and was carrying a sling.

Flavius closed the gate. He helped his wife climb up into the steep-sided wagon.

Gladius then reached for Linus to lift him up, but the young boy pushed the slave's hands away.

"No!" Linus quipped, "I can do it myself."

As Linus clambered up and over the top board, he triumphantly called out:

"Look, Father! I did it."

Flavius grinned with approval. Even for a boy of nearly nine, the wagon was somewhat of a challenge. The triumphant youth made a face at Gladius as the slave mounted the driving box to sit beside his master.

"You drive the oxen," Flavius commanded his slave.

Gladius took the switch from its clasp and goaded the beasts into cumbersome motion. The great wheels began to turn, scattering loose stones under their grinding weight. Flavius' family started their journey from Magdala to Sepphoris.

Although caravans from Damascus often traveled over these hills taking their goods down to Caesarea, the road up from the lake was still little more than a track. The area of Galilee between the lake and Sepphoris was wild, a place where brigands easily hid and channels of communication were slow.

It was rare that Flavius, as commander of the Sepphoris garrison, had his family at the barracks. But Varus, the Syrian governor, was coming down from Damascus. Flavius felt that it was time for his son to see something of Roman Imperial service. The commander believed Linus' idyllic childhood in the vineyards above Magdala was making the boy soft. Besides, Flavius wanted Varus to meet Linus now that the lad was growing up. The only other time he had presented his son to the governor had been shortly after the boy's birth back in the days of King Herod.

Linus needs to understand the importance of these Roman officials if he's ever going to fulfill my dream and become a future governor in the Levant, he thought. *The sooner all Syria comes under direct Roman rule the better. Herod's worthless son, Archelaus, has no control over the affairs of Judea. There's been chaos in the southern kingdom ever since the pharisaic revolt and King Herod's death. Sooner or later, King Archelaus will be deposed.*

Flavius' thoughts were interrupted as the wagon turned a corner by a rocky outcrop just before the descent into the vale of Esdraelon. A shepherd was driving a large flock of sheep toward them. Gladius had no choice but to pull up the oxen until the sheep passed.

Linus picked a smooth stone from the wagon floor and, aiming his thonged sling, hurled the missile at the backside of one of the bleating sheep. It hit the beast with a thud. The hurt animal bleated vigorously as it jumped in the air, and the surrounding sheep scattered.

The shepherd yelled at the boy in Aramaic.

Copernia turned at the shout, but missed her son's prank.

Linus smiled. He had quickly dropped his sling to the wagon floor and avoided his mother's wrath.

Flavius shook his head, but didn't reprimand his son.

As the shepherd passed with the last of the sheep, he glared at the Roman boy and hit the side of the wagon with his crook.

Gladius beat the oxen, and the wagon rolled on, leaving the sheep and the disgruntled shepherd behind.

They traveled most of the day, and it was evening when they reached Nazareth. Gladius stopped the wagon at the well. He lowered buckets for water to refresh the oxen. A curious crowd from among the villagers gathered around.

A local craftsman took particular interest in the wagon, admiring its unusual construction. Flavius had ordered the vehicle to be built on a rural Tuscan design. It was quite different from the simpler kind of cart commonly found in Galilee. Flavius, always ready to share his common love for Galilee with the local population and show his command of their Aramaic language, called down to the curious onlooker:

"What is your profession, young man?"

"A carpenter, sir. A woodworker."

"Ah! No wonder you show interest in my wagon. What's your name?"

"Amos ben Joseph."

"I doubt, Amos, that you've ever seen a wagon like this?"

"No, sir. It's got larger wheels and a much heavier frame than those that we build here, or even in Alexandria."

"You've been to Alexandria?"

"Yes, sir. I lived in Alexandria for six years."

The other villagers stood back, uncomfortable at Amos' familiarity with the Roman and equally suspicious of the Roman's friendly response. Some, even jeered at Amos as the carpenter continued to touch and admire the wagon.

"They're afraid of us," Linus said in Greek.

"They should respect us, but we don't have to make them fearful." Flavius said. "This man's not afraid. I'm purposely encouraging him to admire our wagon. One day, if we teach them how, they'll build wagons like this for themselves. We have to be their teachers, Linus."

"It feels good sitting above their heads. We're really very important people, aren't we, Father?"

"Yes. We are the masters. Their future is in our hands."

But Flavius' patronizing gesture did little to reduce the tension felt between Roman and Hebrew in Nazareth. The other villagers warned Amos by their guarded response that in Nazareth one didn't fraternize with Romans. Some spat on the ground, muttering their disapproval.

Amos stood back from the wagon.

When Gladius had finished watering the oxen, he passed a bucket of the cool water up to Flavius and his family before remounting the vehicle. With a touch of the switch, he brought the oxen to life and they plodded on.

Leaving Nazareth and their mixed reception behind, the family of Flavius Septimus journeyed the last six miles to Sepphoris.

Flavius felt sad as he reflected on the hostility of the Nazareth peasants. They had turned on Amos, one of their own, because he had been friendly. There didn't have to be this difference between the races, even if as Romans they were in charge. They were all in the one Empire. He felt a great compassion for the Jewish people. In this moment of racial rejection, he daydreamed of Esther. His memories were pleasant, but sitting beside Copernia, they, as usual, became tinged with guilt.

* * *

It was dark by the time they got to Sepphoris. The quarters of the commanding officer at the barracks were comfortable for entertaining, but were poorly designed for family living. Copernia had to share Flavius' rather spartan room with views over the central courtyard. Linus and Gladius were billeted in the Centurions' Tower. Although called a tower, it was really a group of rooms used by the officers of the garrison that stretched back on two floors from behind the facade of this inner court. Here, were the officers' baths, the gymnasium, and the armory.

After a simple meal of fruit and bread, Linus and Gladius were taken across the courtyard to a doorway illuminated by two braziers that led into the armory. Linus was fascinated by the rows of gleaming javelins in the torchlight, and noted the oily smell of cured leather. The officers' dormitories were above. There, they were shown to two trundle beds. Apart from the smell, there was a dark, dank feeling to most of the complex.

Linus complained.

"If you'd been on the march or standing in the sun all day in a cuirass, you'd welcome this," Gladius explained. "In the heat of summer, this dark coolness in the barrack rooms becomes a welcome relief."

In the orange glare of the torchlight, they unpacked what they needed and stowed away their heavy traveling box.

Linus was exhausted and soon slept.

At first light, the officers rose for an early inspection parade. The Centurions' Tower was empty when Gladius and Linus made their way down the dark steps from the upper floor to the baths.

The officers' baths had both a cool pool and a hot bath. In chambers around the baths, the centurions and their fellow officers relaxed and received massages from the slaves of the neighboring gladiatorial school. It was here, in the baths of the Sepphoris garrison, that Gladius had first met Flavius Septimus back in the days when the commanding officer had merely been a centurion. Gladius had regularly massaged Flavius, and the centurion had admired him as a gladiator. It was a natural progression that led to Flavius buying him from the gladiatorial school. He took him to Magdala to be his indentured slave. Later, Gladius became a pedagogue for Linus. Thus, the gladiator had become an integral part of the commanding officer's household. Linus learned a great deal from the slave, especially in the field of martial arts. It was Gladius who had taught him his expertise with his slingshot.

The sulfurous odors of the warm bath, enclosed as it was in a vault on one side, permeated the entire complex.

"You have to go in the warm water first," Gladius said. "After soaking, we will become invigorated by a rinse in the cold pool."

They stripped off their clothing.

Gladius took Linus by the hand and led him down the four steps into the warm, bubbling waters. When they spoke, their voices echoed, bouncing off the walls and barreled ceiling of the enclosed chamber.

"When you were a gladiator, did you bathe every day?" Linus asked.

"When you fight you get very dirty, and your muscles become bruised. We first bathed like this in the hot sulfur bath to relax our muscles. Then, we refreshed ourselves in the cooler water. Sometimes, we'd return to the hot water after we'd had a massage. All gladiators learned to massage each other to mend punished muscles. That's how we knew the way to massage the officers. This sulfur spring here is from the same source as the one in the gladiatorial school."

Linus' eyes gleamed.

"Can we go to the Gladiators' School?"

"I'll take you there later today if you like. It's right next door."

"Teach me to be a gladiator."

"It's too dangerous."

"Not for me," Linus said smugly. "No harm can come to me. I'm the son of the commanding officer."

He looked up at Gladius.

"I want to be a gladiator like you. You didn't get killed."

303

"I was lucky. I nearly got killed many times."

Man and boy immersed themselves in the balmy water.

"We mustn't stay in here too long," Gladius advised. "It's very easy to fall asleep. It's so relaxing. If you do, I'll have to pick you up and throw you into the cold water of the big pool."

Gladius looked over at Linus with a curious smile to test the boy's reaction, but Linus was lying back and soaking in the bubbling bath with his eyes closed. Gladius let him relax for a while, but not for too long.

"Time's up," he shouted, his voice echoing off the walls. "We must go straight into the cold pool."

The two of them climbed from the warm water and crossed the pillared chamber to the big pool. Their wet bodies glistened in the sunlight from the atrium opening above.

"Jump in!" Gladius commanded, when he saw the boy hesitating.

Linus threw himself into the pool and Gladius followed. They swam in the clear water.

When Linus climbed out of the bath, the sun again caught his young naked body, outlining it in contrast to the darkness of the dank rooms behind. Swimming playfully toward him, Gladius splashed cold water in his direction. Linus squealed and ran around the pool shouting. His high-pitched voice echoed through the chamber:

"You can't catch me! Try! Try! You can't catch me!"

Gladius got out and Linus stopped to regain his breath.

At that moment, in the shaft of sunlight, the cool marble of their bodies met, and Gladius lightly kissed the youth on his forehead. Gladius trembled in so doing, but Linus showed no emotion. He simply looked up at Gladius and repeated:

"Teach me to fight like a gladiator."

Later that day, as promised, Gladius took Linus to the Gladiatorial School, and from the Spectators' Gallery they watched several training fights in progress. Two brawny slaves were fighting each other with net and trident. Another pair was in combat with mace and sword. There was the smell of sweat and dust, but without the crowds there was no sense of glory. Even in practice, these trained fighters were undoubtedly inflicting pain on each other, and two of them were bleeding profusely. The sight of blood, however, didn't seem to deter Linus.

"After the fight, they'll be the best of friends," the ex-gladiator explained. "They'll enjoy the baths and have a good massage. The surface wounds will quickly heal in response to the oils and treatment."

One of the fighting gladiators caught his opponent in his net. The man struggled to get free, but only wrapped himself further in the mesh. His opponent held up his trident like a javelin and advanced on the tangled net. In a mock gesture of victory, he stood over his opponent, his trident still poised for thrust. He grinned and looked up at the Spectators' Gallery. Gladius grinned back and turned his thumb down. The triumphant gladiator jabbed the trident toward his victim.

Linus gasped.

The struggling man screamed out in genuine fear, but the attacker stopped the thrust within inches of his opponent's chest. He raised the trident again and stabbed it into the earthen floor. The three spikes sank into the packed dust, and the handle quivered. The successful gladiator then set about freeing his friend from the net. He helped him up and put his arm around him. In the closed acoustics of the arena, Gladius and Linus could hear their conversation clearly.

"You should never have taken your eyes off me, my friend. That was your mistake."

The victor then pointed up at the Spectators' Gallery.

"If this had been at the games and those two up there had been our guests, you'd now be dead."

The two gladiators embraced each other and picked up their weapons. They walked out of the arena to enjoy the baths and a massage.

Linus's eyes were wide.

"In a real fight that man would have been killed. Did you always fight to the death?" he asked Gladius.

"Often. I've long since lost count of how many times. I was lucky. I was never pitched against the wild beasts. They usually only put the real criminals in the arena with the beasts."

"You mean lions and wolves?"

"Yes, Linus. Lions and wolves and blood-hungry hounds! I believe, in Egypt they even use crocodiles, although I've never seen those ferocious beasts except on Caesar's coins. They keep some beasts here in Sepphoris for the spectator games. They'll probably use them for the execution of criminals when the governor of Syria arrives."

"When does Father expect the governor?"

"Tomorrow, I think."

Together, the young master and slave made their way down the wooden steps from the Spectators' Gallery into the dark maze of passageways leading through the Gladiatorial School. Here and there, doorways led off to rooms where the weary fighters received their massage therapy or worked to improve on their physical condition.

"What happens if a criminal wins and actually kills a wild beast?" Linus asked.

"It's rare. Usually the prisoners are sent into the arena unarmed. They have to fight with their bare hands. Most of them run for their lives, until the beasts catch up with them. There are occasions when they do send real gladiators into the arena to fight with the beasts. If so, they carry a sword or at least a dagger. A gladiator who wins against the beasts is somewhat of a hero and sometimes is granted freedom from gladiatorial service."

"Are all gladiators slaves?"

"Most of them, but there are many who win respect and freedom from their exploits in the arena. After all, your father bought me from the Gladiatorial School after he had admired my skills."

"Do you ever miss the excitement of being a gladiator?"

"Sometimes. But you must remember that we lose people we like, and are occasionally forced to kill our best friends, all on the wishes and command of those who are watching. We live constantly in danger of being killed ourselves. It could have happened to me."

"I'm glad you weren't killed," Linus said.

Gladius put an arm around the boy's shoulders. They walked out of the Gladiatorial School back to the barracks.

* * *

The next day, Linus rode a small horse beside his father as they went out to greet the Syrian governor. In honor of the occasion, Flavius Septimus was dressed in his most splendid uniform, the gold clasp and great plumes of his helmet matching the bright scarlet of his cloak and the gilt of his breastplate. When Governor Varus reached Sepphoris at the head of his guards, he greeted Flavius with a customary formal salutation. He softened when he saw Linus, however, and winked at the boy. The three of them then rode side by side into the barracks, with the governor's entourage following.

Flavius looked up at the balcony of his quarters. Copernia was smiling with pride when she saw her son, dressed in his very best tunic, riding flawlessly beside his father and the governor. They dismounted in front of the steps leading into the vestibule. Copernia blew him a kiss and went inside to set her hair ribbons and adjust her bodice.

Varus, Flavius, and Linus crossed the dark hallway.

The governor patted Linus on the shoulder as they mounted the stairs.

"You're a fine horseman, young man," he said

Flavius beamed at his son with pride.

"Well done, you Tuscan tiger!" he acknowledged.

The governor paused in front of a marble bust of his likeness.

"I never thought I would have such a distinguished look as is displayed here, Flavius Septimus. I truly believe this bust resembles Augustus Caesar more than me. I think they model all these official sculptures on the Emperor."

"Don't belittle yourself, sir," Flavius said. "The bust shows a fine likeness worthy of the master of the Levant—our governor in Syria."

The two leaders and her young son reached the top of the stairs and entered the brighter light of the living quarters. Copernia bowed gracefully.

Varus nodded in response.

Then they relaxed, and the appearance of official business passed as both men removed their helmets and cloaks. Copernia left to fetch a flagon of wine and goblets.

"What news do you bring us from Damascus and Antioch?" Flavius asked as they seated themselves.

"Flavius Septimus, I know of your keen interest in the affairs of the Levant. I believe your dream may become true very soon. The incompetent rule of Archelaus in Jerusalem will be terminated."

Flavius' eyes lit up.

"I've word from Augustus Caesar himself," continued the governor, "that he thinks it will be wise to send a prefect out to rule in Judea."

"A prefect?"

Varus picked up his concern. "A prefect would of course be directly under my command as supreme governor of all the Syrian Province. In reality, Flavius, that will bring Judea, Samaria and Galilee under direct rule. Your tetrarchs up here have no judicial power in Roman law. They only judge their own people's affairs."

Copernia returned with the beverage. She poured the cool wine into the goblets.

"What will be the future of Philip and Antipas, then?" Flavius asked as he took his goblet.

Varus smiled.

"Flavius, do they govern in Galilee, or do you?"

They raised their goblets together.

"They govern in name only, sir. As you say, they're responsible for internal Jewish affairs, but I'm the real administrator."

The two soldiers quaffed their thirst.

"Good, Flavius. You're my man here. You're the man I'll most rely on to advise the prefect when he's appointed. You have the most Jewish experience of any of us. Our officers in Sepphoris, Sebaste, and Jerusalem will be in charge. Forget the tetrarchs. They mean nothing to Caesar. They're only titular kings out of Caesar's respect for their late father. There will never be a united Jewish kingdom again. Eventually, their land will all be annexed to Rome."

Linus became bored with this political discussion. He ran over to his mother and pulled at her dress. Copernia brushed him aside. She knew this news was important to her husband and their ambitions for Linus.

"But meanwhile, what of Archelaus?" asked Flavius, putting down his goblet.

Varus drank again, then turned a serious face toward Flavius.

"As I said, Archelaus will be removed. He's not fit to govern. Mark my words, Flavius, you'll see this change within the year. It's the only way we can restore law and order to this disturbed province and hold the Jewish revolt."

Flavius caught concern in Copernia's eye.

"Do you really believe that the Jews will continue to rebel?" he asked the governor.

"Hold on to Sepphoris, Flavius. The Hebrew underground is still strong in Galilee. Be prepared for revolt here, too. Despite Archelaus and his inability to rule, there are still deep loyalties to the Herodians.

When the incompetent Archelaus is removed, we can expect resistance and rebellion."

Flavius got up and began to pace. Turning to the governor, he finally said:

"But there's been peace in Galilee for nine years. There's not been serious rebellion here since the attack on the garrison when Quirinius was governor. I was away at the time and returned to see the stretched-out bodies of those crucified by my predecessor. Over one hundred of the Hebrew zealots were put to death, including all the principal leaders. The whole nationalist movement was crushed."

"Yes, Flavius. The garrison did well. But like the Hydra's head, rebellion grows again."

Varus drained his goblet, then got up and strolled to the window. He looked out at the distant blue range of mountains to the north.

"These peaceful hills will harbor further bloodshed. Just be prepared!" he warned.

Looking around, he saw that both Flavius and Copernia were intently staring at him. He turned the empty goblet in his fingers.

"The garrison should remain alert," he said. "We cannot relax until such time as we establish our Roman government firmly over these people."

Flavius glanced at Copernia again with a look that was meant to reassure her. This was, after all, a mixture of good and bad news. There might be some immediate danger haunting their peaceful world, but the final annexing of the land of the Jews to Rome was certainly a lot closer. The end of the Herodians and the establishment of permanent, direct Roman rule had always been the dream Flavius had shared many times with Copernia. Their hopes for Linus, too, were dependent on such political changes.

Flavius smiled.

"Sir, tomorrow we'll celebrate your arrival. I've requested gladiatorial games at the arena, including fights between condemned criminals and our wild beasts. It should be a good spectacle."

Linus, omitted from the adult conversation, had been watching the plumes of his father's and the governor's helmets on the table where they had left them. They were waving in the breeze that was coming in from the open balcony. He looked up at the mention of the games. Excitement spread across his face.

"Will I be able to come with you?" he asked.

"Of course, my son. It's part of your education. Gladius can come with us. He'll be able to explain everything to you."

Linus leaped from his chair.

"Gladius already has. We watched them practice," he shouted triumphantly. "Can I go and tell Gladius?"

"Go," Flavius said.

Copernia shook her head.

"He's still too young. I really don't think he should watch the beasts."

"Nonsense, my dear. Linus is growing soft on the easy life at the villa. He needs to be blooded."

"Whatever you say, Flavius Septimus," Copernia said politely but stubbornly.

She then excused herself on the pretense of domestic duties, and the two Roman officials sat down to discuss more informal matters of Galilee.

* * *

A bright and sunny spring morning dawned the next day, and Linus was far too excited to notice Gladius' overtures of affection as they swam in the baths. Today, he was going to see the real gladiators fight.

The morning dragged on as Varus made rounds of inspection. Even Gladius and Linus were asked to present themselves with the centurions of their dormitory. Breastplates were gleaming, swords and daggers sharpened, helmets polished, and plumes feathered, as the governor passed through. Seeing Varus to be satisfied with the inspection, Flavius then declared the already-known reward that gladiatorial games would be held in the neighboring arena that afternoon.

The entire barracks, along with much of the Roman population of Sepphoris, filled the arena for the games. The Hebrew artisans were noticeably absent, but a few traveling merchants and the occasional Hellenist Jew could be found in the better seats. Fresh sawdust had been strewn on the clay bed of the arena, and wooden boards were fitted around the perimeter, protecting the first tier of seats from the pit. The boards were scrubbed and clean, giving the arena an appearance of innocence. Flags and pennants fluttered from the masts above the highest tier. On either side of the Spectators' Gallery—the area reserved for dignitaries and their guests—the eagles and standards of the Syrian Legion glinted in the sunlight.

There was a cheer from the crowd as the governor's party emerged from the dark of the stairway to enter the gallery. Seats with red velvet drapes were reserved for Varus, Flavius, Copernia, and the master of the Gladiatorial School. Linus, Gladius, and other members of the governor's party, along with guests of the gladiatorial master, took their positions on the gleaming, white marble stepped seats above the chairs. From the gallery they could all look down clearly into the arena.

In a much smaller box, opposite the Spectators' Gallery, four trumpeters blasted a fanfare to mark the start of the preliminaries. A gate in the boards below opened up and the gladiators, their bodies glistening with oil, proudly marched into the arena. They carried their arms—maces, daggers, nets, and tridents—and they were presented in pairs before the governor.

"How many will be killed today?" Linus asked Gladius, leaning forward, his eyes naively bright.

"That depends entirely on how well they fight and on the clemency of the governor and your father."

The performance began with eight pairs of gladiators fighting in the arena at the same time. These fights were not to the death, but were put on to exercise the gladiators' combat skills, acknowledging the high standards of the Sepphoris school. The master of the Gladiatorial School waited for the approval of the governor to signal the start of the death fights.

At length, Varus turned to him.

"They fight well, sir. Begin the games," he ordered.

The master signaled to the trumpeters.

When the trumpets blared a second time, the gladiators ceased to fight. They stood at attention, sweat now mixed with body oils, some bloodied, scarlet in the sun. They acknowledged the governor and left the arena.

Gladius looked down to see the first sign of real action.

"Look, Linus! Can you see that wagon with the cage?"

"You mean just coming out now?"

"Yes! The wagon cage pulled by those men. It contains the criminals. Let's see, I think there are six in there."

Linus' eyes widened.

"The ones that will fight with the beasts?"

"That's right! They're condemned to die anyway, and will almost certainly die unless through great skill and courage they defeat the beasts. But remember, Linus, those prisoners haven't been trained to fight like the gladiators, and they're usually unarmed."

"They really don't stand a chance then?"

"That's right, but then they know their fate. They're only here to die."

Linus looked down thoughtfully at the caged wagon and the doomed men.

"What did they do wrong?"

"I've no idea. They probably killed an innocent civilian and were referred to the gladiatorial school by the courts of the tetrarch Antipas."

"What's a tetrarch? Father was talking about them yesterday," Linus asked, screwing up his eyes.

"A minor king, I suppose. Antipas is the Jewish king in Galilee. He's really not very important, or so your father always says. All the important decisions around here are made by men like your father and the Syrian governor."

"But isn't a king more important than a governor?"

"Not here," was all Gladius could reply, bored by Linus' questions, especially in as much as he really didn't know the answers.

The caged men were led away, having merely been paraded to whet the appetites of the spectators.

When the trumpets blasted again, two gladiators strode to the center of the arena. Cheers greeted their entrance. It was to be a fight with nets and tridents.

With feigned attempts at thrusts and throws, the two gladiators played the crowd, for some time moving all around the arena kicking up the sawdust, but successfully avoiding death play. The crowd began to jeer. At the sound, one of the gladiators looked up.

"Gladius!" Linus shouted. "The other man will get him, just like they said yesterday!"

Copernia turned around and beckoned Linus to keep his voice down.

The net was thrown. It caught the erring gladiator. He tripped and fell in its mesh. His opponent moved in with his trident raised. The smitten gladiator struggled out from under the net. With a quick upward thrust, he slashed the arm that held the menacing fork. The surprised attacker dropped the trident with a thud. The two fighters fell into grappling. The crowd cheered the change of fortune. The close fighting was fierce. Both men now held daggers. They were near enough to each other to inflict fatal blows. They rolled in the sawdust as their daggers flashed. They kicked viciously at each other as they wrestled, and in their writhing rolled toward the net that had so nearly given victory a short while before. As the one lost his dagger, so the other became caught in the net. It gave the unarmed gladiator a moment to reach out for the nearby trident. He raised the pronged fork and thrust it toward his trapped opponent. The man struggled in the net, his left arm now weak from the severe wound that he'd received. There was a deafening roar from the excited crowd.

"He's going to kill him!" Linus shouted.

The struggling gladiator, still caught in the net, crawled and half raised himself in a superhuman effort, only to meet the sharp barbs of the trident as it grazed his chest and pinned at his throat. He lay back to avoid the thrust and felt his opponent's foot land heavily on his belly. As the gladiator kicked his feet, he only became more entangled. Above them in the Spectators' Gallery, the governor consulted with the commanding officer and the gladiatorial master. The governor then turned and raised his thumbs upward. The crowd mixed cheers with boos, but the gladiator knew that his life had been spared.

There was a blast on the trumpets that signaled the end of the bout, and the apparent victor withdrew his weapon to the acclaim of the crowd. He pulled at the net and freed his struggling friend. They stood together, acknowledged the governor, and then retreated into the dark caverns of the Gladiatorial School.

"Lucky for him," said Gladius, as Linus sat in silence, pouting.

"Why didn't he kill him?" Linus asked.

"Because they had an even fight. Both of them fought well, and the final victory was won more through a lucky accident than skill."

"You mean when the gladiator who was wounded got caught in the net?"

"Exactly. The other gladiator had already lost his dagger and in combat probably would have lost the fight but for that net getting in the way. It was a fair decision. He didn't really deserve to win, but unquestionably he was the victor. That's why the governor and your father showed mercy."

In the second bout, a gladiator caught in the net had no chance. He was trapped and lay struggling as the poised trident threatened him.

The crowd was ready for blood, shouting down expressions of their disappointment.

"Kill him!" some yelled, while others chanted the traditional: "To death!"

The governor peered down into the arena while Flavius and the gladiatorial master exchanged opinions.

"He was never a good fighter," the master said. "He's a Gaul sent down here from the slave school in Antioch. I can't do much with him. He has poor timing."

Flavius nodded at the governor, who turned his thumbs down. The crowd roared with excitement. The winning gladiator thrust his trident deep into his opponent's thorax.

Blood spurted and there was a strangled cry of death from the smitten Gaul. His lungs punctured and his heart pierced, the man breathed his last. His opponent stood and acknowledged the spectators' cheers while two gladiatorial slaves raced out into the arena and dragged away the dead man's corpse, leaving a trail through the sawdust.

"They'll feed his flesh to the beasts," Gladius said to Linus. "Fresh blood makes them more ferocious!"

Three more fights followed. Two, fine performances with daggers and shields, didn't end in death, but the third one did. Using clubs and daggers, the victor successfully knocked his opponent to the ground, rendering him unconscious. He held his dagger at the man's throat and awaited a decision from the Spectators' Gallery. His opponent regained consciousness. The signal was thumbs down. The sun caught the glint of the dagger as it opened the victim's gullet. The sawdust soaked up the man's blood, and his corpse was swiftly removed.

"Are we going to see the animals fight now?" Linus asked.

"I expect so. Five gladiatorial fights is about the usual," Gladius said.

The trumpets blared, and a large black bear was let out into the arena.

"A black bear!" Gladius exclaimed. "They're fierce!"

"The bear doesn't look fierce," Linus said.

"Not yet, but he soon will be. Watch now. See…they're letting in two javelin throwers. They'll enrage the bear before poisoning the beast."

The javelin throwers came in from two different entrances, each carrying three javelins. Stalking the docile bear, they simultaneously hurled their weapons at the animal. The bear roared as the sharp and poisoned points ripped into its flesh. Quickly, the swift gladiators raised second javelins and thrust them at the enraged bear, while they themselves retreated. One javelin merely grazed the bear's back, but the other pierced the beast's chest. With a massive swipe of a forepaw, the bear knocked the javelin away, revealing the bleeding gash in its glossy coat. Two more javelins hurtled through the air, stabbing the bear on one side. Then the two javelin throwers, fleet of foot, leaped through one of the gateways that was swiftly barred behind them. The bear, now maddened to fury, raced around the arena in obvious pain.

On the far side, another gate opened. Two naked and defenseless prisoners were pushed out. The men stood there trembling. The bear spotted them and lumbered toward them.

"The bear's going to eat those men!" yelled Linus.

"That's right," Gladius agreed. "They haven't got a chance."

Linus looked away. He caught his mother's eye.

"I don't think you should be watching this," Copernia said. "Let me take you home."

Flavius put out his arm in front of her.

"It's good for him," he said. "It will toughen him up."

Copernia looked away from the arena in fearful anticipation and disgust as the great black bear struck the first of the prisoners. One lash with his paw was enough. The prisoner fell. The bear lacerated his flesh. Amidst its victim's screams, the beast mauled on one of his arms. The bear dragged his quarry halfway around the arena, then severed the arm and tore at the man's entrails. Meanwhile, the other condemned man was jumping with energy borne of madness to try to reach the safety of the top of the paling. In a maniacal effort, he managed to get one hand secure, but the enthusiastic spectators kicked it away. The prisoner fell back down to the sawdust of the arena. His resulting cry caught the bear's attention. Leaving its mauled and now dead victim center stage, the beast charged toward the other man as he struggled back on his feet. Momentarily, the prisoner outwitted the bear and raced to the far side of the arena. The bear charged after him. Ultimately, the prisoner's agility couldn't match the fury of the wounded beast. The animal caught him and mauled him. By the time the bear had finished devouring the flesh of his victims, they were beyond human recognition—bloodied bone and offal.

"This is barbaric. Flavius, I'm going to vomit," Copernia said. "Linus, I'm taking you home."

Linus looked at his father.

"Take her home!" Flavius called up to Gladius.

"Linus! Come and sit beside me."

Gladius left the Spectators' Gallery with Copernia, who held her sleeve to her mouth suppressing her urge to gag.

In the arena, the executions continued.

The four remaining criminals were released. They were swiftly followed by a pack of wolves. Three of the ravenous beasts caught one of the terrified men. They savaged him brutally. His right arm was severed from his body as the man helplessly flailed at them. Pulled down by the wolves, the man struggled as gaping jaws tore at him. Soon unconscious, he was left to die. The wolves moved on to the other victims. The bear, meanwhile, weakened by the poison, but still infuriated by its wounds, made a mad dash at the escaping men. While the wolves barked ferociously, the crowd cheered. The bear attacked the next victim. The mad beast struck him to the ground and trampled him to death. The two remaining prisoners did their best to remain alive, drawing out each last second before the end. There was no escape. The wolves savaged the men. They were left ripped and bleeding. The wolves then went on to attack the ailing bear.

The poison had obviously blurred the bear's vision and reflexes. The ravenous wolves, fresh and thirsty for more blood, attacked the unfortunate animal from all sides. The beast made a noble stand. One wolf went yelping into the air. Two others then leaped at the bear's throat.

Within seconds, losing consciousness, the bear fell to the ground, glossy coat caked in blood and sawdust.

"Father, they're going to eat him up right in front of us!" exclaimed Linus, his eyes as big as silver denarii.

"I don't think so," Flavius replied.

The wolves left the bear's corpse to gnaw at the more succulent flesh of the four dying men.

"The bear was a decoy. These men were sent in the arena to die. They were condemned. The wolves are trained to eat human flesh."

"I feel sick in my stomach, Father," Linus said, looking up hesitantly.

"Then, you must control it. I think it's probably over now. The execution of criminals is usually the end."

The gates opened and the wolves dragged their meat from the arena. Skilled animal trainers, wielding whips, ushered them out.

The governor stood to acknowledge the crowd.

The crowd cheered, satisfied with the afternoon's gore.

After the governor and his party left, the stands began to empty.

Evening cast its long dark shadows over the deserted arena. Hot stone and rows of seats, cooled in the silence, as the moon hung over the edge of cloud.

* * *

The first really hot days of the Egyptian summer struck Alexandria. A muggy, oppressive heat hung over the swamps and reed ponds of the Nile Delta. Often the city escaped the worst of the humidity because of cooling winds blowing in from the Great Sea, but for a few days these winds had not blown.

Joshua returned home from the brick kilns.

After a supper of flat bread and figs, he sat outside on the wall bench with his mother.

"Mother," he said, "are you ever going to tell me who was my real father?"

His words carried no impatience, no anger.

Miriam looked at Joshua. At times like this, he seemed older—more mature.

"Joshua, you don't have a real father. Gabriel, my guardian angel, was your father."

Joshua laughed.

"How could an angel be my father?" he retorted.

Miriam flushed.

"There was a man named Gabriel, too."

"Was he my father?" Joshua shifted his hard body on the wall bench. "Nobody will believe me if I say an angel was my father. The other boys laugh at me. They know Joseph isn't my father."

"A man named Gabriel was the High Priest's first choice for me," she answered. "I met him before I met Joseph."

"Why did you marry Joseph then, Mother? Why didn't you marry Gabriel?"

Miriam looked away. She stared at the Egyptian sky.

"I fell in love with Joseph," she said simply. "Joseph's been a better father to you than Gabriel could ever have been. One day, Joshua, you'll fall in love, too. I was lucky. I really did fall in love with Joseph. It could have been different, because I wasn't really free to choose."

"Why?"

"Because I was brought up at the Temple in Jerusalem as one of the virgins."

"Did that mean you couldn't choose whom you wanted to marry?"

"It was the High Priest's responsibility to find husbands for all of us who were Temple virgins. We hardly knew our own families. I only knew your grandparents for four years, and I can hardly remember them."

Joshua nodded.

"I've never met my grandparents. Why don't they ever come here?"

A swarm of flies buzzed around them.

"What's Nazareth like?" the boy asked.

"I don't know, Joshua, I never lived with them there. I was always in Jerusalem."

Miriam waved her hand to distract the flies.

"According to Judith, Galilee is a beautiful, green place, far away from this oppressive heat and all these irritating insects."

"And that's where Amos and Judith have gone?"

"Yes, Joshua," Miriam answered. "One day we'll go back. We'll take you home to my family."

"If we go, will James and Ruth come with us?"

"Yes, of course they will. We're a family. We'll all stay together."

She watched as the flies gradually dispersed in the cooler evening air. It felt better.

"I think it's time to sleep," Miriam said. "That's enough questions for now. Let's stay up on the roof tonight. It's so hard to sleep in the house when it's this hot."

They went in and collected their pallets. Miriam took Ruth and Joshua up on the roof, while James and Joseph remained talking in the dim light of an oil lamp. When the children were settled, she kissed them both lightly on the forehead. As she bent over Joshua, he gazed up into her eyes with that same quizzical look of concern that he had shown all evening.

"You still haven't told me anything about Gabriel," he said. "Was he my real father?"

Miriam put her hand lightly on the boy's shoulder.

"I will. One day you'll meet the only Gabriel who really matters. One day, Joshua, you'll understand. That Gabriel will always be with us. He's our strength when we feel weak; he's our joy when we are happy and our hope when we're sad. He's up there in the stars above us."

Miriam looked up at the heavens and the rising moon.

"Look! Joshua! He's there!" she said, as she pointed to the crescent in the sky.

The boy smiled. He didn't really understand what she was saying, and she hadn't answered his question, but he could appreciate the beauty of the moon.

"It's time to sleep," his mother whispered.

The children slept easily, but Miriam found it hard to take her mind off Joshua's penetrating questions into the inner secrets of her life. She tossed and turned on the uncomfortable pallet as she thought of Gabriel.

The memory caused a stab of pain as she turned on the straw mattress in the muggy heat. Remorse churned as the memories flooded back. James had told her that a man named Gabriel had been put to death with the High Priest over a Temple riot in Jerusalem that had embarrassed King Herod. She always felt in her heart that this must have been him. He had obviously been close to Zechariah, and somehow they had both been drawn into some political Temple intrigue. Gabriel was probably the one who had caused Zechariah's downfall.

Guilt pains gripped her as she looked at Joshua asleep on his pallet. In his innocence, he just wanted to know the truth, but how could she tell him something so horrid?

Gabriel just might be his father, she thought. *I don't think so, but Joseph always says that the rape could have brought about my pregnancy. I'd much rather believe the angels, though. They assured me my child was to be a son of God. They chose his name. Besides, why don't I get pregnant with Joseph? We've tried. I don't seem to be able to have children. Then, what about the rich men who came to the cave? They knew Joshua was special. They called him the 'Prince of Peace'. We have the box of gold to prove it. No, my child was given to me by God. My angel Gabriel told me in the moonbeams. It was magical. God was all around me. I can't deny that. That was the truth.*

A calmness came over Miriam as she lay there on the roof, listening to the bullfrogs and crickets. Under the vast canopy of stars, she was finally lulled into sleep.

* * *

Joshua's curiosity about his birth continued on successive evenings in Alexandria.

"I miss Judith," he confessed to his mother one hot and humid night as they sat on the wall bench. "She used to share many stories with me."

He looked up at Miriam.

"But I'd rather hear them from you," he said.

Miriam kissed her son on the forehead.

"I miss Judith, too," she whispered. "Maybe I can tell you more. You're certainly old enough now to know a little bit about some of the extraordinary things that happened at the time you were born."

"Mother," Joshua said slowly, examining some work-raw skin on his hand, "Judith always said that we had to come to Egypt because the king wanted to kill us."

He looked up at her again.

"Is that true? Why would they want to kill us? We're not important people."

"The king thought so," Miriam said, seeking a way to explain that awkward and dangerous time. "He wanted to kill us. Remember what James and Amos told us?"

"You mean about the babies being thrown down the well?"

"Yes. All the baby boys in Bethlehem, where we lived, were apparently murdered by the king's soldiers."

"So, you mean if I'd still been there I'd have been killed, too?"

"That's why the old High Priest Simeon wanted us to leave Judea."

"Who was Simeon?"

"He performed your circumcision and blessed you the time that we took you to the Temple in Jerusalem."

"You mean he cut my pee-pee to make me a Jew?"

"Joshua!"

"Well, that's what Amos told me. That's what makes us Jews. Other boys at the brick kilns aren't the same."

Miriam blushed.

"Yes. It is part of our tradition."

The frogs and crickets that always accompanied these hot nights with their evening serenade filled the air with their chorus. Miriam dabbed the perspiration from her neck.

"But why did the king want to kill us?" Joshua asked again with his usual persistence in his quest for the truth.

"I don't know, Joshua. We just learned that we were in danger, and Joseph wanted to protect us by taking us away. Maybe it had something to do with the High Priest's execution."

"Which High Priest? Simeon?"

"No, Joshua," she said firmly. "His name was Zechariah. He was my guardian at the Temple, and he was also married to your grandmother's sister. We were all related through marriage."

"Is that why the king wanted to kill us...because we were related to the High Priest?"

"No, Joshua. I don't think so. But Simeon seemed to think we were in danger after they'd killed Zechariah."

Even after all these years, Miriam found it hard to talk about Zechariah's death. Zechariah had been the closest person to her throughout her childhood, and Elizabeth, his wife, had prepared her for her married life with Joseph. She became silent and sad.

Joshua looked at her intently.

"Judith said you were given to God as a child. She also said that I was a gift from God to you."

Miriam was a little startled hearing this from her son.

"Many people said that, Joshua. It's hard for me to understand and even harder for me to explain. Angel Gabriel told me you were God's child and that you'd grow up to be special, some sort of a leader."

"Was this Gabriel my real father, then, Mother?" Joshua pushed. "You never finished telling me."

"My angel Gabriel? I think so, Joshua," Miriam replied, reaching for the lad and putting an arm around his shoulder.

She drew him to her.

"How can I explain the invisible?" his mother continued. "Sometimes, I see God in all the beauty of nature—in the butterflies and flowers, in the rustling of the trees and the glow of the moonlight. God is everywhere, Joshua, and sometimes, he talks to us through the beautiful things around us. God talked to Abraham through nature. Moses was led by natural wonders. When God sends us his angels, they appear in the beauty around us. That's how they talk to us. That's when Gabriel talks to me, and sometimes, when I feel the angels near me, I see things and hear things that I can't explain. It's like a dream. That's when I hear Gabriel's voice."

"Gabriel is really God talking?" Joshua observed with interest.

"Yes, Joshua! Yes!"

Miriam held her son closer to her.

"You see the moon up above us there?" she said, pointing at the growing orb in the celestial Egyptian night. "Look at his face smiling at us. Every day he's there to look after us. Whatever we do and wherever we go, the moon still looks down on us. Can you imagine God's face there in the moon?"

Joshua looked at the moon and squinted with one eye.

"I can see a face in the shadows. The moon really does have a face. He looks like Joseph when I fall in the mud at the brick kilns. It always makes him laugh. The man in the moon's laughing. Does that mean God's laughing?"

"Maybe Joshua, but the more you look at it, the more real that face becomes. If you shut your eyes and pray, you might hear the voice of God calling to you."

Joshua screwed up his eyes.

"I'm praying, Mother. I'm praying!"

"So am I, Joshua. Once, when I was praying in the moonlight at the House of the Virgins, the trees caused the moonlight to flicker. The shafts of moonlight fell all around me, and I felt like I could touch the moon. Then, I heard him, Joshua…I heard Gabriel, my messenger from God, speak to me."

Joshua was still tense with his eyes screwed up.

"What did Gabriel say, Mother?"

"That's when he told me I'd have a baby and that you would be my son. Trembling in the moonlight, I felt this strange power. I heard a voice crying out to me. It told me I would have a child who would be a son of God. You are that child, Joshua. The voice told me you'd be a 'Prince of Peace' and that you'd be a mighty ruler."

Joshua opened his eyes. Relaxing again, he looked at his mother. Tears were running down her cheeks with the emotion of the moment.

"But I'm not a prince, Mother," he said.

"No. Joshua, you're not a prince, nor am I a princess. You're God's prince, though. God's chosen you for some great purpose, and you can rest assured that it'll be more than making mud-bricks at the kiln. I don't understand what God has in mind for you, but I do know that God gave you to me. That was the most precious gift I could ever receive."

Miriam kissed Joshua. He could feel the warmth of her tears and their salt on her cheeks.

"Joshua, I can't tell you who was your father. I'm not sure myself. Something terrible happened to me before you were born."

She turned away momentarily as if to confirm their privacy.

"It takes a man and a woman joined together in love to make a baby. It's like the animals. You've seen the dogs in the street. In human love, babies are made the same way as the puppies. But the man cannot really be a father unless there is true love between that man and the woman. That wasn't the case with that man named Gabriel, whom the High Priest wanted me to marry. He forced himself on me before I was ready for him and destroyed all hope of us living a happy life together. I don't know whether he made me have you as my baby. I never will know. I never saw him after that."

Miriam held Joshua tighter as fresh tears welled.

"Promise me you won't tell anyone what I've just told you," she said, stroking his hair, "not even Ruth. To me, Angel Gabriel is your father, the angel of the Lord, a messenger from God. So, God is your true father, Joshua."

Silently, they both stared up at the moon.

"God is the father of us all," Miriam continued as she regained her composure. "Perhaps it really doesn't matter who our actual father is, if we allow God to be the father. But you're special, Joshua. An angel brought you to me from God—your Father. Never forget that. You are a son of God."

"Those rich men must have thought I was special to give us that gold."

"They said they knew about us because of a prophecy in the Scriptures."

"Judith used to tell me they came because of the star."

Miriam nodded.

"I think the star might have had something to do with it. It was a very bright star with a trail. You were born when it was directly overhead."

Joshua continued to gaze at the stars and the moon in the Egyptian night sky as his mother continued her reminiscence.

"Both the High Priests, Zechariah and Simeon, thought it had something to do with who you are. Those rich men said they had journeyed under that star for several weeks. They believed it led them to us. But the prophecy in the Scriptures is interesting. Old Simeon also quoted Scripture when we took you to the Temple. He believed the Scriptures tell of your birth."

"Do they?" Joshua said, his eyes still fixed intently on the night sky.

"I asked James about that once."

"What did he say?"

"He said he'd let me know. Later, he found the same passage about the 'Prince of Peace' being born to a virgin. Those rich merchants thought they'd found the 'Prince of Peace' when they came. That's why they gave us the gold. It's for you."

"Then, some people do expect me to be a prince," Joshua said. "I want to be a rabbi. Can a rabbi be a prince, or even a prophet?"

"A prophet for our times, perhaps...Joshua the 'Prince of Peace.'"

Joshua returned his attention from the sky to his mother.

"Do you believe that, Mother? James is more likely to be a great rabbi than me. He reads and writes in Hebrew, Aramaic, and Greek!"

Miriam looked at her son's face in the pale moonlight.

"James is a great scholar, but he's also your teacher. You keep studying with James and maybe you'll learn as much as he has. You'll be a great prophet. Remember that apart from the rich merchants who visited us in the cave, my angel Gabriel told me you'll be a ruler and a leader of our people that night in the Temple garden. Gabriel has taken care of me all my life. Gabriel will also take care of you."

They heard footsteps.

Ruth, who'd been trying to sleep in the house, joined them.

"Can we sleep on the roof again tonight?" she said, heading for the stone steps on the side of the house. "It's just too hot inside."

A breeze came up off the Great Sea, and it felt good.

* * *

Joshua's reading and writing improved a lot after James started taking him to the Alexandrine Synagogue School. He could read some Greek now as well as basic Hebrew and Aramaic. He also had a great capacity to remember the interpretations of the Scripture stories that were passed on to him by the scribes. James could see that his pupil was blossoming, so he thought it would be better for Joshua to work permanently in the spiritual atmosphere of the Great Synagogue rather than wasting his time and talents in the slime and mud of the brick kilns. In the papyrus factory, there were many Jewish boys about Joshua's age. He could start there.

Joseph wasn't so sure that James was right. A pittance though their wages were for slaving in the brick kilns, they were better than nothing. With Amos now gone, he would have to carry the entire burden of providing for his family. But James usually got his way. Joseph let Joshua go.

"Making scrolls for writing out the Scriptures is going to be much more important work than making bricks," Joshua said to James excitedly as they prepared to leave the house for the Great Synagogue. "But how did you always manage to escape working in the brick kilns? Amos had to do it just like Joseph and me. In fact, he often complained that he had to go and you didn't."

"Amos has never understood the importance of my work," James replied. "He's not a very spiritual person, but you are. That's why I like taking you to the synagogue. You're going to make a great rabbi one day, Joshua."

They set off together. As they made their way from the fringe of the city, the traffic got busier and the hustle and bustle became more exciting.

Close to the Great Synagogue, the dusty dirt streets gave way to long, paved avenues. The vast stone edifices of the synagogue complex were built in the Ptolemaic style. The main building was fronted with a simple Hellenistic facade.

Alexandria's synagogue was the real hub and focal point of the whole Jewish quarter. It housed a library second only to the Great Library down by the harbor. Around the Synagogue Library stood a whole series of buildings for the schools of the scholars and scribes.

Before entering the main building, James and Joshua washed their feet and arms in the courtyard pool and covered their heads with the mantels provided as was tradition and custom. Then, they entered through the great doors into the synagogue auditorium.

Joshua could hear the echo of his footsteps as he crossed the stone floor following James to the side door that led out to the courtyard of the library. On the Sabbath, every corner of this building was taken up by loyal Alexandrine Jews who followed the exciting speeches of the great scholars. Today, however, there was just an eerie silence in this hall that had made the Jews famous in Alexandria for being the most learned community within the cosmopolitan city.

The papyrus factory was adjacent to the library. James introduced Joshua to the foreman:

"This is my brother. Remember? He would like to learn how to make the scrolls. Can you put him to work today?"

"I would think so. We can always use another boy."

The foreman looked at Joshua quizzically.

"Joshua?"

"Yes," Joshua replied as he looked around, observing that most of those working at the presses and benches were youths of about his own age.

"Well, let's start over here."

The foreman took Joshua to a pile of reeds.

To Joshua, these reeds didn't look much different from those leading to the mud-brick kilns. They were tall, gray-green stalks, but each bore a large, delicate fanned flower at the top that was different from the familiar bulrushes. One of the boys was slicing them in half.

"Show Joshua here what you are doing," the foreman instructed.

The boy nodded.

In no time, Joshua, using a sharp knife, was splitting the reeds just like his new aquaintance. They beat the papyrus with a mallet to flatten it. The boy explained how they must keep the reeds moist all the time and kept pouring water over both his and Joshua's work.

Joshua enjoyed the change, and it was nice and cool in the papyrus factory. He laughed as he tried to explain to his companion how up until now he'd always worked in the mud, making smelly bricks.

"We must take these over to the weaving table," his new friend said, as he picked up their flattened reeds.

At the table, he showed Joshua how to weave the reeds horizontally and vertically into each other. After beating away the excess water, they placed the woven sheets under a heavy, flat stone. There, after a little while the sheets dried out, becoming pressed, papyrus paper. During this process, Joshua caught his finger under the stone. He flinched, as he often did when his fingers got pinched at the brick kilns. He gasped and pulled away. Joshua stood there sucking on his hurt finger, receiving little sympathy from his colleague. Fortunately, with hardened hands like Joshua's, the pain didn't last.

Other boys were stacking the sheets that had already dried so they could trim them and make them ready for the scribes. Once dry, the papyrus was pliable and had a smooth surface that rolled easily into scrolls.

After Joshua had worked nearly a month in the papyrus factory, James suggested that he might spend some time with him so he could continue the studies that they had begun on those balmy summer evenings of the previous months.

Whenever they could over the next several days, they sat in the sunlit court of the library. James would read to Joshua in Hebrew and then explain the passage in Aramaic. Some days, James took Joshua into the auditorium to listen to the great scholars. Afterward, he always tried to interpret their sayings in a simpler form for Joshua to understand. On one of these days, after they had listened to a discourse on the prophet

Isaiah, James picked up a scroll from the library and unraveled it on one of the trestle tables provided for scholars wishing to read in the sunlight of the library courtyard.

"Do you remember how Isaiah believed enemies would be sent against us because of our sinful ways?" he asked Joshua as he flattened out the appropriate section, holding back the wooden spindles of the scroll with his hands.

"Yes. Foreign kings from far away came and conquered our land and took our people away. We talked about that before."

James looked into Joshua's eyes.

"Although Isaiah prophesied our people's destruction, he always held out a ray of hope."

"And our people did come back from the conqueror's land," Joshua added.

"Yes, but now we need a new prophet, another Isaiah, to inspire us before the Romans take away our identity as a people, just like those other kings of long ago."

"You mean because of the bad kings that we have now? The king that caused Joseph to take us to Egypt? The king who wanted to kill us?"

James smiled skeptically.

"Well, Joshua. Our people are not really ruled by proper kings. The Herodians are not really Jews. They're no better than the Samaritans. They believe in our God—although you would sometimes wonder when you hear of the cruel things they do—but they're not from our tribes. Their forefathers were not our kings. They're not of the Royal house of David. My father, Joseph, is a descendent of David. In that sense, you could say he is a sort of prince. He's at least of the princely tribe. You'd never know it though. For years we've been a very humble family. It's funny, really. In a way, it makes me a prince of sorts."

"Does it make me a prince, too?" Joshua asked, squinting at the sinking sun as it cast its evening beams through the courtyard, leaving long shadows on the slabs of cool marble.

James hesitated.

"Yes, I suppose it does," he said slowly. "I don't think you could ever be a king. Not if my father was not your real father."

James looked affectionately at Joshua.

"Perhaps a prince, but not a king," he repeated.

He put his arm around the boy's shoulder.

"Now, let's get back to Isaiah."

"Read to me, James. What does the prophet say to us today? Is he going to give us a message of hope or a message of further destruction?"

James smoothed out the scroll and began to translate aloud into Aramaic.

"A man will come and shall call on my name. He will walk over rulers as a potter flattens clay. Who told us about this? Nobody did until I told you. I declared it to Zion, and I gave Jerusalem hope. But there was no wise man there, no one to answer. Behold, the citizens of Jerusalem are blind. They don't understand God in their hearts. Behold; look at my servant, the one I am telling you about, my chosen one in whom I live. I have put my spirit upon him, and he will bring justice to the Nation. He will not cry out and shout or make a great fuss about things."

Joshua's brow furrowed.

"That means he won't have to be a real king, then. Real kings always shout and make a fuss," he said.

"No, Joshua, not necessarily a king. Maybe just a prophet."

"They sometimes made a lot of noise, too."

James glared at him.

"No more unnecessary comments! Now, back to the message!"

Joshua smiled mischievously as James continued:

"But, as the Scriptures say: 'He will show us that a damaged reed still does not need to break, and a dimly burning wick will not necessarily be put out. He will faithfully bring forth justice, and He will not fail or be discouraged in the face of great difficulty until He has established His message and all the world follows His law. This is the word of God, who made the heavens and created the earth and all life into which He breathes His spirit. I am the Lord, I have called you and I have led you,' he says of this leader. 'I have given you as a savior of my people and as a light to all Nations, so that all who are in darkness or imprisoned in gloom will understand that I am the Lord. That is my name, and I do not give glory to anyone else, and I give no praise to any graven image.' Isaiah then continues: 'The past is now behind us, and I am telling you about a new era. Before this ever happens I am telling you about it.'"

"He doesn't sound like a king," Joshua commented at length.

"Not a king, but possibly another prophet, like Isaiah himself... a holy man who will be more powerful than any king."

Joshua looked up at James and said:

"More like a 'Prince of Peace'?"

"That sounds like a good description of such a man," James said, patting Joshua on the shoulder. "I like that, Joshua, the 'Prince of Peace'. A prince of God, chosen by God with the spirit of God within him. A man whose power will be a spirit that will give us peace."

"If that man is more powerful than kings and can bring only good things to the world, he would be like an angel. He would be like Mother's Gabriel—the power in the sounds and light of God. Like Mother says, James, that power is in the butterflies, in the moon, and in the sound of the bullfrogs by the reed ponds at night. That power is there if we close our eyes and listen and pray."

"Yes, Joshua, that power is there," James answered. "But that doesn't make a leader of our people. We need a new prophet. I think you've described him perfectly as the 'Prince of Peace'."

Joshua smiled, savoring the words.

"You do?"

James rolled up the scroll in his aesthetic, slender hands. Joshua could almost hear the dust motes dancing in the sunbeams.

CHAPTER THREE

Accident and Revenge

Summer dragged on. Linus was bored. The beautiful villa overlooking Magdala and the lake beyond seemed tame after the excitement of life at his father's barracks in Sepphoris. Linus had liked playing at being a soldier and he had enjoyed the amenities that went with urban life. Whenever he could escape the tedious classes with a neighboring pedagogue that his mother had arranged, Linus roamed the hills in search of excitement.

The youth was adept with his sling and many a sheep or goat had felt the thud of a stone missile against its hide, causing the angry shouts of shepherds and goatherds. But sheep were easy quarry. Linus had now taken to trying to kill doves as they flew among the cotes of Magdala. He would hide himself in the scrub around the rocks just above the Hebrew village and sling his missiles at the passing birds. Usually he missed, but once in a while he scored a hit. The stunned creature would fall to the ground. Then, Linus would sneak up to the bird to see if it was dead. If not, he stoned it without mercy until its life ended. It was a solitary sport, but it pleased his bored and spoiled nature.

From above, through a surrounding screen of tall cypress trees, Magdala appeared small—a village of not more than twenty white buildings that lacked any plan or order. The houses spilled down to the pebble beach that acted as a slip for the simple fishing boats that served the villagers as their main source of income. Nets strewn over posts along the beach dried in the warm sun. Fishermen sat in their boats mending others. Some villagers, like Copernia's maid Leah, worked in the villas up on the hillside, but most ignored the presence of these wealthy Roman landowners. A ring of tall cypress trees formed a natural screen around the village, as if making comment on the segregation between the races.

Linus looked down on the village. Outside one of the outlying houses at the quiet end of the street, two men sat idly chatting. Linus could see them easily from his vantagepoint. One had a dark beard and calculating eyes with a look of maturity; the other was a mere youth, ruddy-faced and smooth-skinned. They were watching a group of Hebrew children who were holding hands as they sang a simple song. Whenever the children came to the end of a refrain, they all fell to the ground, laughing and pointing at the last to be seated.

A dove flew out from the largest of the village cotes. It wheeled above the children before settling to perch on the limb of a dead tree. Linus observed the fat bird. It was an obvious target. He took his sling from his waistband. He placed a smooth stone in the weapon. With a few turns of the wrist he set the missile flying.

He missed.

The dove fluttered frantically as it flew to safety.

The pebble ricocheted off a wall. It struck the head of the smallest child in the playing group. She screamed and fell, her head hitting the sharp corner of some broken masonry in the dusty ground. She rolled over and lay motionless. The other children scattered to safety.

Linus watched the two men run to the child. They picked up her frail body and carried her into the house. Their voices sounded angry. The two men returned. They looked up at the dovecote, then cast their eyes up the hillside. They were looking straight at the spot where Linus crouched.

Linus heard them shouting. He made out the Aramaic word for "Romans!" Frightened, he slipped from behind his cover, running through the cypress trees.

The bearded and more aggressive of the men caught sight of Linus.

"Jonah, there's the bastard!" he shouted.

The two men began to give chase.

Panicking, Linus gauged his distance from the villa. A steep climb was the shortest route. He scrambled up the hillside. The two Hebrew men began to gain on him. Panting, Linus dropped his sling. He climbed through the rocks to the rough track above. His pursuers reached the fallen weapon.

"Here's the evidence!" one of them shouted.

Linus ran on until he reached the courtyard gate of the villa. He pounded on it and screamed for help. Desperately, he listened for the latch board to move. It did. Gladius opened the gate. The frightened boy fell into his arms.

* * *

"Roman bastards! You'll pay for this!" Jonah yelled from below. "You think you can get away with anything. Murderers! Now you've killed an innocent child!"

The gate closed.

"It's no use for now, Jonah," advised the older man. "Let's go back down and collect up some of the others. We'll get the zealots together and take action. We know which villa to attack."

"Burn them out, Judas?"

"Yes, my boy. We'll burn them out. That's the house of the Roman commander in Sepphoris. That boy's his son. The brat's been a pest all summer. We couldn't have a better excuse than this to strike at the heart of Roman power."

"I'll round up the men right away," Jonah said. "We may be able to attack tonight before the bastards make any attempt to escape. At least, if not tonight, let's attack tomorrow."

"Fine, Jonah. Hurry on down. You go to the north of the village, and I'll take the southern end. Let's meet at Esther's."

The two men nodded at each other before making their separate ways down the hill.

* * *

Inside the protection of the villa, Gladius demanded an explanation from Linus.

Linus' face was white.

"It was an accident, Gladius. I promise you it was an accident. I was aiming at a bird. I missed and the stone hit a little girl."

"Was she hurt?"

"She didn't move after she fell, and those men carried her away. I think she's dead. That's why they're so angry, Gladius. I watched the whole thing. They think I killed the little girl on purpose."

"Did you?"

"No, Gladius. Of course not!"

The slave gripped the boy's arm and twisted it behind his back.

"Are you sure you didn't try to hurt or wound the child?" he repeated.

"I told you, Gladius. No! Please! Please! You're hurting me! Stop, Gladius! You'll break my arm!"

"I could break your arm. Remember that I was trained to break arms. I want to be sure you're telling the truth."

"Gladius! Stop! If you don't stop I'll tell my mother about you!"

Wincing, Linus looked up at the slave.

"I'll tell her everything," he repeated.

Gladius released his hold.

"Don't you like me any more? You've acted strangely recently. I thought you liked it when I touched you. Recently, I've felt a barrier between us. Are you afraid of me, Linus?"

"No."

"Don't you like me any more? Tell me the truth, Linus. Remember that I'm your best friend. Maybe I'm your only friend!"

The boy was sobbing, partly in pain and partly in fear. *What if I did kill that girl?* he thought. *If they find me, will they feed me to the wild beasts at the Gladiatorial School? That's what Gladius said: 'Some of those prisoners might have stolen or even killed an innocent person.'*

Gladius felt him trembling and kissed his forehead.

"It's the truth," Linus said. "You are my only friend. I'll do anything you ask of me."

Copernia had already heard her son's cries. She came out into the courtyard.

"What is it, Linus?"

"It's all right, Mother. It was nothing. It was just a game."

"No, my lady. It's more serious than that," Gladius said.

Linus ran sobbing to his mother.

"What do you mean, Gladius?" Copernia asked in agitation.

"Linus has...well he's hurt, perhaps even killed, a Hebrew child."

"What!"

"Yes, but it was an accident, my lady. The villagers are upset. Two men chased Linus back up here. I think we can expect them to return. We'd better be prepared."

"What do you mean?"

"We might all be in danger, my lady."

The authority in the slave's voice startled Copernia.

"What should we do?" she asked. "Why isn't Flavius here when we need him?"

"Nothing for the moment, my lady, but my advice is for us to stay in the center of the house. We're well protected by the outside walls. If they should attack, I think we can hold them back. We'll protect the gate and the terrace, which are the vulnerable places."

"What do you mean, attack us?" Copernia asked.

"They might try to burn us out."

Copernia looked aghast.

"Burn the villa?"

"Yes, but if we are prepared, we can probably outwit them."

Gladius took charge. He had been trained for quick thinking in the gladiatorial schools.

"Linus. Go and tell Leah to start drawing water from the well," he commanded. "Tell her to fill every available jar."

Linus ran toward the kitchen, and in jumbled Aramaic and a good deal of sign language, he delivered his message to the Hebrew serving maid.

Copernia's servant obediently went to the well and began to lower buckets to fetch up the water. Linus assisted by bringing all the available jars in the storeroom to the well.

Gladius and Copernia surveyed the terrace.

"If they try to burn us out, my lady, it's here and at the gate that we'll have to make our stand."

Gladius looked at the bright awnings. He tugged at them.

"We'll need to remove these drapes from the terrace," he said. "Anything that might easily burn should be removed. Hebrew torches won't be able to do much damage if we don't give them any kindling. I'll defend the gate, but Linus might have to defend this area."

"But he's only a boy," Copernia gasped.

"He'll be all right. He's a fighter."

Copernia helped Gladius pull down the colorful drapes and dragged them away, leaving them in a pile on the vestibule floor.

Gladius carried out the wooden seats and tables so that only the bare structure of the open terrace was left. He studied the distance down to the track. It was a sheer drop, almost twice the height of a man. *Depending on numbers, it'll be difficult for these pathetic peasants to climb,* he concluded. *It's the gate that'll be the weakest point for certain. I'll need to defend the gate.*

Darkness fell. Gladius suggested that only the oil lamps in the center of the house be lit so as to make it harder for any attackers to see the villa. He realized that he could be fighting alone against as many as twenty people, but then he had known worse odds in the arena.

Linus staggered through the vestibule, slopping a heavy water jar.

"Let me help you," Gladius called out.

They both carried jars to the terrace and the courtyard gate.

"I'm sorry if I hurt you earlier," the slave said, putting his arm around Linus. "You're a fighter. We'll show these Jews who we are."

They were as prepared as they could be for the expected attack. In the nocturnal silence of anticipation, Linus sat on the wall of the terrace with Gladius. The perfume of the late summer trumpet vines hung heavily on the air. A silvery moon caught the still waters of the lake, making the cypress trees at the back of Magdala form a silhouette.

"They'll come," Gladius whispered. "Keep watching. They'll come."

As they whispered nervously in the darkness, a series of pinpoint lights showed down in the village.

"That's them!" Gladius exclaimed. "They're grouping down there with their torches."

The now-excited old gladiator stood up.

"You stay here, Linus," he commanded. "Listen, this is very important. If they throw fiery torches into this area, try to retrieve them and heap them up in a pile here in the center. From where they'll be, they won't see what you're doing. Make it look like a fire as the torches blaze together. Such a fire will be quite safe. The torches will burn out. On no account throw a torch back at them. If you do they'll only use it against us. They can't carry more than about twenty, and they'll need several to try to burn down the courtyard gate if they know what they're doing. If they think they've successfully set the villa ablaze, they'll pull back. Make it look good, but keep the fire in the center. Maybe we can fool them."

Linus made a thumbs-up sign.

"I'll keep them off. We'll beat them!" he said.

Gladius left to defend the courtyard, experiencing a familiar blood thump to his heart.

The procession of lights moved slowly from the cypress trees up the hillside toward them.

Gladius soaked the heavy wooden gate with water from the large jars placed along the inside of the courtyard wall. When both sides were thoroughly wet, he shut and firmly barred it from the inside.

Clouds had obscured the silvery moon, and the darkness was still and silent.

* * *

There were eighteen men in the attacking force led by Judas and Jonah. They climbed the last fifty cubits to reach the track that led to the Flavian villa.

"It sounds quiet, Jonah," Judas whispered.

"That's good. Nobody about, so they've either left or they're all asleep."

"Jonah, take your men to the gate. If it's barred, burn it down. Go on in and plunder. Meanwhile, my men will have created a disturbance in the front. Hopefully we'll distract the bastards so they're out of your way. We'll teach these Romans whose land this is. Apparently, the commander isn't there, so we shouldn't come up against much resistance. Set fire to anything that will burn."

Judas knuckled his forehead, mocking the manner of the Pharisees. "Good luck!"

Judas took ten of the men with him down the track below the stone walls of the villa. The light of their torches lit up the opening of the terrace and the tracery of the balcony between the marble columns.

Linus stepped back from the light to hide in the shadows.

"Hurl fire torches in there," Judas ordered.

* * *

The first flaming torches landed. Linus was quick to retrieve them. As Gladius had instructed him, he piled them up in the center of the terrace garden.

A torch fell back and hit one of the marauders below. The man cursed in Aramaic then hurled the flaming weapon back. It landed at the base of the wooden balcony. The flames set fire to the structure.

Linus moved for the first water jar. Another flaming missile flew through the air. It struck him on the back. He flinched as the hot beacon set fire to his tunic. Instinctively, he fell to the ground, rolled on his back, and smothered the fire. He wasn't seriously hurt, but he needed to retrieve the offending torch and put it in the center of the terrace garden where it would do no harm. Meanwhile, the fire that had started on the balcony began to crackle and grow. By the time Linus could get to it with the water, it was climbing up toward the rafters and out of his reach.

* * *

Flaming torches gave an orange glow to the area behind the gate where Gladius crouched. The wet wood hissed. Tongues of fire licked through underneath and between the marble lintels.

"The bastards! They've soaked the gate," one of the men outside shouted. "Bring more torches and oil."

Gladius poured more water under the gate.

"Fire the roof!" Jonah shouted.

He pointed out the jutting eaves of the vestibule.

"Throw your torches at that corner up there. It looks as if Judas has started a good fire farther down, so we've got nothing to lose."

Jonah's men tossed three torches up at the overhanging rafters. One torch held. The other two fell back, scattering their ashes and sparks over the stones of the track below. The corner of the roof slowly caught on fire as Jonah watched from below.

Gladius continued to soak the inside of the gate. It was paramount that the attackers shouldn't get through the gate and enter the interior of his master's villa. Smoke and flames shot out from the low-hanging eaves behind him.

* * *

The fires Judas and his men had started in the terrace were taking hold. The roof over the balcony was in flames. The interior seemed to be ablaze. Sparks flew through the air. Their mission had been accomplished, but they hadn't managed to fire the gate.

"They prepared the timbers, Judas. The gate's been soaked," Jonah repeated. "I'll need at least five more torches along with the oil to set it ablaze. We've only these three left."

As they spoke, the timbers holding the roof over the balcony began to give way. Tiles fell to the ground in a blaze of sparks. The corner of the vestibule roofing burst into flames as the fire there took a firm hold. From the track where they were standing it looked as if the whole villa would soon be ablaze.

"All right," Judas shouted. "Toss the remaining torches in to fuel the fire. Maybe those bastards will die in the flames or are already asphyxiated by the smoke. At the least, this will teach those high and mighty Romans a lesson."

One of the men threw up the last three torches. They landed in the burning rafters of the vestibule roof.

"That should do it," he said gleefully.

"It would have been better if we could have got inside and killed the bastards," Judas responded, as he looked up at the conflagration, "including that traitor, Leah."

The men then retreated back to the village.

* * *

Gladius dragged a ladder from the storeroom and climbed up onto the vestibule roof. The fierce fire raged over the balcony of the terrace. Linus was attempting to throw water in the general direction of the flames, but the heat was beating him back and the water wasn't reaching its destination. The fire was too advanced.

Gladius shouted down:

"Leave it, Linus! It'll just have to burn itself out. I need your help here. This is more serious. The vestibule will soon be ablaze."

The fire on the terrace was not as fierce as Gladius had thought. Linus crossed the vestibule. Beyond the smell of burning, there was no indication that the blaze had started in the corner of the roof above. By now, Copernia and Leah were wide awake and well aware of the acrid tang of smoke now spreading through the rest of the house. They ran out to the vestibule.

Copernia saw the scorched tunic on Linus' back.

"Linus! What's happened to you?" she shrieked.

"Nothing, Mother. I must go. Gladius needs me on the roof."

"No, Linus! You can't go on the roof! It's too dangerous!"

Linus paid no attention to his mother and ran out into the courtyard, where he struggled to lift the heavy jars of water up to Gladius.

The draperies lying in the vestibule were potential kindling for the apparent fire above. Leah looked up at the ceiling, fearful of the crackling sound of the fire.

"Leah! You must help!" Copernia shouted. "We must drag these away."

Together, mistress and maid pulled away the orange wool draperies, dragging them out into the courtyard. As they worked, the ceiling plaster at the far end of the vestibule cracked. Smoke and sparks poured through, and the two women coughed and choked before retreating into the yard.

A crash came from the direction of the terrace. More sparks whirled upward. The roofing over the balcony was collapsing. It was burning itself out, just as Gladius had said. There was no danger of the fire spreading.

As the fire struggled to advance along the sodden timbers of the vestibule roof, it, too, lost its strength. Gladius called down to Linus and his mother:

"Bring me up one of those drapes!"

Pulling one free from the pile, Linus hauled it up to Gladius. Gladius folded the material and soaked it thoroughly in water, then used it to fight the fading fire at the far end of the roof. The last flickers of flame were extinguished as the faithful servant thrashed the wet material in their direction. Blackened by the debris and smoke, and exhausted from his endeavors, Gladius climbed down, knowing the villa was saved.

In the light of morning, the real damage could be seen. The basic structure was still sound. It was not until Gladius opened the courtyard gate and saw the burned wood on the outside that he realized how close they had been to disaster. The wood had charred to a considerable depth, and it would have taken little more to have destroyed the gate.

"If those men had got in here," Gladius said, "it would have been necessary to choose between them or the roof. We'd have either lost our lives, the villa, or perhaps both."

"We were lucky, then," Linus said.

Gladius smiled at the boy with pride.

"Yes, Linus. We were lucky, but between us we saved the villa."

That very day, Copernia decided to take Linus to Tuscany. The rebellion that Varus had predicted was coming too close for comfort. They left in the wagon and headed for the safety of Sepphoris.

* * *

Below the villa, at about the same time that day, a girl approximately two years younger than Linus was buried on the outskirts of Magdala. It was a poor and simple grave marked only by a heap of stones. After the burial, Esther the whore, the mother of the dead child, stood with her older daughter close to the grave. There was no father to witness the burial, but Judas and Jonah were there with their band of zealots.

"Roman bastards!" they muttered as they cast the last stones onto the little heap.

Esther wept as she held her nine-year-old girl close to her side. Her thoughts were confused. *He is Flavius' son—Maria's half-brother. It was the Roman's boy who killed my little girl.* Her heart churned with the memory of Flavius Septimus. She knew the day she had conceived, the day he had left her to end his double life. *I was almost surprised to see him. He had been less regular in his visits. I had to tell him to be patient as he pulled at my shift to release my breasts.*

"All is for you, all in good time," I had assured him.

But he couldn't hold back. He stripped me, roaming my flesh, soaking in my sweat with heavy breaths.

"What is it, my Roman soldier?" I called out.

He spread me. He plunged into me.

"I've missed you," he said.

"It's more than that," I had replied, sensing his urgency as I arched myself to him.

But he wasn't listening. He lost himself in me until he spent himself in the dim light of the brothel bench. I stroked his back, running my fingertips down his spine to the pooling sweat.

"My Roman soldier," I had whispered in satisfaction.

Then, he had reminded me of how we had first met. It was on the lakeshore south of the village.

"You exposed your breasts," he said.

"And you spoke Aramaic," I had said.

His laugh was a hot breath against my flesh.

"Not very well, I'm afraid."

"At least you tried," I had noted. "It's much better now, very good in fact."

"I was lonely," Flavius had said.

"So was I."

As he pulled on his tunic after that lustful loving—a session more like I knew with my rough fishermen than my Roman boy—he said to me in a serious tone:

"I'll be leaving tomorrow."

"No more visits," I had replied as I lay back, stroking my breasts.

"Not for a while, if ever. I have to go back to my duties."

"What if I have a child?" I pleaded.

He gave me two denarii.

"For you," was all he said.

That was the last time he came.

Esther squeezed her daughter's hand, then turned from the grave.

The little girl stooped to pick up one more loose stone to add to the pile.

"Leave it, Maria," Esther said, tugging at the child's arm.

They left the gravesite.

Judas and Jonah and a few of the zealots followed behind.

CHAPTER FOUR

Passing Ships

It was already hot. Flies swarmed, and the nighttime crickets and bullfrogs rested from their continuous chorus. Joseph walked in front of his family, pushing the crude handcart he had made for their journey, as they left their mud-brick house on the outskirts of Alexandria for the last time. Ruth and Miriam followed on two donkeys led by James and Joshua.

"We are leaving at last," Miriam said to her fast-maturing stepdaughter.

"I hope I'll like Galilee," Ruth said. "I can't remember anything about Bethlehem."

"You'll like it, Ruth. There are vineyards, trees, and beautiful hills. It's so different from this flat, oppressive land of swamps and bulrushes."

As always, the flies, which loved the mangy donkeys, buzzed around them. Miriam frantically waved her hand to move them from her face.

"And that's another thing, there are less flies!" she said.

The traffic intensified as they came closer to the center of the city, with camels, donkeys, carts, and pedestrians all in a seeming hurry.

They passed the Great Synagogue.

"I'll miss the synagogue," James said to Joshua, looking at the seat of learning that had taken up so much of their time. "The synagogue school in Bethlehem was pathetic in comparison with this great building."

"I'll miss it, too, even the Papyrus factory," Joshua agreed.

Joseph and his family progressed down one of the long streets that led to the waterfront. The character of the city changed after they left the Jewish Quarter. The bustle remained, the odors of camel and donkey dung didn't diminish, but the marble and stone facades of the buildings took on a grace and majesty that made even Jerusalem look plain. Statues, plinths, and fluted columns inlaid with gold, glinted in the sunshine. At the end of the street in a square before the harbor, crowds gathered around orators who spoke with grand gestures from a rostrum. There were cheers and there were shouts of anger. There was movement, color, excitement, grandeur, heat, flies, and dust. Finally, ahead lay the harbor with its galleys and the great lighthouse beyond.

James began to feel his responsibility. The rabbi had given him the name of an agent to get them passage from Alexandria to Caesarea, but he didn't know where to begin to find him. The rabbi had merely told him to seek him out at the waterfront. Every warehouse looked the same.

Black slaves from the upper Nile were loading most of the ships with grain. Broken sacks littered the wharves. At the third warehouse, James plucked up his courage to make inquiries. He approached the foreman supervising the slaves.

"Please, sir," he said, trying to get the man's attention. "Can you help us?"

The man turned.

"What do you want? Can't you see I'm busy?"

"Sir, I have a name from the rabbi. I need to find this man," James pleaded.

"Show me the name then."

James took out the precious piece of papyrus on which the rabbi had written the name of his contact.

"Isaac!" the foreman exclaimed.

He began to laugh.

"I hope you have enough to get around him, he doesn't come cheap."

"Where can we find this Isaac, sir?"

"He should be at warehouse fourteen. Where are you trying to go?"

"We need a galley bound for Caesarea."

"Judea, eh? Well, you won't find any galleys going that way here. These are all bound for Rome and Italia."

"Where is warehouse fourteen?"

The foreman pointed to the other side.

"It's over there. See those galleys? I don't know if they're going to Caesarea and I don't really care, but your Isaac should be somewhere over there."

He turned and resumed shouting at the black slaves.

The family group plodded on in hopes that in the general direction in which they had been shown, they would come across warehouse fourteen and the rabbi's contact.

After sometime wandering aimlessly through the warehouses, they made that contact. Isaac, a rakish-looking man in a striped tunic and with shady eyes, a furtive look and an upturned nose, looked at them suspiciously. He had no details of their passage and brusquely informed James that the fourth galley in front of warehouse fourteen was going to Caesarea and that for a fee he might arrange their passage.

Although James was the man in charge, he looked at his father for guidance.

"Will you take the donkeys and our cart in part exchange?" Joseph inquired.

The agent hesitated. James then repeated his father's offer in Greek.

Isaac looked at the two aging donkeys. He laughed.

"They'll barely get me outside the harbor," he said. "They must be twelve years old or more!"

"Maybe, but they've served us well," James replied. "We can't take them with us."

"What else can you offer?" Isaac asked.

Joseph produced a small bag of Egyptian coins from his waistband. Isaac looked at them.

"That'll take you about half-way with the donkeys thrown in. You'll need more than that."

"Please, sir. We're poor, but we're honest. We could help you load and unload the vessel. We need to make this journey to Caesarea," Joseph pleaded.

Again, noting Isaac's expressionless response, James interpreted Joseph's offer into Greek. The agent, however, merely shook his head.

Miriam tugged at Joseph's sleeve. She pointed to the old studded box that was in his pushcart. Joseph looked at her in disbelief.

"Open it up," she said.

Joseph loosened the thongs on the straps that hadn't been undone for ten years. The lid creaked, but gold glinted inside. Joseph looked at Miriam hesitantly. She nodded at him and he took out a handful of old gold coins. His eyes showed a startled surprise as he saw the reality of this treasure after so long. Miriam smiled triumphantly as her eyes met those of Joshua. The box had been part of their secret—part of the strange drama from long ago when the mysterious rich men had visited them in the cave.

James had never seen the contents of that box. He had never paid too much attention to Joseph and Miriam's stories, but he could certainly see and feel the worth of the gold now.

"Mother!" Joshua cried excitedly as he, too, saw the gold. It was as if all of a sudden the stories that Miriam had discussed with him on those hot summer evenings in Alexandria had become the truth.

"Yes, Joshua. It was all true," Miriam said.

"You knew about this treasure all along!" James said to his father. "We could have used this to our advantage in so many ways!"

"I knew about it, but it wasn't mine to give away," Joseph replied. "This treasure could have caused dissention among us. It belongs to Miriam and Joshua. They must use it as they think fit."

"It belongs to God," Miriam said.

The agent's eyes sparkled at the sight of the gold.

"Poor, eh!"

He took a handful of the coins and examined them. He held one of them up to the bright sunlight and polished it with the sleeve of his garment. Then, he took the coins and weighed them on his scales.

"These are not Roman," Isaac said slowly, "that is not Caesar's head."

Joshua looked at the coins. He looked at the gilded head.

"Is that the same as God's face in the moon?" he asked with a beguiling smile.

"It will be if they buy us passage," Miriam answered.

The agent stroked his dark beard and looked at James.

"I'll give you passage for fifteen such coins. They are definitely gold."

"How about twelve?" James bartered.

"Thirteen!" the agent said.

Joseph reached with James into the old box. Together, they counted out thirteen of the coins. While the men were conducting their business, Miriam took Joshua aside.

"God's face was on the coins," she said, putting her arm around him. "Today our secret's been revealed. You'll always be my 'Prince of Peace'. Whatever God asks of us, we must give back to Him tenfold. We're about to start a new life, Joshua, and we mustn't forget that God gave us this treasure so that we could give our lives back to Him."

Joshua looked at his mother. There was an urgency in her message. Their sojourn in Egypt and his childhood were coming to an end. His young face clouded at the insight.

"We're going home," Miriam said. "Our exile's over. Soon we'll see Amos and Judith and you'll meet Joachim and Anna, the grandparents you've never seen."

"Where did you really get that gold?" James asked sarcastically. "Was it a gift from Gabriel, the man to whom you were first betrothed? Father said he was a rich man."

Miriam had rarely seen James react in such a jealous fashion.

"No," she replied rather uncomfortably, looking at Joseph for reassurance. "I've told you all before. The box was a gift from some wandering merchants who took shelter in the cave where Joshua was born."

Joseph nodded.

"That's enough questions, James. Miriam's right, the box was a gift from the men who came to our cave."

"I've carried this box all these years," Miriam continued, "knowing that some day it would be useful to us. It's helped us today and I'm sure it will help us in the future. It was God's gift to us."

When they got to the galley, they loaded their few precious possessions into the hold, including the old studded box. The donkeys and the pushcart were handed over to Isaac, and by the light of the great beacon at the harbor's entrance, their galley slipped out of Alexandria as evening fell.

Joshua stood on deck with Joseph.

"Do you think Amos will have a working business for us in Galilee?" he asked.

"I hope so. It will be wonderful to have us all working in our own business. Much better than making bricks, don't you think?"

Joshua looked out over the undulating waters.

"My real work will start soon. I want to help people…animals, too. I want to be a healer. Both Mother and James think that I also have some special role as a rabbi—to be a spiritual leader for our people."

"Your mother has always believed you have a special, spiritual destiny. It's what you want that really counts, though. Do you want to be a rabbi?"

"I think so. I'd like to fulfill what those rich merchants said when I was born. I'd like to be that 'Prince of Peace.'"

"You can do anything if you put your mind to it, Joshua. Sometimes, you need to concentrate a little more on what you're doing, but I have great faith in you. Even though you're only nine, I think you will be smarter than James. For all his knowledge, James follows the rules. James never broke the rules. You, sometimes do. Breaking the rules gets us into trouble, but it also can lead to greatness. If we always follow the rules, we become like sheep. To be great, you need to be the shepherd."

The sea moved under the darkening night sky.

"God will show me the way, just as He shows Mother the way."

"I'm sure He will, but when we first get to Galilee we will have to work hard to establish ourselves. I'll expect you to work with Amos and me. You're becoming quite a good carpenter. The three of us should have a good business."

Joshua ran his hand along the ship's rail.

"Have you been to Galilee before, Father?"

"No, never. Before we went to Egypt I hardly ever left Bethlehem."

They looked back at the lighthouse. They could still see the burning beacon on the flat horizon where the starlit sky met the dark sea.

The ship settled into its gentle rhythm, riding the swells.

* * *

At the barracks in Sepphoris, Flavius was surprised when his adjutant, Sextus, informed him that his family had arrived.

"How are they traveling?" he inquired. "I wasn't expecting them."

"They came by wagon, Commander, and they look troubled. Shall I take them to your quarters?"

"Of course, Sextus. Tell them I'll be over there shortly. First, I must address the cohort for Jerusalem. Are they nearly ready?"

"Yes, Commander. They're ready for inspection."

"Good, I'll see them off and then come right on over to the Barracks House. Make sure my family have everything they need."

The adjutant touched his dagger in salutation and left.

Flavius picked up his plumed helmet and walked out into the bright sunlight. He blinked in the brilliance after a morning in his dark office. The heavy helmet felt smothering in the heat of the day. He crossed the courtyard to the barracks parade ground. The cohort was lined up and ready.

Flavius was greeted by the cohort's leading officer. Without hesitation, they commenced their inspection through the ranks. The centurions heading each section called their men to attention as the commander and their tribune passed by.

After this hurried inspection, Flavius addressed the men:

"Members of the Syrian Legion," he said, his strong voice carrying in the bright sunlight, "we have been asked to lend support to the troubled garrison in Jerusalem. At long last, the chaotic disorder of the King of Judea has come to an end. Judea is now fully incorporated into Roman rule. The Roman prefect speaks for the Syrian governor and the Emperor. You'll be in the service of the prefect. The Jews have staged a series of revolts and have attempted to create a state based on their religion. They're divided against themselves, and the civil disorder that has resulted, due to the weak rule of the former Jewish king, Archelaus, has virtually brought the city to a standstill. It has always been the policy of the Empire that we should tolerate the religions of our subject peoples. You are not being sent to Jerusalem to destroy their Temple or any of the institutions of the Jewish religion. Your orders are strictly to keep the civil peace. Carry your standards high."

The soldiers gave a brief cheer and then, under the orders of each separate centurion, the cohort formed into columns and marched out from the Sepphoris barracks.

As the dust settled, Flavius hurriedly returned to the commanding officer's quarters to find his family. His eyes scanned each of them. Copernia looked severe, but calm. Gladius and Linus both had cuts and bruises, showing the scars of their recent fire-fighting.

Flavius took Copernia's hand.

"What's happened?" he asked with concern.

"They burned the villa."

"Who?"

"The villagers. They came up and tried to burn us out."

Shock registered on Flavius' face as Gladius took up the tale.

"There was an accident, Master. Linus was killing doves with his slingshot and accidentally caused the death of a Hebrew child."

"What?"

"It was an accident, Father," Linus' voice rose in anxiety.

"But you killed a child!"

"I never meant to harm anyone. The stone bounced off a wall and stunned the girl. She fell and her head hit some rubble. It wasn't my fault."

"That's right, Master," Gladius agreed. "Linus didn't mean any harm. It was an accident. However, the villagers have been a little edgy recently. They saw Linus and chased after him. Then, that night they tried to burn us out."

Flavius looked stern and angry.

"I've told you before, Linus Flavian, I don't want you harming or killing other people's livestock. Those doves belong to the Hebrews. What were you doing there?"

"Nothing in particular. I was bored. I prefer it here in Sepphoris."

"We are here to help the Hebrews, not harm them or their property. When are you going to learn responsibility? You can't be a successful Roman administrator here or anywhere else unless you learn responsibility."

Flavius turned to Gladius.

"Well, what is the extent of the damage? Is my property destroyed as a result of Linus' stupidity?"

"Not too badly, Master."

"How did you escape, then?"

"We defeated them!" Linus exclaimed, anxious to restore his father's approval. "We saved the villa! Gladius and I...we stopped them from coming in! Part of the roof burned and the terrace is a mess, but we saved the villa. They couldn't burn down the gate and they ran out of torches.

We beat them, Father! Gladius, Mother, Leah, and I…we beat them and they went away."

"That's right, Master. Linus fought the fire as well as any man twice his age," Gladius said in support. "The whole villa could easily have been burned. However, it's not safe for us to stay there."

"And from what I hear, it's not safe for us to stay in Galilee," Copernia added. "There's an uncomfortable feeling here. Flavius, you don't have to hide anything from us. There's rebellion coming, and you know it."

"We are living in uncertain times, my dearest, but that's precisely what I'm here for. Rome will bring order to the Levant, just give us time. But, you're right about current tensions. We are on alert. The underground is active again, and in the wake of the Jewish revolt in Jerusalem, we can expect repercussions here in Galilee."

"That's why we left, Flavius Septimus," continued Copernia.

She addressed him by his full name when she was agitated and making a firm statement.

"It's not safe here, is it? I don't understand you!" she went on. "Why are you so determined to stay out here away from everything civilized? You are so obstinate! What place is this for a Tarquin to grow into manhood!"

She paused. Flavius tried to comfort her as he put his arm around her shoulder. Copernia pulled away.

"Don't touch me!" she shouted. "I've had enough of you, the army, and Syria! I'm taking Linus and Gladius to Italia. Linus needs to see Rome and Tuscany! My father and uncle will take care of us. We'll only return when you tell us that it's safe for us to do so. I hate this rebellious country you love so much. I've had enough of it!"

Flavius stared incredulously at Copernia.

Linus looked up at them.

"Wait, Mother! Father, can't I stay and fight in the Legion!"

The commander shook his head.

"No, Linus. You're much too young. Your mother's right. You need to see the heart of the Empire."

Flavius ruffled his son's hair.

"All right, Copernia," he said, "you're right. Maybe this would be a good time for you to take Linus to Rome. I can understand your fears and it's time Linus received the patrician education you so desire for him.

Maybe I have taken you too much for granted. I have my duty here, Copernia, but I need your love. You will come back, won't you?"

Copernia became more gentle, softening as her desires were healed.

"I'd rather not, but my place is with you. We come from two illustrious families. I will come back, but only when it is safe."

Flavius turned to Gladius.

"You'll go to Rome with them. I'll send word to the Tarquins when all is safe. We'll have an escort take you to Caesarea tomorrow and make arrangements there for a ship to carry you to Rome. The port's busy at this time of the year, so there shouldn't be any problem taking a passage."

He looked at his wife and son.

"Let's get you cleaned up," he said, finally breaking his severity and smiling.

He addressed his slave again:

"Gladius, you did well. You saved the property. You shall be rewarded. Thank you. Take Linus to the centurions' baths."

When he and Copernia were left alone, she broke down and expressed her real fear:

"It was frightening, Flavius," she whispered, the tears welling in her eyes turning to tenderness as she felt the comfort of his arms. "I've never been so scared."

"I'm sure, my dearest," he said, kissing her forehead lightly. "You're safe now. However, it may be good for you to get back to Italian civilization."

Flavius stood back and undid the thongs of his leather cuirass, revealing the belt of his tunic.

"Come, Copernia, if you're going to leave me here all alone, you're not going to leave without celebrating our love!"

He removed the garment.

She turned willingly, opening her arms to him.

"I love you," she said, looking at this fine Roman commander who was her husband. "We will come back."

For an all-too-brief interlude, Flavius and Copernia knew each other and recovered their trust and intimacy, but Copernia could not escape flame-hot memories and their dark terror. She drew her husband to her, cocooning herself in his hard body and tender touch, but fearful for his safety in the Jewish zealot revolt.

* * *

Zealots, Judas and Jonah, prepared their meal as the sun dropped below the horizon. The cliffs on the far side of the lake became a blaze of pink. Judas fed their campfire with pieces of driftwood. Jonah cut open the freshly caught fish.

"They're a strange crowd in Magdala," Judas said as he poked the ashes to bring the fire to life. "They don't have much spunk. They pay lip service to us freedom fighters, but they seem to be afraid to become involved."

"Maybe they live too close to those Romans," Jonah commented. "It was hard to get deep-rooted support even when we had a cause. They followed us in revenge for that whore's daughter's death, but not for the cause. They sell their fish to the Romans. Many of them work in the Roman villas and vineyards. Some say that old Esther even serviced that Roman brat's father! They are too provincial. I shouldn't think any of them have ever traveled more than two or three miles from the village except to fish. In reality, Judas, they wouldn't be worth much to the freedom fighters any way you look at it."

Judas sat back as the fire crackled into life.

"True. I think we might find more life in Capernaum or closer to Sepphoris in the hills."

"I've heard the movement used to be strong in the Nazareth area. The zealots had cells there and also in Cana, in fact in most of those villages up toward Syria. But, you know, Judas, the more I see of this part of the country, the more I realize that it was better in Jerusalem. Why do the leaders think we can be more useful here?"

Judas thought about an answer as he readied the fire. He speared one of the fish and held it over the flaming sticks. The fish hissed in the heat. Its skin peeled back to reveal succulent white flesh. At length, Judas looked up at Jonah, fire dancing in his eyes.

"They possibly think we can do more up here because we straddle the supply lines from Syria," he said. "If we can destroy the Roman power in Sepphoris, the Romans will become isolated in Jerusalem, especially in the winter when the port of Caesarea is closed."

"We should be preparing for next winter now."

"Exactly, Jonah! I'm sure when we meet up with the leaders, we'll find that's exactly what they're planning."

"Then, we need to get to Capernaum as quickly as possible and find out what's going on."

"We'll get there tomorrow," Judas replied.

Darkness found the shores of the lake. The two men ate and rested as the coals of their fire glowed in the black night.

* * *

Flavius sent his family off from the barracks proudly. A chariot carrying his adjutant, Sextus Severus, went ahead of the wagon, while four mounted guards escorted them. Copernia looked radiant from her high seat. Despite the recent events, it was a happy departure. Linus, dressed in a fresh toga and sitting beside his mother, looked back with pride at his father, resplendent in his uniform. As they journeyed, Copernia busied herself, filling her son in with stories about her family and how important they were.

In Caesarea, they stopped at the Temple of Augustus to offer prayers for their safe passage. It was more of a formality than a superstitious religious belief. They burned incense on the altars to the Emperor and Neptunus.

"Who is Neptunus?" Linus asked Gladius.

"One of the sea monsters."

"Nonsense," Copernia interjected. "Neptunus controls the sea monsters. He is the god of the sea. We have to hope he gives us a calm passage."

* * *

At the wharf, they learned that a galley from Alexandria, presently in the outer harbor, would be unloading grain before taking passage with spices and cedar wood for Rome. They sat on bales watching the waterfront scene while Sextus made negotiations with the agent.

Linus felt the excitement of the busy life along the waterfront. He watched with keen interest the mechanics of loading and unloading the busy lighters. A small raft-like pontoon, carrying a few sacks of grain and a group of weary-looking Hebrew travelers came into the inner harbor from the anchored galley. There was a boy with a ruddy complexion in the group, also about nine years old. Beside this Hebrew boy stood an older man, possibly the boy's father, and a pretty Hebrew girl. Another woman and a man with a graying beard were also in the group. Despite their travel-weary looks, there was an excitement in their eyes that showed joy and expectation after a long journey. Linus wondered if his own eyes held such a look as he anticipated going to Rome.

The Hebrew family stepped ashore, carrying their few possessions—a heavy-looking box, some tools, drinking skins, and assorted bundles of linens and rough garments. The bearded man and the young girl stayed with these scattered items while the woman sat on the studded box. The young boy and the other man left them and disappeared into the crowd. The boy interested Linus. He had hard, tough hands and a strong body. What had he heard his father say—he was too soft? *I will become strong like that boy*, he thought.

As slaves started to unload the sacks of grain from the pontoon, Linus felt a strange longing for the young maiden, but she lay in an exciting mystery beyond his experience.

When Gladius had held him close or gently massaged his body, especially in the forbidden parts, he had felt a faint if confused excitement. But his feelings, just watching this Hebrew girl, far exceeded anything he had felt with Gladius.

He smiled at her and screwed up his eyes to obtain a blurred image of her loveliness, obliterating the busy scene that was all around them. She had flowing, reddish hair and deep, dark eyes. He stared at her long legs and then at her thighs, where the hem of her simple and rather dirty-looking shift cut off his gaze. When the young girl realized he was looking at her, she smiled back at him. Linus felt his stomach churn. He didn't know what to do, and he reddened in the hot sun.

Sextus returned.

"The galley will leave tomorrow at sundown," he announced. "I've settled it all with the agent. We can stay at his inn overnight."

Linus was pulled back from hot, strangely exciting thoughts.

He and his family returned to the high wagon, and Gladius maneuvered the cumbersome vehicle through the crowds as the Roman escorts cleared the way. As they left the yard behind, they came to the agent's inn on the outskirts of town. The building was where the new road to Sebaste came down from the hills. There, the family of Flavius Septimus had a meal of lentils and beans, supplemented by fresh pomegranates and grapes, before retiring early, shortly after the sun set. Linus couldn't sleep. He was too excited over the coming journey and the strange yearnings that he had felt for the long-haired Hebrew girl.

The next day, Linus, Copernia, and Gladius set sail for Rome. The galley slipped out of Herod's harbor just before sundown, its sail filling to the fresh breeze, its wooden hull and mast creaking over slanting waves. Their sea voyage had begun.

* * *

Judith was returning from the Nazareth water well late in the afternoon when a noisy caravan approached the village from the south. Dust swirled up in the air from the shuffling camels and hard-pressed donkeys.

Such caravans were a familiar sight on this route to Sepphoris, but the drovers were a nuisance to the villagers. They temporarily fouled the well with their filthy camels and were apt to thieve.

Judith waited for the travelers to pass. She crouched down, holding her water pot and covering the open neck with her headpiece to protect it. The caravan had almost passed when she heard someone shout her name. Looking up through the dust, she thought she saw Miriam.

"Judith! It is you!" the voice called again.

Recognizing the voice, Judith stood up, astounded.

"Miriam! I don't believe it. You're here!" she shouted.

As the dust settled, Joseph and Joshua came into view, and there was James, holding a wretched-looking donkey, with Ruth beside him and running her fingers through her long red hair, trying to comb out the dust.

"They told us this is Nazareth!" Miriam said excitedly. "Oh, Judith, we're here! Where does our family live?"

The last of the camels was pushed on by a noisy drover.

"You've passed the house. It was the first house in the village just down the hill from here. Let me take you all home."

* * *

Meanwhile, Joachim had come up from his daily inspection of his vineyards. He had seen the caravan winding its way up the hillside beside his land. It was not unusual at this time of the year to lose succulent bunches of grapes to these marauding thieves. He opened the worn gate that led into the courtyard of his house and crossed to the porch where Elizabeth was trying to teach young Jon the basics of reading and writing. He went on into the house for a cool drink.

The caravan passed by the gate. After peace was restored, and the swirling dust settled, the gate from Joachim's courtyard had unexpectedly swung open. Judith stood there, shouting excitedly for her master:

"Joachim ben Judah, come quickly! They're here!"

Joachim came out on the porch. Jon joined him. Judith led the strangers over her master's threshold. There was a woman with a rough-looking man leaning on a traveler's stick. The woman pulled back her headpiece, revealing a sunburned face. Joachim immediately recognized her.

"Miriam!" he exclaimed.

The older man with the stick, smiled, his familiar sparkling eyes enhanced by the deep sun-baked wrinkles in his face. He stroked his graying beard with his free hand.

"Joachim ben Judah!" he said respectfully.

Joachim walked over to him.

"You must be Joseph! Of course you're Joseph!"

Turning, he shouted back across the courtyard to his wife and sister-in-law.

"Anna! Elizabeth! Look who's here! They're home! It's Miriam and Joseph!"

Addressing Joseph again, he asked:

"Who else do we have here?"

Joseph introduced the rest of his family.

"Joachim ben Judah, this is my eldest son, James. Back there is my daughter Ruth, and here," he said, putting his arm on Joshua's shoulder, "is your grandson."

Anna and Elizabeth ran out toward them.

"Well, Joachim, don't just stand there," Anna cried, her voice filled with excitement, "let them in!"

The surprised strain of their homecoming broke as they all started to talk at once.

While Joseph learned of Amos' success in establishing their trade, and Miriam became reunited with her family, James monopolized Joachim.

Joshua and Ruth looked around at their new surroundings with subdued awe. This was the finest house either of them had ever seen. Ruth pulled one of the door drapes around her and peered out at Joshua.

"Your grandparents must be very rich," she whispered.

"It's like a prince's house must be," Joshua acknowledged. "It's so grand."

Later, Anna arranged places for them all to sleep. Miriam hadn't slept on cushions since she'd left Zechariah's home with Joseph just before Joshua was born. She sank into them, enjoying their luxurious contours against her tired body. She quickly drifted into sleep. Joseph, snoring deeply, was so tired that he would have slept on the marble slabs in the courtyard.

* * *

While the family had reunited, Jon had sat alone. He didn't want to talk to anyone. He studied Joshua from head to toe with his intense, piercing eyes. He remembered the stories his mother had told him. One story was how his father had been struck dumb prior to his birth and his father's declaration that this had been a sign from God indicating that he, Jon, would be a special child. Jon remembered how his mother had told him that her niece had also had a baby. Jon's father, Zechariah the High Priest, had also declared Miriam's son to be a special child.

Both he and this cousin, whom he was now seeing for the first time, had been considered by their families to be gifts from God. They were expected to dedicate their lives to God in some special way. Jon had stared at Joshua intently. He was looking for something special to manifest itself, but Joshua seemed too worldly as he explored Joachim's home with Ruth, too much like a normal boy, to be a 'chosen one'. Jon felt as if he would have to be the one to make the sacrifice of giving up a normal life to the service of God.

That night, Jon couldn't sleep easily. He was plagued with dreams—interpreted as only vague recollections. He knew they centered on his destiny. Joshua was a part of them, that he knew, but he felt a strange new responsibility. He was to be the future spiritual leader of this reunited family. As he stared wide-eyed into the dark, he felt that this was the moment when he had passed from boyhood to manhood. The weight of the future was on his shoulders. He was God's 'chosen one'.

* * *

Amos honed his chisel on a stone in preparation for another day in his Nazareth carpenter's shop. Doves greeted the new morning as they flew out from Benjamin Levi's huge cote. Amos had gotten used to rising early during those years when they had been sent out to the brick kilns in Egypt. He had always been the one to wake up his father as the dawn broke, and to pull Joshua from his straw pallet on the mud floor of the room where they had all slept. Miriam, Ruth, and Judith had shared the only other room in the house. How he had hated Egypt, but he had continued the habit of rising early. His chisel seemed sharp enough. He picked up his wooden mallet and going outside into the yard, with its open gate on the steet, began using the chisel to plane his timber and hollow the joints. The first of the day's curled wood shavings and dust fell across his forearms. Getting on with his workload, he had quite a lot already accomplished by the time village gossips arrived at the well.

Every now and then, he looked up to see if Judith was out there. She usually stopped by on her way to the well. Amos sensed there was something wrong. Perhaps she was sick. She was always so punctual with her morning visits. Amos buried himself in the business of his trade.

The sun rose higher. Sweat beaded on Amos's brow and back. Fellow artisans called out, "Shalom!" and he kindly replied. He loved being his own taskmaster and not having to work for someone who treated him like a slave.

"Surprise!" Judith shrieked.

Amos looked up. There she was, peering in at him from the street, beaming in the sunlight.

Joseph and Joshua stepped forward.

"Father!" Amos cried.

Putting down his chisel and hammer, he jumped up to greet them, embracing them.

Amos excitedly showed them the carpenter's shop.

"Look, Father! We've got a good business. I've so many orders. You'd be proud of my achievements."

Then he turned to Judith.

"Why didn't you tell me my family was coming home? You didn't say anything."

"I didn't know. I'm telling you, none of us knew. They came with that caravan late yesterday. Everyone's here—Miriam, James, Ruth, as well as Joshua and your father."

"You're back from Egypt for good then?" Amos asked, his eyes moving from Joseph to Joshua.

"Yes, my son, and it looks like we've a great opportunity here. I'm proud of you; you've exceeded my best wishes. Now we just have to teach Joshua more about our trade and we'll have a real family business. What do you say, Joshua? Are you ready to be a full time carpenter?"

Joshua winced.

"Do I have to? I mean, all the time?"

"You were doing so well."

"I don't mind helping out, but I'd rather stay studying with James. I've got more important things to do than whittle wood."

"We are family, Joshua," Joseph said firmly. "Remember what I said. We need to stay together and build up this business. I'm sure you'll have time to study, too. And let me remind you what James told you about pride before we left Egypt. He quoted from the Scriptures."

Joshua looked down at the sawdust.

Joseph peered into the gloomy rooms behind the shop.

"Show us the rest of the house," he said to Amos.

While they were looking around, Judith left them to go to the well and fill her water pot.

Joseph and Joshua followed Amos back into the dark living areas of the old square house that had once belonged to Ahab the Zealot.

* * *

Capernaum was the largest town on the Galilean lake, although the Romans were starting to build a whole new city further south. The zealots, Judas and Jonah, arrived there in the middle of the day, when the sun was at its hottest and the buildings looked their whitest. Capernaum supported a synagogue. It seemed to make sense to them to start their inquiries with the rabbi.

The rabbi looked at them suspiciously. He was a peaceful man, but his eyes were watchful and his lips tight behind a long black beard.

"There's trouble enough in Israel without adding to it, my sons," he said after listening to them. "Our movement here is a passive one. We believe in our pharisaic laws. They allow us to practice our faith under any regime, whether it be Syrian, Roman, Herodian, or Priestly." The beard moved agitatedly as he mouthed his words. "We're not a hotbed of rabble-rousers here!"

Jonah looked at Judas, realizing that there was little official sympathy with their cause. There was a strained silence.

The rabbi began to smile, lightening the mood.

"The man you need to see is Simon the Zealot," he said at length. "He lives close to the water, where he keeps his boats. He's a good man and a hard worker, and he might have the contacts you need. Good luck to you, but make sure you don't stir up any trouble for us here in Capernaum."

The rabbi then turned and walked away from them. His sympathy only went so far.

"Let's seek out this Simon," Jonah said quietly. "We've nothing to lose."

The two men set off for the lakeshore. There, they found a solid square house and in front of it a man about Judas' age. He was sitting down, repairing his nets.

Judas caught the fisherman's attention.

"Excuse us, sir. Are you Simon, the one called 'the Zealot'?"

"Yes," the man replied gruffly, the net held firm in his cut, scarred, sunburned hands. "I'm Simon. Who are you? I don't think I've seen you here before, and you don't sound like Galileans."

"No. We're from Judea," Judas explained. "We fought with the zealots in Jerusalem against Archelaus and the Romans. We were lucky and made our escape. Our leaders wanted us to contact the zealots up here."

"What are your names?"

"Judas, sir, and my friend here, Jonah. Jonah's from Bethlehem. He joined us after his family fled when Herod was king."

"And where are you from?" Simon asked, laying aside his net.

"I'm from Jerusalem. My father was murdered in the early days of the pharisaic revolt. That's when I joined the movement."

Simon looked out at the sunlit water, as if reading its secrets.

"Where have you been in Galilee?" he asked.

"We were mostly in Samaria," answered Jonah, "but we didn't get much support from the Samaritans. They don't seem to care about freedom there. We moved on up through the hill country and settled in Magdala for a while."

"Magdala? That's close by. What news do you bring us from Magdala?"

"Not much. There are a few there who might join. They followed us when we burned out a Roman villa. It was revenge for the death of a child in the village. But it's really very quiet. You're all asleep up here compared with the movement in Judea."

"Not asleep," Simon said, looking up at Jonah, a flash of censure in his almost black eyes, "just waiting. We'll have our moment. God will send us our Messiah."

He raised his eyebrows and stared at his wooden threader.

"What have you really achieved in Jerusalem anyway?" he asked, looking at them, testing their true intentions with a hypnotic gaze. "The rumor that we hear is that the Romans have taken over. What sort of a victory is that?"

"Well, there have been setbacks but, perhaps up here we could cut the Roman supply lines to Judea and Jerusalem," Judas suggested.

"We suffered a severe defeat here some years ago," Simon said gravely. "Many of our best men were crucified. The zealots have been cautious since then, and who can blame them? We keep our heads down in Capernaum. If you really want to join the freedom fighters, you should travel up to the caves. Follow the plain north of here and you'll come to a marshy area and another lake. From there, you'll see high mountains to the north and east. In the foothills of those mountains, you'll find the caves. That's where our men are preparing and waiting. Be patient, our time will come."

Simon the Zealot bent over his nets again, his big, knuckled hands working the threader. He spoke no more.

Judas and Jonah left the shore, a light breeze at their backs, and headed north to search for the caves.

* * *

In his palatial home on the Palatine Hill in Rome, the tall, curly-haired old senator and aristocrat of the Tarquin family looked down at Linus from the folds of his purple-lined toga.

"Ah! Young Flavius' boy," he said as if he was inspecting a new slave who had just been delivered to his house.

Copernia stood a couple of paces behind and delighted in the familiar surroundings of her illustrious uncle's mansion. She felt at home in its opulence and civility.

The senator leaned forward and tapped Linus on the head.

"Look up at me, young Flavian," he said.

The purple-lined toga jostled on its folds.

"Be proud. Your mother comes from a family older than Rome. We created Rome!"

Linus stared, unsure of himself, wanting Gladius beside him, not behind him.

The senator grinned, putting both his hands on the boy's shoulders.

"Linus, I'm going to show you Rome. We're going to visit the Curia, the Imperial Forum, and the Circus Maximus. You're going to learn what makes the Empire work. It's all here."

The Senator pointed to the scene beyond the open balcony.

"It's all between here and the Capitoline Hill. Come, let me show you the heart of the Empire."

Grasping Linus by the hand, his great uncle took him out to the open terrace leading off from the pillared room where they had been introduced.

Copernia and Gladius followed them into the warm sun. The senator pointed across the valley to the hill beyond, endowing the gesture with an almost arrogant flourish.

"See there, that's the Capitoline Hill. That's where Rome began," the senator explained proudly. "And then, just off the Capitoline Hill you can see the splendid Temple of Saturn. Follow the buildings down from there."

His hand moved, rings catching the sun.

"Can you see the triangular facade with the tiled roof?"

"Yes, sir," Linus replied.

363

"That's the Curia. That's where the Senate sits."

Linus pointed at a long gallery of columns.

"And further down, what's that?" he asked.

"The Imperial Forum, Linus. The center of business, commerce, and politics. We'll visit there. I'll also take you to the old Forum of Julius Caesar. See how Rome glistens in the sunlight, Linus. Rome is the center of the world!"

"Will we be able to see the gladiators fight?" the boy asked.

"Gladiators and more, young man. I'll take you to the chariot races!"

Linus looked at Gladius. The two exchanged a grin. At last, it seemed that their visit to Rome was going to be exciting. That long, boring sea trip was going to be worthwhile after all.

The senator kept his promises. In the course of the next few days, he took Linus to all the principal sights of Rome. They visited the Temple of Augustus, sat in on a debate at the Senate, and listened to the poet Ovid at a soiree. They heard speakers at the rostrum, and watched a slave auction in the Forum of Julius. They went to the Palestra and enjoyed the gymnasium and the baths, but it was the chariot races that excited Linus the most.

Linus had never ridden in a chariot before coming to Rome. But in Rome he traveled with the senator in his gilded chariot. It was fun to dash through the streets holding on to the platform rail as the driver whipped on the trotter at great speed. On the day of the races, Linus looked like he owned the world, his toga flowing in the wind as the chariot raced down the Palatine Hill to take the senator and himself to the great circus.

The Circus Maximus was hidden from the center of the city. Hillsides of palatial villas and a corner of Augustus Caesar's palace looked down on the great track. Linus had never seen a building of such size. It would have been easy to get lost. Above the tiers of marble seats, long pennants flew from short masts that marked the top of every rising walkway.

"The pennants are numbered," the senator explained, "so that people can find their way."

Tarquinius, in accord with his prestige and social status, had seats opposite the start and finish line. These were centrally located just below the Emperor's box. Several of his colleagues were already seated in the area roped off for members of the Curia. Linus was introduced to them while the crowds began to fill the stadium.

Vendors sold fruits and souvenirs to the spectators that swarmed through the arches like ants and climbed up the tiers to their seats. It was massive, unreal in scale. There was a hum of excitement in the air.

A trumpet blared from just above their seats.

"The Emperor," the senator whispered in Linus' ear.

Everyone in the stadium rose as one, cheering and shouting: "Caesar!"

"Augustus has been our Emperor for over forty years," the Senator explained. "He's much loved by the people. Never have we known such stability and peace. The plebes have never been so fortunate, Linus. Trade prospers everywhere, and Augustus Caesar is revered as a god."

The people sat down again. After an additional fanfare, the events of the afternoon began.

It was not chariots, however, that emerged from the dark tunnel at the far end of the stadium. A colorful variety of popular entertainers, including jugglers, acrobats, musicians, scantily-veiled dancers, animal trainers, and prancing bears, passed through to the applause of the crowd. All of them stopped opposite the Emperor's box and the Curia stands. There, they raised their right arms with a clenched fist in salutation before presenting a special performance for their royal patron. On and on they came, entertainers from all corners of the Empire, bringing the best of their skills and beauty to the populace of Rome. When the parade was finally over, the trumpets blared again.

Now the chariots came. They entered from the same dark cavern at the end of the stadium. Each one in a long procession circled the track. Some vehicles were gilded like the senator's, but they were smaller, designed purely for racing. There was only room for the driver on the platforms of these racing chariots. The charioteers were dressed in military style, with great plumed helmets and gleaming breastplates. They saluted the Emperor as they passed his box, and each chariot flew a pennant with his chosen colors. The crowds roared with excitement as they cheered their favorites.

The stadium girded itself for the thrill of the coming contest. Altogether, there were thirty charioteers racing in heats of five. The winners of each heat competed in two races of three chariots each. This process selected the finalists in the two-chariot championship. It was at either end of the track that the real competition took place. At these sharp turns, a charioteer could make up valuable time and cut across the path of those behind. This was a dangerous maneuver, as wheels only had to touch momentarily for collisions resulting in death to easily occur. Of the thirty charioteers racing that afternoon, two were killed, thrown from their chariots during such clashes at the turns, trampled to death by those coming up from behind. Five others were severely wounded. But the contest produced its two champions. The final race was ready to be run.

A well-rounded senator brushed past Tarquin and Linus on his way to his seat.

"An exciting afternoon," the man commented, his toga fluttering in the breeze. "It should be a good championship."

Tarquinius smiled sarcastically and muttered under his breath to Linus:

"That's Fabian. He's always been very jealous of our illustrious family."

But Linus was engrossed in waiting for the final spectacular race.

There was a blast on the trumpets and the stadium hushed, awaiting the two contestants. As they emerged from the tunnel at the far end of the arena, Linus and the crowd came alive again with shouts of encouragement. The starter raised his flag and the race began.

In a swirl of dust, the two chariots started up the straight. They were absolutely side by side, chariot to chariot, straining horse to straining horse, when they reached the first turn. As a result of the turn, however, the inside charioteer pulled away and his chariot's dust trail flew up into the eyes of his opponent's horse.

The challenger fought his way through, thrashing out with his whip and pulling up some of the lost distance.

At the halfway mark, they were almost side by side again, the leader holding on to the inside and the challenger taking a wide berth on the outside. The crowds cheered on the underdog, who thrashing out with his whip again, edged ahead to take a short lead. It was vital that he should make the inside track by the next turn. He cut across so that his wheel was close to his opponent's horse, boxing him in on the inside track. But the insider was not willing to slow down to give the lead charioteer the advantage. He let his whip fly and caught the man on the forearm.

The leader jerked in sudden pain. His chariot veered right.

It was a perfect maneuver for the insider, who used the split-second advantage to level up. They raced to the second turn, side by side, wheels almost interlocked. Only inches separated them as they churned up the dust.

Linus and the crowds were standing, yelling their support.

Seeking revenge, the outsider flicked his whip back to strike the inside charioteer across the face. Its thongs, however, hit the driver's helmet and only grazed his cheek.

Spurred on in fury, the insider attempted to move through the narrow path between the center fence and his opponent. Their wheels touched just enough to spin the outsider to the right. The insider made it, increased his lead, and held on to the inside track as they came to the turn.

But the challenge wasn't over.

Still within reach, the outside charioteer laid his whip across the back of the leader. Momentarily stung, the leader pulled on his horse, which reared up as the outsider drew even.

At the turn, their wheels crashed again, deflecting each chariot and sending the one crashing into the central barrier and the other out toward the cheering crowd. This clash slowed them both, so that as the finalists came out of the turn they were still in a dead heat. They whipped their horses on, plumed helmets bright in the sun, pennants snapping on the air, dust and clay flying behind them. They were neck and neck. But in lashing out at one another, their whips became entwined. Their two chariots swerved toward each other. The scene was set for disaster.

With quick reflexes the insider let go of his whip. The sudden release caught his opponent off balance as he pulled to free the tangle. The outside charioteer swerved as the unfortunate man fell, but he bravely held on. There was a thunderous roar from the crowd as the insider pulled away.

Standing again, the outsider tossed the tangled whips to the side and, spurred on by the excited spectators, the two charioteers dashed their vehicles toward the finish line.

The quick reaction of the insider in leaving his whip free had not only avoided an almost certain fatal collision, but had given him a comfortable edge. Racing to the finish, the dust of his chariot again blinded his opponent, who gallantly, but vainly, held on behind him.

There was a winner, and the chariot races were over.

As Linus watched, his lungs aching and throat hoarse from shouting, the victor was presented to Augustus Caesar, who crowned him with a headband of laurels while the enthusiastic crowd hailed the charioteer a hero.

* * *

Shortly after their visit to the Circus Maximus, Copernia suggested it was time to go to Tuscany.

"You need to study, Linus. Your Latin is still atrocious. I'm glad Uncle Tarquinius has been able to show you all these things, but study is more important than chariot races."

"But, Mother, those races were so exciting. That was the best day of my life."

"There will be plenty of other opportunities for all that. I'm arranging for us to travel to Tuscany tomorrow."

The next day, they bade farewell to Uncle Tarquinius and made the journey north to the villa that had been Copernia's childhood home.

This beautiful old house in the gentle landscape to the north of Rome was the place where Copernia had married Flavius Septimus. She introduced him to his grandfather, Cassius Tarquin, and his rather frail grandmother, Prosperine. With his grandfather, Copernia took Linus on a tour around the estate. She proudly showed him the well that was six hundred years old. Later, alone in the vestibule, Copernia pointed at some frescoes painted on the walls.

"These were painted over two hundred years ago, when your ancestors fought with Scipio. If you look carefully over here, you can see some elephants. They represent the power of Hannibal and the Carthaginians. They're running away from Scipio and our Roman forebears. It was a great victory, a turning point in our history."

"Do we have animals like that in Syria?"

"No, Linus. They don't have them here either, unless they are performing in the circus. The elephants came from Africa. Carthage was in Africa."

Linus looked a little bored.

"Everything's so old here, Mother. This house must be **three hundred** years old."

"Part of the house is older, up to five hundred years old."

His mother smiled proudly.

"Our family's been here since that old well was dug."

"And that was six hundred years ago," Linus repeated, matching her smile. "You thought I wasn't listening, didn't you, Mother?"

Copernia warmed to her son, knowing he was making a special effort to listen to her while she extolled her family and their ancient home. She put her arm around the boy's waist.

"I get a little carried away, Linus. I love this place; it's our home. Six hundred years ago this country belonged to the Etruscans. Rome was just an unimportant kingdom of Latins to the south. Our family was important even then."

"How do you know all this?" Linus asked.

"Well, some things have just been passed down in our family but I learned a lot when I was growing up. Your grandfather knew Livy. Sometimes, even today, Livy reads his history in the Forum, but when I was growing up, your grandfather used to invite Livy to the house and he would read to us from his 'History', just like you heard Ovid the other day."

"He was boring. I think I'd have rather heard Livy's stories about our glorious past."

"Well, that's because you found the Latin difficult, Linus. That's exactly why you're going to improve your Latin while you're here. We're arranging lessons for you every day. Important though it is to speak excellent Greek, especially in Syria, right here in the heart of the Empire, you also need to know good Latin. You need something better than the rough Latin used by your father's soldiers and slaves, and that dreadful Aramaic's never going to get you very far outside Syria."

Linus obviously wasn't thrilled at the prospect of more schooling, but he accepted the challenge. In Rome, indeed, ever since they had arrived in Italia, the days had shown him how important his family was. He didn't want to let them down by appearing an unworthy heir. Extensive coaching in Latin started the next day.

CHAPTER FIVE

The Calm Before the Storm

The first cool nights of early autumn descended on the Galilean landscape. Threshing floors were busy and winepresses flowed as the harvest was gathered. It had been yet another good year.

Joachim thanked God for his fortunes. His barns were full. His vines had produced an excellent crop of grapes. There seemed to be no end to the prosperity of his agricultural endeavors. He looked forward to celebrating the feast of Booths. Succot was only a month away. And now, his whole family would be gathered together to celebrate. Never had the coming festival meant more.

"It will be good for all of us to celebrate Succot together," Joachim suggested to Joseph. "We usually build our booths down in the vineyard. I must look for suitable branches."

Joseph was a little in awe of Joachim. Not being a farmer, the feast of Booths meant little to him. He had always ignored it in Bethlehem. In Alexandria, he had constructed a booth out of palm fronds a couple of times for Miriam and Joshua's sakes. He had just built a palm frond wall up around the side bench. The structure had been more of a temporary playhouse for Joshua and Ruth. Only Joshua had ever slept out in it.

But Joseph would play his part. He was a carpenter, after all.

"Where has the year gone?" he responded. "Is it really that season again? I'll help you. How many booths will you want to build?"

"Let me see," Joachim said, turning his thumbs in his clasped hands. "There will be three for my family, including Judith, and I suppose three for yours, if Joshua and Ruth can still share."

"They'll have to. They shared a booth in Alexandria."

"Jon and Joshua could share if Ruth would go in with Elizabeth."

"All right," Joseph agreed.

Joachim did not let Joseph forget. As Succot drew near he called on him to help with the construction of the bowers, and there was no question in the patriarch's mind that they were all going to stay together, giving their thanks as one family.

After the years in Egypt, Joseph was his own master again and not responsible to some foreign overseer. He could work when he wanted to work and take time off as he pleased, knowing that Amos would fulfill all their obligations. Amos had made an excellent start in establishing their family workshop. Joseph loved to encourage him, passing on his skills with chisel and hammer. It also gave him great joy to show young Joshua how to turn a plain piece of timber into a useful item. He hummed as he worked. It was this newfound joy that took some of the age from his kindly old face.

Miriam was pleased to have a house to run again, and Ruth was a great help to her. They were always close to Joachim and Anna. Joachim provided them with everything they needed. They were able to eat an abundance of good fruit, and they were never short of the best grain. It was such a joy after the hardships of Egypt.

James was the only one to regret their settling in Nazareth. He missed his work at the Great Synagogue in Alexandria, and frankly found Nazareth very provincial after the excitement of his Egyptian scholarship. James spoke Greek as fluently as he did Aramaic, but in Nazareth not even the rabbi spoke Greek. James found his conversations with Joachim stimulating enough, but generally too conservative. Joshua was his only real outlet, because Joshua still respected him for his learning and was open to challenges.

On an evening when James and Joshua took one of their customary walks discussing the prophecies they had studied together in Egypt, a Roman horseman passed them on the road north from Nazareth. He wore a simple leather tunic and no insignia of office. The man smiled and greeted them in Aramaic.

"It's unusual for a Roman to speak in Aramaic," James said as they stood and watched the horseman ride on. "They usually only speak Greek."

"But nobody speaks Greek here. It's not like Alexandria," Joshua said.

"They may not speak much Greek in Nazareth, but Greek is the language of our world. The more influence these Romans have, the more we're going to need to speak and write in Greek. Don't forget your Greek, Joshua. One day you'll need it. The Romans in our part of the world speak Greek. You hardly hear Latin."

Joshua watched the Roman as one of the village boys cursed the horseman.

"Why do so many people say all Romans are bad?" he asked.

"They're afraid, Joshua. After all, our teachers in Alexandria were Roman citizens. We live in a Roman world. The majority of Romans don't believe in God, but that's mostly because we haven't taught them about Jehovah. Maybe if they knew how the Lord saved our people in the face of impossible conquest and wickedness again and again, they'd understand why we worship the way we do. In fact, if you remember, Joshua, the school in Alexandria taught that God used the great empires of the unbelievers to teach us His awesome power and make us return to our Law and the purity of our Faith. Do you remember the words of the prophet: 'Who stirred up one from the East whom victory meets at every step?' It was God working through those Persian kings."

With the Roman horseman out of sight, the children of the village turned to games.

"Do you think the Romans will help us to obey our God better, then?" Joshua asked.

"Well, they don't stop us worshipping God, do they? The Romans are sometimes cruel, but they haven't made us slaves, at least not unless we rebel against them. Look how prosperous your grandfather is. The Romans don't appear to have interfered with him. In contrast, however, remember the stories Elizabeth tells of the way Jon's father was put to death by the King of the Jews, or the horror that I witnessed myself when the king's soldiers came to Bethlehem and threw all the baby boys down the well. Jews are sometimes just as cruel as Romans. As long as the Romans don't harm us or interfere with our customs and our religious laws, we shouldn't fear them. So, yes...If they provide us with a peaceful world, such as was the case in Alexandria, so that we can live and worship God without fear, then maybe the Romans will help us to obey God better."

"Then we shouldn't really be afraid of them?"

"A lot of people are. But we weren't afraid of the Romans in Alexandria, were we? So why should we be afraid of them here?"

James smiled at Joshua, who still looked concerned.

"I'm not," Joshua said.

Their conversation returned to the prophecies of Isaiah and their interpretation of those Scriptures.

* * *

Still bright in the late afternoon of a Galilean autumnal day, the sun cast an intense light that built shadows over the familiar countryside. The closer Flavius drew to Magdala, the more flustered he felt. He didn't know what to expect. Perhaps his villa had been burned to the ground after his family had left. Almost certainly, it had been plundered. His vineyards were probably overrun with late summer tares, and only thieves could have harvested his grapes. He was very lonely, his happy Galilean life having become shattered by the real possibility of rebellion. Though he missed Copernia and Linus, duty demanded that he stay in Galilee during these uncertain times. The reality of the ordeal that had befallen his family descended on him as he rode toward the village.

Flavius could see the buildings ahead and the tall cypress trees at the bottom of the hill. Esther came into his thoughts.

In those days, he had shown no fear in visiting the village. Ahead of him, he could see the small square house on the outskirts that had been his source of pleasure and the scene of his marital indiscretion. Staring in that direction for a moment, he tugged on his horse to turn left. He knew he must not dwell on the past and climbed the track that led up to his villa.

The hillside looked just the same. Turning around one more time, as if to reassure himself that he was back, he saw below him the familiar view across the lake to the rough country of the Gadarenes. Fishing boats were coming in to bring their evening catch to Magdala, and the smell of the conifers rose up from the cypress grove. These well-remembered scenes and senses only made Flavius more nervous in anticipation of what he would find. He kicked his horse and rode up the hill to look ahead and catch the first glimpse of his derelict home.

Silence hung over the blackened structure. Gaunt stanchions of the marble architrave that had supported the terrace roof now pierced the skyline; and the charred timbers of the vestibule gable looked somehow worse than the way they had been described by Linus and Gladius.

Flavius dismounted and gingerly led his horse through the gate into the yard. Leaves and debris littered the once-pristine entrance, but he could see that most of the villa was intact. Nobody had burned it to the ground, as he had feared. A lizard, disturbed by the commander's presence, slithered off across the yard, rustling the leaves that covered the marble slabs. Flavius tethered his horse and entered the vestibule.

The building smelled musty. Odors of smoke and burned wood had long since left, but a smell of neglect and decay had taken over. Flavius surveyed the damaged roof and the ruins of the terrace. The beautiful garden that he and Copernia had lovingly planted was wild. Half-burned torches and fallen timbers were still piled where Linus had dragged them. The entire balcony's arbor roof was gone.

Flavius moved on into the dining area, where to his surprise and delight he found that little had been disturbed. The statuettes were standing in their niches, and the lamps and reclining couches were still in place. Around the atrium, Copernia's woven awnings hung down, and the fresh green of the plants growing by the central pool caught the late afternoon light, giving that same sense of tranquility they had given just a few months before. The dank, musty smell continued to pervade the house, and a scum covered the water in the atrium pool; but there was little evidence that smoke or fire had damaged this inner area. *Copernia was right*, he thought. *Linus and Gladius did save the villa.*

Relieved, Flavius sat down in one of the chairs on the atrium porch. He untied a part of his leather tunic. He had ridden all day from Sepphoris, and the added nervous tension had made him both mentally and physically tired. His eyes closed as the autumnal sunlight offered its last burst of warmth. He was drifting into sleep, only to be alerted by the cracking of a jar and the sound of footsteps.

Flavius coiled in a soldier's strength. The sound had come from the kitchen wing and its storerooms. He got up, senses alert, straightened his cuirass and returned to the dining area. There, he saw a young girl, about nine years old, cross to the vestibule. She was dressed in a poor, very simple shift and had the dark features of a Hebrew child. He followed her out to the courtyard, and as she ran she tripped on some debris and fell.

"Don't be afraid," Flavius called out to her in Aramaic as he ran to help her. "Who are you?"

The girl had grazed her knee and the palm of her hand, but she didn't appear to be badly hurt. She got up and stumbled as she looked back at Flavius with big brown eyes. Dark, tangled hair fell from her shoulders.

Flavius smiled back.

"Come here," he said. "Don't be afraid. I hope you didn't hurt yourself."

The girl seemed surprised to hear Flavius speak to her in her own language. She stood and stared at him.

Flavius advanced toward her, slowly holding out his hand for her to reach.

"What's your name, little girl?" he asked.

"Maria."

"That's a pretty name. Why don't we go back in the house and see if we can find some water to wash your knee?"

Maria remained silent, but her stare turned to a smile as she yielded to his kindness and gave him her hand.

There was something about her smile that seemed familiar to Flavius, even her eyes. Esther echoed across his memory. As he led her back through the kitchen wing toward the well, he could see that smile wherever he turned. It gnawed at his conscience. *Could this be one of Esther's children?* he thought, as he removed the cover from the well and cupped his hands in the clear water.

He cleaned and removed the dirt from the girl's knee. The child flinched as the water soaked into her broken skin.

"Have you come here before?" Flavius asked.

"Sometimes."

"Why do you come to a Roman house? This is my house, you know."

"But you are never here," Maria pleaded a little fearfully.

"I don't mind," Flavius reassured her, dabbing at her knee, "but what makes you come up here?"

"I like it. It's quiet and beautiful. Sometimes, I go right up the hill and just sit and look at the lake from up there. I can almost imagine I'm a bird up there. The houses look so small. Everything looks better from up here."

"Haven't you any friends?"

"No, not really. They are not very nice to me in the village. They say my mother is a wicked woman full of devils. They ignore us. I haven't had any friends since my little sister died. That's why I come up here. My mother doesn't like me hanging around our house; she says it disturbs her business."

Flavius flinched. Now, he knew. His conscience pricked him even more as he contemplated the possibility that he might be speaking to his own daughter. It was possible; it had all happened just ten years ago. This little girl was about the right age—the same age as Linus. He found himself searching her face for signs of his own.

"Why do you talk in our language?" Maria asked, bravely looking up into Flavius' face.

"Because it is our language," Flavius said simply. "This is also my home."

"Other Romans don't talk like you."

"No, Maria. But I think they should."

"I like you, you're different. Can I stay up here with you?"

Flavius took the little girl into his arms.

"No, sweet one. Your mother really needs you."

He held her for a moment and could feel the affection flow between them. He kissed her lightly on the top of her head. Taking her hand, he walked her back through the villa.

"Can I come here again? This is my secret place," the girl said, looking up at the commander of the Sepphoris garrison.

Flavius felt her hand, so warm and trusting in his. He nodded at her but said nothing. Carefully, they crossed the courtyard, and Flavius led Maria out to the track beyond the gate.

"You can go home now, Maria. Be careful of the debris in the future."

The young girl hobbled off down the hill.

Flavius watched her until she disappeared.

Sunlight turned to gold, and the lake changed from a deep blue to the silvery sheen of evening. The sun moved lower in the western sky. Long shadows of cypress trees streaked the surrounding landscape.

Flavius returned to the loneliness of the villa and shut the courtyard gate, thoughts of Esther and the guilt of their last night of passion dancing before him.

CHAPTER SIX

Coming of Age

As a young man now almost twelve, Joshua was excited at the prospect of being presented at the Temple and seeing Jerusalem. James had prepared him well. In the caravan on their journey down from Nazareth, James had talked continually with him, testing him on his knowledge by discussing in detail the Prophets and the Books of Moses. They went over all the laws of purification and preparation. Joshua was crammed with knowledge. He confidently looked forward to seeing the Temple and receiving the formal blessing that would mark his move to manhood.

Jon joined them for a while, for he, too, was to be presented at the Temple, but he hardly spoke to them and soon returned to his mother.

Joachim and the women were riding donkeys, while Joseph and Amos led two mules.

Ruth walked along with her father. She had grown tall and lithe. Her long auburn hair seductively caught the breeze.

"Jon doesn't seem to fit in with Miriam's family," she said.

"A bit like your brother, Jonah."

"Father, do you think we'll ever see Jonah again?"

"I've no idea. He might have gone back to Bethlehem, but I doubt it. Like this Jon, he was always a loner. I think we just have to accept he's gone his own way. I just hope he's all right. I look at it this way, Ruth. If I lost my son Jonah, I gained a son in Joshua."

"When we're in Jerusalem, maybe we can go to Bethlehem and find out if Jonah ever returned."

"That might be a good idea."

Joseph stroked his straggly, gray, beard and looked at his daughter. She was more than old enough for marriage.

"God will find you a man soon, Ruth. After we have all celebrated the Passover and we return to Galilee, we must look for a spouse for you."

Ruth blushed. The young men in Nazareth had been teasing her and had admired her long red hair. Even Amos had gone so far as to say that she should take a husband so as to give them more room in the house!

"If you think it's time for me to be married, Father, then I'll be happy to leave you and give you grandchildren. My children will be your first grandchildren."

Joseph smiled.

"Why doesn't James marry? Father, he's so serious all the time. Maybe a nice young bride would liven him up a bit."

"James is different," Joseph said simply.

"Do you think he's good for Joshua?"

"Joshua doesn't work as hard as Amos," Joseph admitted.

Ruth looked up at her father.

"No, because he's always off with James," she said deliberately. "Joshua used to be fun when he was younger, but he's getting more like James every day."

"James is a good man," Joseph answered. "I'm sure he'll make an excellent rabbi. He can't be a bad influence on Joshua. We could never have taught him all the things that James has taught him."

"Well, I'm glad I've got you, Miriam, and Amos," Ruth said, squeezing her father's hand. "I feel like we've lost Joshua, just like we lost Jonah. Joshua doesn't seem the same as us anymore. He doesn't laugh as much. He's becoming too serious—almost mysterious."

"I agree he isn't kin, Ruth, but we've given him a good home, and as I said, God gave him to us. I just think Joshua's very excited and serious about our religion. This visit to Jerusalem is very important to him."

"I suppose you're right, Father, but I wish he would talk to us more. It's bad enough having Jon over there, who never says anything, and James, who talks about things that we don't understand. Joshua used to talk to us, but he doesn't seem to want to anymore."

"He will, Ruth, he's just growing up. When you get married and have your own children you'll see how they change over the years. We can't be one family forever, and I don't think it'll be too long before we find that spouse for you and you'll have your own family to worry about. When that happens, it'll be Joshua who'll come to me and say how much he misses the days when he used to play with Ruth!"

They laughed together. Joseph always made such good, practical, common sense. In some ways, he was a greater comfort to Ruth than Miriam, who now seemed a little unapproachable in the ease of her more wealthy family.

As dusk fell, the Passover moon, not quite full, rose up in the sky, and the caravan prepared to stop and make camp for the night. The early spring air in the high country of Samaria was cooler than in Galilee, and they needed their blankets to keep themselves warm.

The next day, they reached Judea and Jerusalem. The caravan passed through the city gates in the northern wall. Joseph hadn't visited Jerusalem all that many times in the past, but Judea was his home territory. For ten years he'd been away. For Ruth and Amos, Jerusalem was just another city like Sepphoris, Sebaste, or Egyptian Alexandria. But Joachim, Anna, and Elizabeth joined in Joseph's excitement. They had avoided the Holy City for many years, but the shadow of Zechariah's murder by the Herodians had now receded enough for them to appreciate the continued importance in their lives of visiting the Temple and making their sacrifices.

There seemed to be more evidence of the Roman presence than in the days of King Herod. In the west of the city, white marble buildings almost outnumbered the yellow stone structures of Semitic architecture. A new viaduct was under construction. Roman chariots rattled down the streets. It was quite evident that the weak rule of Archelaus had given way to Roman government. There were soldiers everywhere. The people looked cowed and defeated. The pall of black smoke, however, rising up from Mount Moriah, reassured them that God's holy Temple was still intact, and despite the presence of Rome, the faith of the Jews had not diminished.

* * *

Joshua had no comparisons to make between Jerusalem as he now saw it and the city of King Herod's time. Something deep within him was telling him that this city was his city. He had never found anything in his life to be so personal and emotional as this first experience of Jerusalem. He could see that Jerusalem lacked the grandeur of Alexandria, but he knew how important Jerusalem was to the Jewish people, and he felt an extraordinary empathy with the place.

It was as if this was the moment of his spiritual crowning—the moment when he first went forth to greet his people and to taste his role as the 'Prince of Peace'. Images of divine purpose resonated, holy and portentous, as the caravan moved on toward the inner city. There was an ineffable lightness to his being. He wanted to reach out and touch the people and preach the message of Isaiah: 'Unto us a son is given, unto us a king is born.' His vision of service to God became imbued with a love so profound that he reeled in awe. *How can I be that son?* he mused. *How can I dare think it?*

He could hear the sounds of the city, and he could smell the spices of the bazaar that reminded him of Alexandria, but his mind was inundated with a soaring personal awareness. As the camels and donkeys of the caravan moved on toward Mount Moriah, Joshua became swept up further in his vision of his future. He saw the faces of the crowds all merging with arms outstretched toward him. The sounds drifted into a common cry welling up toward him—*'Prince of Peace!'*

Joshua stopped walking. In his trance, he looked up in wonderment. With a warm smile, he held out his hands to those elusive masses. Reality returned as a donkey butted him from behind, knocking him to the ground.

The hem of Joshua's garment became caught by the foot of a passing camel. Momentarily, Joshua feared that he would be trampled to death. This fear, along with the reality of the stench in a street thick with animal waste, and the shouts of those behind him telling him to get out of their way, broke his trance.

James rushed back to him and helped him to his feet.

"What happened?"

"I don't know...I fell."

"Look at you!" James admonished him. "Your tunic's covered in dung, and you smell worse than a camel. You aren't fit to enter the Temple.

Pay attention to what you're doing, this isn't Nazareth, you've got to be careful. You're in the city now. Come on with me or we'll lose sight of your mother and the rest of the family."

"I'm sorry, James, I was just thinking too much and I lost track of where we are going. My mind was back with Isaiah and how he prophesied and preached his message of hope for Jerusalem. He was right here, James, where we are now."

James looked at his prodigy, sensing a new awareness that made him feel both proud and wary.

"Move on!" one of the drovers yelled.

James looked ahead and caught a glimpse of their three donkeys carrying Miriam, Anna, and Elizabeth.

"There they are, Joshua. We must walk fast to catch up with them."

The camel train halted in the area between Mount Zion and Mount Moriah. The long façade of King Herod's Temple wall rose above the squalor of the camel stalls and drovers' tents.

The pilgrims left in all directions, carrying their precious possessions, some heading straight for the great Triple Gate.

Joachim and Joseph got their families together and walked to Mount Zion, where, with the assistance of the caravan agent, they took two rooms in a crowded house.

* * *

After carefully cleaning off the filth, Miriam washed Joshua's tunic. It was still three days to the Passover, and Joachim had decided to make their sacrifices at the Temple the next day. The Temple had been Miriam's whole childhood, and she reflected back on those carefree days in the House of the Virgins as she scrubbed the tunic, beating out the dirt with a flat stone.

Joshua joined her.

"You know, the last time that I was at the Temple," she said, "was when Joseph brought me back to Jerusalem for purification after you were born. It was strange, Joshua, but that was the last time that I saw the young man, Gabriel."

Miriam looked at her son. He was definitely now a young man, and his days of childhood were ending. *My son has grown up as fast as Joseph's Ruth*, she thought. Ruth was five years older than Joshua.

"It won't be long before Ruth will be ready to marry," she said. "She's three years older than I was when I married Joseph."

"Will Ruth be able to choose whom she wants to marry, or will her marriage be arranged like yours, Mother?"

"I expect Joseph will arrange something, but there should be a measure of choice. If I had not liked Joseph after we were introduced, I would have let the High Priest know my feelings. Knowing Ruth, I'm sure she'll let us know her feelings if she doesn't approve of Joseph's choice. We're lucky in a way, because your grandparents are well respected and Ruth will probably have many suitable suitors."

Miriam took the tunic up onto the roof of the house to pin it down to dry.

"It won't dry properly until the sun rises tomorrow," she said, "but at least you'll be able to wear it for Passover."

They came back down the stone steps.

"Let's go back into the other room and join the family."

The Passover moon rose over the holy city and cast its pale, yellow light through the courts of the Temple. It was a completely still night without a cloud in the sky. The turmoil of the daytime streets gave way to nocturnal tranquility.

* * *

In Jerusalem, regardless of the approaching Passover, work continued on the completion of the Roman fortress named Antonia's Tower. The building, which had been started in the last days of King Herod, had remained unfinished during the troubled years of Archelaus. Now, however, with a Roman prefect firmly established in Jerusalem, the work was to be finished. A permanent Roman surveillance would now scan all Temple activities from this tower, which hovered over the very courts of the sacred buildings like a watching vulture.

The House of the Virgins, disbanded during the pharisaic revolt, had been taken over by the Romans and incorporated into part of this fortress, so that the conqueror had control within the Temple itself. The noise of hammers and stonemasons' chisels drifted across the inner courts and reminded the Passover pilgrims that there was a new authority in Jerusalem. The last vestige of Maccabean freedom had vanished from the holy city. The Herodian tetrarchs, however, continued to hold weak kingships in Galilee and the land beyond the Jordan, and under Philip between Galilee and the Syrian Province, but all in the shadow of Rome.

Even Joachim, with his philosophical tolerance of the Roman occupation, was moved.

"It's not the same," he muttered as the family made their way through the throngs of pilgrims in the great Court of the Gentiles. "We are becoming absorbed by Rome, and it's not all for the good."

There were Roman soldiers on duty within the vast outer court, ready if necessary to control the crowds should any pharisaic rebels seek to make trouble during the festival week. Roman guards even stood by the entrance into the Sanhedrin council chamber. But despite this surveillance, Temple business was brisk. The moneychangers were still collecting shekels for the Temple and had increased their commissions. Doves, lambs, and goats were readily available for sacrifice. The prophets of doom and suspect soothsayers mixed freely with the beggars and the maimed. Some things never changed.

Joseph and Joachim purchased the necessary turtle doves for Jon and Joshua's presentations and also selected a lamb for the coming feast. They took the doves to the inner courts.

Thank goodness this has remained sacred, Joachim observed. *At least those Roman soldiers have respected the Court of the Jews!*

At the entrance to the priestly court with its great bronze doors, the men took Joshua and Jon with them for the rite of passage. The womenfolk remained in the Court of the Jews.

* * *

James was not as familiar with the Temple as he was with the sacred Scriptures. He had been presented and received his blessing from one of the Temple priests some fifteen years before, the year that his mother had passed away. Otherwise, his schooling was strictly synagogue, and he had been so heavily influenced by the rabbinical schools in Alexandria that the Temple, with its ancient ritual, seemed archaic.

Joshua's keen sense of learning and remarkable maturity of knowledge had been nurtured by James' constant drilling and training.

Jon looked at his cousin with penetrating eyes as they reached the top of the steps leading into the priestly court. They rarely spoke to each other, but deep down Jon knew that Joshua was special. He'd never forgotten the stories that his mother, Elizabeth, had shared with him about his own destiny and that Joshua would be a part of that destiny. Now, they were both about to dedicate their lives to God in the blessing of manhood.

A Temple priest came out and escorted them to the rooms of presentation. He took the two turtle doves up into the Sanctuary. The room they were left in was musty, dark and sparsely furnished. There was an oil lamp on a stand and a menorah of seven more on a small table. Close by, was a large wooden chair draped with finely woven white material that featured the Magan David, or star symbol, embroidered in a thread of gold. There was a bench along the far wall, and the men sat there with the two boys as they waited for the priest to return.

Jon, who rarely showed any outward emotions, took hold of Joshua's hand. Joshua looked at his cousin and squeezed his heavy, clasped hand in response. The priest returned, accompanied by a large man, the High Priest, who, like them all, seemed taller by the triple crown that he wore. His robes and thummin were encrusted in jewels.

The priest called Jon forward.

Jon stood in front of the High Priest. The huge man had picked up the white shawl and sat before him in the wooden chair.

"Who was your father?" the High Priest asked.

"My father was Zechariah, the High Priest," Jon answered.

The High Priest looked over at Joachim and Joseph as if he questioned the boy's reply.

Joachim nodded, and the High Priest continued:

"Where are you from and what is your name?"

"I am Jon ben Zechariah and we live in Galilee. I live with my mother and her sister's family."

"This is your nearest male relative?" he said, turning toward Joachim once again.

"Er... yes, sir."

Sounding a lot less pompous and genuinely pleased, the High Priest spoke to Joachim.

"Joachim ben Judah! I remember you. You were once a priest serving with me. You left the Temple and retired to private life. My goodness, that was some years ago now."

Joachim smiled. But he'd tried hard over the years to banish from his mind all thoughts of his earlier life as a priest in the Temple.

The High Priest pronounced a blessing over Jon, standing up to his full height, he laid both his hands on the young man's shoulders.

Jon cast an eye at Joshua. His demeanor indicated that he wasn't impressed by such pomp and ceremony.

A moment later, Joshua was also called forward. The High Priest asked him similar questions. When the High Priest asked who was Joshua's father, Joshua replied:

"Gabriel."

James winced. This was not what he had suggested Joshua should say.

"Gabriel?" asked the High Priest. "Of what lineage? Who was your father's family?"

"Gabriel was a son of God," Joshua continued calmly. "My Father has no lineage."

Jon's eyes widened as he studied his cousin, admiring the boldness of his voice.

The High Priest looked back at Joachim and Joseph for some affirmation or interpretation.

"Gabriel was a priest at the Temple!" Joachim blurted out. "That's what Joshua means by 'son of God'. He was a priest, just as we were in our youth."

The High Priest lowered one eyebrow and raised the other.

Joshua hid a smile and quietly avoided the giant man's eyes.

"You are also from Galilee?" the High Priest asked.

"Yes, sir. My family lives in Nazareth."

"Joshua of Nazareth," the High Priest said. "And this man here is your guardian?" he asked, pointing at Joseph.

"He is like a father to me, sir. I never knew my father."

A tear welled in Joseph's eye. He carefully removed it.

The High Priest stood up and placed his hands on Joshua's shoulders. He pronounced his blessing, and then addressing them all, recited the Ten Commandments that Moses had declared to the Jews in the days of their desert wandering. The simple ceremony ended with a prayer and exhortation to the two young men that they should always live their lives in obedience to the laws of the Jewish people as laid down in the

Torah. The High Priest left them, and the other priest escorted them back through the side gate of the great bronze doors to the lower level of the inner court. There, Amos and the women greeted them, and each in turn embraced Jon and Joshua.

* * *

After the Passover, Joachim and Joseph again brought their families back to the Temple. Elizabeth and Anna were anxious to buy souvenirs, as it had been so long since they had been in Jerusalem.

James took Joshua and Jon to the Sanhedrin. He was anxious to listen to a debate and make comparisons with the great theological discussions in Alexandria. They could only stand in the entrance area, as all seating in the great council chamber was reserved for the members. This post-Passover meeting was fully attended, because all the council members were in Jerusalem for the festival. The Pharisees and the Sadducees were having one of their customary clashes in a theological struggle over the passage of the dead.

The Pharisees were the minority among the Sanhedrin members, but they were never afraid to speak their mind. The Sadducees rarely discussed deep theological issues, preferring to debate more superficial matters of finance and Temple housekeeping, but they were the undisputed masters of the Temple. The recent pharisaic movement in Jerusalem, which had been such a political disaster, became a cause for smug satisfaction among the Sadducee Temple hierarchy, yet it caused those pharisaic Sanhedrin members to boldly increase their theological debate.

Joshua listened intently as an eager young Pharisee assured the Sanhedrin that before those gathered at this assembly had time to die, the Messiah would come and the end time would begin.

"When that time comes," the young man decreed with prophetic oratory, "there will be neither death nor birth. All will be gathered into one place to be judged by the Messiah as to their future. Those who have lived by obedience to the full law will see God, and those who have lived their lives solely for their own benefit and without reference to our laws, will assuredly be condemned. There will be eternal life and eternal damnation."

There were shouts and jeers from the Sadducee majority, and the

Roman guards standing behind James, Joshua, and Jon peered inside the chamber to see that there was no potential danger that might lead to rioting. The young Pharisee continued boldly, but order in the Council Chamber, fueled by fear of Roman intervention, was maintained.

"Don't you remember the words of Micah the prophet?" he said. "'Will the Lord be satisfied with thousands of rams, or with ten thousand rivers of oil? Shall I give my eldest son for my sin, my own flesh and blood for the sins that are within me?' Was not this the path that Abraham took, and did not the Lord stop him just in time as he was about to sacrifice Isaac, his only son? No, you know what Micah prophesied: 'What does the Lord require of us, but to do justly and to love mercy and to walk humbly with our God.'"

Jon looked at Joshua. He could tell from Joshua's intensity that he was thinking the same way. The Temple sacrifices did not make much sense to either of them. There was much that this young Pharisee was saying that made sense.

James was uneasy, for although his thinking was open to many intellectual advances, he was a traditionalist. He sensed Jon and Joshua's obvious pleasure at hearing the young Pharisee speak out, and he whispered a cautionary word into Joshua's ear:

"Beware of such loose statements, Joshua. Although the man has accurately quoted from the prophets, remember the importance of Yom Kippur. Our religion has been built up on sacrifice. We must atone for our sins and those of our forebears."

Joshua asked:

"Can we not atone for our sins, James, by keeping the Law without killing animals for no real purpose? Why did we have to kill those turtle doves the other day? We never made sacrifices in Alexandria nor in Nazareth, so why here? Aren't they an equal part of God's creation? Why should we have to sacrifice them for God?"

By now, an elderly Sadducee had stood up and was haranguing the young Pharisee.

"How dare you suggest that we are not the guardians of the Law! The Law that we protect is the Law of Moses, and we protect it in its purity. There is no place in the words of Moses for resurrection and eternal life! Your incessant revision and reinterpretation of the Law has made you blind to the real Law!"

There were cheers from the Sadducee majority, and again the Roman guards peered inside the chamber to check that all was in order. The meeting then ended, and members of the Sanhedrin started to leave the building. Joshua watched as they walked by, but made no attempt to leave, despite James telling him that they must go. He waited until the young Pharisee who had been speaking, reached the door.

"I'm interested in what you had to say," Joshua said. "You mentioned that the Messiah will come before these men die. You mean that the Messiah will come now?"

"Very soon, my son. We are living in the last days. The signs are all here."

Not wishing to discuss the matter with one so young, the Pharisee pushed on past Joshua to go out into the sunlit court.

Joshua followed.

"Please, sir!" he called after him. "Couldn't the Messiah be the last sacrifice in preparation for the end time? You quoted from Micah, but what about Isaiah? Didn't Isaiah mention that God will send his servant and that he will be ridiculed and suffer many things, including death? But in his message many will be saved, and in his death he shall offer up their sins."

The Pharisee looked back at Joshua, and like the High Priest at his presentation, raised his eyebrows at the youth in curiosity and irritation.

"A remarkable quote, young man," he said. "You astound me with your knowledge."

James' pupil had once again shown his training and grasp of the Holy Scriptures.

The Pharisee, however, did not wish to engage in further discussion with the precocious boy and walked on, shaking his head as he muttered to himself.

James took Jon and Joshua back to the crowded stalls of the Temple bazaar to look for the rest of the family.

Joshua underwent a metamorphosis during those days in Jerusalem. Much of the time he explored the streets, often on his own, but increasingly more with Jon, who, for the first time since their meeting in his grandfather's house, was opening up a friendship toward him. Joshua did not realize Jon's admiration for his scriptural knowledge, and he saw the change in Jon as a newfound freedom. The two of them roamed the bazaars and delighted in the bustle of Jerusalem's street life. It was, after all, a lot more exciting than the village square in Nazareth.

They sat on a stone wall together, pulling apart a loaf of bread that they had purchased.

"What did you think of that man in the Sanhedrin the other day?" Joshua asked.

"The one you spoke to afterward?"

"Yes. He spoke of the Messiah. Remember how he said the Messiah would come very soon. Do you think Isaiah wrote about the Messiah? He said our savior would be like a servant. Do you think that a great leader can really be like a servant?"

"If a rich man were to give all he had to the poor, he would be a servant to the poor. Isn't that rather like this loaf of bread? If we had given it to some beggar, we would have been servants to the beggar."

"Right, Jon, but we're not rich."

"But we aren't starving, and your grandfather's wealthy."

Joshua watched the people—a diverse crowd. He chewed on the bread.

"Yes. My grandfather is rich, and he helps us a lot. He's helped us with our business, and because of that we're not poor anymore. Rich men can help poor people, but here in Jerusalem there must be lots of rich people, and yet there are so many beggars."

"Some of them are sick and diseased," Jon noted.

"And because our Law says we shouldn't touch the diseased and unclean, I suppose we can't help them. Sometimes, our Law is stupid!"

"Joshua! You'd better not let anybody hear you say that, especially James."

A silly grin then came across Jon's face as his grudging admiration for his outspoken cousin surfaced again.

"But you're right. Sometimes, the rules and regulations do seem a little strange."

Jon tore off another chunk of bread.

"Maybe the Messiah will make some changes."

"I wonder how soon the Messiah will come?" Joshua asked, looking down at the ground, lost in thought.

"Maybe he's already here," Jon answered, giving a furtive glance at his cousin.

Joshua's eyes lit up.

"Do you think the Messiah will be a king or prince? Or do you think he'll be a rabbi—someone like James?"

"I don't think the Messiah has to be a king," Jon said, wiping his mouth. "I suppose he could be a rabbi, but how will we know he's the Messiah?"

Joshua turned pale and became silent.

"Maybe the 'Prince of Peace' and the Messiah are the same person," he answered.

Jon noticed the change.

"What's wrong?" he asked. "Are you afraid?"

"Nothing, Jon. I was just thinking...Well, yes...I am afraid. Let's go back to the house. I need to pray."

They returned home in silence.

* * *

Joshua spent much of the last two days of their sojourn in Jerusalem alone in prayer. At night, he went up onto the roof. He could see the waning Passover moon and the spring stars. They reminded him of those warm nights in Egypt when his mother had revealed so many strange things to him. At that time, much that she had said had seemed like just fascinating stories, a series of secrets between the two of them. Now, however, he began to see them as possible truth.

During the day, Joshua left his family to visit the Temple so that he could again stand at the back of the Sanhedrin chamber and listen to the learned men. Afterward, he stayed and discussed the Scriptures and the Prophets with council members. Some dismissed him as a precocious child, as had the arrogant Pharisee on his first visit, but many of those with whom he talked became fascinated by him. Joshua was eager to learn from them as much as to surprise them with his schooling. It had not occurred to either Joshua or James that the hours they had spent together could be so significant. They had lived in their own exclusive little world. Here, in Jerusalem, the fruits of their labors really showed, and with astonishing ease Joshua was able to converse with men twice his age and more. At times, his vocabulary lacked sophistication, but his knowledge of all the Scriptures astounded Joshua's admirers, who whispered to each other as they listened. There was an aura about the boy that puzzled James. Joshua spoke with a tentative, new confidence that settled into a calm as he found his voice.

Joshua became so absorbed with this new widening of his horizons that he barely heard Joseph and Joachim when they gave their instructions for the caravan departure. It was arranged that they would set out with the caravan at midday, and so Joshua decided to use the morning at the Temple to sit with the learned men one last time. His little group of admirers had grown, and for them, it was more fascinating to discuss the Scriptures with this astonishing youth than it was to listen to the continued theological bickering between Pharisee and Sadducee.

They sat on the steps leading to the Sanctuary opposite the entrance to the Sanhedrin. It was a relatively quiet area of the Temple's great court, and the portico and walls of the Sanctuary rooms gave shade from the spring sun. Each time Joshua made a contribution to their conversation or gave a scriptural quote, they nodded in a patronizing way, each more proud than the other of their prodigy. Joshua was the center of their attention, and they vied with each other to test his knowledge. At times, Joshua couldn't answer their questions, but on more than a few occasions he asked questions of them that were equally hard for them to answer. The time passed quickly, and the sun rose to its midday height.

Joshua was as surprised as the circle of men around him when James came bursting into their midst.

"There you are! I might have known it. Why didn't you come back?"

The men glared at the intruder.

"Come with me," James continued, paying no attention to the learned men. "We've got to move fast. The caravan's left and is probably already at the city gate!"

"I'm sorry, James. I didn't realize it was already midday."

"Past midday!"

A scattering of laughter came from the men.

"It's well past midday," one of them said, looking up at the sun.

James took hold of Joshua roughly and pulled him away.

"When are you going to learn some responsibility? Your mother and my father are very worried. The women are on the donkeys, so we're going to have to run."

Joshua looked up at James. Joshua's face showed that he was not as sorry as he had sounded. James thought he looked strangely different, mysterious, almost defiant. Joshua looked at James as if he were an equal and not his little brother.

"I've said I'm sorry, James. Let's hurry now. We'll catch up with them."

The two of them left the Temple as fast as they could and dodged through the narrow streets of the bazaar to cut across to the city gates. It was well over an hour before they caught up with the shuffling caravan of pilgrims on the road leading north to Samaria.

Joseph looked stern when he saw them, even though they were covered in dirt and sweat from their effort to catch up.

"Where were you?" he shouted. "Where have you been? Your mother's upset, and we couldn't hold up the caravan."

Joshua said nothing. He was disturbed that he had upset his family, but the morning had been so stimulating that it far exceeded his feeling of guilt. *What if this is my future—'Prince of Peace', the Messiah?* he thought. *My responsibility will be to God, not my family.*

His mother, when her donkey drew up level with them, was less severe on him. Her emotion was more of relief than anger.

"Thank goodness you're all right," she said. "We were really concerned."

Joshua looked up at Miriam.

"I'm sorry, Mother. I didn't mean to be late. I was talking in the Temple with some of the men from the Sanhedrin."

He smiled and looked at her with a penetrating gaze born of memory and insight.

"It was fascinating, Mother. You know better than anyone else how important this was for my future."

"I know," Miriam said slowly before she dismounted.

Other members of the caravan shuffled past. Miriam put her hands on her son's shoulders and looked into his eyes. The donkey brayed.

"I think I understand," she said. "You have a destiny, Joshua. Maybe now you are finding it. One day, you will leave us. I pray that God will guide you. Pray, Joshua, pray, for I am a little afraid for your future. I understand…remember how my angels told me…but yet I am afraid."

Joshua smiled as he saw her fear.

"The moonbeams, Mother. Do you remember how God spoke to me from His face in the moon?"

They laughed. Miriam hugged her son knowingly.

"Thank goodness you're back."

Joseph and James muttered to each other.

Joshua helped his mother remount the donkey and took the lead rope.

* * *

Back in Nazareth, Joseph left Benjamin Levi's house with a feeling of supreme contentment. Joachim's old friend Benjamin had agreed to making arrangements for his son to marry Ruth.

Joseph found it hard to believe how his family fortunes had turned. James had now become the established rabbi in Nazareth. The family business was an unqualified success. People from as far away as Cana and Nain came into the Nazareth shop with orders. They had expanded their business to include bricklaying and stone dressing. Some of the wealthier Jews from Sepphoris had even placed orders with them for their building work. It was a seal on their success, however, that Joseph's daughter, the red-haired Ruth, was now to marry Benjamin Levi's son. It would be a big wedding. The whole village would be there. Benjamin Levi was second only to Miriam's father as the wealthiest and most esteemed landowner of their community.

And Ruth was pleased with David ben Levi. Shortly after their arrival in Nazareth, he had been one of the first in the village to notice her blossoming good looks and striking hair. She liked his reserve, possibly the result of his father's position in the village. He didn't flirt with the maidens as much as some of the others. David usually kept to himself.

James had mentioned him several times at their family gatherings. David had been studying with him at the synagogue, and although he did not have the extraordinary learning power of Joshua, he was a good student. He battled with James, however, over the suggestion that he should learn Greek.

"That's only for the soft Jews of Sepphoris," he had apparently said when James brought up the subject. "We in Nazareth are an independent people. We're not going to succumb to those Roman ways and speak in their language."

James tried to explain to him that the Holy Scriptures had been written in Greek for a long time in the outside world, and that more Jews studied in Greek than in Hebrew or Aramaic. His words were lost, however, for in Nazareth, Aramaic was the only language spoken.

In the village, only a handful of the learned men from the synagogue group could even read Hebrew, let alone Greek, so for the most part the Torah was interpreted in Aramaic. Recognizing Joshua's mysterious belief in himself and his destiny, James continued in his determination to teach Joshua both Greek and Hebrew. James missed the trilingual scholarship of Alexandria.

"Never mind what David says about Greek," James reassured Joshua. "With your ability you may very well need it one day. Whether we like it or not, Greek is going to become the official language of our country. I've heard that they now speak Greek at King Herod Antipas' court in Sepphoris. We might as well accept that Galilee is part of the Roman world."

"I don't question it, James," Joshua replied, "but do you think the Messiah should question it?"

"That's a strange question to ask," James said, looking up thoughtfully. "Do you ask whether I think the Messiah should question the use of Greek or the reality of our conquest?"

"Both, really, James. God's kingdom should be above the kingdoms of this earth. Does it matter to God whether we pray to Him in Greek, Aramaic, or Hebrew? Does it matter to God whether we are ruled by the house of Herod, the High Priests, the rabbis, or the Romans? Do you remember the passage from the prophet Micah, which that man quoted when we were in the Sanhedrin chamber last Passover?…'What does the Lord require of us but that we do justly and love mercy and walk humbly with our God?'"

"It looks like you've answered the question for yourself," James replied. "Maybe the Messiah will not concern himself with our freedom as a nation. Who knows? We have to recognize the Messiah first, and it doesn't look like he's with us yet."

Maybe he is, Joshua thought, but James just carried on quoting from the prophets the theme of Israel's redemption.

It was becoming harder for James to instruct Joshua, but easier for them to debate with each other. Joshua was almost his equal in thought processes and scriptural knowledge. Apart from practice in language skills, their working sessions now became joint ventures in scriptural interpretation and a study of the ever-increasing pharisaic law.

* * *

As the day of Ruth's wedding drew closer, Miriam spent many hours spinning and weaving. She wanted to give Ruth the best possible garments for both the wedding ceremony and her future life with David ben Levi. Miriam felt particularly close to Ruth during this time. She felt like she was losing her only daughter, who was, after all, the only other female in an otherwise male-dominated house. Ruth had been a part of Miriam's life ever since Joseph had first brought her as his bride to Bethlehem when Joshua had been born.

Ruth had also been a tremendous help to Miriam throughout their time in Alexandria and Nazareth. It was now Ruth's turn to make changes in her life. Joachim contributed considerably to Ruth's dowry, and Miriam had also taken a few more gold coins from the old wooden box and added them.

Amos and Joseph played their part in making furniture for Ruth's future home. Sometimes, when he was not with James, Joshua helped. It was a large, square house that Benjamin Levi had put aside for them on the western side of Nazareth. Joshua joined in building a courtyard wall and side extensions to some of the storage rooms. They dressed the best yellow stone for the structure, which gave the house more character.

There was a lot of gossip and talk in the village. This wedding promised to be one of the biggest celebrations of the year. The villagers knew that Joachim ben Judah would provide the best wine and that there would be plenty of feasting and lots of dancing. Some of the young men felt disappointed that such a prize as Ruth was now spoken for, but they joined the spirit of the event anyway and teased Ruth about her husband-to-be.

When the great day came, the whole village turned out to witness the marriage. James performed the ceremony outside the synagogue. Anna and Elizabeth had prepared the chuppah, a large ornately embroidered canopy under which the happy couple made their vows. Ruth's hair was braided in a garland of flowers, and David, when he was led to his bride, was also seen to be wearing a crown of myrtle, so that in their floral headdresses they appeared like a royal couple before the rabbi. Joshua stood with his mother and Joseph. Amos was among the sons of the bridegroom, waiting to cheer the happy couple to their nuptials. Rabbi James held up the cup of wine, which was the symbol that would make them one. The cup was gold and a treasure of the Nazareth synagogue. The bride and groom drank from the cup, which James blessed as he pronounced them man and wife. As they turned around under the canopy to face the crowd of guests, James recited the age-old plea:

"May God whose throne is set in this house rejoice your heart with sons and daughters."

Joshua observed a tear run down his mother's cheek. Joseph had not given her a child. Perhaps it was his greater age that had left her without children during their sojourn in Egypt. Miriam remembered how in those days, too, his attempts to make love to her had been so clumsy and how he had always apologized for his roughness. No, they had not enjoyed the most satisfying sexual relationship, and she had not had the joy of a large personal family, but she was married to a wonderful man. His children had become her family, even if they were almost her age. Only Joshua was hers. She bore such an awesome responsibility for this child whose conception she had never really understood.

As she witnessed the marriage of Ruth to David ben Levi, Miriam's thoughts went back to her own wedding day. There had been no chuppah canopy and no crowd of wedding guests. It had been such a simple ceremony on the hillside below Ain Karim, but as she thought on that simple ceremony in contrast to the pomp that surrounded her now, her tears turned to smiles. *Gabriel was there,* she reflected, *with a host of angels. I wonder if he's watching over us now.*

Miriam stepped forward and kissed Ruth as they started out on their bridal procession. The bride and groom then began to make their way down the main street. Amos was among the men who beat on drums and clashed cymbals as the villagers cheered the newly married couple. Joshua ran after them, clapping his hands. As Miriam watched, a yellow butterfly alighted on the canopy, flapped its wings, and flew on down the street to disappear in the crowd of well-wishers. Soon, other butterflies followed. Miriam watched them dart up and down as they smelled the sweet nectar of the flowers in Ruth's garland crown. Miriam smiled with joy and an inner glow. She took hold of Joseph's hand and looked up into his wrinkled face. His beard was quite gray now, almost white, but he was still strong, although gentle and caring.

"Angel Gabriel's here," she said almost coyly.

Joseph saw the butterflies and chuckled. Miriam had delighted in the butterflies that had attended their simple hillside ceremony. She'd insisted that they were her angels in disguise. Even though they'd had more of a father-daughter relationship than husband and wife, Miriam and her angels had brought joy and comfort into Joseph's rough old life. Happily, they also followed the bride and groom.

For seven days the village rejoiced, and for seven nights there was feasting and dancing in the streets. When it was all over, Joseph held Miriam close to him with his rough carpenter's hands.

"Miriam, our wedding was different, wasn't it?" he said. "I really had no idea why the High Priest was so insistent on our marriage. I only went along with it all because I felt comfortable with you and I needed someone to be a real mother to Ruth and Jonah. You were even carrying another man's child at the time. But, it was all so right. Despite all the early hardships, you've been a perfect mother to my family. God bless you, Miriam. I love you, and may God bless you always."

They wept in each other's arms, and they wished for Ruth and David all the happiness that they now shared.

CHAPTER SEVEN

The Great Rebellion

Jonah the zealot was acting as a lookout over the valley leading to Damascus. He sat on a flat ledge of rock that marked the end of a promontory. Outcrops of rock and tussocks of grass with thorny thickets sloped down from the folds of these northern hills to meet the green valley below. Romans rarely penetrated this area, but the caves were continuously guarded just in case. It had been over a year now since Jonah and Judas had arrived. They had been accepted as freedom fighters, but they found here a very different camaraderie than that in Jerusalem. These northern zealots were more determined. They were not concerned with pharisaic grievances and religious wrongs, but had only one goal—death to all Romans.

The warm spring sun reflected from the rockface, making Jonah drowsy. He was bored with the monotony of his task. On hearing unfamiliar voices close by, he awoke with a start. He saw two Romans climbing the hillside.

The two Romans obviously didn't realize how close they were to the zealot camp. Jonah reached for his slingshot and set a stone. This was his first chance to become a hero. He whirled around the sling and shot forth the missile, scoring a direct hit on the taller man. His winter training bore fruit. This time, he had aimed his shot, not at mountain goats or stray sheep while foraging for the men, but at the enemy.

The Roman was stunned and fell. He rolled down the hillside until he was caught in a thicket. His companion, equally surprised, looked up, then ran down to help his friend. Before he could reach the thicket, Jonah had slung a second stone that hit the man sharply on the nape of his neck. The Roman jerked his head back in agony and fell to the ground his helmet detached and following him down the slope.

Jonah climbed down from the ledge and, when within range of the two men, hurled more stones at their heads. Satisfied that neither man could move, Jonah came closer and took the knives that the two felled men had carried. He kicked their bodies to see if they were dead. The men groaned. They had no further concealed weapons. Jonah then climbed back up on the ledge and ran along the track back to the caves.

"Romans!" he shouted.

The zealots heard him, and in no time a band of thirty freedom fighters formed. They followed Jonah swiftly back to the ledge and scanned the hillside. There was no sign of any other Romans. Swiftly, six of the men followed Jonah down to the place where the unconscious men lay. The blood from the facial lacerations of Jonah's victims had begun to congeal. Insects had already started to feed on its life-giving strength. The men kicked the bodies again. The two Romans were barely alive. The zealots easily bound them hand and foot and carried them back to the ledge. From there, they dragged them to the first of the caves and tied them to a stake.

The flat promontory in front of the caves was somewhat like a gladiatorial school. There were zealots in training fights with each other, some using the weapons of gladiatorial slaves. There were stacks of timber and brushwood for open pit fires. Goats were penned at one end of the flat, grassy area. Sheep wandered freely through the camp. Some donkeys were also tethered to wooden posts similar to the stake to which the two Roman prisoners were now tied.

Clophas, a Syrian runaway slave and one of the camp leaders, spoke to the Romans in Greek:

"Who sent you up here?"

The Roman prisoners made no reply.

Clophas slapped the taller of the two men and shook him.

"Did you come alone? Are there any more of you?"

There was no reply, but the man's bloodshot eyes were open.

Clophas spat in his face.

"Again, are there any more of you out there on the hillside?"

"No!" the other prisoner managed to mutter as his consciousness returned.

"Do you know who we are?" Clophas asked.

"No. Perhaps you're an army of runaway slaves."

"Perhaps. It's no matter, because you two are going to die."

Clophas left.

The day dragged on. There was constant camp training. Most of the zealot rebels were Jews, but there were definitely Syrians among them, as well as a few rebel imports and sundry slaves who had escaped from gladiatorial schools.

Early in the afternoon, fires were lit in two pits where goats were roasted between poles. After dark, the goat meat was distributed. The rebels started to sing songs as they built up the fires again.

Clophas returned to the prisoners.

"Untie him," Clophas commanded Jonah as he pointed at the taller Roman.

Jonah loosened the thongs that bound the man.

"Take him to the fire."

There, they strapped him firmly to a pole. The pole was then affixed to the upright posts. The heat of the fire started to scorch the wretched man's torn tunic. For a while, the victim screamed as flames leapt toward him. Finally, he suffocated before becoming a human torch.

Clophas returned to the other prisoner.

"Are you still sure there are no more of you out there?"

The man shook his head.

"Why were you here?"

The man said nothing.

Clophas cuffed the man and spat in his face.

"Tell me, do any other Romans know about this place?"

The Roman stared back fearfully, but said nothing.

"Jonah, and you others here," Clophas shouted. "Take this man away to the other fire pit. He's no use to us as he is. He will be better dead."

* * *

Roman caravans increased in the regularity of their passage from Damascus into Galilee. Apart from feeding the province with officials and militia, these caravans crossed the Levant carrying the riches of the Orient into the Empire. The late King Herod's plans for Caesarea had borne fruit, and the ports of Ptolemais, Tyre, and Sidon were also booming on the Syrian coast of Phoenicia. The Roman consumer market for the exotic had reached new heights in the overall peace and prosperity of the Augustinian age. In the name of the aging victor of Actium, the central core of the great imperial apparatus was enjoying every aspect of human life to the fullest. From their hideouts in the mountains, the Jewish rebels could see this passage of supplies and the easy quarry that surely would soon fall their way.

At last, the command came. The leaders announced plans to ambush one of the caravans. Judas, from a high lookout, was to signal to the rebels farther down the mountain when he first sighted a regular caravan. He had a large silver mirror close at hand. As soon as he could see the caravan, he would reflect the sunlight off the mirror, sending a signal down to the lower camp.

Judas became impatient. It always seemed that when he expected something to happen, it never did. There was no sign of life in the valley below, and he amused himself by carving patterns in the rock with his dagger.

In this rather complacent frame of mind, Judas was taken by surprise when he noticed dust rising in the distance. He angled his mirror to the lower camp. There was a flash in the sage bushes below as his signal was returned.

The approaching caravan moved toward the ambush.

The Romans considered the road from Damascus to be safe. The troops of Flavius Septimus in Galilee had established solid law and order in the tetrarchies, and the trouble in Judea seemed at last to be controlled. Only a few soldiers traveled as escorts these days to ward off wayside brigands.

The quiet plain with its low scrub suddenly became alive with freedom fighters from the hills, brandishing swords, maces, axes, and lances of all shapes and sizes. The hungry zealots, rapacious for blood, outnumbered and overcame the startled soldiers. They speared and hacked at every human in the train. Roman soldiers, traders, Syrian dancing girls...none were spared. The massacre was complete and devastating. The bandits looted the wagons and burned the remains. From Judas' lookout, only the swirls of dust and the faint cries of battle could be seen and heard, but when black smoke plumes billowed upward, Judas knew they had succeeded.

Only four of the freedom fighters were lost. Two were trampled to death by frightened animals and two killed by the Roman guards. Well over sixty men and women in the caravan lay dead on the roadside. Their scattered bodies were left to rot in the baking sun. The rebels vanished as suddenly as they'd come. They retreated back to the safety of the hills and the secret hiding place of the caves, dragging their dead and wounded with them.

* * *

In time, several reports of such attacks reached Flavius Septimus in Sepphoris. Flavius had considered the Syrian Governor Varus to be too pessimistic in his outlook for Galilee, but he had begun to change his heart. He felt that he would have to request additional protection from Damascus or provide greater security from within. He was frustrated by the fact that the worst attacks always seemed to take place in Ituraea, which was not directly under his control. Philip the Tetrarch was of little help. Flavius even wondered if the petty king secretly supported the zealots. After the debacle in Jerusalem, Flavius questioned the integrity of all Herod's heirs.

Roman troops in Philip's tetrarchy lacked a headquarters like Sepphoris in Herod Antipas' Galilee. They relied heavily on support from Damascus. Many of the towns were free cities of the Decapolis, paying tribute to Rome. But they remained totally independent in government, because they had grown up as trading posts along the caravan routes. It was a hard area to control, even though Philip was under the suzerainty of Rome. The decade of uneasy peace in Galilee was threatened by these violent attacks to the north, and despite the obvious defeat of the pharisaic zealots in Jerusalem, and the full incorporation of Judea and Samaria into the Syrian Province, Flavius was concerned. He dispatched a firm request to Varus for more troops.

To His Excellency, Varus, Governor of Syria, Greeting!

In consideration of the continued attacks on Roman caravans and supply routes into Galilee, that have become all too familiar in recent weeks, I would like to formally request a strengthening of troops in preparation for the probable outbreak of major disturbances within the two tetrarchies. I would like to suggest that the Herodian city of Philippi be brought fully under Roman control. A garrison should be established there to control the Damascus highway and seek out these rebels and brigands who appear to be firmly entrenched in the foothills of Hermon. It would not be prudent for me to weaken my cohorts in Sepphoris, as I never know when the prefect will need further assistance in Judea, although all seems quiet in the prefecture at this time. I urgently request that you consider my suggestion and that Philippi become a frontier garrison for protection against Jewish zealot resistance.

Signed: Flavius Septimus, Sepphoris.

* * *

The leaders of the freedom fighters realized that, now that they had declared themselves, their hiding place would not remain secure. Feeling confident after their successive victories on the Damascus road and knowing their men were now well trained, the leaders revealed their master plan. A spokesman addressed selected men at the caves:

"To strike at Rome now, we need to break the conqueror from within. You are the spearhead of our movement. We will divide you up into small working groups and send you back to the villages and cities of Galilee, where you must rapidly recruit the people to the cause. The largest group will infiltrate Sepphoris, and through careful contact you must gain the support of the gladiatorial slaves. That was where we failed the last time."

Another spokesman for the leaders specifically called forward Clophas.

"Clophas, because of your fluency in Greek, we would like to send you and your handpicked team to the coast of Phoenicia. We need the support of the galley slaves at Ptolemais, Tyre, and Sidon. They will be as anxious as we are to see the power of Sepphoris diminished. They're hard, embittered men whose lot is so despicable that they will easily risk their lives for any cause that will take them from their taskmasters."

Clophas nodded in agreement.

"When the time is right for us to sack Sepphoris we will send word to you in Ptolemais. The rioting that you will cause on the Phoenician coast will divert troops from Damascus, leaving Sepphoris at its weakest. If we can then hold out in Galilee, Damascus will not be able to control supplies to their brothers in Samaria and Judea, because we'll control all the key routes south and to the sea. Clophas, we have faith in you. We know your determination to destroy the Roman presence. Your success to the north will be a vitally important part of our strategy for the revolt."

The crowd of well-trained freedom fighters started to discuss the plan among themselves. There was a buzz of excitement in the caves. Judas and Jonah felt their dreams were about to be fulfilled. They crossed hands and shouted:

"Death to all Romans!"

Their cry was taken up by others, and the caves resounded with the common cry:

"Death to all Romans!"

In the detailed organization that followed, both Judas and Jonah were assigned to the Sepphoris group. The revolutionary cell was to be under the leadership of Jacob, known at the caves as 'The Giant' on account of his physique. He truly was as fierce as the legendary Goliath. His eyes flashed with his hatred for Romans. Throughout the camp, there arose a real forming of camaraderie that they had not experienced during the long months of training. This time, they were determined that the 'Great Rebellion' was going to succeed.

The men were instructed to proceed cautiously and slowly to make sure that they really had the backing of the populace in their appointed areas. Sound recruitment and good planning would be the only road to assured success. In a mood of confidence, after a period of nearly two years at the caves, the freedom fighters disbanded to implement their task.

* * *

After receiving Flavius' request, Governor Varus made the Herodian city of Philippi into a full Roman garrison, renaming the town Caesarea Philippi. It was as if he intentionally wished to remind the Tetrarch who was really in charge. Justin and Spartus, who had served in Jerusalem in the days of King Herod, but missed the chaotic period of King Archelaus, joined the new garrison. After Jerusalem, they had risen up through the ranks in the Syrian Legion. Part of that time, they had spent in Antioch on the Orontes, where they had received their promotions to the rank of centurion. One of the first tasks that they were given was to seek out the bandit headquarters in the Hermon mountains and clear the area of potential enclaves of rebels.

It was a laborious task. The mountain country was rugged in the extreme. The relatively gentle lower slopes gave way to steep escarpments that the two mounted centurions could not directly climb, and it took forever to find appropriate passages to penetrate farther. They were commanding a full century of Roman infantry who were alert and ready to face potential attack. They were determined that the sad record of Roman failure on the Damascus road would not be repeated on this mission. Moving one hundred men prepared for battle was no easy task in these rocks, clefts, and crannies.

"This reminds me of the old Jericho patrol," Justin said to his fellow officer. "Do you remember those days when we'd leave Jerusalem and take that mountain road down to Jericho?"

"This is far worse," Spartus replied.

"Donkeys would have been much better. They are able to scramble up these screes and passages."

"I'm not sure that we wouldn't have been better off on foot all the way. It's hard on the legs riding these steep hillsides."

"I agree!"

Justin massaged his calf from the strain, but his mind was still reflecting back on their Jerusalem days.

"I wonder what it was like in Jerusalem after we left. I heard that Marius was killed, along with Janus and Felix."

"They said the fighting was terrible. The Herodians were no help and those religious fanatics just wouldn't give up. What is it with these Jews?

We don't interfere with their religion. I just can't figure them out. They don't like us because we have taken away their so-called independence. That, maybe I can understand, but this scrapping over religion, I just can't understand that at all."

"Well, maybe it's a good thing we weren't there. Antioch wasn't bad, and Damascus was wonderful. The governor seems to be doing a good job. That whole Parthian nonsense seems to be completely controlled now. In fact, the Parthians have become some of our best friends. You ask a Parthian merchant for something on the side, and if you take care of him, you'll be well rewarded. They're not like these wily Jews. You can't trust the Jews, but a well-bribed Parthian will be your friend for life."

There was no sign of life. Their provisions were getting low, but mountain goats and stray sheep provided sustenance at the nightly camp. The hundred men felt that they had marched to Damascus and back ten times over, their search revealing no signs of a rebel camp. They entered caves only to find the excrement of bats. Justin and Spartus climbed the screes, leading their men to search crags and crannies above. They found nothing and climbed higher to areas where the night air was cold. They were coming close to giving up when Spartus looked down from a height and saw a flat, grassy plateau, backed by sheer escarpments. It would be difficult to get to it, but there was evidence of habitation there.

Justin joined Spartus in surveying the scene. There were broken pens, scattered poles and stakes, blackened fire pits, and heaps of stones.

"We're onto something, Justin—something big. This is no small encampment."

"Let's take about twenty men down," Justin suggested.

"How can we get down there?"

"Send a scout by rope."

A scout was dispatched. He climbed down the sheer rock face for what seemed like eternity. The corps held their end taut with all their strength. Finally, they were able to lower the man to the ground. Justin watched as the scout inspected the animal pens.

The dung and droppings had long since dried. There was no evidence of present usage. The scout looked up. High above him he could see the small figures of his comrades. Next, he carefully investigated the caves, noting discarded items of sundry clothing, worn-out sandals, and carved graffiti on the walls. The graffiti were almost all in Aramaic. The scout knew they had found what they had been looking for, but it was too late. All the inhabitants of the rebel camp had left.

* * *

Clophas, now on the Phoenician coast disguised as a slave dormitory warden, was prepared, and the underground cells in Ptolemais, Tyre, and Sidon had received widespread secret support. But a year passed, and the galley slaves began to show impatience. They anxiously awaited the word.

"You promised us action," a Macedonian whispered at one of their clandestine meetings. "Many of the men are now hoping to end up in Greece rather than stay at these ports. If they are lucky enough to work the Greek galleys, the crossings are shorter and the work and time schedules less arduous. From here, we often have to ship direct to Italia and, even if the wind is favorable, the hours at the oars are unbearable, not to mention the searing heat of the sun."

"It will be soon," Clophas replied. "It's better to be fully ready to take on the enemy than to be poorly prepared and suffer disastrous defeat. Our day will come."

The day did come, but not for yet another two phases of the moon. A small, pathetic-looking Jew from Cana in Galilee, Daniel by name, brought the good news. After much cautious questioning, he was led to the rebel warden.

"Greetings, Clophas," he said as they found an appropriate place to talk, out of the earshot of other slave masters. "Jacob the Giant says all is ready. He'll give you a couple of weeks, and then they'll start the rebellion in Galilee. He hopes the diversion here will take care of any Roman assistance reaching Sepphoris from Caesarea Phillipi or Damascus."

"A month?"

"Yes, that's what they told me."

"We'll have to work fast, Dan. Take the road north to Tyre. Seek out the slave dormitories and ask for Sirach. He's in charge there. You'll find him in this same guise. We've infiltrated into the slave dormitories in all three ports. Just tell Sirach that I've said the time has come. He'll send you on to Sidon and tell you who to see there."

Daniel left as quietly as he had come. Clophas allowed five peaceful days to pass before he gave the signal.

The revolt of the galley slaves began!

By the time that word of the rebellion reached Governor Varus in Damascus, most of the ships in the Phoenician ports had already been burned. The storehouses were looted and destroyed. Drunk on the success of their attack, galley slaves rampaged in the streets. The militias in the port cities were outnumbered by the poor, the oppressed, and the slaves, who joined in the rebellion. For most of them, the attack was the greatest occasion for excitement that they had ever had in their hopeless lives. They had no strong cause of their own, just a promise of adventure and freedom. They didn't look beyond the triumph of the moment, and didn't notice that the rebel leaders had quietly slipped away and deserted them with heartless deception. Even as the slaves' aimless rioting gathered momentum, Clophas and his cell of zealots were moving south, confident that their diversion was serving its intended purpose.

* * *

Varus was satisfied that the new garrison at Caesarea Phillipi had solved many potential rebel problems. There had been no further brigand attacks on the Roman caravans, and although the commander had reported evidence of major rebel encampments in the Hermon mountains, no rebels had been found. The fear instilled into the populace by the presence of troops at Caesarea Phillipi seemed to have worked, and the governor congratulated his old friend Flavius Septimus at Sepphoris for his cunning suggestion.

But Varus now saw he had no choice but to send the Phillipi troops to the coast, along with others from Antioch to the north and Sepphoris to the south. He needed to quell this slave riot as quickly as possible, for as long as the galley slaves brought anarchy to the port cities, Syrian trade and prosperity was being brought to a halt. At least the governor had the consolation of knowing that Judean Caesarea was still open for Damascus trade. He dispatched his orders, and in a giant pincer-like movement from three different directions, the major strength of the Syrian Legion marched toward the three port cities of Phoenicia. There would be no mercy for the slaves and no hope for their success.

Varus was irritated by the disorder that this revolt had temporarily caused, but he had no fear of the ultimate outcome. Feeling sure of his impending success, the governor drew comfort from his thoughts. Little did he know that Sepphoris, the garrison city of the tetrarchy of Galilee, was now under siege.

* * *

Flavius watched in disbelief as he saw the coils of dark smoke drift upward from the burning buildings. From the barracks watchtower it seemed as if all Sepphoris was on fire.

"It happened all of a sudden, before the dawn broke, sir," Festus, his new adjutant informed him.

Citizens were swarming in the streets. Some were cheering and brandishing arms, others were busying themselves with their escape. Only a few were fighting the fires.

The noise of confusion rose up in the morning air.

"Festus! Have the entire fighting force alerted," Flavius ordered as he realized the probable truth. "This is no accident, this is rebellion. In the name of Mars! Why, right when we need them most, are half our men off in Phoenicia? Send a dispatch rider out immediately! Ask for reinforcements from Caesarea Phillipi, and then send him on to Varus in Damascus. This is the start of something big. Get every available man out! Call the centurions over to my quarters immediately!"

"Yes, sir!"

The aide ran down the tower ahead of Flavius to alert the men.

The smell of smoke had already penetrated into the Centurions' Tower. In no time, every available soldier was ready to defend the barracks and to fight for the Empire.

By the time the centurions reached the commander's quarters, Flavius had a much clearer picture of the situation. Roman refugees, tax collectors, bankers, influential Sepphoris Jews, wealthy merchants, and Herodian courtiers with Roman sympathies, were streaming into the barracks seeking refuge. The fire was biting at the feet of these refugees, driving them toward the safety of the Roman stronghold. Almost every building occupied by Roman citizens or their sympathizers had been set ablaze.

Flavius issued his commands to the centurions:

"At all costs we must preserve the barracks, that's our first aim. We cannot save the city from obvious destruction, but we must keep our power base. No more refugees can be admitted. The gates must be firmly bolted before the rebels have time to infiltrate within our own walls. That's an order! Semus! You have the gate watch, go to it right away."

Semus left the briefing.

"Quintus! Sallus! You're in charge of fire fighting," Flavius continued. "I want every rampart protected from the blaze. Man a continuous waterline. We can't fight fire and rebels at the same time. Sabinus! Marcellus! Your men and those of Festus are all we have to defend ourselves. It's essential that we do just that. We'll move into the attack and clean out these rebels afterward, but it has got to be defense first. If we lose the barracks, Galilee will have no center. Now, move! There's no time to be lost."

The centurions left to organize their sections of the defense.

Flavius dressed for battle.

Screams, smoke, pungent smells and appalling destruction drifted ever closer.

The great gates into the barracks closed against the surging tide of refugees. The soldiers had to use whips and truncheons to beat them back. The gap between the doors inched together as a last desperate man tried to squeeze through. He was caught and crushed as the doors finally slammed shut, leaving him screaming on the ground. Bars and latch bolts were knocked into place. The noise of the frightened populace faded. A strange quiet came over the compound. After the bolts and bars had all been placed, two heavy chains were slung across from door post to door post to give added protection.

Semus had his men stationed on the walls flanking the gates and ready to repel potential attackers. Sabinus and Marcellus were busy positioning themselves elsewhere in the barracks, which now became their fortress. The able-bodied of the refugees were put to work with the soldiers to handle spears or be prepared to fight with daggers. The others were taken to the dormitories of the Centurions' Tower and locked within to be safely out of the way of the defending soldiers.

* * *

Judas and Jonah had managed to stay together. They were close to the palace of the Tetrarch, Herod Antipas, a barracks in itself that housed the Herodian guard. The palace had not been torched, as Jacob had considered the possibility that Herod Antipas might be a useful figurehead for the

411

movement when the coward saw the signs of victory. Antipas had not shown any inclination to change from his Roman ways; however, in the confusion it looked like he might well have fled. The gates into Herod's outer court were open, and Judas and Jonah could see members of the Herodian household busily packing up carts for evacuation.

"Shall we go in?" Jonah asked.

"No!" the older zealot replied. "Let's move on to the market and search the Roman dwellings down there. Remember the cry, Jonah: 'Death to all Romans.' Let's not worry about the Herodians yet!"

Dodging falling timbers and choking from the smoky fires, they went from house to house.

"Unless they declare that they are with us, Jonah, they're against us. Slit their throats!" Judas ordered.

They spared no man, woman, or child, who was found in the smoking ruins. In the street, their companions fought hand to hand with the desperate Romans who had fled their dwellings. The gladiators had kept their word. With trident, mace, sword, and axe, the seasoned fighters hacked down their Roman overlords with the same vigor as the embittered Jews. Slaves betrayed their masters and joined the rabble army. They gathered together on every street. There were shouts in both Aramaic and Greek—anti-Roman slogans, always culminating in the universal cry:

"Death to all Romans!"

Ahead of this angry mob ran the stream of panic-stricken refugees. Some were opportunist Jews who had talked their way out of brutal assassination for their Roman association. There were patricians and advisers to the Herodian court; even foreign merchants, caught up in the turmoil of the times. They could not save Sepphoris or their possessions, but they could save themselves.

Jacob the Giant surveyed the progress with satisfaction. Everything was going to plan. The neutral Herodians were not to be feared. The gladiators had easily overcome their taskmasters. Roman slaves, encouraged by stories of successful uprisings in the northern ports, flocked to assist the zealots. It looked like the city itself was secured. Now, it was time for the assault on the weakened garrison. It would be difficult, but because of their good planning it would be some time before

Damascus could get any relief troops to Sepphoris. Jacob commanded that the siege begin.

Rebels surrounded and bombarded the Roman ramparts with stones and anything they could throw. Soldiers watched helplessly as the loyal citizens they had been forced to abandon were caught fleeing and slashed to death. Much of the Roman population of Sepphoris lay dead in the streets. Despite the well-planned massacre, however, the rebels appeared less confident when it came to storming the barracks. The walls were difficult to scale, and there was no easy point to torch with fire.

Judas and Jonah were not in the forefront of this feint attack. They found themselves close by the Centurions' Tower at the rear of the barracks, in the area where the gladiatorial school adjoined the gymnasium and baths. There was less commotion here, and with the aid of six slaves from the gladiatorial school, they hoped to break into the barracks from the rear and set fire to the part of the complex where there was no rampart wall.

The gladiators led Judas and Jonah down a dark tunnel into the depths of the school. They had to force open a grill gate, but it gave way quite easily. Wolves barked and a lion roared. The animals had heard the noise of the crashing grill and were upset by the smoke now permeating the building.

"This must be the area where they keep the wild beasts," remarked Jonah.

"Then, this must be the tunnel entrance for bringing the beasts into the gladiatorial school," Judas whispered in response.

"It must be."

Their voices echoed in the confines of the tunnel.

The gladiators didn't stop at the wild beast cellars, but led the two zealots up another tunnel out into the bright light of the fighting arena. There was a further grill gate at the exit, but it, too, opened easily.

After the dark tunnels and the cavernous animal pens, the light had a disorienting effect. The smoke from the nearby burning buildings caused Jonah's eyes to smart and sting. He rubbed them with his dirty hands, only to aggravate them further.

"Come on!" called Judas. "Keep up with us!"

The gladiators threw themselves against the wooden walls of the arena. Climbing on each other's shoulders, they were able to reach the top of the high paling. The first two stepped into the seating well. They beckoned to Judas and Jonah, who climbed up and joined them. One at a time, they pulled up the others in a human chain. Once in the gallery, they accessed the main part of the gladiatorial school through the back entrance to the gymnasium and baths of the barracks. The wooden door was bolted and heavier than the iron grills.

Judas and Jonah followed, and with the help of wall torches and lamp oil from the storeroom, they set about firing the gate. The fierce heat drove them all back as the flames weakened the door. The choking gladiatorial slaves rammed the obstruction with two iron lamp stands. It gave way. The oily smoke had become so thick it was hard for them to breathe, but the rush of fresher air from beyond the fallen structure felt good. Fighting their way through the flames, the little group of invaders scouted the gymnasium, entered the baths, torched the atrium roof, and prepared for attack.

The flames quickly took hold in the roof timbers. Two of Marcellus' men stationed in the nearby watchtower called for the soldier firemen. Several Roman soldiers in the fire patrol carried buckets to the baths. Others, in succession, carried water to the watchtower. From the tower they poured the water down toward the advancing flames.

In the baths, Judas and his men were waiting. The fire detachment was viciously attacked, and in tough hand-to-hand combat they were overcome by the gladiators and the fierce zeal of Judas and Jonah. Their numbers were even, eight against eight, but because the soldiers were on fire detail, they were not carrying their normal weaponry. One of the gladiators was knifed to death by the flashing dagger of the most agile of the Romans, but the victory for the seven remaining rebels was soon complete.

Judas and Jonah stripped the dead Romans of their military dress.

"Here, wear these!" Judas called out to the other five. "In this way, we'll be able to gain access to more obvious areas."

Smeared in the blood of their recent victims, the seven men disguised themselves as Roman soldiers and moved out into the Centurions' Court. They crossed to the watchtower and climbed up with the firefighters. There, they attacked two of Marcellus' unsuspecting men, throwing the two surprised Romans down into the flames. The disguised rebels then became embroiled in further close combat. The tower was easily won, but the flames from the roof of the baths were licking the very beams of the wooden structure. The victorious rebels retreated and let the fire do its work.

Although the rebels had accomplished this initial task relatively easily, Festus, the Roman centurion, was quick to spot what had happened. It didn't take long for Roman soldiers with battle shields and lances to appear in the Centurion's Court. This time, the rebels were outnumbered and needed to use their guile to escape. The Romans drove them back toward the burning baths.

"Jonah! It's every man for himself!" Judas shouted. "We've got to get out of here! Never mind the others!"

It was easier said than done.

"Keep to the outside!" Judas yelled, seeing his friend take a path directly under the burning roof. "Stay over by the hot bath!"

Jonah looked up and changed course.

As Judas also made a dash for it, a large section of the roofing caved in. It fell with a shower of sparks and splintered fire, bringing with it cracked clay tiles and the burning body of one of the two unfortunate Romans from the tower. The body, hair singed and clothing all but gone, rolled into the water of the cold pool to float on the surface, arms outstretched.

Jonah sprinted past the hot bath and made it to the gymnasium. Judas swiftly followed, leaving the gladiators to fight the lance thrusts of their assailants.

One of the gladiators picked up a piece of burning timber and wielded it like a mace, letting it fly toward the soldiers. A Roman fell, probably blinded and certainly stunned. The gladiator ran in to cut his throat. The Roman died, but almost simultaneously the gladiator was pierced by a soldier's lance.

It was impossible for Jonah and Judas to escape through the gladiatorial school. The fire, which they had started in order to burn down the door, had spread fiercely. Beaten back, they were forced to try to make it to the gymnasium roof, but there was no ledge, nothing on which to climb. They dashed back into the baths and hid in the sulphurous waters of the hot pool.

Judas and Jonah were too tense to notice the relaxing waters of the warm bath. They held their breath in fear, not knowing for certain if the soldiers had left or not. The cavernous stone structure of the sulfur bath protected them from the falling timbers and the worst of the fire. Although the smoke drifted in black swirls, it was above their heads and they could breathe freely. Once the roof and adjacent watchtower had completely caved in and the greater part of the debris had been extinguished, the fire dwindled to a few smoldering heaps.

The fires at the rear of the barracks continued to rage. The gymnasium was now ablaze and the gladiatorial school was an inferno. Judas and Jonah could now escape only if they could find a route over the rooftop. They discarded their soaked Roman tunics and noticed in the immediate area that the roofing was still reasonably sound. It was only a distance of about ten feet up to the timbers that formed a gully between the destroyed roof of the baths and the Centurions' Tower.

"If we can get up there, we can probably follow that around past the gymnasium and cross over the buildings beyond the gladiators' arena," Judas suggested.

Jonah looked around. Seeing the dead bodies of their gladiatorial comrades, he got the idea of using their clothing for a rope. He climbed up on Judas' shoulders and pulled himself up onto the roofing. Then he tied the garments to an open timber and dropped them down to Judas. Judas tugged at the clothing rope. It seemed firm, but as soon as he gave it his full weight, there was a ripping sound and one of the knots slipped. He tried again. The knot held, tightening on itself. He climbed up and joined Jonah.

Judas undid the knot, holding onto the clothing rope.

"We had better throw it back," he suggested. "We know those Romans will be in hot pursuit, and we don't want to leave them a ladder."

"Better to pull it up and leave it here so they can't see how we escaped," Jonah added wisely.

He pulled up the clothing rope and bundled it up in a corner of the roof gully.

"Let's go!"

Half naked, the two friends made their escape.

Roman attention was now diverted to the main gates. The rebellious Jews were trying to ram them with heavy timbers. The gates didn't move despite the battering and many of the attacking rebels were struck down by Roman spears.

* * *

Word on the sack of Sepphoris reached Nazareth late that same day. Escaping merchants described the burning of the city. Palls of smoke could be seen on the horizon. The following day, it was the main topic of conversation. Further reports came in from other escapees. At first, the news was greeted with an excited enthusiasm, but the more intelligent members of the synagogue group had some reservations.

James sounded the shofar. The men came in from the fields and from their daily tasks and met in front of the synagogue.

"Sepphoris may be in ruins," James said as he addressed the people, "but we have yet to experience the Roman backlash. I am no lover of the Romans or a traitor to any cause, but be warned, the retribution will be worse than the deed. What has happened has happened. Because we are the closest village of any size to Sepphoris, we should be especially on our guard. I strongly urge you not to take up arms to join this cause, as some zealots have suggested. It will not profit you to fight the Romans. Of course, there are ways we should assist our brothers, who whether in wisdom or in folly have made this stand. We should care for those wounded who reach us and share with them our sustenance."

"Traitor!" shouted one of the Nazareth zealots.

Others joined in:

"Traitor! Traitor!"

However, most respected the rabbi and his calm way of expressing a genuine fear. There were those in the village, including Benjamin Levi, who remembered only too well the severity of the retribution that followed the last abortive uprising in Sepphoris.

"Remember, my boys! Remember Simon and Caleb," called a voice from the back.

"And David and Matthew," called out another.

Many still remembered these young zealots who had died in the retribution a generation back. Hearing their names sparked some reactions from a few of the older men, but overall the freedom fighters hadn't made much of an impression in Nazareth. It was hard to win over farmers and craftsmen who were enjoying such prosperity. Joseph and his sons had actually built houses in Sepphoris for Jewish artisans. The vintners and corn merchants had all done well selling to the city. Even shepherds were content. The increased population in Galilee had meant a necessity for more livestock, and wool was in high demand.

The Nazareth zealots and rebels were outnumbered, and those who had come into the village during the past year with talk of rebellion had met with little enthusiasm. Indeed, most had moved on. They had cursed the attitude of Nazarenes to their Roman taskmasters, but they hadn't disrupted the life of the village, passing their seed of wrath to only a handful of harmless hotheads. The rabbi seemed a traitor to them, but they knew that James had the vast majority of the people on his passive side.

Despite the news of destruction close at hand, Nazareth slept in relative comfort, awaiting the cock to crow at the dawn of another day.

* * *

Joshua listened to James. He didn't disagree with his mentor's passive ways, but he did see the sack of Sepphoris as a prophetically exciting event. Rebellion against the invader was a symbol of the end time. He reflected on the apocalypse of Daniel and the words of Enoch: *'There will be troubles and tribulations with families divided against themselves.'* The writings say so. *Are we now living in the end time?* he wondered. *Will the Messiah rescue us from such horrors and establish his kingdom forever?*

Joshua prayed.

* * *

The fires had diminished by the second day, and the pall of smoke over the city of Sepphoris cleared to reveal blue skies, but the pungent smell of charred wood hung on the air.

The gates of the garrison had held, and the rebels were losing their enthusiasm. Flavius' disciplined Roman soldiers easily killed off the brave few who still attempted to scale the walls in the bright light of this second day of siege.

Judas and Jonah, their remaining clothing torn and black with the grime of their recent exploits, made their way through the almost-deserted streets in the direction of King Herod Antipas' palace. A distressed mother held a crying baby in her arms as she surveyed the ruins of her home. It was obvious that most of the citizens had fled or joined the throngs of slaves and rebels beating on the garrison gates.

"It looks abandoned," Judas observed when they reached the palace. "Let's go in and find out."

Crossing the courtyard, they climbed the steps up to the king's apartments. The smell of smoke clung to the drapes, but there was no evidence of destruction. The building was neither burned nor looted.

"Looks like the king and his men made good on their escape," Jonah noted.

He picked up a Roman vase.

"Look at this. These Herodians are all Romans at heart."

He hurled the vase to the floor, where it shattered into uncountable shards.

"So much for the Herodians! They're not worth the clay that made this vase."

He looked up at his friend with a satisfying grin.

"Shall we fire the palace?"

"No, let's just leave," Judas answered. "We need to get back to the leaders. I've no idea what we're supposed to do next. We've destroyed the city, but we still haven't gained the garrison. These Roman bastards are still in charge."

After angrily smashing the remaining vases in the king's audience chamber, the two zealots left to seek out the leaders at their headquarters. They found Jacob the Giant in the square house that had been the cell for all their planning.

"Ah, Judas Iscariot and Jonah ben Joseph," Jacob said, peering at them in the gloom. "I hope you're bringing me good news."

"We successfully spearheaded an attack on the garrison from the back and destroyed the baths and the gladiatorial school," Judas answered.

'The Giant' stood up and embraced Judas.

"Good news! Were there many casualties?"

"We lost all the gladiators, but we destroyed the watchtower and have created a weakness in the garrison's defenses."

"That's all right," Jacob said as he sat down again. "You did well. We need to push on with this attack. If we don't break through the Roman defenses today, we may lose our advantage. The bastards will send reinforcements up from Samaria, and we'll be surrounded. Go back to the gates and seek out our leaders there. Tell them that you've breached the back approaches to the garrison. Hopefully, we can mount a rearguard attack."

Judas and Jonah left the rebel headquarters and set out toward the garrison gates.

* * *

Meanwhile, Flavius considered his options. If this rebellion was to be crushed throughout the tetrarchy, he would have to get his troops out of the siege. There were only minimum reinforcements in Caesarea Philippi. He needed to secure Sepphoris and fan out his soldiers throughout Galilee. Inspecting the route through the still smouldering damaged baths and gladiatorial schools, he marshaled his plan.

"Festus! You're to lead our attack," he ordered. "Take your hundred out through the back and surprise the rabble from the rear. Marcellus! Hold on to the gate. It is vital that the rabble still thinks that we are on the defensive. Our plan will only work if we can really surprise them from the rear."

The soldiers near the gates continued to repel the determined rebels as they sought to scale the walls and batter the great doors with a wooden ram. The commander noticed the growing fatigue among the rebels, and a new confidence showed itself among the Roman troops.

Festus gathered his men. They were prepared for street fighting and enthusiastic to leave the beleaguered garrison and move from defense to attack.

When Judas and Jonah reached the street surrounding the barracks, a wall of Roman shields advanced toward them.

"Look out!" Judas shouted.

A few of the more lethargic stragglers in the rebel throng turned at the shout.

"Romans!" they cried with both surprise and fear.

The Roman soldiers continued their advance.

Many of the rebel stragglers were defenseless, no longer carrying arms, but merely tagging on in the excitement of the siege.

The Romans advanced with meticulous precision and soon struck the first of the stragglers. Judas and Jonah dodged through the crowd, pointing back at the potential onslaught and shouting their warning.

A few with daggers and swords sallied forth to halt the enemy. Most pressed on, seeking safety in the massed mob ahead.

It was some time before Judas could see any of the rebel leaders or reach the area of armed fighters.

"There are Romans behind us," he shouted, when he knew that they had reached authority. "We're being attacked from the rear!"

"Where have they come from?"

"I don't know," Judas replied. "The city is deserted. We've just come from headquarters, and we saw no sign of them. They appeared just as we reached the garrison walls. They couldn't have gotten here from Caesarea Philippi so soon."

"They're Sepphoris Romans, Judas!" Jonah exclaimed. "Of course they are. They've come out from the gladiatorial school just the way we got in. The cunning bastards have used our own plan against us."

"What do you mean?" the rebel leader asked, raising his eyebrows.

"We came here to let you know that we successfully breached the garrison in the fire," Jonah continued, anxiously looking back over his shoulder. "We were going to suggest that we send a party of fighters in through the gladiatorial school and the baths to attack the Romans from within their own compound. It seems that they've beaten us to it!"

"We must fight," the leader replied.

He shouted orders, and the rabble ranks began to seek out the Roman onslaught. Then, he addressed the men at the battering ram:

"You men there! Keep up your efforts. Don't slacken in your attempt to breach the gates here. Meanwhile, the rest of you, prepare to meet the onslaught down the street."

The mob turned to face the enemy. By now, however, the soldiers were hacking their way through the undisciplined, tired rebels. It was a lost cause.

* * *

Judas and Jonah retreated just in time when they saw the last gallant efforts of Jacob the Giant collapse in the ruins of Sepphoris. The Romans became bolder. Their sallies out from the garrison with lance and shield were too much for the remaining rabble.

The reinforcements from Caesarea Philippi arrived. The street fighting became fierce. Some of the best freedom fighters from the gladiatorial schools died, and although the fanatical rebels caused heavy Roman losses, it was obvious that the conquerors would win. The Roman shield was the real cause of victory. The Jewish freedom fighters hadn't learned the art of body protection. This was a Roman skill that had eluded them in their combat training at the caves.

The two companions made their escape from Sepphoris by taking a rough cross-country route. They instinctively knew that Roman brutality would follow those traveling the better-known roads and tracks. They headed northwest to the high country around Cana.

They heard about a successful attack on the Caesarea Philippi Romans at Cana that had spread through the region. Once Judas and Jonah reached Cana, they found the place swarming with aimless refugees, but no zealots had grouped around the heroic village. It didn't take long for further Roman legions from Caesarea Philippi to follow, and the carnage that then occurred was devastating. Judas and Jonah found themselves fighting for their lives again. They managed to flee the melee, taking shelter in the remote hills above Cana. They hid at a place called Jotbah.

Jotbah was a very small village. The men were all shepherds and goatherds and hadn't been involved in the freedom movement. There were only a handful of rough stone shelters that made up its cluster of buildings. Judas and Jonah were received coolly, the shepherds making it quite clear that they didn't want any trouble from anyone.

Ostensibly, there was little to mark Jotbah as a Jewish village. There was no synagogue, no rabbi, and the language was a rough Aramaic that Jonah, with his Judean background, could hardly understand. This was a village that time had passed by. In fact, it was more Canaanite than Jewish. The men of Jotbah lived by hunting rabbits and mountain goats, whose skins they crudely cured. They ate wild berries and gathered animal droppings for fuel and fodder. Their garments from the ill-cured animal skins were pungent in the extreme and were cause enough for the village to have remained isolated.

This was a perfect place for Judas and Jonah to escape the wrath of Roman retribution and wait out their time. The freedom fighters became shepherds and goatherds and lived off their wits in this unclaimed territory.

* * *

The rebellion crushed, Flavius Septimus offered Marcus Gustavus, the tribune from Caesarea Philippi, a goblet of wine as they sat together in the commander's quarters. Sitting in his crude camp chair, Flavius took several sips from his own cup.

"You arrived just in time," the commander said. "It really would have been very difficult for us to have held out any longer."

"Mind you, we lost a few men along the way. It's not just Sepphoris, Flavius Septimus," the tribune said gravely. "The whole Galilean countryside is in rebellion. We were savagely attacked in Cana. It's a nothing place, populated by rustic Jews of no consequence, but as if from nowhere, well-trained rebels ambushed us there. I would have had reinforcements here earlier, along with the Samaritan troops, but my first cohort was severely beaten back by these ruffians. It was only our greater numbers that got us through. They are well trained, Flavius. They are not an undisciplined rabble such as we encountered in the Phoenician ports."

"The galley slaves!"

"Yes, Flavius. They fight to the death with no surrender. They're so anxious to escape to freedom, but they have little skill."

"They were easily quelled, then?"

"Oh, yes! They turned more to looting and really had no cause beyond those aspirations of personal freedom and greed."

"Well, we'll have plenty of new captives to take their place," Flavius replied with a sardonic smirk. "The galleys will soon be full of Jews. We have at least a thousand held here in Sepphoris and there are more coming up from Judea."

The tribune took another sip from his goblet.

"What news have you heard from Jerusalem, then?"

"Oh, it was nothing like up here. There was the usual outbreak of Jewish nationalism mixed with religious fanaticism. It was all quickly suppressed. There were a few fires, but nothing like we've experienced."

"Sepphoris seems to have been the worst hit, for sure," the tribune said, looking up at Flavius. He then continued with filial reassurance. "But we seem to have broken the back of it now."

The tribune picked up his goblet and clinked his with the commander's before taking another sip of the excellent wine.

"I must admire the way you handled it, Flavius Septimus," he said expansively. "You kept that rabble at bay for so long."

"It was getting very difficult," Flavius replied. "Our food supplies were very low. In the reconstruction, we must give greater thought to our self-sufficiency here within the barracks. Fortunately, the well held and the water wasn't fouled. Our men kept their heads. They were on strict rations. The refugees that we took in at the start of the siege didn't help either. We kept them under house arrest. If I'd had more men here, we could have mopped it up in the streets, but I could only let out a handful at a time for street fighting."

"What of the Herodians, Flavius Septimus? Do we know of the whereabouts of the Jewish king?"

"That wily old tetrarch fled to Samaria and then on to Jerusalem. He's under house arrest at the Antonia now, but in time Caesar will restore him. We may still need the Herodian role in establishing peace in the province. The Herods are a useful tool, as you'll find out in Caesarea Philippi. They help to bind the people."

The tribune was surprised at Flavius' liberal viewpoint.

"They are pretty ineffective, though," he said.

"Totally. They are merely kings in name. Rome rules here, Gustavus, if I may call you by your name."

"Of course."

The two soldiers raised their goblets again, and entwining their arms, drank to each other.

"Rome will succeed," Flavius said with assurance. "I love this country, Gustavus, and despite the setback of this rebellion, we'll see a great land here yet, believe you me. Actually, I have a villa on the shores of the big lake. It's just above Magdala. I haven't been out there for a long time, not since this rebellious spirit began to show and they burned me out."

"Burned you out?"

"Yes, but it was partly my son's fault. A trivial matter that fired up village passions. When we've cleared all this up I must get back to the villa and make the necessary repairs. Soon, unless Caesar wants me elsewhere, I hope to retire there. You must have passed by the lake. How's it looking? Was there much support for the rebellion down there?"

"Isn't Magdala now known as Taricheae?"

"Yes. You've obviously been getting to know the country. That's now its official name—'the place of the salted fish.' But for me it's always been Magdala. That's what the Hebrews call the place."

"I haven't been to Magdala, as you call it, Flavius, but we passed through Capernaum. Those flat fish from the lake are really good. The people there weren't that hostile. Cana in the hills was our main problem. There's a vicious little stronghold there."

"There are still a lot of rebels hiding out in the hillside villages, Gustavus. They are our next task now that we've secured Sepphoris again. We've got to flush them out. It's a slow, tedious task, but it must be done. We don't really want to destroy the villages because the land is prosperous. We just need to round up the troublemakers."

Marcus Gustavus shook his head.

"Easier said than done, Flavius Septimus. Our men are angry. This rebellion had the makings of a Roman defeat. You can expect some pretty brutal retaliation in the villages. I know how my men feel about Cana. If they go back there they'll crucify them all, every last Jew they find, and Flavius, that'll be with my blessing!"

"I know how you feel. My own men have already sought revenge on the Sepphoris Jews, but we must try to control them. We are not barbarians."

Flavius got up and poured out some more wine.

"To the future!" he said, raising his goblet. "From this phoenix we'll build a new Sepphoris and a new Galilee."

* * *

Refugees passed through Nazareth with tales of the dreadful destruction and the controlled Roman revenge. Among them, was Benjamin Levi's aging brother, Abram, who had grown rich in Sepphoris.

Despite the horrors of which they all heard, Nazareth had remained unaffected by the great rebellion. The fanatical few reported on the successful attack by the Jews of Cana on Roman reinforcements that had been heading to the relief of Sepphoris. This story had become much exaggerated and never took into account the decimation of constructive village life that had now ruined Cana in Roman retaliation.

Joshua was assisting Ruth at the well when a detachment of Romans came riding through. The soldiers found Abram Levi in the square. They turned on him. The villagers fled from the Roman hooves as the old merchant became trapped between the street and the high wall of his brother's house. Joshua held Ruth's hand in frozen fear as a Roman whip lashed out at Abram, who, with a look of terror in his eyes, held up his frail, old, defenseless arms to protect his face.

"I've done nothing!" he shouted. "Leave me alone! I never joined the rebels. My business has been ruined. I'm just an innocent old man."

The lash of the whip stung him again.

"You were an informer—a Sepphoris Jew!" one of the soldiers shouted as the whip flew again.

Abram fell to the ground, and the soldiers dismounted and closed in on him. There was no escape. They kicked him and clubbed him until his cries became muffled in loss of consciousness. They bound him by his arms and, remounting their horses, dragged him behind them in a cloud of dust. He dragged until he became dismembered, and the satisfied Romans cut his corpse free.

Joshua trembled as he and Ruth watched the brutal attack. When the dust settled, the terrified villagers stood stunned and amazed. Abram Levi had never been a freedom fighter. He was one of them, a Galilean Jew who had escaped the fires in Sepphoris and sought refuge with his family in Nazareth. If he had been an informer, they didn't know about it. His only crime seemed to be that he was a Sepphoris Jew.

Ruth began to cry. She buried her head in Joshua's robes. Joshua wanted to comfort her, but he was too angry and fearful for words to come forth.

Some of the villagers began to run after the Romans, shouting and waving their arms, but the Romans did not look back.

Joshua took Ruth into Benjamin Levi's house, and they sought out the old patriarch.

"What is it? What's all the shouting?" Benjamin asked when they found him.

Joshua looked straight at the old man. He was still trembling as he held Ruth's hand.

"They came here," he said, tears welling in his eyes.

"Who?"

"Several Roman soldiers. They attacked your brother. They beat him and dragged him after them."

"You mean Abram?"

"He didn't stand a chance. The Romans have killed him. He must be dead."

"Oh, God! Abram, my own brother!"

Benjamin Levi put his hands on Joshua's shoulders.

"We must go, Joshua. Ruth, stay here with Sarah."

He held the young man close to him.

"Take me out on the road," he said. "We may yet find Abram half alive."

Joshua called Amos to join them from the carpenter's shop. The three of them left the village on the Sepphoris road. Ahead, they could see the crowd of angry villagers who had given the Romans chase. Within sight of the village, they were gathered around Abram's body, which lay severed, covered in blood and dust. His pathetic remains were lacerated to shreds by the stones of the rough roadway over which he had been dragged. There was no sign of life in him, just his almost unrecognizable corpse. The flies and ants had already invaded his flesh and blood.

"He's dead," Joshua said quietly. "I saw the whole thing, Benjamin Levi. Like I said, they beat him almost to death and then dragged him out here to die."

Benjamin leaned over the body to see for himself.

"My brother! My only brother!" he cried, kneeling down to take the tortured body in his arms.

The crowd stood back. A Pharisee shook his head and admonished Benjamin Levi:

"Don't touch the corpse, Benjamin, the body's unclean."

Benjamin looked up.

"Is he your brother? He's my kith and kin! Do you expect me to leave him here for the worms?"

"I've long warned you Nazarenes," the pharisaic fanatic continued. "We shouldn't have anything to do with Romans. Your brother was a Sepphoris Jew, just like they said. He lived in the Roman city and traded with Romans. No good can come to our people if we fraternize with the Romans."

An angry Nazarene stood up to the Pharisee.

"We sell our surplus grain and flax to the Romans. We sell them the fruit of our vines. Do you want to destroy what little we have? Leave him alone!"

They all began to shout at one another in confusion.

Eyes wet with sorrow, Joshua and Amos helped Benjamin Levi carry Abram's crushed body from the roadway. They carefully laid it to rest on the stony ground beside a shady grove of olive trees and began to heap stones over the corpse.

Daniel's 'Son of Man', Isaiah's 'Prince of Peace', Joshua reflected. *The suffering servant and the bruised reed. But our people will survive.* A strange feeling of triumph and fear came over him. *Is this my destiny?*

The villagers broke up and with heads hung low, they returned to their homes.

———— CHAPTER EIGHT ————

Slavery

Marched gangs of runaway slaves and Hebrew riffraff, mostly innocent victims of the recent uprising, had become a common sight to the villagers of Nazareth. Rough Roman soldiers ceaselessly beat the gangs on with flailing whips that sang in the air. Groups of pathetic men pulled themselves along like giant, tired caterpillars united by yokes and chains.

Joshua was becoming nauseated at seeing these lost sheep of Israel and their unfortunate allies being marched to doom. It was all too reminiscent of the oppressed brutality that had led to Abram Levi's death, which still lingered in his mind and caused him to ache with gnawing, gut-wrenching, pain. The sight of a Roman soldier brought fear to them all, and no one was sure if they were safe from the retribution.

Amos honed his chisel. He was working with Joshua on building a new wagon for Benjamin Levi. Joseph stood in the carpenter's shop, watching his son. Joseph was too old for heavy work now, but Amos had proved to be an excellent craftsman. Joshua also surprised him. Miriam's child had grown up. He was not only a scholar, thanks to James, but he, too, had become adept at their business.

"Joshua, I never really believed you would settle down as a carpenter," Joseph said, admiring the young man's workmanship. "Your joints are as smooth as those made by Amos. You really have a great partnership now.

When God took Jonah away from us, somehow he sent us a replacement. God bless you, Joshua, you have become a most worthy son."

Joshua smiled. He had always liked Joseph. He thought back on their days together in the kilns in Egypt.

"I'll bet you didn't think that when we used to make bricks together," he said. "Remember how we were always in trouble? It was Amos who was the worker. You used to say I was a dreamer."

"Well, you still are, Joshua," Joseph said with a warm smile, "but you've become a worker, too."

Joshua put down his hammer and chisel.

"God has given us all a purpose, Joseph. Sometimes, our dreams become shattered, but our purpose lives on. If God wants to use my talents as a carpenter, He will find a way. If not, then I must follow the path that He chooses for me. We never know when God is going to call us, but He's always there, ready to guide us."

"Well, He's not guiding us very well right now," Amos interjected as one of the chain gangs of Jewish prisoners shuffled past in the street outside. "Some people think God led us into this strife with the Romans, and a lot of good that's done us."

"You don't know, Amos. That's what the prophets thought when our people were taken captive, but remember that God used that time to train his new prophets and prepare us in those faraway lands for our triumphant return. God has never abandoned us, and He never will."

"That's right, Joshua," Joseph said, nodding his head in simplistic approval. "God hasn't abandoned us. Look at me...I have a rabbi for a son, my daughter is married to a rich man, and I have both of you to carry on my business in my old age. God sent me Miriam to comfort me when we lived in chaos in Bethlehem, and just as I said before, God sent me you, Joshua, for He knew that Jonah would leave us."

Amos looked up at his father quizzically.

"You still think about Jonah, don't you, Father?"

"Yes, I think about Jonah. I pray for Jonah, wherever he may be. Jonah's our flesh and blood, Amos. He was just like you—one of my sons. God gave me Jonah, but what God gives God sometimes takes away. That's the way life is. Now, when are you going to settle down and think about marriage?"

"Not that again, Father," Amos said with no little frustration.

His father was always bringing up the subject of his need to get married, but Amos had no leaning in that direction.

"Yes, it's most important. It's God's command. I can't believe it. Neither you nor James has considered marriage yet, and James a rabbi, too! You, too, Joshua. We need to seek out someone for you! At the moment, there's only Ruth to give me grandsons. It's time, you know, time for all of you."

Amos sighed, and Joshua started to chuckle. Joseph always sounded so serious when he spoke on this subject.

"Have you been talking to Rachel's family again, Father?" Amos asked, shrugging his shoulders as he half smiled at Joseph with enough seriousness to beg an answer.

"Well it does so happen that Rachel's father saw me recently, and I can't say I'm against the agreement. He has a good business, and I think you would make an excellent match for her. If you don't take up the offer, someone else will contract a marriage with her. Rachel would be a very good wife for you, Amos. You won't do better."

Joshua rolled his eyes and chuckled as he looked up at Amos.

Amos was looking very serious, but when he caught Joshua's gaze he started to laugh.

"All right, Father, bring Rachel around to meet us again."

He then pointed at Joshua.

"Bring her sister Joanna around for Joshua at the same time."

Joshua's chuckles exploded into laughter. Amos had got the better of him.

"Joanna!" Joseph said, a little alarmed. "She's still a child!"

"Yes, Joseph. Do you want me to marry a child?" Joshua asked.

Joseph looked down.

"Your mother was little more than a child when I married her," he said contemplatively. "She's made me an excellent wife, and she's been a good mother to you all. So, why not Joanna?"

"Mother was different," Joshua answered.

He addressed his brother as he picked up some wood:

"Amos, are you ready to start on this wheel?"

Amos caught his father's eye again and slapped Joshua on the back.

"You're getting nervous, aren't you?" he teased.

He felt satisfied that he'd caused this little exchange. Joshua needed to be needled from time to time.

The two brothers began to assemble the wagon's solid and heavy wheels. The sound of hammering filled the carpenter's shop and drowned the noise of the passing column of prisoners. Amos and Joshua became engrossed in their work.

Joseph left them to it seeking out Miriam in the interior of the house.

The frequent movement of Roman soldiers through Nazareth had become so commonplace since the rebellion that nobody really paid it much attention. Occasionally, refugee zealots were seized and taken back to Sepphoris to die as vulture meat on Roman crosses, but for the most part, the villagers of Nazareth remained immune from the worst of the retribution—the vicious attack on Abram Levi being the one exception. Under the pacifist leadership of Rabbi James, Nazareth had not become involved in the great rebellion, and its villagers were more concerned with their own affairs than those of greater Galilee. It was somewhat of a surprise, therefore, when four soldiers in rough leather tunics stood in the threshold of the carpenter's shop.

The soldiers spoke noisily in Latin. The message was clear. They seized both Joshua and Amos. In unarmed struggle, they pulled them into the street. There, they tied them with thongs and yoked them to the passing chain gang. It all happened so quickly, too fast for the village to react. Joseph and Miriam heard the cries of the scuffle. By the time they reached the street, the caterpillar of captured men was being whipped onward toward Sepphoris.

* * *

Joshua's feet ached from the forced march, and his left arm hurt from the slash of the whip. He prayed while Amos cursed.

"Father in heaven," Joshua said to himself, "help us! Protect us!"

The heavy yoke weighed on his shoulders. *Don't let us be crucified,* he thought. *My life is only just beginning. I have a destiny to serve You and our people. I am not ready to die. I don't want to die.* He thought of Rachel and her sister Joanna. *Father wants us to marry. He wants us to give him grandsons.* The thought made him chuckle again, but he was brought back to reality with the sting of studded leather ripping at his arm. Amos stopped cursing and plodded on in the dust, eyes staring straight ahead. Neither of them had even a remote idea why suddenly they had become caught up in the horror around them. Deadbeat zealots yoked and chained, trampling the dust to the flash and crack of the Roman whips, were their fellow prisoners. These were people they didn't know and for whose cause they had never fought.

The rough road rounded the outcrop of rocks, making the last rise before Sepphoris come into view. Closer to the ruined city, stretched bodies of dead and dying Jews hung from crude wooden crosses. The Roman whips continued to sing and crack as the human caterpillar moved on through the gates and into the garrison's central square. At last, the march stopped. A temporary sense of relief fell on the exhausted men, and the coolness of the courtyard felt good after the long exposure to the hot sun.

Amos looked over at Joshua and cast a nervous smile in his direction. Joshua nodded in response as the soldiers began to unyoke the men. The captured zealots were unchained, but with their hands still tied together, they were pulled away and led to the tower in the corner of the barracks court. When the soldiers reached Joshua and Amos, they shouted to one of the plumed Roman officers, who came up to them and spoke in Aramaic:

"You're craftsmen, I believe. Carpenters and builders, if I'm correctly informed?"

Amos spat on the ground at the officer's feet. Immediately, one of the soldiers struck him with his whip handle. Amos flinched and stared up into the officer's eyes.

Joshua made no move.

"You're from neighboring Nazareth, I understand?" the officer continued.

Joshua nodded, and begrudgingly Amos followed his example.

"Your skills are needed here in the reconstruction. You'll be placed under forced labor and will assist with the rebuilding program. You'll be foremen. Provided you fulfill this role satisfactorily, you'll not be harmed. When the work is completed you'll be allowed to return to your village."

The officer, a centurion of the Sepphoris garrison, turned to the soldiers, speaking in Latin once again.

A minute or two later, Joshua and Amos were marched to the corner tower and locked in a long, dark chamber with the renegade zealots. The darkness reminded Joshua of the night. He imagined the stars and the moon. In his imagination, he was back on that wall bench in Egypt with his mother. *Have mercy on us,* he prayed, *all of us. Take care of Mother and Joseph, and Amos, here with me; also, James, Ruth and David—even Jonah, wherever he may be. Mother believes in my destiny, Almighty God. She believes I have a purpose. Her angels told her before I was even born. Spare us! Don't let them crucify us!*

Amos looked at Joshua knowingly. He was used to seeing him pray.

"Do you think God will really answer your prayers?" he said.

They heard the screams of a young zealot being flogged.

"I don't know," Joshua replied. "But I am sure God does not mean us to die."

* * *

Joseph held Miriam close to him. Her hair was matted with tears, and her strength was sapped.

"What will become of them, Joseph? Where have they taken them?"

Joseph remained speechless. He shook his head and held Miriam even closer.

"Why Joshua and Amos, Joseph? None of us have ever done anything to harm the Romans. Even when Abram Levi was murdered, we did nothing in revenge. Why us, Joseph? Why? Why? Why?"

Miriam's sobbing tears overcame her speech.

"Miriam, we cannot understand and we never will," Joseph said softly. "Do you remember how God spared Joshua when he was a baby? Do you remember how we were warned by Simeon the High Priest? How we fled to Egypt?"

Miriam looked up at her husband. Her tears welled again.

"God saved us then," Joseph reassured her. "He spared Joshua from the king's soldiers."

"Yes, but that was long ago," Miriam sobbed. "What now? You've heard the stories. They take them to Sepphoris and they bind them to crosses. They just leave them there to die. That's what will happen to

Joshua and Amos. They'll die hanging on crosses, and for no reason, no purpose."

"We don't know that, my dearest."

"Why else would they take them away?"

"Miriam, where is your faith? You once believed that Joshua had a special destiny. Don't you believe that now?"

"How can I? They've taken my son away. Maybe the Romans are stronger than God. What's the use? These Romans are destroying us."

"They can't destroy our faith, Miriam. Remember how you used to believe that your angel Gabriel was always with you? Gabriel's still with you. You used to say he was in the moon and the stars, and the wind and the leaves—even the butterflies. You believed in him, and you believed he heralded something special for your son."

Miriam looked up at Joseph with clearer eyes. He was bringing back to her all her closest secrets.

"Yes…I did," she spluttered.

"The moon's still there. The stars, the wind, the leaves, they are all still with us."

"That's true, but Joshua's gone. Amos is gone. We may never see either of them again."

Joseph crushed Miriam against him with his rough hands.

"God won't abandon us. Ruth will soon have children. What God has taken away will be given back in the next generation. That's the way it's always been. Didn't God command Abraham to multiply and populate the earth with God's chosen people? No Roman can destroy that command."

"No, but Ruth is your daughter. They'll be your grandchildren. What about my son?"

"He will be all right, Miriam. Remember he is God's son, too. Isn't that what Gabriel told you?"

Miriam looked up at Joseph. She felt renewed strength in his arms. She smiled at him through her tears, knowing he must be right.

* * *

Flavius chose to pardon many of the runaway slaves, but he put them to work on the rebuilding of Sepphoris. The captured zealots and freedom fighters, he had executed, or sent to the galley ports to continue hard labor at the oars. Each day, Flavius surveyed the rebuilding from horseback. The industrious sound of stonemasons and woodworkers could be heard everywhere. Sepphoris was rising from her ashes. Barebacked and dripping with sweat, the Jews toiled to rebuild the city that they had destroyed. Soldiers supervised them to see that the work never stopped. The baths and the gymnasium had already been completed, and the garrison was again fully secure.

It was late in the afternoon. Flavius, accompanied by Marcellus and Semus, was riding down the main street. He felt a pride in what was being achieved, and all in so short a time! He recognized that this was forced labor, but he also understood the industrious nature of these captured Jews. The future land that he conceived, was to be one where the Jews could live in harmony with Romans and a mutual respect be evident to all. Then, ahead, he saw a scene that although familiar disturbed him. A Roman soldier was flailing the raw, sunburned back of a young Hebrew man, little more than a youth. He seemed to be taking a sadistic pleasure in his task. The Jewish lad was strapped to a post and was crying out from the pain. Flavius pulled up his horse and asked Marcellus to dismount and investigate.

Marcellus looked at the soldier admonishing the punishment and raised his right hand. The soldier put down the flail.

"The commander wants to know what this man has done?" Marcellus asked.

"He was idling, sir," the soldier replied.

"Carry on then, see that he returns to his task contrite."

The soldier picked up the flail and resumed the thrashing, but after only three strokes he heard the voice of the commander himself:

"Stop this!" Flavius ordered.

Again, the soldier laid down the flail.

Flavius dismounted and personally approached the youth slumped over the whipping post.

"What is your name?" he asked.

"Joshua."

"You won't idle on the job again, will you?"

"No, sir."

"Good, because if you do you will be punished severely."

Flavius then turned to Marcellus.

"If we beat this young man much more, he will not be any use at his trade. Our goal here is to rebuild this city, and our future goal is to rebuild this land. The man has been warned. Do not now take away his capacity to work and make them hate us more than they already do."

Flavius looked at Joshua.

"Young man," he said, "I'm ordering your release so you can return to your work. Don't believe in the injustice of Rome, but believe in the discipline of Rome. An honest day's work will be rewarded honestly. Now, return to your task."

Joshua was untied and gratefully returned to trimming new beams and chiseling joints. His back stung, but the lacerations were only surface wounds. *Thank you, God,* he prayed. *Don't ever let me have to experience that again.*

Flavius Septimus continued his inspection with Marcellus and Semus.

"Marcellus, try to see that the men are not too brutal with these peasants," he said.

"Is Rome going soft, Commander?"

"We are not going soft, but this time we intend to establish our rule permanently. We're in charge now. The Tetrarch has no power. The Herodians can remain titular puppets as long as they please, but we will be making all the decisions, and we'll govern the Jewish state both in the north and the south."

"Then surely we should rule with an iron fist," Semus interjected.

"We want these people with us, not against us," Flavius reiterated. "We must be firm, but we must be fair."

Marcellus and Semus rode on in silence. They knew no other way but to beat the Semites into place.

* * *

While Flavius observed the fast restoration of the Galilean capital, he drifted into thoughts of Magdala. He looked forward to rebuilding his own villa and longed for the day that he could return with his family to the shores of the lake and prove that Galilee was a safe and peaceful land. He feared that the villa might now be overrun with weeds and be crumbling in decay, but he was more determined than ever to restore it to its former beauty and bring Copernia and Linus home.

He felt Magdala was home. He was a Roman Galilean, just as these men working in the streets of Sepphoris were Jewish Galileans. Together, they would help mold a new province, prosperous and safe for all. He hadn't thought of Copernia and Linus much during the days of the siege and the weeks of retribution, but now seemed an appropriate time to reconsider his obligations. He would restore the villa, and then, when his term as garrison commander was completed, he would travel to Rome and bring back his family.

Satisfied with his thoughts and his actions, Flavius dismissed Marcellus and Semus, who returned to the barracks.

Night fell. Sepphoris was well on the way to being rebuilt.

* * *

Joseph watched from the carpenter's shop as yet another procession of wagons laden with timber and marble wound its way through Nazareth bound for Sepphoris. His back ached from the now-unfamiliar workload that he had to do to keep the family business alive. He could tell that he was not as strong as in the past, but the trail of wagons gave him hope for the future.

Deep down he continued to believe that Amos and Joshua were alive. He realized that the Romans needed craftsmen to rebuild Sepphoris. What other reason could they possibly have had for taking away his sons? It was impossible to get word from Sepphoris to find out. Those who had ventured there had been turned away at the gates. Sepphoris was guarded like a fortress. Joseph was sure, however, that Amos and Joshua were there, and nightly in his prayers he called on God to take care of them.

James visited the carpenter's shop more frequently these days, taking on some of the responsibilities that he felt had fallen on his shoulders. He was now Joseph's only son. His feeble efforts to work with his father, however, were more of a hindrance than a help.

Finally, Joseph confronted James with the truth:

"James, you have better things to do in the synagogue than lend a hand here. You really have no skills as a builder and joiner."

"I know, Father, but I'm concerned about you. Can you manage here on your own? Can't Jon help you? He does precious little up at Joachim ben Judah's house. Maybe you should take on an apprentice, someone from the village... from outside the family?"

Joseph put down his tools.

"James, you are supposed to be the rabbi. Have you no faith? Amos and Joshua will return."

"Father, be practical. Do you really think the Romans will let them go? They may be dead, or working the galleys by now. What makes you so sure that they're in Sepphoris?"

"Faith, James."

James looked at his father with mixed feelings of respect and guilt.

"You do have great faith, don't you, Father."

"Yes. More than the rabbi! I never questioned your desire to learn. You're a scholar, and I'm a simple man. All your studying, however, does not bring you any nearer to God. Whether we keep the Law or not, God is still there. Sometimes, all the rules and regulations make it hard to reach Him. Despite the Romans, I have faith when I see how the seeds grow up each year, how the fields of flax turn blue, and how the doves keep flying above, while the lambs bleat on the hillside. I don't have to look further."

James smiled.

"Father, if all of us could share your simple faith, there would be no strife, no Pharisee or Sadducee. We would all just be Jews, and our power would be far greater than that of any Roman."

Joseph looked his son straight in the eye.

"Have faith, because that day will come."

James left the carpenter's shop, surprised by his father's sudden philosophical outburst. He was soon back, however, when he saw Ruth running across the square toward the family home.

"Ruth! What is it? You look so happy," James inquired.

"I am. Is Father there?"

"Yes, he's in the shop. What is it?"

"I'm going to give him his first grandchild," she said, not able to hold back the news any longer.

James opened his arms.

"Ruth, my little sister! There's nothing that would please Father more! He has such faith. He'll see this as a sign that God has not abandoned us!"

James squeezed Ruth affectionately.

"I think this is a sign, too," he said. "Come on, let's go in and tell him. He'll be so happy."

They went over to the house and announced the news to Joseph, who dropped his work in the carpenter's shop with delight.

Miriam busied herself during Ruth's subsequent confinement. In contrast to Miriam's birthing, Ruth had all the comforts of Benjamin Levi's grand house and constant attention from the village midwife.

Ruth had a son, and David Levi declared his name to be Matthew. James performed the circumcision, and the families of Joseph and Benjamin were truly united.

* * *

By the time Sepphoris was rebuilt, 'Pax Romana' returned to the Levant. The prefect in Judea restored good order in Jerusalem, and prosperity marked that bustling crossroads of Semitic trade. Better roads were being constructed everywhere, and the warehouses in Caesarea Maritima and the Phoenician ports were again stacked with the produce of the Empire and its needs. It was now safe for Flavius to leave Sepphoris and return to Magdala to restore his villa.

Flavius had promised to return the conscripted craftsmen to their villages, but he asked certain ones from the Sepphoris gang to remain as potential hired help for his rebuilding project outside Magdala. Joshua and Amos were among the craftsmen whom he summoned to the barracks for this task.

"You will be paid the standard wage of a denarius a day," Flavius told them. "You will work under the supervision of Demetrius, whom you all know, my Greek Master of Works. You won't find him a hard taskmaster, and you'll note that he speaks good Aramaic."

Amos looked at Joshua. At least, now, they were going to be paid.

"Tomorrow, you'll start loading up the ox carts to take the necessary timber, marble, and tiles from Sepphoris to the lake country," Flavius continued. "You will journey with Demetrius and a small detachment of the guard on the following day. You have done well and I have admired your work—that's why I've chosen to hire you for my personal project. Naturally, at the completion of this task you'll be free to return to your former lives."

There were ten craftsmen in the selected group. One was an expert in mosaics and another in tiling. The others, like Amos and Joshua, were woodworkers and stonemasons who had shown prowess in their crafts.

The next day, a wagon train was prepared to take the initial supplies to Magdala that Demetrius deemed necessary for the task. The following morning, the wagons were dispatched on the road northwest, joining the new Roman road to pass through the plain of Asochis down to the villages of Madon, Arbela, and Taricheae.

* * *

Joshua was thrilled to sense the freedom of the countryside and felt that sometime now, he would see his mother again. His time in captivity and suffering had been a time of reflection and growth. *Peace is certainly better than fighting,* he thought. *The way of fighting has failed, but the way of peaceful co-existence might just be beginning.* He glowed as he thought of his mother's title for him all those years ago—The 'Prince of Peace'. He had much to share with her.

The blue flax always looked so pretty at this time of the year and there was more of it around here than in Nazareth. The vines were still fresh with lucid shades of green. The dust of late summer hadn't had time yet to settle. There was also the exhilaration of personal freedom. He was leading his own ox cart, and the Roman soldiers were not there to whip them, but to protect him and the others from possible marauding thieves and robbers. The sun felt good, and a new sense of hope welled within Joshua.

Movement of the heavy ox carts was slow, even on the new roads. Dusk fell and they stopped for the night outside Madon. The stars were bright, and the moon made a perfect crescent in the sky. Joshua and Amos prepared to sleep, reveling in the sudden change in their daily fortune.

* * *

Maria, the little girl who had liked to play in the ruins of Flavius' villa, was growing up. She gently caressed her right breast and felt her nipple harden. She was proud of the way she looked. Her body was smooth and well proportioned, her hair had the fullness and luster of youth, and she knew that she had the power to attract men. Her mother, Esther, had trained her well and used her insatiable desire to advantage. Esther herself was still plying her trade and carried a comely warmth that left many a man trembling for fulfillment.

Maria's personal pleasure was disturbed when she heard her mother's voice:

"Maria, I need the room."

Esther entered the back room of the brothel as Maria pulled up the folds of her garment.

In the dimness of the single oil lamp, Maria could see that a rough-looking fisherman was standing behind her mother. She cast a dark, piercing look at the man before moving out of the house into daylight.

The sun beat down, drying the fish that had been laid out on the pebbles of the beach. It was almost nostalgic as Maria considered how the fishing industry had changed while she had been growing up. The Romans had developed a liking for the abundant flat fish of the Galilean lake. Ambitious merchants had developed a means of packing the fish in brine for long-distance marketing. The traditional drying, which caused a terrible odor and was wasteful in the resulting loss of flesh, was rapidly being replaced by salt pickling. This way, the fish could be preserved in barrels for long periods of time and the flesh could retain its fullness. The carts from the merchants of Capernaum, where the center of this pickling industry was located, were now commonplace in the village.

Maria heard carts coming down the street, but was quite surprised when they came into view. They were not the salt carts of the picklers, but a whole train of ox wagons escorted by a small detachment of Roman soldiers. The wagons carried building materials. Maria watched them as they left the village and turned to climb up the hillside toward the ruined villa.

They were going toward her place of refuge. She remembered the mosaics on the floors, the big clay jars, and those statues of naked men and women that had first aroused her sexual desires. Her thoughts went back to that day when the Roman commander had found her, and how she had fallen while trying to run away. He had surprised her by helping her when she grazed her knee. Nobody had been near the ruined villa for several years. *Maybe the Romans are going to rebuild*, she thought. *If they do, I won't be able to go there anymore.*

She watched the last of the heavy ox carts trundle by and disappear up the hill.

Her mother's client wasn't long. The smelly fishermen rarely were. As the man left the house, he came toward Maria on his way back to the beach.

Maria smiled at him seductively and cupped her breasts through the material of her loose-fitting shift. The man blushed and hurried on to return to his business.

"You'll come for me next time," she muttered to herself. "I'm better than my mother."

* * *

The gaunt ruins of the facade of Flavius' villa had mellowed over the years. Grasses and vines had taken the starkness from them. The outer courtyard was a jungle of saplings and tares, and the mosaic flooring of the vestibule had become a mass of weeds. Vines had also taken over the inner courtyard, winding their way up the pillars and trellises and poking through the tiles of the atrium roof. The furniture in the atrium had rotted. Many of the earthenware jars in the storage rooms had become cracked and broken, their dried-out contents strewn across the flags of the floor. Demetrius surveyed the scene and set his plan for reconstruction. First, the villa would have to be cleared and cleaned of natural intrusions. The structural soundness would then have to be tested, and only after that could the rebuilding begin.

The ox carts were unloaded and the oxen tethered to graze on the hillside. Footsore from their journey, the craftsmen settled to sleep in the late afternoon sun. Later, in the evening, they shared their rations around an open fire and sang songs that reflected their newfound freedom. The next day, Demetrius set them to detailed tasks, and the work of restoration began.

After the basic clearing, Amos and Joshua were appointed to commence work on the vestibule roof. At first, they removed the debris, hacking away the rotten, burned-out timbers, which brought down large sections of the fragile roofing along with loose plaster.

Amos looked at the ever-increasing revelation of damage.

"Joshua, it's no use," he said. "We might as well take off this whole roof. By the time we've finished there will be almost nothing left anyway."

One of the fragile roof timbers began to loosen. Joshua slipped. Climbing back along a safer beam, he moved closer to Amos.

"Did you see that?" he gasped. "I nearly fell. You're right, this whole section needs to come down. Let's dismantle the roof."

"So God and His angels saved you?" Amos teased.

"Perhaps."

Joshua put down his mallet. *Perhaps God needs to spare me*, he thought. *My destiny is yet to be fulfilled.*

Demetrius agreed to their assessment of the structure's safety and durability. The roof was cleared and during the following few days the two carpenters, known as 'The brothers', set about hewing new timbers and preparing the frame.

Stonemasons busied themselves, restoring the architrave of the terrace and adding new dressed stone where the masonry had fallen. Piece by piece, the villa of the Sepphoris commander was restored.

Demetrius was not a hard taskmaster. There was time to relax, unlike the many months of hard labor in Sepphoris; and there was always the lake in which to cool off and bathe after the day's toil. The prisoners baked their own bread, and fresh fish was available in abundance. Fruits and berries that they had rarely seen in the Sepphoris days were easy to get in the village. It was only natural that given their new freedom, this congenial group of craftsmen would eventually seek out other local pleasures that were, apparently, also a cheap commodity in Magdala.

As they sat one evening after their work, their conversation turned to the subject of those pleasures.

"You had the mother last week?" one of the stonemasons asked a fellow worker with a leering look of recent satisfaction. "You should try the daughter."

Amos looked at Joshua.

"Do you think my father still has plans to marry us off to Rachel and Joanna?" he said, wanting to test Joshua's reaction.

Joshua gave a shy smile. He had put most of his adolescent energies into his studies with James.

"Why does he want us to be married? Why not James? James really should be married, especially as the rabbi."

"Father wants grandchildren, that's why," Amos replied.

"Maybe Ruth has given him grandchildren. Why does he get so concerned over that?"

"It's tradition, Joshua. You know the Law."

"Do you really think God would think any the less of us if we were not married, Amos?"

"Don't you want a wife and a family?"

"I've never really given it much thought. What about you? Would you like to marry Rachel?"

Amos looked a little sheepish.

"She's moderately attractive. I don't see why people say things about her. Perhaps she's a bit big-boned and rather taller than most of the others, but I suppose if it would please Father, and if the dowry was right, I'd consider her."

Their fellow stonemasons were still discussing the Magdala whores.

"Listening to them makes me begin to want a woman, though," Amos continued.

He looked at Joshua directly.

"It would be easy here," he whispered. "Nobody would know us and we seem to be the only two who haven't tried it."

Joshua reddened and turned to look in the other direction.

"You do what you want. I don't think I'm ready for a woman yet," he declared.

The two brothers settled their straw pallets and dozed off.

Two days later, Amos admitted to his sexual adventures with Esther.

"Joshua, you should seriously think about it. That woman's incredible. I've never experienced anything so pleasurable in my life. You should come with me. She'll drive you wild."

"You lay with her, Amos? She's old!"

"Of course! It was wonderful! I really don't know why I never let myself be with the girls in Nazareth. Somehow, it just didn't seem right there. Aren't you curious to have a woman? Esther's a real woman. She has experience."

"It's not something of which we Jews really approve. It's something that the Gentiles do," Joshua replied.

"That's tradition again, Joshua. Sometimes, I think we have too much tradition. Anyway, Esther's a Jewess. Really, Joshua, you should try it."

Joshua looked away. One part of him wanted to share in Amos' joy, but another still nagged at him, saying that it was wrong.

"We'll see, Amos. Maybe..." he said.

The subject was closed, and it was not discussed again for several days. Amos made frequent visits to the small square house at the end of the village. Esther worked her charms on him, and he had fallen for them even though she was so much older than he was.

Amos and Joshua usually went down to the lake to bathe after their hard day's work. On their way back they passed close by the whores' house. One warm evening, Maria saw them coming and, knowing Amos served her mother, she prepared herself in anticipation of catching the younger man for herself. She flashed her sultry eyes at Joshua and with a beckoning smile stood with one leg slightly forward so that it revealed the lines of her thighs and rounded hips.

"Look, Joshua!" Amos said excitedly. "I think she wants you. Why don't you take the daughter while I'm with the mother?"

Joshua couldn't deny he was aroused, but something told him this was wrong. Passages of Scripture were ambiguous on the subject—David, Solomon and other kings had concubines, although they were often foreigners. But thinking of his rough work mates and the fishermen on the beach made him associate brothels with violence and drunkards. He even wondered if the man, Gabriel, of whom his mother had sometimes spoken, had forced himself upon her like the rough men he now knew visited the Magdala whores' house. *It's interesting*, he reflected, *how Mother nearly always turns the subject from Gabriel the man, to the angel she believes protects her. She's afraid to speak of the man the High Priest had first selected for her.*

Maria pulled down the top of her shift to reveal the light olive flesh of her breasts, allowing one bosom to show in full as her hand cupped it underneath. Joshua could see the hardening nipple, and he felt the excitement of youth rush through his body at the sight of Maria's provocation.

"She's yours, Joshua!" Amos repeated. "Try her out. You'll enjoy it. Sooner or later you'll have to find out what it is to be a man."

Joshua trembled and looked at Amos apprehensively.

"What shall I say to her?"

"Nothing, Joshua. Just go up to her and smile. She'll do the rest.

She'll take you into the house. You really don't have to say anything, but be sure to give her a couple of bronze coins when you're through."

Amos reached into his leather purse. He pulled out four Roman quadrans.

"Here, take these. They'll be enough. I'll give you this one."

Joshua took the coins and clutched them in his hand. He hesitated. *God guide me*, he prayed.

Amos stepped back, laughing.

"Go with her, Joshua!" he shouted as he walked away, but Joshua hardly heard him. His heart pounded in anticipation and fear.

Maria concealed her breast once more in the folds of her loose-fitting garment and held out her hand. Her beckoning smile showed a sense of triumph. Joshua fleetingly looked back. Amos was grinning from ear to ear.

Before he knew it, Joshua's hand clasped Maria's and she began to lead him toward the doorway of the square house. She felt the four coins in his palm and worked them into her own. Amos stood and watched as she took him inside.

There was a sticky, sweet smell in the house. It was a musky odor of body sweat, sweet perfume, and burning oil. The lamps were lit in the outer chamber, revealing only a wooden bench and a bowl of wet rags.

Maria deposited the four quadrans in an earthenware pot and sat Joshua down on the bench. She began to wipe the dust from his feet with the rags. She smiled at him and asked him his name.

"Joshua," he whispered through the lump that had formed in his throat.

"My name's Maria," she said. "Do you want me? Would you like to have me?"

Joshua smiled and pressed his right hand against the softness of Maria's breast. Maria moved closer to him and took his hand inside the material so that it rested on her naked flesh.

Joshua felt its warmth, its softness, and the rising excitement of Maria's nipple. Instinctively, he moved his hand over the roundness of the flesh, but he was afraid to look at what he was doing. Maria was staring straight at him, her eyes drilled into his, and an intensity crossed her face that he had never seen in a woman before. Momentarily, she closed her eyes, and then pulled away, taking Joshua's hand from her breast.

447

Esther emerged from the back room followed by a faceless man.

"It's free now, Joshua," Maria said. "Come with me."

Maria led Joshua into the rear. The oil lamp guttered, making patterns of light on the gauze drapes that hung flimsily around the boxed bench which took up half the room. There was a wooden stool and a bowl of water beside a jar of sweet-smelling oil. Maria slowly undid the cord that held her garment at the waist and then loosened the tie that held the shift on her shoulder. The material fell to the ground in folds at her feet. As Maria stepped from it, the glow of the lamp cast a warm light over her naked flesh. She knelt down and picked up the jar of oil, pouring a little between her breasts and rubbing it lightly over her body.

Joshua stood dumbfounded as he stared at her naked beauty, but he made no move to undress himself.

"Take your tunic off," Maria suggested as she put down the jar.

Joshua began to release his clothing, but could not bring himself to remove the garment. When Maria motioned him to the bench, he followed, clothed as he was.

"Lie beside me," she said, losing a little bit of her confidence.

Maria had only been working with her mother for a year, but she felt that she knew all the moves. She knew she had a good body and that she was irresistible to men. No man hesitated at wanting her warm embrace.

Joshua obeyed. He climbed onto the straw mattress, which was swathed in the sweaty linens of Esther's recent passion. He lay beside Maria's beautiful body, but became totally afraid to touch her.

Maria took the initiative. This man was a challenge. She was determined to have him within her power. She took his hand once again and placed it on the firmness of her breasts and then slid it down her oiled body passing over her generous hips. Then, she straddled over him, thrusting her breasts into his face.

The sweet musk of the perfumed oil sickened Joshua. Maria began to pull at his tunic, ripping the well-worn material at the neck.

Further disgusted, Joshua's shy anxiety left him. He became master of his own destiny and with his greater strength pushed the young girl off him. He left her lying naked on the bench as he fled from the house. In his disheveled tunic, he ran for the cover of the cypress trees.

He heard Amos calling after him:

"What happened?"

Joshua didn't answer. He scrambled up to the path that led back to the villa. By the time he got there, the night sky had formed. He knelt down on the grass of the hillside and prayed through the tears of remorse that were gathering in his eyes:

"Lord, forgive me!" he cried. "Lord, forgive me, for I didn't know what I was doing."

Joshua exhausted himself in prayer and then lay down on the ground, looking up at the stars and rising moon.

* * *

Even for Judas and Jonah, who were used to a hard life, the months living with the goatherds and shepherds of Jotbah were rugged. It had been rigorous in the caves at Hermon, but at least the company was good there, and the place offered a lot more shelter than this forsaken village. The houses were no more than semicircular bowers of stones with goatskin roofs supported by posts and guys. Judas and Jonah were strangers, only accepted as two extra pairs of hands to hunt for sustenance. They were isolated, despised, and uncomfortable, but at least they were safe. These strange, cold, men of Jotbah were independent in the extreme.

Judas and Jonah went down to Cana with hides and wool to exchange for skins of wine and other basic necessities. They tried to get some kind of assessment in the village on the safety of the land. They wanted to get back to the prosperous lake country and eventually return south to Judea. Several zealots from Cana had been seized by Roman soldiers in the retribution that had followed the rebellion. The ringleaders of the famous attack on the Roman forces had been caught, along with some innocent bystanders who paid the price for those who had escaped. Crucifixions had followed, and the population of Cana had been bloodily and dramatically reduced. Several months had now passed. Peace seemed to have been restored. Judas suggested to Jonah that it was now time to move on.

"All right, let's go back to the lake country," Jonah suggested. "I could do with some of that good fish again. I never realized how well we ate and lived until we came here. I'm sick of dung cakes, berries, locusts and honey. When do you think we can start out?"

"There's nothing really to stop us, Jonah. They haven't seen Roman soldiers here since winter. Things have settled down. Let's leave at dawn. I'm sick of Jotbah, too."

The two companions slept on it. Early the next day, they traded Jotbah skins and wool for a bundle of coins and, without conscience for the rough community that had sheltered them, moved on.

Still dressed in their smelly goatskins, they kept away from the new Roman roads and followed a path eastward over the hills. They begged and stole what they could when they reached Arbela, hiding their bag of coins. From the village, they could see the blue waters of the lake in the deep valley below. By evening, they had scrambled down the rocks and reached the deserted vineyards of the Roman villas above Magdala.

Judas pointed at Flavius' home.

"Look! I think that's the villa we burned."

"Maybe it's still a ruin," Jonah suggested as he looked in the same direction. "Perhaps it would be a good place to take shelter for the night."

They made their way along the vineyard terraces until they got closer to the building. By now it was dusk, and it was hard to see if the villa was still ruined. They could see an open fire, and when they came close enough, they could hear voices.

"There are people there," Jonah said

"The Roman bastards must have returned. Perhaps we'd better go on down to the village after all."

They passed by the villa, following the track down to Magdala, and made their own camp on the beach, just as they had done in the years of hope preceding the great rebellion.

The next day, they hired themselves out as fishermen and joined the beach community of smelly men who worked the staple lakeside industry. They learned the skills of casting nets and pickling fish. In a short while, they were pulling in fish with ease.

"You're quick learners," one of the older fisherman remarked. "Where are you from?"

"Judea," Jonah replied.

"I could tell you were not Galileans. We're getting a lot of strangers up here these days. This fish pickling has brought a new prosperity to the lake, and there are lots of new hands trying to make good in the business.

You look like you'll do all right, though. You've got good action with the nets, and you don't seem to be afraid of a hard day's work."

"Thanks," Judas said.

Jonah grinned at Judas after the man moved on.

"It's better than those goats and sheep," he said. "The people here are more friendly."

Another of their fellow fishermen, named Joel, recognized Judas and Jonah from the time of the villa burning.

"They're rebuilding that villa now," he said. "We haven't forgotten the attack that night. Those Romans can do what they like as far as any of us care, as long as they don't interfere with our personal lives. They murdered that little girl. Whether it was an accident or not, they deserved what they got."

"That's all in the past now, Joel," one of the others chimed in. "Apparently, the Roman is paying the men up there a fair wage. They've come to us for lots of things. It's a new world now, and we might as well make the most of it."

Joel looked skeptical.

"I think you're all going soft. That little girl was Maria's sister," he said.

The response he got was a snigger.

"Had she lived we might have had another as good as Maria," one of them said as he turned his fish over the embers of the campfire. "Maria's giving old Esther a little competition these days. You two might look her up. If you're in need of a woman, ask for Maria."

They all laughed.

Jonah was ready for a woman. He had lived a celibate life too long, and although in the wasted years back in Jerusalem he had sown his wild oats, he had led a life of abstinence during the time he had shared with Judas.

"That sounds like a good idea. One of these days you'll have to introduce me to this Maria," he said.

* * *

Judas had no interest in women, nor was he really comfortable with the easy attitude of his fellow fishermen toward the Romans. At heart, he

451

was still a freedom fighter, and he continued to dream of the day when the enemy would be defeated.

When Jonah spoke of visiting this Maria, he looked at him with admonishment.

"Return to a life of soft cushions, if that's what you wish," he said, "but don't expect me to be there with you."

Jonah looked down at the ground and dropped the subject of women and whores. But his fellow fishermen didn't let him forget Maria. She seemed to be the talk of the boats, and it was inevitable that sooner or later Jonah would find out for himself. Eventually, he made his own way to the whore's house.

Jonah stepped inside and sat on the wooden bench in the outer room, where Maria made him comfortable, washing his feet and dabbing the dust from his face. He was not disappointed. Maria was even more beautiful than the men had suggested. Her hair hung in great waves over her shoulders, her lips were full, and her skin had the clarity of her young age. Jonah could see the firmness of her breasts and the voluptuous curves of her young body. She oozed sexuality, but it was her eyes that captivated him most. They commanded Jonah's attention, and willingly he obeyed.

Maria led Jonah into the back room and turned to him with a beguiling smile. In no time, he was enveloped in the sweet perfume of her body. They were not long in their tryst, Jonah making up for his lost years of pleasure in a brief, lustful surge of excitement. It was enough, however, to tell him that he would be back for more, and he willingly parted with the small coin that was required.

As Jonah left the dim light of the brothel, he passed Maria's mother bringing in a man close to his own age. Jonah wore a satisfied smile that caused the other man to smirk when their eyes met. Something stirred in Jonah as he studied the man's face, but before he had time to contemplate his thoughts, the man turned away to follow the whore into the house.

Two days later, Jonah saw this man again.

A group of men were bathing in the lake as Judas beached his boat. The men chatted as they helped to pull the boat in. This man was one of them. Again, Jonah caught his eye.

"I know that man," he said to Judas.

"Do we need to fear him?" Judas asked. "It seems that we have such good cover here as Galilean fishermen."

"Did you hear him speak?"

"Not really."

"I did…He's not a Galilean. He's one of us, and I saw him the other day at the whores' house."

"You mean he's from Judea?"

"Yes. And not just from Judea. I'd almost swear that the man's my brother."

"Surely you'd know if he was your brother!"

Jonah stared at the men as he watched them dress.

"It's been a long time, Judas. I was little more than a boy when I left. It must have been about fifteen years ago now."

Judas was becoming bored with this whole subject.

"If you really think he's your brother, go and ask him."

Jonah left Judas by the boat and approached the men.

"Thanks for your help," he said.

The men looked his way.

Jonah now felt sure that one of them really was his older brother, Amos.

"Are you from Judea?" he asked.

"Yes, and I would say you, too."

"A long time ago."

"You weren't from Bethlehem, by any chance? I'm sure we've met before."

Jonah now realized for certain that the other man was just as curious. He took a chance on making a direct approach.

"You're my brother Amos, aren't you?" he said.

"Jonah?"

"I knew it was you!"

Amos embraced his younger brother.

"Jonah! It is you! Where've you been all these years?"

"Well, that's a long story, but what're you doing in Galilee? Is Father still alive?"

Amos turned to one of his friends.

"Joshua, you'll never believe this!" he exclaimed. "It's a miracle, but this is Jonah, our runaway brother."

"Joseph's lost son?"

"Yes. It's a miracle—Jonah, our lost brother!"

Amos and Jonah embraced again.

Joshua couldn't share in their emotion. He had no recollection of his missing 'brother', relying purely on the memory of stories told by Joseph, Ruth, and his mother. Neither James nor Amos had expressed any real interest in the prodigal. They had always portrayed Jonah as a lost cause, but Joshua accepted the current enthusiasm Amos now expressed over this reunion.

For some time, the brothers exchanged random snippets of their lives. As evening brought its shadows, Amos asked Jonah if he would like to join them up at the Roman's house.

"You mean up on the ridge behind the village?"

"Yes. We're all working there."

Jonah stepped back.

"Oh no, Amos! I could never stay there. I'll explain to you one day. I have my lodgings here with my friend, Judas Iscariot."

The brothers parted. Amos and Joshua left the village to set off up the hillside to the camp at the villa.

"It's very strange," Amos said. "Jonah never really did fit into our family."

Jonah made his way across the square to the whores' house. He wasn't sure whether to be elated or distressed by this recent reunion, but he sought comfort in Maria's arms.

Chapter Nine

Freedom

After a year of absence, Flavius was pleased with the increased prosperity he found in Magdala. There were more fishing boats on the beach, and new houses had been built along the lakeshore. The village was growing into a small town, thriving on the pickled fish industry. *No wonder they call it Taricheae*, he thought. But the house at the end of the street where he had sought comfort from Esther all those years ago looked the same. So did the little square where the children played. The cypress trees still sheltered Magdala in their sweeping arc behind the town. Comfortable with the familiar, Flavius turned his horse up the track that led to his villa.

The work under Demetrius looked like it was progressing well. The burned-out terrace gleamed with a new, white marble architrave, supporting a freshly tiled roof. On arrival, he found a fine, new wooden gate leading into the courtyard where the old olive trees grew. The vestibule was restored. The walls were clean and new mosaics laid. Everywhere, the grime of smoky destruction had been removed, and the crispness of the restoration showed.

Flavius expressed his approval to Demetrius and the workers generously. He paid all the men a bonus of ten denarii for their work. Before dismissing the majority of them, he arranged a feast at their camp to celebrate their release and freedom. He asked two stonemasons to stay on and repair the vineyard terraces and suggested some small additions to the original plan. Joshua and Amos found themselves free to go with the others. Flavius presented them with one of the surplus ox carts as a parting gift.

* * *

Joshua thanked God and left the villa with Amos in the afternoon. Despite the kind treatment they had received from Demetrius and Flavius Septimus, it felt good to be free and independent again. They were traveling with more coins than either of them had ever held at any one time. They had a whole bag full of denarii. They hid it among their water skins along with their old straw pallets that were laid down in the cart. They were cautious, aware that many might still express resentment of Romans and rob them out of spite because they had associated with the enemy.

"This cart will be very useful for Joseph's business in Nazareth," Joshua commented as they maneuvered the ox and cart down the track.

"That's if Father and the rest of them are still there," Amos replied. "We may find that we are on our own when we return. It's been over two years now. They'll have taken us for dead."

"They'll really be surprised to see us, then," Joshua continued, quite confident that they would find everything in Nazareth just as they had left it.

"You're always the optimist, aren't you, Joshua?"

"I suppose I am. Remember that it is God who governs all things, and despite the bad times, He will always win through in the end. He's never abandoned His people, and He hasn't abandoned us now. He's just setting us in a new direction."

"You, James, and your faith!" Amos responded, never too happy to discuss religious matters with Joshua.

Joshua had such a superior knowledge of these things and they didn't really interest Amos anyway.

"Where was God when we were seized by the Romans?" he jibed.

When they reached the village, Amos changed the subject:

"Let's try to find Jonah one last time. Maybe he'll decide to come back with us after all. That would be a double surprise for the family."

"He's probably out on the lake at this time of the day," Joshua suggested. "Why don't we stay here one more night and see if we can talk him into journeying with us after he has brought in his catch?"

They set up camp on the beach.

"You stay here with the cart and tether the ox," Amos ordered. "We need to keep a watch on our things."

"Where are you going?" Joshua asked.

"If you don't mind, Joshua, I'm going to see Esther one more time."

Joshua made no comment, but had a disapproving look on his face. He tethered the ox and began to seek pieces of driftwood and scrub along the beach. After he had collected enough for their evening fire, he stretched himself out in the shadow of the cart to enjoy the unusual luxury of an afternoon rest. As he did so, he contemplated on man's lust. *Is this sexual gratification so important? Dear God, what am I missing that others find so important? I felt guilty when I was with that girl. Her beauty excited me, but her actions disgusted me. No, God, I was disgusted with myself. I am here to serve others, not to be served.* He dozed.

He awoke, disturbed to see a small boy trying to climb into the wagon. The boy, seeing Joshua move, jumped down and ran away, Joshua thought it better to move the coins closer to the old straw pallet that he was using as a cushion. Having done so, he drifted back into contented slumber.

The next time, it was Amos who woke him, after he returned from the brothel.

"Have any of the boats come in yet?" he asked.

Joshua looked sleepily along the beach. There were a few older fishermen mending nets, but only two small boats were beached.

"I don't think so," he replied.

Amos shouted at him.

"Wake up! I left you here to watch our things. Have you seen Jonah yet?"

"Don't shout at me, Amos. I protected our money from a thief while you were taking your pleasures with Esther. I'm entitled to a little rest now."

"So you're jealous, huh! I mean you could have had Maria, I think she was free."

"You sound like a Roman, Amos. Is licentious pleasure all that interests you? One of us had to take care and watch."

"So who was this thief?"

"A boy. The beggar ran away as soon as he knew I was awake."

They started a fire. The golden light that bathed the lake with the sinking sun brought the fishermen home. One by one their boats were beached. Amos left to check if Jonah was among them. Joshua began to cook their dough cakes. In time, Jonah's boat came in.

* * *

Judas and Jonah had grown tired of each other. Judas was still a zealot at heart, whereas Jonah was losing his convictions and his wanderlust. On the few occasions that Amos had met them on the Magdala beach, he had discussed the possibility of them all going to Nazareth. But Judas expressed no interest in journeying with them. Jonah quickly made up his mind to throw in his lot with Amos.

Judas and Jonah parted on a quarrel. Judas could never accept that Jonah's brother had been in the pay of the very Roman commander whom they had tried to destroy in Magdala and Sepphoris.

"What do I care?" Judas shouted. "Go to Nazareth. Leave me alone. I'll find a better fishing partner. I'll find someone more dedicated to the cause!"

Judas and he had been together a long time, but Jonah wanted to try a more settled life, and his brother Amos was offering him this opportunity.

* * *

Linus was not of rural temperament. The long periods he'd spent in Tuscany between visits to Rome were eternally boring. Tuscany suited his mother, but the quiet countryside had few attractions for the son and heir of the Flavian and Tarquin families. He loved sport and the organized exercise that he could enjoy at the Palestra in Rome, but in Tuscany he was restricted to idle hunting. He was still skilled with his slingshot and javelin, but it was the competitive edge that Linus enjoyed. In Tuscany, his only admirer was his trainer and servant, Gladius.

Gladius lusted after Linus. As the boy had matured into manhood, Gladius had intensified his advances. Out of loneliness and immaturity,

Linus had put up with the older man's attentions. Gladius had been his sexual predator and had given the youth his only sexual experiences.

Linus tolerated Gladius' tender kisses, although the boy felt no emotion for the older man. He allowed the old pedagogue to press his lips close to his. Gladius would then pleasure Linus. As their interminable confinement in the Tuscan countryside unraveled, so these sessions became more and more of a habit. Their relationship became a seductive dance, with Gladius using the teenager's natural need for sexual release to hold power over him.

Linus lay back in the grassy glade that had become their secret place where Gladius molested him. Linus accepted the sensations of the moment, although his mind was far from the action. He lay back and thought about Rome. As soon as he was satisfied, Linus allowed the revulsion he now felt for the older man to well up inside of him and spill out.

"You're stupid!" Linus said one day. "I hate it here. I want to stay in Rome permanently. I'm going to tell my mother we're going to Rome. I can exercise there at the Palestra every day. I don't need this!"

Later, Linus told his mother that he longed to return to Rome. She understood his need for independence and adventure, and his Latin had much improved. In a few days, Linus was on his way back to Rome to enter a new phase of his life.

There, Linus joined a crowd of elite noblemen's sons. They trained regularly in the gymnasiums and the Palestrae of the city. He rapidly showed his prowess at all the field sports. It was the javelin that he enjoyed most. After a friendly contest at the Palestra when, as almost always, Linus won, a more subdued Gladius waited to give his master his customary massage.

"Aren't you glad we came back to Rome?" Linus said when he came in.

"Linus Flavian, I go where you go. I will admit, though, I really do prefer it in Rome to Tuscany. Your Uncle Tarquinius is a lot more interesting than your grandfather Cassius Tarquin."

Gladius raked the oil off Linus' body and started his kneading massage. He hit a knot in his young master's shoulder, a muscle that Linus had slightly pulled in the exertion of his victorious javelin thrust. Gladius dug his thumb into its heart.

At first, Linus flinched, but he relaxed as the pain subsided.

"You do that so well, Gladius. You're still the best," Linus acknowledged.

"Better than the young men?" Gladius jealously teased.

He knew with some bitterness how Linus had paid attention to his contemporaries in the Palestra follies. Linus had become a hero at these gatherings of idle athletic youths who sought sexual favors from each other as a forfeit in their sports. His young master often had the chance to be pleasured by those whom he had defeated. Here in the Palestrae of Rome, Linus had climbed the ladder in all sports, and he reaped the rewards.

Linus detected Gladius' sarcasm.

"Just pay attention to the massage. The young men are good, but the young women are better," he said.

Linus' Tarquin cousins had shown him some of the other delights of the Palatine hill. The high-class brothels of Rome were full of exotic young ladies from all parts of the Empire, ready to educate the youths of the rich in the delights of the flesh.

Life was not all hedonistic pleasures, however. Linus had become a reasonable scholar, a concerned politician, and a remarkable horseman. He was able to hold his own at the elaborate soirees of the Tarquins as well as impress the militia with his equine skills at the Hippodrome. Under the careful grooming of both the Tarquins and the Flavians, Linus had become one of the more eligible young bachelors of Augustinian Rome.

* * *

During Amos' absence from Nazareth, Joachim and Joseph had made arrangements for James to marry Rachel. It was a quiet wedding, but to date they had no children. They farmed a small vineyard across from Joachim's property, but there seemed to be no real spark to their marriage.

Joseph's house by the Nazareth village square had become a lonely place. There were only he and Miriam left, and Miriam spent more and more time with Joachim and Anna. Joseph was doing his best to keep their business going, but Jon was not much use as his partner. He was very slow with his hands. He continued to be a secret and introspective young man, just as he had been as a child, and his learning ability seemed limited.

Jon's mother, Elizabeth, had withdrawn into herself and did not know what she could do for her son. He rarely spoke and often sounded resentful and rude when he did. But Joachim's house, unlike Joseph's, was still big enough to absorb their various differences, and as a family, they had all come to think of Joachim as the patriarch.

As an old man, Joachim was now a little hard of hearing, but he still had keen, piercing eyes that peered out from beneath his heavy gray brows. In material wealth, only Benjamin Levi rivaled him in Nazareth. They had both reaped the benefits of their large land holdings during the agricultural boom. Benjamin, just a few years younger, frequently came to Joachim's house with Ruth and the baby grandson, Matthew.

The baby was too young to speak, burbling only a few incomprehensible sounds, but for Joachim, Matthew was a representative of the fourth generation, if not by blood, at least by kith and kin. Miriam also doted on her 'grandchild', sharing in Joseph's joy. Their family had increased, even though Amos and Joshua had been so brutally taken from them.

"He looks just like my son David," Benjamin Levi said with pride as he picked up the little boy and held him to his chest.

Anna disagreed:

"No, Benjamin. He's much more like Ruth. Can't you see? Look at his eyes!"

"Yes, but he's got a Levi nose," the proud grandfather observed.

Miriam spoke up for her husband:

"I think both his eyes and his nose are the same as all Joseph's family. He's unmistakably Joseph's grandson."

She went over to Joachim and put her arms around her old father. Looking up into those deep-set, piercing eyes beneath the bushy brows, she asked:

"Who do you think Matthew looks like?"

"You're all correct," the old patriarch answered.

They all laughed and gathered around the infant that had made them a family again. They were so busy chattering away that it took them a while to hear fierce knocking at the courtyard gate.

"Open up!" a voice cried from the far side.

"That's Joseph making all that noise. He's shouting outside the gate," Miriam noted.

She broke away from the happy group.

"It's all right, Joseph. I'm coming," she shouted as she crossed the courtyard. "I can hear you."

Miriam pulled the latch and opened the gate.

Joseph was standing there with such a look of joy on his face that she barely recognized him.

"Look, Miriam! Look who's here!" was all he said.

Miriam saw Joshua and Amos. She gasped. The two men beamed at her with such joy and love. Joshua now had a full-grown beard, and Amos was rougher-looking than at the time he had been taken away.

"Oh, no!" she cried, "This can't be true!"

She rushed to hug her son.

A third man, of rather a disheveled appearance, stepped forward from behind them.

"This is Jonah, my lost son," Joseph said, almost choking with emotion.

Miriam could barely remember what Jonah had looked like as a boy. She certainly didn't recognize him now as she released her hold on Joshua.

"My prodigal son has returned!" Joseph continued.

Jonah smiled sheepishly, peering in at the rich man's courtyard.

Joshua now embraced his mother.

"I have returned, too," he whispered. "The 'Prince of Peace' could not disappear."

Miriam squeezed him, and they held each other for a long time.

"I knew you would come back," she said. "My angel told me you would come back."

Joshua looked into her eyes.

"Gabriel?" he asked with a smile.

But Joseph then took charge.

"I've sent Jon to the synagogue to find James, and hopefully he and Rachel will join us here soon," he said. "Let's go in and meet the rest of the family."

They moved into the courtyard.

Joachim was surprised to see four men enter. At first, he didn't recognize Joshua with his new beard.

"Who is it, Miriam?" he asked.

"Father...it's Joshua and Amos. They've come home, and you'll never believe this, they've brought Joseph's lost son with them. We haven't seen him since we left Bethlehem to go to Egypt."

Ruth heard the news and ran out into the courtyard. She recognized Jonah instantly.

"Jonah!" she shrieked.

"Yes," Jonah replied.

"It's really you, Jonah," Ruth said, wide-eyed, as she stood back to look at him. "After all these years."

Jonah started to laugh.

"Little Ruth!"

He came forward to take his sister in his arms.

"How did you become such a beauty?"

"I'm not the little one anymore! I'm married," she said proudly.

She turned toward Benjamin Levi and her infant son.

"This is my father-in-law, and this is Matthew, my baby," she said, leading Jonah over to the infant. "He's the little one now."

Jonah looked at the baby gurgling in his swaddling cloths. He smiled and put his arm around his sister's waist.

"It's been a long time, Ruth."

Amos stayed with his father.

"Well, Amos," Joseph said, "I always had faith that you were alive, but you must tell us, what happened? Where did those Romans take you? What did you do?"

Amos started to tell his and Joshua's story, and one by one all the other family members gathered to listen. Jonah remained very quiet during this discussion. His story would differ widely from that of his brother.

Later, James and Rachel arrived with Jon. By this time, Jonah was telling aspects of his story that would not rest easily on the shoulders of the pacifist rabbi. James had never cared for his youngest brother when he was a child. He had always considered him to be a bully—a rough one that really didn't belong in the nest. James was decidedly pro-Roman in his attitude toward the rebellion. He felt that those who had taken up arms were ignorant and had plunged the area into an unnecessary reign of terror. *Far better,* thought he, *to coexist with the Romans than to bring on the inevitable wrath of retribution.* To James, Jonah represented in his story the very worst elements in militant Jewish thinking. The other family members, however, were interested, even if their comprehension of events was minimal.

After they had spun their yarns and the shadows of evening began to fall, Joachim rose up to make an announcement. He leaned on his stick.

"Joseph, in honor of this occasion, I would like to give a feast for the whole village. Two days should give us time enough to prepare. We will roast oxen and drink the best wine, for your sons who were lost have now been found."

Joseph's face showed such joy as he sat beside Jonah. This was in such contrast to James, who wore a frown and was obviously disturbed by Joachim's generous gesture.

Joshua could sense the tension, and when the opportunity arose, he spoke with James:

"It's so good to be home again! Why do you look so distressed? Aren't you pleased to see us? Is there something wrong?"

"Of course I'm pleased to see you. I've missed you, Joshua. I've missed our discussions."

"Well, what is it then? It's apparent that a lot has happened since we left. You married Rachel. Ruth's had a baby. And yet, now that we've all come home, you seem displeased just when everyone else is so happy. You don't seem yourself, James."

"It's not you, Joshua. It's me. I've made a success of my life and yet, Father has never acknowledged me. Jonah comes home having achieved nothing in his life, and he's greeted like a hero. Jonah was worthless as a child and he'll probably be a further burden on us now, and yet, in two day's time Joachim ben Judah, with my father's blessing, is going to kill the fatted calf and give a village feast in this wastrel's honor. I suppose not just in his honor, of course, as you and Amos are home, too, but all this fuss over Jonah really hurts me."

Joshua smiled and squeezed James' hand.

"I understand," he said quietly. "You've taught me everything I know, excepting my woodworking skills, but remember that your father has had you all the time. He had lost Jonah and I suppose in his eyes, Amos and me, too. Now he's found us again. Jonah has a chance to settle down and make good, and with all our help he can and will. Nobody can help him more than you, James. You're the rabbi, so why don't you rejoice with us in the reality that God is giving Jonah another chance?"

James put his hand on Joshua's shoulder.

"You should be the rabbi. Hopefully, one day you will be," he said.

Joshua looked at him seriously.

"God has a destiny for me. Mother still believes that."

They prayed a quiet prayer of thanks before rejoining the family.

Miriam and Rachel busied themselves preparing extra food.

* * *

Imperial messengers rode nearly seventy miles a day, traveling on the new roads that radiated out from Rome. The news they carried spread rapidly through the Empire:

"Augustus Caesar is dead, and the Empire has been passed on to Tiberius. Long live the Emperor!"

Horsemen reached Damascus, and from there, the news spread south to Sepphoris and Jerusalem. The long, prosperous, but rather dull reign of Augustus had come to an end, and, with the death of the Emperor, many imperial appointments were no longer safe. The structures would be reviewed by the new Emperor, who would most likely move his own men into the provinces he controlled. In the Senatorial Provinces, the Senate would watch the new political climate before reconfirming old appointees and creating new ones.

In this climate, Flavius Septimus needed to return to Rome if he was going to retire and realize his ambitions for his son. He realized that by now Linus must be taking on the responsibilities and skills of Roman manhood. Occasional letters and dispatches indicated so.

The commander's journey to Rome was relatively uneventful. Flavius took passage from Caesarea to Brundisium and from there traveled along the commercial artery that linked the capital to the Adriatic port. On the way to Italia, his ship had stopped in Crete where Flavius had picked up some excellent Minoan wines. He intended to give these as gifts to the Flavians and Tarquins.

Copernia, instinctively knowing that Flavius would return to Italia on the death of the Emperor, joined Linus in the capital, and was not surprised when a courier arrived stating her husband was traveling up from Brundisium.

They were all re-united at the Tarquin mansion.

Linus, properly dressed in one of his togas, greeted his father in his now deep masculine voice:

"Welcome, Father, I'm so glad you've come! You've arrived just in time for the Coronation Games!"

The youth stepped back as his mother and father formally greeted each other; then, in turn, Copernia took her husband around to meet all the other illustrious Tarquins.

"Flavius, we will expect you to join us at the Curia for Tiberius Caesar's inaugural speech," old Senator Tarquinius said, both hands holding his rather portly stomach. "And of course, as Linus says, we expect everyone to come to the Coronation Games. Linus will be performing. He's very athletic. He really has no rival in athletic prowess amongst the old families on the Palatine."

Flavius looked at Linus, who now drew nigh to his own height, and congratulated his son:

"That's good news. Well done, Linus!"

"It will be a spectacular event, Father, held at the Field of Mars," Linus said excitedly. "The winner will present the Emperor with his laurel crown. If I win, I will be able to crown the Emperor, and I usually do win, Father, so there's a very good chance it could be me."

"How much time have we got before the great event?" Flavius asked.

"Next month, the new one that has lengthened our summers, the one named after Augustus Caesar, that's when they'll hold the Coronation Games. We're all trying hard to be the winner. You should see us down at the Palestra," Linus answered.

Then, he looked up at his father confidently.

"I know I'm going to win, Father. My nearest rival is Vespasian Fabius, and I've beaten him a lot more than he's beaten me. I'll keep training hard. I want to be the Victor Ludorum."

"I'm sure you'll do well, Linus. Keep training. I'm going to leave for some time with your mother. But we'll be back for the games, we wouldn't miss that for anything."

Copernia looked more beautiful in her fine Roman clothes than she'd ever seemed in Galilee. *Here, in Rome, I know why I chose her,* Flavius thought. *In Galilee, I sometimes wonder…She holds herself back, unlike Esther, who gave me her all. It will be different here, though. She will be more relaxed here in her world.*

"My dear, I think we should go to Tuscany for a few days," he said kissing her slender hands. "We have a lot to share and new plans to make. Why don't we leave tomorrow and spend a few days at the Flavian villa?"

Copernia responded tenderly:

"Of course, my dearest, we will journey tomorrow. Your old family villa should be looking at its best at this time of the year. The trumpet vines will be in full bloom, and the honeysuckle should be at its height. It's almost as beautiful as the Tarquin villa, and we can spend a few days alone there."

Later, as he snuggled up to Copernia on plush quilted cushions, he said:

"I'd almost forgotten how grand things are in Rome. Even wearing a toga now feels strange after years in military tunics."

"It looks good on you," she said. "I've missed you."

"And I, you."

As early as possible on the following day, Flavius and Copernia started on their journey north through the rolling hills of the coastal region where the vines spilled down to the Great Sea. Cypress trees stood like dark green soldiers, and ancient stone walls crisscrossed the terrain. The inevitable patches of olives lent a touch of gray in an otherwise luxurious scene sloping up to the brown hills of the Italian spine. It was not so different from the shores of the lake in Galilee. That was precisely why Flavius had built their home in Galilee. It reminded him of this countryside and the roots of Flavian history. As they passed through the village leading to the Flavian estate, their chariot scattered aimless geese, causing them to cluck in protest.

Copernia laughed, her hair blowing in the breeze.

"Ancestors of clucking geese like these once saved Rome," she noted. "Livy used to tell that story at the Mansion in my childhood."

"Really," Flavius replied as he tried to steer the chariot through a group of chickens running after the geese. "There seem to be a lot more fowl about in Italia now than I remember."

"Roast fowl is becoming very popular. There's so much more variety in our food these days."

"The result of prosperity and trade, my dear."

With one arm around his beautiful wife's waist, he proudly steered the chariot into the lands of the old family villa. The great square walls with their classic pedimented doorways hadn't changed, but then why should they have? They'd withstood the test of time and had watched the growth of Rome from gentle beginnings to becoming the hub of an Empire. Flavius had come home to his and Copernia's roots, and those roots ran deep. Lucius Flavian, the now retired Governor of Tuscany, and Flavius' mother were thrilled to see them.

"When you return, we must come back to Rome with you for the Coronation Games," the old man said. "We want to see that splendid grandson of ours win the Victor Ludorum."

"He's training hard with his Tarquin cousins," Copernia noted. "He's very determined.

Roast fowl was served for dinner.

* * *

The death of Augustus Caesar passed by the village of Nazareth. The Roman dispatch didn't even bother to announce it and the proclamation of the new Emperor as he galloped through on his way from Sepphoris to Sebaste. Nazareth's concerns were over daily toil, the seasons, and personal relationships.

Joseph was much relieved to have Amos and Joshua back in the carpenter's shop. Jonah joined them in their partnership. Although untrained in their craft, Jonah learned fast, having much more aptitude with his hands than the slightly retarded Jon. Jon happily returned to Joachim's house where he helped in the vineyards and olive groves and remained in isolation.

Joshua, when he realized that Amos had a reasonable apprentice in Jonah, also abandoned Joseph, spending much of his time with James at the synagogue. He had taken James' suggestion to heart and had decided that maybe he should become a rabbi, at least for a while. They spent long hours together discussing the Law and its pharisaical interpretation. Neither James nor Joshua had much empathy with those who saw blasphemy in every small deviation from the written Law and the growing traditions. One thing that James had learned after they'd come back from Egypt and settled in Nazareth was that a rabbi in Galilee couldn't exercise the same freedom as one in Alexandria or similar Hellenist cities. Conservatism was rife within village communities. A successful rabbi in Galilee or Judea had to teach at the slow pace of those who were his people.

Often Joshua stayed at James' house at the north end of the village. Rachel always welcomed him, although every time he saw her, Joshua could only think of Amos, and how Joseph had really meant Rachel to marry Amos and not James. *How different things might have been if we had not been abducted that day,* he thought.

During one such visit, Rachel had her sister Joanna at the house. Joanna was about three years younger than Joshua. She had long, straight hair like her sister's, and she'd definitely matured while Joshua had been away.

Joshua watched and listened as Joanna busied herself with Rachel, taking care of the ritual requirements of their food preparation.

"Joanna, I think he's watching you," Rachel said.

"You do?"

"Yes, definitely. I don't think he's listening to James at all right now."

"What do you think of him, Rachel? I don't remember him with a beard before. It makes him handsome."

"I like the beard, but he's different in other ways, Joanna. I think he changed quite a bit while he was away. He seems more approachable now. He's still the scholar, like James, but he seems to be very kind as well. I've noticed how he's always very considerate and generous to everyone. James is a little cold at times."

"Maybe I *could* marry him," Joanna whispered. "Let me think about it."

"I can have Father talk to Joseph again," Rachel suggested. "They get along really well."

"If I were to be married to James' brother, we really would be two sisters married to two brothers."

"Yes, but Joshua's not James' real brother like Amos and Jonah. He's Miriam's son. I don't know who his father was, but nobody thinks he was anyone we know. But, if you really like him, what does his background matter?"

Rachel turned and saw Joshua in the doorway.

"He's watching your every move, Joanna. I'm sure he's interested. I'll speak to Father again."

Joanna slowly turned around. She saw Joshua looking in her direction. She felt excited. There was an enigmatic mystery to the man. She smiled, blushed and quickly returned to her chores.

* * *

Later that evening, Joshua had a heart-to-heart talk with his brother.

"James…did Joseph ever mention Joanna to you when he arranged for you to become betrothed to Rachel?"

"You mean for me?"

"No, not for you, but for me or Amos?"

"As a double-marriage contract?"

"Yes."

James shrugged his shoulders.

"He didn't discuss his arrangements much with me. He knew that Rachel had a reasonable dowry in the vineyard, and he saw that we respected each other and felt that we could settle down to a married life together. As far as I know, Joanna was never mentioned. Anyway, at that time Father had no idea where either you or Amos were. Joanna was very young then, too, barely old enough to be married!"

"She's old enough now. Maybe I should think of marriage."

James laughed loudly.

"So this is what you've been leading up to. You have your eye on Rachel's sister."

"Well, a rabbi should be married. Don't you agree, James?"

"Of course," James said seriously. "It is expected. We should raise up sons for God."

He paused.

"Maybe I should talk to Rachel and see how she feels about it. Her father should get together with my father again. I'm sure Joanna would make an excellent wife for any man, especially you, Joshua. I've not regretted marrying Rachel. The sisters come from a good family, but Joanna is more lively than her sister—just like you have more sparkle than I do. Some people here think I'm too serious. I didn't feel that to be a problem in Alexandria, but people are very set in their ways here, Joshua. This is Galilee."

* * *

James spoke to his father about a possible wedding. Joseph offered Joanna's father another mohar, or token of intent, in the form of a small sum of money, to secure a betrothal between Joshua and Joanna. They prayed together and he accepted, and in turn offered Joseph another vineyard beside that given to James. The two adjacent vineyards were south of the village and together would make a workable parcel of land. The arrangement seemed good, and Joseph put the proposition to Joshua.

"Joshua, you are like my son," he said very seriously. "I've spoken to Joanna's father concerning a marriage between you and her. I know that you look on the young girl favorably. So do I. It's certainly time for you to marry."

"Joanna's a very beautiful girl," Joshua acknowledged, hardly able to contain his excitement. "I'm sure I could be very happy with her. But tell me something, Joseph. Why have you selected me over Amos for this match?"

"Joshua, you and James have always been very close. It is as if you are both on a similar spiritual journey. It's only natural that Rachel and Joanna should be married to the two of you. Besides, you're better matched. Amos needs someone more stolid...more like my Martha was—his mother. Give us time, we'll find someone for Amos."

"Well then, I would be happy to confirm your arrangements," Joshua said, before breaking the formality and embracing Joseph.

The two of them held up their hands in prayer:

"God bless Joanna! God bless this house!"

"God bless you, Joseph," Joshua added.

They embraced again and went inside to give Miriam the news.

* * *

During the betrothal, Joshua visited Joanna's family frequently. Grandmother Anna gave him a pin to present to his bride-to-be. Joanna happily accepted the gift, but Joshua wanted to give her something from himself. He had rich relatives living in Grandfather Joachim's house, but his mother and he were still poor.

Joanna blossomed with the prospect of her coming marriage and made herself busy spinning and weaving flax into linen for their needs. Joshua, meanwhile, started to build their new house. He built the traditional square, flat-roofed structure, on a corner of the dowry land adjacent to James' vineyard. Amos helped him with the work. The house looked out across the valley of Esdraelon, with Mount Tabor over to the east. It was the same view that old Joachim enjoyed from his fine house at the southern end of the village. In fact, from the vineyard one could see Joachim's property, and at one point the roadway winding up to Nazareth was all that separated Joshua's smallholding from Joachim's land. Joshua had never paid much attention to the cultivation of grapes and the production of wine and raisins. There had always been plenty provided for their family needs by Joachim. Now, however, he busied himself by learning the art of viticulture. He planned to work both James' and his own dowry vineyards in the years ahead. Joachim generously passed on his knowledge to his grandson, showing him the differences between good and bad grapes for quality in wine.

Late in the year, everything was ready for the wedding. Miriam, with a certain sadness, called Joshua into the old house by the village square. She took her only son into her embrace.

"Joshua, before you leave I have one last thing to give you," she said.

She took him back into the inner room. Hidden in the corner was the old wooden box with its cracked, dried-out leather fastenings—the box the rich merchants had given to her when Joshua was born.

"Joshua, this is yours. This treasure was given to you when the men said that they had found the 'Prince of Peace'. The only times we've ever used it were to buy our passage home from Egypt and provide a few coins for Ruth's dowry. The rest is all still here."

"No, Mother, I can't! That's for you."

"It was given to me to keep for you. One day you may need it."

Joshua hesitated.

"You still believe I'm the 'Prince of Peace', don't you, Mother?"

"What do you think?"

"I'm not sure. I wanted to be a rabbi and a healer. Now I'm about to be married and to become a vine grower. I may not be the 'Prince of Peace.'"

"I believe you are. God will reveal your destiny. This box will always remind you of that."

"Will people follow me to find the Messiah?"

Joshua put his hand down on the old wooden box and looked into his mother's eyes.

"Take it," Miriam said. "It was God's gift to us. Maybe you *are* the Messiah. One day we'll understand why we were chosen."

"You really do believe that we were chosen, don't you, Mother?"

"I can't help it, Joshua. Your birth was surrounded by such mysterious happenings."

Joshua picked up the heavy box. He trembled as he held it.

"It's not my wish to take this, Mother, but nonetheless, if it's your wish, I'll go along with it."

* * *

Later, Joshua loaded the box on his ox cart. When it was rested in place he prayed. *Almighty God, if you truly chose me for a special task, reveal it to me. I am ready to serve You, but I still do not know quite how.* He led the ox down to his new house in the vineyard. In quiet and solitude he then opened the box. The coins still glinted, untouched by time. He put his hand in and picked out seven. *I'll use these for Joanna's veil,* he thought, setting them aside. Then, he dug a hole in the earthen floor to bury the box. If the aspirations of his mother were ever to come true, he would know exactly where to find it, but for the time being he didn't want Joanna to know that he had the treasure. *At least, not until I know my destiny better,* he thought.

He built a cover for the box and sealed it inside. As he lowered it into the hole, which he had lined with flat stones, fear gripped him again. He felt he could sense the spirit of God blowing through the room—the ruah, or rush of mystical wind. He imagined voices calling to him as a cold sweat built up on the nape of his neck. He sensed that he was in the presence of Elijah, the prophet of the end time.

Has Elijah come? he asked himself. *Could I really be the Messiah? Is this the great commission that God has given to me?*

Somewhat trembling, he dropped the box into the hole. Looking up, he could see the sun streaming through the open door. The clammy feeling of mingled fear and spiritual vision left him. Quickly, he filled the hole with earth, trampled it down and smoothed out the floor.

The warm sun felt good when he stepped outside. He walked through the vineyard and contemplated his future. He wanted to make a success of the vineyard and his marriage, but deep down he knew that sooner or later God would call him to other things. Maybe he would be a rabbi as James and he had planned, but he had an uncomfortable feeling that God was calling him for more than a rabbi's role.

Before the wedding, while Joshua asked his mother to help him affix the seven gold coins that he had removed from the box onto a simple headband, he reflected on the treasure's significance.

"What really did those merchants say to you the night I was born?" he asked.

"They were very grateful to share our cave," Miriam replied. "They called you the 'Prince of Peace'. They quoted from Scripture. They confirmed for me the feelings I had when Gabriel first spoke to me. It seemed that everybody at that time thought you would be special."

Joshua looked at his mother affectionately.

"Gabriel?" he questioned.

"Yes," Miriam said slowly, "but then, there was also the strange star. Everybody had ideas about that star—those men, and Joseph and me… we believed the star was about you."

She put her arm around him as she had so often when he was a child.

"You have a destiny, Josh—I believe it still."

The next day, Joshua presented his bride with the band threaded with the coins. On their wedding day, Joanna wore it. It was Joshua's symbolic gift to her, showing his good intent to provide for her, but for him it had greater meaning—it was the treasure of his destiny.

* * *

Amos was Joshua's companion at the wedding that traditionally took place at the bride's house. In the simple ceremony, James, as the rabbi, pronounced Joshua and Joanna to be married. The wedding veil that hid Joanna's face was moved to one side revealing her radiant smile amidst the joyous shouts of the sons of the bride chamber. Jonah, Jon, and

Joanna's two younger brothers, then escorted Joshua and his new bride in a torchlight procession down the street to Joachim ben Judah's house.

Miriam and Elizabeth, along with their old retainer, Judith, and with occasional help from the matriarch, Anna, had prepared the wedding feast. Musicians were ready in the courtyard, and braziers and burning torches cast a warm glow up into the night sky. When the procession arrived, the courtyard filled with all Joachim's and Joseph's friends as well as those from Joanna's family, and those who were not invited guests made their own party outside the gate.

Before the wedding feast began, the guests filed by to greet the bride and groom. Joshua stood in his new linen tunic and white gossamer robe beside his beaming bride. The gold coins in Joanna's headdress glinted in the glow of the courtyard braziers. Silently, Joshua prayed for God's blessing on their union, and God's blessing on his destiny.

Joachim made sure there was food for everyone, including those in the street. There was music and dancing and great rejoicing for another prosperous year followed by a bounteous harvest and a happy marriage feast. Important events in Rome did not seem a part of Nazareth's world.

When Joshua felt it was time to leave, he sought out his mother. Miriam embraced him. She kissed his cheeks and, holding his face between her hands, said gently:

"Take care of her. Joanna is very precious."

Then, dropping her hands, she dropped her head.

"Be gentle with her," she added. "Don't force yourself on her."

Joshua felt her restraint. *Gabriel* flashed through his mind. *Is she thinking of Gabriel? Did the priest rape her?* He squeezed her in comfort.

When Miriam looked up again, her radiant smile had returned.

"I am always here for you," she said.

"And me for you," Joshua added.

* * *

The sons of the bride chamber, led by Amos and Jon, now both well imbibed, followed Joshua and Joanna across the street into Rabbi James' old vineyards. Using their torches, they started a fire in the clearing where Joshua had built the small one-room house against the vineyard wall. Joshua trimmed a lamp in his new home. When their door shut, just enough light spread under the threshold for the sons of the bride chamber to keep their vigil as they passed around another skin of Joachim's wine.

Joshua felt nervous as he heard their raucous laughter. He felt even more nervous as Joanna removed her headdress and freed her long black hair. Amos had told him 'to make her his own' as quickly as possible. 'She's a real beauty,' he had said. 'Make her your own, enjoy her, because you are the envy of the village.' He thought more of his mother's advice, however: *'Be gentle with her. Don't force yourself upon her.'* He took Joanna in his arms and kissed her softly on her forehead. He could feel her breasts against his tunic, but he didn't want to caress them…at least…not yet.

When they lay beside each other, Joshua could feel the smoothness of Joanna's young flesh. Memories of Maria haunted him. Maria's skin had been smooth just like Joanna's, but Joanna's eyes had an innocent sparkle that appealed to him more than Maria's sultry, seductive look. The memory rekindled the musty odor of the whore's bed and the dirty oil of the lamps that had mingled with the sweet balms and perfumes of the prostitute's trade. It was sickly, and the memory faded his enthusiasm to touch or soil his beloved Joanna. He silently prayed. Joanna waited. Outside, the chants and cheers of the sons of the bride chamber grew louder.

Joanna looked at him, sensing his nervousness.

"I want you to love me," she said gently. "We will have lots of children—boys and girls."

Joshua kissed her and started to caress her young breasts. Slowly, he massaged her with his hard laborer's hands until he was sufficiently aroused to make her his own. Joanna gave herself to him, but not with ease. *'Be gentle with her,'* reverberated through Joshua's head. He was. At length, Joanna's discomfort passed and their flesh became one.

Joshua extinguished the lamp. He heard the cheer of the sons of the bride chamber. He knew he was now truly married to Joanna and they had started their life together whatever God had in mind for him.

CHAPTER TEN

Victor Ludorum

The new Emperor, Tiberius Caesar, was a gentle and scholarly man. He was alert to senatorial suggestions and enthusiastic to maintain the 'Pax Romana'. He had pleaded with the Senate within four weeks of Augustus Caesar's death that they should restore the Republic, and he refused to call himself Emperor, preferring the title 'Leader of the Senate'. At his coronation speech, he steered a middle ground, offending nobody, but at the same time creating no excitement among the neat rows of toga-clad senators and their privileged guests.

Senator Tarquinius took Flavius aside as they filed out of the Curia chamber.

"Nothing to worry about there, young Flavius. There was no drama, no great changes forecast. It was all rather dull and matter-of-fact. I think we'll be able to hold our own with him. I say we have 'Status Quo.'"

"Maybe no changes in Rome, Senator, but on the fringes of the Empire, we might see some. I can see the governors getting more powerful while the Emperor relishes in the Roman peace. I've heard a rumor that he's thinking of sending Germanicus to Asia Minor and possibly Fabian to Syria. Do you think he'll keep Varus on in Damascus?"

"You'd know better than I, Flavius."

The Senator looked off into the distance.

"Syria's your province. I can't understand why you're so bent on staying out there. It seems that those Jews are nothing but trouble."

"It's important to us who gets the Damascus appointment, Tarquinius, because I will want to send Linus to Damascus. You Italian Romans don't understand. It's exciting being on the fringe of the Empire. It's a challenge to see our systems gradually bringing order to a chaotic and rugged land. The glory that you all enjoy here is won on the frontier, Senator. That's what the Empire is all about."

"I wouldn't know, Flavius," the proud senator replied. "It's been so long since I've been out of Italia, and I'm too old to start traveling now."

They started down the Curia steps.

"Let's see if this can be the Tarquins' lucky day, Flavius. Maybe your boy will win the Victor Ludorum and crown the Emperor. It may be the closest we will ever get to really crowning Tiberius, but it would be an honor for us Tarquins."

"He's going to win, Senator. He's very confident."

Flavius looked down.

"If he does win, Tarquinius, just remember that Copernia married a Flavian. It will be a great day for the Flavians, too!"

He looked back up at Tarquinius to test his reaction.

The senator grinned. The old man loved to needle the Flavians whenever he had a chance, and Flavius Septimus had risen to the occasion.

"Of course, Flavius Septimus!" he said condescendingly. "I had almost forgotten. Yes, if young Linus wins at the games today, the Flavians can be as proud as us."

They reached their chariot and were driven away, following many of the other senators around the Imperial Forum and out toward the Field of Mars. The streets were busy with a steady stream of plebeians and patricians alike, making their way to the great athletic stadium. There was a holiday atmosphere as the Empire prepared to celebrate Tiberius Caesar's Coronation Games.

The stadium was filling up fast by the time that Tarquinius and Flavius reached the senatorial sector. The Field of Mars was wider than the Circus Maximus, although not as long, and it purveyed a similar atmosphere of massive spectacle. Pennants flew from the thousand poles that topped the rim of gleaming white tiers. Bright awnings hung over the upper seats to shield the occupants from excessive sun. In the center of the senatorial block, just as at the Circus Maximus, the Imperial box was set aside for the Emperor and his party. Tarquinius and Flavius Septimus made their way to the seats that had been allocated to the senator, and there, joined Copernia and the other ladies nobly escorted by lesser Tarquin and Flavian cousins. Lucius Flavian and his wife were already seated and no sooner had Tarquinius and Flavius joined them, and Cassius Tarquin and Prosperine entered the enclosure. They all had an excellent view of the arena and joined the hum of excited chatter that awaited Tiberius Caesar's arrival.

Flavius took hold of Copernia's hand.

"Linus is going to win today, my dearest. He's beaten every one of his closest rivals at the Palestra," he said proudly.

Copernia hoped that her son would win. She certainly looked forward to these games a lot more than the gladiatorial contests that she had dutifully watched in Sepphoris. She returned the pressure on Flavius' hand in acknowledgment of the hopes that they held.

Trumpets blared.

Tiberius Caesar entered the central platform within the senatorial block. Here, inlaid chairs swathed in purple cloth had been set up for the Imperial party, which included the Emperor's wife, Vipsania, and his popular brother, Drusus. The crowds in the stadium rose to salute the Emperor as the hum of conversation hushed. Tiberius, however, was known to hate these events, and if it were not for his need to be seen by the people as the established new ruler of Rome, he would not have accepted the senatorial invitation. When the crowd stood for him, he did not stand with them long, drinking in the moment, but sat almost immediately, waving his hand in a wide, sweeping motion, beckoning the crowd to be seated so that the games might begin.

With a second fanfare, the athletes marched out to line up in front of the Emperor and give their formal salute. With the Emperor's acknowledgment, the Coronation Games began.

Linus became a finalist in each event. He lost the discus-throwing contest to Vespasian of the Fabii. Fabian supporters in the senatorial block cheered heartily when the final disc landed little more than a short arm ahead of that of Linus Flavius.

"It's all going to have to rest on the javelin contest," Flavius said tensely.

"Linus, you can do it!" he shouted, but his son could not hear him above the roar that came from the crowds.

The two contestants prepared to battle it out.

Vespasian threw the first javelin. It was a fine throw and landed beyond the record set by Linus in the Palestra. Linus was going to have to perform a miracle to beat his rival.

"He's got to win this one," Flavius said with concern as the Fabian supporters in the senatorial sector cheered again.

Copernia gripped her husband's hand, and even Senator Tarquinius shouted out for Linus.

Linus began his run. His lithe, almost naked body showed all his muscles pulling for victory as he increased his pace, raising the javelin high to make his thrust. Sweat, partly from nerves and partly from the exertion of the games, poured down from the nape of his neck. He pulled back his right arm and at his maximum pace released the javelin, thrusting it forward and upward with all his might. The long arrow flew through the air, gracefully gliding to its halt in the turf, where it landed with a thud at precisely the same spot as that of his rival. Linus had beaten his record, but the two young athletes would still have to battle for victory.

Vespasian was again the first to throw. He was slightly taller than Linus, and to many among the spectators this would seem to give him the advantage.

Flavius sat on the edge of his seat with the fingers of his clenched fist resting against his teeth. He needed his son to win so that he could gain the favors that were necessary to secure Linus' eventual position as a provincial leader in Syria.

Vespasian ran forward and thrust his javelin. He showed good action and it flew well, but landed short of the previous shot.

Linus slowly walked back to the start, collecting his nerves. He took the javelin handed to him by the referee. For a moment, he stood there breathing deeply. He knew he had to win this contest.

The eyes of every spectator now watched the son of Flavius Septimus.

Linus ran up with his javelin again. Reaching his peak moment, he pulled back his right arm like a catapult and shot the javelin away. It sailed upward, reaching the height of its arc, and then started its downward plunge. The referee's arm went up as the javelin hit the turf. Linus had won. His throw had landed just a short distance ahead of that of Vespasian.

The crowds in the stands stood, instantly cheering the Flavian hero.

A smug smile of satisfaction crossed the young man's face.

"I won!" Linus shouted out. "I am the Victor Ludorum!"

Copernia stood up with Flavius, shouting at the top of her voice: "Well done! Well done!"

Even the old senator, now knowing that a Tarquin victory had taken place over his Fabian rivals, stood to applaud.

Only the Fabians were silent. Slowly, they stood to join the whole stadium in the resounding cry of victory achieved, but their faces told of their disappointment. Vespasian, the Fabian hopeful, had not matched the bumptious spirit of the Palatine hero, Linus Flavius.

The Emperor's face showed that he didn't share the enthusiasm of the crowds, but he was merely bending to forced duty. He left the Imperial box to descend the marble steps that led into the arena while the athletes left to prepare themselves for presentation. A dais was carried out, decorated in myrtle and laurel. Tiberius took his seat there, flanked by his Praetorian guards. Linus and the athletes then returned, now clad in fresh togas. They stopped in formation in front of the dais. They saluted, crossing their right arms to their left shoulders, and unanimously shouted:

"Long live Tiberius Caesar, Emperor of Rome! Hail Caesar!" The spectators stood and repeated:

"Hail Caesar!"

Once again, the disinterested Emperor waved his hand sideways, asking for no ceremony.

The crowd then watched in silence as Linus, the Victor Ludorum, stepped forward with the crown of laurels and presented it to the Emperor.

Tiberius accepted the crown, held it up once, and placed it upon his cropped gray head. At this point, he could not curtail the cheers of the people. He accepted his role in Imperial duty and raised his right hand. There was thunderous applause. The Emperor smiled at Linus, nodding in his direction. Linus stepped back and gave the Emperor his moment of glory.

Flavius kissed Copernia lightly on her forehead.

"He did it, my dearest," he said. "Linus won! What a tiger you brought into this world!"

"A Tuscan tiger, Flavius," she said, looking adoringly at the man that she had missed for so long, "a true Tarquin."

"A pretty good Flavian, too," Flavius retorted. "Linus, the first of a new and illustrious line."

Lucius Flavian nodded his approval.

The senator joined them.

"You are to be congratulated, Copernia, on raising a true Tarquin," he said pompously.

Copernia looked at Flavius before she answered her proud uncle.

"A Flavian Tarquin," she replied.

"Yes, a Flavian Tarquin," her father, Cassius, repeated.

"A Tarquin Flavian," her father-in-law, Lucius Flavian, chuckled.

* * *

The victory at the Coronation Games made it easier for Flavius to gain the influence that he sought for Linus' future. During the next month, Tarquinius kept his ear close to senate gossip regarding the Emperor's new appointments. It became apparent that certain changes might be made in the Syrian Province. The senator reported the news to Flavius.

"Young Flavius," he said in his condescending and irritating way, "it has reached my ears that your suspicions are correct. Tiberius is considering a new appointment to the governorship of Syria. He has apparently approached Questus, one of the Claudians, for this position."

"Not Fabius, then?" Flavius asked, surprised.

The old senator raised his bushy eyebrows.

"That's what I hear."

"That's good news. You know how the Fabians feel about Linus after his victory over Vespasian. Now, do you know this Questus?"

"Young Flavius, I know everybody who's worth knowing in Rome. I knew his father very well. Questus was in Hispania and up in Gaul. Like you, Flavius, he's spent too much time with the legions, but I suppose that's what you'll need out on your frontier."

"You're unbearable at times," Flavius quipped. "However, I have to hand it to you, you are usually right. It sounds like this Questus does have the right background for the frontier. Are you sure he has the appointment, and if so, how soon?"

"I think it's certain, but I'm not sure how soon. These things sometimes take time. I believe Questus still has some unfinished business in Gaul. However, I expect the appointment will be made and Questus sent to Syria within the year."

"Can you arrange for us to meet Questus, Tarquinius? I would like to have the opportunity to introduce Linus to him while we're still here in Rome. If we make preliminary plans now, it'll be easier for me to send Linus to Damascus next year."

"How soon are you thinking of returning to Syria, then?" the senator asked.

"In the spring, as soon as we can make an easy passage."

Flavius would have been happy if they could have left right then and there, but he needed the senator's influential help.

The pompous man slapped Flavius on the back. It hurt.

"Young Flavius, leave it to me," Tarquinius said. "We have plenty of time."

* * *

In the early spring, Flavius booked passage from Ostia for his family to return to Galilee.

The planned meetings with Questus had taken place, and Flavius felt confident that once Questus was the governor in Damascus, there would be a place for Linus in the Syrian Legion. Flavius looked forward to a peaceful summer at his villa and a pleasant start to his retirement. Copernia had decided to bring back more furnishings from the old house in Tuscany, a fact that pleased Flavius—it showed her intent. He had persuaded her to overcome her fears about living in the land of the Jews and assured her that the rebellion was over.

Traveling with them, was Copernia's new maid, Patricia, and their old retainer, Gladius, who came along in his new role as Linus' secretary, a rather bogus title that justified keeping him in the family.

Mild spring weather sped them across the Great Sea in record time. They stopped at Syracuse and Crete. From there, they sailed to Rhodes with its ancient harbor where the legendary Colossus had once stood. After one more stop in Cyprus, they arrived in Ptolemais on the Syrian coast. At Ptolemais, they purchased two large wagons and crossed into Galilee on the new road to Sepphoris. There, they stayed a few days with Marcellus, now the commanding officer at the barracks, and sent a messenger on to Magdala to inform Demetrius of their imminent return.

Marcellus greeted his old commander enthusiastically.

"We wondered when you would return. Things are going well here in Syria these days. Believe it or not, there is actually peace throughout the province," he said with pride.

"We'll keep the peace, Marcellus," Flavius agreed. "Remember how I used to tell you that this land has enormous potential."

Linus was then officially introduced to Marcellus.

"My son, Marcellus...Linus Flavius. He's been away for several years, but spent his childhood here. Would you mind if he takes a look around? He hasn't seen all the changes we made after the siege."

Linus and Gladius were escorted by a centurion instructed to show them the rebuilt baths and the gymnasium.

Marcellus continued to discuss matters with Flavius as they sipped some wine.

"Galilean grapes have produced some excellent wine in the past two years, Flavius," Marcellus said, turning his goblet around in his hand.

Flavius smelled the bouquet before savoring another sip.

"I really think I prefer this to the Greek wines these days."

"You'll be amazed when you see the prosperity in the countryside, Flavius," the new commanding officer continued. "Everything is changing here, just as you predicted. But, tell me, what news do you have from Rome? Everyone's asking the same question. What changes will Tiberius Caesar make? Will we be affected by new appointments here in Syria?"

"I knew you'd ask me that," Flavius said, laughing. "There will be changes soon. Varus is due to retire anyway. I think we will have a new governor in Syria, and the rumor in Rome is that Germanicus will take over Asia Minor. That's hard to believe when he's been so successful on the Gallic frontier, but Tiberius seems to want to consolidate the Empire at this time."

"Any ideas as to who might replace Varus in Damascus?" Marcellus asked, bringing Flavius back to his real question.

"Possibly Questus, one of the Claudian generals," Flavius answered guardedly. "I don't know him very well, but I did seek him out when I was in Rome. He's had a lot of experience in Hispania and Gaul and will probably do well here, that's if he's definite. I think Varus will be here for the rest of this year."

"It doesn't sound then as if too much is going to change."

"Not really, but don't rely solely on me, Marcellus. Remember, I'm going into retirement. I want to grow some of these good Galilean grapes!"

A couple of days later, Flavius and his entourage set off for Magdala. Their two wagons were heavily laden. Apart from the furnishing items that Copernia brought with her, the carts were filled with added supplies that Copernia and Patricia had picked up in Sepphoris. Even on the new road, they were slow moving. It took them all day to make the journey, and it was almost dark when they arrived in Magdala.

Demetrius had braziers and torches burning. The illuminated villa above the lakeside village looked welcome to the weary travelers.

Flavius carried Copernia down from the wagon and kissed her.

"Welcome home!" he said, before proudly escorting her through the gate into the peaceful courtyard.

The orange glow from the braziers tinted the leaves of the olives and bathed the marble paving slabs with warmth.

"Father! I can't believe what you've done to this place," Linus exclaimed as he followed them in with Gladius and Patricia. "Look at the vestibule, and through there... the terrace!"

He went into the terrace court.

"Gladius! Look here! You remember the fire. We saved this villa that night, didn't we?"

"It certainly looks like it," his secretary observed.

All of them wandered through the rooms.

"It's magnificent!" Copernia remarked when they had completed their tour of the restored villa. "Your craftsmen here are as good as those in Rome."

"Maybe better, my dear."

Flavius called for Demetrius.

The steward greeted his master.

"Demetrius, I know you've thought of everything. We're starving. What have you got for dinner?"

"Plenty, Master. I hired two young Hebrew girls from the village. Whenever you're ready they can serve."

"Tonight let's all eat together," Flavius suggested. "Demetrius, you join us, and make sure that there is room for Gladius and Patricia, too."

The two Hebrew maids served them dinner. There were chopped nuts and fish pieces with sweet wine mingled with honey, followed by a stew of lamb and vegetables, and a dessert of fresh fruit.

Flavius took three pieces of the stewed lamb and placed them on one of the braziers outside.

"These are for the household gods," he said.

Flavius had no real faith in the Lares and Penates, but it was a tradition, and he felt on this occasion that such a gesture might aptly express his personal delight that they were all home. He'd created and recreated this villa at Magdala. The place was his. It was neither Flavian nor Tarquin and he was proud of his achievement.

CHAPTER ELEVEN

Love, Lust and Matters of Fish

Joanna stood by the door of the house that Joshua had built for her. The warmth of the early summer sun felt good on her face. This was her favorite time of the year. The winter rains had ceased, and the summer heat had not yet had time to burn up the wild flowers that covered the hillsides. It was idyllic. The vines were growing, even ready to trim; the foliage still had the luster and freshness of spring. She was surprised how well Joshua had taken to his new life as a vinedresser and admired his enthusiasm, grateful that the land of her dowry was giving him so much pleasure.

Her sister Rachel broke her contemplation.

"I don't believe it. We need to grind more corn," she called out from inside the house. "That husband of yours eats a lot of bread!"

"It's Jon," Joanna complained. "We never seem to have enough. Every time I think we've made extra for a day or two, we run out."

Rachel joined her, carrying a rough-hewn box outside in which they kept the grain. As they set about their task of sorting the grains of barley from the tares, Joanna expressed her fear of Jon.

"He's scary," she said. "I'm a little afraid of him. You never know what he's going to say. To be truthful, I wish he didn't spend so much time here. I'd rather have Joshua to myself more."

Rachel picked out a coarse dark grain. There were always a few seeds from the dreaded darnel weed that got harvested with the barley and survived the threshing. These seeds could cause severe stomach sickness if baked into the bread. The darnel seeds were similar in shape and size to barley grains. The only real difference was their darker color. Rachel and Joanna shuffled the seeds back and forth in a shallow basket continuing to pick off the poisonous ones.

When they were satisfied that the grains were all pure, Joanna scooped up a handful at a time and dropped them through the hole in the upper millstone. Together, the two sisters turned the top stone and ground the grain until it spat out through one side of the groove as rough flour. This time, they tried to make sure they ground enough to last for several days. Grinding the barley was not a favorite chore of either of them. Baking was easier.

Back inside, Joanna formed the dough, mixing the flour with water and a little olive oil. Rachel then kneaded it on a wooden board. She added a little leaven from the previous mixing that had now fermented and hoped it would help to make the new dough rise. Meanwhile, Joanna tended the fire in the clay oven Joshua had built for her outside.

When they took the first loaves from the oven, Joanna broke one and handed a piece of the warm doughy substance to her sister.

"This is always when it tastes best," she said. "I love it fresh like this, but after it dries out it loses its taste."

"Joanna! You've been baking bread all your life," Rachel retorted as she pulled her piece apart. "Why this sudden fascination with it now?"

"Oh, I don't know," Joanna replied. "It's different now. I'm baking for Joshua. There's something more personal about it."

"You'll soon get used to that! The blindness of love doesn't last forever!"

Rachel tasted the bread.

"It is good," she agreed. "It's a shame the men never get the opportunity we do to enjoy it when it's like this."

Joanna laughed.

"It's a good thing they don't. There would be none left. Especially the way Joshua and Jon eat."

"You seem to be very happy. Are you really happy?" Rachel asked. "How is it living with Joshua?"

"I'm very happy," Joanna replied, a little surprised at her sister's tone.

"It's easy living with Joshua. He's always so kind and attentive to me. He's not very demanding, but he's very tender in his sexual intimacy with me."

She blushed.

"I just hope I give him all he needs. After all, Rachel, I don't know much about all that."

"Nobody does when they are first married," Rachel said. "Joshua's not too serious for you, then?"

"Certainly not! We laugh a great deal. I would think James to be a lot more serious than Joshua. What about your marriage with James?"

"James is serious. I sometimes wish he'd laugh more. That's really why I asked you about Joshua. He's spent so much time with James. He might even become a rabbi. He told James he wanted to be a rabbi."

Joanna looked concerned.

"Is everything all right with you and James?" she asked.

"I'm comfortable, Joanna. But I'm glad I can come out here and share time with you. Marriage is more than baking bread and hopefully bearing children. It's companionship, Joanna. James is always reading his scrolls or out trying to heal somebody. He rarely needs me as a woman. He treats me very well, but I'm just his housekeeper."

Joanna hugged her older sister compassionately.

"I'm so happy here with Joshua that I've never thought much about your life with James since I left home. How is it really now?"

"He's a very good man, Joanna, don't misunderstand me. There are a lot of benefits from being married to the rabbi, but he's dull."

"Oh, Rachel! I'm sure he loves you," Joanna said, squeezing her in sisterly affection. "Anyway, you know you're always welcome here. Half the vineyard belongs to James, so this is your home, too!"

"What will you do if Joshua becomes a rabbi like James? He's talked about it often enough."

"If he works with James, I wouldn't mind. We'd still be able to live here. But on the few occasions that he has talked about it, he speaks more about being a traveling rabbi, moving from village to village. He speaks of a destiny—of being some sort of wandering teacher. That bothers me. I love it here in the vineyard. When we have a family, I want them to be here."

"If you do, start now while you have this vineyard," Rachel advised, as she put the cooling loaves on a wooden platter. "If Joshua becomes a rabbi like James, there won't be much time for family."

Joshua and Jon came into sight as they walked up from the lower area of the vineyard, where they'd been pruning.

"Here they are," Joanna said. "I've no problems with Joshua, Rachel. I think I have a very happy start to my marriage, but I do find it hard to deal with Jon. Joshua's so patient with him, but Jon drives me crazy at times. He's not normal. He's so slow and moody."

The two men came closer.

Jon had a round but rugged face and a much darker head of hair and beard than Joshua. His strange eyes were too close to the bridge of his nose and gave him a permanent frown or gaze. He had a powerful physique but a slow gait.

Joshua matched his pace to that of Jon, and kept talking to him the entire time it took for them to reach the house.

"Would you like some fresh bread?" Joanna asked, offering them one of the new loaves. "I'm baking more anyway."

Joshua and Jon took the warm bread willingly.

Jon actually smiled. He started to eat his piece, stopped, leaned back and stared at it, then finished it.

"That's the way to eat it," Joshua said, "all warm and gooey."

He put his arm around Joanna's waist and squeezed her gently with affection.

"Rachel, you have a wonderful sister," he said.

"I know," Rachel replied, smiling at Joanna. "I think my sister has a wonderful husband."

Jon grunted and sat down. They all enjoyed a brief moment of relaxation and laughter before resuming their domestic and agrarian tasks.

* * *

Joachim now lived almost as a recluse. Apart from his family, which now included Benjamin Levi, he rarely had visitors and had long since stopped making the annual pilgrimage to Jerusalem at Succot. He supervised those who tended his vines, figs, and olives, and, outside the village, encouraged by Benjamin Levi, he had started to grow a little flax. Joachim was used to Joshua coming to the house to consult him on different aspects of the husbandry of vines. After all, it was Joshua's first season working a vineyard. Joachim was surprised, however, when a cousin from long ago in Jerusalem traveled up north to Galilee, wanting to consult him on the subject of flax.

Nathaniel ben Judah was at least ten years younger than Joachim. He was traveling with his wife, Sarah, their only daughter, Lila, and a steward. Nathaniel had heard about the tremendous growth of the flax industry in Galilee, and having retired from a prosperous position in Jerusalem, he had taken a chance on coming north to see if it might be worth his while to establish himself in the area as a landowner.

Joachim proudly showed him his small fields outside Nazareth and samples of the flax they had recently harvested.

Miriam had done her best to spin the dried-out stalks into fine thread that now waited to be spun into cords or cloth. There was much demand these days for the precious flax, particularly from the Roman buyers who needed large quantities of linen cloth.

"I've only just started growing flax," Joachim explained. "Most of the good flax is grown a little farther north. Cana is becoming the main center. I'd suggest you have a look around that region."

"We'll take our time, Joachim," Nathaniel ben Judah answered. "We have plenty of time."

They returned to the house to find Amos and Jonah visiting from the carpenter's shop and chatting with Sarah and Lila on the porch. Amos and Lila were about the same age, and Miriam had made a point of introducing them to each other in the hope that maybe, at last, they might have found a suitable bride for Amos. Both Amos and Jonah had buzzed around her like bees about a honeycomb.

Lila was an exceptionally attractive girl. She had an air of Jerusalem sophistication about her, and she wore her hair piled up with a jeweled clasp in the Roman style. Her skin was much smoother than that of the hard-working village girls, and her nose was long and refined.

"That's Amos, isn't it?" Nathaniel asked Joachim as they approached.

"Yes, that's Amos and Jonah. They're Joseph's sons, part of my daughter Miriam's family. You met her husband Joseph yesterday."

Nathaniel recalled the aging carpenter.

"Ah! Yes! They are his sons by his first marriage."

"That's right. Miriam only had one child, my grandson Joshua, who has the vineyard across the way and down the hill. You haven't met him yet, or his wife Joanna. You've met Jon, though. He works with Joshua most the time. He's Elizabeth's son—old Zechariah the High Priest's son, and my wife's nephew."

"Zechariah, the High Priest of Herod's time?"

"Yes, that's right. He got mixed up in some unfortunate pharisaic revolt, which led to his arrest and execution. Well, Elizabeth was his wife and my Anna's sister, so we've kept them with us all these years."

Joachim looked around and then continued confidentially:

"Jon's a bit simple."

"I noticed," said Nathaniel.

"Jon's very strong though. We are doing the best we can with him. Frankly, Joshua has had more success in getting through to him than any of us. Joshua's very patient with him."

Later, Nathaniel met Joshua and Joanna when they came over with Jon for the evening meal. It was a family gathering. Amos was continuing to show an interest in Lila, the beautiful young lady who had so unexpectedly come into their midst.

At an appropriate moment, Miriam caught Joseph alone. She put the proposition to him that maybe they should encourage this relationship and make a match between Amos and Nathaniel's daughter.

Joseph stroked his beard. Now that he had a grandson and the likelihood of future grandchildren, his enthusiasm for marrying off his sons had faded.

"Amos is old enough to make up his own mind what he wants to do with his life," he said. "But I won't stop you talking to your father. Of course, I would be delighted to see Amos married, and Jonah, too, for that matter."

"Well, Joseph, I think a word from Joachim to Nathaniel would go a long way. If they are serious about settling in Galilee, why don't we offer them roots?"

Joseph laughed.

"Miriam! When did you learn to become such a matchmaker?"

He took her in his arms and kissed her lightly on the forehead.

"You have such a way of expressing things: 'Why don't we offer them roots?' When did you become such a Galilean?"

Miriam pulled away.

"Joseph! You're mocking me!"

"No, my dear, not mocking you. I'm just enjoying the fresh spirit that you are giving to me. I'm not so young anymore. My eyes are failing and my back aches. That's life, I suppose, but I'm getting concerned about my eyes. Some days are better than others, but today was a particularly bad one."

Miriam looked at Joseph's eyes.

"Your left eye does look a little cloudy. It's grayer than the right one. Maybe you've got some dirt in it," she suggested. "Let me bathe it."

She took some clean water from the jar in the storeroom and returned with a soaked linen cloth. Lovingly, she dabbed the cooling lint over both of Joseph's eyes and gently wiped them.

"Thank you," Joseph said. "That does feel better."

The following day, there was a marked improvement in Joseph's sight.

"Maybe you were right," Joseph said. "Possibly there was just an accumulation of dirt in my eyes."

Meanwhile, Miriam continued with her matchmaking efforts. Joachim assured his daughter that he would speak to Nathaniel and see if he would agree to their way of thinking.

When Joachim approached him, Nathaniel said:

"My goodness, I suppose it does all seem rather obvious now that you point it out. Lila has definitely taken an interest in Joseph's son."

"What's more," Joachim added, "Amos seems to have shown a lot of interest in your daughter over the past few days. For that matter, so has Jonah, but it's Amos that we would like to see married at this time. Joseph needs Jonah with him at the carpenter's shop right now without the distraction of marriage."

"Joachim," Nathaniel said, "why don't I go up to Cana with my steward and look over the land prospects there? Meanwhile, maybe Sarah and Lila can stay here and you can just observe how things develop. I'll come back once I've found a property. Maybe after that, Joseph and his sons can be our builders. Sarah will want to live in comfort similar to yours if we come to live up here. Can Joseph build this kind of a house?"

"Joseph's an excellent builder, and Amos built for the Romans both in Sepphoris and Magdala. You shouldn't have any problem."

Joachim embraced his cousin.

"What a great suggestion, Nathaniel. We would be happy to entertain your wife and daughter here. What an excellent opportunity that'll be to prove whether this match is the will of God."

Nathaniel made the necessary arrangements with his family and set out for Cana. It was a fair day's journey to the north. In passing through parts of Sepphoris, he was reminded of the new sections of Jerusalem. Being one of the more wealthy Jews of Jerusalem, Nathaniel had come to feel at home in a Roman environment with its comforts.

* * *

Linus didn't share his father's enthusiasm for the agrarian life. Tending vines and supervising the building of walls and irrigation channels was not exactly exciting after the thrills of Rome. He missed the physical exercise at the Palestrae and the companionship of the Palatine youths. It was all so dull in Galilee. He couldn't wait for the day to come when Questus would be appointed governor in Damascus and he could leave the Magdala villa.

Linus made his way along one of the new terraces his father had built. It hugged the hillside above a peaceful grove of olives that sloped down to the shores of the lake. The olives provided tempting shade from the scorching sun that beat down on his arms and back. He climbed down the terrace wall to the rocks below and jumped into the shady grove. He stumbled. As he picked himself up, he heard a muffled cry and caught a glimpse of a naked man running off, trailing a linen loincloth. He watched as the man fled toward the shore. Linus took a few steps in the direction from which the man had suddenly appeared. He could hear the shouts of a Hebrew girl cursing. After another step or two, he could see her.

She was naked with her back to him. Long dark curls of hair fell well below her shoulders, and Linus could see her well-rounded buttocks. He stood for a moment, watching her as she continued to curse the man. He was close enough to see that the girl's olive skin was young and supple and that she was probably no older than he. Curious, Linus moved closer. His foot caught a twig. It snapped. The girl turned. Naked, she looked straight at Linus.

At first, she seemed scared. Instinctively, she pulled up the remnants of her tunic to cover herself. Linus stared. The woman's fear turned to curiosity. Her dark eyes softened and a sensual smile came across her face. Linus was mesmerized.

The girl had an extraordinary natural dignity. She was totally in charge despite her recent cursing of the vanished stranger. Slowly, she dropped the tunic and, out-staring Linus, she sat on the recently torn linen garment and beckoned for him to come to her.

Linus advanced. The girl's gaze was hypnotic, and he really had no choice. He knelt beside her as she continued to look at him with dark, powerful eyes. He was drawn in. Instinctively, he reached for her. He kissed her on the lips.

At first, she passively accepted his embrace. Then she pushed him away, taking control once again.

"I know who you are," she said, staring at him with that hypnotic gaze.

"Who am I?" Linus replied in her language of Aramaic.

"I've watched you ever since you came here. You're the Roman's son, aren't you?"

"What's that to you?"

"I know you're the Roman's son because I've watched you working his men as they built the walls."

"Yes! I am the Roman's son," he said, pushing her back on the ground. "I'm the Roman's son, and you're a Hebrew whore."

Linus forced himself on her, grappling with her and running his hands over her body in a frenzy of combined excitement and anger. He pulled at her hair, forcing her to raise her head so that he could again kiss her fully on the lips, and at the same time, he planted his knees on her thighs to stop her kicking in resistance. His free hand roamed over her soft breasts, pulling at her nipples as she tried to push him away with her arms. She didn't scream, however, and instead of the expected tenseness of resistance, Linus met with the soft warmth of her submission. She started to pull him closer to her. She responded to his kissing with a passion that he had not expected. He found himself grinding against her, but she undulated in response. She was still in charge. Her eyes were still in command.

Linus pulled himself away, catching her beguiling smile once more.

"Who are you? Why have you been watching me?" he asked.

"You're the boy who killed my sister, little Deborah. I was there. I saw the stone bounce off the walls. It wasn't aimed at my sister, but at the doves. I always knew you didn't mean it. I've watched you because I want you. I've wanted you ever since you came back to your father's house. If I want a man, I usually get him."

Linus felt trapped. He retaliated with nervous bombastic confidence.

"But why do you want me? Why don't you stick to your own kind? If I want to have you I can, but you can only have me if I want you."

"Do you want me?" she asked seductively, cupping her breasts as she stared straight at him.

"Of course not. You're a village whore."

The woman continued to massage her breasts.

Linus could feel his inner passions rising. She had a beautiful body, and he knew that deep down he did want her, but he was a Roman. If he was to have her, it should be on his terms and not through her artful seduction.

"What's your name?" he asked turning away from her gaze, ignoring her tempting enticement.

"Maria."

"That's a Roman name, isn't it? Why don't you have a Hebrew name?"

"I've always been Maria. Maybe my father was a Roman."

"Don't you know who's your father?"

"No, I never knew my father."

"Who's your mother, then?"

"My mother's a prostitute. My father could have been any one of her men."

"And your mother had Roman men?" Linus asked with surprise, becoming more curious.

"Of course. Romans have often visited my mother. Some have lain with me, too. I've been with Romans several times. Romans often come to our village to buy fish."

"Are Roman lovers better than Jews?"

Maria continued to smile at him in that same beguiling way.

"You can prove that to me. You're a Roman," she said.

Linus was becoming frustrated. He wanted to accept her challenge, but on his terms. He watched her as she seductively moved her hands over her body, inviting him to prove his Roman prowess. It did not take him long to weaken. He discarded his tunic and sank into the softness of her flesh.

Linus had never made love in the open air. He had known nothing other than the scented parlors of the Roman brothels patronized by the rich youths of the Palatine hill. There was a wild freedom to this tryst and a strange majesty that annulled the feeling of master and slave. He knew when he was spent that he would meet Maria again. The boredom of the eternal Galilean summer had at last found a purpose and a new meaning.

* * *

Linus' instinct was correct. During the remainder of the summer, he frequently met Maria in the cool shade of the olive grove beside the lake. Sometimes, they would follow their passion with a swim in the blue waters or sit idly on the stony beach dreaming impossible dreams of their forbidden love. Maria revealed to Linus how she had often visited his father's villa when it lay in ruins and how, for a Roman, his father had shown unusual kindness toward her.

"Why do my people resist you Romans when there can be such tenderness and love between us?" she asked.

"Because we occupy your land. There are many of your people who think that we will destroy your identity as Jews, but in reality, we are protecting you. We protect you from the Parthians and powers to the east, barbaric forces that would overrun your land if we were not here. Look what we've done for you. We've built you seaports and roads, improved your agriculture, and brought you trade."

Linus was describing a foreign world to Maria. She had not traveled more than ten miles from Magdala in her life. To her, there was no Roman Empire—only Romans. She knew the Romans to be people whom many in the village despised, but who in reality did nothing other than buy their fish.

She put her arms around Linus as he described the benevolence of Rome. The sun was catching the ripples of the small waves on the lake, making them sparkle like gemstones. The purple haze of the far Gadarene shore reflected the inner warmth that Maria felt in the security of Linus' touch.

"Isn't this beautiful?" she said.

Linus stopped. He knew she wasn't listening to him. The Hebrew mind couldn't contemplate the Roman world. Their love was a passion that had grown from lust. He despaired as to whether she could ever really share in his life. He kissed her lightly, and she increased her embrace. This was the world they understood, and in each other's warmth they spent their passions.

* * *

Esther's suspicions were aroused as she became increasingly aware of her daughter's absence from the brothel. Some of Maria's regular patrons had started asking her whereabouts, and a few had even taken up with Esther in frustration, not finding the welcome relief in Maria's arms that they had previously known. The assets that mother and daughter had so successfully built up since Maria had come to maturity, were dwindling. Maria was simply not giving herself to her profession.

Esther confronted her daughter:

"Are you seeing a man? You're always out. We've been turning away good business."

Maria couldn't look her mother in the eye. She was breaking the rules with Linus the Roman. She was falling in love. She had given more pleasure in a shorter period of time to that one man from whom she received no payment than she had given to the many who had paid her well.

"Nobody in particular," she said.

Esther took hold of her daughter by the shoulders and shook her.

"You're seeing someone! Is he from the village or a stranger?"

"I'm enjoying a little freedom from the endless days in the gloomy lamplight of the brothel," she answered. "Leave me in peace!"

Esther only shook her harder and slapped her across the face.

"I need you here! I don't need you up in the hills with a goatherd. What man has destroyed you? Who has taken you away from your duty to me and to those who trust us? Those wild men won't bring us any silver or give us any comfort. Remember, we work as a team!"

Esther slapped Maria again, making her fall back onto the raised bench in the dimly lit back room.

"You stay right here where you belong and where I've taught you to work. I forbid you to wander off whenever you think fit."

Maria looked up at her mother.

"This place stinks! I'd rather make love outside, where the air smells of fresh pines and olives."

"So that's it. You do have a man in the hills."

There was defiance in Maria's big, flashing eyes.

"You couldn't give a man half the pleasure that I can. You're growing too old for the trade. Your skin isn't smooth any more. Your face is cracking. If you were to pleasure a man in daylight, he would scream at the prospect. Your day's over, Mother! It's my turn now! I shall satisfy whom I choose, when I choose, and where I choose!"

Maria's words hit home. Esther knew that the bloom of youth had long since passed her. How could she compare now with the beauty that she had spawned? A tear ran down her cheek as she looked at Maria and those captivating eyes. Thoughts of twenty years flashed by, and memories of the comforting visits of Flavius the Roman filled her mind. At one time, she had thought that she loved him, but it was impossible. *Was this the child that had been conceived in our love? Was Maria my Roman child?* She could never know, but as she looked down at the beauty before her, she hoped that it was so. The thought comforted her in her anger.

"You're right, Maria," she said, calming down. "That's why I need you here now. You have all the beauty that I once had. Use it to the fullest, Maria, for beauty such as ours doesn't last forever."

Slow tears rolled from the older woman's eyes, and she wiped her face against the soiled gossamer of the drapes.

"Maria, if you love him, be good to him just as long as you love him."

Maria's secret was still intact.

Later, Esther let a client in to disturb her daughter's peace. She watched from the darkened corner as Maria performed her sexual obligation with perfunctory perfection.

* * *

Although ruggedly independent by nature, Judas Iscariot missed his long friendship with Jonah. He didn't fit in with the fishermen of Magdala. The village lacked either intrigue or commercial zeal, and there was simply not enough to occupy his mind. Judas was an opportunist and a visionary, but he liked practical planning and organization. The fishermen of Magdala merely plied their trade. They caught fish, dried them, and sold them. The more prosperous business of the pickling merchants attracted Judas. If he couldn't channel his energies into political rebellion, then he thought he might as well take advantage of the Romans for commercial gain. That opportunity came for him when he met Zebedee.

Zebedee frequently traveled to Magdala with the fish carts from Capernaum. More and more of the Magdala catch was being sold to Capernaum merchants. Judas listened as Zebedee, a man a few years his senior and more burly in build, told of the success of his fish-pickling venture.

"I have an excellent partner named Simon," he informed Judas. "He's still affectionately known as 'the Zealot' from pre-rebellion days. My sons are also in our business now."

"Simon the Zealot?" Judas quizzically repeated. "I think I met him once. I was in the movement in those days. It was before the abortive rising. Simon the Zealot was our contact in Capernaum. He directed us up north to the caves at Hermon."

"Yes, that would have been Simon," Zebedee agreed. "He sent a lot of men up there in those days. He was clever, though. He never became directly involved himself. He didn't want to cause trouble locally as he could see the potential wealth from our growing business. We started pickling fish just before the rebellion. At first, we sent the barrels to Sepphoris, Sebaste, and Jerusalem, but now we are exporting the fish through Ptolemais and sending barrels north to Damascus and Antioch. It's hard to keep pace with the demand. The Romans love our Galilean fish."

"How many sons do you have?" Judas asked.

"Two working the boats, Janus and Jonas. We buy from the other fishermen and, of course, regularly from you in Magdala, but I really want to build up my own fleet so that we can become our own suppliers."

"Could I possibly join you? I have my own boat. I'm bored with life here in Magdala. Since my partner left, it hasn't been the same. Would you take me on if I bring my catch north to Capernaum?"

"You're the sort of thinking man we need in our expanding business," Zebedee agreed. "I'd be pleased to hire you. We'd be working three boats continuously that way. If you bring your catch into Capernaum, I'll gladly talk business with you."

Judas grinned.

"I think I'll take up the offer, Zebedee. So many of the best fish are wasted here by drying them on the beach. This market's too small for a serious fisherman."

"Smart thinking, Judas. I'll see you in Capernaum."

Zebedee and Judas loaded the fresh fish from Judas' boat onto the salt rocks in Zebedee's wagon. They covered the fish with palm fronds from the Magdala beach.

Zebedee then paid Judas. It was more than his usual pittance. Zebedees' eyes flashed as he looked around, furtively sealing his deal.

"This is to guarantee that you will come to Capernaum with your next catch," he said, clasping Judas' hand as he slipped him the extra coins. "I can make you a rich man in Capernaum."

Judas nodded.

"I'll be seeing you."

Zebedee began to beat on the ox and move his cartload of fish from the beach.

There was a warm glow of expectant excitement in Judas' heart. He had wanted to leave Magdala ever since Jonah had left. Now, the opportunity had come. The thought of commercial prosperity in Capernaum eclipsed his previous reservations about that town's lukewarm commitment to the cause.

* * *

Judas pulled down the simple sail as Thomas, his new apprentice, steered their boat toward the Capernaum beach. More palm trees fringed the stony lakeside here than at Magdala, and many of the buildings in the town rose up two stories. Like Magdala, the place was fringed with tall cypress trees, and beyond, stony brown hills rose upward, dotted with little groves of thorns, olives, and additional cypresses. There were fewer vineyards or signs of cultivation here. The Romans hadn't built villas above Capernaum as they had above Magdala.

The boat beached with the customary grinding sound as the smooth stones took the weight of the prow. Judas had enjoyed an excellent day. A large catch of flat fish lay in the nets piled up in the hull. As the boat came to rest, Judas jumped out and held the prow.

Still looking at the fruits of their labor as the waters of the lake rippled around his feet, he addressed his assistant:

"What a good catch we had today, Thomas!"

Thomas, little more than a boy, had only recently joined the fishermen of Magdala. He grinned.

"You really think we'll do better here in Capernaum?" he asked.

"Old Zebedee made it seem very attractive," Judas said optimistically. "If he was speaking the truth and you stay with me, we could become rich."

Just beyond the palms that bore the gray dust of the long summer, Judas could see the flat square building that he remembered.

"That was Simon the Zealot's house," he said, pointing at the structure on the beach. "I'm sure that was the house."

There were posts with drying nets in front, and Judas could see that there were men working on them.

"Stay here with the boat, Thomas. I'm going along the shore to see if we can meet up with Zebedee and perhaps Simon."

The fishermen didn't even look up when Judas approached. Judas wasn't sure if he'd recognize Simon the Zealot in any case, even if he was there. He brazenly introduced himself:

"Excuse me. My name is Judas Iscariot, and I'm looking for Zebedee and Simon the Zealot. Can you assist me?"

One of the men turned around. He was much younger than Judas, being only about twenty.

"They're inside. Go on in," he said, nodding in the direction of the house.

Judas walked into the cool, dark interior of the stone dwelling. Simon and Zebedee were deep in conversation, but they looked up when Judas entered.

"Judas Iscariot!" Zebedee said. "Simon, this is our new fisherman from Magdala!"

Simon looked at Iscariot. His eyes, unlike those of Judas, were accustomed to the gloom of the interior.

"I've seen you before," he said. "Have you fished off Capernaum?"

"No, sir, but I have met you. A friend and I came through here before the rebellion. The rabbi here sent us to you so you could direct us north to the caves."

Simon looked beyond the door nervously, then smiled sheepishly at Judas.

"Ah, yes! You must have been one of the freedom fighters. Many came through here in those days. We didn't achieve much, did we?"

"No, but we still may."

"Many good men died," Simon answered pensively. "What's your name again?"

"Judas, sir. Judas Iscariot."

"That's right. So you're the man who's going to expand our fleet?"

"I hope so. I've got a good boat and a new apprentice. He seems useful."

"Good. What's his name?"

"Thomas, sir. He's very willing and shows promise."

Simon then embraced Judas.

"Welcome to our family. Come on out and meet Zebedee's sons."

Simon and Zebedee led Judas back into the daylight.

"Janus and Jonas!" Simon shouted. "Come and meet our new partner, Judas Iscariot."

Simon turned to Judas.

"These are Zebedee's sons. We often call them 'the sons of thunder' as old Zebedee here can get a bit bad-tempered at times."

Janus and Jonas laughed. They seemed like very simple, honest folk and really didn't want to say much. Simon was the obvious leader of the group, although Judas had a feeling that Zebedee, despite his apparent reputation for having a bad temper, was probably the real businessman among them.

"Well, sir," Judas said, "you asked me to come to Capernaum, and here I am. How do you want us to unload today's catch? We've done well."

"Let's take a look," Zebedee answered. "If the fish are the right size, we'll pickle them in brine right away to keep them for the markets. They have to be a certain size. If they're too big for pickling, we sell them fresh, and those that are too small we dry on the beach just as you did in Magdala. The fishing's been good recently. We seem to get larger catches all the time, especially if we fish over on the far side of the lake along the Gadarene shore."

They reached Judas' boat, and Thomas excitedly showed them the catch.

"You've done well, Judas," Simon acknowledged. "Let's haul the fish up into the shade and sort them."

They sorted the fish before darkness came. Most of them were fit for pickling.

"The pickling process is similar to that used for preserving olives," Zebedee explained. "The fish are kept in brine, marinated for preservation, and packed in salted barrels to be sold to the Romans."

Judas caught Simon's eye.

"The Romans are paying a price for their conquest, then," he said. "We couldn't destroy their presence in our land, but we've forced them to buy our fish!"

"Don't despair, Judas," the older zealot replied. "We'll win in the end. Maybe we can win more in peace than in battle. Let's bank Roman silver while we can."

They all agreed, cheering their success.

"Tomorrow, we'll put out all three boats, Judas," Simon suggested. "We're partners now—Simon, Zebedee, and Judas."

* * *

Joseph felt the gritty dust in his eyes as Nathaniel walked away from his house. He rubbed them, but he could still only see a short distance. He went inside.

"Are you really happy about this marriage?" he asked Miriam, blinking and rubbing his smarting eyes again.

"Oh, yes, Joseph. Nathaniel's a much-respected man. Amos should be well established."

"That's just what worries me. We've taught Amos to work hard and live an honest tradesman's life. He's a good son. I don't want him to be wasted in an all-too-comfortable life."

"Nathaniel won't spoil him, Joseph. Were you spoiled when you married me, knowing I was a rich man's daughter?"

"You were different. You barely knew you were a rich man's daughter. Besides, you had no time to dwell on your background. No sooner were we married than we had to escape to Egypt and the hard life in Memphis, Gizah and Alexandria."

Miriam laughed.

"You and Joshua at the mud-brick kilns!" she recalled. "You used to come home covered, and we only had one precious bucket of water to wash you both down. But, all said and done, we were always a family—struggling, but close to each other. Remember how James and Ruth took care of Joshua? Maybe Egypt brought us all closer together."

"They're all married now, or about to be married, that is, all except Jonah. He'll be the only one left when Amos goes to Cana. He's a good joiner, but he'll never be able to keep up with the work. With my eyes as they are, Jonah will be the only one of us left in the business. Joshua's become a winemaker, and who knows what James and Rachel are going to do? James used to talk about leaving Nazareth and going to Jerusalem."

"No, Joseph, I don't think they'll leave Nazareth now that Joanna's married to Joshua. Rachel's very protective of Joanna."

Joseph held Miriam tight. He was trembling.

"I'm scared, my dearest," he said. "If I go blind, it will all be over for me. You will be left alone with nobody to care for you."

Miriam patted him on the back as he held her.

"Joseph, you're not going to be blind and Jonah will still be with us. Now, come on back where I can bathe your eyes again. It's the dust. You know how it gets to all of us in the dry summer."

Miriam bathed Joseph's eyes tenderly, but the soothing action failed to help him. The gray cast in Joseph's left eye had spread, and a similar color was building up in his right eye.

"Let's see if James can help us," Miriam suggested. "James has helped many people. Maybe he can help his ailing father now and cure you of any blindness."

"James can bring comfort, but not a cure," Joseph said firmly. "I can only pray that God will cure my blindness, and only then if it's His wish."

"I'll pray, too, but why don't you see James? What harm can it do?

He's our rabbi as well as your son. Speak to him. I'm sure he will offer some relief or a partial cure."

"If you say so, Miriam," Joseph replied forlornly. "I'll ask him if he can help me."

Later, Joseph consulted with James.

James had not realized how serious his father's condition had become. Like everyone else in the family, he had attributed Joseph's failing eyesight to the dust in the carpenter's shop and the Galilean summer. He gently bathed his father's eyes. When there was no improvement, James took some earth, which he moistened with water and spit to make into mudpacks.

James held the mudpacks against his father's eyes.

"In the name of God, may your sight improve," he prayed.

The mud felt gritty, but as it began to dry, James pulled the packs away and gently bathed off the residue with clean water. The treatment seemed to bring relief, the mud extracting the dust particles. For a day or two, at least, Joseph thought that he could see a little better.

CHAPTER TWELVE

A Matter of Wine

Amos blinked in the sun as he stood in the courtyard of the house he had been working on for a year and a half. Nathaniel ben Judah's now-completed home was a comfortable square complex built some way out from Cana in a flat upland area. Amos had hired laborers from the village to assist him. He was proud of their work, but he could also feel the roughness of his own hands as he rubbed them together in satisfaction. He had worked hard, too, and the structure was substantial. Buildings on all four sides faced the courtyard designed around a central well. Two sides of the courtyard rose up to a second story, and a flat roof accessible by stone steps topped the other sides. The entrance, with massive stone lintels, was situated in one of these low sidewalls. Rustic building materials such as a combination of crudely hewn limestone blocks and mud-bricks were used. The walls were plastered in dried mud.

While Amos and his men had worked on the house, Nathaniel had established a farming enterprise. His new fields were plowed into the flat land of the Galilean plateau. During the early rains following Succot, the first flax was planted. The following spring when the late rains heralded the coming dry summer, the seeds had grown up to produce great fields of blue flowers.

In just one season, Nathaniel had transformed the barren upland. The flowers of the flax waved in the breeze. The barley and wheat that he had also planted for next year's bread were already turning yellow and brown. With the coming heat, his laborers would soon be busy with the harvest.

* * *

Nathaniel began to make plans for his daughter's wedding. Lila and Sarah had spent most of the winter at Joachim's house in Nazareth. They were delighted with the progress they saw when Nathaniel brought them north to Cana. Even then, the house had its full form and looked so pretty surrounded by those fields of blue flax.

"Galilee is beautiful!" Lila declared, excitement filling her large, dark eyes. "I think I can be happy here without the bustle of Jerusalem, and in any case, Sepphoris is not far away."

"I hope so," Sarah answered. "Your father has taken a great chance in coming north."

She smiled rather haughtily and looked at her daughter.

"But then, if Nathaniel ben Judah hadn't brought us up here, you would never have met Amos," she acknowledged.

"Are you glad we're going to be married, Mother?"

"I'm sad that I'll be losing my only daughter, but of course I'm happy for you. Amos seems to be a very pleasant young man, and he's definitely a hard worker. Look what he's built for us here from nothing."

They stood admiring the building. It was like an enclosed village in itself. The materials were simple, but the execution was masterful.

"Mother, there's room enough here for all of us to live."

"I think that's exactly what your father has in mind."

"Then, you'll not be losing me, Mother. You'll just be gaining a son." Sarah smiled.

"That's true, Lila. I already feel that Amos is a part of our family. He's been working for you just as our forefather Jacob worked for Laban and the hand of Leah and Rachel. Your father has a great respect for Amos' hard work."

Nathaniel, looking almost more Roman than Jewish with his curled hair and clean-shaven face, joined his wife and daughter in the courtyard. Proudly, he led them to the finished living quarters that would be their future home.

"The far side of the courtyard will be your section, Lila," he said.

"Amos thinks that it will be ready after the harvest is gathered. Maybe we can hold the wedding party right here just before Succot."

Plans were made and, as predicted, in the late summer the final work was close to completion. The wedding was scheduled to take place in the courtyard of the new house just before the High Holy days. Rabbi James was to come from Nazareth to perform the ceremony.

* * *

Joshua was anxious to complete the harvest in his vineyard before the wedding in Cana. With the help of two hired men and the ever-present Jon, he crushed his new grapes in preparation for fermentation. The fresh grape juice flowed from the press and was gathered into vessels so that it could be screened and sieved before storage for fermenting. Joanna liked to drink the fresh grape juice, but both Joshua and Jon preferred mature wine. In the storehouse, the last season's wine had now fermented and matured in leather skins. It was ready for tasting.

After they had finished with their day's pressing, Joshua took Jon and the two helpers into the cool storehouse built into the hillside like a rich man's tomb. The goatskin bags hung on crude pegs in the stonework. Joshua untied one and took a taste of the musty smelling content.

"Good," he said as he passed the skin to Jon.

Jon, dressed only in his loincloth, raised the skin to his lips, his strange dark eyes alight with pleasure. The wine spilled out, dribbling down his black beard onto his muscular torso as he took several mouthfuls of the cool liquid. Then, he passed the skin on to the others. They all became a little merry on the excellent vintage.

"I think this tastes even better than Joachim's wine," Jon commented, wiping his mouth with the back of his large, rough hand.

"Probably...our vineyards are better than his," Joshua replied with a sparkle in his eyes as he took another draft. "Last year must have just been an excellent year for winemaking."

"Let's hope that the grapes we've pressed today will produce as good a wine," Jon said enthusiastically.

"Better! Our vines will get better every year."

When they gathered together everything they thought they would need to take to Cana, Joshua was careful to include a dozen skins of the precious wine. He would give Amos something that he had produced and grown himself. Joanna had prepared the usual sweet cakes and good things for the wedding, and she had cut and sewn three beautiful linen headdresses for them to give to Lila.

* * *

The family gathered at Joachim's house, where, as he had promised, he had prepared a pre-wedding feast with fatted kid, melons, and cucumbers. Joachim served his own wine at the feast. He was proud of the vintage.

Joshua caught Jon's eye as they reclined at the table.

"Not as good as ours," he whispered.

"I helped to make both yours and Joachim's," Jon retorted.

They quaffed from their goblets in a happy mood.

Joanna sipped on the wine, too. She still looked like a young bride in contrast to her more matronly sister.

Rachel sat with James at the other side of the table. Her sad face resulted from her sister Joanna's happiness. She respected James for his straightforward wisdom, but Joshua and Joanna had a personal relationship that she and James had never enjoyed. She had never been able to compete with her sister's good looks and more bubbling personality. She'd often wondered why she couldn't interest James in the same way that Joanna excited Joshua. Rachel remained moody-looking and quiet throughout the evening.

The other sad face at the family gathering was that of Joseph. Despite all James' efforts with clay and spittle, Joseph's failing eyesight had taken a turn for the worse. Even in the brightness of day, faces and figures were now blurred in his vision. With the onset of this blindness, Joseph, who had been a pillar of strength to them all in their small family squabbles and personal problems, had withdrawn into himself. He was silent, and relied on Miriam more and more for all his needs.

Miriam's family's strength was diminishing. Joachim was still the patriarch, but he was no longer robust. Anna and Elizabeth were now both frail. This wedding at Cana might be the last time that they would all be together.

Whatever their personal thoughts, however, all of the family did come together. Ruth and David Levi joined them the following day, and in a caravan of assorted ox carts and donkeys, they set out on the journey to Cana.

* * *

The courtyard at Nathaniel ben Judah's new house was ablaze with light. Great wall brackets held burning torches, and several braziers stood in the open spaces of the big square. In the yard, to the left of three olive trees, Amos had constructed a small dais for the canopied chuppah under which he and Lila would be married. At the other end of the yard, long tables had been set up for the wedding feast.

Nathaniel had stood up his jars of wine in the cool of the storeroom. At the far end of the room were jars of cold water drawn fresh from the well. Two of these were empty. Joshua, anxious to safeguard his secret gift of wine for Amos, looked over the storeroom and, seeing the empty jars, saw the solution. *Those vessels will be perfect to keep the wine for Amos,* he thought. He left the storeroom and went to fetch the twelve skins.

Joshua poured the wine into the two large water jars. *Nobody will help themselves to wine from these water jars,* he muttered to himself. *They will keep it cool, and it will remain separated from Nathaniel's supply.*

All was ready for the great day.

* * *

As the ceremony drew near, the sons of the bride chamber grew merry on Nathaniel's wine, chanting songs and clapping their hands. Ten virgins lined up on either side of the dais, wearing white robes and shaking tambourines. With their other arms, they held up lamps that made this the brightest place in the courtyard. James, dressed in his finest, gold-trimmed robe, took his place on the dais. He looked more like a High Priest than the simple rabbi of Nazareth.

When the bride and groom appeared, a shout rang out from the crowd of guests that included many unknown persons from the village—even well dressed friends from Jerusalem. Lila was dressed Roman style, her hair piled up and held in place by a silver clasp encrusted with semiprecious stones. She wore a headband of myrtle that held up a thin veil that covered her face. A garland of myrtle and wild flowers hung from her neck. Amos joined her on the dais. His face was rugged from long hours of work that he had put into building Nathaniel's house, but he looked happy and rewarded. The great moment had come.

Joshua looked at Joanna.

"This is very different from our wedding day," he said. "Our ceremony was so simple, but I wouldn't have changed a thing."

Joanna had her arm around his waist, and she squeezed it in response.

"My mother used to describe her wedding to me," Joshua continued. "She and Joseph were married out in the fields. There was nobody there other than the witnesses. My mother said that there were more butterflies than people, lots of yellow butterflies."

Joanna looked up at Joshua with her innocent, sparkling eyes. The light of the torches cast a warm glow on her skin.

"I thank God for the great joy that you've brought into my life," Joshua whispered.

The wedding ceremony then began. The bridegroom gave James a simple ring, which he ceremonially placed on Lila's finger. James pronounced the rabbinical blessing and as they turned to each other, Amos opened Lila's veil, casting it to one side so it draped her shoulder. They drank wine from the wedding cup, and then Amos threw the vessel to the ground.

Bride and groom turned to face the crowd.

"Mazeltov!" rang through the air.

The sons of the bride chamber gathered at the foot of the dais as the ten virgins turned to light them on their way to the other end of the courtyard. It was a short procession, but one of meaning as each relative peered, with the curious villagers, to see the happy bride and groom. At the far end, Amos and Lila stood to receive the guests as each one embraced them in turn. Music started to play, and in a short while the feasting began.

The full moon of the month of Elul rose up in the sky, bathing everything in a pale yellow light that merged with the orange glow of the flaring torches and braziers. The courtyard was filled with warmth.

Miriam looked up at the moon. She nudged Joseph, who was sitting quietly beside her, holding his blind man's stick.

"Gabriel's here," she said as she held his free hand. "I can feel his presence, Joseph. The angel of the Lord is smiling down on us this happy day. We're a special family, Joseph. One day God will reveal why, but for the moment let us count His many blessings."

Joseph felt her warm spirituality, but he could not heartily agree with her sentiments.

"God has not cured my blindness!" he said a little cynically.

"Pray, Joseph. He may yet. God does perform miracles."

Miriam put her arm around her helpless old husband.

"Let me fetch you some food. Sarah and Nathaniel have prepared a great feast. Everything looks beautiful here tonight."

Miriam left him to fill a dish with good things for them to eat. Joseph could hear the sounds of merriment and sense the joy all around.

There was so much to eat and drink. The stewards Nathaniel had hired from Cana poured out the wine. Cup after cup of the cool liquid from the jars in the storeroom was drunk. The young men were becoming loud, and the girls from the village, along with the ten virgins, flirted with them. Dancing commenced and the bacchanalian atmosphere reached its height.

Nathaniel's family had been well received by the people of Cana, even though they had come as strangers to the north—Judeans in Galilee. There was no animosity, however. The men of Cana had been happy to work on his building and agricultural projects. Almost everyone in Cana had come to the wedding. Nathaniel had not expected them all, and although flattered, his supply of wine would soon run dry. Eventually, as the party went on late into the night, Nathaniel's steward came to him while he was talking with Joshua and informed him that the wine had run out.

Nathaniel looked at Joshua.

"You're a wine grower, Joshua. What can I do? I have new wine put down for next year, but it's fresh and not fully fermented. It's little more than grape juice. Do you think I can serve such wine to this crowd?"

"At this stage, Nathaniel, you might well be able to serve new wine. Many of the men are more than merry, but leave it to me. I have a surprise for you. I believe I can help you."

Joshua had a twinkle in his eye as he led Nathaniel and his steward back to the storeroom. The water jars stood alone at the far end. Joshua pointed to the last two jars.

"Those are your water jars, aren't they?" he said.

"Yes, sir," the steward replied.

"Go to the two jars at the end and place your finger in their necks."

The steward did as he was told.

"Does that taste like water?"

The steward licked his fingers and drank in the sweet taste of the wine from Joshua's vineyard. He dipped his fingers in again.

"This is wine!" he exclaimed. "These water jars have become filled with wine!"

Joshua grinned.

"Nathaniel, you can serve those two jars to your guests," he said.

"Pour them," Nathaniel instructed his steward.

"Yes, sir," the steward replied. "Not only has this man turned our water into wine, but he's given us the best wine of the evening!"

"God only provides the best," Joshua said with a whimsical smile.

The steward poured Nathaniel a cup. Nathaniel sipped on the sweetness and then asked:

"How did you do that?"

"Maybe your steward made a mistake."

"No, he didn't," Nathaniel said, staring at Joshua. "I checked the wine jars myself before the feast began. There were twelve jars of wine—these empty jars here."

He pointed at the earthenware amphorae.

"The rest were either empty or filled with water for ablutions. The water jars are always kept separate from the wine amphorae, and in any case, look, they are a different size and shape."

Nathaniel took another sip from the cup. He looked up with a wry smile of satisfaction.

"Even if there was a mistake, this wine is different. It's not the same as the wine I served. I hate to admit it, but this wine is far better than what I served."

Joshua took a cup from the steward, who then left with the first heavy jar to pour it for the guests.

"I really have to agree with you. It's excellent wine," Joshua agreed.

"It's a miracle, Joshua! Somebody had to put this wine here. It can't have just come from God."

That whimsical smile crossed Joshua's face again.

"Why not?"

"Come on, Joshua! Do you know where this wine came from?"

Joshua laughed.

"You needed wine, Nathaniel. You ran out. Let's just say that God gave us the wine."

"I know you know where the wine came from. But if you refuse to tell me, then so be it. We'll count it as a blessing from God."

Nathaniel winked at Joshua.

"God has blessed me with many things. I consider this marriage to be a gift from God, too. Let's go out and join the revelers. This really has turned into quite a party."

In the courtyard, the wine was the main topic of conversation. Old Joachim, who was quite the expert on wines, congratulated Nathaniel.

"Why, Nathaniel!" he exclaimed. "Whereas most men serve their good wine first, so that they can water it down later to last longer, you have kept the best until now. This has to be the finest wine I've tasted this year."

Joshua's hard work laboring in his vineyard had paid off.

* * *

Whether it was the wine, the merriment, or just the shared romance of knowing that Amos and Lila were now united as one, Joshua made passionate love to Joanna that night. Afterward, she lay totally satisfied in his arms.

Joshua kissed her gently before she fell asleep, but he remained restless, more so as the effects of the wine diminished. He wondered to whom he should reveal his secret. Nathaniel had spread the word that he had turned their water into wine. He knew that this wasn't so, but he also realized that he had made many people happy and had saved Nathaniel the embarrassment of running out of wine. He wrestled a little with his conscience, for he had reveled in the glory of being a miracle worker. In the twilight moment before sleep finally overtook him, he found comfort in silent prayer.

Thank you, Lord, he prayed, *for giving me the opportunity to use my bounty wisely. I am only the husbandman of my vineyard. You gave me the good grapes. You gave me the right growing conditions. It was You, Lord, who gave me the wine. I just passed on that bounty to others. Use me, Lord. Use me to pass on Your bounty in whatever way You wish. I am Your servant, Lord, Your 'Prince of Peace', and I give You thanks for all that You do for me. May I give back tenfold the blessings that I have received.*

515

Holding Joanna as she slept, he kissed her again on the forehead. *Thank you, Lord, for giving me such beauty.*

---- CHAPTER THIRTEEN ----

Linus and Maria

Linus spent less and less time with Gladius on the excuse of making spurious rounds of his father's estate. Linus was proving to be a reasonable husbandman, but it was not vines and figs that were foremost on his mind. The youth's secret trysts with the voluptuous Maria had become the drive in Linus' life as he waited out the long dry summer.

Linus didn't look on Maria as a village prostitute. She had become his lover. She was as anxious to fulfill her role as he was to take in his. They met frequently in the olive grove and as time went on they became more brazen about their secret. Linus had been seen with Maria walking along the shore. He had also taken her up into the hills overlooking the panorama of the Galilean lake. He had made love to her in countless secret nests, and each time had been as exotic and inviting as the first.

Gladius started to become suspicious of Linus' absences. He laughed at the youth when Linus suggested that he was needed to run his father's estate. Flavius was not short of hired help, and although Linus had taken on a supervising management of some of his father's agrarian enterprises, his position was not essential.

Flavius Septimus also had other ideas. When the time came for he and Copernia to visit Sepphoris, he called his son to him.

"I think it's time for you to get away," he suggested as he adjusted his tunic. "You need to return to military life before you join the Legion in

Damascus. Remember that I expect you to be a soldier who understands the feelings of his men. I don't want you to hold a sinecure as an officer, serving because you are a rich man's son. Our family has been honorable for generations, but we have all served with knowledge. There are too many soft Palatine pueriles serving the Empire these days. That may work for ceremonials, but it won't police the borderlands. Syria's tough, Linus. Questus is going to need real soldiers."

The commander reached for his cloak.

"I know, Father. I won't let the Flavians down. When the time comes I'll train hard, but we've achieved so much this summer. Look at your vineyards and see how your figs grow. I think you need me here at this time."

Flavius stared at Linus.

"This isn't like you. When we first came back to Magdala you couldn't wait to leave for Sepphoris and move on to Damascus. You can't fool me. I'm a man of the world. Something's holding you here and it's not figs and vines! If I'm to believe what I hear, I know what's changed your mind. You can have all the fun you like with the nubile whores of the village, but not at the expense of your duty or at the expense of your future."

Gladius looked at Flavius in a knowing way. By this time, he'd seen Linus with Maria. He'd followed them at a distance, although he had never caught them copulating. When he went to Damascus with Linus they would again be united in a man's world, but here in Magdala they had drifted apart. Linus had become a stranger, distant in his emotional whirl. Whoever this girl was, she had touched Linus' heart. Linus' affair was clearly driving him away from Gladius' power.

"Father, I'll go back to Sepphoris after the harvest," Linus agreed. "I'll discipline myself before Questus calls me. I'll serve Caesar, but if you don't mind, I'd rather stay here right now."

The youth nervously scratched his nose as he looked at his father.

Flavius looked suspiciously at Gladius and then at his son, but he gave in.

"Very good, but I expect the vines to all be cleaned on our return, then," Flavius said. "We have a business here now, Linus. At your request, I'm leaving you in charge. We are not the only producers on the Galilee lakeside. They are building extensively to the south. Romans from Judea are moving up in droves. Tiberias, the lakeside community named after the Emperor, is surrounded by winegrowers and fig farmers. Demands these days for olive oil have also increased. Galilee is becoming a garden of the Empire, but it's competitive."

"Trust me, Father. The work will be done."

Gladius handed Flavius Septimus his helmet. The commander looked Gladius in the eye to reconfirm Linus' statement. Flavius still looked on his son's childhood pedagogue as carrying responsibility, although in reality it was now Gladius who had to march to Linus' orders.

Demetrius had already helped Copernia into the waiting wagon. Flavius joined her, and they left for Sepphoris.

"I am so glad to be returning to the city," Copernia said as the wagon moved away. "I need a diversion from this quiet life at the villa. Sepphoris has much more to offer than this miserable fisherman's town."

Flavius could not help but reflect on his own dalliance with Esther. For him, Magdala, or Taricheae as his friends all now insisted on calling the place, had been his refuge—his escape. Now, however, thoughts of Maria danced before him. *What if she is the mystery girl in my son's life? It is enough that she might be my daughter.* But he consoled himself. *There are plenty of other tarts willing to serve the fishermen; hopefully this girl's just one of them.*

* * *

The days that followed were frenetic for Linus. He met Maria daily, but he had to balance his liaisons with his promised responsibilities. He also had to ensure that Gladius did not follow him to his secret encounters. Work on the grape harvest was nearing completion. The figs were ready and needed picking. The olives would be next. Linus spent his mornings surveying operations and often took advantage of Gladius by putting him in charge of the winepress or the fig pickers. This allowed Gladius to be out of harm's way for Linus' afternoon trysts.

Maria was nearly always there. Now that the great heat was past, Linus sometimes took his cart to their meetings. He would drive Maria along the shores of the lake, farther from the village and the prying eyes of Gladius and his father's hired men. In the warmth of the autumn sun, they would make love in the back of the cart in the relative comfort of a deep bed of straw.

Maria was exciting and challenging. She constantly varied her style and form, leaving Linus always guessing what new joy she could bring.

519

She remained the aggressor, flaunting her beauty and her warmth that Linus found totally irresistible. Their relationship was real. It was a sensuous tumble that had grown into a naive, but compelling love. They both craved their chosen moments, and their emotional attachment clouded the realities of their daily lives. They wove dreams of a future where, as Roman and Jew, they could live together as man and wife, and they forgot the barriers that separated their worlds.

Gladius became more morose, and his loyalty cracked in the wake of his own jealousy. He had pouted too long, and he was driven to emotional distraction. Positive that his suspicions were correct, he followed Linus to the olive grove.

At a safe distance, he watched Linus drop down from the irrigation terrace and make his way into the trees. Gladius continued to follow, climbing down to observe. He saw Linus meet the girl, with her long, curly hair. She was dressed very simply.

For some time, the two lovers sat at the base of one of the old trees. Gladius was too far away to hear them as they spoke softly.

Linus began to fondle the girl. She gave herself to the young man. Linus unbuckled his belt and in no time was naked.

Gladius forced himself to watch the woman fondle Linus' private parts and kiss him.

Linus laughed. Maria's intimate caresses tickled him. He knelt and sucked on her breasts. In a short while, Maria pulled him down onto her. She gyrated and screamed with the joy of fulfillment. A shaft of afternoon sun caught Linus' forehead as he raised his head and shoulders and revealed his tense delight. They tumbled together and turned. Maria straddled Linus, forcing her weight upon him as he kneaded her breasts before running his hands through her hair.

Overcome with jealousy, Gladius withdrew and made good his escape. He ran from the scene, clambering up the hillside back toward the villa.

* * *

Linus did not hear Gladius make this retreat. He and Maria were in their moment of ecstasy. They fell into each other's satisfied, warm embrace. As they came back to their senses, it was Maria who spoke first:

"Linus, I'm going to have your child," she announced.

Linus swallowed hard. The phantoms of impractical romance gave way to reality. Ecstasy drained.

"Are you sure?"

"Yes!"

"Mine?"

"Well, almost certainly. You have been my most constant lover. I fake it in the brothel."

"But you can't guarantee the child's mine?"

"Not in my profession, but I know it's yours. I don't want it to be anybody else's."

"You really mean this?"

"I'm serious, Linus. I'm going to have your baby!"

Linus became thoughtful.

"How long have you known this?"

"For several days."

"Why didn't you tell me before?"

"I wasn't sure... I'm sure now."

Linus had never felt love before he had met Maria. He had only experienced lust. The naïve love that had so recently belonged to them was now threatened by Maria's startling news. He remained silent, stirring the dead olive leaves with his hand.

"What will you do?" he said at length.

"The child's yours, Linus. What do you want us to do?"

"You can't guarantee the child's mine. You said so yourself."

"What use is the child to me if it's not yours? You're the only man I've ever loved."

"Well, you could bring the child up like other harlots do, like your mother brought you up."

Maria slapped Linus across the face.

"So you think of me as your harlot!" she screamed.

"No, Maria! I'm sorry...It's been different between us...I know that."

"Then take me with you, Linus. I can become a Roman. Men come and men go, that's the way it's always been, but you are my only friend."

"I'll work something out, Maria. I'll take care of you somehow, but I think you'd better go now. Meet me here tomorrow. I've got to think. Please...let me think."

Maria put on her robe.

Linus fixed his tunic and brushed off the dried olive leaves.

"Tomorrow," he said, and turned to leave her.

He didn't look back, but made his way steadily up to the vineyards and on to the villa.

* * *

Inside the villa, Gladius was waiting. He heard Linus open the gate and come into the vestibule. Gladius took a slurp of his master's wine. Then, he attacked Linus, knocking the youth down and pinning him to the ground so that Linus could neither move his legs nor arms. Gladius had not totally lost his fighting skills.

"I'll show you who really loves you!" he said with a slur.

With the smell of the wine reeking on his breath, Gladius kissed Linus firmly on the mouth. Linus tried to bite Gladius' lips and tongue and wrestled with all his might. Linus was strong, and although not as artful in combat as the ex-gladiator, he was able to wiggle an arm free. He forced Gladius' face away and hit him with a heavy blow to the head. The jolt freed one of Linus' legs, and the two men became embroiled in fierce fighting on the mosaic floor. Gladius pummeled the younger man, but Linus managed to land another massive blow to Gladius' head.

"You tiger!" Gladius leered. "Hit me all you want, but love me!"

Linus hit out harder as he continued to be battered by Gladius in return. Only through kicking Gladius firmly between the legs was Linus able to free himself. Gladius, in great pain, tried to stand. Linus exploited his servant's weakness and landed a forceful fist in the man's face. The old warrior fell back and hit his head on the hard floor. He became unconscious.

Linus left Gladius lying where he was to recover and sober up. He determined, however, that this was the end for Gladius. Later that day, he dismissed the long-standing retainer from his service.

The following morning, Gladius was alone, walking the rocky road to Sepphoris in great discomfort, no longer the faithful servant of the family of Flavius Septimus.

* * *

Stiff with bruises from his fight with Gladius, Linus took the path down to the olive grove as he had arranged the day before. Maria was already there and seemed frightened and disturbed.

"You did come!" Linus cried as he limped toward her.

Maria lowered her head as he approached.

"You asked me to come," she said.

"Yes, I know, but you might have changed your mind, or maybe you thought that I'd change my mind."

Maria looked up.

"That certainly worried me. Have you?"

"I don't know, Maria. I told you I don't know what to do, but I'll find a way. I will take care of you."

"Even if you're not the father of my baby?"

"How can we ever know?"

"We never will know, but you're the only man I've ever loved. I take everything I can get from men and I give as good as I get, but I've never *loved* anyone else, Linus."

Linus kissed Maria and wiped a teardrop from her cheek.

"You're going to come back to the villa with me. My mother and father are away, and I've dismissed my servant."

Maria hugged Linus. The pressure hurt his bruised body, making him pull away in pain.

"I'm sorry, Maria. It hurts. I'm bruised."

"What's happened to you?"

Linus thought for a moment.

"Gladius saw us, Maria. He's been my servant since childhood. He was incredibly jealous. He loved me, Maria, but I never wanted to return his physical love. When he saw us so happy together, it must have been too much for him. He tried to rape me. That's why I dismissed him."

"He raped you? What do you mean?"

"Some men in our world think nothing of it, Maria. Men love one another just as they love women."

"And some women, too!" Maria exclaimed. "Don't think it hasn't happened to me in my profession."

Linus fondled her breasts as if to reassert his bruised manhood.

"I never let him love me, Maria. I knew he wanted me, but I never thought he would react to my love for a woman the way he has."

Maria responded to Linus' touch.

"I love you," she said.

"I know, but my father will never condone our love. You're a Jew and I'm a Roman. I'm rich and you're poor. Jews and Romans don't mix any more than rich and poor."

"We seemed to manage pretty well up to now. A lot of our clients are Romans, too."

"That was our secret, Maria. It can never be. My father has set great hopes on my career in the Syrian Legion. How can we be man and wife? My family will never accept you."

Maria stepped back, the sun streaking through the olives and catching her dark tresses.

"So, what will happen to our baby, Linus?"

The breeze caught the leaves above.

"You took the risk, Maria. The baby's yours! You can't prove the baby's mine."

"I know the baby's yours, Linus. What will I do during my confinement? What will I do when I can no longer pleasure men?"

Linus remained calm and assertive.

"What did your mother do? Your mother had many men, including Romans, so you say. You even said your father might have been a Roman. Your mother managed. You'll manage as well."

Maria turned away from him.

"Have you no heart? My mother suffered, and now you want me to suffer, too. The villagers shunned my mother when I was born because they thought I had a Roman father. Many know that my sister Deborah was killed by you, Linus!"

Linus flinched.

"They will probably do the same to me or to my child," Maria sobbed, "if they suspect that a Roman was my lover. Maybe they already know. Your servant knew, so why not the gossips from the village?"

Linus came up behind Maria and put his arms around her waist. She turned to him.

"I told you I would take care of you, Maria," he said. "I will. Come back with me to the villa. We'll confront my father when he returns, but meanwhile stay with me at my father's house."

Maria melted into his arms and cried. She needed Linus' protection.

Linus dabbed her eyes with his tunic's sleeve.

When they arrived at the villa, Demetrius, came out from the storerooms.

Linus addressed the retainer:

"This is Maria. She is to remain as our guest until my father returns. Make sure, therefore, that Leah prepares food for both of us tonight."

Demetrius turned pale. He did not dare question Linus' orders.

Later, after they had eaten and were left alone, Linus took Maria to his room.

"If the village didn't know before, they will certainly know now. Leah won't keep this quiet," he said.

They had never made love with the comfort of linens and cushions, but in the soft glowing light of the oil lamps they embraced each other and fulfilled their passions. They had all night to celebrate their love, and they used every precious moment to exhaust their desires, Maria, carefully caressing Linus' bruised body.

* * *

Gladius knew that he had let his passions get the better of him, but he also knew that Flavius Septimus was the only person who could help him. He covered the ground on the road to Sepphoris as fast as his injuries would allow.

At the barracks, Gladius was kept at the gatehouse to await Commander Marcellus' clearance. He asked a messenger to deliver word that Gladius wished to speak to Flavius Septimus.

Gladius was escorted in by the messenger who took him to Flavius Septimus' quarters.

"Please forgive me, Master Flavius," he said, "but I had to come to you."

"Why? What's the matter, Gladius?"

"It's Linus, Master. He's dismissed me. He's playing around with a Hebrew woman and when I found out, he attacked me, then threw me out of the house."

"Linus threw you out because you knew he was poking some Hebrew girl?" he repeated, chuckling to himself.

"Yes, Master. He's serious about this woman. I've followed them many times and they're very definitely lovers. He's not amusing himself at a brothel, Master. He has seriously taken up with a most unsuitable girl—a Hebrew of the lowest class."

Flavius began to grasp the seriousness of Gladius' message. Such a relationship could impede his plans for Linus.

"Will you come back with us? I won't restore you to service with Linus, but I'll need your testimony, and I'll see what we can do for you."

"Thank you, Master."

Gladius and the guard left. Gladius felt a deep regret for his actions. He realized how different life might become without the patronage of the Flavian family. He was being treated almost as a stranger within Marcellus' barracks, where he had enjoyed all privileges and freedoms as Linus's pedagogue in days gone by. Possibly, this lonely feeling could be a taste of things to come. His rash move, driven by personal passion, might have ended the good days forever.

* * *

The next day, Gladius drove Flavius and Copernia back to the villa in the old ox cart. Copernia had laden the wagon with goods and provisions from the merchants of Sepphoris. It was already dark when they reached Magdala.

Passing through the village with its familiar smell of drying fish, Flavius could not help noticing the brothel at the end of the street. His conscience rose within him once again. *How can I admonish my son for having an affair with a Hebrew girl when I paid Esther for pleasure so many times in those lonely days before Copernia joined me in Galilee?* His guilt feelings increased as Gladius struggled with the ox and cart in the pale nocturnal light, trying to keep them on the path upward. *What if that little girl was our child? I am no better than my son.*

Gladius opened the gate and let Flavius and Copernia in. A brazier burned in the courtyard, and inviting lamps lit the vestibule. Demetrius heard them coming and swiftly went out to greet them.

"Master! Welcome home!" he said, wiping his hands on his tunic.

Gladius and Demetrius had never liked each other. He gave the caretaker a look of self-satisfaction.

Gladius entered the atrium first, followed by Flavius and Copernia, with Demetrius in the rear. Linus stood up to face them.

"Fa...Father!" he faltered, pretending to be both pleased and surprised to see him. The presence of Gladius made him nervous.

"Linus, is everything all right here?"

"Er...Yes, Father, of course."

A young Hebrew woman was reclining on the atrium couch. She looked familiar to Flavius. *Somewhat like the little Hebrew girl I found here, only more mature,* he thought. *The features of her face are the same.* She looked nervous and fearful, but Flavius detected a hint of that beguiling smile he had so often seen on Esther's face. His worst fears rose within him as the face of that little girl danced like a ghost before him. *Linus could be physically involved with my daughter—his half sister. How can I tell him and not let Copernia find out?*

"Father, I would like you to meet Maria," Linus said, using Aramaic so that Maria could understand.

Maria smiled. Flavius swallowed hard as he saw her beguiling radiance. Every instinct told him that this had to be his illegitimate daughter.

"Maria..." he repeated slowly. "Did you come here as a little girl to play in the ruins?"

"Yes," Maria answered, her head hung down in fear and embarrassment.

"Then, I've met you before. I helped you when you fell and hurt your knee."

Linus caught Maria's eye with a look that conveyed relief and confidence.

"Do you remember me?" Flavius asked.

"Yes."

Copernia couldn't follow their conversation. Her Aramaic was very limited and what little she had picked up when she had first come to the Levant she had lost during the intervening time in Rome. She relied on Demetrius with his Greek to be her household interpreter.

"You've met Maria before?" Linus asked.

"I met Maria about eight years ago, when you first went to Italia. She came up here to play in the ruins."

Maria's genuine smile only bothered Flavius the more. He now intentionally spoke in Greek so that Maria wouldn't understand. His tone changed, as did the expression on his face.

"What is she doing here, Linus? Explain yourself! Why is a Hebrew peasant girl at ease here in my house and obviously at your behest and pleasure?"

"Because I invited her to stay here, Father. Maria is my lover; she might even be carrying my child. It's my duty to take care of her."

"What! When have you ever cared about duty toward the Hebrew people? She's your whore, isn't she?"

"I can testify to that, Master," Gladius added. "They are lovers. I've seen them together many times. That's why I came to you, Master. Linus wouldn't listen to me. He wouldn't take my advice. He dismissed me because I stood against this relationship. He attacked me when I suggested that this was wrong."

Linus couldn't believe the blatant lies that Gladius was telling.

"Father! Don't believe him! He attacked me! He attacked me because of his jealous passion for me! Gladius couldn't control himself. He couldn't stand the truth that I had no desire to be *his* lover. The reality was too much for his self-control. Maybe he did see me with Maria, but it was his jealousy that caused him to attack me like a madman. I had no choice but to dismiss him."

Flavius looked at Gladius. The old retainer still seemed composed and comfortable. *Linus has often been boastful and deceitful,* he thought, *I want to believe him but...*

"Is this true?" Flavius asked Gladius, but before Gladius could make his reply, Copernia stepped forward.

"What do you mean when you say this woman might be carrying your child, Linus? Is she, or is she not?"

"I don't know, Mother. Maria has had many other lovers. That's been the misfortune of her station in life. But we love each other, and I intend to stand by her now to protect her and her baby."

"Oh no you won't!" Flavius said in fearful anger mingled with his own inner guilt. "I forbid you to see this girl ever again! You get her out of my house!"

"You can't forbid me, Father! I'll do as I want! I'll go with her."

"Oh no, my son! You're off to Sepphoris in the morning. You have a career, a duty to Caesar and to the Flavian and Tarquin families. If you refuse to serve your duty here we'll send you back to Rome, but your days in Magdala, 'Farmer' Linus, are over."

Flavius paused as he looked at Maria. She was frightened by his tone although she couldn't know what he was saying. Then, he continued admonishing Linus.

"So, you've spent your lust on this Hebrew whore. That's fine, but don't talk of love. Get her out of my house, now! Tonight!"

Copernia's face was an ashen hue.

Flavius glared at Linus as his son made no move to speak.

"You heard me, Linus. Take the girl with you, now! I forbid you to ever bring her back to this house again. This is the end of this sordid affair and your sojourn here. Prepare yourself to join the Legion in Sepphoris."

Flavius looked at Maria one more time. He felt a fearful hatred that mingled with tortured love as he saw her beauty. He could fully understand how his son had fallen for her charms and luscious curves. His stomach ached with his guilty memories of Esther, and the more he looked at Maria the more he felt convinced that he was looking at his own daughter. He felt a strong desire to hold her in his arms and welcome her, but deep down he knew that there was no way he could do so. *I have a duty to Copernia, a duty to Linus, and a duty to the Empire,* he assured himself. The torment tore at him.

Linus had no choice but to obey. He took Maria by the hand and escorted her out to the courtyard.

"They're sending me to the Legion," he said. "I'm never to see you again."

He kissed her in the rising moonlight.

Maria barely responded, a calculated coolness coming over her presence. In the practical reality of the evening's disaster, her passion had fled. She bowed her head, afraid to look Linus in the eye.

"I'll find a way," Linus promised. "One day we'll be together again."

Maria made no response, turned and walked out of the gate. She had ventured into a forbidden world. It was her fault. Her place was in the village.

"Romans!" she muttered.

CHAPTER FOURTEEN

Time for Elijah

The bountiful harvests and many years of prosperity that had smiled upon Nazareth and its surrounding countryside came swiftly to a halt during the winter following Amos and Lila's wedding. A silent but deadly scourge, bringing choleric conditions to its unfortunate victims, gripped Galilee.

Joseph could hear the rumble of a cart crossing the open square as he sat on an old bench. Following the cart, he could hear the all-too-familiar wailing sounds of the bereaved. Another child had obviously died, and another family had been saddened.

"Miriam! Who is it?" he asked. "Is it anyone close to us?"

Miriam, who had been sitting beside her blind husband, stood up, peered at the passing cart, and looked pitifully at the mourners.

"Nobody close to us, Joseph," she answered. "It looks like one of the families from the north end of the village, some of Benjamin Levi's neighbors."

The mourners made their way down to the land near Joshua's vineyards where an emergency burial ground had been established. The graves were shallow pits marked by piles of loose stones that covered each corpse. Most of those who had died in the early days of the Galilean plague had been children overcome by the cramps and weakness of the cholera. As winter drew on to spring, however, almost daily, adults were joining them in the graves.

The cholera attacked suddenly with excruciating stomach pains and a high fever. This was followed by chronic diarrhea that left the victims too weak to fight. Their struggle for life was painful, and few had recovered.

* * *

Joanna began to feel such cramps in the afternoon shortly after the same little funeral procession had passed by on its way to the graveyard.

Joshua was afraid. He had returned from Joachim's house, where he had been pressing olives with Jon. Joshua found Joanna lying down. The twisting pains that she described sounded too much like those of all the others.

"Do you think I'm going to die?" she asked, holding Joshua tightly in her arms.

Joshua winced and prayed.

He tried to bravely reassure his wife:

"Of course not, dearest. It's probably something you've eaten—tares or darnel in the barley you've used for the bread flour. You know how easy it is for the bad ones to slip through."

Joanna gave a little smile as she clung to Joshua.

"You're always such a comfort," she said, looking up into his eyes.

But her smile gave way to another wince as the pains in her stomach gripped her in a spasm. Joanna doubled up in agony and then crawled to the door, where she vomited violently.

Joshua washed her face and held a cool linen rag to her brow as she lay back down on the straw pallet.

But Joanna found it hard to stay still. The cramps increased and induced the dreaded diarrhea.

"It's no use, Joshua. I've got it! I've got the plague!" she cried. "I'm going to die!"

"No, Joanna. God is good," Joshua said comfortingly. "You won't die. Hold on to me. Let me be your strength."

Joshua stayed with her. He prayed earnestly to God that Joanna would be spared. With the diarrhea, however, Joanna only weakened more and Joshua saw no response to his prayers. He could smell only the rising stench of sickness in their home. A feeling of helplessness came over him. There seemed so little he could do. Joanna's fever was raging and her discomfort was ever mounting. He didn't want to leave her, but he knew he had to go and get help.

"I'll be back as soon as I can," he assured her. "I'm going to fetch Mother. I'll see if James and Rachel can also come down."

He kissed Joanna on the forehead, but she barely noticed as a delirious haze filled both her vision and mind.

Joshua hurried into the village, praying as he went. *Surely God will not abandon me*, he thought. *God must answer my prayers if I am His 'Prince of Peace'*. He found Miriam at the carpenter's shop. She was sitting with Joseph while Jonah was busying himself with hammer and chisel.

"Mother!" he cried. "I need your help. It's Joanna. She's sick. I think she's got the plague. She's feverish, she's vomiting and she's got these terrible cramps."

Miriam squeezed Joseph's old hand and let it go.

"Not Joanna!" she exclaimed. "God wouldn't take Joanna! Let me come back with you. Maybe she's eaten something. I'm sure it will pass. Let's see what we can do."

"Mother! She's really sick!" Joshua implored. "She needs all the help we can give her. Let me call on Rachel and James. James has had experience with this disease. He's cured some. He'll cure Joanna."

Miriam looked at her son.

"Joshua, we'll go to her right away. You go up to the synagogue and fetch James and Rachel. Pray, Josh, remember it is God who heals."

She took charge.

"Jonah, take your father to Joachim's house. When you get there, send Judith over to Joshua's place with linens."

Jonah put down his tools.

"Come on, Father, we're going for a little walk," he said as he put Joseph's familiar stick into his father's free hand before leading him out into the street.

Joshua watched. Tears overcame him.

Miriam looked at her son.

"Go!" she commanded. "Fetch James and Rachel! I'll be on my way, and I'll see you at your house."

Joshua left to look for Joanna's sister and the rabbi, revisiting his prayers of supplication. Miriam picked up extra linens.

Miriam passed Joseph and Jonah as they shuffled down to Joachim's house. She didn't stop longer than to remind Jonah to ask Judith to please come on over to Joanna's house as quickly as possible. There was no mistaking the sickness when Miriam arrived. She peered through the doorway into the gloom. Before she could even see where Joanna lay, the smell of human excrement, vomit, and disease, pierced her nostrils.

Softly, she called out into the darkness:

"Joanna! It's Miriam!"

As her eyes became accustomed to the dim light, she could make out Joanna tossing and turning on her straw pallet. Joanna's once-beautiful hair was matted in her own vomit and her shift was soiled in the uncontrollable waste from her frail body.

"Oh, Joanna!" Miriam cried as she came over and placed her hand on the sick woman's brow. "We must get you well again. Rachel and James are coming and Judith will be here soon. We'll have you well again in no time."

Joanna's head pounded with the fever.

"Elijah!" she called out. "Elijah! You are coming! Take me, Elijah!"

Miriam, now able to see a lot more clearly, went to the storeroom to get water. She trimmed a lamp. She returned and bathed Joanna with the cool water and linens as best she could, soothing her as she cleansed away the vomit and excrement.

Joanna became momentarily more calm and stable.

Joshua returned with Rachel and James.

"How is she?" he called out.

"She's very sick, but she is responding."

James put up his right arm and thanked the Lord:

"Blessed be God forever!"

Joshua looked on in silence.

Miriam called out to Rachel:

"Fetch more rags and fresh water from the storeroom. Judith will be bringing others soon, so collect up whatever's there. Joanna needs constant cooling. She's burning up with the fever."

When Rachel left, Miriam looked up at her son.

"It is the plague, isn't it Mother?" Joshua said.

"I'm afraid so. It looks like the same colic condition that has been sweeping through the village. We must do everything we can. Do you have some clear, clean water? The water in the storeroom jars isn't very clean. If not, do you have some cool grape juice? We must try to get Joanna to drink."

Rachel returned with more rags and another water jar. Along with Miriam she tried to bathe Joanna and force her to drink, but the water became fouled by their attempts to clean her and in her delirious state Joanna rejected it and spat it out.

At length, Judith arrived with good clean linens from Joachim's house. She pointed to the empty water jars.

"Let me take these," she said. "I'll fill them from the cistern."

Meanwhile, Joshua brought out a fresh skin of grape juice. He tried to squeeze some into Joanna's mouth. Much of it dribbled from the corners, but with effort she swallowed a couple of times as Miriam and Rachel held up her head.

Joanna hadn't spoken, being only semiconscious. When she saw Joshua holding the skin up to her, she seemed to recognize him and a faint smile came across her face.

"Elijah was here, Joshua," she said, before closing her eyes and leaning back against Miriam and Rachel.

For a while, she slept.

James led them all in prayer as they asked God to spare Joanna from the shadow of death.

The shaft of evening light faded from the doorway. Darkness descended and filled the landscape. They waited, watched, and prayed.

Momentarily, Joshua stepped out and looked up at the stars. He was reminded of that night in Egypt long ago, when his mother had implored him to see God in the face of the moon and stars, and to pray. *What if Joanna is dying?* he thought. *What if God has another destiny for me?* He could make out his vines in the shadows of the night. *What if The 'Prince of Peace' means more than marriage, family and vines?*

"Dear God," he cried out. "Not my will, but Thy will be done."

But the thought was no consolation for the tears that welled. After a period of silent petition, he returned to his beloved.

The next morning, as dawn broke, bringing white light to the hillside of dormant vines, Joanna stirred on her pallet. She hadn't slept long, having remained restless most of the night. In that first light that streamed in through the doorway, she smiled at Joshua with his rugged strands of unkempt beard.

"Joshua," she said weakly, holding out her hand and clasping his, "I saw Elijah. He was here."

Momentarily, there was strength in her hand.

God Almighty! Don't take Joanna from me, Joshua prayed as he watched her intently. *Please, don't take Joanna away.* He squeezed her hand. *Dear God, I ask that you give me power to make her live.* Joanna gazed into Joshua's determined eyes.

Then, she released her hold and lay back as if to sleep.

By the time Judith and Miriam approached with wet linens to bathe the sweat beads from Joanna's brow, the aches had returned to her body after that brief peace. She tried to vomit, but she had nothing left to lose. The pains twisted in her stomach again, and she doubled up in agony. As Joanna became more feverish and dehydrated, Joshua tried to get her to swallow more grape juice, and with Judith's help, he was able to moisten Joanna's lips. She wouldn't swallow, however. The weakness of her drained body and high temperature inhibited her ability to function.

The hours passed. There was no sign of improvement or relief. While Rachel baked them all some fresh bread, James and Joshua took a short walk in the vineyard.

"You needed to get away from there," James said. "I know I'm not helping much. This plague is not within my power. Demons and devils I can admonish, blindness I have been known to cure, although I've had little success with Father, but this silent sickness is beyond my ability. It's a curse on us, Joshua. I believe Joanna is going to die. I know no cure."

He put his arm around Joshua's shoulders.

Joshua tried to hold back his bitter tears.

"Deep in my heart I know that, James. It's not your failure. It's not the care of Mother, Judith, and Rachel that has failed. God has sent a curse on us, a silent scourge. We are no more immune to it than any other family. God gave us plenty for many years, but there comes a time when we are tested. Wasn't Job a rich man? Didn't Job have everything? Yet, piece by piece, God took everything away from him to test his worth. I've been thinking, James."

He looked at his feet as he walked, then at the vines.

"Maybe God doesn't mean me to stay tending vines here in Nazareth any more than He expects you to stay the rabbi of this little village. We believed in our personal destiny once. That was before we became comfortable here in Galilee. Remember how Mother used to say we were special—chosen people? Maybe she's right. Maybe we have a destiny that is greater than family here in Nazareth. Maybe that's why God is taking away our family."

"This is hardly a time for philosophy," James replied, patting Joshua's back. "It's a time for prayer."

"I prayed all night, but it would seem to no avail. She's no better. It would take a miracle for her to recover now."

"God doesn't always grant us miracles, Joshua. Maybe we are praying for our own ends. Perhaps we should pray more for God's power to direct us wherever He needs us. Perhaps you're right. God is testing us. It is not our will but His will that will be done."

As they spoke, Jon came running up from Joachim's house.

"Joshua!" he called out when he saw the two men in deep conversation. "Joshua! Come quickly. It's Mother! She's also sick."

"What!" Joshua answered. "You mean Elizabeth is also sick at Joachim's house?"

"Yes, Joshua!" Jon said, panting for breath as he reached them. "Mother has awful stomach pains and she's vomiting, too."

Joshua looked at James.

"The plague is spreading," he said. "Take Judith back to Joachim's house with Jon. I must stay here with Joanna. You've done all you can here. Mother and Rachel will do their best for Joanna. You take care of Elizabeth. She's much older and more frail."

"I'll be on my way," the rabbi answered. Then, turning back, he grasped Joshua's hand. "Remember, it's not our will, but God's will that will be done," he repeated.

"I know," Joshua answered, embracing his lifelong mentor and friend. "May God be with Elizabeth."

Jon fetched Judith from the house, and with James they hurried off through the vineyard toward Joachim's house.

Joshua went inside to Joanna. She seemed unconscious. She was lying very still on her pallet.

"She's restful now," Miriam said. "She's very weak, but she's more at peace."

Joshua took Joanna's hand. She made just the faintest response, and there was the glimmer of a smile on her lips. He sat holding her hand for what seemed an eternity as Rachel and Miriam applied cool, damp linens to her head.

At length, Joanna opened her eyes.

"Elijah!" she said as her smile broadened. "Elijah, you came!"

Joshua squeezed her hand harder.

Joanna closed her eyes and lay still for a while longer.

Miriam tried to feed her a little water, but Joanna's lips wouldn't part.

Sweat beads formed on Joanna's neck and forehead once again. The fever rose in intensity. For a while, she twisted her body weakly, but then gave up the struggle. She lay still only to open her eyes one more time.

"Joshua, it's all right," she said, eyes bright and momentarily coherent. "Elijah came!"

* * *

Joshua buried Joanna in the vineyard just below the wall adjoining the house. He dug a good, deep grave, and covered her body in soil and stones. Miriam and Rachel stood beside him as he fulfilled his task.

Rachel wept at the loss of her sister, but Joshua calmed her:

"What the Lord gave us, the Lord has taken away, Rachel. But all of us have been the richer for what He gave."

Rachel stared at Joshua.

"I loved your sister," he continued. "I will spend the rest of my life proving to you that this was God's will. Joanna and I were meant to be together, albeit for so brief a time. The happiness that God gave me through her I will pass on to others. Joanna may be gone, but the joy that God gave in her, lives on."

Joshua embraced Rachel.

"Don't be afraid. We must thank God for Joanna and all that she gave us."

Joshua then turned to Miriam, who had remained profoundly silent.

"Mother, it was God's will. Thank you for trying to save Joanna's life, and if it had been the Almighty's wish, your efforts would not have been in vain."

He took his mother in his arms.

"I love you, Mother. You give me such strength."

He kissed Miriam on the forehead, no longer able to hold back the tears of grief welling up in his eyes.

"God's still with us," she said.

Slowly, the three of them walked back up to the house.

* * *

Elizabeth's death was almost as swift as Joanna's. The old lady hadn't the stamina to fight the plague, despite the efforts of Joachim's servants and Anna's helpless assistance.

Jon sat looking at the clouds scurrying across the spring landscape. He had coolly watched as his mother slipped away. He couldn't understand his emotions. After she was buried, he had almost felt a sense of relief—a new freedom. His childhood dreams of destiny resurfaced. He was now his own master. *Joachim is not my father. Joshua is not my brother. James does not even have to be my rabbi.* He considered his destiny.

I have been commissioned by God, he thought, *Nobody expected me to be born and my father was struck dumb until I was. He believed that I would be great. Maybe he was right. Maybe I do have a destiny beyond this village and these hills.*

He watched as a hawk swooped down to pick up its prey.

God will pick us up and snatch us away just like that. We won't know when or how. It'll be sudden, just like the plague that took my mother and Joanna. Are we ready to be taken away in death? Are we ready to be judged by God?

After a flurry and some squawking, the hawk rose again. It carried its prey back to the rocks from whence it had come. The landscape returned to silence.

Jon sat there until the cool of evening descended, and he returned to Joachim's house. The brightness and the warmth seemed artificial to him. He reflected on the landscape that had been his inspiration.

I do have a destiny, he thought. *I must prepare us for the day when the Lord will come.*

* * *

Maria felt totally alone. Esther had rebuked her for her indiscretion more out of fear than honor. She had forced her to drink concoctions made from herbs and boiled fish heads in the hope of getting rid of the child, but Maria wanted to have her baby. She wanted to keep her brief moment of freedom with Linus as a treasured memory. She couldn't hate the Roman youth or despise his father for his actions. But, it was her mother's revelation, after all attempts at inducing abortion had failed, that finally exiled Maria.

"Your child will be cursed!" Esther said with a dreaded horror. "Haven't you guessed that you were probably the Roman's daughter? It was my folly that caused you to be born the daughter of a Roman. Your lover's father was my lover! You have probably spent your lust on your own half-brother! This child you are carrying will be a Roman filled with devils...an inbred madman fit only to be cast out into the wilderness to take his chance with the wild beasts."

Maria saw the hatred welling in her mother's eyes. It was hatred of herself mingled with fear and guilt.

"Your child will be the son or daughter of your sister's murderer! Your little sister was killed by the Roman monster you call your lover!"

Maria stopped listening as her mother trailed off into a tirade against Romans in which Esther tried to purge her own guilt.

Linus is no murderer, Maria thought. *He was my lover. He stood by me and promised to take care of me at great risk to himself and against his family. Circumstances went against us, but it doesn't make me think any the less of him. What did he say? 'I'll find a way. One day we'll be together again.' There wouldn't be a way.* She knew that, but she believed he had sincerely meant it.

She turned her thoughts to his father. *I wonder if he knew I might be his daughter, and how can my mother be so sure I was his daughter? She had so many men. But if he knew, or even suspected this, it would account for his sudden outburst and rejection of me. His anger may have just been like hers, a tirade to cover up his own guilt.*

"Your child will be another Roman bastard just like you!" Esther shouted as she paced the room. Maria barely heard her. She was almost in a trance.

I want to believe that my child was the result of our love. I told Linus so, but how can I prove it when my mother forced me to lie with all those

fishermen and strangers that came to our house through those long summer
months? I can't prove it any more than she can prove I am Linus' father's
daughter.

Her mother's voice harangued her:

"If you want to live with the Romans, go to their cities. You can't stay
here. You've made yourself an outcast, Maria!"

Maria couldn't hate her mother still unleashing years of guilt upon
her. Maria felt no emotions. She only wanted to protect the child now
growing in her womb. She packed up a bundle of ragged garments and
left the village. She followed the shore of the lake, the only landscape she
knew, passing by the olive grove that came down to the pebbled beach
where she had shared such happiness with Linus. She was aware that if
she kept walking south along the lakeshore, she would eventually come
to the new Roman town that Linus had visited and that was common
gossip among the fishermen. She left the confines of her summer's love
and faced a brave new world.

* * *

Maria had never seen a true Roman city. Tiberias was a revelation to her.
She had no idea that there was such a place on the shores of her lake.
Villas, more majestic than those where Linus lived, dotted the hillside
above the blue waters. Everywhere, builders were at work. There were
carpenters, stonemasons, and busy laborers constructing columns and
architraves, pediments and arches quite foreign to Magdala. Maria was
awestruck by the grandeur of it all. Why, even the streets were paved in
white marble slabs! She had never known anything but dust and stones.
The marble felt cool and delightfully smooth under her sore feet.

Nobody seemed to scorn Maria's presence in Tiberias. She walked
freely through the streets, sensing a feeling of friendship, almost a
welcome, from these Roman strangers. She was conscious of the glances
that they cast in her direction, and more than once she instinctively
smiled at an admirer. If she was rejected by her own people, she saw no
reason, now, not to settle with these people.

At first, Maria slept rough on the beach, not knowing what her destiny
might be. She didn't know anyone and had no means to live in shelter.
By day, she walked around, watching the construction and drinking in
the sounds and smells of this foreign world. For food, she had to rely on

scraps from the open stalls in the marketplace or the berries and fruits of the surrounding autumnal countryside.

Maria rarely heard her native language. The Romans all spoke Greek or Latin. She was startled, therefore, when she did hear someone call to her softly in Aramaic. It was a female voice.

"Where are you from?" it said.

Turning around, Maria saw a Hebrew girl about her own age. She was dressed like a Roman, her dark hair cropped and ribboned, but the girl wore no clasps or Roman jewels.

"From Magdala," Maria replied with a smile.

"My name's Delilah. I've noticed you here the past few days. You must be alone. You look tired and hungry."

"I am. I have nowhere to go."

Delilah took Maria's hand.

"You are not alone now. What is your name?"

"Maria."

"Maria of Magdala," Delilah repeated. "Come with me. I can find you a place to rest and eat."

Maria followed Delilah up a narrow, paved street that led off the market square. It was stepped, with periodic arches opening in the sidewalls where various tradesmen plied their crafts. Eventually, they came to a large, marble lintel and a great wooden door.

Delilah pushed the door open.

A white marble passageway led into a bright courtyard in complete contrast to the dark street outside. A fountain played, and men sat on benches in the shade of a portico. All around this portico there were small rooms, their narrow entranceways shut off by bright orange drapes. Delilah led Maria across this courtyard down a narrower passageway into another atrium. The space was much smaller, with an overhanging tiled roof much the same as that which Maria remembered at Linus' father's villa. Sitting here, was an older, Roman lady, with her hair piled up on her head and held in place by richly decorated clasps and pins.

Delilah spoke to the woman in broken Greek:

"This is Maria of Magdala. She needs shelter and food, and I believe we can use her to our advantage."

The Roman lady stood up and walked around Maria. She gave a smile of approval.

Weakly, Maria smiled back.

"Ask her what experience she has had with men," the lady requested in Greek.

Delilah grinned, as if she could tell just from Maria's sensuous looks that she knew the answer.

"Have you been with many men?" she asked.

Maria began to suspect into what she had just walked. Although not as pungent as her mother's parlor, she had caught the drift of perfumed oils as they had crossed the larger court. Delilah was asking her to join a brothel. Maria couldn't help but open up her whole beguiling smile.

"Many!" she replied. "Ever since I was a child I have pleasured men."

Delilah relayed Maria's answer to the older woman.

They spoke a brief exchange in Greek, enough for Delilah to understand that she was to take care of Maria and that she would be rewarded. She was to show her where to sleep, give her food, take her to the baths, and then put her to work.

Delilah took Maria in as her partner. Maria shared her small room that the matron had provided off one of the narrow streets. The room was little more than a cavern in a vaulted archway and was furnished merely with pallets and a lamp.

Maria was more than grateful in her loneliness to have a place to sleep and some companionship.

Delilah was very beautiful. She was tall with that dark, curly, beribboned head of hair. Her features were sharp and sparkling, and her body was firm and exquisite. Her breasts were small compared to the voluptuous bosoms that Maria shared with her men, and her buttocks were very firm, smooth and round. She had the classic looks of a Greek goddess and had apparently long been a favorite with regular patrons at the Tiberias brothel. When Delilah initiated her into sharing their bodies in tender affection, it was easy in Maria's loneliness for her to respond.

Delilah's touch was so different from that of their over-eager clients. She kissed Maria tenderly, never bruising her lips, but gently caressing the soft rim of their protruding flesh. At times, she quietly nibbled on Maria's ears, using only her lips and pulling lightly on the lobes. Maria had never felt the sensations that this action summoned. No man had ever gently kissed her ears. The excitement of that simple action sent tingles through her whole body. Together, they caressed the warmth of each other's flesh and lightly massaged each other's breasts. Their touching was so gentle. Their nipples hardened, but their bodies remained totally relaxed. Maria and Delilah bathed in the pure pleasure that they administered to each other in the soft glow of that single lamp that lit their simple home. They rarely spoke as they explored each other. The sensations were so strong and so intimate that their minds seemed to fall into a trance. Never in her life had Maria felt so relaxed. They lay for hours in each other's arms, gently soothing away all the pains of the world.

They worked alternate days at the brothel, and on the days that Delilah was working, Maria would scout for food at the market to have a welcome dish waiting for Delilah when she returned. The brothel matron paid her girls well for their labors, so Maria and Delilah could purchase all their needs. They didn't bother to bake their own bread, as fresh loaves were always available from the bakeries. Maria also found herself drawn more and more to the pomegranates that the Romans loved.

On each day off, she would buy herself three or four pomegranates and take them down to the beach, where she spat out the seeds while looking over the water. In the distance, she would see fishing boats and be reminded of the rough men that used to visit her mother's house in Magdala. She remembered the stink of rotting fish that permeated from their skins. Somehow, she preferred the Roman men who had now become her principal clients. Their requests were sometimes a little bizarre, but they were cleaner and generally more tender lovers. As she sat on the beach one afternoon spitting out those pomegranate pips, she considered her condition and how it might threaten this new life.

I must be nearly three months pregnant now, she reflected. *Sooner or later I'll have to reveal my condition to the matron. She won't want me at the brothel then. I wonder if she'll let me stay with Delilah until my child's born? I wonder if Delilah will be able to keep us while I'm not working?*

Later that night, as she lay gently caressing Delilah's body and bringing her relaxation and relief after her day in the brothel, Maria revealed the truth:

"Delilah, I'm going to have a baby. I'm nearly three months along."

Delilah sat up and stared at Maria.

"Three months! That's impossible. You haven't been with us for three months."

"I know, Delilah. I was pregnant when you found me. I spent the summer with a Roman boy. I'm sure it's his baby."

"Oh, Maria. When the matron finds this out she'll expel you. Nobody's allowed to stay in the brothel when they're pregnant. We have to be so careful. That's why she always makes us take that hot herbal bath before we leave each day."

"I like the hot baths."

"So do I, Maria, but the purpose of the bath is to wash out any possible pregnancy. Sometimes, the hot baths don't work. When that happens the matron just dismisses the girls. She'll dismiss you, Maria."

"Can't you talk to her, Delilah? I can't because I don't understand Greek."

"I can try, but I don't think it'll do much good. Maybe she'll be more lenient on you. Our booth is one of the most popular with the regulars, and that's not all because of me. If I can explain that you were pregnant before you ever came to the brothel, it might help, but maybe not. That might go against us both, because in a way I deceived her when I brought you in. I didn't know you were pregnant. How could I have known?"

Delilah softly caressed the underside of those voluptuous breasts, and Maria's nipples responded. She hugged her friend, pulling her close as they sat facing each other, their legs entwined. She gently caressed Maria's back.

"You don't look pregnant," Delilah whispered. "Are you really sure?"

"Yes, Delilah. For two months, and now I've passed my time for a third month."

"Now that you say so...yes. Why didn't it occur to me? No wonder you've been able to give so many days to the brothel. I should have guessed."

Delilah kissed Maria tenderly on the lips.

"I'll bet you'll have the most beautiful baby. Such a beautiful woman could only have beautiful children."

Maria smiled.

"Will you help me?"

"Of course, Maria...I love you."

* * *

A bright summer moon rose above Nazareth. The scourge of the plague had worn itself out. Depleted families were picking up their shattered lives as they returned to the busy toil of their land.

Joshua had spent many lonely evenings in the vineyard, looking across the valley. He missed Joanna terribly. Their brief time together had been such a happy interlude, but deep down he felt the stirring of that new beginning, perhaps formed in the crucible of Joanna's constant love. As the summer advanced, the work of thinning the grapes commenced. He needed Jon to assist him.

Poor Jon, Joshua thought as he cut a cluster of shriveled grapes from a succulent bunch. *Who is going to look after him now? His mother and father are both gone and it will not be long before Joachim and Anna will be too old and feeble to care for him. My mother has enough on her hands with blind Joseph. I suppose in reality, Jon's now my responsibility.*

Jon moved into Joshua's house so that they could more easily share the work in the vineyard. He was restless. Joshua guessed that he was carrying some secret. One evening Joshua broached the subject.

"You're hiding something from me, aren't you?" he suggested. "There's something occupying your mind. Your heart's not in your work in the vineyard as it used to be."

Jon remained silent for a moment and then looked up at Joshua.

"I had a vision," he said. "I have a mission from God. My father said so all those years ago. He said I was a special child given to my mother by God. Joshua, I believe the time has come. I may not be clever and I might be clumsy, but I can point the way. I've thought about this ever since the plague swept through the village."

"Thought about what?"

"The plague came suddenly, like a thief in the night. It will be like that, Joshua. It will be sudden. God will come down swooping like a hawk, and only those who are prepared will be saved."

Joshua was astounded. Jon had never been party to his theological debates with James and the synagogue group. Neither James nor he had ever considered Jon to be intelligent enough to engage in such discussion. Jon was backward. He was strange, his mind not strong. Yet now, this same moody and slow-witted burden on his family was speaking with great authority.

"How long have you felt this way?"

"For a long time, but I've never understood. Now, seeing my mother die and the way Joanna was so suddenly taken from us, I'm beginning to understand. There will be a terrible judgment, Joshua. Only the good and honest people will be spared."

"Who's been talking to you?" Joshua asked.

He really wasn't sure how far he could pursue this conversation when he knew that Jon had no learning, no intimate knowledge of the prophets and the true destiny of their people.

"God talks to me, when I'm alone" Jon said. "God has frightening power. He moves the clouds, roars the thunder, pours down the rain, and gives us the heat of the sun. He's always watching us, Joshua, and one day He will take us, just like He took Mother and Joanna. We must be ready for Him. We must be ready to meet God when that time comes."

Joshua felt disturbed. He was witnessing a side to his cousin that he had never seen before. There was an earnest sincerity in what Jon said, even though Joshua was not sure that he agreed with him. Joshua was afraid to pursue the discussion further, as it made him uncomfortable. It reminded him of his own fears for the future. He thought back to his childhood discussions with his mother and considered again the strange circumstances behind the buried treasure that was still under the floor of his house. *Is Jon, in his innocent, unknowing way, guiding me on?* he thought. *Is it now the time for me to take up a new destiny and become that 'Prince of Peace'?*

"We should all be prepared," Joshua answered Jon. "You're right. We'll never know when our time will come. What was that expression you used...'The Lord will come like a thief in the night'? It's good, Jon. God comes into our lives when we least expect Him, but not necessarily to destroy us."

Joshua remained in thought for a moment and then smiled before changing the subject:

"We had better get down to the lower part of the vineyard, Jon. I noticed yesterday how the weeds are taking hold there."

Jon and Joshua spent the rest of the day pulling at the tares and cleaning out the root areas around the vines. Jon became rather quiet, withdrawing into his moody old self. Joshua remained in deep thought.

In the evening, Joshua sought out Miriam. Jon had set him thinking and he needed to talk with her. He was excited as well as disturbed. He felt on the verge of a new destiny.

Miriam sat with him in the courtyard at Joachim's house as they looked out over the darkening landscape of the vale of Esdraelon and watched the moon rise.

"Mother," Joshua said, "I've been thinking a great deal since Joanna died. Jon spoke to me today in a very lucid way for him. He described Joanna's and Elizabeth's deaths as visitations from God that came without warning, 'like a thief in the night.'"

Miriam looked at Joshua with a puzzled expression.

"God will take us all in His own time," Joshua continued. "Sometimes, we have time to prepare, like your father or Benjamin Levi. Even Elizabeth had some time to prepare, as she was a fair age. But for many, like Joanna, it can be sudden. Death can come through an unexpected illness, childbirth, or a simple accident. When we die, are we ready to come face to face with God? If we are not ready, what will become of us?"

"Most of us won't know when our time will come," Miriam answered.

"Tell me, Mother, why do you think I have been chosen by God?"

Joshua looked at Miriam with penetrating eyes.

"Do you really believe all those stories you told me long ago?" he said. "Do you believe that I shall be a 'Prince of Peace' leading our people?"

Miriam sighed.

"Joshua. I knew that one day you would become serious about this. I've never really known what to say to you. It was easy to tell the stories to you in your childhood, but it is much harder now, as I really don't understand God's purpose myself. You were so happy with Joanna. You seemed so pleased to live with the family here in Nazareth. I really haven't wanted to face you with my true feelings, but now I have to be honest. I have never believed that the life of a grape grower is your path. I still believe that God gave you to me for a higher purpose. You are more than a vinedresser or even a rabbi, Joshua. I believe you are a son of God. I believe you were born for a special purpose. You have been chosen by God, Joshua. I believe you have a destiny of great importance to all our people."

"Do you mean…to be a prophet, like Jon has suggested…who must warn our people to be prepared to meet God when they die?"

"Possibly a prophet…"

Miriam looked at him, then added:

"A great rabbi could be a prophet, or even one of the High Priests."

"What do you mean?" Joshua asked, taking hold of her hands.

"Joshua, from the moment you were born you have brought me endless surprises. There was the star with its trail of light right above us in the cave outside Bethlehem. Then, there were those rich merchants. You have the treasure that they left us. They did believe that you were some kind of a prince, but I have never thought of you in that way."

"But you believe that I am a son of God? That could be more than a prince," Joshua noted. "Sometimes, you say you don't know how you conceived me…what do you mean by that? You said you thought that Gabriel the priest was my father. You must know in your heart."

"I don't know what I mean, Joshua. But it was my angels who told me you were a son of God. It was just something I knew. It was something I sensed."

Joshua raised his eyebrows as he heard her standard answer.

"No, Mother," he continued, pushing his point. "Who could have been my father if it wasn't Gabriel the Priest?"

"Joshua, I used to say Gabriel was your father."

"Yes, Mother…your angel friend. But, was Gabriel the priest my real father? Was I part of a marriage contract that went wrong? After all, Mother, we have always known that that's what the rest of the family thinks. That's what James thinks, and I really think that deep down that's what Joseph thinks, too."

Miriam stared at Joshua. Her face was stern, almost afraid, and he could see that behind this brave front his mother was about to burst into tears. Something deep inside her had lain hidden all these years. Joshua realized that he was on the brink of finding out the truth.

"Gabriel tried to rape me!" she said as the tears burst forth.

Joshua took his mother's head in his arms.

"He tried, Joshua. He even entered me, but I thought I freed myself from him in time. I never wanted to believe that you were the result of that frightening encounter. It was something that was too terrible to ever explain to anybody. I never even told Zechariah the High Priest."

Miriam broke down into choking sobs.

"It's all right, Mother. I'm the only person who ever needs to know the truth, whatever other people may assume."

"I know it didn't happen then, at least not spiritually and emotionally. It really was impossible. I had kicked him away. But, Joshua, apart from that horrifying experience, I never lay with Gabriel, and for that matter I have never lain with any man other than Joseph, and God love him, that was never very often. My marriage was arranged. You were already kicking in my womb when I married. I really don't understand who your father was, but I knew that you were going to be born long before I knew that I was pregnant. Something happened."

"Tell me what," Joshua said, wiping the tears from her face.

"Emotionally, I believe I conceived on the night before I left the House of the Virgins at the Temple. I was in the moonlight praying, as was my custom. I was afraid. I knew I had to leave the shelter of my home. As I stood in the courtyard that night, I could feel an incredible oneness with God. The moonlight was like a ladder to heaven. I could imagine the angels flickering up and down as they did in Jacob's vision, but in my vision I could hear a voice that I have never forgotten. It said, 'Don't be afraid, Miriam, for God has chosen you. You will have a son, and he will be a leader of our people and a son of God.'"

Joshua was listening intently. Miriam had never told him of this vision at the House of the Virgins. She had alluded to her angels many times and to her belief that Gabriel, her favorite angel, had told her that her son would be special. But this lucid description of his mother's vision was something new.

"What do you think this means?" Joshua asked.

"I believe your conception was a miracle that happened that night. I don't know how else you were conceived. I only know that somehow God taught me through my angels that you are His chosen one. You have a destiny, Joshua. You are to be a great man—more than a man—a son of God. I can not explain it; I can only feel it. Nobody would believe me then, so why should they believe me now?"

"You really have no doubt, Mother?" Joshua asked. "Are you absolutely positive that I was not conceived from your ordeal with Gabriel?"

"No, Joshua. I can never be completely sure. But, even if Gabriel the Priest is your physical father, I still believe in my vision. God commissioned me to bring you into this world and you must now fulfill the burdens that I believe He has laid upon you. God spoke to me from the heavens that night. I know that with as much certainty as that we are sitting here now. If your conception was an accident of that attempted rape, it was an accident arranged by God."

"Do you think Joseph might believe all this?"

"Not really. He always shied away from the subject. Like you said, I think deep down he does think that Gabriel the priest was your father. But God love Joseph, he's never held that against us. He's been the best—a loving and caring father to us both. Like I said, Joseph has been more of a father to me than my lover. He's guided me through all our hard times. I would have been lost without him when we first went to Egypt." Miriam's speech faltered as she struggled for words, wiping a tear from her cheek. "Oh, Joshua... I hate to see him like he is now. Poor Joseph! He cannot see and he has become so helpless, and now I'm the one who has to do everything for him. But then, that's the least I can do after all he has done for us."

Joshua thought back to those days in Egypt. He remembered Joseph stooping all day making mud-bricks at the kiln. Joshua had loved him then more than anyone. *Joseph was always so patient and always laughed, unlike Amos, who never shared a smile, but stolidly got on with the job. We had fun together in those days*, he thought.

Joshua comforted his mother.

"Joseph's a wonderful man," he said. "He has always treated me as his son, and both you and I have been blessed. You know something, Mother, Joseph may be blind and helpless now, but the love he shares with us both we will carry forever. It is as if the spirit of God shone forth from him all these years. He shared with us his Divine love."

Miriam leaned against Joshua and sat in silence, staring at the yellowing moon over the vale of Esdraelon. Then, she looked up as he held her.

"Maybe that's what you can give to the world, Joshua, your own Divine love. If an angel of God announced your conception, then why should you not shine like an angel? Why shouldn't the light of the angels and the glory of God shine forth from you?"

Fear moved through Joshua.

"You are suggesting that I should spread the light of God? Do you think that men should see God in me? Mother, that's blasphemy!"

"Maybe we see God in all things. Sometimes, however, we become blinded by the world around us and can no longer see that love and hope. Maybe God chose you for this purpose. You're not a freedom fighter like Jonah was—you'd be hopeless as a soldier. You are a scholar like James, but you have a better way with people. You make everyone feel wanted and special. If my Joseph spread Divine love, I believe you do even more so."

Miriam kissed her son's forehead.

"Maybe this will be the strength of your greatness. Maybe this is what will make you a son of God and the 'Prince of Peace.'"

"Mother, I can only be myself. If I can spread a little Divine love, as you call it, I will have served my purpose."

He put his arm aound her.

"It's getting cool now. Don't you think we should go back inside? Joseph will be needing you."

As Miriam stood up, Joshua embraced her one more time.

"Mother, you have helped me so much. Thank you."

Miriam smiled, exquisitely serene, ageless in the moonlight.

* * *

Joshua shared many thoughts with his mother as the summer drew on. However, he was reticent to discuss these things with James.

James was a great scholar, but not much taken with mysticism. James saw the role of Judaism within its historic concept, and the Jewish people as an example of ordered living within the gentile world. He was neither bound by nationalism nor spirituality. His was a straightforward faith, interpreting the Law sensibly and practically through the Nazareth synagogue. He missed the tools of interpretation in Nazareth, however, which was stifling his scholasticism. He missed the synagogue library at Alexandria and the stimulating debates of those days. He was becoming stale and bored in the Galilean village.

"It would be good for us to study again," Joshua said to James when he was ready. "Jerusalem is the center of our faith. Both of us need new stimulation. Besides, James, I have lost interest in the vineyards. I don't have Joanna to share in my work and joy anymore. I need to leave

Nazareth for a while and think things out. There are all sorts of ideas in my head. I need a new purpose and a new life. I don't think I'm going to find it here in Nazareth, and I don't think you are finding it either. If I go, would you consider coming with me?"

James thought for a moment.

"I long to visit Jerusalem, but I've Rachel here and her family. Then there's Father, too. He's old and blind."

"I know, James, but Mother will take care of him. She does now. We don't contribute much to his comfort."

"What about Jon? He needs constant help and guidance. He has done so well with you in the vineyards. He trusts you, Joshua. Jon needs somebody to look up to and trust."

"I think Jon might come with us. Jon has talked with me quite a bit this summer. He's not as backward as we think. His learning skills are slow, but he gets there in the end. Since his mother died, he has a new determination. The change may do him good. I think he needs to be exposed to more of life. We've kept him locked away here too long. He thinks he has a destiny. We should let him find out for himself."

"You're determined, aren't you, Joshua."

"I've decided we need to go to Jerusalem. If you won't come with us, Jon and I will go without you. If we leave after the grapes have been harvested and the wine put away for next year, we might still get there for the High Holy days and Succot. It's so long since we've made a pilgrimage now that the older family members can't travel. We owe it to God and ourselves."

"Let me think about it," James mused. "I would like to get back to serious study and listen to the Sanhedrin debates, but I will have to consider Rachel's feelings. I have a premonition that if I do go to Jerusalem as you suggest, it might be for some time, maybe even forever... not just a pilgrimage."

Joshua embraced James.

"I know it. There's a whole new world waiting for us. We must follow our destinies."

Rachel prepared them a meal of fruit, bread and honey. As they ate, they did not discuss the matter any further.

* * *

As the summer drew to its close and the grape harvest began, Joshua suggested his plan to Jon.

"You want me to come with you to Jerusalem?" Jon asked excitedly. "It's a great idea. It'll be wonderful. There'll be James, Rachel, you and me. I can't remember Jerusalem. It's been so long. But if we're the 'chosen ones,' Joshua, we need to go to Jerusalem. That was my father's city. It's where I belong."

"In a way, Jon, Jerusalem's where we all belong. The city has been the center of our faith for a long, long time."

"How soon do you think we can leave?"

"Not until all these grapes have been harvested, pressed, or dried and all the new wine is put up in skins and jars. We still have a lot to do. Remember, we had the best wine in Nazareth last year, even better than Joachim's. Maybe this year our harvest will be as good again."

They returned to their task, cutting the ripened bunches of grapes and putting them into big baskets. They would take them to the press and squeeze out the grape juice ready to ferment it for the next year's wine, then dry the excess bunches to make raisins for winter use.

* * *

The harvest over, James and Rachel continued to be undecided, but Joshua and Jon were ready to make their journey.

Joshua dug into the floor in the corner of his house where he had buried the box of treasure. His stomach tightened when he saw again the leather and studs of the fasteners that bound the wood. He cleared away the soil from around its edges. Slowly, he eased the heavy box out of the hole. Setting it down, Joshua opened the thongs and raised the creaking lid. The gold coins were still there, a mass of glistening medallions. Carefully, he closed the lid again.

I may well need this now, he thought. *Mother always said I should keep it to use when I needed it to fulfill my destiny. I could give it all to the poor, but Nazareth already has Benjamin Levi and old Joachim for such charity. Who knows where or when I will need it, but I'd better keep this with me. These coins were the proof to my mother that those old men from the East knew that I was called to be a son of God.*

Unexpectedly, as Joshua held the box, Jon came in from outside.

"What have you there?" he asked.

"Gold coins, Jon."

Joshua felt a little embarrassed that he had been caught looking at the treasure that he and his mother had denied themselves for so long.

"Are they yours?"

"Yes, but only in trust. They're only mine if I use them wisely."

"What do you mean? Where did they come from? Did old Joachim give them to you, or did they come from Joanna's father?"

"No, Jon. It's a mystery that I've lived with all my life. The treasure was given to my mother when I was born. Travelers from the East, rich merchants, gave it to her. If you remember your mother's stories, Jon, we were both born in the year of the bright star with the trail of light. These rich merchants told my mother that the star was a sign from God and that they believed that I was a 'chosen one'. That was why they left me this box of gold. Apparently, they also left us precious stones and incense balm, but they have long since gone, sold for household expenses and our passage money from Egypt. Mother kept this box of gold coins for me. She never lost faith that one day, maybe, I would fulfill those rich men's hopes. Perhaps the time has come, Jon. I'm going to take this box with us to Jerusalem. It's my legacy—the legacy of a star."

Jon's eyes glistened.

"We really are going to make a new beginning."

Joshua looked up at Jon as he tightened the thongs on the heavy box.

"Help me carry this out to the cart. I want to take it over to old Joachim's house until we are ready to leave on our journey."

Jon helped Joshua.

"This could make you a rich man," he said.

"Don't tempt me, Jon. These gold coins are for use in the service of God. Remember what we've discussed. We're going to Jerusalem to learn how to serve the Lord better. We need to be at the center of our faith. We are buried here in Nazareth, where nothing spiritual ever happens. Remember, Jon: 'We are the chosen ones.'"

They laid the box down in the cart. Joshua put an arm around Jon's shoulder.

"All right, Jon, do you want to lead the mule? Let's get back to Joachim's house. We've completed everything here. You've been a great help with the harvest. I think we became the best winemakers in Nazareth, but from now on, it will be up to Joanna's father to keep these vineyards."

Jon pulled on the mule and the cart began to move.

Joshua hung back momentarily, looking at the neat rows of vines and the little house with its cistern and storeroom that he had built for Joanna. There was a lump in his throat, and he felt he could hear Joanna's voice and see her smiling face.

"Thank you for the good times we had here, Lord," he said. "I hope that wherever You lead me, I can be half as happy as I have been here."

His eyes were smarting, but he turned and slowly followed the cart. Deep down, he knew that his time as a winemaker was over. Jerusalem and an unknown future in the service of the Lord lay ahead.

THE HASMONEANS

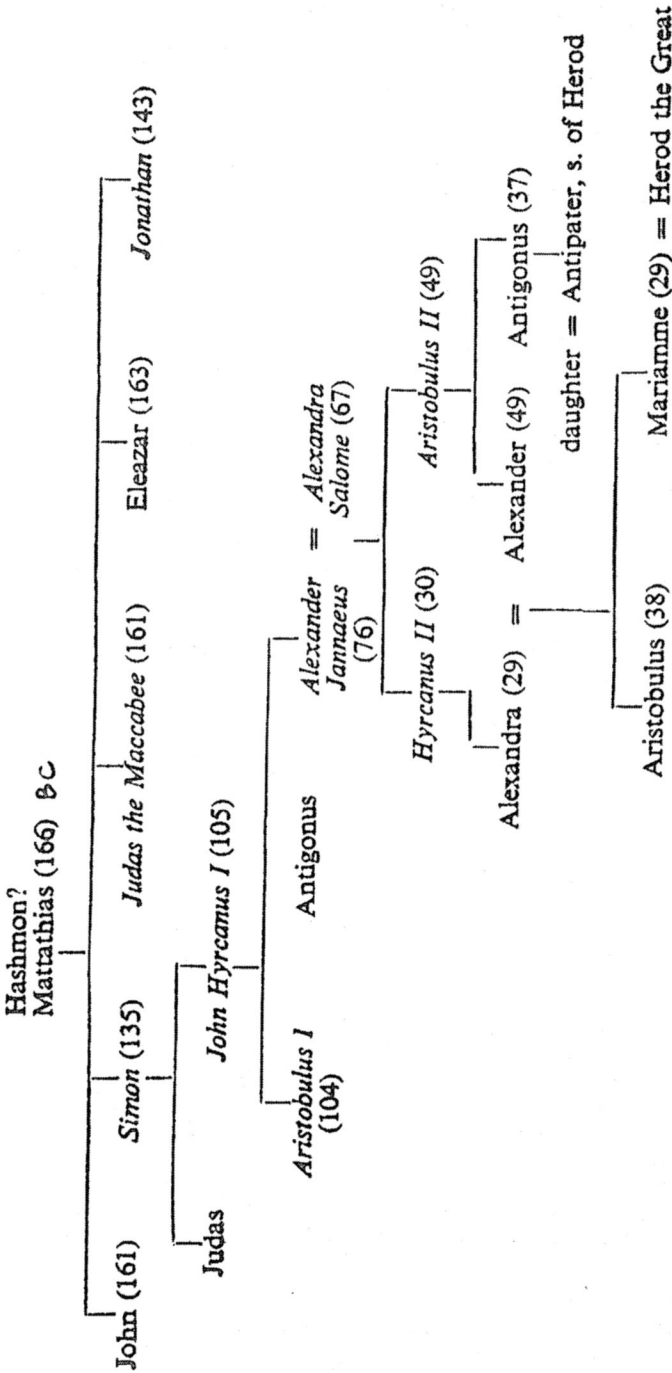

Hashmon?
Mattathias (166) BC

John (161)

Simon (135)

Judas the Maccabee (161)

Eleazar (163)

Jonathan (143)

Judas

John Hyrcanus I (105)

Aristobulus I (104)

Antigonus

Alexander Jannaeus (76) = Alexandra Salome (67)

Hyrcanus II (30)

Aristobulus II (49)

Alexandra (29) = Alexander (49)

Antigonus (37)

Aristobulus (38)

daughter = Antipater, s. of Herod

Mariamne (29) = Herod the Great

High Priests and Rulers are in italics: dates of death are in parentheses.

557

HEROD'S FAMILY

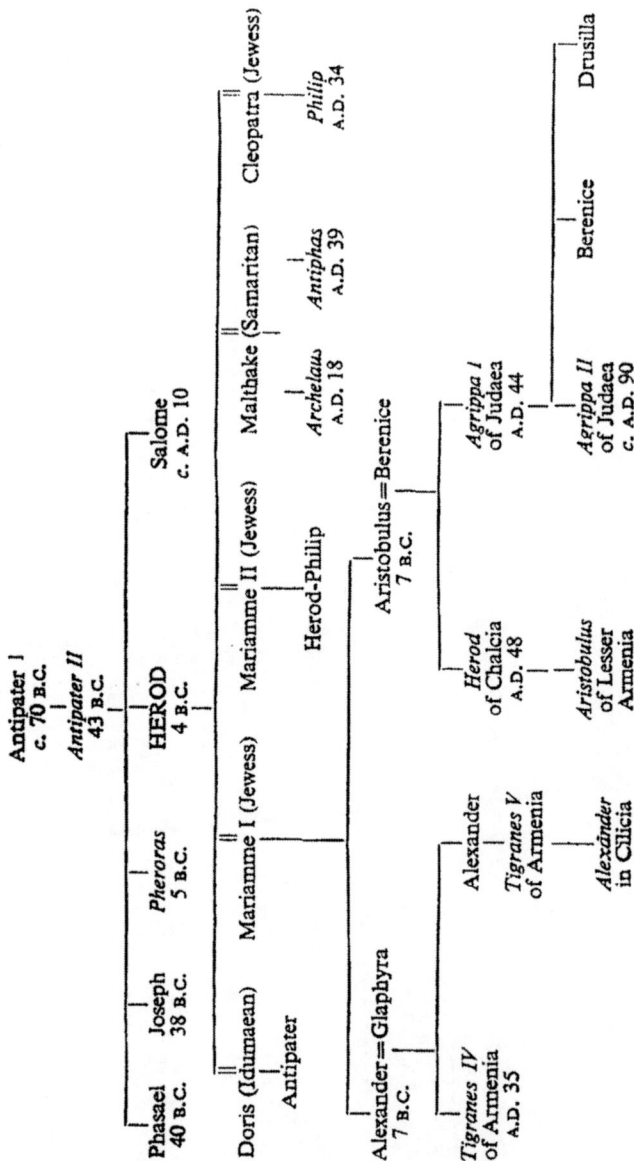

NOTE: This table is not complete. Herod married ten wives, by eight of whom he had issue, fourteen children in all, nine sons and five daughters. The names given here are those which come into this story. Rulers recognized by Rome as Ethnarchs, Kings or Tetrarchs are in italics. The dates below each name are those of death where known. Herod-Philip, Herod's son by Mariamme II, first husband of Herodias and father of Salome, who is mentioned (thought not by name) in the Gospels as having demanded the death of John the Baptist, is to be distinguished from Philip, Herod's son by Cleopatra of Jerusalem, who from 4 B.C. to A.D. 34 was Tetrarch of Ituraea, etc. It was their half-brother, Antipas, who was Tetrarch of Galilee in the days of Christ.

Antipater I
c. 70 B.C.
|
Antipater II
43 B.C.

Children of Antipater II: Phasael (40 B.C.), Joseph (38 B.C.), **HEROD** (4 B.C.), Pheroras (5 B.C.), Salome (c. A.D. 10)

Herod's wives: Doris (Idumaean), Mariamme I (Jewess), Mariamme II (Jewess), Malthake (Samaritan), Cleopatra (Jewess)

Doris — Antipater

Mariamme I (Jewess):
- Alexander = Glaphyra (7 B.C.)
  - Tigranes IV of Armenia (A.D. 35)
  - Alexander in Cilicia
    - Tigranes V of Armenia
- Aristobulus = Berenice (7 B.C.)
  - Herod of Chalcia (A.D. 48)
  - Agrippa I of Judaea (A.D. 44)
    - Agrippa II of Judaea (c. A.D. 90)
    - Berenice
    - Drusilla
  - Aristobulus of Lesser Armenia

Mariamme II (Jewess):
- Herod-Philip

Malthake (Samaritan):
- *Archelaus* (A.D. 18)
- *Antiphas* (A.D. 39)

Cleopatra (Jewess):
- *Philip* (A.D. 34)

THE FAMILIES OF JOACHIM AND ZECHARIAH

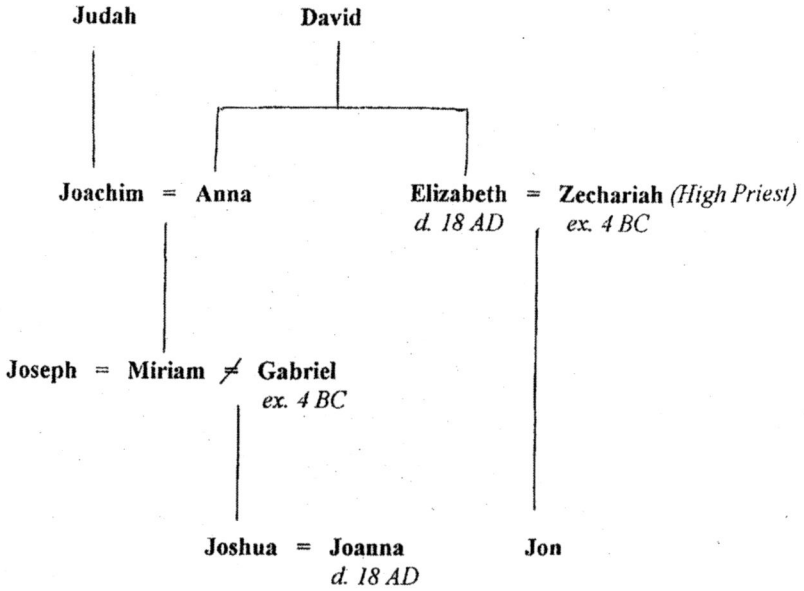

```
     Judah              David


   Joachim  =  Anna              Elizabeth  =  Zechariah (High Priest)
                                 d. 18 AD        ex. 4 BC

Joseph = Miriam  ≠  Gabriel
                    ex. 4 BC


        Joshua  =  Joanna              Jon
                   d. 18 AD
```

THE TARQUIN AND FLAVIAN FAMILIES

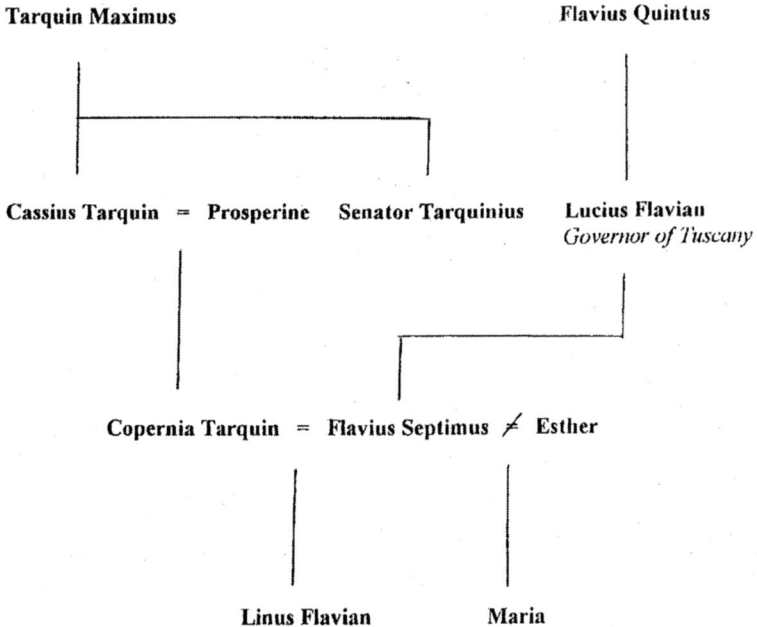

```
Tarquin Maximus                          Flavius Quintus


Cassius Tarquin = Prosperine   Senator Tarquinius   Lucius Flavian
                                                    Governor of Tuscany


      Copernia Tarquin  =  Flavius Septimus  ≠  Esther


        Linus Flavian              Maria
```

MAP OF THE PROVINCE OF SYRIA

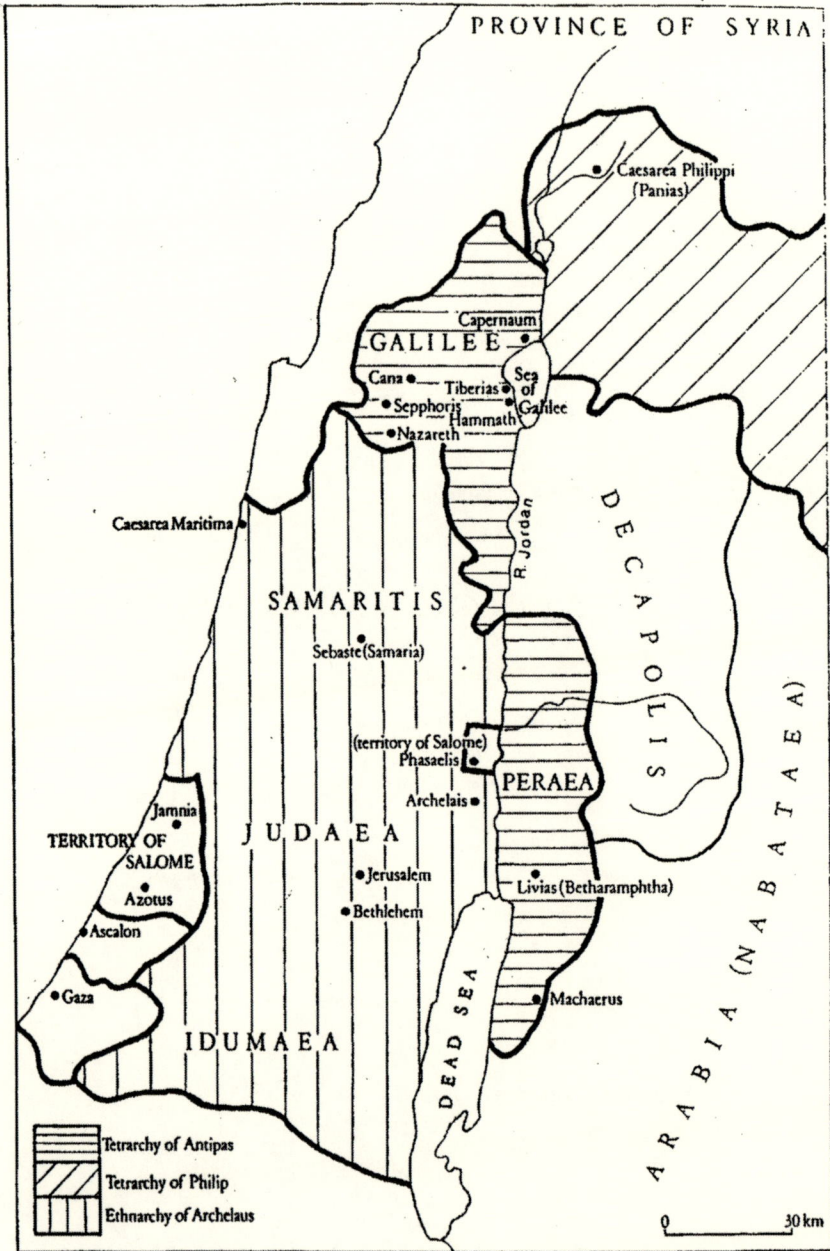

Judaea under Herod's sons

MAP OF JUDEA AND THE LEVANT
IN THE FIRST CENTURY

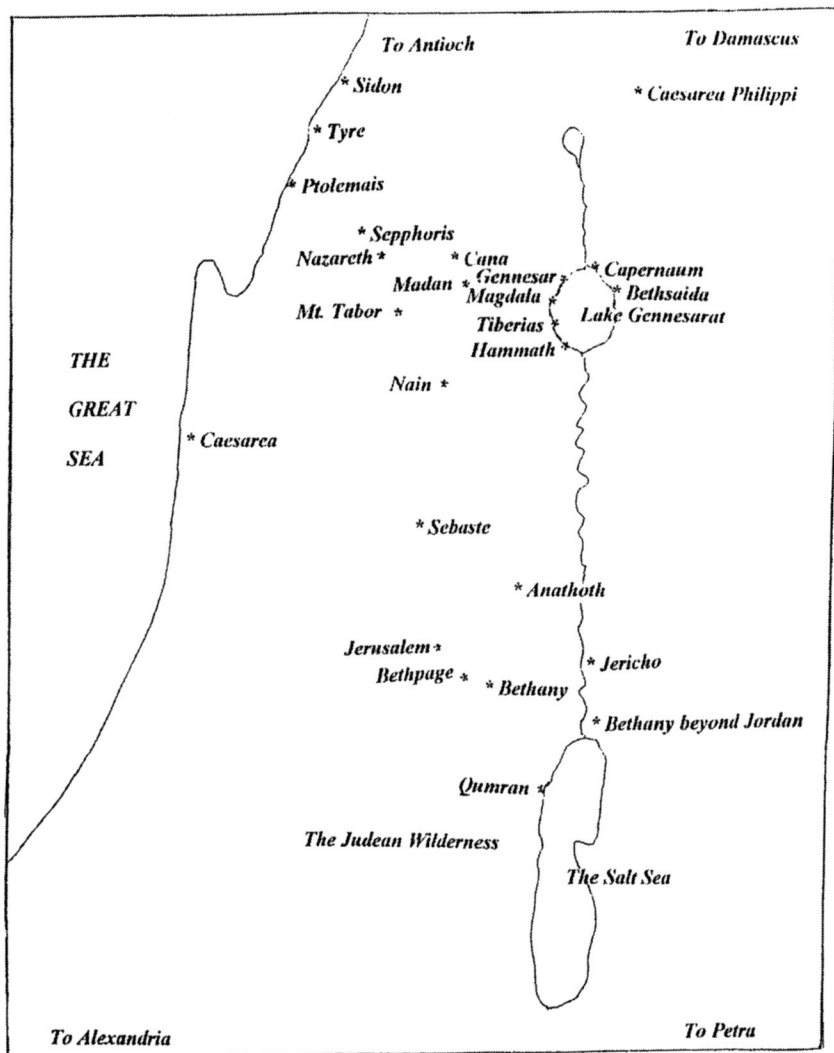

To Antioch

To Damascus

* *Sidon*

* *Caesarea Philippi*

* *Tyre*

* *Ptolemais*

* *Sepphoris*

Nazareth *

* *Cana*

Gennesar *

* *Capernaum*

Madan *

Magdala

* *Bethsaida*

Mt. Tabor *

Tiberias *

Lake Gennesarat

Hammath *

THE

Nain *

GREAT

* *Caesarea*

SEA

* *Sebaste*

* *Anathoth*

Jerusalem *

* *Jericho*

Bethpage *

* *Bethany*

* *Bethany beyond Jordan*

Qumran *

The Judean Wilderness

The Salt Sea

To Alexandria

To Petra

MAP OF JERUSALEM

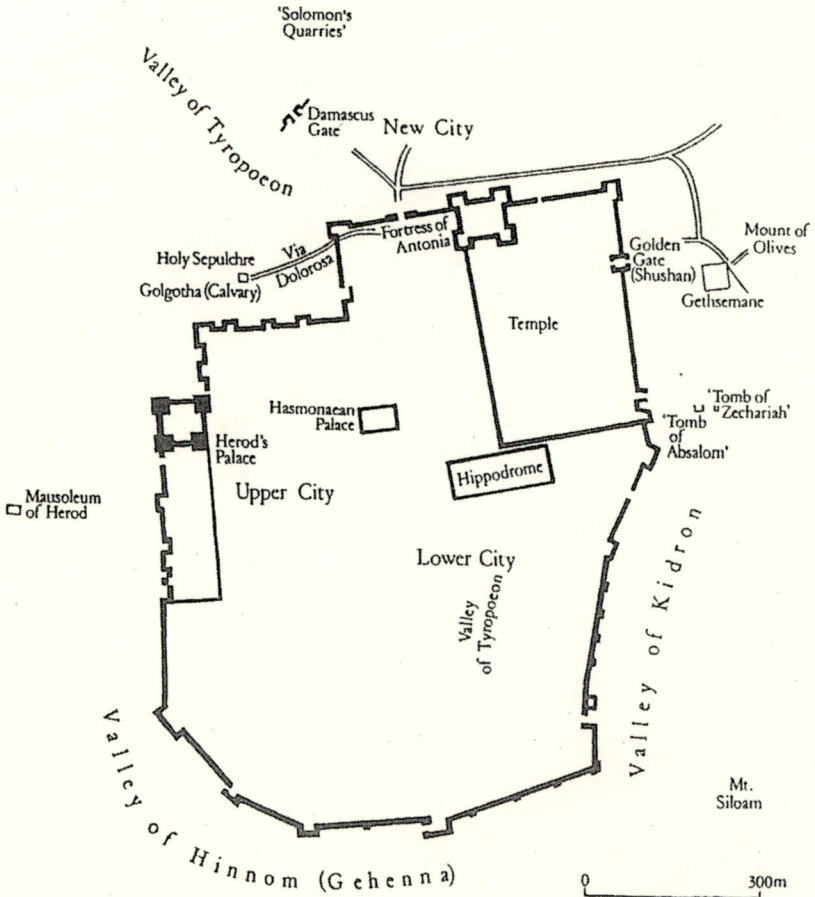

'Solomon's
Quarries'

Valley of Tyropoeon

Damascus
Gate   New City

Fortress of
Antonia

Holy Sepulchre   Via
Dolorosa

Golgotha (Calvary)

Golden
Gate
(Shushan)

Mount of
Olives

Gethsemane

Temple

Hasmonaean
Palace

'Tomb of
Zechariah'

'Tomb
of
Absalom'

Herod's
Palace

Mausoleum
of Herod

Upper City

Hippodrome

Lower City

Valley
of Tyropoeon

Valley of Kidron

Mt.
Siloam

Valley of Hinnom (Gehenna)

0   300m

PLAN OF THE TEMPLE

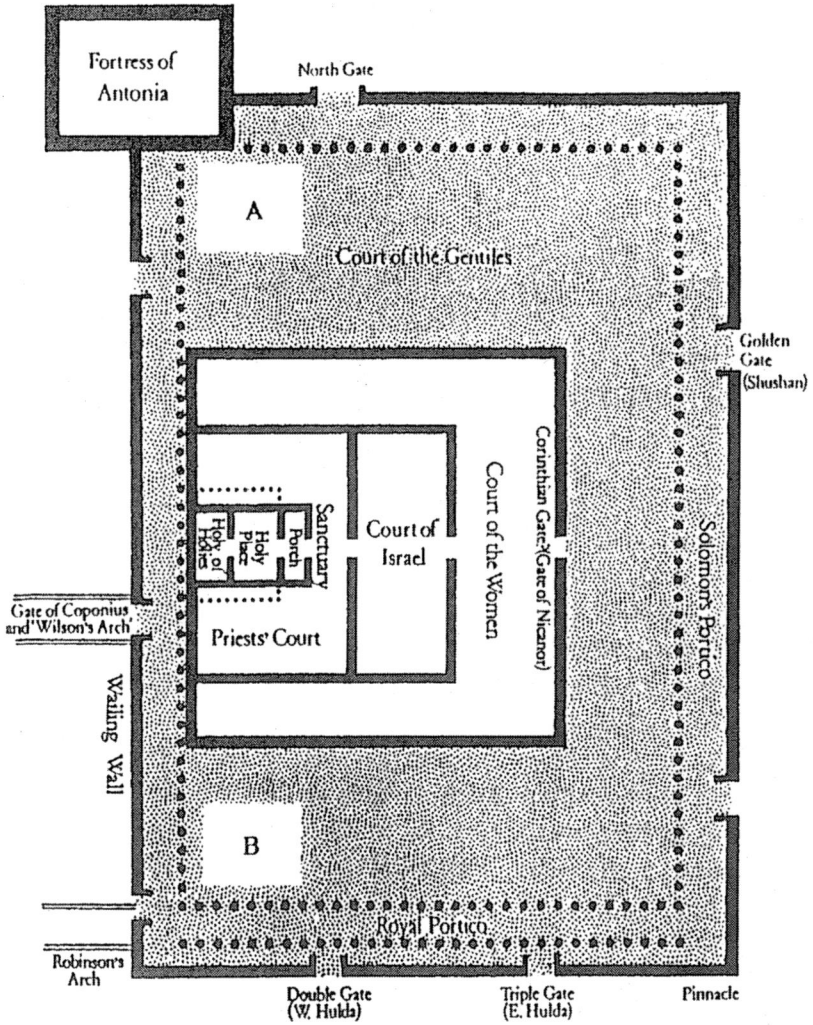

Fortress of Antonia

North Gate

A

Court of the Gentiles

Golden Gate (Shushan)

Gate of Coponius and 'Wilson's Arch'

Wailing Wall

Sanctuary

Holy of Holies

Holy Place

Porch

Court of Israel

Court of the Women

Corinthian Gate (Gate of Nicanor)

Solomon's Portico

Priests' Court

B

Robinson's Arch

Royal Portico

Double Gate (W. Hulda)

Triple Gate (E. Hulda)

Pinnacle

A   The House of the Virgins

B   The Sanhedrin

Printed in the United States
221326BV00001B/7/P